Praise for *Hell or Richmond*

**Winner of the American Library Association's
2014 W. Y. Boyd Award for Literary Excellence in
Military Fiction**

"*Hell or Richmond* is an American epic, a prose *Iliad* of the Civil War. It is stunningly well researched and beautifully, poetically written. No other book I have read conveys so forcefully and eloquently the physical and moral challenges faced by the soldiers who took part in the Civil War."
—Dr. Guy MacLean Rogers,
author of *Alexander: The Ambiguity of Greatness*

"Swift-moving . . . harrowing . . . [Peters] writes with a fine balance of historical accuracy and drama."
—*Kirkus Reviews*

"A towering work of historical fiction, majestic in its ferocity, strangely beautiful in its expression, [and] cold-eyed honest in the truths it tells about men at war."
—William Martin,
author of *The Lincoln Letter* and *The Lost Constitution*

"Firmly grounded in the historical record, *Hell or Richmond* recounts the horrific bloodbaths of the Wilderness, Spotsylvania, and Cold Harbor with the skill of an accomplished novelist. Peters's narrative unfolds with gripping you-are-there urgency. This is enthralling historical fiction of the highest order."
—Gordon C. Rhea,
author of *The Battle of the Wilderness* and *Cold Harbor*

"Another triumph of meticulous scholarship, compelling characterization, and exciting, page-turning combat action. *Hell or Richmond* is not only storytelling at its best, it is also astonishingly accurate . . . down to the weather for a given time of day. Superbly crafted . . . and brought to vivid life by a writer at the top of his form." —Jerry Morelock,
editor in chief of *Armchair General* magazine

HELL OR RICHMOND

RALPH PETERS

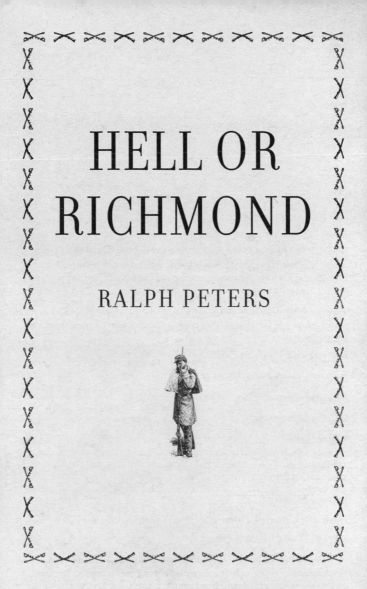

A TOM DOHERTY ASSOCIATES BOOK | NEW YORK

This is a work of fiction. All of the characters, organizations, and events portrayed in this novel are either products of the author's imagination or are used fictitiously.

HELL OR RICHMOND

Copyright © 2013 by Ralph Peters

All rights reserved.

Maps by George Skoch

A Forge Book
Published by Tom Doherty Associates, LLC
175 Fifth Avenue
New York, NY 10010

www.tor-forge.com

Forge® is a registered trademark of Tom Doherty Associates, LLC.

ISBN 978-0-7653-6823-2

Forge books may be purchased for educational, business, or promotional use. For information on bulk purchases, please contact the Macmillan Corporate and Premium Sales Department at 1-800-221-7945, extension 5442, or write to specialmarkets@macmillan.com.

First Edition: May 2013
First Mass Market Edition: March 2015

Printed in the United States of America

0 9 8 7 6 5 4 3 2 1

To the flesh-and-blood men who struggled,
before we turned them into bronze and marble

Key Characters

UNION

AYRES, Romeyn B. "Rome," Brigadier General. Commanding First Brigade, First (Griffin's) Division, Fifth Corps.

BADEAU, Adam, Lieutenant Colonel. Military secretary to Grant.

BARLOW, Francis Channing, Brigadier General. Commanding First Division, Second (Hancock's) Corps. Descended from old New England blood; first in the Harvard class of 1855; successful lawyer before the war; a ruthless fighter.

BEAUDRY, Louis Napoleon. Chaplain, Fifth New York Cavalry, and temperance advocate.

BILL. Manservant to Grant. Freed slave.

BIRNEY, David B., Major General. Commanding Third Division, Second (Hancock's) Corps.

BLACK, John D., Captain. Aide to Barlow.

BROOKE, John R., Colonel. Commanding Fourth Brigade, First (Barlow's) Division, Second Corps.

BROWN, Charles E., Sergeant. Company C, 50th Pennsylvania Veteran Volunteer Infantry Regiment. Canal boatman before the war.

BURKET, Daniel F., Captain. Commanding Company C, 50th Pennsylvania. Canal harbormaster before the war.

BURNSIDE, Ambrose E., Major General. Commanding Ninth Corps (initially a separate corps, later integrated into the Army of the Potomac).

BYRNES, Richard, Colonel. Commanding Second ("Irish") Brigade, First (Barlow's) Division, Second (Hancock's) Corps, after Smyth transfers to Gibbon's division.

CHRIST, Benjamin C., Colonel. Commanding Second Brigade, Third Division, Ninth (Burnside's) Corps. His brigade includes the 50th Pennsylvania.

DOUDLE, John, Corporal. Company C, 50th Pennsylvania. Canal boatman before the war.

FRANK, Paul, Colonel. Commanding Third Brigade, First (Barlow's) Division, Second Corps. German immigrant.

GETTY, George Washington, Brigadier General. Commanding Second Division, Sixth (Sedgwick's) Corps, at the start of the campaign.

GIBBON, John, Brigadier General. Commanding Second Division, Second (Hancock's) Corps. Occasionally serves as deputy commander to Hancock.

GRANT, Ulysses S. "Sam," Lieutenant General. General in chief of the Union's armies.

GRIFFIN, Charles, Brigadier General. Commanding First Division, Fifth (Warren's) Corps. Old soldier with a great affection for his troops and a genius for profanity.

HAMMOND, John, Lieutenant Colonel. Commanding Fifth New York Cavalry.

HANCOCK, Winfield Scott, Major General. Commanding Second Corps, Army of the Potomac.

HILL, Henry, Private. Company C, 50th Pennsylvania. Canal boatman before the war. Cousin to First Sergeant William Hill.

HILL, William, First Sergeant. Company C, 50th Pennsylvania. Canal boatman before the war.

HUMPHREYS, Andrew Atkinson, Major General. Chief of staff, Army of the Potomac.

UPTON, Emory, Colonel. Commanding Second Brigade, First (Wright's) Division, Sixth Corps. Abolitionist, fervent Christian, martinet, and budding military genius.

WAINWRIGHT, Charles S., Colonel. Commanding the artillery brigade, Fifth (Warren's) Corps. Brilliant gunner, brave soldier, scalding personality.

WARREN, Gouverneur Kemble, Major General. Commanding Fifth Corps, Army of the Potomac.

WASHBURNE, Elihu, Congressman. Member of the powerful Ways and Means Committee. Radical Republican and abolitionist. Early backer and protector of Grant's.

WILDERMUTH, William, Private. Company C, 50th Pennsylvania. Canal boatman before the war.

WILSON, James H., Brigadier General. Newly appointed commander of the Third Division, Cavalry (Sheridan's) Corps. "Western" officer brought along by Grant.

WRIGHT, Horatio G., Brigadier General. Initially commanding First Division, Sixth (Sedgwick's) Corps; subsequently assumes command of the corps.

CONFEDERATE

ALEXANDER, E. Porter, Brigadier General. Commanding artillery, First (Longstreet's) Corps.

ATKINSON, Edmund N., Colonel. Commanding 26th Georgia, Gordon's Brigade, Early's Division.

BERRY, Thomas J., Lieutenant Colonel. Commanding 60th Georgia, Gordon's Brigade, Early's Division.

EARLY, Jubal A. "Old Jube," Major General. Commanding Early's Division, Second (Ewell's) Corps.

EVANS, Clement A., Colonel. Commanding 31st Georgia, Gordon's Brigade, Early's Division.

EWELL, Richard S. "Dick," Lieutenant General. Commander, Second Corps, Army of Northern Virginia.

GORDON, John Brown, Brigadier General. Commanding Gordon's Brigade, Early's Division, Second (Ewell's) Corps. Forced to leave his college to reorganize his family's coal mines in northwestern Georgia, but retained his passion for rhetoric over the years. One of the rare "born commanders."

HAMPTON, Wade, Major General. Commanding a cavalry division under J. E. B. Stuart.

HENAGAN, John W., Colonel. Commanding Kershaw's Brigade, First (Anderson's, formerly Longstreet's) Corps.

HETH, Henry "Harry," Major General. Commanding Heth's Division, Third (Hill's) Corps.

JENKINS, Micah, Brigadier General. Commanding Jenkins' Brigade, Field's Division, First (Longstreet's) Corps.

KEITT, Lawrence, Colonel. Commanding 20th South Carolina and, briefly, Kershaw's Brigade at Cold Harbor. Pre-war firebrand, pro-slavery politician, brilliant, resolute, and pigheaded.

KERSHAW, Joseph B., Brigadier General. Commanding Kershaw's Division, First (Anderson's, formerly Longstreet's) Corps. Former commander of Kershaw's Brigade.

JOHNSON, Edward "Alleghany," Major General. Commanding Stonewall Jackson's old division.

LAW, Evander McIvor, Brigadier General. After removal from command by Longstreet, returned to command of Law's Brigade by Lee in mid-campaign. His brigade includes the 15th Alabama.

LEE, Fitzhugh "Fitz," Major General. Commanding a cavalry division under Stuart.

LEE, Robert E., General. Commander, Army of Northern Virginia.

LEE, William Henry Fitzhugh "Rooney," Major General. Commanding a cavalry division under Stuart.

LONGSTREET, James "Peter," "Old Pete," Lieutenant General. Commander, First Corps, Army of Northern Virginia.

LOWTHER, Alexander A., Major. Intermittently second in command of the 15th Alabama.

MARSHALL, Charles, Lieutenant Colonel. Military secretary to Lee.

OATES, William C., Colonel. Commanding 15th Alabama. Before the war: a not quite murderer, a runaway, a schooner crewman, a vagabond, a teetotaler, a ladies' man, a lawyer, and part owner of a local newspaper. Ferocious in war and peace.

PERRY, Edward A., Brigadier General. Commanding Perry's Florida Brigade, Anderson's Division, Third (Hill's) Corps.

PERRY, William F., Colonel. Acting commander of Law's Brigade, Field's Division, First (Longstreet's) Corps, in the absence of Evander Law. His brigade includes the 15th Alabama.

POAGUE, William T., Lieutenant Colonel. Commanding Poague's Battalion (artillery), Third (Hill's) Corps. Arguably the true savior of the Army of Northern Virginia on the morning of May 6, 1864.

STUART, James E. B. "Jeb," Major General. Commander of the Cavalry Corps, Army of Northern Virginia.

TAYLOR, Walter, Lieutenant Colonel. Assistant adjutant general to Lee.

VENABLE, Charles, Lieutenant Colonel. Aide to Lee.

Peace is despaired,
For who can think submission? War, then, war . . .

—JOHN MILTON, *Paradise Lost*

PART I

STARS ON THEIR SHOULDERS, AND STRIPES ON THEIR SLEEVES . . .

PROLOGUE

March 10, 1864
Brandy Station, Virginia

Rain. Thudding on canvas like bullets on flesh. Imagining a different sound, he rose and opened the tent's flap.

Merely a courier passing by, fighting the mud for mastery of his horse. Not the visitor. Another man might have felt reprieved, but that was not his nature.

Would he be able to hear the train? Or the band when it struck up down by the siding? Would he have a last few minutes to prepare himself?

The rain only dirtied the day, leaving the stripped land as colorless as the uniforms south of the river, the fouled garments of the men he had learned to kill. And to respect.

He coughed.

Letting the sodden flap fall, he turned back to the emptied headquarters tent, a domain of maps and papers, of lingering human scents. The stove reeked of damp wood and ancient ashes. He had ordered the plank floor scrubbed, but the effort was futile. With each tread mud oozed up between the boards.

Determined not to make things worse, he sat down, jarring old bones. But he was not in command of himself this day. He soon got to his feet again, fussing with his uniform as he paced the canvas cage. Was *that* the rumble of the train from Washington?

The heavy rain obscured all other sounds. He had refused to let Humphreys site the headquarters close to the station, with its smoke and stink and noise. For the first time, he regretted that decision. This wait was abominable.

He wiped his nose with a handkerchief hard used. In the old days, before the madness of the war, he had been particular as to the freshness of his handkerchiefs. Now such matters seemed laughable.

Damnable illness, a vicious living thing in the lungs and throat. He had thought himself quite over it that morning. But the pestiferous cold without would not let go. Nor was it honest Philadelphia cold, but a damp wickedness crawling into the lungs and clawing the sinuses, assassin of consumptives. No wonder more soldiers died in camp than in battle. Even the weather aligned against him now, another enemy.

At least it did not seem to be a return of his pneumonia. The politicians and their favored generals had tried to employ even his health against him, declaring him unfit on that count, too. Yet, he had won battles, and they had not, an achievement that would never be forgiven.

Plagued by nerves and temperament, he opened the flap again. The landscape lay drear and dead, with no hint of spring. The war had passed over it many times, impoverishing its poverty. If the men across the river were fighting for this wretched dirt, he was not. At the start of the war, he had served a noble idea and kindled ambition. Now he fought because it was too late to stop, too ignoble after such a torrent of blood. He still believed in the justice of his cause, in the sanctity of an undivided Union, but the fine words that once had passed his lips were gall. What mattered now was the debt owed his dead and holding fast to his honor. The thought of defeat, of quitting, was unbearable.

But the choice had been taken from him. He knew what was coming on that special train: not just a man, but a sentence.

He made a fist at the air, embarrassing himself. The Committee on the Conduct of the War was a damned disgrace, a cabal of drunkards trafficking in lies. He hated politics, had always hated them. Now he was mired in their filth. There were times, black times, when he wondered if his government merited saving. Scoundrels were permitted—nay, encouraged—to undo the reputations of decent men.

The rain, the rain. Let the spring come and the marching into battle. Even if he would no longer be part of it. Let the sun warm the shoulders pressing forward in blue columns, let someone force this horror to an end. Even if that someone could not be him.

He dropped back into a camp chair, sour and heartbroken, yearning for a chance to show them all, to frustrate his accusers. He believed he was still the man to lead this army. He knew how to fight the men south of the river. But he lacked the skills to defend himself against the press and hireling politicians.

He had to do the honorable thing, he understood that. Today of all days, it was vital to remain a gentleman, to speak faithfully and betray no emotions to his career's executioner. His family seemed ever destined for disappointment: his father, now him. Yet, he had done much, giving them all the victory they needed, that victory and more. . . .

Only to have a low cabal poison Lincoln against him. *Liars. Devils. Whoremongers.* Intimating, in the wake of Mine Run, that he sympathized with the Confederacy, that he was unfit to command, even that he was cowardly. All because he would not squander thousands of men to no purpose. Oh, yes. Had he overruled all military judgment, common sense, and decency and ordered Warren to attack, had he sacrificed five thousand soldiers in an act of folly, he might have been forgiven. But powerful men never spotted near a battlefield had seized upon his refusal to charge Lee's entrenchments, coiling like snakes to strike his reputation. Their ardor for slaughter repelled him.

Perhaps he was better off being relieved. He could put this filth behind him, this infinite human vice of cold ambition. He could not understand how men could tell a public lie and then stand by it. He was not made for the politics of command, not for politics of any kind. He knew that his notions of honor seemed quaint, even laughable, to the likes of Sickles, Hooker, and Butterfield. But he could not imagine a life lived another way.

It would have been best to remain a corps commander. Or merely the commander of a division. The leadership of this army had brought with it more threats from the rear than from the Confederacy.

He wiped his nose, wet linen on raw skin.

Soon, soon, blessedly soon he would return to Margaret and the children. Taking pride in what *he* knew he had done and leaving the vultures to feast on the country's carcass. Damn them all. Let them have their misbegotten war. . . .

Yet, even as he railed against the world, his heart declared against his going home. He longed to finish what he had begun, then to go back to Philadelphia in triumph, not odium. The unavoidable speeches of praise by aldermen and consolation banquets at the Union League would only prolong the pain. He wanted to stay here and *fight*. But the choice was not his to make.

Another fit of coughing dragged him back to the front of the tent. He hacked up what phlegm he could and spit into the mud. Still nothing. Only more rain. Preferring to do things properly, he would have liked to post an honor guard at the station. He felt no resentment toward the man himself. But the rain made the prospect of troops on parade a travesty. Only an ass would give soldiers a needless drenching. The war had taken decent men beyond that. He had settled for a few bandsmen and a lean retinue selected from the staff.

A mighty burst of rain assaulted the canvas, conjuring Gettysburg: his hour of glory, of triumph. The smoke, confusion, and carnage had calmed to reveal his army victorious. Lee had been *defeated. Lee!* His elation on that July afternoon had soared beyond all words, beyond his deathly exhaustion, and he had thought, mistakenly, that all might be well thereafter. Only to spend the night wrapped in an oilcloth, sitting on a rock amid the mud, under a tree that channeled the rain into torrents. Every roof had been required for the wounded his victory cost.

The wounded, in their legions. Damn Washington, and damn the New York papers. None of the men in frock coats and cravats understood the human side of an army. How they had howled—and were howling still—because he had not chased Lee like an ill-trained dog. They refused to hear that three hard days of battle had left tens of thousands of wounded men in his care and thousands more as prisoners on his hands. They did not want to hear that his army, too, had been mauled and thrown into confusion, that officers had been slaughtered by the hundredfold, that ammunition pouches and caissons had been emptied, that entire divisions had nothing to eat and no water untainted by blood, that the corpses of the brave baked in the sun, or simply that he had done the best he could. The Army of the Potomac had worked a miracle, sending Lee home in shame, but it had not been wonder enough for the stay-at-homes.

Now their spite had caught up with him, with an innocent man their instrument, and he would be replaced by Baldy Smith, a rude and cranky fellow. It was humiliating. But he was determined to bear it as a gentleman.

The rain retreated abruptly, leaving a rear guard of droplets. Perhaps the change of command would bring the army better weather. And dry the damnable mud of "Old Virginny." His men needed to escape the stench of their hovels and the diseases crowding bred. The sick rolls and the tally of the dead were simply appalling. The men needed the warmth of the sun to quicken their muscles and fresh air to lift their hearts.

He sneezed and felt his beard for snot. It was vital to maintain his dignity. His visitor had soared above them all. He remembered the fellow from Texas and then Mexico: sun-reddened and rusty-haired, otherwise nondescript, of medium height and build, earnest and amenable, the sort of lieutenant you called upon to make up a fourth at cards. He always had seemed a lonely man, but they all had been lonely for their wives and sweethearts in those Texican days when the war refused to come. He himself had been a staff engineer, the other man a chafing quartermaster. At Monterrey, they had been thrilled by war, young men eager for accolades and brevets. It was grotesque to remember it now, how even he had viewed war as romantic. And the sad, silver-jangling Mexicans obliged them.

He had not heard the train or any warning fanfare, so the ruckus of horses slopping through the mud close by surprised him. He stood, straightened his uniform, and fixed his hat on his head. Stepping out onto a walkway of planks, he scanned the powder-smoke mist.

His visitor rode ahead of the others, as if he knew exactly where he was going. The man had always had a good seat on a horse, had set some sort of equestrian record at West Point. Or was that someone else? At times he feared his memory would betray him. Forty-eight? Not so old. But old, too. War wanted the young. He cleared his throat and— just then, of all times—the damned fleabites on his calves began to itch.

He might not miss this, after all.

The visitor rode close, dropped easily and carelessly into

the muck, and strode toward him. Splashing defiantly, determinedly, as if no mud would dare hold fast his boots. The other horsemen held back, fixed to their saddles.

There was no saluting, no formality. The visitor pulled off a riding glove and extended his hand.

"General Meade," the man said in an easy western voice. "Sweet weather, ain't it?"

Meeting the visitor's cold flesh with his own, Meade replied, "Lieutenant General Grant, sir. Welcome to the Army of the Potomac."

Coffee?" Meade asked, prepared to call for an orderly.

Grant shook his head. "Best get down to business." His face was set, emotionless, the common jaw outlined by a close-cropped beard.

Meade gestured toward a camp chair. "Please."

Retaining his plain soldier's overcoat, Grant sat down. The coat filled the tent with odors of old tobacco and wet wool. It wanted laundering.

Meade remained standing, posture erect, though not to parade-ground extremes. He wished to appear respectful, but not pompous. It was such a damnably awkward situation.

"Sir, if I may?" he began. He had prepared his speech, a schoolboy facing chastisement and hoping to salvage his pride.

Slump-shouldered and inscrutable, the newly made general in chief gave a single nod.

"General Grant . . . I understand that you may wish to name your own man to command the Army of the Potomac. I should regret that, of course. I should regret it a great deal. But I do not believe that the feelings or ambitions of any officer can be allowed to stand in the way of . . . of our efforts to end this war. What I mean to say is . . . I will neither protest nor resist your decision, whatever it may be. There will be no politicking, no underhandedness. We've had enough of that." He breathed deeply, careful not to let it sound like a sigh, and forced himself to conclude. "The Union matters. I don't. You may count on my . . . comity. And my full support, sir."

Grant's pale eyes remained inhumanly steady, but he gestured toward the chair nearest where he sat. As if he, not Meade, were the host. Suppressing a cough, Meade obeyed. His throat felt raw and his calves itched. He truly did feel old.

The younger man, arbiter of his fate, drew a pair of cigars from his overcoat. He bit off the end of one and extended the other to Meade.

Why not? Meade decided. Damn the old lungs. And damn this weather. Damn all of Virginia.

Grant struck a match and lit his cigar, but let Meade light his own.

Just say it, Meade thought. Finish me off. The way you would a lame cavalry mount.

Grant sat back, puffing. The overcoat bunched around him, as graceless as a blanket. "Jealous of you in Mexico," he told Meade. "Staff engineer seemed a high and mighty creature. Envied you being in on things with Old Zach." A smile ghosted by. "Beat you at poker, though."

Their minds had run close, perhaps inevitably. Mexico was what they had in common. That and West Point. "I was just thinking that you remind me of General Taylor," Meade said.

Grant brightened. "I take that as a compliment." The Union's first lieutenant general shifted in his chair, as if he had his own itches to resist. "Wasn't just porch talk, Old Zach. Knew how to make men go, how to reach right into them." Assessing his cigar, not Meade, he continued: "Different business now."

Glad to take refuge in memories, Meade asked, "Do you

remember how it struck us when Major Ringgold died? How unbelievable it seemed? These days," he went on ruefully, "a major general's death would hardly be noticed." The cigar Grant had given him was of fine quality. He addressed it with care, determined not to fall into a coughing fit. "One thing I certainly envy General Taylor is the freedom he had. To do what needed to be done. Such liberty seems unimaginable now." Meade shook his head. "The bane of my command has been modern communications, the damned telegraph. And proximity to Washington. The amount of contradictory direction I receive daily all but paralyzes this army."

"That so?" Grant asked. His tone had become impersonal again. That voice was not unfriendly, but neither could Meade detect warmth in it.

Never a patient man, he decided to have his say. Grant could choose to listen to him or not.

"General Grant, if you want your commander of the Army of the Potomac to succeed, you must stand between him and Washington, all the damned busybodies. Just let him fight. This is a fine, fine army, a *fighting* army. I tell you, it's at the peak of its capabilities: nearly a hundred thousand men, spirited and ready. More, should the Ninth Corps join it. But it cannot be commanded and fought from Washington."

"Noted," Grant said.

"And I hope you'll permit my successor to execute the corps' reorganization. Oh, I know the arguments against it . . . too many divisions for one general to control, the unwieldiness. But the damnable thing is that I have only three capable corps commanders to offer my successor. Not four or five. And it's only three if Hancock's wound doesn't invalid him out again. He'll be back with the army any day, but the surgeons seem to have made a thorough mess of things."

"Win's a tough bird," Grant said. "Other two Warren and Sedgwick?"

"Yes, sir."

"Warren up to a fight?"

"Yes, sir."

Grant flipped the stub of his cigar onto the planks and crushed it with a boot heel: a raw man of the West, another breed. His lips suggested a smile, but none appeared. "Fine work at Gettysburg. Been waiting a while to tell you that. Ignore the committee. And the newspapers. Only difference between a reporter and a fifty-cent prostitute is that the latter has to be moderately presentable."

"Your Vicksburg campaign was remarkable, sir."

Accepting the tribute as fair, Grant nodded again. He rummaged deep in his overcoat and produced a leather wallet of fresh cigars. Meade had allowed the first smoke to go out. He declined the offer of a second.

"Be the death of me, these things," Grant said, lighting up anew. "Couldn't afford 'em back before the war. Now they send them to me by the crate." He took his time with the match, letting the flame approach his fingertips, seeking an even burn on the cigar. "Folks in Washington tell me Lee isn't much more than a reputation nowadays, that he has no spunk left."

Meade's hands balled into fists. "I know what's said. I've heard every word and whisper. But let me tell you something outright, General Grant: You're going to find Lee a formidable opponent. And his soldiers are tough nuts. Don't underestimate them."

"Tougher than ours?" Grant asked sharply.

Meade caught the testing tone. "No. Different. Wilder. They don't quit when you expect them to. We're better-drilled, better-equipped, morale's far better than Mr. Greeley would have it . . . but Lee's men keep coming at you like Florida cottonmouths." He gestured southward, across the Rapidan. "Of course, they're fighting for their homes. But it's more than that. They *like* to fight."

"We don't?"

"We fight . . . from a sense of duty. Oh, some men revel in it. Hancock. Barlow, this Harvard buck. Gibbon, Carroll. Young Upton. But you understand me, I think."

"You don't think Lee can be beaten?"

Meade stood up. Affronted. He had not said any such thing. It was suddenly a struggle to master his temper.

"Certainly, he can be beaten. He *has* been beaten. But this army needs to be allowed to fight him, and to fight him with every man and gun it has. It can't defeat him decisively if entire corps are stripped away in mid-campaign because some congressman heard a noise in his back garden. This army . . . you have no idea of the restrictions under which I've had to act. It's . . . it's . . ." The foulest language he knew almost escaped him. "Criminal."

Grant shrugged, a gesture tamed by the bulk of his overcoat. But he smiled truly at last. With brown teeth.

"You're lucky you didn't have to answer to Old Brains. Way I did before he came east. Told me everything but how to saddle my horse, and he was getting around to that." Grant, too, rose to his feet, compact and uninterested in the impression he made. "Talk me through those maps. Tell me what you'd do, if you had the run of things, with no interference."

The smoke in the tent burned Meade's lungs and throat, and he fought back another cough. But he was on firmer ground now. He knew the land, knew how to fight on it.

They labored at the maps for over an hour, talking of roads and fords, of rail lines and the supplies required by an army on the move, of food and fodder, artillery trains and the army's real strength available for duty. They spoke of officers who could be depended upon to fight, and of those who wanted watching or replacement. For a time, all other concerns receded as their profession gripped two old soldiers.

At last, Grant asked: "And your preferred course of action? When the roads dry out?"

"If Richmond's our objective—"

"Richmond won't be the objective," Grant cut him off. "Lee will be. I mean to break his army by this summer."

The man's confidence stopped Meade's breath. Recovering, he continued, "Lee's army will always shield Richmond. The way to get him to fight is to threaten Richmond."

"Go on," Grant said.

"I still favor the eastern axis. Cross at the fords above Fredericksburg and move south fast. Washington's covered, so you won't have to split off a corps or more to keep them feeling snug back along the Potomac. Supplies can be shifted along the coast as the army advances. Shorter lines of communications all around."

Grant kept his eyes on the map, and Meade could feel the man's gaze settle on Chancellorsville.

"Been tried," Grant said. "Hasn't worked."

"The army's never been properly *led* when it was tried." Meade undid the top button of his uniform. "Oh, why not say it? Burnside wasn't fit to command this army. We could've won at Fredericksburg, I was there. My division broke their line. All for nothing. You've never seen such a needless, senseless, damnable debacle. And Chancellorsville. Hooker froze like a hare cornered by a rattlesnake. We could've won at Chancellorsville, too. Even after Jackson embarrassed us. We *all* wanted to attack, all the real generals, to hit back hard. Even Dan Sickles was for attacking, God help us, and he was Hooker's creature through and through. Lord knows, we had the numbers. We could've destroyed Lee's army then and there, it was split in two and disorganized." He felt the need to cough, but growled instead. "And what did we do? We just quit. It was . . . it was despicable." Infuriated, Meade let his voice rise, abandoning his gentlemanly decorum. "This army's *never* been allowed to really fight by its commanders. Little Mac, Burnside, Hooker . . . damn the whole business to Hell. We've wasted *years*."

"It was allowed to fight at Gettysburg," Grant said.

Abandoning society manners, Meade spit into the tobacco fog. "They didn't have a damned choice. They were shitting themselves, imagining Stuart was going to ravish their women and cut their throats in the night. They were glad to give me free rein then. Oh, weren't they just? And look what it got me. The damned committee—you know I've got to report again tomorrow? I'm interrogated in public like a criminal." Furious now, he towered over Grant. "I tell you, if this war is lost, it'll be lost in Washington, not by this army. This is a *great* army. It just needs the politicians to let it *be* great." Abruptly, Meade sagged. "I've done the best I could."

"Sit down, General Meade," Grant ordered. The words were spoken calmly, but intently. When Meade, ruing his temper, had settled himself in his chair, the general in chief said, "You seem to be under a misapprehension."

Meade looked up and met those opaque eyes again.

"I'm sorry?"

"This business of you being relieved of command. I expect you to stay at your post."

"But . . . General Smith?"

"I'll find something for Baldy to do. Probably give him a corps. You and I are closer in line than Washington would have it. And, frankly, you know this army, it respects you. You're the only man who gave it a victory. More than one. Bristoe Station, that Rappahannock business . . ." He snorted. "We don't fit together right, I'll put you out to pasture. But I'd be a fool to do it now and start off on the wrong foot with every man in the Army of the Potomac." Relaxing now, Grant grinned. "Oh, my western boys would like to see a clean sweep of every officer east of the Appalachians, they're pissing fire. But you just stand your ground, and they'll calm down."

"I'm honored, sir. Positively honored." Meade caught himself. It didn't do to sound groveling, after all. But his relief was immeasurable, nearly of the extent he had felt on that last afternoon at Gettysburg. *He had not failed.* At least, not yet.

Grant stood up and stepped back to the maps. Meade didn't move. He sensed that Grant had more to say.

"As for me," the general in chief resumed, "I have no intention of being trapped, bagged up and skinned at a desk in Washington. My headquarters will be with your army. If you can't bear the thought of me looking over your shoulder, tell me now." Grant's eyes turned cold again. "I don't intend to count your bullets for you, or wipe your nose for you. I'll tell you where I want you to go and let you decide how to get there. I'll tell you when I want you to fight, but let you figure out how to do it. If that arrangement suits you, we can go forward."

"Yes, sir."

Grant cocked his head above the overcoat's collar, sizing up a horse he had just purchased. "Now take me around and introduce me to your staff, let them have a sniff. Early tomorrow, I'm going back to Washington, then back out west for a time to tidy things up." He forgot his cigar as he thought on distant matters. "I'll miss some of those men . . . good men, fine men . . ." He grunted. "Some of 'em I can't say I'll miss at all, though. Listen, you might as well ride along with me tomorrow. Since you've got that committee business. No sense taking separate trains like we're the emperor of France and the king of Prussia. And either call me 'Sam' or just plain 'Grant.' Way it was in Mexico. Doesn't do to make everything sound like a speech."

As the two generals stepped out into the rain, Meade said, "I'm afraid you'll find Virginia a forlorn place, Sam."

"Going to be a sight more forlorn when we're through with it," Grant told him.

March 11, 1864
Orange & Alexandria Railroad

As the train clacked along the rails, with Meade a few rows back working on his testimony, Grant turned his face from the staff men and the guards. Hidden behind the collar of his overcoat, he smiled through the window. The look on Meade's face yesterday! On a devilish whim, he had tossed his cigar butt on the planks, just to see how George Meade would react. The Philadelphia patrician's look had been priceless. Old Meade standing there in full uniform, bags under his eyes that could have held a peck of potatoes each . . .

Well, they'd get past the fussiness. Meade would be reminded soon enough that not every man born west of Pittsburgh picked his teeth with a knife.

Baldy Smith had, indeed, been in the running for command of the Army of the Potomac, but Meade had said all the right things and seemed to mean them. If his performance disappointed, he could be removed. Meanwhile, Meade would do as he was told and see to the details, leaving him free to run the wider war.

As for Lee, Grant rejected the notion that the man was invincible. Oh, they all had admired the dashing Lee in Mexico, where he was Scott's pet, but that had been a very different horse race. Grant intended to break Lee as soon as campaigning weather came to Virginia. All that was needed was to hit Lee good and hard, shockingly hard, and not let go of him. Just keep hitting him and hitting him. The South couldn't stand that for long.

If he could smash Lee's army and Sherman could take Atlanta, the war would end. As for the great and glorious Generals Butler, Banks, Sigel, and their ilk, if he had to keep them in command for election-year reasons, he would not let them jeopardize his purpose: The upcoming campaign in Virginia and Sherman's match with Joe Johnston down in Georgia would be the combination to kill the Confederacy. Everything else was free eggs.

As for Meade, the man had fight in him, but he was, in the end, an eastern general who believed that wars could be fought as they had been waged by the great captains of the past, with a battle followed by a pause that allowed the enemy's army to rest up. There was still too damned much Jomini in the East, all highfalutin angles marked on maps and too little grit or even common sense. Grant intended to bring this burgeoning colossus of an army to bear in one decisive campaign, no matter how long that campaign might last, and not let it rest until Lee was crushed. If George Meade needed prodding, he meant to provide it.

To his surprise, he had *liked* Meade, who was far from the bumbler malicious tongues implied. He remembered only scraps of the man from Mexico, but didn't recollect Meade as a bad fellow, just old before his time with all that eastern, old-blood gravity of demeanor. And Meade had struck the proper tone in their meeting: His selflessness felt genuine. As for any haughtiness, there'd been a good sight less in Meade than George Thomas displayed.

How he wished Cump Sherman were on hand, though! Cump would have loved the tale of the cigar butt.

A captain thrust his head into the cabin. The guards

tensed and gripped their weapons. It gave the railway officer a start.

"Anybody for Warrenton Station?"

A few additional officers had jumped a ride on the train.
Two shuffled forward, carrying dispatch bags. Grant returned his attention to the world beyond the car: the raw
morning, billows of steam, and burned-out ruins around
a muddy station yard. Ragged whites averted their eyes,
going about their business. With their darkies gone, they
looked lost.

That called to mind his father-in-law, in the fine house
in Missouri. He, too, would be lost without Negroes to do
for him. Grant's experience had been of a different kind,
working beside loaned slaves in his fields at Hardscrabble,
teased by other whites for his indulgence to them. But as
the darkies sweated at his side, Grant had grasped that
even a slave needed a reason to work for a hard-up white
man whose kin saw him as a failure.

Grant sighed. Plenty of soldiers stood guard at the junction, so many it seemed a waste. Fearful men in Washington had warned of partisan rangers, as if guerrillas might
swoop down and tuck the train in their saddlebags. Stanton himself had insisted that a company of infantry travel
with him. Grant had not resisted the gesture, but he was
sick to death of other men's fears.

With a great metal groan and shrieking wheels, the train
pulled northward again. In the soiled light, the landscape
appeared ravaged by a power greater than man: Scrub
growth encroached on desolate fields and most of the surviving houses were shacks. He might have been on another
continent, rather than a few hundred miles from the Ohio
Valley and fat farms of his childhood. Even his father's tan-
nery, whose gore had appalled him, seemed a lusty affair
compared to this wretchedness.

These people had wanted war, and they had gotten it.

As the train rattled over a bridge, the major in charge of the guard detail approached Grant.

"Your pardon, sir, but you might want to move from the window. Wouldn't want Mosby's men to get a shot at you. They've been playing Hell up the line."

Grant didn't move.

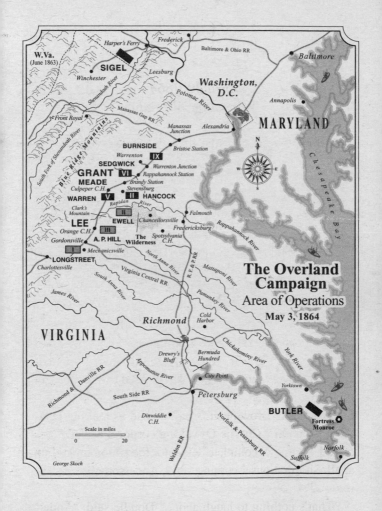

ONE

Lord in Heaven, Old Abe's a desperate man," Bill Wildermuth said. "Lifting Brownie up to be a sergeant. *This* army ain't scraping the bottom of the barrel, no, sir. We're reaching down *under* that barrel." He leaned over and gave Brown, his old workmate, a blow where a corporal's stripes still graced a sleeve. "Ain't that right, boys?"

Scattered on stumps and scavenged chairs set out in the wonderful sun, the old comrades drew their pipes from their mouths to offer up mock dismay at the coming promotion. Recruits new to the company smiled cautiously.

Apple blossoms feathered down around them. Promotion or not, Corporal Charles Brown told himself, the world went on, and the war went on, and one man no longer counted for very much. Yet, he was pleased by the prospect of adding a stripe.

"Promoting Brownie ain't half so bad as making Doudle a corporal," Charlie Oswald, a corporal himself, declared. "I predict complete defeat for the Union in no time at all. Short rations a-coming, boys, Andersonville's a-calling. . . ."

"That's nothing to laugh about," Doudle said. "Andersonville, I mean."

"But you do agree it's a grave . . . a grave and desperate measure . . . making you a corporal and Brownie there a sergeant," Wildermuth insisted. He cackled and tapped the ashes from his pipe. "I fear for the glorious Union, boys," he told the new recruits. "You'll be crying for your mothers, if they ain't crying for you. Between Brownie, Doudle, and U. S. Grant, it's a-going to be something."

A quiet man, solid as oak, Private Henry Hill startled them all. Not only by speaking, but by the force in his tone: "Nobody's 'making' Corporal Brown a sergeant. He made himself a sergeant. And you know it."

Hill meant well. He always did. But solemnity wasn't in season. A mood as fine as the afternoon—all green and gold and blue and free of rain—had captivated the men. The teasing continued amid the drifting blossoms.

Wildermuth stretched like a sun-warmed cat and turned back to the new faces. All of the gathered soldiers, green or veteran, had been canal boatmen back home. Except for Sammy Martz, the Pottsville blacksmith, who could not be deterred from joining their fellowship.

"Boys," Wildermuth resumed, "it's hard enough for a man to tell you four Eckerts apart. I mean, I don't know if you're brothers, cousins, uncles, or everything at once. Fellow gets to wondering what all goes on back home on Eckert Hill. Tell you this, though: Private Hill there might be the first sergeant's confessed and proven cousin, but him and Brownie got some relation they ain't admitting. Can't hardly separate 'em, can't hardly tell 'em apart. Same great big inky-head targets for the Johnnies, same jut-out jaws just a-begging for a fist." He stretched again, smiling as if he knew all and would soon tell all. "Only difference I see is that Henry there got black eyes fit for a gypsy gal. Which sets a man wondering in a new direction entirely."

Thrilled by spring, two birds swooped overhead. Delighted to have an audience still unwise, Wildermuth went on: "I figure it's all up with us now. Over and done. You new fellows joined up at a terrible time, just terrible. Before you know it, 'Sergeant' Brown's going to be running the company, if not the regiment. Then you look out! Yes, sir! General Burnside himself won't be able to save a man among you."

Surfeited, Brown spoke for himself at last: "Bill, if words were bullets, we could point you south and there wouldn't be one Reb left alive come Sunday. And First Sergeant Hill might have something to say about who runs the company."

"Not for long," Wildermuth said. "I hear they're going to make him a lieutenant any time now. And lieutenants never do nothing."

"He'd make a good officer," Doudle said. "What say, Henry? Pair of shoulder straps for Cousin Willie?"

Hill shrugged. His first loyalty, as all the veterans knew, was to the soon-to-be sergeant. Henry Hill and Charles Brown had not been close back home on the Schuylkill Canal, but war had bound them together in the odd way it had with men.

Sensing, as old soldiers do, that the call to form up was coming, Brown rose and said, "You Eckerts. You there, Martz. Line up, let me have a look at you. I'm not going to have you embarrassing this company."

The new men fumbled about, but got themselves into what passed for order. Brown was struck, yet again, by how young they appeared. There would be, at most, two or three years' difference between the survivors of old Company C and the new recruits they'd collected during their reenlistment furlough in February. Yet, the men who had left their barges and mule barns in '61, who had fought from Port Royal to Knoxville, looked a decade older to Brown's eyes.

He thought of his elder brother, dead of a simple sickness and buried at Vicksburg, above a river whose breadth stunned men bred on the humble Schuylkill. The regiment had moved from north to south to the west and back again, staking claims to strange earth with its dead. Now its flag drooped on a Virginia field. They had gone in a circle, blindfolded mules in a mill.

Flicking away a blossom that called to mind women and private things, Brown tightened the belt on one of the Eckert boys, asking, "You're William, right?"

"No, Corporal. I'm Johnny. That's William." Dutchie as could be, the new man pronounced the names as "Chonny" and "Villy-yam." The Eckerts were their own breed. In more than one way, folks said.

Brown grunted. Of the four Eckerts in the company now, the only one he could be sure of naming right was Isaac, who had been with them from the beginning. Standing off to the side, Isaac Eckert did not take a protective or helpful attitude toward his relatives, but let Brown straighten them out.

"I have a thing I must ask you, please, Corporal Brown," the next Eckert in line said. His accent was thick as lard on farmhouse bread.

"What's that?"

"Them Rebel girls, the ones in town there?" *Dem Reppel kirlz, ta˙wuns in tawn dare?* If Brown sometimes had trouble understanding the speech of Reb prisoners, he was sure the Johnnies wouldn't know what to make of the Eckert boys or the other Dutchmen in the 50th Pennsylvania.

"What about 'em?"

"They are all so *verdammt* mean? I try to make polite . . . but when I lifts my cap, *die kleine Hexe* looks like I am the snake and she wants for the hatchet."

"The ladies of Warrenton have seen their fill of Yankees," Brown told the boy. He thought about the matter for a moment. "You just do like I told you and stay away from those darkey gals who come around of evenings. Or you'll go home with something you won't be proud of."

Henry Hill spoke again. Twice in an afternoon was something of a milestone.

"First sergeant just stepped out of the captain's tent."

He spoke to Brown as if no one else were present.

"All right, then," Brown said to the new men, straining to remember his canal Dutch. "Try to look like soldiers out there. *Stramm und still, versteh'? Mach doch keine Schweinerei.* And keep a crimp in your knees, the way I told you. Any man passes out in front of Captain Burket, he'll have guard duty for a month. Let's go now. *Los geht's.*"

Company C of the 50th Pennsylvania Veteran Volunteer Infantry Regiment had not gone in for an excess of pomp of late, but the captain wanted to put martial spirit into the new recruits, to make them feel part of something big and important. So the day's two promotions, which otherwise would have been handled in five minutes by the first sergeant, would occur in front of a company formation.

Good day for it, anyway, Brown thought. It looked as though they might have a dry stretch. Virginia had put on her best green dress, decorated with pink and purple blossoms, thick with scents that put hopes in a man. This field of tents just north of Warrenton—a hard Rebel town, if ever a hard one there was—had almost a fairground atmosphere, crowded with men as thoughtless as bees in the warmth. Yet, every man who had a campaign behind him sensed that they would march to battle soon, knowing it the way veteran soldiers just knew, sensing that this fellow Grant was out to get an early start on the season, that General Burnside and their Ninth Corps were about to be swept along behind the Army of the Potomac. The veterans knew the awfulness of it, too, the pain and death that waited, yet good sense could not overcome their excitement at the prospect of marching forward, of heading southward one more time, of *doing* something. If war made men of boys, it could also make boys of men.

Charles Brown had long ago stopped trying to make sense of war. He had listened for years as his fellow

soldiers, his fellow canal men, complained endlessly
about army life, the folly of generals, the bad food and
poor equipment, the marches to nowhere. They claimed,
endlessly, that they'd give anything to go home, and to
Hell with the war. Nonetheless, the survivors of Company
C had reenlisted almost to a man. War was a woman you
hated but couldn't let go.

All of the high-flown purposes were gone now. There
was only the rough ache to win that they all shared, and
the being together like this, the queer feeling when faced
with death that even those who survived would never be
so completely alive again. Men learned to treasure the smell
of campfire coffee and a shared tobacco pouch. A soldier
repaired another fellow's boot and made a friend who
would die for him. If he lived—and Brown hoped to—he
knew he would never be able to explain it.

He had not chased promotions and looked down on those
who did. Yet, men had always turned to him for orders,
back on the canal and then at war. In barely twenty-three
years of life, he had been forced to lead in countless ways,
starting back when he was just a boy. So he did his part,
and a little more, and tried not to lament what he could
not change.

Thinking about the great, big things led nowhere. The
regiment had been camped right here in 1862, below the
defiant town up on the hill. Now they were back again. And
what difference had all the bleeding and dying made? The
young darkies who had not run off expected less these days,
although they still flattered, begged, cajoled, and stole,
while the older Negroes just kept at their doings. You saw
them leaving their shanties in the dawn, shuffling up to the
fine brick houses to start the stoves and fireplaces, just as
they had been doing all their lives. As for the white women
of the sort who had startled that Eckert boy, their once fine
dresses were faded now, but they carried themselves as high

and mighty as ever. If anything, they'd grown haughtier. Except for the destruction and the slaughter, Brown was not sure that very much had changed. Or ever would.

It had been jarring to go home for a month. It was good, because it was home, but unsettling because home had changed. After Knoxville, the regiment had endured its worst experience of the war, not a battle but a winter march through the mountains into Kentucky. Knoxville had been a horror of wicked cold and savage fighting with frozen hands and feet, but the worst came afterward, when the regiment, shy of winter garments and shoes, had been issued nothing but uncured hides in which to wrap their feet for a march of two hundred miles. The footwear they stitched and tied together had hardly lasted a day, and the regiment had left bloody tracks on the snow. Had the men of Company C not reenlisted the autumn before, the number who would have signed on again might have been a sight lower after that march.

But ordeals end for the lucky men who survive them. They had been fitted out again, then carried home in railroad cars. After the ravaged Southland, it was a shock to see the prosperity of the North. When their train pulled into Schuylkill Haven, the men were amazed at the furious work behind the *Turnverein* band and the hollering families. Boats and barges jammed the canal basin, all but blocking the channel, and new construction had risen wherever there was dry land along the river. The rail yards, sprawling over the Flats, seemed greater now than those of a Southern city. In many ways, the war had been good to the town at the bends of the Schuylkill, with the Navy's hunger for anthracite coal and industries begging for it. Schuylkill Haven was the point where the coal region ended and barges were filled for the trip to Philadelphia. It had always seemed a busy place, but never frenzied like this.

There was money for those who had not gone to war.

But there was a price, too. There were more rough-mannered Irishmen now, taking over the shacks on the Eck, where Brown had passed a brief and broken childhood. Louts in packs roamed Dock Street in the evenings, and sullen women in shawls cursed at Dutch grocers. The new men on the canal were surly, anticipating accusations that they belonged in uniform themselves. Unasked, they loudly damned the war and the nigger, in brogues as foreign as their red and ready faces, willing to fight in any saloon, but not on a field of battle. It grated on Brown to see the lack of care they took with the boats and their even worse care of the mules. It bothered him more than it had a right to do to see busy towpaths left in disrepair and the brass fittings at the harbormaster's station left unpolished. When Captain Burket had been harbormaster before the war, each last buckle on a mule's belly had shone. Now it felt as though nothing mattered but making money today, tomorrow be damned. The town was home, and it wasn't.

Yet, for all the rawness and brute collisions between the Dutch and Irish, home still had a decency Brown missed in the South. Here, in Virginia, there were great houses and shanties, with little between them. In Schuylkill Haven there wasn't one building as grand as the plantation house down the field or the mansions behind the courthouse on Warrenton Hill. Back home, men lived in a world more evened out, with due respect given but no sense that one fellow was a king and his neighbors dirt. They were different worlds, North and South, and Brown wondered, as he had often done, if they belonged together.

On the last fair day back home—kind weather for early March—he and Frances had fled her family for the orchard west of the river, seeking an hour of privacy amid trees months shy of flowering, and he had felt they understood each other. He was good enough with words with other men, but women wanted something more, and he was not sure that he possessed that something. Frances didn't seem to mind. She just smiled. Her presence beside him on that bright day had been thoroughly, wonderfully good. He had wanted, terribly, to ask her to marry him then. But he held back. The war had made widows enough. Nor did he want her to be a cripple's nurse. He would ask when the war was over, if he returned a whole man. It was the only decent course he saw. And if Charles Brown no longer believed in high and mighty causes, he had come to believe in decency all the more.

For now, he labored over letters to her, conscious of his defective spelling and wishing, for her sake, that he had more education. Most of what he had learned he had taught himself, at the cost of candles sold three for a penny, the sort that smoked and stank. He had been sent out, a small boy, to work in a tobacco factory for twenty-five cents a week, by a miserly father afraid to end up in an almshouse. The Lord's own joke, his father had died of cholera, without telling even his wife where he hid his money.

Laboring at the stacks and racks had been hateful work, its only lasting effect his dislike for tobacco. He had grown strong early and, at thirteen, went to work on the canal, driving mules and caring for them, doing the chores the regular boatmen avoided. He didn't mind. The air was fresh, and as for the mules, they were never worse than men and often better.

Hardly had he moved up to a man's job aboard a coal barge when he did a foolish, foolish thing that the men around him misunderstood as bravery. The doing had been no more than the act of an ignorant boy who might have gotten a bullet or worse for his trouble.

He had been present at the last, feeble gasp of the Schuylkill Rangers, the canal pirates who came down from the mountain hollows to steal for their livelihoods. Everyone had believed them to be finished off years back, part of the local history and no more, but a few broken-toothed young fools had attempted to rob a coal barge Brown was aboard. They were not far from Port Clinton when the fuss began, with a shot fired in the air and cries that this was a robbery. The would-be-brazen voices quivered with fear, though, as if a game had gotten out of hand. The pirates were such novices that they didn't know that a coal barge headed south to Philadelphia offered nothing practical to steal: The prizes were on the goods boats pulling northward.

The Rangers fired their only gun at the outset, shooting into the air, and the shot failed to frighten the bargemen or even the mule boys. The fighting didn't last long, but Brown plunged into the brawl with a young man's fury. The result was that he killed a man—a boy, really—with a shovel blade brought down on the fellow's skull.

He worried that he might be charged with murder, but the constable and the justice of the peace hailed the deed as a good one. The dead lad was criminal filth, not worth a thought. His accomplices were hardly worth pursuing, although they would be taken in good time. The constable expected that the thieves had learned their lesson, but the law was the law and the county would see to matters. Annoyed at the interruption of his sleep, the frock-coated lawman raised his lantern a last time and shook his head.

Staring down at the corpse stowed on the deck, Evans the justice told the bargemen, "Look you, boys, I'll not waste public money. Put him in a hole, if so you're minded, but throw him in the river if you're not. And be it a warning."

That was when Brown did the foolish thing.

By first light, he inspected the fellow he'd killed, bewildered by the gash in the skull, the jagged bone, and the drying slop of brains, the blood like set molasses. A dead man was as dead as a dead mule. But there was a difference, too. He saw what he had to do without true thinking.

Everyone knew where the folk who had spawned the Rangers hid. They crawled about the north folds of First Mountain and were said to have bred among themselves at a speed of two generations to one in the valley. An unholy mix of Dutchmen shunned by their brethren and lawless Scotchmen who'd wandered in and stayed, they were hardly considered human by the citizenry. Borrowing a mule, Brown roped up the body and led the beast into the hollows up behind Port Clinton, asking as he went for the dead lad's family.

No men appeared, but more than one woman warned him to go home and let things be.

It took most of the day to discover the right trail. It led up a steep ravine where the world ran queer. In time, he smelled fires, but not proper cooking smells. Then all grew quiet, as if the birds and animals had run off to join the men fearful of the law.

Materializing from thickets, a pack of slatternly women and girls closed off the path behind him. He had not had the least sense of their presence.

They didn't say a word, but there was something not right about them. Their faces were numb, their features daubed with soot as if on purpose. More than a few were simple-looking, while others were sharp-boned and spook-eyed, the sort who practiced the rites in the Fifth Book of Moses.

They looked Brown over, then, after shooing the flies, applied their claws to the corpse. Brown had wrapped the dead youth's wound in rags to keep the brains in. As the women untied the body from the mule's back, the cloth fell away. Brown gagged at what spilled on the trail.

The women gave no hint of sorrow. There was no weeping or even one cry of grief. They just dragged off the body. As if this were a common task in their world.

A filthy girl big with child turned back to Brown. "Go

on with you now," she said. The hatred in her eyes wasn't just for him, but for all living things. "I told him he were a fool. Men do na listen."

She spat a gob and followed the other women.

The men who thought he had done a brave thing did not understand that he had not had a choice. And bravery was about choices.

A fusillade of orders slew his memories. Corporal Brown was about to become Sergeant Charles E. Brown. He had not had a choice in that matter, either.

Stevensburg, Virginia

Francis Channing Barlow threw his saber on his cot. "It's unspeakable," he said. "Simply damnable. I don't see why Gibbon can have a man shot, but I can't."

Hancock listened in exasperation. The twenty-nine-year-old brigadier general not only looked like a boy, but sounded like one at the moment. Yet, Barlow was the most aggressive division commander in Hancock's corps, a born killer.

"This isn't the time to be shooting our own men," Hancock said. "Anyway, the president disapproves. It's an election year. 'Clemency' is the watchword of the day."

"I shouldn't think it's his business," Barlow pouted. "Rainey's a repeat deserter, yellow as butter. Condemned by a proper court-martial. This 'mercy' is a damned insult to every man who does his duty properly." He snarled, showing crooked teeth. "How on earth can Lincoln pardon the shirkers? Then send good men to die?"

Hancock raised his hand. It was a warning: *Enough is enough.*

"Forget the president, then," he told his subordinate. "*I* say you're not going to shoot anybody. Frank, I can't have you breaking down morale when we're going to march any day now."

Barlow perked up. "Heard something, sir?"

Hancock shrugged. The movement awakened the pain in his thigh and he winced. His Gettysburg wound had ambushed him again.

He mastered himself. "Same as you, same as everybody," he told the brigadier. "Everything and nothing. But Humphreys has the staff working late at night. Weather's good, roads are dry . . ."

Barlow sniffed. "Anything's better than this endless parading."

Hancock smiled. "I thought you seemed rather proud at the corps review."

"Proud of my *men,*" Barlow said quickly.

"The men you want to shoot? Frank, listen to me. Your men respect you. They respect the Hell out of you. They'll follow you and fight for you and, damn it, they'll die for you. The veterans who know you think you're the bravest man on earth. But they don't *like* you."

"I don't care whether they like me. I want them afraid of me. You know what Frederick the Great said."

Exasperated anew, Hancock sharpened his tone. "Yes, Barlow, I know what Frederick said. But you're *not* Frederick the Great, and this isn't the Prussian army. They're volunteers, Frank. Citizens. 'United States of America.' Remember?"

"If I could just shoot Rainey, as an example . . ."

Hancock rolled his eyes. He yearned to dress down the young brigadier, to pour fire and brimstone into one of Barlow's ears and watch it flame out the other. But, he reminded himself, it was better to have division commanders who had to be reined in than generals who were afraid to apply the spurs.

"If you want to shoot some poor bastard for cowardice after the next battle, we'll see about it then. But right now you're not shooting anybody who isn't wearing a gray uniform. For Christ's sake, man, you've got the biggest and best-disciplined division in this army. And the lowest desertion rate. Ease up. There'll be killing enough, soon enough."

Praised, Barlow changed his tone: "Do you believe Grant will fight, sir? Really fight, I mean? After Lee gets a piece of him?"

"Mind if I sit down?"

"No, sir. Of course not." Barlow gestured at the tent's sole camp chair. "Mother would chastise me for my lack of manners."

Hancock lowered himself, carefully, into the seat. The damned leg hurt like Hell. Barlow, too, had been wounded at Gettysburg, even more severely. But the younger man didn't show it. Frank Barlow had been badly shot up at Antietam as well, after his regiment's charge saved the day at Bloody Lane. Yet, he couldn't wait to get back in the thick of it.

Ah, youth, Hancock thought, feeling the burden of his forty years.

"I'm told your mother was quite the belle in her day," the corps commander said. It was a relief to escape the subject of executions.

Barlow displayed his lopsided, snaggletoothed smile. It made his long face seem longer. "She still is. Mother's quite fine, you know."

"I'll have to meet her one day." Hancock cleared his throat. "And the other Mrs. Barlow? I hear she's a splendid nurse, your wife. I trust she's well?"

"She's fine, thank you, sir. Marvelous, in fact. She's quite a brave girl."

"My regards, when next you write."

Mrs. Francis Channing Barlow might, indeed, be brave, Hancock thought, but she was hardly a girl. He had been bewildered upon meeting the woman during one of her camp visits. She had to be a decade Frank Barlow's senior. Side by side, they looked more like mother and son than husband and wife. Odd match, strange. You'd think a young man, a fighter . . .

You never knew about men and women, Hancock warned himself. And probably best not to know. He'd been damned lucky himself. Almira. Born to be a soldier's wife, that one.

"But back to Grant," Barlow said, moving his sword and settling his rump on the cot. For a slender man, the young brigadier was broad-hipped. "He hardly seems the conquering hero sort. At the review, he looked like a vagabond."

Hancock eased his posture, wondering if the butchers really had gotten the last metal out of his thigh. At inconvenient moments, pain shot to his skull.

"Don't judge Grant by appearances," Hancock said. "Christ, if people judged generals by appearances, *you'd* be back in a Harvard dormitory, conjugating Latin and fucking your mattress. Grant will fight." He grunted to mask another stab of pain. "And I'll tell you *why* he'll fight. He's the opposite of Georgie McClellan, in all his grandeur. Grant has nothing to lose. He'd already lost all he had before the war . . . reputation, commission, livelihood . . . everything but his wife. She sticks to him like a carbuncle. And now he's playing for once-in-a-lifetime stakes, with other people's money. Or their blood. And that man loves every minute of it, if I'm any judge."

Hancock massaged his thigh, the swollen meat of it. "Grant may look untidy, but he's a tough sonofabitch. Only knows how to go forward. Because he remembers what's behind him and doesn't much like the thought of it catching up. Problem won't be getting Grant to fight, but getting him to stop when it makes sense to. George Meade's going to age ten years before the summer's out." The corps commander lifted his hand to his face, as if the pain had moved there. Hurting or not, he chuckled. "Maybe we all will. Sam Grant and old Marse Robert are going to come as a shock to one another."

Barlow had lowered his gaze, but Hancock could read him: Frank Barlow was thinking about the upcoming fighting the way a glutton pondered a heaping plate. Barlow was an odd bugger: number one in his class at Harvard and pals with all the great brains of New England, a lanky, slump-shouldered gent who appeared eternally bored, with eyes that looked as if he were always drowsy. But let him hear the sound of the guns, and he'd light up like a battery of rockets.

War drew out unexpected talents in men, or so they said. Hancock suspected it was less a matter of talent than of brilliant, burning insanity. Killing well was the darkest form of genius. And, God help them all, the greatest of earthly thrills.

He often wondered what he would do when the war was done. Even the Army wouldn't be the same. And Barlow: Could *he* go back to the settled life of a fine society lawyer?

"Well"—Hancock picked up the thread again—"soon enough we'll be headed to Hell or Richmond." He grinned. "And Frederick the Great won't help us, I'm afraid."

"No, actually, he won't," Barlow sniffed. "It's been idiocy to resurrect his tactics." The younger man's condescending tone made Hancock want to slap him. "His approach to discipline made perfect sense, but consider those famed oblique attacks of his: The way our generals and Lee's bunch have been struggling with his method is simply ridiculous. It only worked for Frederick because the range of the weapons was minimal. With modern, rifled arms, the oblique attack with infantry in line only begs for slaughter. It's plain mathematics." He held up his hands, then slowly brought them together. "It's all about contracting the deadly space and limiting our exposure." Clapping his hands shut, Barlow concluded, "*You* must see that."

Hancock told himself that he'd give the notion some thought when he found the time. But the candle had already flared: This blue-blood Harvard shit-ass was dead right. And it grated on a West Point man who'd served a hard apprenticeship. Eventually, Barlow managed to grate on everybody.

Yet, Hancock could not help himself. He had to show that he, too, had an intellect.

"Plodding through Carlyle, Frank?" Hancock had never read a page of Carlyle in his life, but had heard that the fellow was publishing volume after tedious volume about Frederick the Great.

"Oh, no," Barlow said. "I mean, I had my London bookseller send the available volumes. But Carlyle's insufferable."

Hancock raised his hand again: *Stop.* "We'll have to take that up another time. I do have a corps to command." He hoisted himself—painfully—from the chair. It nearly tipped over. He really did have to take more care of his weight. The flesh and the spirit were constantly at war.

Barlow leapt to help him. A glare from Hancock put a stop to that.

"By the way," the older man said, "General Meade sends his regards. He was quite impressed by your men at the review. Miles' brigade in particular."

Barlow's expression darkened and Hancock grasped his mistake. By singling out one of Barlow's brigades for praise, even at a remove, he had just made the next several days pure Hell for Barlow's other subordinates. Barlow's interpretation would be that if Miles alone had been complimented, the rest must have been deficient.

Good Christ, Hancock told himself, going into battle will be a relief for the poor bastards. He took up his hat and riding gloves, anxious to escape. Barlow was best taken in small doses.

"Oh," he said, "I almost forgot. George Meade sent his regards to each of your other brigade commanders, as well. He said that Miles set the standard and, by God, the others matched it to a man."

Barlow brightened a shade, but suspicion lurked in those hooded eyes of his.

"Good," the younger man said. "That's good. My thanks to the general."

Hancock settled his hat on his head and slapped his gloves in his left hand. "I'll pass that on. Meanwhile, Frank, try not to shoot anybody."

Barlow watched his corps commander walk toward his mount. Hancock tried to hide his limp, but gave himself away at every fourth step. That worried Frank Barlow. He didn't want his corps commander invalided out. Hancock was the man under whom he meant to serve until the final shot. Or until the stupidity of his peers drove him to resign. Suffering and death were to be expected, but incompetence merited hanging, in Barlow's view. The general mediocrity appalled him.

The Freedmen's Bureau position remained a temptation. "Helping darkies out of the darkness," as poor Bob Shaw once put it. Arabella didn't believe he'd quit—she laughed and said he'd miss the war too much—but there were days when he had a mind to surprise her.

Whatever happened, he was damned well never going to serve under a horse's ass like Howard again. And God save him from more German troops than his division had at present. Deplorable as soldiers, execrable as men, they were bound to dilute the good native stock of the country.

The Irish were beastly, too, but the bastards fought.

Yet, even as he swore to himself, he felt the old twinge return: not pain from his wounds, but the deep, unspoken, unspeakable knowledge that it hadn't been Howard or the Germans who had blundered that day at Gettysburg, but him.

Never show doubt, he reminded himself. And never let another man witness your pain. His own wounds ached more often than not, and a lingering toothache pushed him halfway to madness. But nobody knew how bad it was, even Bella.

He was going to punish the Confederates for what they had done to him at Gettysburg. They were going to pay and pay. He intended to grind their misery into their snouts.

Barlow watched Hancock's bulky figure grow smaller: The corps commander rode more carefully now. But if Hancock was in pain, Barlow knew some others who were going to feel pain soon enough. Hancock hadn't fooled him one least bit. He'd let the cat out of the bag, and it wouldn't be coaxed back in. Meade obviously had been displeased with the appearance and marching of the brigades of Smyth, Frank, and Brooke. And Frank, a worthless Teuton, had no business leading a brigade in any case. Nor was Smyth all he should be, although he and his Hibernians did show spunk. Even Brooke could stand to improve his performance. If orders to march did not arrive first, the division was going to have an early morning. And the world would see who could march in step and who couldn't.

He considered calling for his provost marshal to discuss the disposition of Private Rainey, but stepped back into his tent for a moment alone. Carlyle? He didn't believe Hancock had ever cut the first pages of one of his books.

They all made so much of his standing at the top of the

Harvard class of '55, but had no idea how utterly worthless his education had been. Barlow smirked. Nor did they know what jackasses most of his classmates were, destined for safe Unitarian livings or privileged positions amid family fortunes. He had been amazed at the naivety—not just on the part of the students, but the professors as well. He had arrived at Harvard Yard with rather more knowledge of the world than even the two sorry whore-chasers in his class. What were their names? Couldn't even remember, they were inconsequential men. Probably safe at home after purchasing substitutes, or off on grand tours that would last through the end of the war. Collecting art in Paris and syphilis in Rome.

He had Brook Farm to thank for his own knowledge, tawdry but useful. *The Blithedale Romance* did not half capture the farce he'd been subjected to as a boy. All the sententious idealism and the grave communal sanctimony had collapsed into a swamp of petty jealousies and recriminations over who was to do the laundry. And his beautiful mother had been in the thick of it, not for the better. Even a lad still missing teeth could tell the arrangements were cockeyed. And yet . . . there had been lovely days before the mood turned vicious, and idyllic memories intertwined with embarrassments that came later. Before he was ten, he not only had learned the practical things that eluded his Harvard classmates, but knew how it felt to be expelled from Eden.

And thanks to his mother's vapid and wan admirers, he'd had quite enough of "the life of the mind" to last him for eternity. Now he took pains to conceal the extent of his reading from those around him: It had been an indiscretion to blather about Frederick to Hancock, who was just a marvelous blue bull turned loose in the Rebel china shop. Barlow despised men who lived in books, the august figures of his New England childhood, who said much and did so little of any consequence.

Was there anything more disgusting, more useless, than a man devoted to fondling his own intellect? A man had to *act*. Even Emerson had become too much to endure, an "uncle" who once had seemed a beacon of brilliance. His self-adoring nonsense struck Barlow as morbid now. Emerson could plead all he wanted, but he would never return to New England. Manhattan might be sordid, but it had *life*.

Damn the black-clad gentlemen his mother had needed to please after his father went mad and ran away from his wife and three young boys! The shame of certain things she had done, the beggarly things to which he had seen her stoop, would rankle him until his dying day.

If Boston's self-congratulation had become odious, he had not found a home in uniform, either. Having turned his back on those who spoke *ad infinitum* without acting, he now found himself among active men incapable of speech. He never had a proper conversation. Except with Arabella, when she visited.

His smirk was his armor; he wore it as his custom. He found the human species absurdly limited. No doubt that rogue of an Englishman was right and they were all descended from apes. Although the proposition seemed hard on the monkeys.

He sat down in the camp chair Hancock's bulk had threatened to crumple. About to call for his orderly to help him with his boots, he decided that he preferred to extend his solitude. Carefully, he worked the boots off himself and felt, simultaneously, the relief of cool air on his damp wool stockings and the attack of the infernal itching that wouldn't leave him.

Rolling off the stockings, he examined the peeling,

flaking skin that led down to his toes. It was a wretched business. He'd seen doctors. Their succession of salves seemed to help for a time, as did the salt baths mixed like alchemist's potions. But the damnable itch always, always returned. One ass of a doctor in New York had prescribed a summer at Newport, where Barlow could go barefoot and bathe his feet in the sea each morning and evening.

Barlow did not doubt that his feet would get wet as the weather warmed. But it was going to be from the mud of Virginia's swamps, not the great salt ocean.

"Orderly!" he bellowed. *"Orderly!"*

The man appeared at the double-quick. He was new at the work, a replacement, and wonderfully terrified.

"Bring me a bucket of water."

"Hot water, sir?"

"Cold."

"Yes, sir."

The corporal eyed Barlow's exposed feet, and Barlow caught it.

"Sir . . . if you don't mind my saying . . ."

"I *do* mind, Corporal."

"Yes, sir."

Barlow believed that Hancock had it wrong. Whether or not this was the Prussian army—and it damned well wasn't, more's the pity—he believed that Frederick had been absolutely correct that the men should fear their officers more than the enemy. Look at the rabble they were putting in uniform these days. Oh, the old veterans were fine. He still loved to visit the men of the 61st, his first real regiment, down in Miles' brigade. But the drafted lot, and the Irish, the bounty-jumpers. They hadn't the mettle. The gaps in his division had been filled with the scum of the earth, he didn't see how a sane person could deny it, and the only way to get such men to face the bayonets to their front was to place even sharper bayonets at their backs. And the only thing worse than a cowardly soldier was a cowardly officer.

Barlow had never quite understood the importance men attached to their puny lives. Certainly, he preferred life to death. That was ordained. But evaluated by a man of sense, life wasn't to be taken all that seriously. As far as commodities went, human lives sold cheap. The politicians could spout their praises of the common citizen, but many a man wasn't worth the food he stuffed in his maw at dinner.

He just could not understand the fear men felt on the verge of battle or in its midst. There was nothing on earth more exhilarating. Certainly, it was an incalculably greater thrill than intimate association with a woman, an enterprise much overpraised by poets. Of the many causes for his appreciation of his wife, not least was Arabella's sense of proportion.

The orderly returned, announcing himself before entering the tent. The bucket the man carried was sloshing full.

"Your pardon, sir, but Colonel Miles is trotting up the way."

"Put down the bucket. Outside, put it outside, man. And come back here."

"Yes, sir."

Sentenced to suffer, Barlow drew on his stockings again.

The corporal stepped back under the canvas. He looked at Barlow's now clad feet. Doubtfully.

"Don't stare, you ass." He could hear Miles clopping up. "Help me with my boots."

"Yes, sir."

"Move."

The man moved. He was deathly afraid. That was good.

Fully clad below the waist again, Barlow stood and said, "Now get out of here."

His feet burned, damn them. He dreaded the coming summer.

And yet, he relished the suffering, too, and knew he did. He took a fierce pride in treating hardships casually, in living rough, in enduring more than the Irish toughs and the muscle-clad farm-boys still not dead of dysentery. In winter, he wore an overcoat only when the cold became truly unbearable, a rare thing in Virginia. He intended to be more spartan than the Spartans, more stoic than the Stoics. He relished humbling other men with their weaknesses.

Barlow stepped outside as Miles dismounted. They had served together, on and off, since the Peninsula. If there was any officer Barlow trusted, it was Nelson Miles.

"Well, Nellie!" he said. "You look like a damned Red Indian. Careful of that Virginia sun, old man." Feet be damned, he was happy to see Miles. The fellow was not just a fighter, but almost had a brain.

"Drilling," Miles told him. "Have to put the new men through their paces. Your skirmishing evolutions."

"Meade sent down a compliment for you. Regarding the review. He thought your brigade looked splendid. Now come into the tent, for God's sake. I could bear losing you to a bullet, but not to sunburn. What's on your mind? Drink?"

"Just water. For now, sir."

As Barlow poured from a pitcher, Miles looked about. "I see the new saber arrived."

"Here. At least the well water's decent in this godforsaken place. Nice blade. Good and heavy. Whack a coward with the flat of that one, and he'll think twice. Sit down, sit down. Hancock was just here. Not sure his leg's all it should be."

"Any news?" Miles took the camp chair, weary and forgetful of decorum. Barlow let it go.

"He thinks we'll get marching orders any day now."

Miles looked around. As if he could see through the canvas. "Shame to waste this good weather. Rather fight now, before the heat sets in. Listen, Frank"—in private, they were "Frank" and "Nelson" or, when Barlow was in the spirit, "Nellie"—"maybe you should address the men. I know you don't go in for that sort of thing . . . but all of the other division commanders are doing it. They're hollering up a storm fit for shouting Methodists: 'God bless the sacred Union . . . our holy cause triumphant . . . damnation to the Confederacy . . .' You know the sort of thing. The men expect it."

Barlow's grimace took his jaw a good inch out of alignment. "If I'd wanted to preach from a pulpit, I would have pursued a different vocation." He thought of Coriolanus, the much maligned. "All the men need to hear from me is 'Fix bayonets!' and 'Charge!' And, really, only you and the other brigade commanders need to hear that much. The men need clear orders, not rhetoric."

Barlow abhorred and dreaded public speaking. Even as a lawyer, he had preferred settling things in chambers. Fighting a battle was easy compared to addressing a throng. He had sat through enough pandering lectures in churches, parlors, assembly halls, and classrooms to know exactly what speeches were worth, and what a shabby thing it was to plead for the mob's approval.

"Frank"—Miles tried again—"you've got the old Third Corps men disgruntled that they've been resubordinated to Second Corps. And everyone's grumbling—company commanders included—about your order to strip the men's packs of everything not on your list. At least show them you're human."

"They've been loading themselves like donkeys. Lighten the packs, and we'll have fewer stragglers. I want men on the firing line, not lining the damned roads and playing possum." He folded his arms. "The Johnnies don't carry gewgaws into battle. That's why they move so fast while we bump along."

"Oh, Christ, Frank! It's as if you're *determined* to make them hate you. And they want to like you, they really do. The veterans understand what you're after, and they tell the new men what's what." Miles leaned toward him. "They do look up to you, you know. But soldiers want to like their commanders, too."

"I don't need them to like me," Barlow said. "I just need them to fight."

TWO

May 4, late morning
Gordonsville, Virginia

Colonel William C. Oates watched the two sergeants fight. Although he wasn't a gambling man, he did like a good match. Didn't mind taking part in one, either. He'd have to rely on brawn, though, if it came to fisticuffs. He wasn't going to do much dancing around with his shot-through hip. He could move just fine again, no need of crutches, and could even run when the spirit was upon him. But he wasn't fit for a quickstep anymore, whether with a belle or knuckles up.

As each blow landed, the onlookers yipped and yowled, hollering out encouragement to the sergeant they preferred. It was quite a go-to, scattering sweat and blood. Under a blue sky clean enough for churchgoing. Or for sweet-saying a woman, a matter of fond recall. Here and now, the ladies weren't for touching. And he wasn't about to risk what health he had with one of the mammies who came around selling fried chicken. Nothing here to occupy a man but the infernal wait for the Yankees, the wondering over what the next days would deliver. At the hospital pavilions behind the rail stop, idle surgeons lurked like vultures atop a fence: The sick, of which there always was aplenty, weren't much pleasure for a sawing doc.

They wouldn't have to wait long to bloody their aprons. Oates felt it. The Federals would come splashing across that river, hell-bent on getting to Richmond this time, and the fighting would be a sight worse than this brawl.

The match had been set up to settle some paltry grievance, with his permission as the regiment's colonel of some duration, a tenure interrupted only by the annoyance of a wound. Law had sought to make him a brigadier, but Longstreet put Law under arrest—out of shame and malice—so none of Evander Law's favorites was going to see higher rank for a good, long time. As for Longstreet, Oates had turned against him hard after Tennessee, when he struggled back to the regiment in March and found it run-down as a poor-white's hogpen, fewer than four hundred men present and a passel of the best left dead at Knoxville. The living had been half-frozen and hungry enough to eat dirt. Old Pete had made a mess of things and, instead of facing his failure like a man, had tried to relieve or arrest his division commanders and any unlucky colonels who caught his eye, shifting the blame like a tramp caught stealing a pie.

Longstreet hated Law's Alabama Brigade, he'd tried to leave it rotting in Tennessee. But Lee had thought better of things. Longstreet's revenge, when the Alabamans returned to his command, was to place his own man, Colonel Perry, over the brigade while Law stood aside under charges. Oates' willingness to serve as his old brigade commander's attorney, if it came to a trial, had been the worst of treasons in Longstreet's eyes.

The army was worse than the red-clay politics back in Alabama. He would have liked to have Old Pete right here in this ring of soldiers. Then they'd see which one was the proper man.

The fight turned sluggish and cruel. Both of the Company I sergeants, Jimmy Ball and Clarence Morgan, were wearing down, painted with blood and welts. For years, the two had been the best of friends. But something had happened out there in Tennessee, something neither of them cared to speak to. Now they were fit to kill each other. Oates watched the proceedings with a sharpened eye: He was going to need both men. Hell, he was going to need every man, halt, lame, or blind. The return of wounded veterans had brought the 15th's roster back above four hundred men, but that wasn't even half the authorized strength.

If Old Pete were to ride up, Oates knew, he'd lose his command for letting the fight go ahead. But Alabama men had their own way of settling matters, and they didn't need some jackass fool of a West Point martinet to come around to judge the quick and the dead.

Oates took in the downright glee on the faces of the men watching the fight. For these few carved-out minutes of manly violence, they had forgotten their troubles, their old complaints, and their own long-standing grudges, captivated by bloodshed not their own. Out of all the beasts in the fields and all the birds in the air, a man was the strangest creature: When the fight was done—and he meant to end it soon—these men would be all kindness to victor and vanquished alike.

He wished he had been at Knoxville with them and not a pampered guest in a plantation house. Nothing against Colonel Toney and his family, who had treated him like a son and nursed his wounds. The gentlemanly old fellow had anticipated each of a young man's needs and had even sent a gal around on the quiet, warm skin shining like saddle leather. But no loin-quickening memory could free him from the ghosts of the men who had died during his absence: Frank Park, John McLeod . . . so many of the first volunteers from southeast Alabama, men with whom he had shared many a misery. It wasn't as bad as Gettysburg, where he'd lost his brother John to those Maine sonsofbitches, but it came near.

Ball landed a blow that sent Morgan reeling. Big for his

kind, the Welshman didn't go down, but staggered. To the
extent he could maintain a direction for his unwilling feet
to follow, Morgan aimed back toward Ball. The two sergeants were mean-fighting men, Hell on the Yankees. Oates
needed them to save some meanness up.

"That's enough," he barked, stepping into the circle of
ragged uniforms. "Fight's over, hear?"

He and Ball made eye contact. Ball had heard him all
right. But the sergeant turned back to his opponent, who
was struggling to hold up his fists. Ball thrust a straight-
armed punch at Morgan's jaw.

The Welshman went down.

Oates strode up to the sergeant. Just as the victor turned
his way again, Oates let go a widow-maker that put Ball
down beside the man he'd bested.

"You ever disobey an order of mine again," he told the
unconscious figure, "you'll get a damn sight worse."

Big, black-haired, and black of mien, Oates knew his
effect on others. He straightened his spine and glared at
the crowd of soldiers, every one of them silent now.

"Any other man got his spite up, save it for the Yankees.
Going to be plenty of those sonsofbitches coming this way
soon." He growled like a feral hog, as if he might lunge at
any man within range. "Now get these two fools out of here,
before something makes me madder than I am."

Men leapt to do his bidding, and a smile threatened his
face. The ease with which he put fear into others was a precious thing. Not that he didn't know what fear was himself: Still a boy, if a big one, he'd run off far and fast, sure
the law was coming to Oates's Corners to fetch and hang
him. He'd taken a hoe to a grown man who deserved it and
left him lying dead. Or so he'd thought. He slipped on down
to Florida, where he hawked cigars, then signed on aboard
a schooner. Quick to dislike the sailor's life and its disre-
spectful nature, he made his way bleak-bellied from the

French stink of New Orleans up to Shreveport, where he dallied a night too long with a slave dealer's daughter and nearly killed another man before running hard for Texas. There'd been hungry times and worse before his younger brother, John, tracked him down in Henderson and told him he could come home, that the dead man was alive and the law had more than William C. Oates to fuss about.

Running from the law let a man see its uses, though, and he set himself to clerking for an attorney. After passing the bar, he put up a shingle in Abbeville, near enough to home, but not so close he'd have to live with his mother's ever-angrier love of the Lord. She was a haunted woman who had the sight, but could not see her own way. He always kept his vow to her never to touch alcohol, but as for religion, the war had thrashed it out of him. He went through the motions for the sake of his men, since many a fine soldier had been caught up in the revival over the winter, desperate to believe in a Providence Oates just could not see. The death of his brother up in Pennsylvania had shot his faith through the heart.

His mother had foreseen John's death, but said nothing of his own fate. Questioned, she just went back to her Bible and silence. On his dark days, he wondered how much she really saw. Mostly, though, he left it. Some things didn't bear too much thinking over.

He remembered John as a jolly boy, the two of them kicking their way down a dusty trace, eyes peeled for snakes, walking through heat thick as wadding to sit just beyond the circle of whiskey-suckers down at the cross-roads store, men of varied provenance, slight ambition, and the occasional suspect hue, a profane congregation met to swap tales of Pike County and the wide world. Even a boy could tell they all were liars, but listening made you dream. And now he dreamed of John, fixing him in childhood for eternity. Ambushed by visions, Oates saw his brother squatting in the dust like a waiting Indian, but sweet-eyed and soft-mouthed, wearing a smile wise beyond his years as he listened to the corn liquor talk through the mouths of men who had become its slaves, niggers to a jug. It still seemed an impossible thing that such a fine, bright soul could be no more, reduced to a rotten corpse in Pennsylvania.

There were some things that could not but be thought over, things a man just could not leave behind. He did not know what he could have done to save his brother on that rocky hillside, but he knew he should have done whatever it was.

John. Sweet, loyal John. Never really meant to be a soldier.

With the fight crowd dissolving, Oates spotted Billy Strickland, newly made a captain.

"Walk with me, Billy," Oates said.

They strolled beyond the regimental camp, following a farm lane. The fencing was gone, used for firewood by soldiers who had preceded them. Didn't matter much, since there was no livestock, or none worth the notice. Even the spring greenery seemed poor, as if nature, too, had tightened up on rations. Virginia had been humbled by the war, its grand houses set to mourning. The landscape still had a gentility Alabama never quite reached, not even Montgomery, but it wasn't like to last if the war chewed south. And that was about what the Yankees had in mind. He was pretty damned sure that he and his men would not see Pennsylvania again. They'd be lucky enough to set eyes on Alabama. Hard times were coming, hard fighting. What pleasure there had been in war was gone, replaced by a muddle of rage and desperation.

"Should I take away Ball's stripes, sir?" Strickland asked.

Oates shook his head as they walked, feeling that little

click in his hip, bad bone. The pain was bearable, local as an itch. But it was there.

"Leave him be," Oates said. "He just had his blood up."

Before their boots, flies rose from an ancient cowpat.

"Think the Yanks are ready to come on?" the captain asked, passing the time.

"Just been waiting for the roads to get good and dry. They'll want to move fast. That polecat Grant. I had enough of that bastard at Chattanooga."

Between Lookout Mountain and the river, blue uniforms had appeared out of the mist, too damned many for one regiment to manage. He had been hit in the hip and thigh.

"Wish I could've been with you boys at Knoxville," Oates said. He tracked a bird's flight, as if he meant to shoot it. "Damned shame."

"Wasn't much to be done, sir," Strickland told him. "Just all bad, beginning to end. Not sure any one man would've made much difference."

Oates almost said, "Unless he'd replaced Longstreet." But that wasn't the way to talk in front of subordinates.

Instead of ranting, he smiled, spreading his black beard. It was one of his queer smiles, though. "Man can't help but feel guilty, that's the thing. Laying up in a fine house like Colonel Toney's. Laying there in a poster bed, fearing his men aren't going to be properly handled."

"They were glad to see you, when you turned up, sir." The captain paused, choosing his words carefully. "We didn't know if we'd ever see you again."

Oates grunted. "I suppose I looked a sight. Back on the river."

"Yes, sir. Mad-dog angry, too."

"God almighty. Look at that horse there. Wouldn't be worth the killing for the meat."

"That's how the cavalry mounts all looked at Knoxville," Strickland told him.

"Just hard to believe," Oates said, going back to his musing. "There I am, living in luxury and dandling babies, every need provided for. Like there wasn't a war at all, not anywhere." He paused. "I wanted the feeling to last, tell you the truth."

"But you came back, sir."

Oates nodded, thoughts shifting again. "I grew up hard, Billy. Don't know if I ever said. *So* hard. You know what it's like in the backcountry. Might say it made me what I am, but I'd as lief not go through that ordeal twice. And there I am, lying up in that big, fine house . . . oh, I wasn't thinking about the war every single minute. No, sir. Not even thinking about the boys as much as I should have. I was thinking I'd like to have me a house like that."

He laughed. "Wouldn't make a plug of difference, I suppose. Even if I struck it rich, or married some high gentleman's spinster daughter—which I don't have a mind to do—even with that big house and all, there's a kind of fence they put up. They ask you along on a hunt, but it's really your dogs they want. No, there's always this fence. And they aren't going to let you jump it, because folks like you and me aren't welcome behind it." He slapped at a greenbottle. "Lawyer? Officer? That's no mind. Not once this war is over. It'll all go back to being the way it was. Men like you and me, we'll never be fine. We might be respected in a middling way. Might even wind up in the legislature. But we won't be fine."

"Were they rude, sir? The people who took you in?"

Oates laughed. It was a big sound in the meadows.

"High folks are never rude," he said. "That's part of the bundle." He laughed again. "Where you and I would make a fist, they just lift them an eyebrow. I wasn't speaking against old Toney, now. I'll be grateful to that man and his family until the day I die. I'd been robbed of every penny I had down in the train yard, lying there wounded and crazy with fever, and thank you for your service to our great Confederacy." He swung his head like a bothered horse. "Colonel Toney took me into the bosom of his family. Out of kindness, nothing but. Another man might donate a gold piece or two to some sanitary commission, but isn't like to open his doors to a wounded man who's not blood kin. No, sir. Old Toney treated me handsome. I was talking on the principle." He stopped himself. "But I do talk on. And I still haven't got 'round to what I had to say to you, Billy."

"Sir?"

Oates kicked a stone. His boot leather was so thin his toes felt the hardness. In the strange way a man had of doing things, just below the level of true thinking, he had hoped the gesture would lengthen out his bad leg, making the thigh right again.

"Best turn around," Oates said. "Don't want to get too far from the regiment." He twisted up a wormwood smile. "Can't have Major Lowther overtaxing himself in my absence. Can we now? Listen here, Billy. You're a captain now. It's a different job. You know it, but I'm going to tell it to you anyways. Your job is to control your company. And dead men don't control a pile of shit. Inspiring your men is just fine, all that preaching and praising and getting them riled up before they step off. But your main business is to *control* them when we go forward. I don't ever want to see Company I or any damned company in the Fifteenth Alabama go to pieces the way we did at Gettysburg. And I will shoot the man who lets it happen. Hear?"

They walked a few steps in silence, letting the heat of the words cool on the air. At last, Strickland said, "I remember how thirsty I was. That's what I always think about. How thirsty I was."

"You just keep your hellions together, doing what they're meant to do. This war's going to get even uglier, mark my words."

As he spoke, it struck Oates that, above all, he was speaking to himself. Strickland needed to hear this counsel. But William C. Oates was the man who needed to take it to heart: When he got in a fight, he just wanted to *fight,* to go at the enemy with gun, sword, knife, knuckles, teeth, anything at all. He was the one who had to control himself.

They walked back toward the temporary camp. They had been there but one night and the men had not yet had time to render it foul. The air smelled of spring, not mankind.

"Funny thing," the captain said to his commanding officer, "as much as they complained about the work, the men enjoyed the review the other day. Once they got to it. Never saw them so proud. More spit than polish, but you saw how they stood up proper."

"Complaining," Oates said, "is the soldier's one inalienable right."

"And General Lee . . . ," Strickland went on. "I do believe every man present would have died for him right there."

Oates snorted. "They're going to get the chance."

Lee. A fine man, no doubt. But a man. Having knocked down the God above, Oates wasn't looking for a substitute on earth. He was willing to fight for Robert E. Lee. To die for him, if dying was required. But he wasn't about to worship any creature that walked on two legs or four.

Lee's magic had touched him, too, though, on that splendid afternoon: the erect old man in his unsullied uniform, riding his fine dapple gray, with his daughter in a borrowed carriage behind him, spine as straight and face as stiff as her father's. The men had cheered their throats raw. Oates only hoped that Longstreet hadn't imagined that any of the cheers were for him.

Lee's daughter now. Fellow would be afraid to marry her, even if he took an interest. Which seemed unlikely, given what Oates had seen of her: plain and prim, with not one hint of pleasure anywhere near her. With a few startling exceptions, white women had never been sporting enough for his tastes: The ones who weren't outright slatterns had too little joy about them and a bushel too many worries. Every one of them thought too much. He'd take a brown girl for pleasure any day: They lived in the moment, the way he did himself. Women, good women, had always been powerful fond of him, but he had no interest in subsequent domesticity, with all the do's and don'ts, the ifs and buts and maybes. When the war finished up, he meant to buy himself the finest piece of tail in Alabama and shut the door. Maybe old Toney would sell him that pleasing missy with whom he had developed an acquaintance. Cheekbones of a Cherokee and the rump of the devil's dam. Or if Toney didn't have a mind to sell her, perhaps he'd put her out to him on loan. For services rendered to the glorious Confederacy. The way the old man had given him William for a manservant in the field.

It was a fine thing to have a nigger to clean your boots.

Thinking about all that put him in the mood for a woman's company, for the rut smell of just one of them, even though nothing would come of it. If the Yankees held off a few days, perhaps one of the local families would ask the brigade's field officers in for a dinner. He could tolerate that nicely about now.

They were being held in reserve, well south of Ewell's Corps and Hill's men. That meant hard, fast marching to get to the battle, when it came. For now, though, there was no danger and the sentries ahead stood slackly. He decided not to upbraid them, but recalled another concern.

"Billy, I hear two Texas boys got smallpox, they put 'em in one of the pesthouses back of town. You make sure nobody goes wandering off where they don't need to be. Yankees are bad enough."

Belatedly spying Oates, the pickets straightened. As he

stepped close, arms were presented and proper salutes rendered. The men had come a long way back from the despondency he had found them in at Bull's Gap.

Parting, Oates told Strickland, "You go on now and look in on Morgan and Ball. If Jimmy's come to, you let him know how goddamned close he came to losing those stripes." Oates winked at the captain, a man who had been but a boy when the war began.

Strickland saluted and started to turn away.

A rider burst from the stand of trees where the road ran. Galloping from the town toward the encampment. Waving his cap and hollering, he was still too far off for his words to make any sense.

"Now what the Hell?" Oates asked the air.

The regiments closer to Gordonsville came to urgent life as the rider passed. Refusing to gentle his hip, Oates stepped off sharply to intercept the horseman. Soon enough, he made out the rider's words.

"The Yankees are moving!" the man cried. "Git ready to march!"

Midday
Clark's Mountain

Lee thanked the Lord that his soldiers could not see the Rapidan Valley from the signal station. He had ridden up to the mountain to observe the Union movement with his own eyes, to measure its scope and intent. And what he saw was daunting: Bereft of crops this year, the landscape had grown an army of fearsome size.

Across the river, long blue columns wound along the roads amid billows of dust, their seeming slowness a trick of the distance as they advanced southeastward. Lee could tell those men were marching hard. Dark blurs in the dirtied air, battalions of guns pursued the brigades and divisions they would support. Behind the marching men and jouncing cannon, the white ribbons of supply trains stretched for miles, their bounty immense. Lee knew he was outnumbered two to one.

The commanding general of the Army of Northern Virginia lowered his field glasses, careful not to let his expression reveal his dismay to the members of his staff. Before detouring to the summit on his way forward, he had set Ewell and Hill in motion on parallel roads to the east, but had hesitated to summon Longstreet's reserve corps and had ordered Hill to leave a division behind, in case the Federal movement was a ruse to cover a thrust down from the west. But the spectacle before him made his opponents' intent plain. Within minutes of his arrival on the mountain, he had ordered Longstreet to come up as swiftly as possible on the army's right. There was no mistaking it: Meade and Grant were moving the entire army south by way of Germanna Ford and Ely's Ford. They had stolen a march on him.

He needed to make up in resolve the time he had spent on caution. But he could not be as daring as he would have liked, not with such legions against him. Nor was it only the numbers. This blue-clad army gleamed, supplied and supported with all the wealth of the North, while his own men covered taut bellies in rags.

Oh, after he had gone begging—*begging*—time and again to Richmond, the authorities had grudgingly issued uniforms and shoes. But they never sent enough. The government he served was parsimonious with goods, but spendthrift with men's lives, and his interviews in the capital demanded an increasing level of self-control. More than once, he had felt his temper pressing him, threatening an ungentlemanly outburst against self-important officials or even President Davis. At a low point in midwinter, his men had been reduced to a quarter pound of wretched meat a day, mostly rancid bacon. Unpaid for months and left to their own devices, his officers had turned to cajoling their own men to share out their rations. But Lee had yet to encounter a famine-struck table in Richmond, nor did any man at a desk above the James wear the malnourished, beggarly look of his soldiers.

To be with his men and of them, he had done a foolish thing with good intentions. Although he never barred his subordinates from accepting the hospitality of local families for their winter quarters—Powell Hill had taken up residence in the grandest mansion in Orange—Lee had insisted on living in a tent on the Bloomsbury grounds. And when Mrs. Taylor sent down treats from Meadow Farm, he had shared them with the soldiers. But his gestures had not eased his soul or helped his men. Instead, they had only let his chest pains grieve him, while his digestion remained an embarrassment.

Mrs. Taylor's generous gifts of buttermilk, jars of jam, and fresh-baked bread had pleased a few men, no doubt, but neither the cold he shared in goodwill nor the delicacies passed down had staunched the flow of deserters. Nor had it escaped him that more of his own men sneaked north to surrender than Federals came south. Desertions plagued the army, and he had needed to have men shot as examples. But he did what military law allowed to discriminate between cowards and shirkers on one hand, and the many who had gone southward to their homes in the hope that they might eat their fill and sleep warmly for a few months before returning to the ranks when the weather turned.

The winter had been terrible. But spring had come, as it always did, and the April rains left May a shimmering legacy. Ragged or not, his men stood straight again.

Not a week before, he had reviewed Longstreet's returned corps in the first fine weather. The sight of the men raised his spirits and broke his heart. They were so few, barely ten thousand of all arms, the size of a division a year before. The soldiers had burnished their leathers and polished the brass that remained to them, they had washed themselves and brushed their threadbare uniforms. Their cannon gleamed. But for all that, and for all their heartfelt, heartening cheers, those brave men had looked like tatterdemalion vagabonds. And still so very many went unshod.

But they would *fight*. He knew he could depend on them for that.

They would have to fight with an even graver ferocity now. Contemplating the campaigns to come, he had bleak days when he feared he had displeased God, or that the South had sinned against the Lord. Each visit to Richmond discouraged him anew, as President Davis demanded ever more, speaking with a grandiosity to which Lee could respond only with temperate silence. Richmond was so near, yet so painfully far from the reality of this army. He endeavored to make the president understand that there were not men enough to take the offensive now, and that those still in the ranks had to be supplied. In turn, the president offered empty assurances. Mr. Davis still believed that the continental powers could be enticed to support the Confederacy, if only Lee delivered one more great victory.

Lee no longer believed that. He struggled to keep faith with President Davis, ever careful to demonstrate his subordination to the civil authorities. But he understood that the last hope of the Confederacy was to frustrate the Union here on Virginia's soil, to make this war so costly to the North that, come autumn, those people would elect a peace candidate who would allow the South its freedom. He would have to fight as he never had fought before, to always be the one to choose the ground, to set the terms of every battle, to send the Federals reeling. And he could not afford to match Meade and Grant in losses, not in soldiers on the firing line or in the generals who led them.

Thankfully, his Old War Horse was back, the best of the generals left to him now. But chastened by disappointments in the west, Longstreet ached to redeem his reputation, and that worried Lee. He wanted Longstreet to be aggressive, but not to risk his person out of vanity. He had too many generals obsessed with their reputations, from Stuart to Hill, and he worried that, on a fateful day, one of them would behave foolishly. He needed them in command, not in their coffins. Bravery took many forms, and leaders had to have the strength within to choose the right one.

He could not afford to lose Longstreet, for all the man's testy squabbling with his subordinates. Longstreet was the only man he had left fit for corps command, who could think beyond the battlefield in front of him. Had he had good replacements for them, Lee would have removed Hill and Ewell, the first a man not meant to command more than a division, the second an erratic leader who, on his bad days, seemed spent. But there were no replacements. The casualties of the past year had been appalling, the loss of Jackson above all. Each day, Lee felt the absence of the one man who could wield independent command.

How he missed Tom Jackson!

It was an odd thing, Lee mused. When Jackson had been at his side, he had never called him "Thomas," and certainly not "Tom." Yet, that was how he thought of Jackson now, as if they had been boyhood friends.

Grim 1863 had been disastrous, with even the early victory of Chancellorsville blighted by Jackson's wounding and death. Then came Gettysburg and Vicksburg. After a glimmer of hope at Chickamauga, Chattanooga had become another debacle. And after that, Knoxville. The best he himself had been able to do was to dig Meade to a standstill at Mine Run.

A recent remark of Longstreet's troubled him as deeply as the sight of those columns hurrying across the Rapidan. At the sparse repast to honor his review of Longstreet's corps, Lee had said, "When those people cross the river, we will have to strike them very hard, to drive them back and gain a month or two."

Longstreet's good humor—so rare a thing these days—had fled the tent, leaving the corps commander almost funereal.

"Grant won't go back," Longstreet told him. "I know him. Once he gets his teeth into our leg, he'll never let go."

What if Longstreet was right? How could they endure?

The best hope, Lee believed, was to prove his senior corps commander wrong, to thrash Grant and Meade so severely that they saw no choice but withdrawal, as stunned as Joseph Hooker had been at Chancellorsville.

But what if neither man proved to be a Hooker? Meade was not one to panic, that much he knew. Had he been, he would have ordered his men from the field that first evening at Gettysburg. As for Grant, it was said he was given to drink. But the men who held forth on his vice seemed not to have met Grant. Longstreet knew him. And Longstreet did not count the bottle their ally.

How much, in the end, could be known of any man?

A courier rode up in a plume of dust. Lieutenant Colonel Marshall intercepted the man and took his dispatch. The military secretary scanned the note to ensure its contents merited troubling Lee. They did. Features drumhead tight, Marshall approached him.

"From General Ewell, sir." Marshall held out the paper, in case Lee wished to review it personally, but summarized its contents: "He sends his compliments and requests permission to call up Gordon's Brigade."

So many decisions seemed difficult now. Age? The weariness of the spirit that no mortal sleep could cure? The only time when decisions came easily anymore was on the battlefield, amid the cacophonous butchery and terrible thrill of war. Then he could make decisions in an instant, possessed by a greater spirit, perhaps by grace.

"General Gordon may withdraw his brigade from the river. There will be no movement on our left by those people. He will rejoin General Early." Something irked Lee, though. There was an admonition to add to the message. He took a step back toward Marshall. "You will stress to General Ewell that he is not to become engaged . . . not beyond any skirmishing forced upon him. I do not wish any part of this army to excite a battle, not until Longstreet is up. We will not have a repeat of Gettysburg."

Speaking that fateful name brought Lee up short. It would not do to single out Ewell for such an admonition, since Hill bore far more responsibility for stumbling into the meeting engagement that began that dreadful ordeal in Pennsylvania.

"I wish the same counsel to go to General Hill," Lee added. "He is not to become inextricably engaged. We will conduct ourselves with restraint until this army has closed up and we have chosen the ground on which to greet our visitors."

He had been thinking about a battleground not merely for hours, but for months. And still he found himself plagued with indecision and had to force himself to issue orders. It was essential to move quickly, to wrest control of developments from those people. They would be well into the tangles of the Wilderness this day, with at least one corps past it tomorrow and the remainder of their army strung out behind. If he caught an exposed portion of their force in there . . . taking them on the flank . . . it would deny the Federals use of their artillery, given the restricted fields of fire. Lee had learned at Malvern Hill, then doubly so at Gettysburg, to respect the Army of the Potomac's guns. On the other hand, a major attack in that labyrinth would break down in a shambles, a brawl that would defy all attempts to control it. It had been a blessing that those people had not grasped how disordered Jackson's men had been in the wake of their triumph the year before. No, the Wilderness would not be the place to fight a full-scale battle. Not without Jackson. But it had to be used gingerly to delay the Federals, to divert them from their purposes and help him regain the initiative.

He saw it now. His opening gambit would be to surprise an isolated corps on terrain where skill trumped numbers, to play havoc with the strategy of his opponents, then disengage before they could bring the weight of their numbers to bear. He could threaten their lines of retreat to the fords, while Stuart embarrassed their trains. And he could always withdraw to the entrenchments along Mine Run, if things went awry.

Still, he would take no irrevocable action until Longstreet brought up his corps. His men would need to march hard.

As Marshall wrote out the orders on the little board he carried in his saddlebag, Lee turned his back decisively on the spectacle across the river.

Speaking with more heat than usual, he said, "Colonel Marshall, you *must* stress to Generals Ewell and Hill that they are *not* to do more than reconnoiter carefully, not until I am present. Write forcefully, sir. We cannot afford to have a misunderstanding."

He would have to fight those people within days, but he did not mean to—could not afford to—rush into it headlong. For now, the cavalry could annoy their forward elements to delay them. But he needed more information to craft a plan in detail and bait the trap. He would refuse battle tomorrow, if he could. The day after that was a question mark.

For all his concerns, his heart leapt at the prospect of fighting again. Lee smelled powder the way a horse smelled oats. There were things he dared not discuss with other men, matters he preferred not to think on too much himself. He loved war, that was the wicked truth. God forgive him, he *loved* it. Worse, this army had become his greatest love. It was a terrible thing for a man of faith, or any man, to recognize.

When he told himself that he loved his wife, he found himself insisting that he *still* loved her, as if effort were required. He felt a growing dread of his visits to the rented home in Richmond, where the beauty he had courted so long ago, when he had served under a different flag, kept to her bed with ever greater lassitude, surrendering to the temptations of the invalid. He treated her with tenderness forced by guilt: First he had taken her from a wealthy home, now he had seen that house turned into a graveyard. But that weight was nothing before the guilt of the soul.

As for his children, he loved them dearly, of course. His conduct attested to that. He was proud of his three sons, each of them in uniform, and his daughters adored him, rushing to serve with devotion almost unsound. He worried for the safety of the boys, especially Rooney and Rob, but knew not what to make of the lives of his daughters. Not one of them had married or shown a will to do so. And "Daughter" was nearly thirty years old; Agnes, what, twenty-three? And was it two years since Annie, a tender thing, had died of typhoid, a mockery of fate in the midst of war? Millie was still little more than a girl, of course, but it had been a delight to have her by him at Longstreet's review.

The girls needed suitors, husbands. Well they might care for their mother and honor their father, but at what cost? What lives would be left them? Even if this war left *beaux* enough? A parade of widows darkened Richmond's streets, but at least those women had known the wonders of matrimony. What of all the unmarried women and girls? What would be left for them, if this slaughter continued?

It was time to mount and ride down to the fields, where he would order to their deaths the men ten thousand spinsters would never know.

Dear Lord, he prayed, forgive me.

General Ewell's dispatch rider tore off, followed by a courier headed for General Hill down on the Plank Road.

Lee felt the impulse to turn again, to take one last look at the Federal columns and the wealth they dragged behind them. In Mexico, he had thought Scott's army magnificent, certain he'd never see the like again. Never had he or his brethren in arms dreamed of so great and fierce a war as this.

Forbidding himself that last glimpse toward fate, Lee turned to the officers who had accompanied him to the mountaintop.

"Gentlemen," he said, "let us go down to the men and see to our duties."

THREE

The man's a damned swine," General Humphreys said.
Another column of soldiers trudged up from the ford
and passed the headquarters tents: Sedgwick's first division. In the heat of the afternoon, shoulders drooped and
feet dragged, and more than a few blankets lay discarded
along the roads, but if the men were not as brisk as they had
been at daybreak, they still maintained good order. Now
and then they even mustered a cheer, sometimes at the
sight of Meade, but more often for Grant, who sat impas-
sively on the porch of a derelict house across the road.

"Lawyer, my foot," Humphreys went on. "If that cur can
spell his own name, he'll leave me spellbound."

"It doesn't matter, Humph," Meade said. "Forget it." He,
too, had been infuriated by the tirade Grant's chief of staff
had just inflicted on them. With everything going brilliantly, Rawlins had still found reason to mock and gloat,
and not without his usual flood of obscenities.

"Grant may or may not be the second incarnation of
Alexander," Humphreys seethed, "but he's a damnably
poor judge of character. And what's old Washburne doing
here? He ought to be in Washington, stealing the Treasury
blind with his fellow congressmen." Bitterness carved
lines around his mouth. "Grant's staff is more circus than
military establishment. Complete with a Red Indian."

"Just let it go," Meade repeated. "Take down the banner, put up the old flag. It hardly matters. You and I have greater matters before us."

But it *did* matter. With all the complex marches and daring river crossings gone off without one flaw, this should have been a day for pride all around. Yet, no sooner had Grant and his staff caught up with Meade's headquarters— Grant cantering across the pontoon bridge on his big bay horse—than Rawlins stormed across the road, pushing his way through the ranks of marching troops, face set in that venomous manner of his, with a hardhearted grin breaking out of his beard and murderous eyes above.

He had pushed up to Meade without a salute, waving his paw toward the splendid new swallow-tailed banner donated to the Army of the Potomac. The flag, all silk, bore a gold eagle wreathed in silver on a magenta field. Meade thought it striking.

"Know what Grant thinks about them coon drawers you got on that pole?" Rawlins had barked for the world to hear. "Know what he had to say? I'll quote you just what he said." The man's eyes glittered with the joy of malice. "He said, 'What's this, what's this? Is Imperial Caesar anywhere about?' Hah! I was you, I'd haul down that hoor's petticoat this minute."

Meade had been mortified. He had expected congratulations on the day's achievements. Rawlins was a rude, raw man, but, given that he was Grant's personal confidant, Meade had been careful to treat the man with courtesy. And Rawlins had not seemed ill-disposed toward him.

Meade could only stutter, "If . . . should General Grant find our new flag inappropriate—"

Rawlins cut him off. " 'Inappropriate' may be the gentleman's word, but I'd say he finds it downright mule-fuck preposterous."

Choking on dust and bile, Rawlins suffered a coughing fit. It climaxed in a burst of blood-flecked phlegm, and that

only added to the fellow's outrage. Without the hint of a
compliment about the army's performance, the former
country lawyer who had clamped himself to Grant from
the war's first days—and now wore a brigadier general's
star—strode off to curse a battery to a stop so he could
amble across the road at his own pace, waving his arms in
anger at the miasma kicked up by a marching army.

"Just take it down," Meade told his fellow Philadelphian
a last time. But that was not enough. He turned from the
endless stream of troops whose passing had tanned their
uniforms with dust. Feeling a rush of warmth toward his
chief of staff, he said, "It's only jealousy, I think. Those
western men wouldn't mind seeing us fail. But we carried
it off, and handsomely. Thanks to *you*, Humph."

It was only true. Meade had given the orders. But Andrew Atkinson Humphreys, whose naval architect grand-
father had designed "Old Ironsides," was the man who had
labored for weeks to calculate how to swiftly march a massive army over a patchwork of country lanes, how to sneak
hulking pontoon trains into hiding places close to a river
line guarded by the enemy, how to push out the cavalry
and seize multiple fords by surprise, how to move and protect the largest supply train in history, how to herd along ten
thousand head of cattle to feed the men, and how to time it
all perfectly. The stay-at-homes wished to hear of epic
battles, but few had a sense of the labors that delivered an
intact army to the fight. When the history of the war's campaigns was written, who would remember the commissary
wagons?

The problem was that Humphreys detested his duties as
chief of staff. He longed to return to a field command.
Meade had been compelled to refuse his requests to go back
to the troops again and again. There was no one to replace
him: Humphreys was a man of genius who wanted an av-
erage job.

Watching his army pass in good order—thanks to Humphreys' skill—Meade understood what his old comrade was feeling, that irrepressible soldier's desire to lead men into battle, instead of scribbling orders back at headquarters. For his own part, he judged Humphreys to be the only indispensable man in the entire army, himself included. George Gordon Meade had come to the conclusion, through hard experience, that a great commander would fail without an able chief of staff, while a great chief of staff could save almost any commander. Humphreys would have to wait awhile before he rode at the head of troops again.

Another veil of dust settled on the violets by the roadside. The determination of the tiny flowers to thrust up their colors reminded him of soldiers who would not quit. Lee's soldiers. This march was one thing, the coming battle another.

"I'd like to thrash that lout," Humphreys grumbled, aiming all his pent-up frustrations at Rawlins.

Meade laughed. He couldn't help it. Even though there really was nothing to laugh about. Nor was he given to laughter by his nature. Wiping tears and grit from his eyes, he turned from the pageant on the road to face Humphreys full on. He could hold a grudge himself, but did not want to end up on Humphreys' bad side, that was certain.

"Humph, I think the world of you. But Rawlins just might be your match."

"He's a damned consumptive and can't face up to it."

Plagued by the dust he had devoured while laughing, Meade coughed himself. "Well, Grant believes he needs the man. So bear with him. All in all, Grant's been a decent fellow. He's given us all we've asked for, he's kept Washington off our backs . . . he does seem a man of his word." Meade constructed a smile. "As far as I'm concerned, the occasional visitation from John Rawlins, Esquire, is a trivial price to pay."

In an uncharacteristic gesture, Meade patted Humphreys on the shoulder. Beige smoke rose from blue wool. "If the worst they can do is to find fault with the taste of the best-bred ladies of Philadelphia, I'd call the day a success."

The two men spotted Sedgwick trotting up from the river, urging on his corps and waving his hat. A good, grizzled man on a fine white horse, even Uncle John smiled today. And just before Rawlins' intrusion, a dispatch had arrived from Hancock, stating that his trail division was crossing the Rapidan ahead of schedule and that Barlow, whose division had led the way at Ely's Ford, had already reached the objective for the day's march. Meade felt a burst of confidence and pride: Perhaps Grant was right. Perhaps they'd conclude the war in a matter of months, even weeks.

"I still say the man's a swine," Humphreys muttered.

Dusk
Chancellorsville battlefield

Holding the skull at arm's length like an actor playing Hamlet, Colonel Frank declaimed, *"Wer darf das Kind beim rechten Namen nennen?"*

Oh, do shut up, Barlow thought. Without dismounting, he said, "Put down the skull. And set a proper example for your troops by saluting your superior officer."

The colonel tossed the skull away, further angering Barlow. The remains belonged to a soldier who had fought upon this ground a year before. Barlow had been there. And while he didn't subscribe to the fuss that glorified any ne'er-do-well the moment he donned a uniform, Barlow believed in a show of respect for the dead. If only for the sake of his living soldiers.

The colonel drew himself up and saluted. Barlow returned the gesture.

"I am just quoting Goethe," the colonel said. "I cite a famous line, 'Who will call the child by its proper name?'"

"I know what it means," Barlow said. "I've had to learn no end of worthless drivel. Have you been drinking?"

The colonel shook his head. "No. Not drinking. One *Schnaps*. To celebrate."

"You have nothing to celebrate. Win a battle. Then you can celebrate. Meanwhile, I'll relieve you of command of this brigade if I find you drinking again."

"But . . . I have not been drinking. It is only—"

"This is not a Berlin debating society, Colonel, and I don't measure degrees of inebriation. Now double your pickets and see that a capable officer's in charge, not the butt of some regiment's jokes. This division will *not* be surprised."

"But . . . the Rebels are not here, I think."

Barlow exploded. "That's what I heard a year ago. On this very ground. See to your brigade, man, or I'll rip those eagles off your shoulders myself."

Barlow pulled his horse about and spurred it. At his back, the colonel muttered, *"Gott im Himmel."*

A part of him hoped he would discover Frank falling-down drunk in the morning. He ached to relieve the man, had little faith in his leadership, but Hancock insisted the popular German's removal would be impolitic. "Make it work," Hancock had cautioned. And the colonel was sly: In the morning, he'd be preening at the head of his brigade, breath reeking of peppermint wash.

As he rode on toward the Irish Brigade—another story entirely—Barlow wondered if his distaste for Germans and all that went with them hadn't to do with his longing to purge any lingering trace of Emerson's woolly nonsense from his brain. New England's Transcendentalists had afflicted his youth and his student years with the works of lumbering German seers and mordant Frenchmen. Their

very inanity made the French less bothersome, but the notion that Americans had anything to learn from bilious Teu-
tons had become as repugnant as vomit. He had pledged
not to open another tome of Hegel's, and that was a promise he certainly meant to keep.

Arabella, bless her, shared his disdain for the cabbage-
eaters, whether the turgid philosophers or the commoners
with their beer and maudlin tastes. And their bilious
effrontery. Barlows had been in New England for two
centuries, yet a creature such as *Herr Oberst* Frank
walked down a gangplank, drained a glass, and thought
himself the equal of any American. Stir in the Irish and it
seemed clear the country was going to Hell, with the war
the least of it.

As he followed the archipelago of campfires, Barlow
heard laughter. The sound came as a relief. Upon reaching the day's limit of advance, he'd been furious at Humphreys and Hancock for holding up his division on a
mockery of a graveyard. All around the bivouac site, white
bones thrust from the earth; elsewhere, rain had uncovered
entire skeletons, all of them macabre remembrances of the
debacle a year before. It was a grisly place, and his first
thought beyond disgust had been that it must have a bad
effect on the men's morale. But he had failed to appreciate their fatalism, the humor that better served a man than
anything in Feuerbach or Herder. The veterans made rough
jokes, and the new recruits followed their lead. With shoes
off and pipes lit, his men had become almost jovial.

Barlow was anxious to remove his own boots and bathe
his feet. In the excitement of the day, his feet had behaved
themselves, no more than a sneaking bother lurking in ambush. But as soon as his division coiled in, the itching had
flared unbearably.

He wriggled his toes, loosening their sweat-grip on one
another. It only made matters worse. The feeling that his

toes and feet were trapped was maddening. It took all the self-control that he could muster not to stop and scratch right through his boots.

The itching faded again as his hackles went up. And not because of the pale litter of bones. No matter what the cavalry and his own patrols reported, he could feel the Confederates out there. How near, he couldn't say with useful precision. But he sensed their vitality, their menace.

He expected fighting the next day, whether the grand plan called for it or not, and whatever Humphreys, Meade, or Hancock told themselves. It had the inevitability of a physical law, of chemical combinations in a laboratory: Lee would fight.

He could almost see gray columns in the dark.

And here he was, with his division halted in a poisoned spot where the stink of old defeat lingered all around. The thickets and scrub trees seemed to have grown even denser than they had been the previous year, fertilized with the blood and meat of the fallen. It was no place to fight, a worthless expanse of near jungle his division could have marched through to open ground. He understood the need to keep the army compact, the need for each corps to be in position to support the others, but some risks were worth taking, and seizing good terrain topped the list of reasons. God help the men who had to fight in these brambles.

As Barlow understood the order of march, the Rebels would strike Warren's corps initially, since Lee's men would be marching from the west and Warren would be smack in front of them—and watching his flank, Barlow hoped. Tonight, though, the threat arose from Stuart's cavalry, who would love to pin the tail on a Union donkey again. Barlow did not mean to be that ass. And Fitz Lee's horsemen had been spotted outside of Fredericksburg, which raised a nice proposition: If Robert E. Lee's nephew attempted some dashing *coup,* it would be charming to take the fellow captive. Or kill him.

That was a pleasant fantasy and no more, Barlow understood. The twilight hours fostered that sort of musing. But tomorrow would be a very different story. Brigadier General Francis Channing Barlow had no doubt that he and his men would be drawn in, if the armies clashed in the Wilderness.

And if it came to a fight, he was damned well ready.

Challenged by a picket, he gave the parole and steered his mount between the Irish Brigade's campfires. As ever, Smyth's tenors wailed. Drunk or sober, the Irish were always singing about their abandoned paradise. If it was such a bloody heaven, Barlow wondered, why had they left in the first place? Ireland had to be madder than Rhode Island.

A dark shape in the purple night, Colonel Smyth appeared.

"General Barlow, me fine man," Smyth called out, "all's well from County Cork to Donegal. What can we do for ye on this fine May evening, sir?"

"Have you been drinking?" Barlow asked.

Late evening
New Verdiersville

Lee's hand quivered as he sipped the buttermilk. He had been fond of the beverage since childhood, but the richness did not always agree with him these days. It would have been poor manners, however, to decline the offering from the Widow Rhodes. She had delivered the drink in a cut-glass goblet that was, he was certain, the pride of her household goods. Approaching him directly, she had presumed to renew their acquaintance of the past autumn, when the grounds of her house had harbored his headquarters tents in another desperate hour.

As the widow watched him drink, awe shone in her fire-lit eyes, the same near reverence he met too often now, a look akin to idolatrous love and the expectation of miracles. But Lee knew that he could not give them miracles, no more than he could digest this yellow poison.

"Be good for you, that will," the widow told him. "You drink that up and you keep healthy for us'n."

"Yes, ma'am," Lee answered dutifully. "It's a kindness. And I am grateful."

She smiled, and motherly interest tangled with something less selfless. He thanked the good Lord that he was known to be married; otherwise, who knew what the endless parade of widows and aging maidens might expect?

"Well now," Widow Rhodes picked up again, "there'll be more of that in the morning, start you off right. And I told that Colonel Taylor how our Heraclea's fetching a nice smoked ham for y'all. Just takes a mite of digging, Yankees coming and all."

The poor woman froze, alarmed at the prospect that she had offended by implying that she expected those people to come, that she lacked faith in his protection.

"I'm glad, Mrs. Rhodes," Lee told her, "that the brave women of Virginia show such foresight. We must conserve what we have and shun needless risks. Now . . . if you'll allow me, I must tend to the army's affairs." He held up the barely touched glass of buttermilk. "I will take this delight slowly, the better to savor it." He turned with the crispness of the young officer he once had been. "Colonel Marshall! My cup, if you please. I dare not expose Mrs. Rhodes' fine glass to the hazards of war."

Taking off his spectacles, Marshall moved with haste. The secretary knew as much about his general's ailments as Lee revealed to any man but his surgeon. Steeling himself, Lee sipped a last time from the tinted glass. His hand trembled anew as he passed on the goblet to Marshall to transfer its contents. The show of frailty embarrassed him, but he did not attempt to mask it. The South, he now believed, had hidden too much from itself, for too many years. The time for truth-telling loomed.

But truth, as Mary had pointed out shortly after their wedding, is never an excuse for unsound manners. He let Marshall pour the buttermilk into a tin cup, but when the colonel moved to return the glass to the widow, Lee intervened and took it from his hand. With a delicate flourish, he passed it back to the widow.

"The generosity of our Virginia ladies," he told her, "never fails to stimulate our courage."

As she accepted the goblet, their fingertips touched. He feared that she would make too much of that, take unwarranted pride in it. They all had lifted him too high, and he worried not only that such an elevation offended the Lord, who asked of his children humility, but that he took too much satisfaction in it himself.

War endangered body and soul. And the threat to the soul was graver.

Sensing, as lonely women learn to do, that her welcome had expired, the widow trailed off across her untended lawns, heading back to the house she shared with a Negro girl.

Surprising Lee, the widow turned a last time, calling from a distance, her voice raised above the level of good breeding.

"Now don't you forget that ham," she ordered.

He would not forget the ham, but he would forgo it. Let the members of his staff enjoy a treat. Ham—seductive, salt-cured Virginia ham—was yet another of the pleasures denied him now. His stomach did best with chicken, sometimes eggs, and, on occasion, fresh beef, if it was cut finely.

He worried that the end of the war, when it came, would find him as much an invalid as his wife, imprisoned in that house on East Franklin Street, where the variety of her days was but the shift from a bed to a wheelchair. The first time he had seen her walk on crutches, he had wept.

How could he doubt that he loved her? Or believe he loved this faithful army more? There were so many varieties of love. It would not be measured or weighed like tobacco or cotton, nor would it hold still. Certainly, what he felt for the tiny woman brought low by rheumatism and a medical roster of additional ailments differed from what he had felt toward the round-faced beauty with oiled hair and the mischievous look that had taken his heart by storm. But it was, indisputably, love. Was it not?

Poor Mary. She was younger than him.

As for *his* mortal coil, the decay was plain. His fifty-seven years had become a punishment. How long would he have the strength to lead the army, with no man he could trust as his replacement? His heart pains threatened betrayal, as if the organ wished to desert his chest, and his digestion was traitorous always. Nor had the outward man been spared. In three years of war, gently graying hair had turned the color of ashes and his beard had grizzled. As a youth, he had been vain, if quietly so. Now his only pride lay in his skill at commanding men on their way to their deaths.

He had sacrificed much for the South, for his Virginia. He had betrayed the oath he had sworn to the country and the army he had abandoned. Ennoble it as men might with splendid words, he had conspired in butchery. Yet, he felt a sinful degree of pride, clinging to it, unable to relinquish this last passion, this all-consuming, unquenchable mistress, War. He feared that his final sacrifice would be his immortal soul.

He prayed with all the humility and propriety he could

muster, struggling to suppress the thoughts that plagued him, the guilt no man could see. He sought to lead a righteous life, but worried that he shared the pride of Lucifer. Were Mary's pains a curse upon *his* head? Even his recent readings in the Book of Job seemed prideful now, any mental comparison a sacrilege. And what had become of Job's daughters, after their father's death? The daughters who tended the old man in his dotage? Had they married? Or had they squandered their lives on a selfish father?

Surrender took as many forms as love.

Lee stopped himself. He had to concentrate on the impending battle. As for the fate of his soul, God would decide.

"Colonel Marshall," he said, "I would be grateful if you would see that Mrs. Rhodes' buttermilk does not go to waste." His smile struggled and faltered, but, as always, he drove on. "You might share it with Venable, if he's still about. He has an abiding affection for the beverage."

Glad of a hint of humor after a grueling day, Marshall answered, "Mrs. Rhodes hasn't forgotten Charlie's predilections, sir. She's been pouring that stuff down his gullet since we got here. A fellow could begin to suspect her intentions."

The witticism did not sit well with Lee. No better than did the buttermilk. A gentleman did not mock a widow's conduct.

Marshall read Lee's face and dropped the matter. He sipped the buttermilk, though.

The evening was warm for May, yet Lee felt the impulse to walk over to the fire the men had got up. Walter Taylor approached before he could move.

The assistant adjutant general said, "No further word from Stuart, sir, but Fitz Lee confirms Union cavalry moving east. It's still a muddle, at least to me. We have reports of infantry moving south, away from us, and of infantry moving west, almost toward us. Other dispatches suggest Fredericksburg as Grant's objective."

"General Grant will have grander things in mind. He'll want a fight, not a stroll into a town that's his for the taking."

"Yes, sir."

Lee turned to look past the paleness of the four tents that sheltered his headquarters, staring into the dark and toward the east, in the direction where those people must be encamped.

"I do so want to hear more from General Stuart," he continued. "Do Grant and Meade foresee a race to Richmond? Or do they covet the Mine Run line even now? I cannot refresh my orders to General Longstreet until I have a better sense of things."

"Well, they've already lost the race to Mine Run, sir. If that's their purpose. General Ewell has Early's Division beyond it. And General Hill's just a stretch from the old entrenchments, with cavalry out."

Lee shuddered from a chill unfelt by others. "Those people moved well today. General Meade must be pleased with his army. And Grant with Meade, I should think."

Taylor paused a few seconds, then pushed on with his summary of developments: "Generals Ewell and Hill have their amended orders, sir. Both corps move forward at dawn."

"And they understand that I want them to *annoy* those people, if they find them still in the Wilderness? But that they must avoid decisive engagement?"

"Yes, sir. I put the order in General Ewell's hand myself and watched him read it. And General Hill had no questions when he was here."

Lee crossed his arms. "There are times when I prefer that General Hill *does* ask questions. Go on."

"During their marches, Generals Hill and Ewell will

coordinate with each other, with Ewell's advance regulated by Hill's. If the Federals move in strength against either wing, both corps are to withdraw to the Mine Run entrenchments. Then we—"

"I *want* those people to come on," Lee interrupted. His plan had been developing through the day and he was thinking aloud now, something he permitted himself to do only in the presence of intimate members of his staff. "General Grant will have high expectations of himself, after his successes in the west. He will be confident, eager to prove himself here. We must make use of that. I expect Generals Ewell and Hill to tease those people, if the word is not too frivolous. We must lure them back to Mine Run and give General Longstreet an opening to flank them. As General Jackson did. Do we know if General Burnside is still above the Rappahannock?"

"Mosby's people report Ninth Corps troops leaving Warrenton around noon. So General Burnside could have a division across the Rappahannock tonight, if he pushes hard. That would put the Ninth Corps south of the Rapidan late tomorrow."

Lee looked toward the fire. The flames outlined familiar silhouettes. "General Burnside is a deliberate man by nature, made more so by experience. He will move slowly." Lee permitted himself a temperate smile. "He will not be to General Grant's taste, I fear."

Burnside's corps would not be up to support Meade's three corps before the following night, Lee was convinced of it. And Burnside's corps would be weary from the march when it arrived. Those thirty thousand troops could not influence the battle until the day after tomorrow, at the earliest. There was opportunity in that delay.

Longstreet had promised to be up before the next afternoon was out. That would leave precious hours when the numbers would not be so terribly unequal. If Grant and

Meade could be lured back to Mine Run by late afternoon, if pride led them to commit their forces piecemeal . . . if Grant drove Meade to squander his best men against entrenchments . . .

Lee turned back to the main headquarters tent, where Marshall sat making clean copies of the day's orders. Suicidal moths attacked his lantern. Taking care not to smear his work, the military secretary brushed a tiny corpse from the document at hand. Even paper was precious now: Nothing could be wasted.

"Colonel Marshall? We must send another dispatch to General Longstreet. Tell him he *must* honor his promise to join the army by late afternoon. Further orders will follow with details, but he must come up." Lee tapped a finger at the corner of his mouth. "I would not wish him to construe silence from this headquarters as suggesting a lack of urgency."

"He's got a devil of a march to make, sir."

"General Longstreet assured me he can do it." Lee almost smiled. "But even generals want reminding."

"Yes, sir."

Lee knew Marshall's biases. The military secretary was a brilliant mathematician with a knack for calculating time, distance, and the possibilities inherent in a soldier's legs. As a rule, though, Marshall preferred orderly marches that let the men arrive in condition to fight. He did not like too much risk. Normally, Lee appreciated that quality. He needed men around him who could check his sudden impulses. And those closest to him sought to do so, with sometimes comical discretion. But tonight was not a time to take counsel of fear.

Longstreet would keep his promise and be up. After all, Jackson had marched farther and faster many a time. And if the generals in blue could be lured into folly, he and his army would deliver a telling blow to the reputation of the great General Grant, conqueror of Vicksburg and purported savior of the Union. Lee allowed himself the vanity to believe that he was not the mild opponent Grant had found in Pemberton or Johnston. And, ragged or not, the Army of Northern Virginia was composed of the finest soldiers who ever had marched into battle.

He needed sleep, but still had to write to the president in his own hand, to keep the strictest confidence between them. The Federals were active on the Peninsula again, and menacing the Valley with another force. Sherman was stirring in northwestern Georgia, and there was activity west of the Mississippi. Grant clearly intended to overwhelm the Confederacy, and he could not be allowed to maintain the initiative. Instead of striking the Southern armies from every side, those people must be beaten in detail. Grant's proposition had to be turned on its head.

And he needed Pickett's division to rejoin Longstreet's command. It was an infernal frustration that men who faced trivial threats inflated them when they spoke to President Davis, leaving him afraid of spooks when real dangers were present. He had to make his case in logic even Jefferson Davis could not dismiss.

It would be another long letter, and he would get too little sleep again. War was for the young.

He turned back to his adjutant. "All right, Colonel Taylor. Let me know if word comes from General Stuart. Wake me, if necessary. And tomorrow, if the Lord sees fit to bless our enterprises, we will trouble those people in the Wilderness, then beat them at Mine Run." He smiled and, despite his weariness, this last smile was a full one. "I would offer you some of Mrs. Rhodes' excellent buttermilk, but I fear Colonel Marshall had no inclination to share. Good night, gentlemen."

It would not be a good night for Robert E. Lee of Virginia. He would dream, terribly, of the long blue columns he had watched from the top of the mountain. In his dream, they would be everywhere.

Night
Germanna Ford

I'd like to get out of the Wilderness," Meade said. "It's a wretched place that's only fit for bushwhacking."

Grant leaned toward the fire, scratching the ground with a stick. "Think Lee wants to fight in there? That what you're saying?"

Ever wary of unfriendly ears, Meade glanced around. All of the staff men had kept a proper distance, allowing the two commanders a private parley. Beyond the fire, the faces of Rawlins and Congressman Washburne haunted the shadows, though. Their heads together, the two looked like conspirators, glancing now and then toward the generals. Meade imagined them snickering: He found all politicians suspect. The blasted Committee on the Conduct of the War was a grotesque display of the corruption that blighted every effort to defeat the Confederacy. His public shaming gnawed at him, and he didn't trust a single elected official. Not even Governor Curtin. Or Lincoln, who allowed himself to be swayed by boastful frauds.

Still, Meade warned himself, Washburne was Grant's advocate and protector, and the man had nothing to do with the committee's disgraceful shenanigans. The congressman had yet to show any hostility to him, and Meade meant to keep it so. Careful not to descend into obsequiousness, he took pains to be courteous and helpful. Even if he would not make Washburne a friend, he did not need another foe in Washington.

"I don't think Lee wants to fight in that tangle, either,"

Meade explained. "But we'll see blood, if we delay. Given the opportunity, he'll try to draw us out, try to get us to attack him at Mine Run. That's what he wants, I'd bet my shoulder straps on it. And if Lee calculates that he has to bloody our noses to provoke us, he'll come on fists up."

"Good," Grant said.

Meade stiffened. "But . . ."

Grant tapped the ground, then cocked his face toward Meade. The man's eyes were impenetrable but glowing, a trick of the firelight.

"Recollect what I told you, George." Grant's voice was quiet, but firm. "Where Lee goes, there you'll go also. I mean to get at him, and sooner's better than later. And once we get him by the tail, I don't mean to let him go."

"All well and good, Sam . . . well and good, of course . . . but Humphreys' plan is sound and I'd like to stick to it. We have to march hard tomorrow. To outflank Lee. If he takes up the Mine Run line, we need to be in position to envelop him. A frontal attack would be murderous. We need to adhere to the plan and resume the march."

Grant put down his stick and fished out a fresh cigar. This time, he failed to offer one to Meade. "Plans get you started. That's about all they're good for. I don't want this army stretched out like a concertina, that's asking for trouble. I want to be ready to hammer Lee the moment he leaves his hole. I want Burnside up, the entire force together. I mean to hit Lee with everything we have."

"Well, you won't be able to do that in the Wilderness, Sam. A fight in there would be a drunkard's brawl. Wait until tomorrow, wait until you see the ground for yourself. Lee could hold us up with a handful of regiments. Oh, I'm all for consolidating the Army of the Potomac. And with Burnside, too. I don't want to move rashly. But I want to get through that hellhole. And the Ninth Corps won't be here for another day, at least. We can't let General Burnside delay this army."

As Meade waited for a reply, a leaping flame made it look as though the derelict house in the background were ablaze. Meade declined to believe in omens.

Taking his time about lighting his cigar, Grant said, "Burnside will be here tomorrow afternoon. I have his word."

"He won't be. He *can't* be. His men don't have their campaign legs yet." Meade hoped to leave it at that. He had to be careful not to appear too critical of Burnside, whose corps remained independent of the Army of the Potomac, thanks to Burnside's seniority on the rolls. It made for a damnably awkward chain of command, with Burnside ordered to cooperate with Meade, but receiving his orders only from Grant's headquarters. Meade hoped the arrangement would work, but had his doubts.

"A fellow tells me something, I take him at his word," Grant said calmly. "Until he shows me that his word's no good." Cigar still unlit, he canted his head, looking at Meade the way he might have looked at a horse he still wasn't quite sure of. "I want you to get everybody tied in proper. Figure out where it's best to hold up Hancock's advance tomorrow, then have him reach back and tie in to Warren's left. And Warren should reach for Hancock, as soon as he makes Parker's Store. Sedgwick's corps can link into Warren's right, when he comes up. I want an unbroken front, if Lee comes on. Or if we have to go for him."

"Lee won't just let us arrange ourselves. He's not like that," Meade warned. "He'll start in skirmishing to throw us off balance. He'll probe for a weak spot and try to delay us, buy himself time. He'll test you. Based on my own not altogether pleasant experience, I'm convinced he'll want to draw us toward Mine Run. The place is a fortress for him and a waiting slaughter pen for us. And all the while his cavalry will be out, looking for a way into our trains and stirring confusion." Meade grunted. "Stuart loves to read about himself in the Richmond papers."

Grant's voice remained quiet, but his cigar stabbed the air. "If Lee wants a fight, he'll get one. If he comes up, you're to pitch into him. Wherever he may be. Attack *him*. *Before* he attacks you. Get your teeth in his leg and chew."

Meade felt queasy: Grant didn't understand this battlefield. Or Lee. He saw the plan, their fine plan, collapsing around them.

"Yes, sir," he said. But his voice was empty.

"As for cavalry"—Grant eased his tone back toward friendliness—"you've got Sheridan angrier than a stepped-on cottonmouth. He thinks it's a mistake to detail two of his cavalry divisions to guard the rear, with only Wilson to cover the army's front." The unexpected mirth of Grant's expression threatened to explode into a laugh. "Of course, I'm cleaning up his vocabulary considerably."

"If General Sheridan has a complaint, let him bring it to me."

Grant chuckled, fighting back the insistent laugh. "Oh, he will, he will. Have no doubt of that. Phil's got him a temper shorter than the man himself. His last dispatch burned my fingers. I had to pass it off to young Badeau."

"General Sheridan will always get a fair hearing from me," Meade said stiffly. "But I think I know how to handle my own cavalry. Stuart's not to be trifled with, Sam. Sheridan's about to find that out."

"Bedford Forrest wasn't to be trifled with, either," Grant told him.

An aide approached and offered them fresh coffee. Meade declined, but Grant accepted. And he finally lit the cigar.

Meade had grown more than unsettled. The heat of the fire had begun to make him dizzy. It was a hot night, more

July than early May, and bad for the troops, who would discard even more of their blankets.

Grant seemed unaffected. He even had his tunic fully buttoned, which wasn't his habit.

"How long will Lee wait?" the general in chief asked. "Before he moves? I don't mean just skirmishers."

Meade looked into the firelight, as if it held the answers. He did not want to reply lightly and pay for it later.

"I'd say . . . we have a day. Or the better part of one. Longstreet's corps was in bivouac between Gordonsville and Mechanicsville. He'll have to march forty miles, if not more. He won't reach Lee before tomorrow night. *If* he moved promptly today. And given the numbers against him, Lee will want to have Longstreet up before he risks a general attack."

"You think it's going to take Pete that long? After all I've heard about Jackson's Foot Cavalry?"

"Jackson's dead."

Grant let out a mouthful of smoke. "And Longstreet isn't his equal?"

Meade warned himself to step carefully: Grant and Longstreet were known to be old friends.

"Longstreet moves . . . with more precision," Meade said. "Anyway, I don't believe he can reach Lee before tomorrow night, not in any effective condition. And Lee won't want to get into a major fight without Longstreet's corps on hand. He learned that lesson at Gettysburg, I think."

Grant drew heavily on his cigar, as if smoking it were a pleasure and burden at once. Exhaling, he smiled that troubling, close-lipped smile again.

"That so? And what did you learn at Gettysburg, George?"

"I learned," Meade told him, "that Lee never has to be taught a lesson twice."

PART II

WILDERNESS OF BLOOD

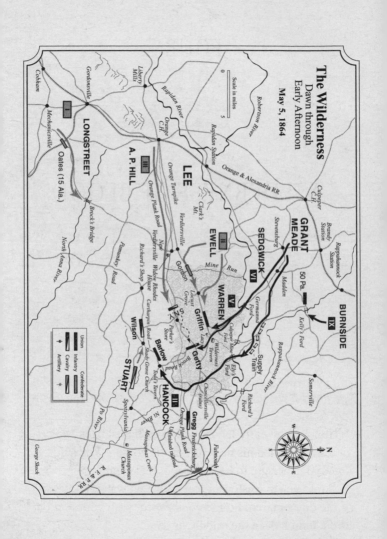

The Wilderness
Dawn through
Early Afternoon
May 5, 1864

FOUR

May 5, dawn
Kelly's Ford

W̶here you going, Private?" Sergeant Brown demanded. He had spotted the boy slipping off in the mist that rose from the river. If the shorter of the company's two John Eckerts meant to empty his bowels, he was headed in the wrong direction. And if he didn't intend to have a squat, he had no excuse to go anywhere. "And where's your cap?"

Rumpling pale hair with an awkward paw, the private said, "I was just going down for to wash my feet. I think I don't need no cap, Sergeant Brown." The boy pronounced the rank and name as "Sarchint Brawn," his Dutchie accent thick as mashed-up beans.

"You wear your cap everywhere, Private. And what did I say about washing your feet? Stand up proper when you talk to me."

Hunched by early labors with pick and shovel, the private straightened his back as best he could. "You said . . . you told us we got to keep our feet real clean."

"I told you to wash your feet with cold water. At the *end* of the day's march. I told you *never* to wash your feet before a march or in the middle of one. "

"But they hurt me."

Brown took a deep breath. It was like trying to explain mathematics to a mule. "They're going to hurt worse. You'll get used to it." He looked the boy up and down. Five foot two, with some stretch put in. But the lad had shoulders broad enough to carry the weight of the world. If he didn't get killed in his first fight, he'd do all right. "Didn't you wash your feet last night?"

"No."

"That's 'No, Sergeant.' "

"No, Sergeant."

"Why not?"

"I was every ways tired."

"Well, you're going to feel worse tonight. Just buck up." He considered the bovine stupidity that infected new recruits, leaving them stubbornly helpless. "You eat your breakfast? Or are you waiting to be told that, too?"

"I et some."

The private looked as though he expected a beating. Justice took a practical course back home on Eckert Hill.

"All right. Just go back and put on clean stockings, get yourself ready to march. You can wash those feet tonight."

Around them, the rough encampment had come to life. At any moment, the bugles would be unleashed, to the groans of the men from companies less alert. The hapless would hurry to do the things left undone the night before, and the laziest men would attempt to cajole hot coffee from their betters. Brown liked his own men up early and properly fed. You could get a Dutchman to do most anything if you kept his belly full.

"I can't," the private said. As if the words cost pain.

A shaft from the rising sun reached the boy. For an uncanny moment, John N. Eckert, private, Company C, 50th Pennsylvania Veteran Volunteer Infantry, wore a golden halo.

A horse whinnied. The regimental officers were up and interfering.

"Why can't you?"

"Because I only got the one pair of stockings now."

Brown was bewildered. Dealing with the Eckert boys wasn't like schooling a mule. It was worse. "When I turned out your rucksack in Warrenton, you had two pair. What happened?"

The boy shuffled his body without quite moving his feet. "Isaac said we have too much we are carrying, we must throw away unneeded things that make heavy the pack."

"Damn it, stockings don't weigh a thing."

The boy squirmed again. "But Isaac said—"

"I don't give a damn what Isaac says. He may be your cousin, but I'm your sergeant. Sergeants outrank cousins. You listen to what *I* say, understand? *Versteh' mal?*"

Down by the ford, a battery began to cross the Rappahannock on a pontoon bridge. The procession was barely visible through the mist that clung to the river, but the sounds confirmed its identity. Dangling their chains, the gun carriages, limbers, and caissons creaked slowly over the span and dozens of hooves clopped on the shifting planks. Engineer sergeants tending the site cursed the gunners on principle, their language riper than any heard on the Philadelphia docks. Brown considered himself a war-toughened man, but their vivid descriptions of men and women, of mothers and sons, and of various nationalities made him feel like a spinster who blushed at the word *begat* in the preacher's Bible.

"Do you understand me?" Brown demanded.

"Yes, Sergeant."

"Where are those stockings now? Where did you leave them? Back in Warrenton?"

"No, Sergeant. I give them to Isaac. He said it makes him no difference to carry them, he knows to march the right way."

"You gave Isaac Eckert your stockings?"

The boy shrugged. "He gives me Reb tobacco for them.

He wishes to be fair, since I am *verwandt,* the same in the blood."

"Come on," Brown ordered. "You come with me."

As the two of them marched across the raw encampment, Bill Wildermuth attached himself to the party.

"What do *you* want?" Brown snapped.

"Just limbering up my legs, Sergeant Brown. I been watching Isaac watching you two parley, and I figure there might be a skunk under the porch. Thought I might help you catch him."

"I'm not in joking spirits today," Brown warned him.

Isaac Eckert stood waiting for them, face stripped of emotion. He held a tin cup in one hand, a bit-off cake in the other.

"Give him his stockings," Brown said.

Eckert nodded, but the gesture had no agreement in it. "We made a trade."

"Give him the stockings. For Christ's sake, Isaac. His feet aren't toughened up. And he's your relation."

Isaac charged himself with a swig of coffee. "Fair's fair, Sergeant. Me and him made a trade. Them down-the-hill, dumb-Dutch Eckerts don't count as close blood, anyway. I mean, look at him. That hair. True Eckerts are dark-favored."

"I don't care if he's a total stranger. Just give him the stockings. So the boy at least has time to put them on. It's going to be a hard day, and you know it."

"Yes, sir!" Bill Wildermuth put in. "Going to be some *hard* marching today, the boys'll be dropping like flies. They won't stop us at the Rapidan, neither." He turned to the younger Eckert. "Son, the generals play with their peckers and forget what time it is. Then they remember there's things they got to get done, and we have to run like the cholera to catch up."

"Shut up, Bill," Brown said. He turned back to Isaac. "I gave you an order. Give the kid his stockings."

"That's not no legal order, I know my rights!" Isaac cried. He splashed the dregs of his coffee on the ground. "We made an honest trade! I want a hearing from Captain Burket, he'll say what's fair and what ain't."

"Captain Burket will listen to First Sergeant Hill. And the first sergeant will back me up. And if you think you're testing these stripes on my arm, you think again. Or we can discuss what I caught you doing at Knoxville, you shit-dripper. And that talk won't be with Captain Burket, but with Colonel Christ."

Brown was furious. He wanted to knock Isaac Eckert to the ground, but preferred not to lose the stripes he had just sewn on.

The first bugle call beat the others by a few seconds. In moments, the world seemed a madhouse of blaring trumpets and barked orders.

Henry Hill, the first sergeant's cousin, emerged from the patch of brush that had been given over to personal business. Whether or not he had heard one word of the exchange over the stockings, he seemed to sense the way the matter stood. His somber face was set.

Hill walked up to Isaac Eckert and punched him in the stomach. The blow had such force it dropped Isaac to the ground, where he groaned like a gut-shot dog.

Hill stood over him.

"You do what Sergeant Brown says."

And Hill walked away.

"I was you," Bill Wildermuth told the crumpled private, "I'd listen."

"Bill," Brown said, "you get the stockings off him. I've got things to tend to." He raised his voice. "Formation in five minutes, everybody." Turning, he saw that John Eckert had retreated a few steps. "*You*. Come with me. And you listen here. We go into battle, you don't step back from a fight, you jump right into it. Unless you want to be stupid and dead together."

The boy's reaction to the trivial violence worried him far more than the stockings fuss.

Private Eckert obeyed and followed after him. With time running out, Brown headed for the spot where he had slept out the short night. His well-trimmed rucksack and haversack leaned against a tree, watched over by Sammy Martz, the Pottsville blacksmith who clung to the canal men.

"I was going to bring your things to you, Sergeant," Martz told Brown.

Brown nodded and knelt down to unbuckle his pack. The one indulgence he allowed himself was a small hoard of clean stockings. Irate at God and Man for making him disorder his possessions and cheating him out of time for a last dose of coffee, he pulled out the first pair of stockings he could find. Frances had made them herself and had given them to him before the end of the company's leave back home.

"Get those shoes off quick," he told the Eckert boy. "And put these on. And if you so much as fall one step behind today, I'm going to take a stick to you. You understand me? And you're going to wash these good and give them back."

He lingered just long enough to glimpse the boy's bare feet. They were already blistered and bleeding, Private Eckert's first taste of war's reality.

There would be more to come, and it would come soon. For the first time, the weight of his sergeant's stripes struck him fully: He was responsible for so many lives now, for men and boys with whom he had labored on the canal, whose meals and bedding he had shared even before they went off to war. His soldiers had wives and children, sweethearts and families, back home, and he knew them all, man, woman, and child, by name, knew their kinships, legitimate and shaming, acknowledged and not, and the family secrets that never stayed kept in a small town. If they died because of his errors, how would he ever face the people back home? Would he have to wander the earth like the soul of Judas? How would he face Frances? Or live with himself?

He had weighed these matters in his mind, but now they pierced his heart.

Even as a corporal, he had done his best to prepare the new recruits, to convince them that it wasn't all a grand lark. At the end of their leave, the company had gone to Camp Curtin in Harrisburg to rejoin the regiment. Then the regiment was ordered to Annapolis to join its brigade and division. The new recruits had been full of brag and bull, ready to show the reenlisted veterans how to win the war without even sweating. So Brown had taken his charges for a walk, leading them past the grounds of the vast convalescent hospital, where thousands of men in bits and pieces of uniforms were learning to live without arms or legs or eyes. Boys imagined fine, brave deaths as a storybook romance, but never thought of the forms survival took. The spectacle of cripples loitering in the hundreds had sobered the new recruits, if only briefly.

From Annapolis, they had gone south to Warrenton, moving by a series of trains, still protected from war's temper. The forced march the day before had been the new men's welcome to a soldier's life.

Brown shouldered his rucksack, looped his haversack over his head, and stepped off to take up his rifle. He considered sending the Eckert boy back to ride on the company wagon, given the condition of his feet.

But softness killed. And no matter how bad the boy's feet became, he'd forget the misery as soon as they went into battle. The flesh had a remarkable gift for sensing what really mattered.

Brown heard First Sergeant Hill's familiar bellow, calling a company formation. Corporal Doudle rushed past him, chiding Privates Sharon and Hoffman to tighten their leathers and straighten their packs and hurry the Hell up. Doudle was clearly enjoying his new corporalcy. As he himself enjoyed being a sergeant, Brown had to admit.

"Come on, come on," he shouted to the laggards he passed on the double-quick. "Bobby Lee's waiting. Being late's bad manners."

Dawn
Orange Turnpike

Brigadier General John Brown Gordon was as pleased as a sow in a mud pit. He loved his Georgia boys, and they were fond of him and his ways, and there was nothing like a well-turned speech delivered on horseback on a fine May morning.

Straight as a mast, he rose in his stirrups, pulled off his hat, and gazed beyond the assembled ranks of his infantry, staring through the sun-gilt mists that ghosted over the fields, staring into battles immortal and glorious fame eternal. He said:

"Damnation, you boys look ready for a fight! *Georgia! Are you ready?*"

His soldiers roared. Surely, Gordon thought, surely this multitude must be heard where the Federals held Virginia's soil in thrall, these voices must be heard and set men trembling.

"Boys, you know me. And I know you. You know I don't believe, never have believed, in showing the enemy my back. My motto is *'Forward!'* But, Lord bless me, since I took command of this fine, this brave, this impeccable brigade . . . boys, I have been shamed. Yes, shamed! And shamed again. You heard me right, just still those murmurs right now. You hold your tongues and listen. You've shamed your commanding officer, a man who always led the way in the face of the enemy, and do you know why?"

Gordon surveyed the beautiful, tattered, willing ranks before him. Without dropping his rump down into the saddle, he let his mount step along. The men knew the rules and patterns of his performances and he could feel them waiting for the kicker.

"I'll *tell* you why you shame me, boys." He let his face expand in a mighty smile. "Because, once y'all get going at the Yankees, *I can't keep up with you!* You make your general look like a shirking skedaddler, like a shade tree do-nothing. *God bless Georgia!*"

A thousand voices and a thousand more howled, cheered, and bellowed their approval.

"You jest watch us, Genr'l," a voice called, piercing the hubbub. *"Even that horse a your'n won't catch us up."*

"Oh, I don't want to slow you down," Gordon responded to his bearded interlocutor, to them all. "No, gentlemen, no! I wouldn't want to be the cause of sparing those Billy Yanks one mite of the terrible blow this brigade is set to deliver upon that pusillanimous blue multitude. So . . . I'm just going to do my best to keep up with y'all. I want you boys to go at those blue devils like a high-summer hurricane and send them running back to Hell or Boston, whichever's closer."

He paused, letting the renewed cheers dissipate and scanning the ranks before him. His horse pranced and Gordon preened. Wishing Fanny were there to admire him, as she had that sweet gift of doing. He was grateful for every glimpse of the woman, for every breath she took.

Men said he loved to hear the sound of his own voice,

but Gordon didn't mind. It was the Lord's own truth. He loved to stand up and speechify, and his men loved to listen and play their parts in the spectacle. The trick, of course, was to know the men, to reach past their desires to get at their needs. Once you knew the audience, you knew the words to say, and all you had to do was to say them proper.

Softening his tone, but making his voice carry like an actor on the best stage in Savannah, Gordon told them, "Think now of those dear hearts at home in Georgia, fearing the depredations and monstrosities infernal the invader proposes for the defenseless fair . . . think of the indignities those hellish legions would gladly visit upon your wives and daughters, your sweethearts and your frail, beloved mothers. Win here, boys, win this battle that's coming our way . . . vanquish the iniquitous foe, these vandal-like invaders, this barbaric horde . . . and the flimsy efforts of the Federals infecting a small corner of our state, our beloved home, will be as nothing but air. Drive out Useless Simpleton Grant, with his coon-dog Meade at his heels, and all their hellish stratagems will fail. Here . . . perhaps on this very day . . . here in Virginia . . . *this* is where we defend Georgia's sacred soil." He lifted his hat, extending his arm to the full. His horse nickered. And with all the force his powerful voice could muster, Gordon called, *"Georgia, are you with me?"*

This roar was the mightiest response of all. A good speech never failed to spunk up the men and set them marching hard.

But Gordon's poetic idyll was destined to end. He saw a rider galloping from the direction of Early's headquarters. That messenger would bear the order to march.

The general gestured for quiet. And when the multitude had calmed, he told them, "Let us pray. . . ."

"Glory hallelujah, Jesus is Lord!" a voice called.

"Hallelujah," another seconded, followed by a third.

Gordon waved down the voices and deepened his own, pushing it to the extreme that had worked so well back in his college debating society, the sonorous timbre that would have served him beautifully as the valedictory speaker, had not his father's misfortunes put too soon an end to his education.

"Oh, Lord of hosts . . . God of battles . . . great Jehovah, who taught the armies of Israel to smite thine enemies . . . Lord, we call upon you and your only begotten son to bless us this day . . . to give us strength in the rightness . . . in the *righteousness* of our cause . . . to guide us to do your will. Let us bear your blessing into battle . . . into battle against those who, if not heathen in their faith, are become heathens through their wicked acts. Spread out your shield before us, and raise your fiery sword against the iniquitous. Look with favor upon our plea for victory in thy name . . . and dispense your endless mercy to that earthly rival to Eden, the blessed, beloved, and bounteous State of Georgia. Amen."

No congregation had ever answered with an "Amen" greater.

Gordon had calculated perfectly, as he was wont to do. Just as the amens echoed off across the glistening fields, the messenger covered the final stretch and reined in his mount by the general.

"It's all right, son," Gordon told him. "Georgia's ready to march."

Gordon liked to think of himself as a shepherd to his men, but knew that his brigade was a pack of wolves. And that was all right. Alexander had conquered the known world with lesser soldiers. And if he had gotten too late a start in military affairs to become an Alexander, that was all right, too. He preferred to cast himself as another Ulysses, courageous, but wise in guile and a skillful orator. He only hoped *his* homecoming would not drag on for ten years.

His Fanny was a warm, loving woman who deserved a husband by her side every single night of the year. Nor was there a better place on earth than in his Fanny's arms. When his wife held him close in their blessed bed, it mended the world's deficiencies. She made him laugh and laughed at him when he needed to be laughed at, but did it as though she were petting a favored dog. As fair as Helen, she was Penelope in her fortitude and loyalty. Brave as an Amazon, too. Not content to visit him in the lulls between campaigns, she followed the army in the field, whenever she could come by a team of horses. His Fanny. Had ever nobler woman lived, the Attic bards would surely have made her immortal.

Gordon was a happy man, if a sane man could be happy amid a war. He had his moods, as did everyone, but relished the joys to be found each given day. And on those hard, rare days when not one jot of pleasure was to be had, he reveled in memories of other, better times. He loved a well-roasted chicken, well-made whiskey, and well-bred horses, his wife's affection and the baked-bread smell of her, and war had only intensified his pleasure in common things. He found battle exciting and had a gift for leading men through the Valley of the Shadow. He could fight.

But he never forgot that every war ends—even the walls of Troy had fallen at last—and he thought beyond the day when peace would come. If the Lord permitted him to survive, he meant to plunge into politics as furiously as he had plunged into every battle, determined to win at all costs. If the Confederacy fought its way to freedom, the heroes of the war would be invincible at the ballot box. Not even a low-country congressman by birthright would be able to steal enough votes to beat a veteran. And if the South was humbled in defeat—a possibility that had to be faced quietly—Georgia would need her heroes to raise her up again.

Politics would suit him, he believed. He loved adulation, and was man enough to admit it: The cheers of his soldiers were worth any risk to his life. He envisioned himself as a governor or senator, a tribune of the people, a generous Caesar. And when he passed on, at a patriarchal age, throngs of mourners would respond as did Shakespeare's Cleopatra to Antony's death: "The odds is gone and there is nothing left remarkable beneath the visiting moon."

"What say, General?"

"Just thinking out loud," he told his temporary adjutant, "just thinking out loud, son."

"Going to be a hot one, sir." The captain lifted his hat, fanned himself, and covered his head again.

"Virginia hot," Gordon said. "But not Georgia hot."

"Sir?"

"Yes?"

"Put a question to you?"

"You may, lad. And I may, or may not, answer it."

They rode past a black child sucking its thumb by the roadside and marveling at the circus the fates had delivered.

"Sir, what do you think Sherman's going to do? Where's he going to aim at? In your opinion?"

"You mean what's he going to *try* to do. Before General Johnston lures him unto defeat and degradation."

"Yes, sir. Pardon. My folk are out of Dalton, you know."

"General Sherman will never reach Dalton, Captain. He shall not glimpse the spires of her churches."

"And that's what you really think, General?"

Gordon spit beyond his stirrup, willing his mouth clean of the endless grit. They were marching at the tail end of the division and the clouds of dust looked a quarter mile high.

"Hell, boy, I don't know. Sherman's going to do his best to march right down to Atlanta, and old Joe's going to do his best to stop him. The Lord and the guns will decide."

"I wish we were down there, sir. To give Bloody Billy the licking he deserves. Rather than up here, where we can't help none."

"Here or there," Gordon said, "it's the same war." He urged on his slowing horse and returned a much-diminished company's greeting with a flourish. "Everything's going to be fine," he told the adjutant, "just wait and see. We win this battle coming on and, the good Lord willing, everything will be fine. Now ride on back and see we don't have any stragglers."

But Gordon wondered, as he rode along, how he would feel if his kinfolk lived in Dalton.

Nine a.m.
Orange Turnpike

Brigadier General Charles Griffin was an abstemious man with a barroom temper, and he didn't like what he saw. The commander of the First Division of Warren's Fifth Corps was loved by his men for a number of reasons, some of them unreasonable, but above all because they sensed that he would not waste their lives, if he could help it. That morning, as he watched dust clouds on the Turnpike resolve themselves into Confederates, he knew that a battle had come to him, just not where anybody had expected it. And lives would be wasted indeed.

"Where the fuck-all is the cavalry?" he asked in the gentlest tone he would use all day. "Those sonsofbitches were supposed to be picketing that road, the worthless pissants."

None of his aides or couriers proposed an answer. Avoiding his eyes, they pretended to calm their horses.

But there they were, Reb infantry in at least brigade strength, not a mile away and going to ground on a ridge Griffin damned well didn't want to charge. And a Reb brigade meant a division was behind it. A division meant a corps.

He drew a notebook and pencil from a pocket of his tunic. His horse shook and settled again. As Griffin wrote, he glanced up now and then, monitoring the arrival of his enemies, and said, twice, "Warren's fucked for beans." The second time, he added, "I suppose the damned plan took account of every last thing but Robert E. Lee."

When he finished writing, he handed the dispatch to an officer he trusted. "You get this to General Warren, if you have to carry that fucking horse on your back, boy. If you can't find goddamned Warren, go right to General Meade."

As the captain galloped off, Griffin watched a knot of Reb horsemen pause on the high ground down to the west, looking toward the Union force just as Griffin was measuring them.

"Fuck me to blue blazes," he said.

Skirmishers pecked at the morning.

Griffin began shouting orders to couriers to race up the forest track that veered from the Turnpike and along which the bulk of the corps had been advancing, like idiot Texans strolling right into a Comanche ambush. His brigades were to halt their marches, to hold where they were, face right-front, and get to work on field fortifications, in case the Rebs intended to come on and not just dig ditches up along that ridge.

The general spurred his horse forward, deeper into the field, barking that he wanted a battery placed just there. Cursing himself for his oversight, he sent another rider forward to inform the corps' lead divisions about the appearance of Reb infantry on their right flank. Raging and impatient and feeling cornered by fate, he turned to the nearest artilleryman too soon for his query to make any sense and barked, "Schuyler, where the fuck-all are my guns?"

Before the dumbfounded redleg could answer, the division commander spurred toward his nearest brigadier.

"Bartlett! Get some of your boys out, prod 'em. See what they're up to. Don't get into a goddamned wrestling match, just find out who we're up against. I need some fucking numbers. Warren's going to be pissing all over, and we can't just scratch our asses."

As Griffin rode along his lined-up regiments, the men cheered. And when he snapped, "I don't see one goddamned thing to cheer about, you dumb bastards," they cheered more heartily.

His men, his boys. In dusty blue or the faded costume-ball outfits of Zouaves. *His boys*.

"Fucked for beans," he muttered to himself.

Ten a.m.
Orange Plank Road

Approaching the dismounted cavalrymen from behind, the chaplain called, "Fear not! For if the Lord hath granted them a multitude, he hath given unto you the Spencer carbine!"

Lieutenant Colonel John Hammond dashed across the Plank Road toward the chaplain, who was standing erect as Minié balls split the air.

"The Lord's judgment shall be visited upon the infamous brethren of Joseph, who enslaved the cherished son . . ."

Louis Napoleon Beaudry had been captured just after Gettysburg and had suffered for months in Rebel prisons before being exchanged. Since the preacher's return to the regiment, he had put the fear of God into his charges and the Fifth New York Cavalry had the lowest court-martial rate in the mounted arm, but Hammond had come to question the man's soundness.

As the colonel cleared the open ground, a bullet smacked into a scrub oak right in front of him. Hammond yanked the preacher to his knees. Clutching his Bible in one hand and putting right his spectacles with the other, Beaudry looked affronted.

Behind the man of the cloth crouched Sergeant McManus, waiting for Company K to pass back through so he could sport with the Rebels again. The sergeant fondled his carbine with the affection he might, under other circumstances, have displayed toward a woman. Face soiled by hours of fighting and scarred by years of hard living, he grinned at Hammond's discovery of the preacher.

Yelling over the din, Hammond told the chaplain, "I ordered you to the rear an hour ago."

Even on his knees, the preacher held his spine upright. He would bend in prayer, but not to the dross of the world. His calling was more Old Testament than Gospels, with a great deal of smiting heathens recommended.

"The men of the Fifth New York are a flock in my keeping, sir," the chaplain announced. "I must not abandon my sheep this day, no more than you would desert your command, Colonel Hammond."

"Chaplain . . ." Hammond wondered if the man really understood that there was a definite border between life and death. "I just had to leave Captain McGuinn behind. Terribly wounded, maybe dead. I don't want—"

"The Lord will look fondly upon Captain McGuinn."

"Chaplain, listen to me. I'm giving you a *second* direct order: Go to the rear. Comfort the wounded. And tell Lieutenant Hayward to send ammunition."

The one curse of the Spencer, with its seven-round magazine and high rate of fire, was that the ordnance system had not caught up with the increased ammunition expenditure. Hammond considered himself an honest Christian, but he had broken a decalogue of military commandments to amass extra rounds for his regiment. Even so, the length of this running fight had drained his stock.

The chaplain didn't move.

"Chaplain Beaudry . . . do *not* defy me."

The chaplain lowered his eyes. In dismay at mankind's folly. "I answer to a Higher Power," he said.

Hammond had no more time to spare. The Confederates threatened to overrun Company K in its forward outpost. Captain O'Connor should have pulled back minutes before.

Hammond hoped O'Connor hadn't fallen. Company K needed a commander, and its surviving lieutenant wouldn't do. He would have to go forward himself and see them extricated. A dozen tasks competed for his attention. And here he was, debating with a preacher.

Another volley tore through the trees and shrubs, ripping leaves from their branches and splintering wood.

"*Damn* you, Chaplain!"

Ignoring the death that filled the air, Beaudry got to his feet. A prematurely wizened man, as scrawny as starvation in the flesh, he possessed eyes ablaze with faith and a voice made for the pulpit. He stared down at the colonel with a look to curdle the milk of human kindness.

Sheepish, Hammond rose and stood as well. Knowing it was idiocy.

"John Hammond!" the chaplain bellowed in his tent revival voice. "What would your dear wife and children say . . . if *they* knew you had disgraced yourself by profane language in the face of eternity?"

Sergeant McManus—who had not signed the chaplain's Temperance Union pledge—rolled half over and cackled,

"You school that colonel, Chaplain. For we'll all be in Heaven or elsewhere before nightfall." The sergeant turned back to his business, aiming his carbine down the road, finger caressing the trigger in a manner to evoke lascivious thoughts.

Moments were precious. Hammond's regiment had delayed the Rebel host for over three hours, parrying a Confederate brigade. And mighty dust clouds rose behind that brigade. Leapfrogging backward from one position to the next, clinging to each until it was about to be overrun, his cavalrymen had pulled off an earthly miracle. Thanks, as the chaplain had noted, to the Lord and their repeating carbines.

They had fought for every yard. But the yards had turned to miles. Parker's Store, where they had spent the night, was far behind the Secesh infantry now.

"I'm sorry, Chaplain," the colonel said. "Forgive me." Even as he spoke, he knew it was bedlam mad to waste time on such things in the middle of a maelstrom. Lifting his cap, he wiped the grease of sweat and dust and powder from his forehead. His eyes ached. "But you still have to go to the rear. Do you want to go back to Libby?"

A grisly chance at redeeming the situation thrashed out of the dwarf pines. Two troopers were making a rearward run, with the arms of a wounded man over their shoulders.

"*There's* something you can do," he told the chaplain. "Comfort Billings, help him to the rear."

But Beaudry was already on his way, rushing to alleviate the burden of the quick and the nearly dead.

He was a remarkable man, Hammond had to admit. The chaplain had convinced over two hundred cavalrymen to sign his Temperance Union pledge. Nearly as many had signed a pledge not to curse. The piety of the Fifth New York Cavalry had given General Kilpatrick no end of amusement, before the general was removed by a higher hand—not the Lord's, but General Meade's, which came close enough.

Helping to lug the wounded man along, Beaudry bellowed: "Show them, boys! Show those heathens how Christian soldiers fight!"

Hammond got considerably closer to the ground and told the sergeant, "McManus, I'm going forward to see what the devil's the matter with Company K. Try not to shoot me. And send a man to tell the horse-holders to pull back a hundred yards."

"May you fly on the wings of the angels, sir."

"I'll settle for my horse, if no relief comes."

Clutching a fallen trooper's carbine, Hammond set off at a run. The regiment's major was off to the rear, and he had no couriers left. Each of those men had been sent to the rear to beg for a relief force. He was losing troopers right and left, and even repeating rifles could not keep off the swelling hordes that came screaming down the road and through the brush.

A round tore the air so close to his eyes, it briefly stole his vision. He stumbled, failed to catch himself, and plunged into the scrub growth.

Terrifying moments of dizziness froze him where he fell.

After seconds that seemed a small eternity, his vision came back in a blink. Two troopers lay on their bellies in front of him, staring. When they realized he had not been shot, one held up an empty magazine and said, "We're out of rounds, Colonel. We can't do no more without no ammunition."

"Fall back and rally at Company H's position. Wait there for your officers."

He knew the two men. He knew each man in the regiment and could readily put a first name to nine out of ten.

But in battle only the wounded were addressed by their Christian names.

"Get out of here. *Go!*"

The troopers dodged to the rear and Hammond thrust himself forward through the brambles. His uniform was torn like a beggar's rags and his flesh burned with scratches from hours of scrambling through this foretaste of Hell, but he'd call it luck if that was the worst that happened.

Arriving at the heart of the forward position, he shouted, "Captain O'Connor? Where's Captain O'Connor?" Ripples and crackles of rifle fire competed with the raw voice that remained to him.

"Here, sir! Over here!" O'Connor was on the firing line on the other side of the road, but the Rebels were too close now for a man to survive a dash across the open ground. "They're coming around on both flanks," the captain added.

"*I know.* Pull your men back." He waved: *Withdraw.* "Get out of here." He almost said, "Get the Hell out of here," but the chaplain's spirit hovered.

"We got a prisoner. One of Hill's boys."

That meant a Confederate corps was on that road.

"Just get out of here," Hammond shouted. "Rally on Company H. Tell Barker I expect to pass Company D through in twenty minutes."

Wretched with dust, his throat was parched and torn. His canteen was not only back with his horse, but long since emptied. The heat had begun early and gotten worse. He tasted powder and smoke, mixed with belly acid. "If Barker doesn't hear from me, he's to take command and hold as long as he can."

The captain was already moving, shouting to his troopers. Hammond wondered how much the man had heard.

He risked a look straight down the road and saw

gray-clad soldiers, at least a hundred, preparing to charge. And on they came, with a maddened Rebel yell.

He hoped the withdrawing troopers had some rounds left. They were going to have to fight their way to the rear.

Hammond knelt by the roadside, aimed, and fired, then went on firing until the weapon had emptied. Around him, the rapid report of other Spencers chattered and bit the on-coming Rebels. Company K still punched. The impromptu attack faltered.

But the problem of withdrawing hadn't been solved. Hammond understood that the charge had been a display to draw their attention away from the flanks.

"Out of here! Now!" he shouted.

His voice didn't count for much against the racket.

The men ran pell-mell. Hammond raced off, too. A boy fell at his side. The colonel swooped to help him, but the lad—Private Timothy Owens—had been shot in the back of the head. Blood and brains clotted the dust.

Inserting his last magazine tube as he ran, Hammond sensed a fusillade and threw himself back into the trees. Massed rounds ripped the air.

How could a man know such a thing would happen? And why didn't every man know? Even the chaplain would have no answer to that. Unless he pleaded destiny, which was the Presbyterian excuse.

"Keep going, keep going!" Hammond yelled. He fired three rounds toward the approaching Confederates, then ran again.

He just wanted to buy more time, a little more time. Until someone at some headquarters came to his senses.

As soon as they could safely do so, the troopers with Sergeant McManus put out covering fire. Even with the carbines, it was no more than a plinking compared to the Secesh volleys.

The good thing, if there was one, was that the Rebs were

tired, too, and weren't aiming closely. Hammond could tell: They were just laying down fire, a mechanical act.

Instantly, he prayed he hadn't doomed himself by thinking that. He could almost feel a bullet in his back.

It was time to stop playing captain and become a lieutenant colonel again. He had to organize further defensive positions, to command what remained of his regiment, not just a stranded company. And he had to send yet another message to the rear. What did he have to do, write it in blood?

Didn't they *see*? Didn't they understand? His dying regiment had hardly another mile at its back before it was pushed past the crossing of the Plank Road and Brock Road. Hammond didn't know everything about the army's plans, but he had become enough of a cavalryman to recognize that the crossroads was the key to the army's position. If the Confederates took it, they'd split the army in two.

This war of fighting dismounted with repeating rifles was ugly and new, a far different business from drawing sabers to cut through Confederate horsemen at Orange Courthouse or playing cat and mouse with the villainous Mosby. They had gone from a certain glory, if a grim one, to grinding murder.

Hammond dropped to his knees beside Sergeant McManus. Gasping.

"I suppose them angels skedaddled on you, sir," McManus said. "You'd best catch your wind."

"McManus, I may court-martial you. Just to remind my officers how to hold one."

The sergeant grinned. "As long as I don't have to take me no temperance pledge, sir."

McManus went back to firing, choosing his targets coldly. He was far from a godly man, but a very good one.

Still out of breath, Hammond rose and scurried back to

where he'd left his horse in a private's care. He needed to ride at a gallop now, to choose more fighting ground amid the brief stretch between his firing line and the crossroads. And he needed a count of the remaining ammunition.

What had Wilson been thinking? Hammond had known that his regiment was too small a force to be left to cover a prime route for the enemy. Worse, the new general from out in the West had left the northern road, the Turnpike, completely uncovered. It was no way to screen an army.

He calculated that Wilson had his hands full himself now, though. Cannon had been sounding to the south, away from the main army, but just about where the general and his horsemen would be.

It was all a mess. A *damned* one.

At least his mount was waiting, his lovely black stallion. Restless and nickering, the horse seemed about to explode with animal energy. When it saw him, it tried to pull away from the horse-holder and come to him.

Before he could lift himself into the saddle, Hammond spied the chaplain hurrying up the road again. In blunt defiance of Hammond's orders, Beaudry led a detail of dismounted troopers. They lugged the small, heavy crates that held rounds for the carbines.

As Hammond approached the sweating men, three things happened:

First, another Rebel yell went up, a powerful one this time.

Second, a corporal blurted out, "'Tis the last of it, sir. I told the chaplain, didn't I? This is it."

And third, the preacher laid his hands on the nearest wooden boxes, raised his eyes to Heaven, and cried, "Lord, let it be as with the loaves and fishes!"

"Amen," Hammond said.

FIVE

L ee and Hill rode past the bodies of two more Union cavalrymen. A wounded mount grazed nearby, favoring a hind leg. The sight of the horse pained Lee. Not because of the ugly gash on its hindquarters, but thanks to its evident health in other respects. The animal had been well fed, and the gleam of its coat was more than the sheen of sweat. His army's cavalry mounts and the teams that drew his guns were lean and weakened. Half-starved themselves, the men who rode or drove those horses would have to make up their deficiencies with courage.

How much could valor do?

Skirmishing rattled the morning and light smoke marred the sky. Hill had Kirkland's men deployed ahead, pushing along the Plank Road toward the crossroads, while Ewell's soldiers watched the Federals to the north, along the Turnpike. A struggle here would contest the roads, Lee knew. The terrain between his two forward corps was a low forest mad with brambles, a grim place that warned men away. He could not ignore it, but lacked the numbers or the inclination to fight in it. The essential thing now was to divert those people from a movement south, without getting caught in a grip he could not escape.

"Just up there," Hill said, pointing. "Up by that shanty. Best spot to place your headquarters for now, sir." As they turned their horses into the rising field, he twisted his scarecrow's shoulders to face Lee. "Can't see much, but it's better than seeing nothing. My people call this 'poison land.' Don't even like passing through."

The generals dismounted near the crest, at the edge of an unkempt field, and walked into the shade. Staff officers scurried about, while enlisted men led off the horses to cool them down. Walter Taylor brought Lee his binoculars.

Lee scanned the horizon. And saw nothing. Where the trees began, several hundred yards away, a realm of secrets waited.

He heard a swell of firing well to the north. If the maps ran true, Ewell's men were nearly three miles away, with only a few vague trails linking them to Hill's corps. There would be no swift reinforcements, should the fighting explode. Each corps would fight on its own. Until Longstreet came up.

With handsome timing, Sandie Pendleton appeared. Whenever he saw the young man, Lee felt a twinge. The long-faced, graceful major sparked thoughts of Jackson, who had favored the lad.

Pendleton dismounted, saluted, and approached Taylor first. The adjutant nodded, authorizing the major to speak to Lee.

Saluting again, Pendleton said, "General Ewell's compliments, sir. The Federals are gathering to his front. It's the Fifth Corps, General Warren's. General Ewell believes they'll attack. Our position is sound, sir, but more Federals have been moving to the south and southwest, into the forest. General Ewell awaits your orders, sir."

"My orders stand," Lee told him. "I prefer that General Ewell not become inextricably engaged. If he can maintain his position without discomfiture, he should do so. If he finds himself pressed, he may withdraw to Mine Run." Lee glanced at Hill, whose long hair clung to a cadaverous face. He feared Hill's illness was haunting him again.

"Any such movement will be coordinated with General Hill and his corps, of course. We must act in unison."

"Yes, sir." The young man saluted and turned toward his mount.

"Major Pendleton?"

The boy pivoted. "Sir?"

"You may not need a rest, but I recommend you grant your horse a few minutes. He will be hard used this day."

As we all may be, Lee told himself.

Lee and Hill had ridden ahead of the main body of the Culpeper native's corps. Hill knew the ground as well as any of Lee's generals. Which was to say imperfectly. The Wilderness was not a place to hold men's interest in better times, and past campaigns had rushed through it, gripping the roads. Even Jackson had only pierced its edges, leaving these brambles and swamps an unknown world.

Lee consoled himself that the generals in blue suffered ignorance worse than his own. He counted on that to render them wary and slow.

If Longstreet was still many miles to the west, another welcome face appeared in his stead. Waving his hat and its long widow's plume, Stuart encouraged his mount to prance up the slope toward Lee and his staff. The man was incorrigible. But his theatrics tricked a faint smile out of Lee.

With the grin of a naughty child, Stuart dismounted, saluted all present, and strode toward Lee and Hill.

"My compliments, gentlemen." Instead of saluting, he tipped his hat. "General Lee, sir, General Hill. Lovely day. Bit warm. Hot, actually. D'you know that Wilson? Grant's new boy? Not Sheridan, the other one. Engineer fellow they gave a division of cavalry? Insult to the mounted arm, as far as I'm concerned. Well, we just gave young Master Wilson a spanking he'll remember. Fellow had the nerve to stand and fight. He'll learn, I s'pose." Stuart laughed merrily. "Oh, it was splendid!"

Lee suspected that it had not been splendid at all, but deadly and ugly. The Federal horsemen had improved much over the years, and their numbers were daunting. But Stuart was Stuart. The man would laugh at his funeral. And call for a banjo tune.

"I've got cavalry to my front," Hill told Stuart. "New York boys. Scrappy."

"Like me to see to 'em?"

"Oh, I expect we can handle them. Just wondering why your boys didn't run 'em off earlier."

Lee felt compelled to enter the discussion. "Perhaps," he told Hill, "we might press them a bit harder now. Since General Ewell reports troops moving southward. We must possess the crossroads."

Alert to every gradation of Lee's tone, Hill said: "Yes, sir. Kirkland hasn't been slouching, I didn't mean that. The Yankees have been giving a fair account of themselves." He glanced at Stuart. "Up here, at least. But I'll see to it that we finish things up right now." He strode off to give orders to an aide.

It was always a difficult thing, finding the correct words and the precise tone to make men do what had to be done without exciting their tempers or wounding their pride. A hint that a man had faltered turned bravery spendthrift. And men had a genius for hearing what they wished to hear, be it for good or ill.

But the crossroads up ahead had to be seized and held, if the army was going to fight upon this ground. Hill had been too slow, content to await the arrival of more men. Should they be forced to withdraw to Mine Run before Longstreet arrived, the crossroads could be held by a rear guard, preventing those people from mounting a strong pursuit and creating disorder.

Time, it was always about time. It was the factor in war that had no give.

Grant and Meade just needed to allow him a little time now. If he could fix them, hold them passively before him, until Longstreet appeared . . .

Around him, staff men who had not slept lay in the shade to rest. Orderlies groomed horses, while others started a fire for the coffee Lee no longer dared to drink in quantity.

At least his bowels had been merciful this day. And his heart beat painlessly.

Good omens? He prayed the Lord would let him survive to see his duty through.

Stepping from the shade into the sunlight, yearning to see more of the fight than the undergrowth allowed, Lee asked: "What other news have you brought us, General Stuart?"

Belatedly drawing off his riding gauntlets, Stuart said, "Hancock's down on the Catharpin Road. Same as earlier, sir. Sedgwick's back between Warren and the river, just plain crawling along the road down from the ford. His men are packed thick as fleas on an old shuck mattress, I'd love to have a few batteries up there."

"General Burnside?"

"He's across the Rappahannock, but still well north of the Rapidan. He won't be worth much until tonight." Stuart smiled. "Maybe not then, either."

Lee's mien grew earnest. "I need you close now, General Stuart. Parry their cavalry, blind them. The southern flank must be held open for General Longstreet. His approach must not be detected."

"I was thinking, General, that I might have a go at their trains in the meantime. Fitz could do it. Just another brigade or so, bring up his numbers a little."

"No. Not now. I need you to safeguard our flanks. And to keep me informed. We must not be embarrassed by General Grant in our first encounter."

"Man's a famous drunk. He won't get any farther than Joe Hooker."

Lee let the remarks pass, but he was tired of such flippancies. He knew too well the cost of underestimating an opponent. As he had George Meade at Gettysburg.

Eastward, along the Plank Road, the firing expanded. Hill's aide had delivered the general's message forcefully. The crossroads soon would be occupied. And they would see to the next order of business.

Hill rejoined Lee and Stuart. Pretending mortification, he said, "Jeb, you're sweating, boy. I didn't think a cavalryman ever broke a sweat."

Stuart doffed his hat and bowed. "You will note, General Hill, that I am dismounted at present. Thus—to my immeasurable sorrow—I must be counted among the infantry. And I have observed that infantrymen sweat copiously, sir. Indeed, their perspiration is extravagant."

Hill shook his head and his grin showed a broken front tooth. "Stuart, I swear. This war ends, I'm going to stuff you for a peacock and charge admission."

Lee felt the heat strike suddenly. A wave of it swept over him, its effect almost prostrating. He turned to step into the shade, but was stopped by a sight that astonished him.

Not two hundred yards away, a blue skirmish line emerged from the gloom of the trees, headed straight for the generals.

Lee thrust out his hand and gripped Stuart's forearm.

"Gently," Lee said.

Turning his back on the Federal troops—who advanced with bayonets fixed—Lee forced himself to walk slowly. But his heart beat like a drum calling men to arms.

"Gently," he repeated as staff men rushed toward him, betraying alarm. "Colonel Taylor, let us go quietly. We must not appear troubled."

He kept on walking down toward the road without looking back. Taylor called softly to an aide to bring Lee's horse.

Still no shots, no shouts.

Hill's man, Palmer, galloped past to hurry forward any troops he could find. Behind himself, Lee heard shouted commands and whinnying horses as the staff men tried to decide whether it was wiser to put up a fight or just get away.

Good Lord, Lee thought, veering as close to harsh language as he ever did, were they to take him, Hill, and Stuart at one grab . . .

Still no shots. Lee could not understand it. But he would not, could not, turn. Those people must not recognize him.

Where had they come from? Federal troops weren't supposed to be anywhere near. They could only have forced their way through the heart of the Wilderness.

The realization chilled him.

An orderly brought up the horse and saw Lee mounted. He was about to spur the mount into a gallop when Stuart overtook him.

The cavalryman was laughing.

"Yankees hightailed it," he said, speaking through his mirth. "They were just as surprised to see us as we were to see them. Somebody shouted, 'Right about!' and off they went like rabbits. Probably in Philadelphia by now. "

The relief Lee felt was real enough, but had a queerness to it. His spine softened and he slouched like an old man, an indulgence he never allowed himself in the presence of subordinates of any rank. It was almost as if he had relished the danger, had wanted something to happen, something definite, permanent, and had been disappointed. The sensation was new, and he did not understand it.

Lee corrected his posture. "I feared a grave misfortune," he told Stuart. "This army could not spare you or General Hill."

The young man riding beside him laughed again. He loved to laugh, to play the cavalier. But Lee could feel the days allotted for merriment running out.

"Oh, they never would've caught up with Powell Hill or me. My man Boteler was dead asleep under a tree, though. Should've seen his face when he woke up. Yanks would've bagged him sure."

Lee felt a surge of temper. It was not a joking matter. Tragedy had been averted only by the mercy of the Creator. He needed Stuart to comport himself sensibly now, to avoid theatrics and unwarranted risks.

Before Lee could speak, the first troops of Hill's main body came into view. The weary men cheered at the sight of him.

Eleven thirty a.m.
Brock Road

Brigadier General George Washington Getty never lost his composure in front of his men, but there were times when he came close. This was one of those times.

First, his division had been stripped of one brigade. Then Meade's bald-headed schoolboy, Lyman, had arrived with orders for him to make a forced march to the Brock Road and Orange Plank Road crossing, which had been left undefended, except for a handful of jockeys off in the wilds. The folly of failing to cover that crossroads was insufferable. Even on the crudest map, a beardless lieutenant could see the junction's importance.

Now his division's men were marching hard, racing two miles from the rear in a frantic effort to arrive before what might be an entire Confederate corps. And Hancock apparently was so far south of the action that he might as well have been off fighting Seminoles.

Getty held his frustrations inside as he galloped ahead of his troops, accompanied only by his staff and some couriers. He was a Regular, a veteran of Mexico and of Florida's endless swamp fights, and he did not intend to fail his army today.

At last, he could see the crossroads in the distance. There was heavy firing ahead.

What happened next further strained his self-control. A gaggle of blue-clad horsemen streamed back through the junction, riding as if the devil were at their heels. Careless of Getty and his staff, they thundered past, raising dust and flinging up clots of dirt. One called:

"Rebs are up that road. Thousands of 'em."

A captain came on at a slower pace, barely a canter, accompanied by a handful of his troopers in fair order. Getty waved him to a halt.

Keeping his voice low and stern, he demanded, "And where are you going, Captain? Shall I help you find the enemy? Who's your commanding officer?"

The captain was not daunted. "I know where the Rebs are, General. I'm from the Fifth New York, and we've been holding them off for five hours. We're out of ammunition, and we've been out. Take it up with Colonel Hammond, if that's your pleasure." The horseman grew angrier. "If you want to know where I'm going, tell me where you and your fancy-boys have been."

Getty waved the captain off and spurred his horse forward, shouting to an aide to ride back and order his men to come on at the double-quick.

Five hours? Even allowing for heat-of-battle exaggeration, it suggested infernal neglect. What had Meade's staff been doing all the while? And then to send Lyman down with a flurry of commands, jumping the chain of command and sending his division to fix the mess made by the neglect of others . . .

Getty gave his horse the spurs again, letting his officers keep up as best they could. A few more horsemen passed them, galloping for the rear. Blood marked more than one man. A crimson-pated sergeant could barely stay in the saddle.

Five hours? Even had it been only three, or even two . . . why had nothing been done? Cavalry couldn't be expected to hold back infantry that long.

He rued his tone toward the New York captain.

Getty reined up in the middle of the crossroads. His horse lifted its forelegs at the hard tug on the bit, then settled down. The general's staff filled in around him.

There were no more blue-coated cavalrymen to be seen, but a few hundred yards down the road there were plenty of men on foot. They wore gray uniforms.

How far back was his first regiment?

"Gentlemen," Getty said, raising his voice just slightly above the fuss, the horse jangle and gunfire, "my orders are to hold this point at any risk, and I always obey my orders. Arrange yourselves to my left and right, as if preparing to charge. Color sergeant to me."

"Sir . . . you're not really going to charge them?"

"No, Major. But *they* don't know that."

His officers and a pair of couriers nudged their horses forward to Getty's flanks, filling up the crossroads as best they could. It made for a meager offering.

Bullets tore past as Rebels paused to fire. The men in gray advanced carefully, unsure of what might be waiting for them, of what the Yankees might have up their sleeves.

Let them pause over their doubts, Getty prayed to the old god of soldiers. Let their imaginations course with possibilities. Let them feel a twist of dread at each step.

"Steady, gentlemen," he said.

Clipped by bullets, small branches fell, their new leaves brilliant even in the shade. An orderly gasped and folded onto his horse's mane. Blood burst from his mouth.

"Steady," Getty repeated. "No man moves, except at my command."

The general considered drawing his saber, but decided against it. A display of confidence was of more use than bravado.

"General," an aide said, "at least move back yourself."

"The division will arrive shortly, Major Wolcott. Meanwhile, our place of duty is right here."

The Rebels were gaining confidence, moving more quickly. The blessing was that fewer paused to fire.

They know, Getty thought. The bastards have seen through the bluff.

Where were his troops? He felt a surge of rage. But the expression on his face remained unchanged. And he did not mean to change it even in death.

He beat down the anger, reminding himself that his troops were good men, as good as could be found, and they were doubtless moving as fast as they could.

A round caught the division's flag, tearing the silk. But the color sergeant righted it again.

Getty could make out Confederate faces now, their beards first, then their features. Men as lean as he was himself, as fierce. Brave men. But his own must be braver this day.

He could feel the tension in the men beside him, the awful waiting for death or a terrible wound. Miraculously, all but the orderly remained untouched.

"Steady, gentlemen. Just hold steady."

A few of the Rebs got a cheer going, another version of their banshee's wail. Some dashed up the road now, as if toward a prize.

"Gentlemen, your pistols," he said. But he did not draw his own. As rounds snapped off on either side of him, Getty continued looking straight ahead. Staring down his opponent in the ultimate poker game.

Was this the start of a momentous battle? Or would he and these men be sacrificed for a diversion that would be forgotten in days? What did soldiers ever die for, really, if not for the call of soldiering itself? Was every glorious cause a mere excuse?

His officers and men soon emptied their pistols.

The leading Rebels had come within fifty yards. If they paused to fire now, their rounds would tell.

"Don't reload," he ordered. "Just keep pointing your pistols at them. Bluff them."

Struck by a ball, a horse became unmanageable. The rider fought to keep it in the line.

It was a matter of seconds now. And the race would be lost.

Nothing Getty had ever heard sounded finer, more purely beautiful, than the cheers that rose at his back. And the manly cheers—deep Northern cheers—were followed by the pounding of hundreds of feet coming on at a run.

Frank Wheaton rode up beside him, leading his Pennsylvania Volunteers. The veteran soldiers knew what to do. Without command, they formed in line in front of the waiting horsemen.

Shortening his commands to the essentials, Wheaton barked, "Front! Fire!"

The first volley was a ragged one, but it told. Balls met the advancing Confederates, sweeping the road and scouring the brush.

The balance of fate had changed. The Confederates were outnumbered now, at least for the present. And they recognized it. Shouting curses, the shabby men withdrew, some of them pausing to shoot in a show of defiance.

Others refused to bolt into the bushes, keeping to the road they had briefly possessed, suicidal in their courage and rage.

"Nicely done, Frank," Getty said. "Now push your men out a little, would you? We're on our own until Hancock decides to show up."

The nearest Rebel dead lay within thirty yards.

Eleven thirty a.m.
Orange Turnpike

Meade found Warren beyond the shabby plantation house. Surrounded by his mounted staff and hangers-on, the Fifth Corps commander was arguing with Griffin, a tough old soldier.

Damned society ball, Meade thought as he aimed his mount into the crowd. He could not see or hear one sign of the attack he had ordered Warren to make hours earlier. If anything, the skirmishing had dropped off on Warren's front.

Warren and Griffin broke off their exchange at Meade's approach, but their faces told the story: Warren wore the look of a truant caught out by his teacher, while Griffin's expression remained hot and defiant. Meade thought Warren a fool for allowing subordinates to entertain themselves by listening to generals bicker. It was like a blasted minstrel show, with gunpowder for blackface.

"All of you," Meade snapped, "clear out."

The staff men and the merely curious nudged their horses off in every direction, toward an idle battery, or to the rear, or, in a few cases, closer to the troops gathered down in the pasture.

General Griffin did not go.

Meade mastered his temper as best he could, but spoke

curtly: "I wish to speak with General Warren privately. If you don't mind, General Griffin."

Throwing invisible sparks, Griffin saluted and kicked his horse into motion.

When they were alone—as alone as they could be in full view of hundreds of onlookers—Meade said, "Damn me to blazes, G.K. How many orders to attack do I have to give you?"

"George—"

"You should've been at them hours ago. Grant's fuming."

"I'm trying to—"

"Our reputation's at stake, man. Here. Now. *Today.* Grant's been told over and over that the Army of the Potomac doesn't fight. And here we are, the first damned time he orders an attack, and I might as well be giving commands to Chinamen."

It was a struggle not to tear Warren into pieces, but the curious did not need to know any more than they already did, and he did not want to undercut Warren's authority. Enough was enough, though. Back on the hill where Grant had chosen a stump for his headquarters, Rawlins had roared to all the saints and sinners in Creation, "I told you, I told every one of you: These eastern fellas won't fight."

Meade almost had to wonder if Rawlins was right.

"George . . . General Meade . . ." Warren seemed amazed that he might be allowed a word. His bird's face was sharp with nerves, not fortitude. "I'm doing all I can. You told me Sedgwick would be up on my right, but there's no sign of him. I've recalled Crawford, but he has high ground he doesn't want to give up. And Wadsworth's division is strung out in the undergrowth. You have no idea how bad this ground is, how difficult."

"I think I have some idea," Meade snapped. "What about Griffin?"

"He can't attack alone."

"He could have. Had he done so when first ordered."

"George . . . we don't know how many Confederates are out there, just that they're Ewell's men. We could be facing his entire corps."

"I'll damned well tell you how many Rebels are out there," Meade said, temper bucking. "More of them every minute, that's how many." Sweat burned his eyes. "Could Wadsworth support him, if Griffin attacked now?"

Warren shrugged. "They're not tied in, not properly. I have entire brigades moving Indian-file in that . . . that labyrinth. I'm trying to coordinate an attack that won't be sheer chaos."

Meade sensed that, at least on this day, Grant had been right, that the proper action would have been to pitch right into Lee, first thing in the morning, with the forces at hand, and damn the risk. Now Warren's pursuit of an engineer's perfection and Griffin's reluctance to spend the lives of his troops had given the Confederates time to get ready. Warren liked well-organized set-piece battles, and Meade was not entirely without sympathy. But those days were going, if not gone. From here on out, it would be about who landed the first and hardest blow on the enemy.

And there was sense in Grant's approach, given the taste Lee had developed for entrenching. A morning attack might have been bloody, but an attack delayed would be costlier. One had to be made, though. And every minute lost only strengthened the enemy.

He wished the order of march had been different, that Hancock had been here in Warren's place. Had Win had Gibbon's or Barlow's divisions on this field in the morning, the only problem would have been holding them back. G. K. Warren was a brilliant man, but, for the first time, Meade wondered if it was possible to have too fine a mind to command effectively. What if intelligence only inflated dangers, while clouding opportunity? Hancock was no dunce, but no one would have mistaken him for a professor. Warren would have suited the West Point faculty.

Nor did Grant seem possessed of a shining intellect. But he won battles.

"If we wait a little longer," Warren resumed, "I'm convinced we can get the Confederates to attack us. Then we'd have the defense's advantages. The way we did at Gettysburg." He gestured toward his waiting regiments: The men were digging entrenchments.

"It's a different war now," Meade said. "Delays only add to the casualty rolls. Order Griffin and Wadsworth to attack."

"Griffin just wants to wait until Sedgwick comes up," Warren pleaded. "He's ridden forward to see things for himself, George. He says the Confederates overlap his right, that even if he's successful, he'll be enveloped." Warren pawed his mustaches, a sad and friendless gesture. "Possibly on both flanks, if Wadsworth's men can't make it through that undergrowth. And there's an open field a mile out, with Ewell's men dug in on a ridge. Griffin says it's a natural butcher's yard."

Meade saw the danger of being drawn into Warren's endless arguments. There were always logical reasons not to do anything. Yes, the attack might fail. And thanks to the morning's delays, it would damned well be costly, whether it worked or not. But it had to be made. And he needed to return to headquarters, to find out where Sedgwick's lead division had gotten to and confirm that Hancock had reinforced Getty down on the Plank Road. It seemed that the only men in his entire army who'd shown their mettle had been a handful of New York cavalrymen.

Lee was probably gloating.

And Grant just sat there on his stump, whittling a stick

and smoking his cigars, watching everything and saying nothing, letting Rawlins do his dirty work.

"You will attack," Meade told his subordinate. "Immediately."

SIX

One p.m.
Todd's Tavern

Hancock saw Frank Barlow riding up in his checkered shirt and knew exactly how their exchange would run. Barlow's reactions were as reliable as a rich man's watch.

Young Barlow would never make a cavalryman, and that was certain, too. He sat a horse well enough to lead an infantry division, but an old soldier could tell at a glance that the New Englander had never ridden the plains with the old dragoons before the war. And the saber that dangled off his thigh appeared made for a giant. It would have excited ridicule, had it not been employed so earnestly. Barlow's face was set hard, though, and his gracelessness on horseback somehow made him seem more determined and ruthless.

Riding up to Hancock's position between the crossroads and a poor-man's tavern, Barlow stopped his horse, saluted carelessly—as if he were the superior—and patted the animal's neck. The beast's mouth foamed. Barlow was hard on every living creature, and Hancock wondered how the boy got on with his matronly wife. Stonehearted Frank Barlow, with his crooked teeth and prodding talk? Did Barlow, too, have a soul behind those close-set, wintry eyes?

Before Barlow could speak, Hancock said, "Got your men turned around?"

The brigadier nodded. "They have orders to move as soon as the road's clear behind them. What's this about, sir?"

Hancock nodded toward the north, away from his interrupted line of march. Barely audible rifle fire rankled the afternoon. "Bobby Lee didn't wait for our grand plan to come to fruition."

"I don't hear any cannon," Barlow said. "If it was serious, there'd be artillery."

Hancock shook his head. "Not artillery ground up there. No fields of fire, except along the roads. If George Meade's going to fight in that damned jungle, he's going to do it with infantry and little else."

"Sir . . . I've been given orders to bring up the rear of the corps."

Hancock beat down a smile before Barlow could see it. "You were in front, now you're in the rear. I'm just turning this leviathan around as fast as I can. Before George Meade falls down dead with a heart attack." Hancock stopped himself. "That was unfair. Meade's doing the best he can. With Grant looking over his shoulder every minute. Christ, I'd hate that."

"Sir, if you held up Mott's division and let mine pass, my men are better marchers. . . ." Barlow took off his cap, exposing sweat-plastered hair, and wiped a dirty sleeve across his forehead. Hancock wore a starched white shirt each day, his one indulgence. "I'd like to get into the fight," Barlow continued. "Mott could bring up the rear."

Barlow was as predictable as the stink on an Indian. The instant he smelled a fight, he wanted to join it.

"No. I *want* you to bring up the rear. Longstreet's out there, think it through. If Lee's trying to fix us in the Wilderness, what do you figure he's up to? If I know Marse Robert, he's going to try to swing Longstreet around our flank and pull off another Chancellorsville. And he'll come at this flank, if he comes at all."

A passing regiment cheered at the sight of Hancock. The corps commander waved his hat in return.

"Longstreet's not in front of me," Barlow said. "I had scouts out, my own men. Since the damned cavalry's nowhere to be found."

"He may not be in front of you now, but he'll show up all right."

"Mott could watch the flank as well as I could."

"No. You've got my largest division. I need you on the flank. If Longstreet tries to hit us, I want him to come up against something that's going to hurt him back. Something that can stop him, until we sort things out. You hold the lucky number, Frank."

"The damned cavalry should be out there, doing their proper work." Barlow swept an arm toward the countermarching troops. "None of these contortions would be necessary."

"Oh, they're out there," Hancock said. "Just not necessarily where we'd like 'em to be. I could hear a fuss off in the woods this morning. I figure our boys and Stuart's bunch are playing tag with each other."

A passing band struck up "Camptown Races," but their playing was ragged and weak: dry throats and parched lips on a hot day's march.

"Won't win any prizes at the Academy of Music, that's for damned sure," Hancock said. "Well, now that we're all pissing in the right direction, I've got to get up to the fight. Meade's goddamned courier got here late and things sound a little unhinged. Just pull your men back and take up a blocking position along that rise. I don't want to give up this crossroads until I know what the Hell else is going on."

As Hancock turned northward up the Brock Road, his color sergeants kicked their horses to life and fell in at his stirrup. His staff, in turn, joined the cavalcade behind the flags of the corps. It made him feel vividly alive to ride into battle, and he savored the sensation every time.

Whether Longstreet appeared on the flank or not, Barlow would be exactly where Hancock wanted him. If a flank attack materialized, Barlow would fight his division to the last man. And if Longstreet showed up elsewhere, Barlow would be downright rabid to get into the fight by the time his division was needed, and God help any Rebels who got in his way.

Trotting forward beside a brigade column, Hancock called out to his game, dust-sucking infantry, "Come on, boys, come on, step out now! There's more Johnnies up ahead than bugs in a whorehouse shitter on Sunday morning. Step along, let's go!"

Two p.m.
Saunders Field

It was every bit as bloody a damned mess as Griffin had feared. But his boys were in it now, and fine they were. He had never seen them braver.

Ignoring stray rounds, he galloped across the high field to Rome Ayres, his West Point classmate and the commander of the brigade engaged north of the Turnpike.

Shouting above the roar of the battle, Griffin asked, "Rome, can you hold that flank?"

Ayres turned a grimed and sweating face toward him. "Did you see them, Charlie? Did you see my men go in?"

Griffin realized that the sweat on Ayres' face mingled with tears.

"I saw 'em. Goddamn thing of beauty. Can you hold that flank, Rome?"

Ayres nodded. "Do my best. Hell with them, the sons-ofbitches. Damned if they'll get through, I've got the Regulars over there." He shook his head. "You should've seen the Forty-fourth New York go in. And the Hundred and Fortieth."

"I saw 'em."

"Now just look," Ayres said.

The two brigadiers stared out across the field. Gauzed with smoke, their lines of sight came and went, but the first results of the charge were clear. Speckled with the dead, the low ground crawled with the wounded, some in plain blue uniforms, others in the flared pantaloons of Zouaves. Here and there, fires gnawed the brush, nipping at the fallen. Down in the swale that broke the field in two, soldiers who could not or would not go forward gripped the earth, hoping to make themselves small. To the left, a section of guns blazed away, but Griffin, an old artilleryman, doubted they could identify useful targets. The Rebs were deep in the trees, deep in a wild undergrowth that had swallowed hundreds of men. Somewhere in there, north of the road, the survivors of Ayres' brigade were fighting hard, by the sound of things. Had they not been, the Confederates would have counterattacked by now. Still, the situation on the division's flank was growing perilous.

Sedgwick? Wright? And their promised supporting attack? Shit for the birds. It was just as he'd predicted. The Rebs overlapped his right, and now, with not a man of the Sixth Corps in sight, the crisis was no more than a matter of time.

"You just hold that flank, Rome," Griffin said. "Bartlett's got a lodgment on the other side of the road and his boys are punching through them."

"We'll hold," Ayres said. His voice was firm again. "My boys will hold. Charlie, I need to get back on that flank myself, see what can be done."

For a pained few minutes, Griffin had been worried about Ayres, afraid he would need to relieve him after the shock of the slaughter his old classmate had just witnessed. But Ayres was an old gunner, too. He had snapped right back.

"Just give 'em the devil," Griffin said. "I've got to find goddamned Warren. If he has the brains and the balls to send in Robinson behind Bartlett, this shit of a day might not turn out so badly."

A great wool-headed, brush-bearded man, Ayres saluted and pulled his horse around. His adjutant, Swan, a man loyal to the death, mimicked the brigade commander's action. Griffin didn't believe the flank could be held indefinitely, but he thought it likely to hold for thirty minutes. Rome Ayres would buy him that much time. And it just might be enough.

Where the Hell was Sedgwick, though? All those promises of support had been no more than a pimp's oaths to a whore.

He had last seen Warren amid the long line of ambulances backed up along the Turnpike. Warren had known how bad it was going to be. At least he had the decency to care about the wounded.

As Griffin, one aide, and his color sergeants rode parallel to the rear of the attack, the party had to weave between wounded men walking rearward and those helped along by healthy soldiers glad of an excuse to leave the battle.

The best men were the soldiers out there now, dying by the hundreds in the most slovenly excuse for a proper battle that Griffin had ever witnessed. If any good was done this day, it would be thanks to those boys, not to any general.

Two cannon blasted away into clouds of smoke. Warren had ordered them forward to a position no artilleryman would have chosen, exposed and useless. It had infuriated Griffin, who knew how to employ guns, but he had cautioned himself that even the possible loss of a few field-pieces was trivial compared to the greater matters at hand. He needed the corps commander to think about greater things. And to act.

He recognized a member of Warren's staff galloping along. The man was too damned careless of the wounded in his path. Nor did he appear much interested in Griffin.

The division commander flagged the rider down. Reluctantly, the officer reined in his mount.

"Where are you going, Roebling?"

"Message for General Sedgwick, sir. It's urgent."

"Well, you won't find him out that way. Ride past General Ayres' brigade, and you'll be off to Libby Prison. If you live."

Roebling looked befuddled. He had been some sort of civilian engineer, a man who expected logic to rule the world. "Then how do I get to General Sedgwick? Or his lead division, sir?"

"Christ if I know," Griffin said. "I'd like to find him myself. Where's General Warren, back at that house?"

"No, sir, he's forward. Just beyond those trees."

Griffin decided to do the young officer a kindness. "Roebling, if I were you, I'd ride back past that line of butcher's carts. Meade has his headquarters just off the road back there, you must know where it is. Ask around the royal court if anybody knows where Sedgwick is taking the waters. But stay out of—"

The staff man's horse reared, neighing madly. Roebling fought to stay in the saddle. Blood from the animal's rump sprayed Griffin's trousers.

He had no more time for the messenger's dilemmas. Spurring his horse, he launched himself and his party across the shot-swept road. Toward the corps commander's supposed location. He, too, grew careless and almost rode down a boy with a blood-covered face. The lad had been blinded and wandered the field, veering away from noises and stumbling along.

To his right, across the murderous ground and beyond the tree line, the smoke rose at a notably greater distance.

Against the odds and at terrible expense, Bartlett's brigade had broken through the Rebels. Bartlett had damned fine regiments, if much-reduced ones, the 83rd Pennsylvania, the 20th Maine, and their like. Men who were out to get their own back from the Johnnies any way they could. Ayres' men were every bit as good as Bartlett's, but they had drawn the worse terrain in the war's hard lottery. The next time, Bartlett's boys might be dealt the death card. Luck played as great a role in battle as skill.

When Griffin found Warren—surrounded by enough staff men to form a cavalry troop—the corps commander looked glum. When he first met Griffin's eyes, there was something close to apathy in evidence. Griffin figured that Meade had been hammering Warren hard. As Meade, no doubt, was getting pounded by Grant.

"General Griffin," Warren said, voice faint in the din, "I find matters unclear."

Disciplining his language, Griffin answered, "Bloody mess on the right, sir. Rebs are on Ayres' flank, just like he warned us. But he's holding, and his New York boys made it into the far woods. Look at Bartlett's front, though. Look how far the smoke's moved. Wadsworth must be into them, too. Damn me if we don't have a chance to break Ewell's corps."

"Yes," Warren said dully. "Bartlett."

"Sir, he needs to be reinforced. Now. For God's sake, send in everything you can. Bartlett's punctured their line, this is our chance."

Warren shook his head. As if even that were an effort. He did not meet Griffin's eyes.

"Damn it, sir! You've got a division sitting on its ass. Send in Robinson. Right behind Bartlett. We could break them."

"I can't," Warren said.

"Sir, you *have* to. You have to do it."

"I can't."

"Why? Don't throw this chance away."

It was Warren's turn to lose his temper. Eyes flashing, he turned his raptor's face on his subordinate.

"Goddamn it, Charlie, I *can't*. I told you. Robinson's being held as the army reserve. Until Sedgwick comes up."

"Sir . . . for the love of God . . . order Robinson up. Break Ewell's corps, and they'll forgive you anything."

"I can't. Robinson's the army's reserve. Meade would never release him."

A shell screamed overhead. The Confederates still had artillery somewhere along their line. The explosion sounded just to their rear, followed by the shrieks of wounded horses. The ambulance train had been hit.

"Sir . . . ," Griffin tried, "what's a reserve for? You have to move *now*. Before the chance slips away."

Warren's look veered toward doubt. "What if the right flank collapses? We'd need Robinson then."

"Ayres will hold. Long enough. Ewell won't be thinking about our flank, if we're crushing his balls. Sir, this is what Meade wanted, what Grant wants." Desperate, he said, "At least send in one of Robinson's brigades. Just give me one brigade. Even that might do it."

"General Griffin," Warren said coldly, distantly, a man of kaleidoscopic moods, "I cannot act without General Meade's authorization. Robinson is the army reserve. It is not my decision to make. You should understand my situation."

"Goddamn it, sir. It's *your* decision. You're the man on the spot. I *beg* you. . . ."

Warren stared into the distance, toward the unseen slaughter in the woods. "It would take too long to bring Robinson up through that forest, anyway. Bartlett will have to do the best he can."

Tempted for the first time in his career to strike a senior officer, Griffin said, "Then damn you to Hell."

He pulled his horse around and spurred it forward. Back toward the slaughter of his men.

Two p.m.
Orange Turnpike

The trickles of wounded men and skedaddlers turned into a stream. Wise to the folly of confronting soldiers from another man's command, Gordon left it to his staff to admonish the shirkers. Riding at the front of his brigade, he kept his face straight to the front, eyes on the smoke rising from the treetops a mile ahead and ears alert to the shifting sounds of battle. The noise of rifle volleys and distant shouts seemed to leap toward him.

The day was hot, the march had been hard, and the little news he had gotten had not been good. Now a rider approached him at a gallop. For the second time in one day, Gordon did not have to hear the words a courier would speak. It would be an order to come on at the double-quick, to quell a crisis. Or, perhaps, more crises than one.

As he limped rearward, a black-bearded soldier with a torn cheek called a warning to Gordon's men: "Y'all goin' to ketch it now, boys. Yankees coming on thick as flies on shit."

"You could pass for shit yourself," one of Gordon's men responded. "This here's the Georgia Brigade."

"I can smell that much," the limping soldier hooted. "You'll see who's shit soon enough, Peach-head."

Gordon pulled his horse to the side so the courier wouldn't break the march's rhythm. It was Major Daniel, Early's aide. He kicked up enough dust to choke a company.

Breathless, the aide called, "General Gordon, sir! You're

to bring up your brigade as fast as you can. Yankees put a hole in the line. Genr'l Early's compliments, and he says he needs you right now."

Belatedly, the excited young man remembered to salute. Daniel was normally well composed. It had to be the devil's own mess up there, Gordon realized.

"Major Daniel, do me a favor. You ride back and give the word to my regimental commanders to come on at the double-quick. I'll ride ahead for a look."

"Yes, sir. You'll see Genr'l Ewell's flag smack in the road. He means to make a stand."

Good Lord, Gordon thought. A dozen questions leapt to mind, but there was no time for chatter. Without another word, he spurred his horse, leading his staff and his colors toward the battle.

Even above the pounding of dozens of hooves, he soon heard cheering, all of the wrong kind. It was baritone Yankee huzzahing, with none of the yip and howl that marked his side's triumphs.

The stream of wounded men and quitters became a river. At least a brigade, perhaps more than one, had broken.

There would be no time for eloquent speeches now.

In minutes, he spied a familiar group of horsemen. Someone had, indeed, planted a battle flag in the middle of the roadway. A motley collection of soldiers guarded the generals, who were milling about and shouting curses at runaways.

General Early trotted back to meet him. "Gordon, for God's sake! How far back are your men?"

"Ten minutes away, sir."

Early glanced over his shoulder and his hair threw sweat. "I don't know if we have ten minutes. Jones is dead, his brigade's collapsed. Battle's brigade pulled back without orders and they're a goddamned shambles." Dancing his horse about, Early pointed into the thickets south of the Turnpike. "Can't even say what's holding up the Yankees. Unless the bastards have squirreled themselves around in there. Worst damned fighting terrain I've ever come across. You get your men in there as fast as they can go, just plunge on in at, say, a twenty-degree angle from the road here. Then you give those goddamned Yankees a fucking."

"Yes, sir."

Gordon saluted and rode out to look at the ground. Stray rounds flirted. From the forest, he heard ragged volleys and unusual, terrified wails, as if the Cyclops had emerged from his cave to eat men alive for his dinner.

Even in those urgent moments, Gordon remained conscious of his appearance, sitting so upright in the saddle that he almost tilted backward.

Breaking out of the undergrowth, two men carried a third who swung from their shoulders. Instead of legs, the wounded man had shreds of blood-soaked trousers and one white thighbone visible, striped like a barber's pole painted by a drunkard. The soldier's head lolled every which way, and his youthful face, beyond pain, was golden and beautiful.

" 'Covetous death takes a thousand forms around us,' " Gordon recited, " 'and flight brings no man safety in this hour.' " Homer knew, he *knew*.

But Gordon didn't know what the devil was in that tangle of undergrowth and scrub pine. Fighting in there would be little better than brawling on a night without a moon. Some of the gunfire sounded terribly close, the only consolation that the volleys were those of much-diminished companies, not full regiments, of the enemy.

He decided that all he could do would be to put his men shoulder to shoulder in two lines and order them forward.

General Early caught up with him again. "You said ten minutes, Gordon."

"It hasn't been ten minutes, sir. What about the other flank? Will it hold?"

Instinctively, Early looked north of the road. But a man could see no more than thirty feet into the brush. If that.

"We've got the bastards flanked up there. But they're not for quitting today. Killing a right good number of them, though."

General Ewell left his frantic staff and joined his two subordinates.

"Where's your brigade, Gordon? We need you now, not tomorrow."

"If, sir, you would kindly turn your eyes . . ."

On they came, thirsty as out-of-pocket Irishmen, tired as washerwomen on Saturday night, and mean as a wild sow defending her litter. Hurrying forward at the double-quick, they didn't cheer. They were saving that, Gordon knew, marshaling what voices they had left after eating dust for the last eight hours. They were building up their ability to howl and terrify the way they husbanded ammunition.

"Lord be praised," Ewell said.

"Get in there, John," Early told him. "Get in there and tear the guts out of those bastards."

"As Achilles avenged the death of beloved Patroclus," Gordon told his superiors. He kicked his horse to meet his rushing men. Some of them raised their rifles from their shoulders, lifting them in one hand in a slapdash salute. For all the rigors of the day and the dangers just ahead, a goodly proportion of his boys were grinning to split their cheeks. It was a grand, inspiring sight, although their smiles could not be described as "ivory."

And now for the topless towers of Ilium, Gordon thought. Or those goddamned bush pines, anyway.

The 26th led the march. Straightening himself like a Spanish grandee posing for a portrait, Gordon yelled to the regiment's colonel, "Eddie, plant your left on the side of the road by that broke-down limber. Form two ranks, just shy of a quarter turn to the right."

"Yes, sir."

Colonel Evans of the 31st, the next regiment in line, rode up to join them, but Atkinson of the 26th had already turned to his task.

"Clem," Gordon shouted, "you form to the right of the Twenty-sixth. Two ranks, shoulder to shoulder. Just align on Eddie's boys. Be quick now."

Evans saluted and hastened back to lead his men from the roadway into the brush. The men of the 26th streamed around Gordon, water rushing around a rock, and a soldier called, "Genr'l, you'd fright the Yanks just to look at you, I swear."

Against his will, Gordon lost control of his features. He grinned at the dust-crusted faces hurrying past. "Then I shall be as the Gorgon!" he declaimed. The boys wouldn't have a scrap of an idea what he was talking about, but he knew that they just liked to hear him talk.

He rode back to give orders to his four following regiments, drawing his sword to point at the spots where he wanted them to go in.

The fighting sounded impossibly close now, a monstrous, invisible beast in the hot, dark labyrinth.

"Thirty-eighth Georgia! Align on the Thirty-first. Get into those woods, boys. Get on into those woods. . . ."

The crashing and thrashing of his men was complemented by imaginative curses, brief prayers hollered as at a camp meeting, and dry-spit challenges to the unseen enemy.

In a matter of minutes, Gordon had his brigade in a swaybacked line that thrust deep into the brambles. The formation was the best the hour allowed. Forcing his horse through briars and stray wildflowers, he rose in his stirrups and bellowed:

"Georgia! For*ward!*"

The Rebel yell his men had been saving up tore the air like a volley unleashed by the gods. In response, disorganized but heavy fire erupted from the undergrowth. Rounds ripped leaves and knocked down Gordon's first casualties. When a clot of men stopped to return fire, he waved his sword toward their enemies.

"Just go at 'em, get on 'em. Wait till you get your muzzles against their bellies."

But it was the way of soldiers to fire back when fired upon. And the tangled growth was, indeed, a terrible place. As the last wave of Rebel yells faded off and the men got down to killing, Gordon forced his mount back toward the 26th.

"Where's my bull, my Minotaur?" he called. "Spivey, you answer up! James Ervin Spivey, answer up!"

A wild halloo, a scream like the triumphant cry of Death himself, erupted from the thickets. Spivey's unearthly howl had become a signature of the brigade.

The Yankees had come damned close. Barely a hundred yards from the road, the blind volleys turned to private tussles with bayonets and rifle butts wielded as clubs. Disregarding the squalls of lead, Gordon rode along his line, if line it could still be called, urging on his officers and men, driving them, adding his strength of will to their animal rage. Off to the left, a stretch of the forest had caught fire, but his men just veered around it.

Gordon's horse shied mildly at the first Union corpse it met. Thereafter, the number of blue-clad bodies and struggling wounded multiplied. His own men were not unscathed, though. One soldier sat against a tree, clutching the belly of a bloodstained shirt. With more blood greasing his chin, the lad called out, "I'm a-going to catch up with you, Genr'l." He puked gore. "I'll be catching on up now."

"God bless you, son," Gordon told the boy.

The musketry grew deafening. As one of his men, bloody-shouldered, nudged along a string of captured Federals—threatening them with what Gordon would have bet was an empty rifle—Gordon could only tell an abashed Union captain, "Fortunes of war. . . ."

His men were a wonder to him, now and always. They kept on going, unwilling, even unable, to stop. Sometimes, he would ride fifty yards and see little but flashes ahead. Then he would come to a scramble of bodies, the living and the dead, intermingled and tangled. Crazed, a man from the 38th bayoneted a Yankee body over and over again, pulping the meat. Gordon knew enough of war to pretend he did not see. When a man was in such a state, you just left him alone.

His men needed no more encouragement, no ringing speeches, now. Victory was more stimulating than the finest store-bought whiskey, a close horse race, and a pliant woman together. His problem would be stopping them, if it came to that.

On their own, his men raised another yell, as if they shared one mind, a great gray beast. The most effective measure Gordon could take was just to ride back and forth behind the advance, showing himself and admonishing men to maintain their ranks where the infernal grove allowed.

Another string of prisoners passed on their way to the rear. A copper-haired Yankee sergeant, red of face, demanded of Gordon, "Where the Hell did you sonsofbitches come from?"

When one of the guards raised a rifle butt to club the insolent man, Gordon waved him off.

"We come, sir, from the verdant fields and sylvan groves of an earthly paradise mortal men call 'Georgia.'"

"Lord awmighty," one of the guards said, grinning black-toothed at Gordon. "I don't know what language you're talkin' in, General, but it sounds a heap of pretty."

A volley from the brush struck the herded prisoners, dropping two. It was impossible to say which side had fired.

"Get them out of here," Gordon barked. He was all for killing men in arms, but did not wish to injure a captive foe.

He gave his horse both spurs, but it did little good. A horse could not get through where a fawn couldn't pass. He had to guide the animal around a natural barricade of thorns. Then he came up against a wall of pines and the body of one of his men with its head blown open.

A wave of soldiers appeared from an unexpected direction. They were his men, strayed off. It was impossible to keep one's bearings in the thickets.

Gordon waved his sword to correct their direction. It struck a tree. After sheathing the blade again, he pointed with a gloved hand and bellowed, "That way. Follow the sound of the guns."

A few yards on, he found the colonel of the 13th extricating his men as stubborn Yankees fired from an embankment beyond a marsh. Gordon let the colonel do his own work and pushed on to find a way around the obstacle. But his men had solved the problem for themselves, and a wild mob of soldiers in gray—from the 60th, he figured—swept the Yankee line from right to left.

"Keep together now, you men, you keep together!" Gordon shouted. "Close on the center regiments!"

One of his lieutenants lay facedown and unmoving in the muck. Gordon could read the rank, but not see the features. And there was no time for courtesies.

His attack had come so far so fast that he worried it would dissolve from its own success, disintegrating into little bands of soldiers wandering about, as the Yankees who had come the farthest had done. He rode back toward the left, to gather in the 26th and tighten what passed for a line now, but Colonel Atkinson met him on the way.

"General, we've got Yankees on our left. We're in so deep they're just about behind us."

"Do they know we're here? If they're behind us, we're behind them, too, Eddie. Leastways, that's the way I'd prefer to look at it."

"Well, there's a plenty of them, either way."

A welter of musketry rose on the right, a perfect, unwanted bookend to the dilemma.

"I would say," Gordon told the colonel, "that we have effected a successful penetration of the Army of the Potomac. In fact, we may have been a mite too successful."

Dirty-faced, Atkinson grinned. "Gave 'em the devil, though. Busted up the nigger lovers good."

"Eddie, gather your men in. Tell Clem to contract his lines toward the center, too. And get ready."

"For what?"

"More fighting. You just go on now, I'll call for you."

Gordon made his way along the line a last time, spooling in his brigade, careful not to go astray himself. Finally, he summoned all of the regimental commanders to meet behind the 13th. And he called for Private Spivey.

"Gentlemen," Gordon began amid the revelry of death, "I make out that we still have a few stray Yankees to our front, their famed and feted Iron Brigade on our right, and a moderately worrisome collection of unknown interlocutors to our left. Eddie, you are going to wheel the Twenty-sixth left and charge straight into them. Colonel Berry will lead his Sixtieth in a simultaneous charge to the right, supported by the Thirteenth and Sixty-first attacking on his left and right obliques. We'll see if we can't collect a few black hats today." He turned to the commander of the 31st and said, "Clem, I want you to keep on attacking straight ahead, in case anybody out there's getting ideas. The Thirty-eighth will remain with me as a reserve."

"General . . . sir . . . you're attacking in three directions. With one brigade. That does make for interesting odds."

"Mathematical speculations were never my favorite pastime," Gordon said. "The signal to attack will be Private Spivey's *basso profundo*. Back to your regiments, gentlemen."

"John Gordon, you are crazy as a loon," Clem Evans said. "Well, it's been an honor to serve under you."

When Gordon's men renewed the attack, they broke two Union brigades and took three hundred prisoners.

Two forty-five p.m.
Headquarters, Army of the Potomac
and the general in chief

Meade faced one disheartening report after another. Warren had been right. The attack had been as ill-conceived as it was ill-prepared. But Grant had left him no choice. And, to be honest, he had wanted to impress Grant with the army's ferocity. Now he stood in the shade and read the scrawled messages couriers delivered. The attack in the north, along the Turnpike, had failed at every point. It would be up to Hancock, down on the Plank Road, to advance the army's position. And save its reputation in Grant's eyes.

John Rawlins strode about, casting blame in the intervals between his coughs and outbursts of obscenity. Grant sat on his stump, from which he had moved only to take a cup of coffee, then, a bit later, to relieve himself of the drink's consequences. The general in chief whittled one stick after another, making nothing, simply shaving away peels of wood and shredding the knitted gloves he wore. Grant seemed unaware of the condition of the gloves and appeared only mildly interested in the affairs of the army. But Meade was certain the man took everything in.

Grant's quiet was unsettling.

What slight calm there was amid Rawlins' eruptions soon came to an end. Charlie Griffin rode up, face smeared and angry, accompanied by a single officer. He leapt to the ground and came on shouting at everybody.

"Goddamn it to Hell, my men just drove Dick Ewell three-quarters of a mile. We broke the goddamned sonofabitch, we goddamned broke them all." Griffin's rage was all-encompassing, not aimed particularly at Meade or anyone else. The man was a shotgun blast, not a rifle shot. "Where were those Sixth Corps bastards, tell me that? Goddamned Wright, the worthless sonofabitch. No support from anybody, and damned well not from Robinson's cunts sitting there doing fuck-all. And my boys are dead and bloodied to Hell and we can't even get back the wounded, they're goddamned burning to death." He rounded on Adam Badeau, blameless in the day's affairs and guilty only of bearing the same given name as the first man to sin. "Do *you* know what happens when a wounded man burns to death, sonny? When he can't crawl away? Or can't crawl fast enough? It's not some holy martyrdom like Joan of fucking Arc." He turned from the mortified staff man and surveyed the collection of men on the little hill, all shocked into silence. Even Rawlins gaped. "You're worthless as a wet shit," Griffin concluded. "You killed my boys for nothing."

And he stalked off, not bothering to mount his horse, just striding back toward his battered division. His mustering officer followed with both mounts.

On a delayed fuse, Rawlins exploded. "That man ought to be court-martialed. He's a disgrace to the uniform, to the entire army." He glared and scanned the collection of officers, settling his fevered eyes on Meade. "Goddamned lucky no newspaperman was here, I'll tell you that. Every word that came out of his mouth was mutinous, downright mutinous. He has to be relieved and placed under arrest. Today. Immediately."

Grant laid down his whittling knife and rose to his feet.

"Who was that?" he asked.

"General Gregg," Rawlins answered.

"No," Meade corrected him, surprised at his own calm tone, "that was General Griffin. His division led the attack today."

"You ought to arrest him," Grant said.

Meade shook his head. "It's only his way of talking."

To the end of his days, Meade was never clear as to why he did what came next. He walked over to where Grant stood disheveled and doubtful, and gently buttoned his superior's tunic. He tugged the garment straight and patted down the lapels as a mother would.

Grant reeked of tobacco and stale breath.

"Griffin's a fighter," Meade said. "We're going to need him."

SEVEN

Three p.m.
North of the Pamunkey Road

I'll tell you where we are, if you want to know," Oates said. "We're damned well lost. Longstreet doesn't know his head from a mule's behind."

"Ain't that the gospel truth," a fellow regimental commander agreed.

New to command of the Alabama Brigade, but not to the ways of the army, Colonel Perry refused to be baited by his embittered subordinates.

"Orders change," Perry said. "And when they do, we carry them out. Anything else, gentlemen? If not, get your men turned around."

"All this ass-over-elbows business," Oates put in, "we're just wearing out our boys before a battle." Oates was prepared to do what had to be done. But there were times when a man just had to say a thing.

"I'm sure your men will be ready for a fight, Bill," Perry said.

Perry was doing all he could to break through the men's anger at the arrest and replacement of the brigade's old commander, Evander Law. Oates understood the fix Perry was in, and Law's removal had not been Perry's doing. But a man had to spit out certain things before they ate up his insides. Once he got them out, he'd be all right, though. They'd all fight well for Perry, when the time came. But the man lacked Law's sense of people. For one thing, nobody called William C. Oates "Bill." He went by "William," and didn't appreciate anybody taking liberties.

The commanders dispersed, barking orders as they went, and soon the brigade snaked onto a rough-made farm track pointed north. It was the second time the entire division had been pulled up and turned back that day. The first instance had occurred when someone figured out that the local guide didn't know his local business. Now this.

The cold truth was that marching toward a battle unsettled Oates. He didn't mind the fighting itself, which was a lusty matter more often than not. Fear had never been powerful in his makeup. But the getting up to a battle teased out memories. And those memories got all mixed up, good and bad, until the good ones made the bad ones harder to bear. The memories were always of his brother, John, last seen dying on that hillside in Pennsylvania, bleeding and lost amid tumult and disaster, with Oates choosing his duty as commander over his desire to stay with his brother to the end. He had met John's eyes a last time, and perhaps his brother's eyes had been past knowing, but they accused him here and now, asking, plaintive as a hant-spooked boy, *You just going to leave me here?*

The march to that useless, hopeless fight had been brutal, hotter than this, and made for the most part with empty canteens and bellies flushed by the camp trots. Oates had not learned the name of the nearby town, Gettysburg, until well after the 15th's fighting was done. It was all a heat-crazed, kill-a-man march, with good men falling away before they saw the first Yankee, a long march made at a brutal pace, with Hood himself riding up and down the column, railing at them to move, move, move, and who's that coward straggling? That march had been murderous but straight until near the end, when the division had marched and countermarched as Yankee cannon tried the day in the distance, getting ready for them, and there never was a damned explanation of where the devil they were, just "Git on along there! Pick up the step!" followed by a few shreds of formal orders issued on unfamiliar ground, with the brigade and regimental officers unsure of what they were meant to do beyond going forward and let's just see what comes of it.

Law had been fuming, burned like a sulfur match, unable to get a fair look at the ground the brigade was to cross, unsure if it could be crossed to good effect, and then, just after Oates had sent a detail to fill the men's canteens, the division moved forward, and the brigade moved forward, and Oates gave the order to his regiment to move forward, and the unappeased thirst and fiendish heat just made the men grim and mean, ready to kill any living thing that crossed them or just looked at them cockeyed. The Yankee artillery down on that flank had peculiar fields of fire, butchering some regiments while sparing others entirely, and the 15th just passed through most of that fuss at a quickstep amid drifts of smoke as stink-sharp in the nostrils as unwashed quim. Then word came down that Hood was badly wounded and Law had the division. Oates never knew if the next order to his regiment was Hood's last or one of Law's first. The courier just pointed in the direction of the two hills off to the right and front, and said, "Colonel Oates, you're to move off at the oblique and take care of the Yankees on that hill," and then the man was off, without clarifying which of the two hills he meant.

The big hill came first, steep and strewn with boulders, but at least there was shade for most of the going up. Exhausted, dead-eyed soldiers grew twitchy as fighting cocks and discovered the down-deep strength to keep pushing on, maybe because stopping would have required a decision they were too dogged out to make, men too weary to fall down and just quit, just doing by rote because that was the easiest thing. Expecting a fight, expecting the Yankees hidden in the trees up there to open up just any old time at all, but there were no Yankees on that higher of the two hills, just rocks and trees and a view that made Oates wished he commanded the entire army for one drop-jawed moment, because he knew just what he'd do with it: He could roll up the goddamned Yankees like a rug when the fiddles came out.

He held his men there, high up on that precious ground, as the battle raged and hammered and shrieked below, and he sent a runner—just a boy who looked like he might not fall down dead from the day's gathered heat—to beg for guns to be manhandled up that hill, for cannon and more men, at least a brigade to plunge behind the Yankees and tear the heart out of their blundering, blue-bellied army, but all he got back was word that there were no more troops, that there was no damned time to bring up any artillery— and why hadn't he obeyed his orders and pitched into the Yankees on that hill?

Well, at least he knew which hill they meant now, and he ordered his withered regiment forward, northward, down through the boulders that played Hell with their alignment before rupturing it entirely, him yelling in a dry-husk voice, "Keep together, damn you, align on the colors." And he stumbled and cracked his elbow on a boulder as he almost fell, winning himself a sharp white pain like snakebite, but he refused the pain and the very notion of injury the way you slammed the door in the face of a drummer who knocked while you were addressing a woman. His body was defiant, though, and his left arm did its best to refuse his orders. And that just made his rage worse, rage at everybody and everything, and the regiment arrived at a poison-green saddle between the hills and, Jesus Christ, the Yankees were dead in front of them, up on a lip of ground, and their first volley made the regiment quake like a hurricane wind up from the Gulf had struck it.

"Charge! Charge! Charge!" was all he could yell, all he cared to yell, all his voice was good for, and he regretted now that he had not taken two minutes, or maybe three, to put his men in some kind of order, but that was not his way, nor theirs, and they plunged toward the Yankees in that terrible green place, a grove sweated sickly cool in the treacherous evening, and the goddamned Yankees just blistered them.

The first charge failed. But the men didn't run, they just gathered up back in the rocks, catching their wind, making sure they were still alive, and this time he made their captains and lieutenants give them proper orders, and the sergeants bullied the lines straight, and down the slope they ran again, dodging trees and tripping over the rocks, and the Yankees didn't wait long to open up this time, but fired the way veterans do, fast and aiming low. Some of his men made it right up to their line, stabbing and clubbing wildly until they were slaughtered, and a passel of the Yankees hollered, "Maine, Maine!" and at first Oates thought they were yelling, "Mean, mean!" and he thought to himself, You want mean, I am going to show you mean, you sonsofbitches.

They made five charges in all. Later, some men claimed six, and a few said only four, but Oates remembered five. And each time he led those boys from the rough-tempered towns and break-a-man farms he knew all too well, each time he led them back into the fight, they were fewer and fewer. But damn if they didn't rush up that body-strewn bank another time for him. By the last charge, Oates had been maddened to a rabid state, determined that those Yankees, those bastards, were not going to hold him at bay, and he wished agonized deaths upon them all. He had tried flanking them, tried everything his scorched mind could think up, and nothing worked, and all he could do was hope the Yankees were tired, too, and maybe low on ammunition, or maybe just Yankees, men accustomed to being whipped, so that last time he ordered his men to concentrate on the jut of their line, to punch right through the blue-coated bastards right there and nowhere else, and to shoot their damned officers, starting with that mustached sonofabitch waving his sword.

And in they went again, with their special Alabama yell, unstoppable and indomitable, but the Yankees must have been reinforced, or hiding part of their strength, and they came sweeping down out of the trees with bayonets fixed, just swinging around like a dead cat tied to a stick, smacking into his enfeebled regiment's right flank, and that was too damned much, and his fine men broke, and those who didn't run were shot down, clubbed, bayoneted, or taken with their hands thrust up in immeasurable shame, and when Oates looked about, one of the last to fly, he caught John's eyes, John down and already more dead than alive, propped against a boulder, and William C. Oates knew only two things, that he was obliged to command what remained of the 15th Alabama, and that no worthless Yankee sonofabitch was going to take him prisoner. So he looked away from John, fired his pistol into an Irish face, and ran, slowing only to shoot a Yankee who somehow had gotten ahead of him. No damned Yankee was going to . . . .

But they had John. Still alive, most like. Alive for a pinch of time yet. His little brother. Did they rob his pocket watch while he was still breathing but unable to resist them? How much cruelty was in them?

The last, terrible thing he recalled was the cheering of the Yankees to his rear.

Now Oates hated marching into battle. Marching gave a man too much time to think. Killing was better.

Three thirty p.m.
North Bank of the Rapidan

With his immediate duties done, Sergeant Brown scooped his tin cup into the bucket of coffee, thanked the boys who'd cooked it up, then joined Bill Wildermuth, the company's most talkative man, and Henry Hill, the least apt to say a word, under a shade tree whose leaves had been dulled by dust. Out on the road, other regiments marched down the cutaway bank to the crossing site, and every so often Brown heard cannon boom in the distance, faint as thunder across Second Mountain back home. He had no idea why they had been stopped and turned off the road, after which the entire brigade had waited for almost two hours for further orders. It was the sort of doing an old soldier simply accepted.

"Well, boys . . . ," Brown said by way of greeting.

Hill and Wildermuth looked up at him with the same wait-and-see expression. It was a common look among the veterans, a mutually agreed statement about the way of the world that spared them the need for speech.

"Coffee just gets worse and worse," Bill Wildermuth said. "A man can't drink this mule piss." As soon as he had spoken, he took another swallow. "Sit on down there, Sergeant. Rest those big, old feet."

Brown chose a place between two sprawling roots. The coffee was god-awful, Bill was right. But it was better than no coffee.

He glanced back toward the gathered Eckert clan, making sure that young John Eckert heeded his order not to remove his shoes until the day's march was well and truly over. The Eckerts were a strange bunch, no way around it. Isaac was already back in the good graces of the others, after what had fallen just short of an outright theft of his cousin's stockings.

"You know," Brown said, "I still can't figure why Isaac reenlisted. For that matter, I find it hard to say why the man joined up in the first place."

"Hah!" Wildermuth said. "You knew his wife, you'd know. Most Eckerts just sort of match themselves up right inside the family, but Isaac, he made the mistake of marrying out. And he got himself one great, big, wicked Dutch gal, mean as stink." Wildermuth took another swig of coffee and made a jester's face. "God almighty, this is awful stuff. Isaac's probably afraid to go home, probably hopes the war's going to last till doomsday."

"That a fact?" Brown said. Just to help the conversation along.

"A fact indeed. Yes, indeed." Wildermuth alerted, the way a dog will. "Oh, here we go. Looks like the colonel just got a message from Jesus and his archangels." He shifted his backside, as if ants had got at him. "Guess we'll be moving. And I was just getting fond of this place, all nice and far from the battle."

Abruptly, Henry Hill said, "Sergeant Brown, I've just got this queer feeling." Even in front of Bill Wildermuth, the oldest of comrades, Hill insisted on using his friend's new rank.

"Taking sick, Henry?"

"No. I didn't mean that."

A bolt of alarm shot through Brown's chest. He'd known a number of men to have premonitions, and it was uncanny how often they foresaw their deaths.

"Worried? Anything in particular?" He didn't know how forthcoming Hill would be in front of the other man. Henry Hill was the most private being Brown had ever known, as solid as an oak tree and about as likely to display his emotions.

Hill deciphered Brown's meaning. "Not that. Nothing like that. It's . . ." Hill searched for words. "It's that something's different now. About the war, I mean. I don't know."

Wildermuth jumped in, as he usually did: "I know just how you feel, Henry. Yes, I do. Oh, there was dying enough before, Lord knows, but right up to Vicksburg and even a while after, it was all kind of a lark, to be plain honest."

"I wouldn't call it 'a lark,'" Brown said.

"You know what I mean, though. Then, at Knoxville—"

Hill cut him off. "I wasn't talking about Knoxville. Shut up for a minute, Bill. I mean the war. I can't say exactly, but something just feels different. Like it's going to get worse, a whole lot worse. I don't know. It's all just . . . so big now. It isn't man-size anymore." He shrugged. "I guess that's fool talk. I can't explain it right."

For Henry Hill, that had been a speech comparable to a sermon for the ages.

"It's not fool talk," Brown said. "I think we all feel something on those lines. Even Bill here. Though he does have a knack for overtalking matters." He drank the last, cold dregs of coffee, wishing that Wildermuth were not present. He and Henry had things to share that the other man would just cut down to jokes.

"Captain's on his feet," Hill said.

Brown turned, saw, rose. They would be moving again.

"I better let some of this coffee back out," Wildermuth told them, and he turned to face the tree.

What Brown wanted to say was that, yes, there was a new ugliness in the air, and a sudden decrease in the old fool talk that made light of earnest things. Even Bill had eased up on his mockery. There were no shining daydreams left, no expectations of glory. The world had become a darker place, as if winter lingered on in the hearts of men.

Brown's problem wasn't exactly with the war, it was with himself. Maybe it was the effect of his feelings for Frances, but he asked himself, again, if it were possible to remain a good man through all this. He had done things so shameful that he didn't know how to measure them. Forgiveness fled his heart and forbearance weakened. He had become a harder man, with a toughness grimly different from that of the lad he had been when he killed the Ranger. He feared he might not be fit for the soft things in life.

Virtue was something he had not pondered before. He had assumed he was good enough, normal, imperfect, but a worthy companion to others. Now he longed to be virtuous and good. Not in some tent revival way, spouting Bible verses and preening. Damnation in the afterlife didn't worry him, though he knew it should. He just accepted that, in the wake of this war, the Lord would judge them all as he saw fit. But it had become a matter of grave concern to be a good man on this earth. Not merely a man who would make his Frances proud, if indeed this war let her be his. And not a man drunk with pride at the things he abjured. He wished to live and live well, to love and be loved. But he just wasn't sure he knew the how of it anymore.

The kind of goodness fixed in his mind was about far more than the daily care of the men given into his charge, although that was a serious thing. He could not explain his longing, no more than Henry could find words to capture his altered feeling about the war. Brown wanted to be honest inside and out, but it was more than that. When he spoke to himself of goodness, he did not mean meekness or show-off public kindness. Nor could he say he wanted to do no man harm, since he was sworn a soldier and obliged to kill. But in a world that held beings such as Frances, a man had to find a proper way to live. And neither honor nor riches had to do with it. Not fame or glory, either. The riddle was how to stay upright marching through Hell.

Henry's cousin, First Sergeant Hill, bellowed for the company to fall in. But even after the lines were dressed and the men had faced right to form a marching column, they were held up to keep the road clear for someone else, a brigade or perhaps a battalion of guns urgently needed ahead. But the road remained empty. The sky even cleared of dust. A few stragglers came up, and that was all.

It was just another pointless delay that would never be explained or even remembered.

At last, the order came down from some all-knowing general, passed on by colonels to lieutenant colonels and downward to the captains who led the companies:

"Forward, march!"

Four p.m.
Junction of Brock Road and
the Orange Plank Road

Getty, don't be an idiot," Hancock said.

Getty stiffened. Hancock might sit upon his stallion in all his majesty, but Getty had been fighting and Hancock had not.

The division commander resisted the urge to ask the corps commander what had taken him so long to bring up his corps. And Hancock remained unready and disorganized even now, his men still streaming in.

"I have my orders," Getty said, "and I always follow my orders."

"But . . . this is folly. Don't be pigheaded, George. Just hold off until Mott closes up behind Birney and I can support you. You told me yourself you're already short a brigade. If you advance your division unsupported, you know what will happen."

A few hundred yards from the crossroads, skirmishing rattled the woods. Smoke prowled.

"I have my orders. As you have yours, General Hancock.

Meade has directed me to attack 'immediately.' I shall do so."

"Getty . . . for Christ's sake . . ."

Bulky and grand, Hancock did indeed resemble the war god praised in all the newspapers. And Getty knew that Hancock was correct, tactically speaking. He would have preferred not to attack without Hancock's divisions on his flanks, he had made that clear to Meade's pink-pated errand boy, Lyman, a society creature got up in a tailored uniform. But that had been the extent of Getty's protest.

He was an old soldier and, he believed, a good one. Earlier in the day, he had followed his orders to rush his division to this place and hold it, and he had held it. He had cursed Meade, but he had done so to himself, not to other men. And Meade had been right, he had been needed exactly where he was sent and precisely when he got there. For all he knew, Meade would be right again this time.

But even if George Meade was wrong, the order must be obeyed to its last letter. The greater point was obedience. An army could not function if the orders of its commanders went ignored or were amended to each subordinate's liking. George Washington Getty had never disobeyed or delayed the execution of an order in his life. He believed his fellow officers respected that.

Of course, he yearned to make excuses, to blame others, to agree with Hancock, to delay his attack until he had a full division up on either flank to step off with his men. He feared that this attack would squander lives. But soldiers did not make excuses, nor did they fish for sympathy. Soldiers followed orders.

"General Hancock," Getty repeated, "my orders are to attack immediately. I can no longer delay."

Even Hancock's horse appeared disgusted. The animal backed away, prancing and snorting.

"Then be it on your head, you damned old fool," Hancock told him. "You're throwing away your division."

Getty saluted and turned away to see if his brigade commanders were ready.

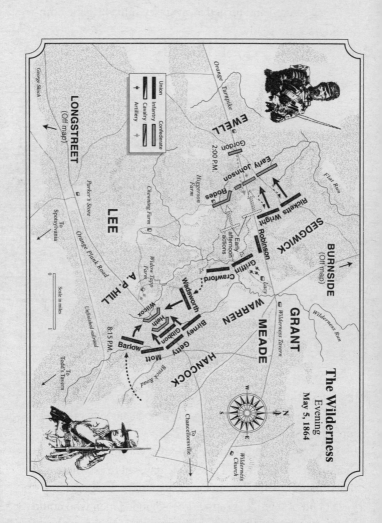

The Wilderness
Evening
May 5, 1864

EIGHT

Seven p.m.
Tapp Farm

W e're holding them!" Powell Hill could not wait, but had to shout his tidings over the hoofbeats of his horse and the storm of gunfire. "By God, sir, my boys are holding them!"

Lee passed over the use of the Lord's name. Hill's two scant divisions were, indeed, holding their lines. They had been driven back, but they refused to be driven farther. It made him proud unto sinfulness.

He could not see the fighting, which had been veiled by smoke. Even with little artillery in play, the roar of ten thousand rifles and more made the fouled air quiver. Men howled and cheered in masses. Still, he heard Hill's flinty voice as the corps commander reined up, panting and sweated through his blouse, deprived of his hat by war.

"Hancock's men . . . they just come on and we pile them up, just pile them up."

Lee sensed the butchery wrought within the smoke. It had been and still was a desperate day, but his soldiers had been magnificent, a wonder.

Not all of them, of course. The wounded men who could walk streamed back and shirkers infiltrated the ranks of the brave. There always would be a few, Lee knew, men pleading, if challenged, that they were out of ammunition or seeking to locate their units. Other men wandered open-mouthed and open-eyed after something cracked inside them. But the cowards and weaklings were few today, as if all good men sensed the desperate hour.

"My compliments, General Hill," Lee said. "Your men have done splendidly."

"Any reinforcements coming from Ewell?" Hill asked.

"I have asked him to spare us any strength he can."

"We could use help now, sir. They do keep coming. Hancock's got at least one Sixth Corps division added in."

"I know."

"Longstreet?"

Lee's stomach churned unpleasantly. "There have been delays. The march is long."

"Sir, we *need* him. With two divisions, I can't—" Hill broke off and stared at Lee. Hound-eyed and reproachful.

"You must hold until dark, General. By morning, General Longstreet's men will relieve you."

"Morning . . ."

Hill's proud spirits were plunging by the second. Lee did not want that. He knew what Hill longed to say, but dared not. Would they still be here in the morning, he and his men? What if Hancock gave them another hard push? The fighting had been savage, the men were exhausted. Many an ammunition pouch was empty. But they had to hold on. He could not let it be otherwise, would not think it. Grant could not be allowed an early triumph.

"Your soldiers will not let you down," Lee said. "And you will not let me down."

"No, sir. Of course not. But . . ."

Hill would have to be satisfied with such praise as he had given him. Lee's mind drove on.

"I can't understand it," he said. "I cannot fathom it."

Hill's fine stallion nickered, eyes straining, as uneasy as its master. As if it had only now discovered fear.

"Sir?" Hill said. His lank hair clotted to his face, rendering Lee's fellow Virginian as ill of aspect as he was in body. Earlier, Lee had feared that the effects of Hill's youthful indiscretion would incapacitate him before a battle again—as illness had at Gettysburg—but this day had been a triumph for Powell Hill. Never had he performed more bravely or finely than in the face of Hancock's onslaught. But there was still much to do before nightfall spared them.

What had Wellington said? "Give me night or Blücher"? His Blücher, James Longstreet, still struggled along country roads. It would be night, or nothing.

"I do not understand," Lee said, "the piecemeal nature of General Hancock's efforts. It isn't his practice." He looked at Hill. "General Grant, perhaps? Might he be impatient?"

Hill considered the matter, but said nothing. Both men sensed that it was time for Hill to ride back down to his troops. It was remarkable how soldiers understood certain things between them.

"Express my gratitude to Generals Heth and Wilcox for their labors today," Lee said. "Your corps never did this army finer service." Anticipating Hill, he raised a salute and dropped it. His hand was heavy, the knuckles swollen.

Hill spurred his mount and pounded back down into the battle's miasma. His sweat-heavy hair broke free and streamed behind him, as if daring his aides to grasp a lock.

How long? How long until those people ceased fighting this day? Two hours? Surely they could not fight in those hideous thickets in the darkness? An attack would dissolve into chaos.

Jehovah had stayed the course of the sun for Joshua. Now Lee wished the Lord would speed it along. The thought was insolent, blasphemous. But it was there. He wanted the Lord's attention, hope, a sign . . .

Meade and Grant seemed taken by surprise, there was that much. All day, their moves had been awkward and incremental, meeting successive repulses. Ewell's front, to the north, along the Turnpike, had been quiet for hours, the killing grown desultory. But Hancock was a bulldog.

Lee's own plan had gone to pieces. There could be no withdrawal to the Mine Run position now. Despite this day's severity and loss. The hasty barricades and rifle pits his men had thrown up here, in this . . . this wilderness, indeed . . . were nothing as to the entrenchments to their rear. But such would have to do. The battle had been joined, against his will . . . perhaps against wills on both sides . . . but Lee knew that he had to fight here and now, that Grant could not be allowed a victory in their first encounter. He had to be taught a lesson, his expectations frustrated, his army bloodied and its commander shamed. Grant had to learn here, on this field, that there would be no easy victories anymore, that the army he now faced was not the hapless foe he had known in the West. No matter the cost, the Army of Northern Virginia had to hold its ground, to command it.

Meade had to be beaten, but Grant had to be shamed.

Walter Taylor cantered up. Lee waved the adjutant off. He needed a moment. And had the matter been vital, Taylor would have come on at a gallop. The members of his staff knew him by now, even the inflection of such a gesture: *Not now . . . unless the business cannot wait.*

Ewell had won the day along the Turnpike, and Lee had heard that Gordon—an officer on whom he had long had his eye—had performed brilliantly at the decisive moment, carrying all before him. But here on the Plank Road the matter remained doubtful. Bravery, as he had learned so painfully at Gettysburg, went only so far.

The firing beyond the hill, down in the gunsmoke, swelled again.

All his life, Lee had scorned selfish prayers. But now he prayed:

"Lord, let it be night."

Seven thirty p.m.
Brock Road

Morgan!" Hancock barked to his chief of staff. "Ride down and get that Harvard sonofabitch. I need him *now*."

His chief of staff smiled and tipped a salute. Morgan liked a battle, the little bastard. West Point hadn't spoiled that one. Told hilarious stories about riding herd on the Mormons with Sidney Johnston.

"Wait a minute, Morgan," Hancock bellowed. "Waste of goddamned time, I'll—" He whipped about. "You there, soldier. *You*. Turn your ass around and get back in the fight, that's no fucking wound." And turning again to his chief of staff: "Tell Mott to get those twats of his back in the fight, they're not here to spread their legs for Robert E. Lee. I'll deal with Barlow myself. Walker, you come with me. And two couriers." He pointed. "You two. The rest of you stay put, including flags."

He spurred his horse, and a streak of white-fire pain shot from thigh to brain. Damned wound had been a bother all day. Just had to ignore it. Gettysburg. Finest hour. Bullshit, all of it. Just more slaughter. Now this mess. Getty pig-headed as ever, with Frank Wheaton moaning that his men were exhausted. Sweet Christ, they were all exhausted. And poor, damned Hays, dead as bones. Meade pushing him to attack, attack, attack. Not Meade's way, either. Hancock felt the heavy hand of Grant behind all that. *Attack, attack!* And he had attacked and attacked, first to keep goddamned Getty from annihilation, then, as more of his men arrived, drenched in sweat, painted with dust, and throats as dry as your grandmother's tits, because he had just enough success to make it worth continuing. "In you go, boys." And out they came. Bloody mess. Mott's men falling back in droves. All of them, his boys under Mott as well as Getty's mob, backed off by two raggle-taggle divisions under Hill, the walking skeleton, and Longstreet not even up. Where was *that* sonofabitch?

"Walker," he called behind him as he rode, "if you can't keep up, I'll get a damned aide who can."

Goddamned Barlow. He'd have that cocksure look on his schoolboy face. But he was the man for this now, the little piss-cutter. Hancock wondered if the stories were true about Barlow's mother whoring her way through New England society to keep her brood fed and clothed, with the father Bedlam mad and off to the races. If the rumors were true, Sir Frank wasn't quite so fine as he let on.

Might explain his delight in killing, though. Shame had never made any bugger kinder. No matter how well concealed the shame might be. Was that the case with Powell Hill, with his plugged-up cock and his gal lost to Georgie McClellan, of all people?

Soldiers, some wounded, others not, leapt out of his way. Stripped to the waist and working like navvies, enlisted men shoveled up earthworks along the road and chopped down trees to open fields of fire. Still others meandered, shocked by battle or dumbstruck with the heat. Hard enough for a man to breathe in the smoke, and damned near impossible to hear. The battle raging to his right reminded him of ocean storms pounding on the California rocks. So long ago it seemed. California. Worthless place, and keep the gold for your troubles. But once you'd taken it over from the greasers, you damned well couldn't return it and say, "Sorry."

Hancock's fury preceded him. A battery struggling up the road hurriedly drew to the side to let him pass. That only angered him more. He didn't need more guns, he had no place for them. He needed infantry, damn it. To replace the infantry sacrificed in the utter absence of a sensible plan. Terrible damned place to fight. Favored the defender in every way.

But Grant wanted a fight, that much was clear.

And now he had one.

The trees fell away on the left. Hancock spotted Barlow up on a hillock, in front of his guns, high on a white horse, his damned high horse, as cool as if he'd never had to shit.

As always, Barlow's men looked ordered and ready.

When Barlow saw Hancock, he cantered down to meet him. He didn't gallop. Just cantered.

But there was an expectation on Barlow's face.

"Barlow! Ready to go in, damn you?"

The white-faced—pasty-faced—boy pulled up, the two of them horse's nose to horse's ass.

"Of course, sir."

"Then go in, damn it. Mott's made a Mexican whorehouse mess of his attack. I need you on the left. Just up the road."

"I know where Mott went in, sir."

"Just follow the goddamned bodies. Christ, Barlow . . . we were breaking them! And I don't know what happened. Oh, I do and I don't. The bastards dig in so fast. And you can't see a thing until you're right on top of the sonsofbitches. Despite all the fucking interference from headquarters, we were pushing them like the devil's broom in Hell. Then they dug in their heels, and now we're shit for the birds." Hancock stroked his agonized thigh. "Just shore up Mott on the left. Turn them, if you can. Do what you can before dark." Hancock looked to the sky, its light already fading. "Can't let the day end with those bastards thinking they've screwed us. Don't want Deacon Lee feeling all holy about today's sermon." Before Barlow could speak, Hancock added, "Leave one brigade here. In case something does turn up along the road."

"I'll leave Paul Frank. His men just closed from the tavern. Miles and Brooke are the men I want now, anyway." He looked straight into Hancock's eyes, unblinking as a snake. Not much subordinate feeling in Frank Barlow. As if he were God Almighty and Commodore Vanderbilt wrapped into one. "What about Smyth, the Irish?"

"You'll get Smyth back later," Hancock told him. "We'll have to wait until after dark to untangle things up there. Well, what are you waiting for? Teacher to ring the bell?"

Barlow smiled, then grinned. He had an ugly grin, all crooked teeth. The expression transformed the schoolboy into a murderer.

Turning to his own aide, Barlow called, "Black! Tell Brooke and Miles they're to form their brigades for battle. Immediately."

Eight fifteen p.m.
Below the intersection of the
Plank Road and Brock Road

Forward!" Barlow shouted. He lowered his saber, pointing it at the enemy. Out there in the brush and smoke.

If any of his subordinates had failed to hear the command amid the din, they saw the saber drop. His colonels aped the gesture. Bayonets fixed, the blue lines moved into the undergrowth, with Miles' brigade forward on the right, four of five regiments on line, and Brooke trailing slightly on the left, refusing the flank just enough to address surprises.

There was no cheering. His men had seen enough from the battle's edge to realize this was a bitter sort of fight, close and grinding, with men fed between the millstones. Nor was there any parade-ground nonsense, with weapons held at right-shoulder-shift to the last. His men went in with their rifles leveled at their sides, ready to charge.

Ahead: Ragged rifle volleys, shrieks, and curses unintelligible but distinguished by their tone. His skirmishers were out, alert, in their groups of four, trained specially for their task over the past month. He listened as majors and sergeants, captains and gaping lieutenants, chastised soldiers who fell one step behind. The lines would not remain unbroken, the terrain, the green and smoldering rottenness of it, would not allow it. But Barlow wanted them held together as long as possible. Each step counted. His orders were that no man was to fire until they were atop or among the enemy. He had had enough gentlemanly idiocy *à la* Fontenoy. There were to be no pauses, no premature volleys that did little more than immobilize his men as targets. And when the lines inevitably came apart, his soldiers had some training now in open-order fighting.

This would be a test. Of course, every battle was a test. And it bewildered Frank Barlow that any man was ever willing to fail.

But plenty were. Along with the wounded, stumbling, gruesome, or glad of a crimson excuse to make for the rear, other men just trod rearward, most still with their rifles, quitting, as if they had merely reached the end of their shift at the foundry.

Had it been up to him, every one of them would have been shot.

He took the flat of his own sword to the back of a limping sergeant, one of his own men, who had not quite kept up with his charges. Applying the saber soundly to the man's back, Barlow snapped, "Get moving, or I'll tear off those stripes myself."

The man stepped out at the double, catching up to his men in a scatter of seconds. He still limped, but not as slowly.

The first corpses materialized, dark forms in the fading light. And the immobile or crawling wounded became an annoyance, pleading to be carried off or succored by men who had other tasks before them. His own ranks began to buckle, encountering stands of scrub pines and impenetrable briars. His officers did all they could to enforce alignments.

Other swathes of undergrowth had been trampled or broken off in the previous fighting and he was able to ride a jagged course behind the ranks of Miles' leftmost regiments. In hardly a minute, he reached the brigade commander.

"Nellie, just don't stop. Don't let your men stop. They won't be expecting us this late." He glanced instinctively toward the sky, as Hancock had done. "Make the bad light a friend."

"Rebs must be tired," Miles said. "They've stuck, though, say that for them."

What did he, Francis Channing Barlow, have to say for the Confederates? Nothing for their cause, which he believed odious. But wounded—mortally, they all thought—and taken prisoner at Gettysburg, he had liked their officers better than his own comrades. Their courtesy was as good as a cold drink on that July day, the manners of the officers courtly to quaintness. Even their ragamuffin rank and file had shown a respect toward superior officers that simply did not exist in the Union's armies. All of them had been unexpectedly kind, and all things being equal— which they were not—he would have preferred to serve beside such men.

But the nation's soil had to be rid of their "peculiar institution," and the Union had to be saved. Both matters were givens. So Barlow would kill the men he liked with undiminished enthusiasm.

Battle was better by far than any sport. And the prizes were worth immeasurably more.

"If they're tired, they can be panicked," he told Miles. "If they panic, don't let your front ranks stop to take prisoners. Don't give their reserves a moment to react. If a soldier stops to loot, I want you to shoot him."

Miles laughed. "Looting won't be a problem. The Rebs have nothing worth stealing."

But they did. Tobacco. An officer's watch. Some of the men the North recruited now were inveterate thieves. And worse. Barlow wanted *those* men to go forward, to take the bullets in chest and loins, sparing his precious veterans.

That was never the way it turned out, though. The brave and best died first.

His horse danced across a corpse. It was hard to spot even living men in the dense vegetation. Barlow tugged the mount back toward Brooke's trailing brigade, but didn't get far. Brewster, one of Mott's brigade commanders, found him. The man was disheveled, his horse dripped blood, and old blood crusted the side of his aide's face.

"Thank God," Brewster said. "My men need relief immediately."

"Those who haven't run away," Barlow said coldly.

Brewster stiffened.

"Oh, bugger it," Barlow told him. "Who's up ahead?"

"You mean from my brigade?"

"I don't give a damn about your brigade, Colonel. *The enemy.*"

"North Carolina boys. Lane's crowd, I think. Tough as nails."

"We'll see," Barlow said, and he left the brigade commander to his own business.

As he passed his 26th Michigan, Barlow warned its colonel anew not to let his men stop to fire volleys. An approximation of night had come to the fern glades and briars, and men from Mott's division cursed as Barlow's ranks passed over them where they lay, stepping on limbs and hands.

It would be but moments now.

Before he reached Brooke, a mighty shout erupted from his men, followed by massed firing. Barlow pulled his horse about.

His men were running forward, charging. Well, Brooke would know what to do. Remaining mounted, Barlow followed the fight, ignoring the maelstrom of lead. Calling, "Keep going, forward, *forward!*" and waving his saber, he kept up with his second line of troops, riding around obstacles and between men stricken with wounds.

"Keep going, get at them!" he yelled.

His troops had already rushed in among the Confederates, with men firing point-blank into each other's torsos and clubbing each other with gun stocks, most still shy about using the bayonet, even hard men queerly timid about thrusting a blade deep into human flesh.

To his right, he saw Nellie Miles, a shadow on horseback, driving his men into a nest of Confederates.

Rebels appeared right at his side. Disarmed men. Herded rearward. But the firing hard to his right flank intensified.

An aide to Miles rode near, struggling through tangled flesh and vegetation.

"What's happening?" Barlow demanded.

"Orders to the Hundred and Sixteenth Pennsylvania. Move to the right flank. Hot fight over there, sir."

Well, he trusted Miles' judgment.

A sergeant approached him, bearing a captured battle flag. Grinning as wide as Galway Bay in the gloaming.

"You!" Barlow said. "Give that to a private. Get back to your men."

They'd take any damned excuse. . . .

He almost took his saber to a soldier headed weaponless to the rear. Then he saw that half the boy's face was missing.

The lines kept moving, but the darkness thickened. Outraged at nature itself, that nightfall might deprive him of a triumph, Barlow cursed viciously.

Alarmed at the expression on their general's face, the soldiers nearest him hastened toward more Confederates.

Another cluster of prisoners. Sullen men. Filthy. Faces blackened by a day's worth of powder, dark now as the men they had enslaved.

A gray-clad youth wept in shame as he approached.

"What's your unit?" Barlow demanded.

Responding instinctively to the tone of command, the boy said, "Seventh North Carolina, sir."

"You don't need to tell that sumbitch nothing," another prisoner said.

Why had Hancock waited so long? Graced with just another twenty minutes, Barlow believed he would have rolled up the entire Confederate flank. But the dark favored the defender, who could stay put, not the attacker blundering forward. Soon, too soon, he would need to call off the hounds.

He rode over Confederate corpses and whimpering wounded. They lay interspersed with the fallen from his own army. The ratio seemed a good one, at least here.

More prisoners. Officers among them. Broken men.

The twilight had progressed so far that muzzle blasts turned into hundreds of monstrous fireflies. Patches of brush set alight by discharges made ghostly silhouettes of antic men.

Miles found him. "Frank, we've got to halt. We're blundering about."

"So are they." His voice was remorseless, cold even to his own ears.

"General Barlow . . . Frank . . . we've done all we can tonight. We must be four hundred yards in advance of the corps. Maybe five. . . ."

And those bastards were too lazy, weak, and oblivious

to catch up, Barlow thought. He would've cashiered Mott, had it been in his power. Even Birney, if it came to that. The fight had to be to the death. Didn't any of them understand that basic principle?

He felt victory slipping away and had to subdue an impulse to lash out at Miles, to reach across the space between their mounts and slap the man's face. Not because Miles had done a single thing wrong—he had performed handsomely—but because he was the nearest living thing, other than his horse. Barlow wanted to hurt things, to destroy worlds.

But Miles was right, and he knew it.

Before he could give the necessary orders to re-form and consolidate their position, one of Hancock's aides, Billy Miller, found him.

"Compliments, sir. General Hancock says well done, very well done. He desires you to break off the attack and align with the rest of the corps."

"Withdraw?" Barlow was livid.

"To adjust the lines, sir. It's a matter of asserting our position."

"The last time I bothered with a dictionary, Captain, 'asserting' implied going forward, not retreating."

"Yes, sir."

Miles said, "It's not Miller's fault. He's only carrying the order."

"And your men are to be relieved as soon as practicable," the captain added. "So you can re-form on the corps' flank. In your previous position, sir."

Barlow shook his head, a narrow shadow in the smoke-thickened night. "So we were only out for a stroll in the woods? Was that it? I might as well be back in goddamned Concord."

Neither Miles nor Miller dared speak.

"Oh, bugger it," Barlow said, breaking the spell that battle had cast upon him. "Colonel Miles, give the order to your men. I'll pass it on to Brooke myself." But he could not resist saying, "Sonofa*bitch*." Had he been afoot, he would have kicked the turf like a surly child.

As he rode southward toward Brooke's brigade, he passed another band of prisoners herded toward the rear at bayonet point, cursed along by voices native-born and Irish, united in pleasure over their own survival and delighted at the predicament of their enemies. Oblivious to the pleas of the wounded and measuring the decline of the fighting by the diminishing gunfire, he felt the wondrous exhilaration return.

Really, it had all been splendid. Too short. But utterly splendid.

Francis Channing Barlow could not understand how a man could prefer a woman to a war.

Eleven thirty p.m.
Near Wilderness Tavern

Grant sat on a stool in front of his tent, smoking a pipe in place of a cigar. Hours before, he had ceased whittling and discarded his shredded gloves to give Meade orders for a general attack in the morning. No bits and pieces or hesitations this time, Hancock's corps, reinforced, would strike along the line of the Plank Road, while Burnside brought the Ninth Corps in on Hancock's right, driving a wedge between the wings of Lee's army. Both Warren and Sedgwick would attack in support in the north, on the Turnpike line, to immobilize Ewell. Somewhere, there would be a weak spot. And Lee would break.

He tapped out the pipe, anxious for it to cool sufficiently for him to refill it. He had come to prefer cigars over the pipe that had been his companion in poverty, but sometimes, even now, he needed a change. All day long, he had revealed as little emotion as possible, watching Meade and his men perform—some of them, like Warren, disappointingly—but he had been churning inside. The responses to orders within the Army of the Potomac had not been as crisp as he would have liked, although he sensed that the men were fighting well. Meade had been right about that: The men were fighters. Even if some of their leaders might be wanting. What troubled him was an awakened sense of Lee, a foreboding that not all of the warnings had been exaggerated, a sense that things were different here indeed.

He had never encountered such tenacious resistance in the past. Meade's attacks had gone in hard. Yet, at best, the day was a stalemate. In the west, Confederate armies had collapsed or just plain quit when he hit them hard enough. Oh, they were dandy at yipping their way through a sudden attack. But when the tables were turned, they had always folded. At Donelson. On the second morning at Shiloh. At Champion Hill and Missionary Ridge.

This felt different. Even Rawlins' mockery had grown subdued as the day burned into evening. Grant thought of Shiloh, of that first night, of Cump Sherman coming into his own, wildly capable on the battlefield, commiserating by a fire that, yes, the day had been hard, but they had held that last line above the river. And Grant had said to his friend, yes, it had been a hard enough day. "Beat 'em tomorrow, though."

And they had done it. Attacking, when the Rebels had expected to renew their own attack. Rage had grown overnight in the blue ranks, and his vengeful men had broken the hopes of the western Confederacy. But today he had been the attacker, as he preferred. And each attack had failed or fallen short.

Beat 'em tomorrow, though.

"I still think you ought to cashier that bastard Griffin," Rawlins said. The chief of staff sat facing Grant, with Congressman Washburne rounding out the trio on camp stools placed in front of Grant's tent. All other parties had been alerted to keep a respectful distance.

"What's that?" Grant said, rising from his thoughts.

"Griffin. The one who went on a tirade. He should be court-martialed."

Grant shook his head. "Meade said he's a good man. Claims he needs him."

"It was a public affront. To you."

Again, Grant shook his head. Slowly. "Man was riled. That's all."

"At least, order Meade to give him a dressing-down. And a damned good one."

"Meade's no fool. He'll talk to the man."

Grant's first sponsor in Washington and a mighty power back home in Illinois politics, Elihu Washburne entered the conversation: "What *about* Meade?"

"He'll do," Grant said. He began reloading his pipe.

"For now?" Washburne asked.

"Maybe longer. Meade isn't the problem."

"Then who is?"

"Lee. Near as I can tell."

"Meade's all right," Rawlins put in. "I give him the devil. Poor bastard needs it. Stiffen him up. Wouldn't admit it to his face, but he's one of the few West Pointers I'd give you a nickel for."

Grant smiled. "John's in a generous mood. I feel my own worth climbing toward ten cents."

Washburne looked to Grant. Haunted by distant firelight, the congressman's face was a mask of shadows. "That's good. About Meade. I've been thinking about your political future."

A sharp exchange between skirmishers raised a

commotion off to the west. None of the three men paid it any attention.

"I've told you," Grant said. "I have no interest in politics. Not suited for it."

"And I've told you, wait and see," the congressman said. "Never burn a bridge or slam a door."

"I agree," Rawlins said. "It's a good thing if Meade's kept on. Don't want this army and all the voters in and around it to feel slighted. They may not love him all the way to the shitter, but Meade's their own."

"Exactly," Washburne said. "If you run for president, Sam, you're going to have to carry the votes of *all* the veterans and their families. And Meade would bring in Pennsylvania. Can't win a national election without Pennsylvania."

"I'm not running for president. I told Lincoln I support him, and I meant it."

"We're talking about after the war," Rawlins said.

"Exactly," Washburne seconded. He leaned closer to the general in chief.

Grant lit his pipe anew. "I'll never run for president. Or mayor. Or alderman. Meanwhile, boys, I've got a war to fight. In case you've forgotten."

"Even in that regard," Washburne told him, "I'm glad you don't feel a need to relieve George Meade. At least, not yet. Oh, he's got enemies aplenty. But he has friends, too. He should only be relieved by popular demand. Which, of course, can always be arranged." The congressman chuckled. "He could be damned useful, if a catastrophe came upon us. He'd be just high enough to take the blame and leave your record clean."

"There won't be a catastrophe," Grant said. "And I'm not about to lay blame on George Meade. Unless he has it coming." He couldn't say he liked the man particularly, but he had found Meade to be one of those rare officers who never seemed to connive, not even for his own advancement. Grant valued that.

"But if an unfortunate turn of events *was* his fault . . . ," Washburne continued. "It's his army, after all. *Ergo* . . ."

Grant lowered the pipe. "The day may come when I tell Meade to pack up and go. But I'm not going to saddle a man with blame that ain't his." His voice was as firm as an oak stump.

"Dear God," Washburne said, "you really may not be cut out for politics."

The congressman and Rawlins laughed. Grant smiled along.

A shriek rose from the road below, where ambulance wagons rumbled through the darkness.

Grant winced. He did not like to think of wounded men. And he did what he could to avoid seeing them. He did not like blood. His meat had to be charred to a crisp before he could lift it to his mouth. He did not like the sight of suffering, whether of man or beast. A general could not think of such things, he knew: War was slaughter, and only when enough slaughter had been done did any war end. But he did not care to dwell on a battle's aftermath.

Grant puffed fiercely on his pipe, as if its smoke might suffocate his thoughts.

The congressman slapped his knees. The sound was as sharp as two quick shots. He asked, "What about tomorrow? Think you can smash up Lee's army?"

"Like to," Grant said. "He may have a say in the matter."

"Meade's people are worried about the Ninth Corps, you know," Rawlins told him. "About Burnside. They don't think he'll be up in time to do his part."

"He told me he'll be up," Grant said.

"Nobody else believes it."

"We'll give him a chance. I never was one for execution before trial."

"Burnside has a constituency in Washington," the congressman warned Rawlins. "He's a likable man. And well liked, accordingly. The very opposite of Meade, with that snoot-in-the-air attitude of his."

"Burnside's a fat-assed dandy," Rawlins said. He turned exclusively to Grant. "I don't like this arrangement. Senior or not, Burnside should be directly under Meade. This is a damned mess. 'Unity of command,' ain't that how you put it?"

"Can't do it," Grant said. "Not yet. Army rolls. Matter of pride for Burnside."

"*And* for his people in Washington," Washburne added. "We want Burnside and his allies happy. Right through November."

Grant turned to Rawlins. "Maybe you could go a little softer on Meade, John? And Humphreys? In front of others? Given how you're always lawyering for him when it's just you and me. . . ."

"No," Rawlins told him. "Meade needs to feel the pressure. Humphreys, too."

"Good man, Humphreys," Grant said.

"That's not the point, Sam. They need driving. All of them. And that's *my* job. You're the big chief who don't take scalps himself. I'm the dirty sonofabitch with the knife. Near as I can tell, it's the one true duty of a chief of staff." Grown excited, Rawlins coughed. He felt wetness on the fist he pressed to his mouth, but refused to examine it. "Damned smoke," he said, clearing his throat and spitting. "One thing I never get used to is the smoke. And the stink. You don't get a sense of *that* from the illustrated papers. Everybody charging in perfect rows, flags waving. And not one sorry mick bastard squatting to shit."

Grant winced. Unreasonably, the image had called up the worst ordeal of his life, a memory that often plagued him out of the blue. It had been worse even than his failure in the Northwest, his fateful weakness, his humiliation, the agony of missing Julia. The trial had come suddenly, during his passage to California, while he led a train of soldiers, women, children, drovers, and mules across the isthmus. Cholera had struck them, and the deaths, not least of the women and their little ones, had been as gruesome as anything seen on a battlefield, ladies who had stood primly on their dignity in the morning shitting and puking themselves to death at noon. Nothing had ever been as grim as their flesh blackening in the heat before they could be hidden in shallow graves. And all he could do was to drag along the survivors. He remembered—could never forget—one captain's wife, headed to San Francisco to join her husband. She had been fair, with chestnut locks and the features of a princess in a fairy tale. The last time he had glimpsed her she had become a corpse, three-quarters naked in a shit-covered shift, her face set in an open-mouthed rictus and coated with the rice-pudding cholera spew, a hideous death of agony and shame. Nothing was ever as bad as that. *Nothing.* He had begun drinking afterward.

"Tell you what," Washburne said. "Sam, you finish off Bobby Lee tomorrow, we'll give Old Abe a second term, then put you in the White House in '68."

Grant had had enough of such talk. He needed the grand attack in the morning to work. He could not allow Robert E. Lee to feel superior in any sense, to judge himself the master of this battlefield. Even if the Army of Northern Virginia could not be destroyed on the spot, Lee's will had to be weakened, he had to feel doubt, to know that he had a tougher opponent now, one who would not relent. Lee had to learn to fear him. The onetime captain of engineers whom they had all admired in Mexico had to sense that this was the beginning of the end of things for his people and that continuing the war was naught but futility.

"Got any more of those cigars you were smoking?" Washburne asked him. "I'm all out."

"Bill?" Grant called over his shoulder. In seconds, a black face—blacker than the surrounding darkness by a full degree—popped out of the depths of the tent.

"Suh?"

"Bill, fetch the congressman a handful of cigars. The good Havanas."

"Yassuh."

"That reminds me," Washburne said. "Ferrero. His division. The Colored Troops."

"What about them?"

"Careful how you use them. We can't have another Fort Pillow. If the Confederates massacre those darkies, Lee won't get the blame. The abolitionists will blame you, Sam. You're the name in the papers now. And they're still sore about that business with the Jews. They'll claim that you used the Colored Troops as cannon fodder. Greeley and Stevens and the whole damned lot of them don't really want their little black pets to fight, they just want them to march around bright and shiny."

"Well," Grant said, "they're guarding the army's trains. That's about as safe as I can keep them. May get to a point where I have to use 'em, though."

"Try not to. Really, Sam. I mean, you don't really expect them to fight, do you? Against white men? They'd probably run at the first shot."

"From what I hear, the Fifty-fourth Massachusetts didn't run," Grant said.

"And what did they accomplish? Sam, this is a political matter. And you just went on about how you don't want to fiddle with politics. Trust me on this."

Grant chose not to argue the matter further. He respected Washburne, was grateful to him. But he was not going to take military advice from the man. He turned to Rawlins:

"Heard anything from your bride, John?" He felt great affection for Rawlins, who had been one of the few to believe in him back in Galena. Now he worried about the country lawyer who had come so far beside him, worried about the cough that suggested consumption—the disease that had killed John's adored first wife—and worried that his second marriage, to a Yankee girl they had discovered stranded in Vicksburg, might have proven a disappointment. Grant thought he understood the weight of the loss of a much-loved wife. His long separation from Julia, those grim years in the desolate Northwest, had given him a taste of it. He could not imagine how he could go on, were he to lose her forever. He was not certain that any war, or the fate of any nation, was as important as the existence of his living, breathing, gently chiding wife. She, too, had believed in him when others did not. Years before John Rawlins and Elihu Washburne had come along.

If a man needed anything, it seemed to Grant, it was for others to believe in him. When they did, he could believe in himself at last.

Bill delivered a fistful of cigars to the congressman, who skillfully avoided the Negro's touch. Washburne rose, followed by Rawlins.

"Think I'll retire to my lavish accommodations," the congressman said. "After this, I'll have some advice for Mr. Willard."

"I need to see what Humphreys has cooked up while we were visiting," Rawlins said. "Won't come waking you, unless it's a thing that matters."

Grant nodded. He didn't rise. Just didn't feel like it. Not yet.

He watched his two closest friends descend the back side of the knoll and fade into the darkness. Out on the roads, the commotion continued: supply wagons, provost men, redirected infantry regiments, and the endless ambulances. Curses, cries, and commands.

He believed in getting what sleep he could. A few hours, anyway. Weary men made poor decisions. And the days ahead would be busy ones.

His manservant came back out of the tent, carrying a shirt he'd been mending by lantern light—an excuse for listening in, Grant knew—and ready to receive the day's final instructions. A freed slave, Bill had attached himself to Grant early on as well. He, too, believed in the "general in chief." But not quite as unreservedly as the others. Life had taught old Bill a degree of skepticism a white man rarely attained, and the fellow had the biggest ears of any man Grant had met when it came to listening to every whisper around him. Even Washburne was a babe in the woods compared to his manservant. Or his "valet," as Julia always wanted him to call the poor devil. Whatever folks might call the darkey, Grant enjoyed the man's presence.

"Well," Grant said, "did you give the congressman the good cigars this time?"

Bill shuffled a bit, fussing with the garment in his hands, then said, "No, suh. I give him the pretty good cigars, not the *good* cigars. That man don't never know the difference. Them good cigars comes to you, ain't nobody sent 'em to Washington."

"You're supposed to do what I tell you, you know."

"Yassuh. I knows. I'm supposed to do 'zacly how you says, just like every man in this here army supposed to do 'zacly what you says."

Grant's lips spread in amusement. "Meaning . . . they don't?"

"Some does, some don't. That General Meade now, he do what you say, just like you say it. 'Least, he trying to. Downright pitiful, watching how hard that man try."

"Think I'll need one more of those good cigars myself.

But hold on. Put the shirt down and sit down. And tell me something. What do *you* make of Meade, Bill? What do you really think? Given that you haven't missed a word that's been said since the day I brought you east."

Bill laid the shirt, half-folded, on a camp stool. But he didn't sit. "Not my place to say, suh. Not 'bout a general."

Grant enjoyed their routines. Many a day it was the only play he had, the only enjoyment, other than his cigars, that he could allow himself.

"Well, then," Grant said, "that suggests it isn't my place to ask you. Do we have to go through this every time?"

"Yassuh. I reckon we do. That's how we keeps things right."

"So give me your honest opinion of General Meade. That's an order."

Bill pretended to think hard on the question. As if he had not been pondering it for well over a month. "Well, suh, that man has him a powerful temper, terrible powerful. But he wants to make things be right, that's all, and some things are all mule and no filly. When he's not blowing his head off his own shoulders, he's got him all the fixings of a true gentleman."

Grant smiled again. "And I don't?"

Bill feigned deep thought. "Well, now, Genr'l, I been knowing you years on years now. And I knows you got the soul of a gentleman, and the spirit of a gentleman. You just wasn't born with the fixings."

Grant shook his head. "Bill, you'd make a better diplomat than Secretary Seward. I'd be downright fearful of dealing with you."

"Nawsuh. You ain't feared of nothing but Miss Julia."

"That a fact?"

"You has *concerns*. That's a different thing, Genr'l."

"That I do. I have concerns. The congressman and every biscuit-grabbing journalist in this camp think I should

wrap up things with a nice big bow and do it all by suppertime tomorrow. What do *you* think?"

"Ain't my place to go telling nobody what I thinks about
manhandling this here army. That's your paid business.
Like mending shirts is my business."

"You do more thinking than half the generals I know."

"Ain't much of a compliment, Genr'l. If that's what
you're intending."

Grant laughed out loud. It was the first time he had
laughed properly that day. The first time he had known reason to laugh. "Well, I'm appointing you a brevet major general. Commission to expire in five minutes. So tell me: You
think we'll whip Marse Robert tomorrow? And be done
with it?"

Bill hesitated. Grant knew the man didn't fear an outburst of wrath. This was just the way they played the game.
Bill's opinion had to be courted. Even though he was
swollen with opinions. You almost had to bring him flowers. Or let him "test" a fair number of cigars when things
were slow.

Another skirmish flared up in the distance. It was an
uneasy battlefield this midnight, crowded, uncertain, unclear, a place of the lost, of small and fatal blunders. He
refused, again and adamantly, to think of the suffering.
The price had to be paid. He had to get at Lee, and keep at
him, until there was no more Lee left, no will left to fight
on the other side. The army was a great blue hammer, and
he would not hesitate to wield it.

"Go ahead," Grant told his manservant. "Before you bust
open with not saying what you want to say."

Bill shook his head. "There's that song, suh. One of them
songs to make fun of the black man, like white folks
do. . . ."

"You know I can't tell one song from another."

Bill shook his head in exaggerated mournfulness. "Ain't the singing part, Genr'l, just the words."

"Which words?"

" 'Richmond am a hard road to travel.' "

May 6, twelve thirty a.m.
Grant's headquarters

As he lay on his bed of pine branches and blankets, Bill was glad the general had not asked him about the use of Negro troops. He might have spoken his mind, really spoken it. Saying as how the general needed to let them fight, let them do what they hurt and ached and just plain wanted to do, to settle debts of a hundred years and more. Would black men fight? Near as he could tell, only army discipline was stopping them from fighting.

The general was a good man, easy, half nigger himself after the low way he lived back in Missouri, back in his bad times. That man knew what it was to be shamed. But even he didn't understand it all, no white man could. Mostly, they got it terrible wrong, body and soul, especially the ones who meant to do black folk good, the abolitionists. He had his letters solid, and he had thought over some of their writings. Heard them talk, too. And they were good Christian men and women, no denying. But it was like that book they all loved so much, *Uncle Tom's Cabin*. Poor little white woman didn't understand slavery at all, not one little bit. All that fuss about whipping. Wasn't all that many niggers got themselves whipped, not even downriver. And half of them who did were like to deserve it, for one thing or another. No, it wasn't the whipping. Bill had never seen a master take a lash to a black man's body, although he'd heard tell. Anyway, whipping just wasn't a mighty doing like folks said. Ugly and unwelcome, surely. But whipping was an outside thing, like a bad storm come by, and it passed over, maybe leaving its mark, maybe not. The hell-fire evil in slavery was the inside, everyday part of it, the mountain piled up from little bits of shame and insult, the way a man was lifelong caught between the place of an animal and that of a man. Scars on a black back were one thing, but the true scars were the ones white folk couldn't see, the scars of shame, the un-ableness to stand up on your hind legs and choose ways for yourself and be admired for what you made of this span on earth—God's blessing—and not for what you could steal, or how well you tricked white folks, or just for your sin-loving.

"You let the black man fight," he had wanted to tell the general, shout at him. "You just let them niggers fight out all the meanness they got built up in them, and you're like to see what fighting really is. Just turn those black men loose, Genr'l, turn those black men loose. . . ."

But he had held his tongue. He had spent a lifetime holding his tongue. Even with a good man like the general, there was a limit, clear as the words of Jesus Christ, past which no sober black man was going to step. Even with Grant, he affected a degree of coon speech because that was expected and easier. Safer. A black man who spoke well worried a white man. Any white man.

Nor was he always honest in other things. Truth-telling every minute was a prideful matter even most white men couldn't afford. And when a white man told the plain-dealing truth, the way that fireball, hellhound Griffin done told them all what was chewing on him that afternoon, he just got everybody riled up and no good come out of it. Take that General Meade, the fellow General Grant was always weighing in the scales, even when he claimed he wasn't. Wouldn't tell a lie, that man, and it hurt him like a sharp pain in the belly to pretty up the truth even a little.

Anybody could see it. But all it did was make folks walk on tippytoe around him and say hard things about him behind his back. General Grant, now, he was wise as a church elder in his quietness. He understood the black man's law that there was a lot to be said for not saying a lot.

And he didn't mind if a good cigar turned up in a Negro's mouth every now and then.

Nearing sleep, Bill smiled. The hard, brute world was fading, the crack of gunfire a distant lullaby, the occasional screams no worse than he'd heard before. He'd told the general a little lie this very evening, though for the general's own good: He hadn't given Mr. Washburne the pretty good cigars. Those were for the general, too, way he went through them. He'd given that high congressman the not-too-bad cigars, the way he always did. Man was so deep in love with himself, he never noticed one bit.

Let the black man fight! Let him carve out justice for himself. Don't hand it to him like a Christmas gift. Let him take it. Bill was too old for that nonsense now, nearly too old for the other, private, close-up, young man's doings. But, just once, he wanted to see a black man with a foot on a white man's back. A dead white man, if he had his druthers.

Meanwhile, it didn't trouble him to see white folk kill each other by the bushel.

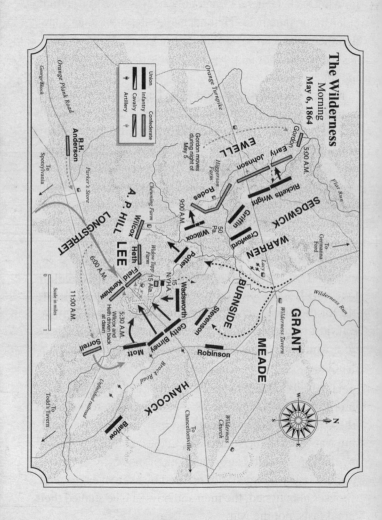

The Wilderness
Morning
May 6, 1864

Union
Confederate
Infantry
Cavalry
Artillery

Orange Turnpike

Flat Run

To Germanna Ford

Wilderness Run

GRANT

MEADE

Wilderness Tavern

SEDGWICK

EWELL

Gordon

500 A.M.

Gordon moves during night of May 5

Higgerson Farm

Early   Johnson

Ricketts Wright

Rodes

900 A.M.

Griffin

Crawford

Chewning Farm

WARREN

50 Pa.

Willcox

Parker's Store

Orange Plank Road

George/Block

To Spotsylvania

R.H. Anderson

A. P. HILL

LONGSTREET

LEE

600 A.M.

11:00 A.M.

Scale in miles

0   1

Willcox

Heth

Field   Kershaw

Widow Tapp Farm

15 Ala.

Willcox

Potter

BURNSIDE

Stevenson

Lacy

NYHA

Wadsworth

5:30 A.M.

Wilcox and Heth driven back at dawn

Getty Birney

Mott

Robinson

Sorrel

Brock Road

Orange Plank Road

To Todd's Tavern

HANCOCK

Barlow

To Chancellorsville

Wilderness Church

N

W   E

S

NINE

May 6, five thirty a.m.
Northern flank

The smell of the coffee enchanted Gordon. No parsimony had degraded its preparation; the men who brewed it were spendthrift with the beans. The fragrance was so rich it was nigh on lascivious, enticing as the Sirens. He would have liked to stroll right over and help himself to a cup.

The problem was that the coffee belonged to Yankees.

It was an amazing, bewildering, breathtaking situation, so perfect for his army's purposes that he could scarcely believe it. As he lay on the ground in the underbrush, peering through branches parted by a scout, the Union troops behaved as though safe in the rear: Their entrenchments were slapdash, their weapons rested by the low dirt parapets, and their leaders appeared unconcerned. The early morning firing along the corps' line had sputtered out, and these men had not been engaged in it, anyway. The fighting was miles to the south now, a constant roar from down by the Plank Road. Here, the flank of the Army of the Potomac simply dangled, not refused by even one regiment. Blouses unbuttoned, the men and boys in blue studied their breakfasts, not the war.

He ached to attack immediately, to deliver a blow that would send Grant and Meade and their self-righteous minions reeling. But he and a scout made an insufficient force.

Still, the prospect before him was a gift, and he felt a thrill so rich it bordered on sin. His lack of sleep was nothing now, overpowered by the vision of what he knew could be done to these careless men. He foresaw his greatest moment of the war.

In the black hours of the night, his brigade had been shifted from the corps' right to its extreme left, to guard the flank of the Army of Northern Virginia. Upon arrival at the new position, a clean place beyond the infestation of corpses, he had sent scouts out past his picket line immediately, unwilling to let weariness suborn duty, preaching to his men on the virtues of diligence. And yet, he'd been cranky himself when they awakened him, until he heard the news the scouts had brought. They swore the Yankees were nowhere to be found to the brigade's front, that his men could have lined up and marched straight forward.

He knew what that meant, but didn't believe it possible. His enemies, veterans now, could not have made such a blunder. But he also knew he would get no more sleep that night: The report would gnaw at him until he confirmed it.

He sent out another brace of scouts, his best men, before dawn. They returned with an identical report, adding that they had located the end of the Yankee line off to the right.

Thereafter, a cavalry patrol reported to him: There were no Union troops to the north, either, not even a cavalry screen. Nothing stood between his brigade and the road to Fredericksburg but a supply train and a crawling procession of ambulances.

He *still* had been unable to credit the news, so he set off himself with a scout who had been with him since his captaincy of the fur-capped Raccoon Roughs at the start of the war. They rode, unchallenged, for miles through the forest, and it might as well have been peacetime. Birds trilled and chirped with confidence, and though a scent of powder marred the air, the reek of death had not yet come so far.

At last, the scout led him, afoot and then on their bellies, to the vantage point where the two now lay, within pistol range of their enemies. And Gordon was ravished by the aroma of coffee.

He heard the Yankees speak of petty concerns—even complaining about the drink he envied—while he envisioned how the attack would be executed. The plan made itself. His brigade stretched a quarter mile beyond the end of the Union line. The Yankees had exposed not the mere heel of Achilles, but the leg right up to the hip. His brigade could simply advance and wheel to the right, hitting the Union flank at a right angle. Achieving surprise, his men could collapse the Union line like a squeezebox, spreading panic and pushing on at a left oblique to allow the other brigades of Early's Division to connect with his right flank and sweep down to the Turnpike, where the rest of Ewell's corps could finish the destruction of at least half of the Army of the Potomac.

It would be a victory greater than Chancellorsville, more lopsided than Fredericksburg, and more powerful than either in its advantage to the Confederacy. It would make him. He'd gain a division command, Lee would have to create an opening. The old man's sense of justice would demand it, as would the public. He would sew on his second star—if the war even continued after Grant, the North's great hope, suffered such a disaster. In any case, his reputation would be indomitable. In war he could pick his command, in peace he could choose his office.

He would give the Yankees the licking they needed, as surely as mighty Caesar subdued the Nervii. He foresaw the blue lines breaking, dissolving, men running madly, others throwing down their rifles and raising their hands, and just enough of them making a stand to polish up the glory. His men would lay dozens of captured flags at the feet of Robert E. Lee.

No finer opportunity had presented itself in the war. For the Army of Northern Virginia. For the Confederacy. And for John B. Gordon.

In wonderful spirits, Gordon regaled his staff: "I almost walked on over there, grabbed that coffeepot, and drank right from the spout in a fashion most barbarous. Gentlemen, I tell you, the perfume of that beverage was pure Elysium. Surely, Helen herself was no more desirable. . . ."

Shaded from the blood-red sun by the trees, he squinted at his map again, wishing he had a better one. But the plan he'd committed to paper was sound, of that he was certain.

"We'll git you your coffee, sir," a captain from downstate said. "Missed it for breakfast, but you'll have it rightly for dinnertime. Lord, I'd pay gold dollars to be part of this."

"Just ain't right," another man said, "how Grant sent off his sutlers. Boys feel cheated."

"Well," Gordon said, "tonight they shall revel in plenty."

Rather than dashing to headquarters, he had dispatched his aide to alert General Early. He wanted his plan down in writing before they conferred. A document in his hand, countersigned, would guarantee that the credit could not be purloined.

Almost finished, he straightened his back and told his warrior band, "The incautious foe shall perish as did the legions of Varus, defeated as were the mongrel hordes of Persia by Alexander." He wasn't sure any of them understood even the reference to Alexander, but it didn't matter. They liked to hear him declaim as much as the soldiers did. He made them smile. And smiling subordinates would die for you in a blink.

Anyway, his mood was so fine, so ebullient, that Gordon could not restrain himself from the innocent joy of speechifying. He was a happy man, almost as delighted—almost, but not quite—as if he were returned to Fanny's arms. Had he needed to glower like Zeus, he could not have done so. Today, even Mars wore a grin.

Hoofbeats. Coming on fast. That would be Jones, his aide, coming back from Old Jube. But there should have been other horses, too. Gordon had flattered himself that Early would be so elated by his news that the division commander would ride straight down to praise him.

It all began to collapse.

After dismounting with a hangdog look, Jones glanced around before he dared say a word. Like a child fully expecting to be spanked.

"Well?" Gordon said. "Speak, winged Mercury!"

"Sir . . . General Early says you're to hold still and stay put. He says . . . that you must be mistaken, that General Burnside's entire Yankee corps is out there in front of us. He says we'll be lucky if we can hold our own flank."

Gordon opened his mouth to speak, but, for once, he found that events had robbed him of words.

At last, he muttered, "I . . . we must inform General Ewell. . . ."

"General Ewell was present, sir. With General Early."

"And did he share our division commander's opinion?"

"Seemed to. Just cussing a blue streak, the way he does. About the morning's fighting down thataway." Jones shrugged, making himself small. "It's settled down, but folks are feeling gruff."

"And General Early's tone . . . was so dismissive?"

"It was one of rebuke, sir. Said he didn't care to be pestered no more. And that's a quote."

"Damnation."

Gordon could see it well enough, though. Early in one

of his fits of spleen and Ewell enclosed in some momentary ire, hugging his bitterness the way a child clutched a doll and deferring to Early, only half listening to Jones. Gordon served two cantankerous men who would fight like lions, then lose a battle for spite.

He turned to his staff. "Gentlemen, if the mountain comes not to Muhammad, Muhammad must go to the mountain. Major Jones, if you'll accompany me?"

I was out there myself," Gordon said. There was a plea in his voice now. "I saw it for myself. There's nobody. Not for miles. It's quiet as a church at midnight."

In one of his invincible grumps, Early told him, "I don't know where exactly you rode, Gordon, but it takes a man of high ability to miss an entire Yankee corps to his front."

Wounded men passed on their way to the rear, scrapped by the morning's fighting. Those capable saluted or at least nodded toward the generals on horseback, but there was a sullen face or two as well.

"Cavalry reports had Burnside on the Germanna Road last night," Ewell put in. His wooden leg was an awkward thing to behold stretched from saddle to stirrup. "Ready to come down on the flank of this corps."

"And that flank would be you, Gordon," Early said.

Already straight-backed as a Quaker chair, Gordon stiffened further. Warning himself not to give his temper rein.

"Gentlemen," he said, "it may be that the Union Ninth Corps, or part of it, was on that road last night, but I swear to you upon my honor that it isn't there this morning. That flank is just dangling, like the hem of a stepped-on petticoat. They're spread thin, too."

"They're spread thin," Early said, "because there's a whole goddamned corps right behind them. They're not worried, and for good reason." He spit an imaginary gob of tobacco. "What you saw was just a goddamned skirmish line."

"Just listen to that." The corps commander gestured toward the south. "Hell of a fuss down there. Sounds like Powell Hill's fighting for his life. I can only hope that some of the commotion's due to the arrival of General Longstreet."

Early smirked. "Old Pete got him another case of the slows. Same as Gettysburg. Lee may think that thickheaded Dutchman's the Lord's own gift to this army. . . ."

Ewell said nothing, but clearly did not mind criticism of his rival corps commander.

"If we attacked . . . ," Gordon tried again. "Hit them now, when they don't expect it . . . that would take the pressure off of Hill. Longstreet or no Longstreet. With their northern flank collapsing, they'd have to go on the defensive."

Early snorted. "Until Burnside comes in on *our* flank. And drives through you and the rest of us like a steel plow through a shit-pile."

"Burnside isn't there. For all we know, he could be reinforcing Hancock."

"General Gordon," Early said, "I just told you where Burnside and his whole damned corps happen to be. You border on insolence."

Ewell tried again to change the subject. "Bloody damn mess this morning. Got the jump on Sedgwick, beat him to the races. But we just didn't have the punch. . . ." He looked at Gordon. "John, we're spread thin as boardinghouse butter up here. This corps has no reserve. Things went wrong on your end, we couldn't answer."

Gordon almost said, "Jackson would've taken the risk in a blink." He longed to say it, to throw it in both of their faces. But he knew he didn't dare. Ewell and Early were hardened in their jealousy. Of the living and the dead.

"Paid the sonsofbitches in full, though," Early put in. "They drove us back, no denying it. But, Hell, if we didn't give them twice the punishment when the fuck-a-doodles tried to break *our* lines."

Ewell wouldn't be cheered. "We can't break their line, they can't break ours. It's all going to be decided by Hill and Longstreet."

"If Hill isn't sick again." Early snorted. "He's dainty as Miss Sallie with the cramp."

"But we *can* break their line," Gordon insisted. "We could collapse it like a Chinese fan. Just let me hit them with my brigade, my one brigade. Have Hoffman and the rest of them ready to come in, if what I say proves true."

Early narrowed his eyes. They were not the eyes of a likable man, or of one who had enjoyed much success with women. There was no streak of joy in any part of him, ever, and not much in Dick Ewell, either. Gordon was wary of such men: At the banquet of life, they squabbled over crusts.

"Gordon," Early said coldly, "I am telling you, once and for all, that I want you to hold still. Right where you are. Your brigade will not move one inch. That's a direct order, and General Ewell is my witness. You just stay put, boy. You'll have plenty of chances for glory when the entire Ninth Corps comes for your behind."

Gordon looked at Ewell in a last, forlorn hope.

It was clear from the expression on the corps commander's face that he had no intention of overruling Early.

But Ewell did say, "General Gordon, I understand that you're convinced of what you say. You believe we're forgoing a grand opportunity." He glanced southward again. "But this entire army is at risk, and we can't add more risks on top of what General Lee's already got to deal with. Nonetheless, I promise you that, when I can find the time, I'll have a look at that flank of yours myself. Will that satisfy you?"

No. No, because opportunity is fleeting in war. No, because a chance such as this may never come again.

Gordon said nothing.

The torrent of noise from Hill's portion of the field became a deluge.

"Something going on, all right," Early said. "And Gordon here thinks he can save us all single-handed."

Ewell touched his fingers to his hat. "Gentlemen, I'd best see to this corps' other flank." He gee-upped his mount.

When their superior had gone, staff trailing behind, Early smirked at Gordon. "You just think you know every last goddamned thing. Don't you, John?"

Gordon remembered his division commander on the previous afternoon, begging him to save the collapsing corps. And he had done it. Gratitude had a shorter life than a mayfly.

He could not believe that the opportunity before them would not be seized. Nor was he ready to give up. There was no progress to be made at the moment, but he'd try them again in a few hours. And hope that the Yankees had not grown any wiser.

"Just every last goddamned thing," Early repeated.

Five thirty a.m.
Orange Plank Road

His men fled. Ignoring his pleas, they ran past, only the best of them pausing to meet his eyes before running again.

"You must stop!" Lee shouted, his tone harsh beyond custom. "Halt and re-form! Stand to your regiments, men!"

For the first time in his experience, soldiers ignored him. He rode among them, fierce of heart, alternately pleading and nearing profanity. It did no good.

"You! Captain! Form your company."

The officer slowed, wild-featured, and shook his head. "I got no comp'ny, sir." And he moved on. The Plank Road had flooded with such men, the heroes of the afternoon before, of the sanguinary evening.

Lee looked down the road, past the shameful exodus, yearning to see Longstreet. The man's latest promise had been to arrive with the dawn. Now defeat swelled around a dying army and Lee could not see so much as a dust cloud.

His fault, his fault, he knew. He should have ordered Longstreet up immediately when Grant and Meade began to move, should not have placed him so far to the south, and should not have attempted a complicated plan. Surely, Longstreet had done his best. Surely. Yet, the anger was there, a thrashing anger. At Longstreet. At Hill, so afflicted today he could barely sit his horse. At these long-brave men made cowards by the numbers applied against them. And, always, at himself.

He had behaved foolishly, forbidding Hill to reorder his lines in the night or to set the men to work on better entrenchments. He had been so confident that Longstreet would come to Hill's relief that he had chosen to let the men sleep a few hours. But war held no brief for mercy.

"Soldiers! Halt! You must re-form! Form on those guns, men!"

His words accomplished nothing.

He spotted General McGowan leading a fragment of his brigade to the rear. Lee nudged Traveller through the throng toward the brigadier.

"My God!" he cried. His voice surprised McGowan. "Your splendid brigade . . . are they running like geese?"

McGowan glared, but his answer was not uncivil. "General, my men were surprised, not whipped. They just need a place to form. I get 'em formed, they'll fight as well as ever."

Then Major General Wilcox appeared, face streaked with tears.

Lee felt a burst of anger and turned from the man. He knew the action was unjust, that Wilcox was not to blame.

But Wilcox would not be deterred from delivering his message. "Sir," he reported, "my men can't hold much longer. They're flanked on both sides."

Lee turned on him. "*Your* men . . . your men have *not* held, sir. They're fleeing all around us. See to your division, man."

Mortified, Wilcox saluted—as stiffly as an automaton—and turned back to the debacle.

He had been unjust, unjust. But his temper had leapt the fence and would not be penned again.

Turning to his aide—who was threatening men with his sword to no effect—Lee snapped, "Longstreet *must* be here. Colonel Taylor, go bring him up."

Obedient ever, Taylor steered into the human flood.

"And ready the trains to retreat," Lee called to his back.

Better to die. Better to die than live with such ignominy. That Grant . . . a wretched creature too small to retain in his memory . . . that such a man would humble him like this. Defeating him after but two days of effort. Lee raged against the shame.

Better to die.

He guided his horse back into the rising field, toward the line of guns by the ravaged farmhouse. Poague's batteries stood alone against the blue swarm about to erupt from the trees around them.

Some of his men still fought. They only wanted aid. Wilcox had tried to tell him that. He had been unjust to Wilcox. But who could bear this? Even faith in God availed nothing now.

A wave of gray fugitives burst from the far trees, running for all they were worth. Powell Hill had given up trying to rally his men. Ill or not, he had dismounted and stood by Colonel Poague. They were arguing furiously.

Lee looked to the east again and saw *them:* the first blue lines, bowed and uneven, but dauntless. Victory fed victory. So oft before, *his* men had been in pursuit.

A wave of dizziness stopped him. The early heat, his bowels. Gathering himself as best he could, he rode over to Hill and Poague in time to hear the artilleryman say, "I can't fire across that road. Our men are mixed in with them."

"I order you to fire now!" Hill shouted.

Newly aware of Lee's presence, Poague looked up at him. Lee nodded: *Do as Hill says.*

A bullet dropped a nearby cannoneer.

Poague leapt to his task at once, screaming to be heard, ordering his right battery to manhandle their guns to sweep the road.

They were everywhere now, those people. Swarming south of the road and to the north, slowed by the guns, by the terrible cost of advancing across open ground, but pressed on by the masses to their rear.

Lee resolved not to move. He would die here.

Some of the Union infantry paused to unleash volleys toward the artillery on the ridge. And gunners fell. But the cannon kept blasting, with Poague rushing from piece to piece and directing his left battery to swing northward.

Through new smoke, Lee spotted Hill wielding a swab, the work of an artillery private. Hill, too, had made his resolution to stay.

How could he have harbored anger toward such a man, blaming such a one as that for ancient indiscretions and ill health? He suspected that one of his last sights on earth would be of Powell Hill in a flannel shirt sweated black, hair flying as he shouted commands to the gunners still on their feet. Hill had begun as an artilleryman, and he would end as one.

Colonel Marshall edged his horse up to Lee's side. The military secretary said nothing, but removed his spectacles and put them in a pocket of his coat.

"Why doesn't Longstreet come?" Lee said softly, careless of whether the other man caught the words.

Marshall said nothing. There was nothing to say. But he waited for the end beside his chieftain.

With a hurrah, the Union troops south of the road burst through a last pocket of resistance. To the north, Union regiments had re-formed for a final assault on Poague's guns, barely half of which were still manned and firing.

Those people had grown confident enough to call up drums to regulate their advance. As if they meant to parade across the field.

Straight ahead, blue ranks left the tree line at the double-quick, while the long lines in the north stepped out to a drum's tap. Flag-bearers waved their banners in the absence of a breeze.

A bloody sun shone through the smoke behind the advancing enemy. It was a fitting sun for a last morning, suited to an apocalypse.

Lee's hand tightened on his sword. His last guns barked. And he caught another glimpse of Hill, face blackened and gleaming. Perhaps he, too, would welcome death.

Marshall reached over and touched Lee's sleeve.

Turning, Lee saw the head of Longstreet's column.

As the lead brigade formed a hasty front to charge, Lee spurred his horse up to their commanding officer. He did not recognize the man.

"General, which brigade is this?"

"Texans," the hard-eyed officer said, bellowing to be heard. "The Texas Brigade."

"I'm glad," Lee said. "Oh, I'm glad! Go in and give them

cold steel. Don't let them stand and fight. You must charge them, sir."

"Yas, sir. That's just what we're aiming to do."

Lee turned to the men around him. "The Texas Brigade has always driven the enemy . . . always. . . ." He spoke to their brigadier again, trying to recall this new man's name. Gregg? He wasn't certain enough to speak it. "Tell your men, General, that they fight under my eyes today. I will be with you. Every man must know."

Gregg rose in his stirrups, roaring out his commands. "Brigade . . . attention. Y'all listen here. The eyes of General Lee himself are on you now. *Texans! Forward!*"

Wet-eyed, Lee tore off his hat and waved it. "Texans have never let me down," he shouted. "Texans always move them."

The brigade howled as it advanced, a thousand coyotes bred with a thousand wildcats.

"We'll skin 'em alive, General Lee," a soldier called.

Lee rode forward with them. Willing, almost wanting, to die, rather than be vanquished. Even now the issue remained in doubt. He did not know if these first brigades would be sufficient to halt the blue hordes until their comrades could join them. When a defeat began, it was difficult to stem. And he would not live on, if it meant being humbled.

They had reached the center of the field, with bullets scouring the air and Texans falling, when the men about him realized that he meant to join their charge.

The soldiers nearest Lee wavered, then stopped. The colors paused, disordering the advance.

"Go back, go back!" the soldiers cried. "General Lee, go back!"

Lee felt the sun upon his hair, his scalp. His vision blurred.

"We ain't a-goin' on, less'n you go back," a soldier told him.

"Go back!" a sergeant seconded.

Men reached for his bridle, but Traveller reared his head.

The brigadier—yes, it was Gregg, that was the man's name—rode up and snapped at him, "Go back, sir. You're delaying my advance."

Coming up from the rear, his aide, Venable, called out, "General Longstreet's yonder. He's waiting on you, sir."

Lee still felt dazed. But the words had penetrated.

"Yes," he said. "Yes, I will go back."

As he turned his horse, the Texans howled and charged.

Longstreet. The man's face shone with sweat. Lee did not remonstrate with him. There was no point: Done was done. And he was here now, evidently full of fight. Suddenly, Lee felt the weight of his exhaustion. But he did not relax his spine.

"No time for fancy work," Longstreet told him, with the battle's renewed pandemonium a few hundred yards away. "Gregg's boys are in, and Rock Benning's. Perry's coming up, I'll put him on the left. Just need to hold 'em off until I can form up for a proper counterattack. Down that road looks about right."

Lee nodded. His thoughts were a muddle, veering between the accusatory and feelings of relief, of gratitude. He did not quite trust himself to speak, unsure if his voice would obey him or yield to his spleen.

"I'll take care of this, sir," Longstreet said, with a glance toward Venable. As if the two had conspired in some matter. "Give me a free hand, and I'll restore the line. And more, God willing." His Old War Horse grinned, yellow teeth strong in a mighty beard. "But I do think we'd best leave this spot. It's not quite comfortable."

"Yes," Lee said. At first, he allowed Venable to nudge him rearward. Then he took command of himself, gripping the reins and touching Traveller's belly with his spurs.

More and more of Longstreet's men were coming up. Where there had been a drought, there was a flood. The Lord was merciful, after all.

Even at a distance, he heard Longstreet shouting commands, his voice as powerful as his will.

Back on the knoll by the line of guns, Lee met a litter carrying off General Benning, badly wounded. The man had gone in only minutes before. Much hard labor remained, more blood in tribute to sway the fortunes of war. But there was hope now.

Lee felt a burst of elation so unreasonable it alarmed him.

He watched the developing battle from the ridge. Soon, he began to issue clear orders again.

Another brigade was forming up to wrest back the field's northern edge. Lee rode over to them and asked, "What troops are these?"

"Law's Alabama Brigade," a soldier hollered. "Law's men," yelled another. "Alabamans," came a rash of shouts.

Their commander looked taken aback. Then Lee remembered. "Law's Brigade." But it marched under Colonel Perry. Longstreet had arrested Law. It had not been a popular move. Perry was a good officer, and he would do his duty. As would these men. But Lee decided to speak to Longstreet about Law after the battle. The army could not afford to demean its best officers.

Lee put a good face on it all. "God bless the Alabamans!" he called to the men. "All I ask is that you keep up with the Texans. Surely, Alabamans can do that. . . ."

"More!" men cried. "We'll go right on to Washington," a stick of a man hollered. Lee felt the old adulation again, the gorgeous warmth of it. He nodded at Perry, who raised his sword in salute. It caught the sun and flashed lightning.

"Alabama," Perry bellowed, "at the double-quick . . . *forward!*"

As the brigade advanced, a black-eyed, black-haired, black-bearded lieutenant colonel on foot caught Lee's eye, a man with a look as menacing as a devil. The officer threw off a quick salute, as if even Lee didn't matter one bit now, as if all that mattered were getting on with the killing.

"Oates," Lee remembered.

William C. Oates couldn't say whether he'd ever seen a sight grander than Lee on his fine gray horse, surrounded by his staff on that little hill, nodding as the 15th Alabama passed. "Like a god of war," Oates told himself, instinctively repeating the phrase he'd heard used to describe Lee, "just like an old god of war." For an instant and no more, he believed he had caught the army commander's eyes.

Then it was all business, all done in a hurry, with Yankees somewhere down in the trees a few hundred yards along, at the rough field's border. Colonel Perry hollered orders, doing just fine for all the deep bad feelings, and Oates bellowed to be heard above the cannon, riflery, and titanic howl of men bent on doing harm. Marching backward, ass turned to the enemy, Oates pointed with his saber wherever he wanted his men to straighten the line, but they were all right, his boys, all right, just marching forward angry as wild country sonsofbitches cheated at cards in town.

Already hot. And the smoke stink, the burn in a man's lungs. Entrails and death for a welcome. All the tiredness of the long night's march, with its dead-end paths and inexcusable blundering, blew away like dandelion fluff. Nothing perked a fellow up like the prospect of killing others and being lauded for it.

The field sloped down, gently, the only gentle thing left in the world. Heel gripped by a varmint's hole, Oates almost stumbled. Cursing hard, he turned to face the enemy lurking ahead. He had no intention of marching behind his men, or in between the ranks. He was in a going-forward mood.

The 15th advanced on the left flank of the brigade. Looking down the long lines, with battle flags pawed at by whore-lazy smoke and bayonets bright as gold teeth in a pimp's mouth, Oates just felt an itch to *do,* to flail at the earth and sky in untempered wrath, to leave death and awe in his wake. There was nothing grander than this, not one thing finer. Not even a high-yellow woman after a creek bath.

The Yankees were down there all right. Firing now. Bullets slopping up the air, trying to slow things down. Oates couldn't see his enemies for the sun's glare, like jagged glass in the eye. Allied with the Yankees, thick smoke gripped the low ground, hiding death, while his men advanced over open land in raw light.

Be there soon enough, he told himself. Then we'll see who's king of the hill today.

"Steady, Alabama, steady!" Oates barked. "Major Lowther, address the second line."

Lowther was back, in time for whatever glory he could steal. Oates didn't trust the man, never had, but Lowther had friends in high places.

The 47th Alabama, off to the right, hit the trees first and paused to shoot, with their officers yapping at them.

"Nobody stops, nobody shoots," Oates shouted, throat already smoke-bit.

Yankees shooting plenty, but not aiming worth a damn.

By echelon from the right, the brigade's regiments dropped into the trees. The way they went in, it was clear the gentle slope turned sheer in the undergrowth. Made sense. Fields ended where a man couldn't plow any farther. Should've figured that out back a ways, Oates told himself.

Before the 15th hit the trees, a courier from Colonel

Perry reached him. The young man, Cadwallader, did not fancy riding in front of the advancing ranks.

Saluting, the boy said, "Colonel Oates! There's Yankees up on a rump of hill yonder, up ahead on your left. They're shooting down into us, we're caught in a swamp down there." The lieutenant gestured into the morbid greenery.

"Acknowledged," Oates said. And the boy rode off.

He halted the regiment, ordered a left face, and ran to the head of what was now a column of twos. Sword flashing, he called, "Forward. Follow me!"

Splitting away from the brigade, he plunged down the bank through tangled brush, pushing forward regardless of the clawing thorns. Before he poked a boot into the pig marsh at the bottom of the bank, he spotted the blue-bellies. Up on a spur where the trees were thinner, thick ranks of men in dark coats, lined up almost too perfectly, sent volleys down into the wet ground where the 15th's sister regiments had gotten their cracker behinds stuck, with more Yankees ahead of them and these sonsofbitches firing down from the flank.

The brush and trees thinned between the narrow marsh and the enemy, as if the soil couldn't nourish anything more. That would expose his men, but it also revealed the Yankees.

He splashed and slopped his way ahead, confident the long gray snake of men behind him would follow. Let them get their feet wet, too. Just make angry men angrier.

He noted a gap between the Yankees gone head-to-head with the brigade and their comrades up on the spur. No time to charge through it and turn their lines, but the gap meant the bluecoats up on that high ground wouldn't get much support. And they were about to need a passel of help.

With the enemy shooting down at him and missing—men shooting downhill shot high, more often than not—and hollering insults and curses in his direction, Oates leapt up on a speck of dry ground, halted the regiment, and immediately ordered, "Left face! Forward! Right wheel!"

It was a thing of beauty. Morass or not, the regiment pivoted as crisply as if on parade in Montgomery.

Pointing his sword at the enemy up on the spur, Oates shouted, "Charge! Fire on the move!" He drew out his revolver as he ran forward, cocking the hammer with his thumb.

The 15th Alabama went up the hill like a pack of hounds after a three-legged fox. Some of the Yankees didn't even pause to fire again, but thinned their own line by running. The remainder gave off a doubtful feel.

"Give 'em the bayonet!" Oates hollered. But his men were screaming to wake the dead and he doubted he was heard. Mostly for the benefit of the Yankees, he added, "Kill any bastard who doesn't drop his rifle."

Even with time slowed down the way it did when men started killing each other, it still seemed but seconds before his men were in among the Yankees, shooting them belly-wise with leveled weapons, smashing in heads, and, here and there, using bayonets. In a brace of minutes, there were more Yankees with their hands in the air than cottonmouths in Pike County.

Oates came face-to-face with a lieutenant begging his men to rally. He shot him in the center of the chest. The soldiers the boy had gathered up dropped their rifles and raised their paws.

The Yankees were got up fine, with uniforms unravaged by campaigning, the color of their blouses still darkest blue.

Coming up on his major, who didn't seem to be doing much other than tagging along, Oates said, "Lowther, you pull the boys back, get 'em organized again. Most quick. Hear me?"

"I'm shot," Lowther said, calm as a fellow reporting indigestion. "In the foot. I have to go to the rear." And he strutted off.

Oates didn't mind seeing the bastard go.

A string of disarmed Yankees came by, with Sergeant Ball shoving them along. Oates grabbed one by the arm, a boy hardly of shaving age, and yanked him out of the gang of bewildered bluecoats.

"Talk to me, boy. What's this here unit of yours?"

Terrified at the sight of Oates, at the death grip of his hand, the boy stammered, "F-Fifteenth New York Heavy Artillery, sir. Fifteenth New York Heavy—"

Oates released him. What the Hell? Were the Yankees so desperate they were plugging artillerymen into their battle line? Explained the worthlessness, though.

His hip reminded him of last year's wound. It just made him feel meaner.

The 15th New York Heavy Artillery? Christ almighty. Probably couldn't tell a rifle's muzzle from a pig's ass. Took a lot of the polish off the business. He would have preferred to whip a veteran regiment.

Re-forming his men as quickly as he could, Oates spotted Cadwallader, Perry's aide, splashing through the marsh toward him. The lieutenant was on foot and speckled with mud.

Pride comes before a fall, Oates thought with a smile.

"Colonel Oates! Colonel Perry needs you to rejoin the brigade quick as you can, sir."

"Tell Colonel Perry we're about to hit those Yankees of his in the flank."

The lieutenant looked doubtful. "The colonel hasn't authorized that movement, sir."

"He will when it's done," Oates told him. "You go along now."

The lieutenant saluted and plodded off. Oates was never

fond of messenger boys. In his experience, they found you too late and delivered instructions that no longer made sense.

He ordered every man to reload, then led them off along a saddle on the Yankee side of the marsh. He had that gap in mind. Indeed, nobody had come to the aid of the pressed artillerymen. The other Yankees hadn't even been aware of what was transpiring.

"Sergeant Morgan," he called. There was no time for the chain of command to relay orders.

Face still showing the beating he'd taken two days before, the Welshman rushed up and saluted, open-palmed, the way the English did.

"Take a few men yonder, along the ridge there. Stop when you see the Yankees and before they see you. Let me know how the ground lies. We'll be coming right along."

"Yes, sir."

"Well, move, man!"

Morgan had a way of prowling that came naturally to some men, while others could never learn it, hard as they tried. Oates believed in attacking fiercely when you weren't sure what you were facing, but he didn't mind knowing.

It had not been a half hour since they had marched by Robert E. Lee.

As the column advanced through the brush, Oates turned and snapped, "Y'all hush. Officers, keep your men quiet."

Ahead, a battle raged, but the regiment moved along in a pocket of silence. Oates wondered if those Yankee artillerymen had just been forgotten by their army. Devil of a business, war. Like dice, but with worse odds.

At one point, Oates could peer down the trough of the marsh. The brigade was still mired. A few thousand men on either side fired at each other, unable to see much of anything, just loading and shooting and hoping. That kind of fighting didn't appeal to Oates. He believed that fighting was about doing, not just waiting for something to be done to you.

Movement in the trees: one of his men returning from Sergeant Morgan.

Fleet as a deer, the private stopped just a breath from Oates and pivoted to march beside him. The boy talked hot: "Sergeant Morgan says they got no idea we're here, they're all just having themselves a time shooting at the brigade. He said to lead you over to where he is."

"You go ahead, son. And don't run."

The hip, the leg. His body's untimely recalcitrance enraged him.

The distance remaining was nothing. In less than five minutes, he had the regiment ranked and ready behind the crest of another low ridge that overlooked the Yankees. They had neglected to outpost the rise, figuring those defrocked artillerymen had their flank well covered. They were going to pay for it.

Oates glanced down the silent ranks of his regiment, allowing himself a few seconds to savor the beauty. The world crackled with death. Smoke sneaked around like a no-good woman's fingers.

He kept his voice low: "Regiment! Forward!"

At the tenth step, he called, "Halt."

On their twelfth step, the men stood ready. Overlooking a maddened nest of men in blue, thick as ants on cornmeal, every last damned one concentrated on killing the men in gray trapped to their front.

Not twenty yards away, and they hadn't heard a thing.

A blond-bearded Yankee looked their way at last. The man's mouth opened.

Oates opened his mouth, too: "Aim, fire! Fire at will!"

Some of his men got off second shots before the Yankees cottoned to their predicament. Then the blue-bellies howled. Like one big, wounded creature. And men began to flee.

"Colors to me!" Oates cried. *"Charge!"*

With a screeching, biting, terrifying yell, his men leapt forward, the old veterans able to trot along and reload as they went down the slope. Other men raced forward to grab a Yankee or a flag. Moments later, another great Rebel yell arose, the Alabama version, and the rest of the brigade joined the charge, splashing forward, banners high and catching in branches.

After that, it was nothing but hounds and hares.

Ride with you, Micah?" Longstreet asked Brigadier General Jenkins. Longstreet maintained a steady aspect for the world, but inside he was glowing. That morning, he had redeemed his reputation.

"The South Carolina Brigade would be honored, sir," Jenkins told him. "As I am myself."

Longstreet rode close. "You know, it would not be taken amiss if you—"

The highborn son of the Low Country cut him off. "I'm fine, sir. Just fine."

But Jenkins wasn't fine. The dashing young man looked twice his age this morning. Longstreet knew that the brigadier had been carried to the battlefield in an ambulance, flat on his back, and had managed to mount his horse only at nearby Parker's Store.

"And you understand what you're to do?" Longstreet said.

The pale young man smiled. "Not the most complicated order I've received, sir. Straight up this road. Take the junction and hold it. Finish what Billy Mahone and the rest got started. My congratulations, sir."

Yes, Longstreet felt, congratulations were in order all around. But he said, "Save those sentiments until we've finished with Hancock. We're only partway there."

"From what I hear, it's a good partway," Jenkins said.

Hancock! God, what a fine morning it had been. After two days of wretched roads and trails, of error-riddled maps and incompetent guides, and of constantly changing orders from Lee and his staff . . . after all of that, he had arrived in the nick of time, able first to blunt Hancock's grand attack, next to contain it, and then to grind it back. After which Moxley Sorrel, bless him, had brought word of a railroad cut on the right, a perfect thoroughfare to channel a force hard onto the flank of Hancock's penetration and roll him up. It hadn't offered a deep envelopment as originally foreseen, the scheme of attack up the Brock Road from Todd's Tavern. But today, a shallower flank movement had to do.

And it *did* do. Guided by Sorrel—who was in his glory—Billy Mahone's Virginians, with Wofford's Georgians abreast, had slammed into the left wing of Hancock's advance, and one Union brigade after another had disintegrated. Then entire divisions began to collapse. Mahone had swept all the way across the front, crossing the Plank Road to the north at last report.

It was as brilliant a maneuver, Longstreet believed, as Jackson's flank march at Chancellorsville had been. And the strategic consequences might prove greater. If Hancock's entire corps could be destroyed . . .

Longstreet's pride had been wounded again and again, first when he was blamed for Lee's blindness at Gettysburg, then, after a too-brief glow of triumph at Chickamauga, for the defeat at Knoxville. But this . . . this must lift his reputation high.

Longstreet refused to dwell on the blow to Grant, his old friend and a man fools underestimated. Nor did Meade leap to mind. His goal was to complete his rout of Hancock, the Army of the Potomac's battlefield lion. Destroy Hancock's Second Corps, and the remainder of Meade's army wouldn't count for much. There was glory to spare in laying Hancock low.

Arms of smoke wrapped around the marching column, but the clamor of the fighting ahead had been tamped down by the drubbing the Yankees had taken.

Long lines of Union prisoners trudged rearward along the roadside. Now and then, one of Jenkins' soldiers heckled them, but most men let them be.

Jenkins coughed.

When Longstreet looked at him a mite too sharply, the brigadier forced a smile and said, "You know, sir, I had been losing faith. In our ultimate victory. I'm not ashamed to admit it. But this"—he gestured toward the stream of prisoners, ignoring the shoals of casualties—"this restores my faith. You have won a great victory, sir."

Yes. A great victory. Again, Longstreet said, "You just hold on to those sentiments, General Jenkins. By the grace of God, we'll have something to toast tonight."

As the head of the column entered an acrid cloud, an aide rode up beside Longstreet.

"Sir . . . don't you think you're a trifle exposed?"

"That," Longstreet snapped, "is our business."

"Yes, sir." The aide, Andy Dunn, let his horse slip back among the staffs of the generals. Kershaw, too, had joined the party, telling jokes and laughing at them himself, ecstatic.

It was a good day when Kershaw laughed. A very good day. Longstreet felt a fresh wave of satisfaction.

Of course, Dunn had a point. His tone toward the aide had been too harsh. But it would not do to turn around just yet. Nor did he want to. With more officers joining their party every few yards, it had become a triumphal procession. They rode not between prisoners now, but amid the amassed dead and twitching wounded. *This* was war. And the aim was to ride past the enemy's dead, not the enemy past yours.

It had been a *brilliant* morning. When Longstreet first met him on the field, Lee had been as unsettled as he had ever seen the old man, his voice quaking from a soul on the edge of an abyss. But Lee was himself again now, posing on his horse and enjoying the cheers of any men marching by. Lee might put on a stone face, Longstreet knew, but the old dog loved adulation.

Well, he would not begrudge Lee that. Or anything else. Today, there was glory to spare.

The roadside undergrowth smoldered and smoked, adding to the miasma of blown powder.

"Glad I just have to follow the road," Jenkins said. "Can't hardly see a thing."

Ahead, some fighting lingered on. But it barely seemed a skirmish compared to the uproar an hour before. An army in collapse made a terrible noise.

"Be grateful for that smoke," Longstreet told his companion. "Yankees can't see a thing either. And they've got a sight more to look out for." He scanned about for landmarks, though, trying to remember how the terrain ran. One stretch of scrub pine and brambles looked much like another. Even the dead and wounded bore a sameness, although far more of them wore blue wool hereabouts.

"Take that crossroads for me," Longstreet said, "and you'll win another star. I want South Carolina men to be the first to cross the Brock Road today." He chuckled. "Only thing worries me is those new uniforms your boys have. You dye 'em with charcoal? Don't want the boys confusing you with Yankees."

"Sir, we'll be so far in front of everybody else . . ."

Longstreet smiled. "All right. I reckon another hundred yards, and you'd better put your brigade into line of battle. No need to take chances."

A volley exploded from the woods on the left. So close

it hurt Longstreet's ears. He yanked the reins, turning his horse, ready to take action. But he could not see who was firing.

The men of Jenkins' lead regiment broke ranks and rushed to the roadside, shooting into the smoke and foliage. In moments, the firing on both sides became maddened.

A voice shouted, "Show your colors!"

Up ahead, a figure ran into the roadway. The man waved a Confederate battle flag.

Our own men.

Kershaw saw the flag, too. He wheeled about and drove his horse into Jenkins' soldiers, screaming at them to stop firing. "Friends!" he shouted. *"Friends!"*

The firing continued.

Longstreet turned to order Jenkins to control the regiment. Just in time to see a bullet punch a hole where Jenkins' forehead curved into his temple. The brigadier sprawled backward and fell from the saddle.

Appalled, Longstreet spurred his horse forward to stop the firing. But something happened that passed his understanding: He felt a blow as if struck with a steel hammer. Felt it, yet didn't feel it. Of a sudden, he was unsure of the world around him. All things, great and small, slowed and receded. He gasped. There was shouting, screaming, on every side. But it was far away. Far, far away, and yet he knew it was near. He wished to speak, but could not form words. His body began to quiver. He could not control it. Then his flesh bucked like an unbroken horse. Something had splashed him, he was drenched. He fell forward, struggling all the while to keep himself upright.

His horse rebelled. What was wrong with his horse?

Hands gripped him. Yankees? No, no. He remembered. *His* men. His men had been firing at him.

Chancellorsville. The thought put ice in his bowels. Was this Tom Jackson's last joke from the grave?

This could not happen . . . not today . . .

What day was it? Who was speaking? Why couldn't he move?

He felt himself falling again. Falling and falling. But no. There were hands upon him. His great weight was falling. Like the Mexican cadets tumbling from the battlements at Chapultepec. . . .

He choked. With all the strength he could muster, he managed to raise one hand—only one obeyed him—to clutch his neck.

Wet pulp. He let the hand fall.

The firing had stopped. He believed the firing had stopped. Hadn't it? They had to stop firing. His men were shooting at each other. That red flag . . .

Was he dying?

Men laid him down. The earth was hard.

"Ride for a surgeon!" someone cried.

Jenkins didn't need a surgeon. The man was dead. Shot through the forehead. Didn't they know?

Why wasn't Jenkins attacking? Finish the business. Hancock. "Jenkins!" he tried to call, to order him to attack at once. Jenkins was dead, but he had to attack . . .

Strange matter blocked his mouth and strangled his tongue.

Attack, attack . . .

Why wasn't Jenkins attacking?

Hancock. Kill him myself. Bare hands.

Tom Jackson. Laughing.

The world had lost its color, its shape. Black shadows, gray confusion. Was it night?

Had to attack immediately . . .

"He's choking on his own blood," someone said.

Who? Who was choking? Jenkins? Jenkins was dead, surely. . . .

Hands grasped him again, raising him, dragging him.

They placed him against something hard. Holding him up in a sitting position.

He gagged, spewed.

In an instant, he was lucid again. Remembering all.

"Can you . . . hear me?" he said. Bubbles crowded his throat.

"Yes, sir. But don't speak, you mustn't try to speak."

"Tell . . . General Field . . . he must take command. . . ."

"Yes, sir. General Field. Yes, sir, we hear you. We understand."

"Press the enemy . . . tell Lee . . ." He recognized Moxley Sorrel. "Report to Lee . . . what accomplished . . . continue . . . attack . . . success . . ."

"Yes, sir. We'll do it all, everything you want. But you need to stop speaking now."

Longstreet felt a burst of anger. He was not about to be told what to do. Not now. Not ever.

He managed to fix his eyes on Sorrel's. "*You* . . . tell Field . . . attack with everything. Take Brock Road. Break Hancock. Don't stop."

Sorrel tried to clean him with a handkerchief, and Longstreet watched a crimson rag retreat.

"Victory," he said.

TEN

Nine a.m.
Wilderness Run

The new men of Company C ate little during their unexpected pause for breakfast. They had just gotten their
first look at a battlefield.

"You wish for *mein Speck,* Sergeant?" Private Eckert,
the shorter of the two John Eckerts, offered. Since the commotion over the stockings, the boy had attached himself
to Brown.

The bacon drooled fat on a foul tin plate. It was clear
why the shriveled meat didn't tempt the recruits. Marching
into the battlefield's depths, they had passed not only the
usual scattered bodies, but corpses blackened and twisted
up by fire, creatures from a sermon on damnation. Private
Martz had broken ranks to puke, soon followed by others.

"Force it down, boy," Brown said. "Could be a while
before you get cooked meat again."

Eckert shook his head. "I can't *fress* nothing."

"Then put it in your haversack. You're going to be hungry."

The private looked doubtful.

Brown, too, had his doubts, but about larger matters. He
could not understand what the regiment or, for that matter, the brigade and division were doing. No veteran expected every maneuver to make plain sense, but he couldn't
figure the reason for their dawdling. They should have been
in the fight by now.

The regiment had set off in the dark, marching into the common clutter of war: wagons rolling in contrary directions and batteries waiting for orders, couriers on frothing horses, the straying wounded, and a legion of shirkers. After that, it was stop and start until they reached the rump end of the battlefield, with its clusters of do-nothing officers and sergeants who had figured out the army. A Fifth Corps flag drooped by a hard-used house and war-stained regiments pulled back to reorganize, their bleak-eyed men stunned wordless by their survival. All that was normal as turd piles on a mule path.

The brigade had been ordered forward, still in column. They followed a farm trail down a field strewn with dead.

"Looks like we kilt ten Rebs for every one of us," Sam Martz announced.

"And pussy grows on trees," Bill Wildermuth told him. "We gather up our own and leave the Johnnies."

The veterans were mostly quiet. Those who had seen the elephant read the noise. Off to the right, the skirmishing was heavy, but still only skirmishing. A mile or so to the left, though, a battle raged. They were thrusting between the skirmishing and the slaughter.

"Turning a flank, that's what they got us doing," Corporal Doudle blurted out. He spoke what the regiment's old-timers were thinking.

"We'll see what Bobby Lee has to say about that," Wildermuth responded.

Nobody laughed.

Stray shots pecked the morning, just enough to make the new men wince. As they entered a woodland, the farm trail narrowed. The burned men waited there, white bones revealed by flesh peeled back and teeth grinning through black lips. The stink was worse than dead snakes.

The vomiting began. Commands grew harsher.

Abruptly, the column halted amid scrub pines and shallow rifle pits. Brown expected orders to face left from the trail and form lines of battle, to fix bayonets and advance toward the fighting. They'd feel for a flank, all right. And, most likely, blunder into the Johnnies. He steeled himself for the effort to come, every nerve taut as a tourniquet.

You got used to some of it. But you never got used to all of it.

Instead of swinging into the battle, the regiment was ordered to break ranks and cook breakfast. Brown couldn't make sense of it. Was the fighting going so well that they weren't needed? It didn't sound that way.

He posted his own pickets, pairing a veteran with a new recruit on either side of the trail, and the rest of the men got up cooking fires with a speed that would have amazed them all a few years back. When the officers gave you a chance to eat and cook coffee, you ate and cooked coffee.

Henry Hill crushed coffee beans using the hilt of a knife. Henry made fine coffee and always had some roasted-up beans in his knapsack. Other than Brown, he was the only man in the company who wouldn't trade beans for tobacco with the Rebs when things were quiet.

"Tell you this," Bill Wildermuth said, "Old Burnside may have his faults, but he knows men have to eat. I'll take a fat general over a skinny one any day."

As the smell of bacon pushed back the stink of war, Private Eckert said, "I don't like this place."

Stepping away from his talk with Captain Burket, First Sergeant Hill barked, "Form up, form up! Get those fires out. Let's go!"

"You heard the first sergeant," Brown told his men. "On your feet!"

The first sergeant formed them in two ranks along the

trail. Brown figured the order to advance would come at last. But regiment had decided that the roll had to be called again. The first sergeant backed up against a bush and read:

"Agley . . . Baker . . . Berger . . . Berger . . . Bowsman . . ."

Midway through the roll call, a black snake reared up in front of the first sergeant. Brown had seen plenty of snakes in his canal days, but never one that rose straight up like that.

The snake startled the first sergeant and he stopped reading. Brown and Henry Hill stepped forward and beat the snake down with their rifle butts.

"Guertler . . . Haines . . . Harner . . ."

The snake reared up again, closer this time. As if about to strike the first sergeant's loins.

This time, Brown and Henry Hill beat the snake to death.

The first sergeant ordered the company to ground its knapsacks and haversacks by the trail. Their quartermaster detail had not caught up and unwatched knapsacks wandered off immediately, so a four-man guard was chosen to stay behind.

"That Doudle," Isaac Eckert complained, "he always gets the feather-pillow duty. Me, I never once get picked."

"That's because you'd steal everything yourself," Wildermuth told him.

That drew a laugh from a few men, but it faded fast.

The battle off to the left flared up again. Everyone tensed. This was it, they'd be going forward now. But another unexpected command caught Brown and the other veterans off guard: The regiment was ordered to face right, to form a column again.

"Forward, *march!*" The shouts echoed down the line, setting men in motion. But they went only a few hundred yards before halting, still hemmed in on both sides by the forest. Listening to the voices repeating orders, Brown realized that the brigade was incomplete, that only the 50th and one or two other regiments remained on the trail. Had the others kept going when they stopped for breakfast? Had they already been sent into the fight? Why split them up?

"Regiment!"

"Company!"

"Riiiight . . . *face!*"

The greenery in front of Brown looked thicker than the swamp growth north of Vicksburg.

"This don't make no sense," Bill Wildermuth said.

"Shut up, Bill," Brown ordered.

"Fix . . . bayonets!"

Steel left leather, steel met steel.

"Rifles at the carry . . . forward . . . *march!*"

They pushed into the undergrowth. The new men shied from a corpse in Confederate rags.

"Close up," Brown said. It was hard from the start to maintain orderly ranks.

The regiment wheeled left—westward, Brown thought—and advanced parallel to the trail along which they had marched.

All right, Brown decided. Up the trail, that's where they'll be. Just waiting. Probably had their scouts out in the brush, watching us all the while we were gorging on fatback.

There was no line advancing on the 50th's right flank. You had to hope the colonels and generals knew what they were doing.

"Close up," Brown repeated mechanically. "Rub elbows with the next man. Keep it closed up, boys."

Shafts of sunlight pierced the trees. The glimpsed sky shone flat blue, hard as cheap paint. Brambles gripped sleeves and trousers. They scraped through a raspberry thicket yet to bud and dropped into a mire. Well, old canal men were used to getting their feet wet.

"Keep looking out ahead of you," Brown told the new men. "Keep your eyes open."

For all that, canal men didn't *like* getting their feet wet. The mud tried to steal Brown's shoes.

He just didn't want the Rebs to pop up while the company was stumbling through the stretch of muck. If he had to fight, he wanted firm ground under him.

Bowing and splitting, the line moved slowly forward. As men splashed and stumbled, curses profaned the silence. When they reached the end of the slop, the regiment reformed amid the thickets and pushed forward another two hundred yards or so.

Light. Up ahead. *Bright* light, sharp and raw as a bought woman. That meant open ground.

"Close up now," Brown said.

Thirty paces. Maybe. Then a field.

That's where they'll be. He glanced at Henry Hill. Grim-faced now, his friend knew what was coming.

"You new men, listen up," Brown said. Just loud enough to be heard. "You hear an order, you do what it says. Don't go to thinking."

Fifteen paces . . . ten . . .

After the gloom in the brush, the sunlight dazzled.

Confederate cannon opened fire as the regiment broke from the trees.

"Steady now . . . close up."

They marched into the field. The Rebs were less than a quarter mile away, atop what passed for a hill in Virginia's lowlands.

Lieutenant Colonel Overton ran to the front of the ranks, holding up his sword, its grip in one hand, the tip of the blade in the other, signaling to his officers and sergeants to dress the ranks.

The Rebs had only two cannon pointed their way, but

they did immediate damage. Captain Burket called the first sergeant forward, but as he dashed up a shell burst at his feet.

Blood splashed as far as a man could throw a rock.

One of the new men shrieked and spun around. A long piece of bone, the first sergeant's bone, jutted from his face.

There's no time to form, Brown wanted to shout, *just charge, if we're going to charge.* The colonel needed to shit or get off the pot.

Brown glanced toward Henry Hill to see if his cousin's death had shaken him.

Hill's face remained impassive.

Lines far from perfect, the regiment advanced. An order to charge rang out.

A round shot struck Sam Martz, cutting him in two in a flash of red. Freed of its cage, Sam's heart hopped along the ground.

"Look to your front," Brown shouted. "Look straight ahead!" He reached out and slapped John Eckert on the back of the head. "*Move!* Let's go, boys. *Charge!*"

The Reb infantry loosed a volley. The advancing lines shivered, then pressed on, leaving a claim of bodies.

If there was some clever plan, Brown couldn't see it.

More men fell.

They reached a streambed, all but dry. Some men sought shelter in the small depression, while others paused, as though at a wild river, firing up the slope at the Confederates.

"Let's go, *let's go!*" Brown shouted.

Company C pressed forward. Mike Reilly, a veteran, toppled. Brown realized that only his company had pushed beyond the creek.

The Reb cannon blew more holes in the regiment's lines. The brigade was even weaker than Brown had feared. At most, two regiments had made the charge, far too small a force. He recognized the flag of the 20th Michigan to the left, but the field beyond was empty.

Without waiting for orders, soldiers began to fall back. Brown looked about for an officer and spotted Captain Burket behind the creek, arguing with Lieutenant Colonel Overton. Overton stalked off, shouting words few men could make out.

Company C had stopped of its own mind. The men fired gamely up at the Confederates, but their feet were done moving forward. Isaac Eckert, always trouble in the rear, stood ahead of the rest, leading a charmed life, the fastest reloader and shooter in the regiment.

The Rebs had got up low barricades, but hadn't had time to really set themselves in. For a long few minutes, men on both sides just shot one another.

The new men were firing. That was good. Brown doubted they were hitting anything, unless by dumb luck, but just getting them to stand and shoot was a start.

He spotted at least a few companies of Rebs working down the wood line to their right, trying to encircle them.

They had to pull back, it was the only thing that made sense. Get back in the trees and organize a fighting line. But he didn't have the authority to order anything that big. For once, he wished he wore an officer's shoulder boards.

What remained of the attack was going to bits. On the left, the Michigan boys began withdrawing, some of them running, and through the smoke Brown saw Johnnies on that flank, too.

The order came down—from God knew where—to retreat. Captain Burket appeared at Brown's side, shouting to the men to stay together, to keep fighting as they withdrew. Brown fixed his eyes on the men he thought might run.

"Sergeant Brown?" the captain said. He was greased

with sweat and panting, beard wet as a mop. Some of the
wet was the blood of other men.

"Sir?"

"You're first sergeant now."

"I don't have rank."

"Doesn't matter. Help me get these boys back."

The captain lunged to the side, catching a new man
who'd caught the panic. Burket made him stand straight,
load, and fire. Then he let the boy join the retreat.

It became a rout. Aware at last of how badly they were
outnumbered—and nearly surrounded—even good men
ran. Brown had to give up. All he could do was try to reach
the trees himself.

Men dropped with bullets in their backs. Henry Hill
caught up and ran beside him.

"You're first sergeant now. I heard him."

"Henry, I'm sorry. . . ."

"Don't matter."

A soldier dashing past threw down his rifle. Brown
grabbed him by the collar, snapping him back.

"You pick up that gun."

Mad-eyed, the boy did as he was told. Then he took off
running again, but held the rifle to his breast the way a man
in a flood clutched a floating board.

Brown was in a fury. The attack made no damned sense.
Where was the rest of the brigade? The division? Fighting
was one thing, stupidity another.

Gaining the trees, he shouted for his men to stop. But
the companies were intermingled, just mixed up as Hell,
and even some of the officers were running. The goal now
was just to avoid being taken prisoner. The regiment had
never broken like this.

He saw the hopelessness, even the foolishness, of his effort, and he called instead for the men to rally behind the
marsh they'd crossed a fair stretch back. He hoped the

officers would grasp that the ground behind the swamp was the place to hold.

Brown turned a last time to see if any wounded men were struggling along behind him, anyone he might have time to help, or just any lost souls.

All he saw was Henry Hill standing beside one of the few proper trees, firing toward the approaching lines of Rebs.

"Henry, for God's sake . . . come on."

Hill finished reloading, picked a target, fired, and began to reload again.

"Henry—"

His friend looked at him. "I'm not of a mind to run today," he said.

Brown took up a position behind a tree a few paces away. Picking a target, a flag-bearer, he fired, too.

The man dropped. Brown wasn't the world's finest marksman, but sometimes things went right.

Hill stepped into the sunlight, aimed, and shot. Then he dodged into the shade again.

The Johnnies stopped cold. Brown heard the orders given for a volley.

"Henry!"

But Hill had already made himself as small as a big man could behind his tree. Brown turned sideways, too, and closed his eyes.

The ragged crack of the volley left them standing amid flying bark and falling branches.

Hill took aim and fired again. Brown did the same.

It was the craziest damned thing. The Rebs, a regiment or more of them, had just stopped dead.

They were reloading.

"Get ready," Brown warned.

Hill nodded.

Miraculously, the second volley spared them, too. The

only harm done came from a wood splinter that drove through Brown's trousers. He yanked it out and felt warm wet on his leg. Not a gush, just slime.

"Surrender, you Yankee sonsofbitches!" a Reb called. Other Confederates took up the shout, chanting, "Surrender, surrender . . ."

Brown wanted to do something bold, perhaps shout, "*You* surrender," back at them. But his mouth, tongue, throat, and just about every other body part refused to take his orders.

Henry Hill leaned out and shot a Rebel officer off his horse.

That was a mistake. An outraged howl rose from the Rebel ranks. They weren't interested in exchanging polite volleys now. Brown could feel them about to charge, whether ordered to or not. Mercy would not be included in their behavior.

"Henry, we have to go *now.*"

Hill looked at him, jaw still set. But he nodded his agreement.

The two of them took off on the wildest footrace of their lives. Hundreds of rifle balls chased them through the greenery, and loyal Virginia briars tried to hold them. But they burst through every obstacle, each man faster than he thought he could go.

Furious shouts and flurries of bullets pursued them. Once, Brown heard a voice all too near snarl, "Get those sonsofbitches!"

They reached the marshy ground, where Virginia mud went to war with Yankee shoes again. And a mighty cheer went up. To their front this time. Blue uniforms rose from the earth and hats came off.

"There they are, there they are!" Brown recognized Bill Wildermuth's voice. There was pure joy in it.

Perhaps it was the sound of Yankees cheering up ahead,

or just sensible orders to re-form, but the noise of thrashing Rebs behind them faded.

Brown and Hill scrambled up an embankment and blue-clad arms embraced them. Men cheered and slapped them heavily on their backs. Captain Burket was there. And Lieutenant Colonel Overton.

When the celebration had calmed enough for a man's voice to be heard, the colonel spoke for everyone to hear.

"Your stand . . . that stand was about the bravest thing I've seen. . . ."

The two friends looked at each other and started to laugh.

Men from the 1st Michigan Sharpshooters established a picket line along the marsh, and the remnants of the 50th Pennsylvania plodded back to the trail. For all the blood spilled and the brethren lost, the veterans were delighted to see their knapsacks where they had left them. A soldier's life was one of small consolations.

As he set about re-forming the men, Brown mourned First Sergeant Hill. They had been together since the company's first muster. September 9, 1861. He remembered the day had still been August hot. Apples burdened the trees behind the field where they tried and failed to march in step before the eyes of forgiving spectators. Even the town's bad boys had kept their mouths shut. Bill Hill had taken the volunteers in his grip, putting them through their paces again and again. Brown recalled the innocence, the enthusiasm, even the silliness he had shared with his comrades, young men freed from their drudgery on the canal and thrilled at the prospect of a grand adventure.

So many were dead now, so many. Less than three years, and it seemed at least a lifetime.

He felt overwhelmed and uncertain of himself, struggling to remember all the things he had known the first sergeant to do after a fight. Order up ammunition, that was

number one. Call the roll, mark the known casualties, record the names of those who had witnessed the deaths
or wounding or capture of men left behind, write down the
names of the wounded sent to the rear . . . see about
water . . .

Lieutenant Eckel helped him. Eckel was a decent man,
a Dutchman from Tremont who had been promoted from
quartermaster sergeant back in March.

"I feel spitted up and turned over the fire," Brown said.
They sorted through the first sergeant's pack for the roster Hill kept wrapped in oiled cloth.

"You'll do fine, Brownie," Eckel told him. "Just let them
know you're in charge right off, and you'll do fine after
that." He added, "I'll see to the ammunition for you."

Calling the roll was painful. But he got through it. Then
he called together all of the new men. He wanted to talk
to them apart from any heckling from the veterans or smart-
mouth from Bill Wildermuth or the likes of Isaac Eckert.

"Crowd around," he said, putting beef in his voice, "I'm
not going to shout."

The new men closed in obediently. Authority, even newly
conferred, still impressed them.

"All right," Brown began. "You're all veteran soldiers
now. You've been in a battle, you know what it's like. The
way things went wasn't your fault, you did your duty." He
searched for words. "We just got put in a bad way. That
happens sometimes. Not so often, but it happens. War's a
messy business, not like some picture book. And the day
isn't over. Don't make faces. The day isn't over, and we're
like to go in again. Whether back there, or someplace else.
And when we do, it's going to be *our* turn. We're going to
pay the Johnnies back. That's how it works, we'll get our
turn. You'll feel better then." He didn't know how to end
his speech, so he continued, "Well, you're alive, be glad
of that. It means you followed orders. Following orders is

the best way to stay in one piece." That didn't quite work, either, so he decided to finish up on the practical side. "If you need to take care of your private business, you go do that now. But don't stray off, I want to see your heads above the bushes when you squat. Then be ready to move. You're dismissed now."

When he finished speaking, Brown realized that he was swimming in sweat, as if he had been through another charge. He turned and found Bill Wildermuth waiting in ambush.

"First Sergeant," Bill said, grinning, "that was one steaming pile you fed those boys."

"Kiss my backside, Private."

But he couldn't help smiling: Wildermuth was right.

A bit later, Captain Burket called him over. The way he used to summon First Sergeant Hill. It felt strange, the way a dream could feel false and true at the same time. The captain led him a few steps away from the men.

"Well, First Sergeant," he said to Brown, "it's been a Hell of a morning."

"Yes, sir."

"The new men didn't do badly. Under the circumstances."

"No, sir."

"Everything all right?"

"Yes, sir. As much as it can be. After . . ." He opened his hands before him, releasing an imaginary bird.

The captain sighed and looked into the underbrush. "After that bloody damn mess. I feel the same way, Brownie, a captain's bars don't change that." Burket fooled with the end of his long black beard. It was still matted with the blood of others, as was the man's tunic. "I suppose I shouldn't tell you this . . . but . . . oh, damn it all. Our attack? It was a mistake. General Willcox just wanted us to push out a little and guard the division's flank."

Across the woodlands, the battle swelled again.

Two p.m.
Brock Road

Hancock couldn't understand why Lee had stopped. Confederate troops still pecked at his reorganizing lines, but Longstreet's men had been rolling him up like a wet carpet, sweeping from south to north to stunning effect.

Then they just stopped. On the cusp of inflicting a catastrophe on him and a third of the army. It wasn't like Lee, and it wasn't in Longstreet's nature to halt like that. For whatever reason, they had spared him, though, giving him time to rally disintegrating regiments and brigades, even broken divisions. Wadsworth had been reported mortally wounded, if not already dead, and left in Confederate hands. Getty had been carried off the field. And Baxter was wounded, too. Carroll was bleeding, but clinging to his command. Winfield Scott Hancock had been within a half hour of suffering one of the war's ugliest defeats, a fact he would have had to live with for the rest of his life. And the Confederates stopped.

He could think of no explanation for it. Despite his losses, Lee had men enough to keep driving forward. Longstreet had not committed his last brigade, if reports were true. And Hill's men would have regrouped well enough to add weight to the attack. Was it possible that Lee and Longstreet didn't know how close they had come to smashing him? Had they, for some madcap reason, lost their nerve? Had they judged the day victory enough? Had he bled Lee that badly earlier on?

It wasn't their way, it wasn't their way. . . .

If Hancock lacked answers, he wasn't short of anger. Once again, Burnside had not come in when he was supposed to attack. The blustering stoat had learned nothing since Fredericksburg, the man couldn't lead a temperance procession. And now Meade expected *him* to support Burnside's belated attack, if it ever came off.

Worse, he had put Gibbon in charge of his left wing, and Gibbon, of all people, had disobeyed orders. And that snot Barlow. Had he brought his entire division forward as ordered, Longstreet would never have been able to pull off his goddamned stunt. Instead, Barlow had sent him one brigade, and Paul Frank's brigade at that.

His thigh hurt. Awfully. He longed to dismount. But it would be hours before he could leave the saddle. The Rebs would come again. Surely. He looked out past his barricades and the hastily made abatis, past grimy, surly soldiers, and into the smoke and wreckage of the day. You could almost walk on the bodies, they had come that close. Now the woods were burning between the armies, and wounded men shrieked as they roasted in broad daylight.

Careful to keep his expression firm and confident, he watched regimental officers putting men back to work, trying to make up for their earlier failures, deepening entrenchments, felling trees, and piling up more wood in front of their rifle pits, working—at his insistence—on a second line of earthworks behind the first. Lee had had his chance. Hancock did not mean to grant him another one.

But damn Gibbon! And damn Barlow! With his lines taking proper shape again, it was time to deal with those two. He fantasized about relieving them on the spot, imagining their shocked faces. Gibbon, with that Philadelphia snootiness he shared with Meade, the two of them men for whom Norristown wasn't close enough to Rittenhouse Square. And Barlow, that little prig. Wouldn't they be surprised if he ripped off their stars?

Of course, he knew he wouldn't, couldn't, relieve them. Gibbon and Barlow were the best fighters he had. For what that was worth. And he lacked the power to take away their ranks. But those two bastards had almost cost him the battle this fine day.

"Morgan!" he called to his chief of staff. "Ride down and fetch Barlow. Don't send Walker or Miller. Go yourself and escort the bugger. I'll be with Gibbon, we're going to have a prayer meeting. Bring Barlow."

Morgan dug steel into his horse's belly, making the weary beast leap onto the road.

Saving his fury until he had things reorganized, Hancock had restricted himself to sending Gibbon terse orders to get things done. Now it was time for a reckoning. He rode the short distance through the splintered woodland, between troops gilded with sweat and useless batteries. At a hastily got-up field surgery, the wounded lay packed together like tinned fish. The usual pile of limbs lay near enough to warn men what to expect.

He wondered if he should have let them take off his leg and have done with it. Had he been one of these poor bastards with no rank, the butchers would have hacked it off at once. But generals rated above common humanity. Other men died while a general's limb was saved by surgeons who dropped everything else. But the ghosts had their revenge: The pain from his thigh approached an unbearable level.

Spotting Gibbon astride his horse, Hancock turned to his flag-bearers and staff. "This is generals' talk, stay back. Walker, find out why I haven't heard fuck-all from Stevenson."

Hancock nudged his horse forward. Gibbon rode a few dainty steps toward him and saluted. As if condescending to do so.

Be fair, Hancock warned himself. But he just couldn't do it. He needed to unload some canister on the men who had let him down.

"You fucking bastard," he said by way of opening the conversation.

Gibbon paled. His mouth opened. No words came out.

"You know you almost cost this army the battle, you son-ofabitch? I want an answer, damn you. Why didn't you send Barlow's division forward when I ordered it? Was it *you* who decided to send me just one brigade? Or was that pissant Barlow making decisions for all of us today? I put *you* in charge of my left wing, not him. Why didn't you send me his goddamned division when I asked for it?"

"Gen-General Hancock . . . ," Gibbon stuttered, something Hancock had never known him to do, "I . . . I never received such an order. You called for one of Barlow's brigades, not his division."

"That's a goddamned lie!"

Gibbon blanched. But Hancock saw fire rising in the other man's eyes, too. Gibbon was a fighter, both of them wounded within a stone's throw of each other on that ridge at Gettysburg.

"General Hancock, your messenger asked for one brigade. At which point I ordered Barlow to dispatch a brigade immediately."

"I ordered you to send me his *division*. Between you and Barlow and Burnside, we might as well just surrender to goddamned Lee."

Barlow galloped toward them, big saber clanking. He wore no hat or uniform blouse, just his usual checkered shirt and a bow tie askew. Morgan rode at his side.

The brigadier reined in, saluting.

Hancock turned first to Morgan. "Charlie, take yourself off."

Morgan eyed the three generals, saluted sharply, and left them.

"You piss-cutting bastard," Hancock said to Barlow. "What have you got to say for yourself? Did you, or did you not, receive an order to advance your division?"

Barlow was startled. "When was the order given, sir?"

"You goddamned well know when it was given. This morning, damn you."

Bewildered, Barlow told him, "I received no such order." He looked at Gibbon, then back to Hancock. "I was directed to advance one brigade to support the attack's left wing."

Weren't they both just too smug? Society boys. Hancock yearned to take them down a peg. "And who do you send, at that? Goddamned Frank, a drunken sauerkraut gobbler. Do you know he ran away? Left his men and ran?"

"I've already relieved Colonel Frank, sir." Again, he looked to Gibbon. "With General Gibbon's approval." Left unsaid was that Hancock had prevented Barlow from replacing Frank in April.

"General," Gibbon said, "you can't blame Barlow for the confusion. He obeyed the order I sent him, which relayed the only order I had from you on the subject."

Hancock refused to be placated. He lashed out at Barlow again. "And why send Frank? The worst brigade commander . . ."

"His troops were fresh. They weren't in the fight last night. And I wanted to keep my best brigades together, sir. I *expected* you to order me to attack."

"Then why didn't you?" Hancock knew he was being completely unreasonable. Even making an ass of himself.

"Because I was never ordered to do so, sir."

Barlow's tone was unafraid, almost cocky now. And that wouldn't do. He had meant to put the fear of God and W. S. Hancock into the little piss-cutter, and here was Barlow turning the tables on him.

"Sir . . . ," Gibbon tried again. "Win, please . . . Barlow did precisely what I ordered him to do. If there's a fault, it's with me."

"Damned right it is."

"But I swear to you that I never received an order to advance Barlow's division."

"Well, that's the order I sent. And I'll damned well prove it, we'll see what I wrote. . . ." But Hancock's guns were running out of powder: He wasn't at all certain he could prove anything; he was blustering and he knew it. It had been a terrible day, made worse by its spectacular beginning.

"General Hancock, I received a *verbal* order," Gibbon said. "To forward one brigade."

"Well, I damned well didn't have time to write you a formal invitation. I was trying to hold this goddamned corps together. With that bastard Longstreet up my ass."

How he regretted his early morning euphoria, when his attack had overwhelmed Hill's shocked men, driving them more than a mile down the Plank Road. He had told Lyman, Meade's little spy, "Tell General Meade we're driving them handsomely." Hardly an hour later, Longstreet's men had been doing all the driving, herding Hancock's men toward calamity.

Barlow cocked an eyebrow. "We might ask the messenger, sir. Maybe he confused things. Who was it, why don't you send for him?"

Hancock felt himself heating up again. With the pain in his thigh a torment. "He's dead. It was damned Roberts. He was killed riding out after Wadsworth."

Barlow curled his lips. " 'Rosencrantz and Guildenstern are dead,' " he muttered.

Hancock turned on him again. "*Goddamn you!* I don't know what the devil you're talking about, Barlow. I never do. But I know insolence when I see it."

"My apologies, General. The remark wasn't so intended."

They were so smooth, so sleek, the two of them. White-glove boys.

Suddenly, all of the air went out of Hancock. He wanted to lie down, to put all this behind him and rub his thigh with alcohol. But any rest was a long way off, and it was time to get back to business. He felt completely drained, but the Confederates would be coming at least one more time and he had to meet them. The day was still too young for Lee to quit.

"Barlow, goddamn it, just go back to your men. We'll sort this out later. Get your men ready to fight. Bobby Lee and Pete Longstreet won't let us off so easily."

"My men are ready, sir." Barlow saluted and pulled hard on the reins. Too hard. Hancock sensed, belatedly, how much of a struggle it had been for Frank Barlow to keep his temper. Christ. Of course, Barlow would have wanted to get into the fight. What had he been thinking?

Yet . . . Hancock was certain he had called for Barlow's division to come up. Gibbon must have misheard. Or the messenger had misspoken. . . .

In a voice almost penitent, Hancock said to Gibbon, "All right, John. Tell me about the men over here. Are they up for a fight?"

"Some of them. Some of them are angry as hornets. Others . . ."

"Others?"

"Others are just plain broken. They won't be worth a damn until they've slept. Maybe not until we get out of these woods."

Hancock nodded and stared down past his stirrups. "We came so close. We *had* him. Lee. Hill's corps was broken, utterly broken." He met Gibbon's eyes. "Then they had us. The Second Corps never folded like that before. It was shameful to watch."

"Well, their boiler ran out of steam. And just in time." Gibbon tried to bandage things up between them, adding, "Don't worry, Win. If they come again, we'll hold them."

Hancock nodded. Thinking about the victory he had almost won that morning.

A courier rode up. Colonel Morgan intercepted the man, who drew a paper from his dispatch bag. The horseman looked agitated, anxious.

Not more bad news, Hancock thought. Good Lord.

Morgan rode forward. Slowly. Testing his welcome.

Hancock waved him on. One storm, at least, was over.

The chief of staff held out the unread paper, but said, "Confederate prisoners say Longstreet's been badly wounded. Maybe dying."

"Well," Gibbon commented, "now we know why they stopped."

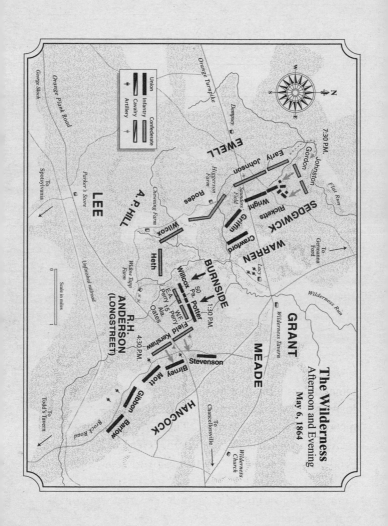

The Wilderness
Afternoon and Evening
May 6, 1864

ELEVEN

May 6, three p.m.
The Wilderness, northeast of Tapp Field

Oates thought: Well, we do have us an abundance of high-flown officers name of Perry.

He said: "General Perry, sir . . . Colonel Perry . . . I've been out there myself. There's more Yankees in those woods than maggots on a dog been two days dead."

"Indeed, Colonel Oates, indeed," General Perry responded. "Those are Wadsworth's men. Their general is dead, they've been sorely tried. I doubt they'll trouble us." He offered Oates a smile that felt well practiced. "Trepidation must not be our downfall."

Oates thought: A man can either talk fine, or he can talk sense.

He said: "My men go forward the way you say, we're going to pass a lump of high ground on our left. When we do, we're going to catch it. And—all respect, sir—your Florida boys are going to get it, too. Those Yankees aren't beat."

"An advance has been ordered," General Perry said. "And we shall advance." He let his bearded jaw play back and forth, swishing his next words around before he spoke them. "We must not let General Longstreet's misfortune deny us victory."

Oates knew that the Massachusetts-born Floridian was a brave man. And he knew that Edward Perry was an educated man. He even knew that this particular Perry had read the law in Alabama, as Oates had himself, before

becoming a Florida man by choice. But he wasn't convinced the transplanted Yankee was a wise man. Oates just
couldn't take to the fine-looking fellow's nasal twang, a
sorry concoction of up-north flint and studied-up, high-
flown drawl. It was as if some coon-hugging New England
preacher tried playing a Southern gentleman on the stage.

As for Longstreet, Oates didn't revel in the man's wounding, much as he disliked him. He even hoped the man might
live to enjoy a long convalescence away from the army. Fair
was fair, and a man who went down in a fight deserved
good wishes.

The worst part had been the leaderless muddle that came
in Longstreet's wake, a do-nothing waste of hour after hour
while the rest of the generals stuck their hands down each
other's pants to see whose stick was bigger. High chances
were squandered, openings bought with good men's blood
that morning.

Now this: an attack in the wrong damned direction. With
Yankees piling up just to their north, the two understrength
brigades under General Perry were set to attack due east.
Might as well poke your bare ass at a rattlesnake.

Oates read the look that Colonel Perry shot him: *Quiet
down and let me handle this.*

Simmering, Oates backed off half a step and pawed
sweat from his beard. Truth be told, Colonel Perry had done
fine so far. The man was no Evander Law, but he'd fought
to win. Oates kept his mouth shut. For the moment.

"General Perry," Colonel Perry began, "the Alabama
Brigade and I take pride in serving under your command,
sir. Florida and Alabama, united, must be formidable. . . ."

Bill Perry, too, had studied for the bar—sometimes it
seemed to Oates that he served in an army of lawyers—
but the elder Perry had then pursued a career in education,
rising high.

"So if I may hazard a thought . . . let my brigade advance

at an oblique from right to left, with Colonel Oates prepared to defend our flank. I've given him the Forty-
eighth Alabama, in addition to his Fifteenth, and propose
that—"

"That will be fine," the general said, impatient to start
his attack. "Your brigade may advance in echelon of battalions, at forty-pace intervals. Will that do?" Without waiting for an answer, he turned to Oates. Their eyes met
without fellowship. "I'm sure Colonel Oates won't allow
the foe to embarrass us."

Oates let an eyebrow climb and said: "Heaps of them
out there, sir." He just couldn't help himself, had to give
this peacock a last warning.

"Indeed," the general told him. "Heaps of their dead. We
shall add to them, Colonel Oates, I expect we shall add to
them."

General Perry began the attack before Oates got back to
his men. He had to run like a damned fool, shot hip feeling like it might crack in two. Wounds to the body, wounds
to his vanity, he'd had a surfeit of both.

"Form your men!" he shouted as he passed the 48th.
"Commanders to me!" Reaching the 15th, he repeated the
order and planted himself where the regiments brushed one
another. "Captain Shaaf, get up here. *Now!*"

There wasn't much get-ready needed: Calloused inside
and out by years of fighting, the men arranged themselves
for battle under the eyes of their sergeants. As Shaaf trotted up, Oates told him, "Don't even stop. Turn around and
take your company out as skirmishers. Wheel right and advance."

But Shaaf did stop, bewildered at the order. The rest of
the gathering officers were startled, too.

"Shaaf, just do what you're told, goddamn it. You know
what's out there, and I know what's out there. Just go."

The captain was so taken aback that he forgot to salute. But he turned to his task.

Oates looked over the other officers, some of them bloodied up in the morning ruckus but unwilling to leave their men while they could stand. Young Billy Strickland had a rag tied around his head.

"All right," Oates said, "there's no time for pissing on each other's legs, just do how I tell you. Forty-eighth, right wheel and advance by battalion at the left oblique, forty paces off the Forty-fourth. Fifteenth follows on the left, advancing the same way."

"That's mad-dog crazy," a captain said.

"Well, bite yourself some Yankees," Oates told him.

When the officers had returned to their positions, Oates allowed himself one deep breath, then ordered the 48th forward. He counted the regiment's paces like a schoolboy doing his sums with corn kernels. Sharply at their thirty-second step, he barked, "Fifteenth Alabama . . . forward . . . *march*."

As the 48th Alabama's front rank landed its fortieth step, the 15th stepped off. Oates figured it for the last orderly action of the afternoon.

No sooner had they pressed into the undergrowth than shots splashed to their front. Shaaf and his boys were in it already.

"Jesus Christ," Oates muttered. "Jesus damn Christ."

His front rank passed the mound from which he'd spied swarms of Federals half an hour earlier. Doubtless, the Yankees had skirmishers up there now, men too savvy to open fire too soon. They'd wait until his men reached the low ground where Shaaf was fussing around and the blue-bellies could bring massed fires to bear.

The only hope was to surprise the Yankees in turn, to wheel left and attack straight into their snouts, to shock them with crazy daring and gain some time.

Oates pushed ahead of his men. He had to see things for himself.

Just as he passed through his first rank, hundreds of rifles roared on the left.

Men fell around him.

The Yankees were so thick that the brush couldn't hide the half of them. Seemed to be twice as many, at least, as he'd seen on his earlier prowl. Momentarily stunned by the mass of Federals, Oates expected a charge that would swamp his regiment.

But the Yankees didn't charge, contenting themselves with a turkey shoot. Shouting orders to change front, he looked about for anything that resembled defensible ground. There wasn't much.

His vision of a charge of his own evaporated. The numbers out there were just too overwhelming.

Shaaf's skirmishers stood their ground, buying time with lives. Oates sent a runner to the 48th to halt and change front, too, tying in with the right of the 15th. All they could do now was hold as long as possible.

Under fire, Oates organized his line, anchoring it on bumps of earth that hardly counted as "high ground." It was worthless dirt by any sane account, but all he had.

His men scrambled to throw together barricades of fallen trees and branches, hacking off scraps of shrubbery that gave a man no protection but let him feel better kneeling down behind them. Tough as bear hide, Shaaf and his boys refused to quit their scuffle out in the killing ground. The captain knew what was at stake: He understood fighting the way a good hound took to hunting.

To the right and back a throw, an uproar of volleys and shouts worsened their prospects. Peering through the brush, Oates sensed as much as saw a dark blur as Union troops surged forward on his flank. They were going after the rest of the Alabama Brigade and General Perry's Floridians.

The Yankees had been handed a gift that was sweeter than a kiss from a rich man's wife.

His men dug madly with bayonets and spoons, with rifle butts and bare hands, waiting for the *hurrah* that would signal a Yankee attack against them, too.

"Folger," Oates said to one of his runners, "go on over and see how Colonel Perry's fixed. You tell him I can't advance, but I have a mind to hold, if that suits him. Tell him I just don't want to be cut off, hear?"

"Yes, sir."

The corporal took off at a run, doing the best he could to bust through the undergrowth.

Oates heard the fateful, expected shout, heralding the onset of a deluge.

Shaaf's men dashed back. One after another, they leapt over the low barricades their comrades continued to strengthen even now. The captain came in last of all his company.

Oates grabbed him. "Get your hellions gathered back up and wait in that dip yonder. You're my reserve."

Out of breath, the captain nodded. He forgot to salute again, but Oates could forgive a great many breaches of military decorum from a man who fought like he meant it.

"My God," a man said in a voice of wonder. "Oh, my God and Savior . . ."

Years before, Oates had seen the Gulf shore during a storm. It was like that now. A huge wave rolled toward them, with another right behind it. And other blue waves followed that.

"Stay down," Oates bellowed as he paced his line. The men were brave, but that went only so far, unless you were crazy. The body did its own sums, overtopping the calculations of the mind, and legs made their own decisions to up and run. Oates had to challenge the men's pride to whip down their fears. And that meant parading around like a fool until he could let them take solace in pulling triggers. "Stay down now. Nobody fires until I damned well say so."

If the Yankees behaved as usual, pausing to exchange volleys, he had a chance. If they showed unusual enterprise and came on, he lacked the numbers to do much more than sting them.

Corporal Folger reappeared. Crouching like that Hunchback of Notre Dame, expecting Yankee bullets to ring his bells.

"Sir," the soldier panted, "the colonel begs you to hold . . . while he re-forms."

"Florida Brigade?"

"Just broke to pieces, broke all to pieces. Yankees hit 'em every which way. General Perry's wounded."

Oates thought: That didn't take long.

"All right," he said. "You stay by me now."

The Yankees were a hundred paces off. They overlapped his command on either flank. He hoped they weren't aware of that advantage yet.

Oates turned, quickly, to his runner. "You see where Captain Shaaf's tucked in?"

The corporal nodded. "Run right by him."

"Good."

Oates thought: Lord God of hosts, my mama's your devoted servant, even if I've gone my way apart. For her sake, stop those sonsofbitches short.

His mother, with her gift of the sight: She had foreseen his brother's death. Had she dreamed of this day and kept her silence?

The Yankees halted. Fifty paces out.

As the Federals shouldered up to unleash a volley, Oates screamed, *"Fire!"*

The Yankees just stood there in what passed for open ground, exchanging volleys as if they were in no hurry.

Despite their numbers, the Federals were not finding matters to their advantage.

There was a cost, though. Calvin Whatley, who had been with Oates' old company from the first, took a bullet in the eye, and John Stone, another of the old bunch, was laid out flat, pumping blood and no way to stop it. Plenty of others went down, too.

No longer standing upright, Oates worked his way past a stretch of smoldering brambles to Sergeant Ball, who maintained a delicate trigger finger, despite his brawler's paws and gutter habits.

"See that Yankee officer there?" Oates asked, half-shouting.

"Which'n?"

"Watch now. Kind of weaves in and out. Dozen men left of those flags."

The Yankees let go another volley. Bullets bit the air.

"Can't see him. Damned smoke."

"Keep watching. Left of the flags. Knows everybody's aiming at the colors, so he set himself off to the side. *There.* Waving his butter knife."

Ball's grip tightened on his rifle. "I saw him. Ain't there now, though."

"Just wait. Wait until that sucker pops out again. And you kill the bastard."

Ball looked up at Oates with a happy smirk. "Know what I like about you, Colonel?"

"Not sure I give a purple damn."

"You're not a gentleman."

"No," Oates said.

A moment later, Ball dropped the Yankee.

Oates thought: Now or never.

He stood up and shouted, "Bayonets! Fifteenth Alabama! Forty-eighth! *Charge!*"

* * *

Drifting smoke nagged at Brown's lungs as he and the men of the 50th Pennsylvania double-quicked forward, following a trail beaten down by thousands before them. They were headed into the depths of the fighting this time, with their cartridge pouches refilled and hearts grown hard. After the shock of the morning's losses, meanness had taken hold of them, rearing up like that black snake in front of First Sergeant Hill, an appetite for cruelty worthy of Bible stories.

From a distance—just as they started south through the woodlands—they had heard encouraging Northern hurrahs amid the volleys. Closer now, they caught a Rebel yell.

"We'll have them hollering something else," Doudle shouted. Others called out their agreement. It never ceased to be a wonder to Brown how war worked on men: Those who had run from the enemy hours before now ran toward that same enemy with their hearts on fire. And Doudle . . . John was a curious man. He would stand for as long as needed in the front rank, loading and firing, seemingly fearless. But he would not go one step in front of the rest of the regiment: His fear of capture was famed within the company. Doudle seemed resigned to possible death or mutilation, but rumors about Andersonville unnerved him.

Brown dropped back beside Henry Hill.

"No more craziness, all right? Once was enough."

"All right," his friend said.

The smoke stuck to their sweat as they hurried forward, greasing their flesh and making the heat still hotter. Lower faces blackened with powder, the men looked as though they wore bandits' masks askew. Few uniforms were buttoned up, fewer still unstained.

Brown's crusted undergarments chafed his thighs. For

a few paces, but no more, he let himself dream of a bath in a cool, clean river.

The clamor of battle rushed toward them. Wounded men appeared, clutching shattered arms or bloodied faces, some staggering and on the verge of collapse, others not displeased at the nicks they'd received.

"What's happening up there?" Brown asked a soldier who seemed merely sobered by the damage done to him.

"Same old story," the private said. "We start out whupping them, they end up whupping us."

Men in shameless flight came next, a few strays first, then knots and clots of skedaddlers.

Bullets gnawed the treetops. One of the rounds chased a brown snake off a limb. It dropped into the column, slapping the back of one of the Eckerts, who jogged on unaware of what had happened.

"Like goddamned Mississippi," Bill Wildermuth griped.

The column halted and the front ranks of the 20th Michigan collided with the rear of the 50th Pennsylvania. As junior officers and sergeants sorted things out, the captain waved Brown to his side. Soldiers who had had enough edged past them.

"Stay with the men," Burket said. "Don't let them fall out. I'm going forward to see the colonel, find out what I can."

"He'll be with Colonel Christ, sir."

"I know."

Neither of them said what Brown knew both of them were thinking: They'd seen the brigade commander in the saddle an hour before, working hard on his whiskey flask.

The captain added, "Only two choices. We either shore up the line, or we attack."

Recalling Christ's reddened face, Brown said, "We'll attack."

The company commander nodded. Then Burket smiled.

"It's all on your head, Brownie. You're the one who lugged him back in at Antietam."

They giggled like mischievous boys. There was nothing else to be done.

The captain hurried along the column of companies, and Brown turned back to the men who were now his charges. Trying to recall each step First Sergeant Hill had taken before an attack, he called out, "Corporal Oswald! If we ground knapsacks, you stand guard. Pick two men for the detail."

There were fewer packs to watch over now.

Next, he inspected the weapons of the recruits, checking that muzzles weren't gritty or barrels fouled. When he reached the Eckert boys, he told John the Shorter, "After this fuss, you're going to wash those stockings good and give them back."

"Teacher's pet," another Eckert muttered.

Brown ignored it. He wanted the boy and the rest of the new men thinking about anything but what waited ahead. It was queer: When men were moving forward toward a fight, especially moving at the double-quick, they acquired a fierceness of outlook that no one had ever managed to explain to him. But let them pause for even a peck of time, and their minds roamed off in all the wrong directions.

The captain returned along with the commanders of the trail companies. Each man's face was grim.

Before the column resumed its march, the battle approached again. Brown and the veterans understood: They were needed and they'd be going straight into it.

They pushed on for a hundred paces before their officers turned them into the brush. Fighting raged to their front, glimpsed as muzzle flashes and shapes in the smoke. Instead of deploying in two battle lines, the regiment formed four deep. It made sense to Brown: Better chance of keeping the men together in the undergrowth and general confusion.

Between their left flank and the right of the 20th Michigan, a thicket blazed. The heat had become dizzying. Brown hoped the new men had not drunk up their water. It shamed him to think that he had not checked their canteens when he'd had the chance. Overwhelmed by all he suddenly had to do and ruing how much he had to leave undone, Brown was far from certain he could replace First Sergeant Hill.

Dismounted now, Lieutenant Colonel Overton announced, "The Rebs up ahead pushed our boys back, but they're about played out. We're going to teach them a lesson." He raised his sword so every man could see it. "For the good old Keystone State!" he cried.

"Pennsylvania never done shit for me," Isaac Eckert whispered.

Bill Wildermuth told him, "Guess that makes you and Harrisburg about even."

The inevitable order came. And the men of Company C, 50th Pennsylvania, started forward. For a small eternity, Brown feared a repeat of the morning's debacle, with only the 50th and the 20th Michigan making the attack, but as the regiment neared the front line, other regiments rose from behind hasty barricades.

"Let's go, let's go!" Brown shouted, just as thousands of men broke into a cheer.

Oates had driven his regiments as far as they could go, surprising himself with what he had achieved. For his part, Colonel Perry helped worthily, pushing up the 44th Alabama under Major Carey, giving Oates command of a third rump regiment. Together, they had sent maybe three times their number of Yankees reeling backward. But just as Oates meant to bring some order to his strewn command, the Yankees burst out of the forest again, fresh Yankees, as though the sonsofbitches had factories turning out men as quick as a foundry made railroad spikes.

"Rally on the colors!" Oates shouted, voice nearly gone. "Rally on the colors of your regiment!"

His soldiers edged back before the renewed onslaught. Few men on either side would close with bayonets, and rarely when exhausted. The threat of cold steel had worked in his favor for the past half hour, but only New Orleans cutthroats really hankered to gut other men. A soldier might club a head in with a rifle butt and do it merrily, but the bayonet worked differently on the mind. Almost as if men thought, Do unto others . . .

"Rally, boys!" Oates called. "Fifteenth Alabama, hold this ditch."

The men nearest him obeyed, and others joined them. They got down in the trough of a drying creek, using the waist-high banks for their protection, and fired into the Yankees as fast as they could.

Oates expected the Federals to halt, as usual, to trade volleys. But this bunch just kept pushing. When they got within thirty paces, Oates pulled his men back, firing as they withdrew. The Yankees seized the creekbed and briefly turned it to their benefit, propping elbows on the bank to aim at withdrawing Confederates. Then the blue-bellies climbed out of the ditch again, on the near side, coming on hot. Another Alabaman toppled backward beside Oates, and a blue-clad flag-bearer clutched his belly and staggered. A ready Yankee caught the flag, yelling words in a dialect thick as molasses.

"Rally on the high ground," Oates barked. Or tried to. His voice was dry as wood shavings.

He launched Folger with orders for the 48th Alabama, but the corporal dropped before he had gone twenty feet and lay there twitching. Smoke from volleys on the left rode a hot gust into the 15th Alabama. Brushfires thickened the swirls and donated cinders.

"Rally! Captain Strickland, to me!"

It took an eternity, at least thirty seconds, for Billy Strickland to reach him.

"Got a grip on your boys?"

The captain nodded.

"You hold them sonsofbitches up," Oates told him. "Just give me two, three minutes, till I can get us back where we started and under some shape of cover."

"Yes, sir."

If the young captain had doubts, he didn't show them.

"Fifteenth! Withdraw! Back to the barricades. . . ." He ran along his broken line to pass the order to the 48th. As for the 44th on the left, Carey had a quick eye, he'd figure things out for himself.

With another hurrah, the Yankees surged again.

Oates wondered whether anything was left of the Florida Brigade, or if the Alabamans were on their own. The rest of the army had as good as disappeared.

The 48th was fighting handsomely, contesting every bit of ground with the Yankees. Oates sent a private back to tell Colonel Perry he meant to try to hold where he'd first changed front, adding that they were under attack by at least one fresh brigade and maybe two.

Cursing, Oates passed wounded men in the uniforms of both armies, all begging to be taken along before the brushfires reached them. Pity was all he had to spare, not time. Not even time to help the men he recognized. He would have let them all burn to death in the bottom pit of Hell if it meant he could whip the Yankees.

The men of Company C leapt into the ditch the Rebels had defended. Some paused to aim and fire after the Johnnies, but Brown soon had the last of them scrambling up the far bank and back in the chase. Billy Eckert was hit and dropped to his knees, but the other Eckerts kept going. Everyone's blood was up. And the Rebs didn't have the numbers they had feared. The morning's situation had been reversed.

Here and there, a Johnny dawdled too long getting off a last shot and the boys caught up with him. If the Reb didn't drop his weapon and raise his hands fast, he didn't fare well. Running ahead in a fit of mean, Isaac Eckert locked rifles with a Johnny inches taller but plank thin. Seconds into their smoke-wreathed duel, Isaac sidestepped and swept his stock up into the other man's face, stepped back, and thrust his bayonet into the staggering Johnny's belly. The Reb convulsed and collapsed. Crowing like a rooster, Isaac smashed in his skull.

Sometimes the clashes went the other way.

But the 50th kept shoving through the brambles, slowed only by the patches of crawling flames. Brown could tell that the Johnnies they faced had been fighting awhile. Their moves were tardy and they fired low, forearms quivering under the weight of their rifles. Their shoulders would be bruised and painful, too, no matter how much experience they had.

The puffed-up generals with mighty plans never fired rifles and had no idea what one could do to a man in one hour of fighting. At the very least, a soldier's aim went off as he coddled his shooting shoulder.

Brown saw Henry Hill advance with an air of determination, judging when it was time to pause and shoot, and taking careful aim before pulling the trigger. He was a model of how a veteran moved. The new men needed talking to, though, since most of them fired before choosing a target, just blasting in the direction of the enemy.

"Keep together!" Brown shouted. A gulp of smoke made him cough and gasp, but he continued giving orders, pausing to fire only when he believed he had his men in hand.

He glimpsed Isaac Eckert's blood-spattered grin and mad eyes.

The Rebs dug in their heels at a string of barricades, none worth much except as a marker of where they meant to fight. More men in gray and brown rags rushed up from the enemy's rear, just enough fresh blood to give the defenders hope.

The advance slowed and the firing thickened. At a command, the 50th stopped and formed lines, angering Brown: He was sure they could have run right over the Rebs, even with that handful of reinforcements.

The two sides traded volleys. Killing each other at close range because the officers didn't know what else to do. Someone had ordered the 50th to halt, because someone else a half mile along had ordered a halt, and the order had just ricocheted down the line.

Walking behind the ranks of shooters and loaders, Captain Burket spun around and tumbled.

Brown froze.

In moments, the captain got back up, holding his side and wheezing. He had lost his cap, but held on to his pistol.

Brown rushed toward him. "Sir?"

The captain grunted. His eyes strained, seeking nothing in particular. Then he came around, at least partway, and declared, "I'm all right. It's all right. See to the men . . . the men . . ."

"You have to go to the rear, sir," Brown told him.

Clutching his ribs with one hand and the revolver in the other, he shook his head. "They'll have to do a damn sight worse than that."

There was no blood in his spittle. That was good.

"See to the men!" Burket snarled. "Damn it, Brown, do your duty."

Brown turned back to his soldiers. Walking the firing line as the captain had done, patting men on the shoulder, cautioning the new recruits to take time to aim. Stepping over the dead and wounded.

It was blundering idiocy now. Just standing there, saying, "Shoot me."

But they all stood there.

The Rebs had to be low on ammunition and getting jumpy. The 50th could charge them, Brown was certain. More lives would be saved than lost.

But he had no say in it. All he could do was to steady his men and encourage them to be good targets for their enemies.

Another order came down the line. Not to charge, but to take what cover they could and keep up the fire. Instead of welcoming the order, most of the veterans cursed. They all sensed what they could do, given the command.

Once they dropped down, the Johnnies behind the barricades slackened their fire. Yes, Brown thought, they're happy as drunks in a brewery. We could have had them. And we stopped like fools.

He picked out a target, a Johnny's head crowned by a misshapen hat, but he missed.

More smoke rolled in, thick as river fog.

Crouching, Brown worked along the line, telling the men to fire only if sure of a target. He didn't want them wasting their cartridges and ending up in the same state as the Johnnies. You could win a fight or stay alive because you had one round left when a Reb had none.

He could tell from behind that one of the new recruits had pissed his pants. Well, men had done worse.

They were tired from their trot through the woodlands and their angry charge, from their earlier fight and their night march, from the weight of their dead and the terrible load of their thoughts, more tired lying on the ground than they would have been standing and charging. Weariness was a bushwhacker, waiting for a chance to strike from behind.

The firing on both sides dwindled to odd shots, then to almost none.

"You men drink water," Brown told the recruits. "But don't lift up to do it, you stay down. And don't drink all of it. We're not done."

The line grew almost silent. Men heard chiming in their ears and the thunderous breathing of others. You could almost hear the smoke drift by.

A Southern voice rang out: "Hey, Yanks! Who you boys with?"

Proud, angry, and stupid, one of the new men answered: "Fiftieth Pennsylvania."

"Never heard of y'all."

"Who're you, then?"

"Fifteenth Alabama. Got some 'baccy, if you want to come over and get it."

Brown scrambled over to the new man and yanked his sleeve. "Shut up, boy."

But Bill Wildermuth took a turn, unable to resist: "Trade you some cartridges for it, Johnny. I figure you boys are out."

"Go to Hell, you Yankee sonofabitch."

"Go to Hell yourself, Johnny."

"Already been. Place was full of Yankees, so I left."

Several men in Company C laughed out loud despite themselves. Any Reb who could best Bill Wildermuth in a war of words was a worthy enemy.

Brown looked around for Captain Burket. And saw him a stretch back, kneeling low with Lieutenant Colonel Overton and a gaggle of other officers.

Maybe, Brown thought, just maybe they've figured it out.

Somebody had. The officers crabbed back to their companies and passed the word: "Get ready. We're going to rush them. Don't stop to fire until you're over their barricades."

Brown felt the soldiers, new and old, tense up.

Rustling and rattling swelled to the rear and he turned his head to look. A fresh regiment was advancing to support them. The Johnnies had to see it, but held their fire. That convinced Brown beyond any doubt that the Rebs were either out of ammunition or low enough to give them cause to bolt.

"Pennsylvania! Charge!"

Brown leapt to his feet and gave in to the thrall of the wild rush. As if he were a corporal, or even a private, again. He didn't bother with malingerers, but raced ahead with his rifle leveled, howling like an animal.

"Pennsylvania! Pennsylvania!" men screamed.

The Rebs broke. They got off a few last shots and just plain ran. Brown saw a big, black-bearded officer, a chesty bear of a man, standing and waving his men back, encouraging them to run, to save what was left of their regiment.

With his men under way, tearing off like rabbits-in-arms, the big officer finally loped after them, moving as if slightly hobbled. Then he, too, sped up to an outright run.

Brown stopped, aimed his rifle . . . then didn't fire, after all.

There'd been killing enough.

The regiment halted just beyond the barricades. Soldiers cheered.

"Pennsylvania . . . Pensylvania . . ."

Instead of pushing through to pursue the Rebs, the fresh regiment behind them stopped as well. Brown figured there'd been an order he hadn't heard.

Captain Burket said, "Organize your men, First Sergeant."

"Yes, sir. Are you—"

"Scratched rib. Maybe cracked. No real damage. See to the men."

The veterans had begun to pick through the meager

possessions on Rebel corpses. As Brown summoned them to re-form for whatever the officers had in mind next, Bill Wildermuth passed him.

"Jokers didn't leave any tobacco, after all," he said.

Oates ran. He was in a fury, but refused to be ashamed. His men had done all they could, and he wasn't about to see them slaughtered or captured to no purpose. He had ordered them to run like the dickens and forget about keeping order. And they did.

His rage deadened the pain that haunted his hip. The Alabama Brigade had *never* broken, not once in three years of war. But they'd been left hanging out like bait forgotten by the fisherman, just begging to be swallowed by a blue whale.

He ran as madly as he had run as a boy, when he and John raced, or when he went after somebody who wanted a thumping. The difference now was that he had a man's deep anger, not a boy's blow-over heat. He cursed in words his mother forbade within a mile of her door. Then he progressed to language even his father had likely not known, wicked epithets gathered in his itinerant days.

No, he was not a gentleman.

Sergeant Ball lay dead, shot thrice in a moment.

No gentleman.

He and his soldiers scurried, crashed, and man-galloped through the brush for a good four hundred yards, until they broke into a field and saw gray lines ahead.

Instantly, they slowed to a walk and were hallooed in by their comrades.

Colonel Perry was still fighting somewhere, but General Perry, the self-declared Floridian, appeared with his shrunken staff. Oates was ready to tear the bastard's head off. Then he saw the blood and bandages, the ruined uniform, and the man's struggle to stay upright in the saddle.

The general broke protocol to salute first.

"Colonel Oates," he rasped, "you were correct . . . I was in error. I . . . thank your brave men for doing . . . all that mortal men could do." He slumped and Oates feared he would fall off of his horse. But the brigadier clung to the saddle. An aide rushed up and whispered words close to Perry's ear. The Floridian straightened again.

"Yes . . . ," he resumed. "I forget my duty, Colonel. Form to the rear, at the far edge of the field." He thought for another moment, loss-of-blood dizzy, struggling. Then the general added, "God bless Alabama."

Brown was angry. Shortly after dispatching details to gather up their wounded, the 50th Pennsylvania had been ordered to fall back a quarter mile. The regiments stacked behind them fell back, too, along with all the forces on their flanks. The ground for which they had fought and bled was worthless.

They had to consolidate their lines, officers explained. Old soldiers understood that "consolidate the lines" was a secret code among generals for "We're not sure what to do next."

Brown was angry, but not disheartened. He had accepted long before that war was a contest of idiocies, and the least idiotic behavior won by a hair. Slumping rearward, the company paused to take up its knapsacks again. Corporal Oswald apologized: Several had been grabbed by skedaddlers he couldn't catch. Soon after, the company took its place in what passed for a line in the undergrowth.

Step by step, the bitterness passed and memories of their success crowded out the frustration. Brown heard a new man tell a comrade, "I got one of their officers. I really did. I saw him go down."

"Amazing shooting, son," a veteran said.

The boy brightened.

"Amazing," the veteran continued, "since I saw you close your eyes every time you fired."

"Dass war alles nur Quatsch und Dummheit," one of the Dutchmen remarked to no one in particular.

All nonsense and stupidity. Brown understood that much Pennsy-German.

And yet . . . there was more to it: That intoxicating thrill, born of mortal terror. The way a man became part of something greater than himself, part of a mighty creature made up of many men, a company's worth, a regiment's, a division's. The way you soared to a place no one could name and you didn't know you were there until you weren't there anymore and you were dazed by the hollowness afterward. When you warmed all the way back to life and sense again, you sought out friends who also had survived and who would be friends for a lifetime if they lived through the fights to come, and you made little jokes that avoided the unspeakable. You mourned together, you mourned alone. Then you got up and marched somewhere else, and you dreaded and hungered for what was coming toward you, what you knew was coming sooner or later, until, at last, your feet just ached and your belly was empty and your throat had gone dry as dust, and that was what you thought about, if you had the strength left to think any thoughts at all, and the part of you that craved being so alive again went numb while you sat down to a feed of beans.

There were no beans this night. Not even coffee, since fires had been forbidden. Men shared what rations they had left in their haversacks. The ammunition would come, all right, but they would not see cooked food until God knew when.

Brown called the roll, wincing each time no one answered, and reorganized the company around the surviving sergeants and corporals. He sent a detail loaded with canteens in search of water and did not ask its source when they returned. After selecting men to rotate on guard duty, he kicked recruits awake to clean their rifles. Even the veterans were too weary to search each other for ticks.

And what would Brown remember of that day? Later on, in the dark, as men tried to sleep against the cries of the wounded burning alive out in the undergrowth, listening to their garbled pleas and the *pop-pop-pop* as cartridge pouches exploded in the flames to gut men dead and alive, listening to all that and to the barking snores of his own soldiers, Brown sat up pondering, wondering, empty of answers to any question that mattered.

A shriek of horror rose from the midst of the sleeping men.

Instantly alert and fully awake, Brown rushed toward the cry.

Wails and weeping trailed the shriek, the uncommon sound—rare even in war—of a grown man crying piteously.

Men cursed the noise that woke them.

In the starlight that pierced the undergrowth and smoke, Brown found John Eckert, the boy who had his stockings. He was all but naked and crying to beat the band.

Brown tried to think what the problem might be. He'd seen soldiers old and new fight like lions, then go to bits when things were quiet and safe. Like ropes and cables on the canal back home, men had different strengths.

The boy howled again. Someone snapped, "Shut the Hell up." Others shared the sentiment in rougher language.

Brown said, "If you're worried about your cousin, his wound isn't bad."

"It isn't that, it ain't that," the boy cried.

"You wounded?" Some men failed to realize for hours that they'd been shot.

The boy shook his head, pale in the gloom, and howled again.

"What's wrong, for God's sake?" Brown demanded. His temper, too, had grown frail. "You'll wake the whole damned army."

John Eckert raised his face to Brown. Even in the dark, his anguish was frightful.

"I got the poison ivy," the boy said.

TWELVE

Lee rode north. Hoping that something might be done on that flank. A last attack on the Plank Road had failed, after exciting false sentiments of triumph. As the men stormed forward, wind-whipped flames had driven Hancock's soldiers from their earthworks. Remembering their fallen general, the furious soldiers of Jenkins' Brigade had plunged through the inferno's gaps to plant their battle flags along the Brock Road. Only to be shot down, captured, or thrust back. Too few had reached the Union line, and their lodgment had been fragile: bravery practiced uselessly against numbers. The southern flank was played out and Lee had no gambit left him but a last, bold move by Ewell.

As Lee and his small cavalcade passed them on a farm trail, the men of Ramseur's Brigade raised their hats and cheered. Lee saluted with a hand raised barely to shoulder level. He could not see a reason for their high spirits. Taylor, who had an eye for such things, believed the army's casualties for the two days of fighting might reach ten thousand men. Listening with a guarded expression, Marshall had removed his spectacles and looked away, feigning other concerns. Lee understood that his military secretary feared their losses would be even higher.

The dozen horsemen narrowed their column to a single file to pass through the next stretch of woodland, a clean space untouched by battle. Peeved at Taylor and

Marshall—their calculations came too near his own—
Lee had brought along only Venable and a few guardian
horsemen. As if attempting to ride away from his thoughts.

Ten thousand men. Or more. Lost to no advantage. The
army could not afford to bleed so wantonly. Worse, the loss
of Longstreet was disastrous. Even if his Old War Horse
lived, the man's abilities would be denied to the army indefinitely. And Hill . . . after fighting brilliantly the previous day, then desperately that morning, ready to die beside
him in a simple gunner's role, Hill had gone brittle again,
ghost pale, succumbing to his old sickness, that shameful
business. Lee didn't know if the man would be well enough
to remain in command of his corps.

Who would be left him? Ewell? An irascible, awkward
man, though one of experience.

Jenkins dead. Jones gone. Benning badly wounded. A
half-dozen other generals bleeding from wounds, struggling to remain with their battered brigades . . .

When Lee's party reached Rodes' Division, those men
cheered him, too. That morning, the soldiers' cries had
been sweet music. Now they stung his ears.

He *had* to bring off something to humble Grant. Ten
thousand casualties or more . . . and those people still
held the crossroads in the south and their advanced position in the north. His own men were back on the lines
they had taken up as the battle began. It didn't matter
whether the Federals had suffered markedly higher casualties, as Taylor insisted and Lee preferred to believe. The
Union had men enough, men and all else. What mattered
was the need to savage Grant in this first encounter, to
sweep away his aura as a victor. The Army of Northern
Virginia had little beyond rags and reputation. It could
not afford to sacrifice the latter.

And courage. His men had that, too. Despite the morning's near collapse, the soldiers' fortitude was undeniable.

Rodes cantered up and joined Lee, guiding him to Ewell's headquarters in the trees beyond the Turnpike. Except for the usual serenade of skirmishing, the Second Corps' front was quiet, almost restful. Lee regretted his inattention to his left wing that day. Had opportunities been missed? Ewell had said nothing, had not requested permission to attack since a brief fight that morning. Had Dick Ewell grown too cautious? Had he lost more than a leg over the war years? Lee had pondered the matter ever since Gettysburg, but always returned to the fact that he had no one fit to take over the corps.

The visit surprised Ewell, who greeted Lee bareheaded, tin cup in hand. Had the man expected him to be off in Richmond? And Early, a shadow to his corps commander, surely should have been with his division?

Lee cautioned himself to be civil. When he felt worn, his stomach filled with bile and his temper with acid. Self-control had cost him as much effort as anything in the war, but he prided himself on how seldom he'd been ungentlemanly.

He reminded himself of Ewell's superb performance the day before. And if Ewell had shown no initiative today, neither had Lee pressed him to renew the battle.

Dismounting, Lee took special care, worried his bowels might betray him. Dignity was essential.

"It's good to see you, General," Ewell said. "Coffee?"

Lee shook his head. "Thank you, no." He looked at Ewell as if really seeing him only now: an eager man, often cranky, balding, swinging about on his wooden leg with the gait of a music hall sailor. Lee's heart bade him say, "Richard, you and I are too old for this young man's sport." But he did not, would not, say such a thing. Nor would he call the man "Richard." Such intimacies only made command more difficult.

"Hard fight down there," Ewell said. "Sorry to hear about Longstreet. Terrible thing."

At Ewell's shoulder, Early nodded along.

The gathered heat pressed down on Lee. "Might we sit, General Ewell? The day has been long, and not without tribulation."

"Of course, sir. Come in the shade. Right over here." The lieutenant general waved a hand at his bevy of aides. It was a nervous gesture, almost feminine.

Men scrambled to accommodate the men who wore the stars.

"General Rodes, General Early, please join us," Lee said.

"Shall I roust up Johnson?" Ewell asked.

"Let us talk for a moment. Gentlemen, there is nothing more to be done this day on the right." He looked at Ewell, introducing a measure of coldness to his expression. "Might nothing be done on this flank? To discomfit those people? I am loath to leave them the field."

Ewell twitched. "Way I see it, General Lee, they're not any more in command of the field than we are. We can't go that way, they can't come this way." The corps commander inspected Lee's face for a reaction, but Lee revealed nothing. Ewell decided to talk on and said, "Given the disparity in numbers, I'd say we haven't done less than fairly, all in all."

"The men," Lee said, intoning each word distinctly, "have been splendid."

"Yes, sir," Ewell said. He bent to scratch his wooden leg, a gesture that always seemed unsound to Lee. "Yes, sir, that's true, that's true. I was thinking . . . in the night, we could withdraw to the Mine Run line. Better ground. Much better."

Lee almost admonished the man, tempted to remind Ewell of his orders the previous morning to refuse battle.

Certainly, Mine Run was a preferable battleground. But the choice no longer remained to them.

"We will not retreat," Lee said.

His tone carried a warning, but Ewell was flustered and said, "I wasn't talking about a retreat. . . ."

"We cannot leave this field. Grant and Meade must abandon it. We dare not permit them a supposition of victory."

"No . . . no, sir," Ewell responded. "I see that. I was talking through my hat."

Lee turned his gaze on each of the division commanders, then shifted it back to Ewell. "Is there nothing to be done here, General? Nothing?"

A brave but calculating man, Early leaned forward. He reached the edge of speech, then paused.

"General Early?" Lee said. "Have you something to offer us?"

Early looked at Ewell, then back to Lee.

"Gordon's been pestering me all day. Insisting Sedgwick's flank is hanging out, that the Yankees left it dangling. I told him Burnside's corps was out there, but—"

"General Burnside has been engaged elsewhere," Lee said sharply. Warning himself against a display of temper. "He is not on this flank."

"Yes, sir, true enough. But Gordon was just too big for his boots this morning, talking all sorts of nonsense—he can be an impetuous man, General—and we didn't know where Burnside was for certain. All I had was word from your own staff, and your people had Burnside on the Germanna Road. Later on . . ." Early waved a hand, shooing a fly. "Well, I figured Gordon was talking hogswallow by then. The Yankees must've tucked their flank in proper and fixed things up. Even if Gordon was right first off, they wouldn't have left it like that."

"Find out," Lee said.

Seven p.m.

The sun rushed to meet the horizon; minutes had grown more valuable than gold. At last, Gordon had the order to attack. All day, he had been as Tantalus, yearning for grapes of victory but a short grasp away. Then, cruelly late, Early galloped up, impatient for Gordon to do what he had begged to do since morning.

To add weight to the charge, his superior gave him Johnston's Brigade as well. Early even said Pegram's Brigade might follow, *if* Gordon delivered success. The division commander's tone was urgent and peevish, suggesting a story waiting to be told. Gordon ignored the rudeness and leapt to his task.

He ordered his own men to leave behind anything that might rattle or creak and give them away as they approached the Yankees. Johnston's Brigade would be a help, but it was a hindrance, too. Bob Johnston turned thickheaded when Gordon explained his plan. More time was consumed as Johnston passed his own instructions to his subordinate officers. One frustration had piled atop another as the bright evening softened toward dusk.

There was no time for rousing speeches or even a flourish of prayer.

But they were ready at last, three thousand men sneaking through the woodlands, Johnston on the left and ordered to drive into the Union rear. Gordon's own men would strike the Yankee flank directly and roll it up. And if Early did send in Pegram's Brigade, much could still be accomplished.

Gordon's vision of a complete rout had faded, though. The attack should have been made by two divisions in the morning, not two brigades at nightfall. Despite that, he refused to be pessimistic. He had gotten his chance, how-

ever flawed, and he meant to make the most of it. He re
mained confident that he and his men could deliver a blow
their opponents would never forget.

It seemed impossible—downright amazing—that the
Yankees hadn't detected their advance. The light had weakened, further limiting vision through the woodlands, but
strive for quiet as they might, thousands of men made a
certain amount of noise. And Gordon and a number of
other officers rode their horses, contributing snorts and
whinnies.

Still the men in blue suspected nothing, derelict even in
the duty of posting pickets at a proper distance. The gray
brigades covered the final stretch, the last fateful yards
where they might have been challenged.

Gordon saw Yankees cooking their supper, carefree as
if having a race-day picnic.

He looked down the shadowed ranks of his men, all of
them champing like thoroughbreds, and glanced through
the mesh of treetops to the heavens: There was no time to
waste on straightening lines or etiquette.

He drew his sword.

"Georgia! Charge!"

His men swept forward with a wild yell, flying from the
undergrowth like demons. Gordon rode among them, calling encouragement, sword flashing back the light of cooking fires. At first, the Yankees did nothing, utterly stunned.
By the time the first bluecoats leapt to their feet or lunged
for their rifles, Gordon's men were already behind their
worthless entrenchments, firing point-blank at men fool
enough to resist and grabbing dumbfounded prisoners by
their blouses.

"Push on! Drive on!" Gordon shouted. The dusk was already deepening into the gloaming that heralded night. If
only . . . if only the order had come at breakfast, not supper. . . .

The enthusiasm and delight of his men made his heart swell. The advance was nearly bloodless. The soldiers simply trotted along, collecting befuddled Yankees and telling them, "Walk on back thataway, Billy Yank, you git along now." And the prisoners obeyed.

Other Federals just ran. The better-handled Yankee units struggled to get up a defense, but had no time. Regiment after regiment collapsed, as Gordon had promised all day.

He couldn't see as far as Johnston's men and could only hope their success had been as great. Certainly, there was no sign of firm resistance.

Looting was a temptation: The boys had little enough to adorn their lives. Yet, all but a few kept chasing the Yankee hares.

The light was dying.

" 'Dying, Egypt, dying . . . ,' " Gordon recited.

"We got us a general! We got us a general here!" a pack of soldiers cried.

Captive generals were always welcome, but the attack's very success was breaking up what remained of Gordon's ranks. He ordered Clem Evans of the 31st Georgia to get his boys back into a semblance of order. Clem saluted, but Gordon was not sure how much could be done. He rode along his advancing, dissolving regiments, telling the men to rally to their flags.

There was more fighting now. They had gone a good half mile, he estimated, and some of the Yankees had started to figure things out. It grew dark enough for muzzle flashes to capture the eye and blot a man's vision. Shadows wrestled in front of cooking fires, and a human torch ran off into the night.

"Tom," he told the commander of the 60th Georgia, "keep 'em in what order you can, but don't stop pushing. Make this a night the Yankees will never forget."

"I believe we already have, sir."

Herds of Yankee prisoners passed to the rear like sheep, with hardly a guard in evidence. There had to be hundreds of them.

A lieutenant approached Gordon, calling for his attention. "We got us *two* Yankee generals, sir. One's Shaler. And somebody else."

Shaler commanded a brigade, Gordon believed. Or *had* commanded one.

"Fine, son, that's fine. You get on back to your men now."

Ahead: Ripples of fire announced a Union line standing its ground. His own men howled and, amid the confident, angry, exuberant shrieks, Gordon heard the bull call of Private Spivey.

What, besides a glorious love, filled the heart as fully as triumph in war? Homer knew, he *knew*. . . .

That afternoon, of all times, a letter from a creditor back in Georgia had caught up with him, threatening to sue over promises broken, all to do with the family mining concern. Well, let the man try to drag him into court. No one was going to fare well against a hero.

He wished Fanny could see him.

"You're driving them, boys," he called, waving his saber again. "You just keep on, don't let 'em form up."

But as the night robbed his ranks of their last coherence, the Yankees did form up. His men moved in packs now, like wolves. Martial order was a bygone thing.

Unexpectedly—and unhappily—he heard a great commotion on his right flank, heavy firing where none should have been. He spurred his horse through the wreckage of Yankee encampments to see to the matter.

Clem Evans met him.

"Christ almighty, the damned fools have been firing into our flank."

"Who?"

"Our own men. Back in our lines. Nobody told 'em about

our attack, I guess." He caught Gordon's bridle. "Eddie's seeing to it, don't get yourself shot. We're a damned mess, anyway. Can't tell our men from the Yankees, for all the smoke and the dark."

Yes. Darkness. What did Milton speak of? "Darkness visible."

Up ahead, the fighting had grown fierce, with volley fire resounding. And that would not be coming from his men. His boys were still screaming to wake the dead, though, never ones to lack spirit.

Darkness visible. Hail, brazen arms of Chaos!

Heart sinking, Gordon realized there was little more he could do.

Early and Ewell had both acted like damned fools. Had he only been allowed to strike sooner, even by an hour . . .

He had hurt the Yankees severely. He attempted to console himself with that. But a brace of shattered brigades was not the destruction of a corps or an army.

Gordon refused to give up hope. His brigade had done all it could, but he might ride back and persuade Pegram's men to make one more attack, to see if they couldn't tip the Yankees end over end, after all.

If Jack Pegram hadn't been wounded in the earlier fighting, he would have agreed to extend the attack at once.

If, if, if . . .

At the edge of his advance, the firing declined. When he heard Union troops hurrahing, it struck like a fist.

Searching for Pegram's men, he encountered two soldiers who'd called it quits after fighting for nearly a mile. They were picking through abandoned Yankee treasures. When they spotted Gordon, they ceased rifling knapsacks and stood up straight, caught out.

By the light of an abandoned campfire, their faces shone with perspiration and powder. They were of the sharecropper class, earnest and lean; Gordon knew them by sight.

Their expressions were doubtful now, expecting chastisement. They were men who had done what could be done and knew, perhaps better than he or the other generals, what could not be done.

As he reached the firelight himself, astonishment froze the expressions of the two soldiers.

Gordon realized his face was covered with tears.

Eight p.m.
Headquarters, Army of the Potomac

As the lieutenant colonel ranted on, Meade folded his arms and tucked in his chin.

"You've got to flee," the man pleaded. "The Sixth Corps is all broken, the Rebs are in behind us. All the generals have been captured, Shaler, Neill, Sedgwick . . ." Eyes burning fever-bright, he seemed about to grasp Meade by the coat and drag him away.

"Nonsense," Meade said. "General Sedgwick was just here."

The lieutenant colonel, a Sixth Corps man named Kent, paid no attention and raved on: "It's a total collapse . . . you must save General Grant. . . ."

The noise of battle to the north was already fading. Meade spoke calmly, if cynically: "And those brigades Sedgwick told me he could spare? Are they doing nothing? How about Upton?"

"I don't know, sir."

"So . . . I may expect no more fighting from the Sixth Corps in this campaign?"

"I . . . I fear not, sir."

"Kent, you're an ass," Meade said, and turned away.

Under the fly of the headquarters tent, Humphreys was at his duties as chief of staff, invigorated by the urgency of the moment, but no more flustered than Meade. He looked up at his superior's approach.

"Well?" Meade asked.

"Neill's solid. Sedgwick's moving up more men. Upton led a couple of regiments into the fight on his own initiative."

"That'll be it for the night, then. Lee couldn't sustain an attack in the darkness, they've done what damage they could." He paused, then added, "What do you make of it all, Humph?"

"When they didn't attack all along the front, I stopped worrying. Not that we haven't had a blow."

"Who got hit? Which brigades?"

The chief of staff shrugged. "If the dispositions I have are accurate, Shaler and Seymour got the worst of it."

Meade smiled wryly, casting a glance toward the cacophony to the rear of the headquarters, in the forest and on the roads. "*That's* the worst of it. Teamsters, hostlers, quartermasters . . . they panic at a sneeze."

Humphreys let a ghost of mirth cross his face. "Shitting bricks. Like Gettysburg."

Yes, like Gettysburg. When the rear echelon had collapsed in a fit of terror while the men behind the wall and the fence stood their ground and shattered the enemy.

"Tell Patrick I want him to get all that sorted out. Quickly."

"He's already at it, sir."

"And let Sedgwick know that I never want to see that man Kent at this headquarters again."

Humphreys almost forgot himself and grinned. "If *any* of us ever see Kent again. . . ."

Meade had been careful from the first to show no sign of alarm, and the men of the staff, at least, had patterned themselves on his comportment.

"Teddy," he called to Lieutenant Colonel Lyman, a fellow whose discretion Meade trusted completely. "Go down there and let Grant know how things stand. Tell the general in chief I'll join him shortly."

"I'm surprised Rawlins isn't up here tearing into us by now," Humphreys said in a voice intended only for Meade's ears.

"I'd better go down and see him. Grant, I mean. He's been all right." Meade thought for a moment, then said, "You and I may not agree with all of his decisions—"

"That's putting it mildly. He fought this army piecemeal."

"*We* fought it piecemeal. Following his orders."

"We threw men away."

"Humph, listen to me. I know you're angry about how things have been handled. And Kent or no Kent, we've just had a bit of a scare. But credit Grant with one thing: He accepts responsibility for his actions. The man hasn't tried to cast blame when things disappointed him." Meade thought again of Grant's whittling and his silence. "I'd say he takes setbacks with remarkable aplomb. I rather wish I had his even temper, I'd be better off."

Humphreys grunted. "Grant may sit there like a wooden Indian, but I'll bet he's been jumping every which way inside. And I wouldn't trust Rawlins or Washburne for an instant."

In the background, the shooting had died down to occasional pocks, but the self-inflicted uproar in the army's rear continued to make an appalling noise: crashing wagons, braying beasts, and the wails of terrified men. The provost marshal had his work cut out for him.

"They're Grant's men," Meade said. "Naturally, their loyalty goes to him, not us."

Humphreys gave an ungentlemanly snort. "Washburne's

loyal to Washburne. George, the man's a politician, for Heaven's sake. Haven't you had enough of that sort of creature?"

"He's Grant's man."

"That's not the way he sees it. He thinks Grant's *his* man." Humphreys smirked. "Watch Grant's face. From a distance. When Washburne starts wagging his finger."

"Speaking of Grant . . ." Tired or not, he had to relate the latest developments to the general in chief, who had remained down in the hollow where his tent had been moved in the hopeless hope of quiet.

On his way down the path, Meade passed Lyman coming back.

"How is he?" Meade asked quietly.

"Odd, sir. He's been so calm the past two days. But he strikes me as somewhat agitated tonight. I believe this last fuss got to him."

"About-face, Lyman. Come along. I may want another set of eyes and ears."

Stepping off again, Meade guided on the campfire ahead. The racket out on the road truly was a disgrace, the sound of fear.

As Meade emerged from the darkness, Rawlins and Washburne had been taking leave of Grant. They decided to stay.

Meade was about to report that Uncle John Sedgwick had things under control when a major Meade didn't recognize crashed through the brush toward them.

"Great God!" the man cried, spotting Grant. "General, you must retire!" Out of breath, the major wheezed. "I know Lee's methods, he's going to throw his army between us and the Rapidan, he'll cut us off from our communications—"

Shocking everyone, Grant exploded. Tearing the cigar from his mouth, he said, "You shut up, damn you." He stamped the earth, a stubborn, outraged child. "I'm heartily tired of hearing what Lee's going to do." His eyes were cold no more, but blazed with fury. "Some of you seem to think Lee's suddenly going to turn a double somersault and land in our rear and on both flanks at the same time." He stepped toward the major. "*You, sir!* Go back to your command. And try to think what we're going to do ourselves, instead of about what Lee's going to do."

Chambers emptied, Grant went quiet. Unable to raise his eyes from the fire now. No one dared speak.

The major disappeared.

When Grant shut himself in his tent, Washburne led Rawlins aside for as much privacy as the circumstances allowed.

"Is he all right?" the congressman asked.

"I think so." Rawlins considered how much else to say. "It's all been a shock of a kind. You heard what he said earlier. This isn't like fighting Joe Johnston."

Washburne gripped the brigadier's forearm. "Don't let anyone give him liquor."

"You don't have to worry. Not about that. Not yet. He's been on his best behavior. And Bill would let me know if he saw trouble coming."

"I don't trust that darkey."

Rawlins laughed, coughed. "You don't trust anybody, El. You've become a Washington man."

"Strikes me there's more politicking right here in this army."

"It's no worse than out west."

The woods and roads had calmed to the common sounds of an army's rear.

"Listen to me, John," Washburne said. "I'm not sure how much longer I'll be staying with the army. Battles have to be fought in the capital, too."

Rawlins smiled. "Spooked?"

"You know better."

"Well?"

The congressman took a deep breath that was almost a piece of rhetoric in itself. As if he were about to address the House. But his voice, when it emerged, was hushed.

"About those murdered U.S. Colored Troops? That report?"

"Ferrero's men."

"You need to quash it. Knock heads, if you have to. Work through Humphreys, he's got more political savvy than George Meade."

"Word may already have gotten out."

"No. It hasn't. I sounded out Cadwallader. If he hasn't heard anything, the other newspapermen haven't."

"Hard to keep the cold-blooded execution of two dozen prisoners quiet. Whatever the color of their skin," Rawlins said. "Still, it's hardly Fort Pillow."

"It's bad enough. Listen to me. Grant has enough problems piling up in front of him. We can't afford to have Greeley and every holier-than-thou abolitionist from here to Bangor screaming for vengeance and making things worse for Lincoln. And our mutual friend."

"Ugly business, El."

Washburne swept a darker-than-the-darkness arm toward the battlefield. "Compared to this? There are thousands of *white* men dead out there. And there'll be more to come, that's clear enough. Tell me exactly how much a few dozen darkies weigh in those scales?"

"All right," Rawlins said. "I'll do what I can." He imagined the bodies of the captive Negroes in blue uniforms, lined up and shot by Confederate cavalrymen. It bothered him, and he was hardly a firebrand. But Washburne was right: They didn't need pressure from stay-at-homes to make the war less merciful than it was.

He came back from the dead men: "What else?"

"Meade."

"What about him?"

"Is he right?"

"About what?"

"That this isn't working. That the army has to fight Lee on better ground."

"Of course he's right. These damned woods. This isn't war, it's two mobs pounding each other bloody."

"Sam can be stubborn. Once he starts in at something."

"No, I think he sees it."

"He won't want to go at Lee again tomorrow?"

"He may feel their lines, see if there's any weakness. But, like I said, it's been a shock to all of us, him included. Johnston would've collapsed after two days of this. If he lasted two days. This is a new kind of war, takes some figuring out."

"In the meantime, we've got to look out for him. As regards Meade now . . . what would your response be if you heard someone . . . say, one of those newspaper people . . . suggest that Meade just wanted to retreat? And Grant had to overrule him? To put fight in this army?"

"I'd say he's a damned liar."

"Would you? Think about it."

"For Christ's sake, El. Meade *wants* to fight. He just doesn't like throwing men away." He put his hands on his hips and stretched his back. "Nor do I, for that matter."

"You're not in question. Meade is. Listen to me, John. The people back home . . . the voters . . . have high expectations of our friend. *Very* high expectations. At least half of them think he should be in Richmond before next week is out." Washburne rubbed pale hands together, as if he needed to warm them. "Do *you* think we're going to be in Richmond before next week is out?"

"No."

"And the casualty lists. When the newspapers publish

the casualty lists from this . . . this bloodbath . . . and then the lists from whatever comes after . . . there are going to be questions."

"There always are. That's natural."

"And it's also natural enough to want someone to blame, if things go wrong. Would you prefer the people blame Grant or Meade?"

"El, you can be a real bastard."

"And so can you. I've seen you, time and again. The way you've torn into Meade in public. You've got people thinking you're the devil incarnate."

"I'm just trying to keep them in harness. They all need to know who's boss, including Meade. But to be fair, he's done everything Grant's asked."

"So does a well-trained dog. Meade's inconsequential. Compared to what you and I could make of Sam. What we *have* made of him." Washburne grinned, teeth pale in the darkness. "As for being a bastard, I'm unashamed. I haven't managed to stay in Congress by ladling out porridge for orphans. And I look at you, John, as the brother I inexplicably failed to have, a fellow bastard." He patted Rawlins' upper arm. "Between the two of us, we're going to put Grant in the president's house four years from now. But not if the public blames him . . . should matters with this army go awry. George Meade may be useful in more ways than one."

"Meade's a man of honor."

"They're the easiest to ruin."

Rawlins shook his head in the darkness. "I'm not sure I could do that."

"Oh, you could. You can. And you will, if need be. Fair chance, though, that we won't have to ruin the man, just take him down a peg. Hear me out. I'm not asking you to *do* anything. Nor have I undertaken anything. Not yet. Perhaps such a necessity won't arise and Meade can prance home to Philadelphia on his charger, hail the conquering hero! What I propose is merely that . . . if one day you should be asked to confirm that Meade proposed to retreat, while Grant insisted on defeating Robert E. Lee . . . all I ask is that you say nothing at all. Be enigmatic, you can do that. Let whoever might raise such a wicked query infer what they will from your considered silence." He chuckled, inviting Rawlins to join in and be friends, as always. "After all, what's one man's reputation against the preservation of our Union? Or the presidency?"

Yes. What *was* one man worth? What, after all, did any of them matter? No more than those dead darkies by the roadside. . . .

"You really believe . . . ," Rawlins said, fighting down a cough, "you're *that* confident about Grant being elected president?"

"If you keep him off the whiskey. And let me handle the newspapers."

"I told you. There's been none of that. He hasn't gone on one of his binges in months."

"Then I only have to worry about the newspapers." Washburne chuckled. "And now I think I'll find myself another cup of that government-purchased coffee. I fear I may have to investigate the purveyors. Say hello to Mrs. Rawlins, when you write."

And Washburne was off.

Rawlins was tired. The smoke clogged his lungs fearfully. He made his way back toward his sleeping tent, erected in line with Grant's, but not too near. By the campfire, he picked up a glowing splinter to light his candle. Bill, Grant's grizzled Nubian, watched him from a stump.

After yanking off his boots, he took a long swig of water, coughed his throat clear, and bent to the battered trunk that held his belongings. He drew out a small wooden box containing an object wrapped in black velvet. With great delicacy, he unfolded the cloth. And he stared at the oval image in the gleaming silver frame.

It was a photographer's rendering of his first wife.

Grant wept.

He had given orders to his manservant that he was not to be disturbed by anyone. Then he had dropped the flap of his tent and thrown himself onto his cot. He had wept more than once in his life. The years had not handled him gently. But he did not recall weeping with such abandon since the night after handing his letter of resignation to his commanding officer out in the Territories. The alternative had been a court-martial.

He was paying for his pride now, for his brash abundance of confidence. He might find a thousand faults with the Army of the Potomac, picking at one officer for this and another for that, had he a mind to. But the truth was that he had underestimated Lee. The result had been slovenly butchery out in those woods.

And there would be more butchery to come, he saw that now. He still hoped to break Lee and his army by the summer. But he recognized that the cost would be higher, the effort required greater, and the risks more daunting than he and the men he trusted most had believed.

He assumed that Lee was reveling in his embarrassment, gloating about fighting him to a standstill in their first match. Nothing Grant had done, no order Meade had issued at his behest, had moved Lee. At least, not for long. The man's skill and resilience were unsettling.

His weeping slowed, leaving the bedclothes beneath his face as sodden as a consumptive's. He *would* defeat Lee. It would just take a bit longer. And it would be bloodier. And so be it. If he had to bleed the South to death, he would.

He yearned for a smashing victory over the man once idolized by the old Army in which he had failed. Whatever sorrow he felt over the men who lay dead or maimed, he knew he would pay the price it took to win. That was what soldiers did. He would destroy Lee for the sake of President Lincoln and the Union, and for himself. Whatever it took, he would break the Virginia grandee like the head of a china doll bashed on a stone.

He was done fighting here, though, in this hopeless place.

Grant wept a little longer, easing toward sleep. But before he drifted off, he made his decision: Come morning, he would order Meade to ready the army to march.

South.

PART III

A NEW KIND OF WAR

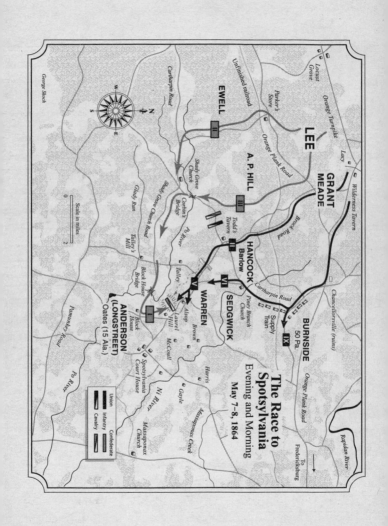

George Stock

Carthapin Road

Locust Grove

Unfinished railroad

Parker's Store

Orange Turnpike

EWELL
II

LEE

A. P. HILL

Orange Plank Road

Lacy

GRANT
MEADE

Wilderness Tavern

Shady Grove Church

Shady Grove Church Road

Corbin's Bridge

Po River

III

Todd's Tavern

Brock Road

HANCOCK
Barlow

Glady Run

Talley's Mill

Block House Bridge

Talley

WARREN

VI

Piney Branch Church

Carthapin Road

Chancellorsville (ruins)

Supply Train

BURNSIDE
IX
50 Pa.

SEDGWICK

Block House

ANDERSON
(LONGSTREET)
Oates (15 Ala.)

Laurel
Brown

McCoull

Alsop

Pomunkey Road

Harris

Spotsylvania Court House

Gayle

Ni River

Massaponax Church

Massaponax Creek

Po River

Orange Plank Road

To Fredericksburg

Rapidan River

The Race to Spotsylvania
Evening and Morning
May 7–8, 1864

Scale in miles
0   2

Union
Confederate

Infantry
Cavalry

THIRTEEN

May 8, nine thirty a.m.
Shady Grove Church Road

Young gals in their Sunday best, sweet as wild honey, went their way afoot against the flow of trudging men. Demure, laced tight, and bonneted, the quality sort made their way along in bright-eyed detachments of sisters, followed by old men poking canes in the dust and joyless matrons with handkerchiefs pressed to their mouths. All buggy horses had long since been requisitioned for the army, so the middling sort and better of the succulents were as sweat-stained as the poor whites, heading to church, or maybe home from it, on the hottest day yet of the year, stepping as handsomely as they could through the dust of an army. Their fashions had not been renewed, Oates had the eye to tell that of a woman, but the only purpose of a skirt, after all, was to be lifted waist-high by a bold man. He would have liked to draw one black-haired creature, especially, up behind his saddle and ride off.

His men were respectful, admirably so, with the girls who looked properly raised, but when they came upon a chippy or two, they called out a range of greetings, most of them amiable. They were a weary, ragged bunch, his men. He still had the 48th Alabama under him, in addition to his 15th, but together they didn't make one proper regiment. Their march had begun deep in the night, with but one stop for cold rations, and men who had not slept three hours in three days, men who had fought bitterly, plodded along as gamely as they could, first through the puke-up death-stink of the battlefield, then, startlingly, bewilderingly, through green and peaceful country where, despite the tattle and rattle of distant musketry, these ribbon-waisted Baptists and Presbyterians, equal before God in their virginity, intact or feigned, were all close to equal in beauty when judged by sunken-eyed men got up in the blackface of powder, men with dust glued to their flesh by sweat, foul and fouler, but awakened to high delight at the sight of bounty made flesh in a young gal's form. A smile from one such slaked a thirst no water would ever vanquish.

Oates was never too worn to regard a woman. And that black-haired gal, perhaps not the best in virtue, nor perfect in her complexion—indeed, almost with the look of a French-talking slut come in from the bayous to a New Orleans house—that woman-gal's imagined scent stayed with him as he rode another mile, his morning enriched by a dream of supple flesh. He let his fantasy roam, returning from the war to find her willing.

But if he burst to life at the sight of those perspiring angels, and if they made the men straighten their backs and step smartly, it was funny and crying sad at once to watch the lasses and their watchful families struggle to mask their shock at what *they* saw. And what they smelled. An army of black-mouthed ragamuffins stumbled along, not only trailing a shithole stink, but sending it out to precede them. The noble young ladies sought to bear up, committed to taking pride in their brave army, resolutely declining to bring *their* handkerchiefs—this one adorned with violets, the next embroidered with roses—anywhere near their nostrils, unwilling to shame the men marching along, but, oh, their eyes, their eyes betrayed them, appalled eyes, eyes that said, *But this . . . surely these men . . . the novels never . . .* , and, scrapping along behind, the little boys who once would have saluted and emulated their marching now pinched their nostrils shut and made idiot faces. The old men were angry and wet-eyed.

"Unfurl the flags," Oates called back over his saddle.

The rags for which men die. Let them take note: We are still proud. But, oh, he wished to kiss that raven-haired missy's lips, to press his mouth to hers and then do more.

Men collapsed by the roadside, ruined by the heat and the hour still short of noon. But he knew his men, they'd come along when they could. Those who remained in the ranks would remain to the end, or until killed or shredded unto uselessness. Oates smirked. Except for Lowther, of course. His major had convinced a surgeon to dispatch him to Richmond for medical treatment for a wound that was no more than a bruise to his foot. Well, good riddance. Lowther wasn't worth a damn, present or gone off larking. The man had pull, though, at home in Alabama and in Richmond. Oates couldn't quite figure it, but for all his sick leaves and even one murky letter of resignation, Lowther kept reappearing when things were easy, then disappeared again when a scrap got going. And for all that, Evander Law himself, the best of men, had ordered Oates not to chastise the major or put him on report.

Christ, it was hot.

At least they had pride of place this morning at the head of the division. The dust was wicked enough at the front of the column, pity the sorry devils who marched in the rear.

The churchgoers thinned, then disappeared, gone to their prayers and hymn singing, but no bells marked the hour or called the faithful, all their pealing sacrificed on the altar of Tredegar, melted down for cannon, and his mother, boiled in belief, able to bear the loss of a beloved son because she knew she would see him again eternally, young John, sweet John, his mother who could barely write had scratched out a letter mourning the loss of the slap-tin bell from the ramshackle church past Oates's Corners half a mile, the only complaint she had made through all the war, aching to hear that most unmusical bell on a Sunday morning, her Gideon's trumpet, or, perhaps, the voice of Jesus metaled over . . . how could she believe, how could those fine, sweat-bothered, unknowing, good people off to church or chapel, how could they believe, Oates wanted to know, in a merciful God after three mad years of this? He liked to fight, didn't mind killing, but, damnation and worse, there was nothing godly he could see in this war. Sometimes it delighted him, exciting his blood as powerfully as any woman had done, more powerfully even, but he could not reconcile sermons with the slaughter. Mixing war and religion struck him as the blasphemy of blasphemies, redolent of unforgivable sin even to one who did not believe a whit. His mother's faith, once bearable from a distance, now seemed naught but the frothing of a rabid bitch in Helldirt. *He could not believe.* And he would not believe. Once, he had wished he might find faith, but now he had no interest in a parson's tales. Better a kiss from that black-haired gal, one kiss, than eternity on a cloud where neither fist nor cock was of use to a man. When he killed men, he killed them, and he didn't need a Bible verse to excuse it.

And yet, he knelt when his men knelt. Not out of respect for God, but out of care for those who fought beside him.

All the grand and eloquent speeches, all the books and pamphlets extolling the nobility of their cause—of any cause—even the scrawls and scribbles he had committed on the newspaper side of his lawyering, all of it had less value than a turd, which might at least fertilize a few inches of furrow. They weren't fighting for their rights. They were fighting because they damned well had wanted to fight, because it had just come time to fight, and fighting had seemed like a mighty fine idea.

Now this, they had come to this: filthy men whose odor made young girls ill. And those men were the fortunate ones.

Yet, he would fight until he could fight no longer. Because that was what he was formed for, from sacred clay or bloody jissom, no matter. He would fight. But he would not beautify blood-glutton deeds with lies.

Gunfire. Lots of it. Cannon, too. To the left, a mile or so off, almost behind the marching columns now. For hours, quick, hot fights had pecked the morning, always to the left, but first ahead, then alongside the marching column, and now, queerly, behind the bent shoulders of the marching men. An accident of how the roads bent? Oates wondered. He had no map, no familiarity with this stretch of Virginia, with its deep-down creeks that weren't quite rivers and fields that looked plowed by womenfolk, even the earth grown war-weary. All he had was the name of a more-or-less destination: Spotsylvania Court House.

And more gunfire. A serious to-do. He could feel his men quicken behind him, their pace the same until commanded otherwise, but blood coursing through them, eyes opened all the way.

A rider came back from Colonel Perry's party, which had gone on ahead. The courier hardly got his yap open before the colonel himself galloped back to Oates.

"Hard doings yonder," he said. "Stuart's been delaying the varmints all morning. Kershaw's up with him now, holding a ridge north of town, but Yank cavalry are pawing around the courthouse. Behind our boys."

Oates waited for the orders that must follow.

"You take your men," Perry continued, "and go fast. There's a lane to the left a quarter mile on. Get up it as fast as you can and go in where Stuart wants you. I'm going to pay off those blue-bellies at the courthouse."

Why, surely, Oates thought. We'll run us a happy old footrace. Fresh and full of spunk, every last one of us. . . .

But that was just the surly side of his nature, an amusement even to himself, so he saluted and turned a hot face to his nearest officers and the skeletal regiments trailing them.

"That there firing," he hollered. "Yankees are overstepping again. Boys up there need help." He gathered his breath. "At the double-quick . . . *forward!*"

Wondering how many men he'd lose to this Hell-heat before they fired a shot, this infernal, wet, worse-than-Pike-County heat, for his men were tired beyond biblical measure, beyond four score and ten years' worth of weariness.

They hadn't a cheer in them, not yet, not without Yankees plain to their front, but the men growled through mouths full of dust and picked up to a dogtrot, and Oates knew just how much he was asking of them, their canteens doubtless empty or nigh on it, so he steered his horse to the roadside and waved up his nigger, who shambled along as if born for the heat, blood of ape ancestors cooked by the African sun, and Oates dismounted and said, "You take care of this horse now. Lose him, boy, and I'll whip you from here to Montgomery."

"Ain't never us lost no horse, Marse."

But Oates had already turned, pain-bitten by his bad-dog hip, one of the wounds that had shocked him with the knowledge that he was not invulnerable and might not be immortal upon this earth, and that hip hurt infernally, but he marched on afoot, beside his men, every step a small misery and a pride.

"Colonel, you ought to ride that nag of your'n, that's what he's for," a soldier called. "Leastwise, till the ruckus comes on."

"Horse needs a rest, I don't."

He waved to Captain Shaaf, who had not possessed a horse of his own for months. The commander of Company A stepped up and strode next to him.

"We get to that lane where those limbers sit, and we're going left and on in. Be ready to move your company out as skirmishers, once we get our bearings."

"Would've been right disappointed, had you asked somebody else, sir," the captain told him.

"See how you feel come nightfall."

No sooner had they turned into the lane than they found themselves amid the castoffs of battle, stray wagons, emptied caissons, cavalry mounts husbanded from danger, and officers on horseback humming back and forth like bees 'round a hive, all these things set upon a field bright with wildflowers.

Pretty as a lady, if a bearded one, General Stuart cantered up. He wore a barn-dance grin and waved his hat. A black plume lofted.

"Colonel Oates, if I do not misapprehend?"

Oates stopped. Feeling his hip grind. Saluting after his fashion.

"In the nick of time," Stuart said, "indeed, in the nick of time, Colonel." He pointed into the rising smoke. "That grove of trees, on the left. Yankees mean to flank us. I'd take it as a courtesy if you'd deny them the opportunity."

Oates nodded. Stuart smiled again, turned his horse, and rode back to his merriment.

"Captain Shaaf!" Oates shouted, taking up his trot again. "Skirmishers forward. Get in those trees up there."

Shaaf waved an acknowledgment and hurried his men forward. Weary, stumbling, willing men, men whose rifles had grown to be part of their flesh.

Litter bearers and cowards helped off casualties, some of them men in cut-short cavalry jackets, bloodied now. Oates recalled the old quip, "Who ever saw a dead cavalryman?"

Up ahead, along a gentle ridge, a few guns in battery supported a busy gray line. The Yankees were out of view, down the far slope. Amid carnage, Stuart pranced. As if no bullet dared touch him and spoil his uniform.

"Fifteenth, by battalion, to my right!" Oates shouted, and heard the order echoed. "Forty-eighth, left and forward!"

His hip hurt like plain Hell.

Sword nothing but a bother, he let the blade rest and drew his pistol as they approached the grove. On the right, men shouted as cannon tore holes in the morning. Just before his soldiers reached the trees, he caught a glimpse—one glimpse—down the far slope of the not-much-to-it ridge. It looked as though the whole Union army were gathering.

Shots. One, two. A dozen. Dozens. Straight ahead. Shaaf and his men. Yanks had come a good way in. But not far enough.

"Skirmishers! Recover!" Oates shouted. Determined to be heard. He turned his back to the enemy and, just at the edge of the woodland, slowed his men, letting them firm up their ranks. The moment he wheeled about to face his enemies again, he saw blue forms hasten up between wide-set trees.

"Halt!" he shouted. "Fire by battalion." And he let the captains and lieutenants who led his shrunken companies do their work. Ripples of flame and the clap of fires stopped the Yankees short.

"Bayonets!" Oates barked. He wanted the Yankees to hear him, as well as his own men. When the bayonets came out, the side that was weaker of will tended to give way before any steel met flesh.

The scrape of the long blades fixing to muzzles called to mind his father grinding a knife to butcher a hog. That sound it was, multiplied by many hundreds.

"Charge!"

Now his men cheered. The Alabama banshee call sharpened the edges of the Rebel yell, and down the broken ground they ran, weapons leveled at their waists or held across their chests, exhausted men kept upright and moving by war's fury alone. The grove was a cleaner, better place than the ground over which they had fought two days before: They could see their opponents clearly, as they themselves could be seen. It only increased their appetite for slaughter.

The Yankees fired a volley, flame-spit and smoke. Oates saw Jep Brown, a fine soldier, clutch his breast.

"Kill the sonsofbitches!" Oates howled. "Give 'em the bayonet."

That was the playacting part of leading men, the threat of the bayonet more potent to an enemy than the glinting reality. The brief bayonet duels in the Wilderness had been shocking, and Oates knew men well enough to believe that no one wished to repeat those contests. A soldier might stand and fire into an enemy's belly from three feet away and feel just fine, but ramming home the steel took a special hardness.

Sure enough, the Yankees drew back, the better men loading and firing as they went. The blue-bellies transited a ravine and crossed a ridge spur deeper into the trees. Oates' men followed, the ranks breaking down into clusters of soldiers pausing to fire, then pushing on. Men fell on both sides, but the Yankees, despite what looked to Oates like greater numbers, kept pulling back. They moved like damaged creatures.

For one instant that could not and would not last, Oates felt a flash of sympathy, sensing that those men he meant to kill or wound might have marched even harder than his own boys. He glimpsed their flesh-and-bloodness.

Then they were just his enemies again.

Billy Strickland came up. "I think we hit the flank of their attack, sir. There's nothing out on the left."

"Maybe not now, but you watch that flank for me, Billy. I don't need any surprises."

When they had driven the Yankees a good two hundred yards, the trees thinned and the companies on Oates' right pushed beyond the grove. He dashed over to see what they were up against and got his first full view of the contested slope. The ground out there was speckled with dead and twitching Yankees, some in red Zouave drawers, while ragged formations struggled up the hill toward Stuart's line. It looked like a fool-crazy, piecemeal attack, the sort for which a general ought to be horsewhipped.

"Sumbitch," Oates said. He'd spotted Yankee reinforcements headed his way and realized that he and his men were far ahead of and fully detached from the Confederate line. He cursed his taste for brawling, his raw, joyous enthusiasm for a fight, most any fight, telling himself yet again to behave like the commanding officer of two regiments, not an idiot captain out to get himself mentioned in the newspapers.

The Federals coming on looked tight and determined, a good regiment adding weight to the nothing-much brigade his men had driven.

"Order your lines!" Oates shouted, running back toward his other flank. "Officers, get your men back in line!" He wanted them under control when the Yankees reached them. "Hold where you are. Halt and hold your ground, align right and hold your ground. . . ."

The Yankees came on fiercely, their formation compact and aimed right at the juncture of his two regiments. Oates knew his boys wouldn't hold.

Had to give the Yankees a blooding, though.

Instead of shouting, he hurried along the rear of his roughed-out line, with bullets punching the trees around his head. He told each company commander he meant to give the Yankees two volleys, then pull back to the ridge spur they'd crossed and hold there.

But the Yankees came on faster and harder than he had anticipated. Before he could organize a crisp withdrawal, the Federals were at them. Not with the bayonet, but willing to trade volleys at rock-throwing distance. And the blue-bellies Oates had embarrassed were rallying now.

Soon, the men were fighting from tree to tree. His boys were better shots, but they were worn out, even the juice of battle quitting on them. But the Yankees were tired, too, sure enough. Heat-sick, exhausted men stood and killed each other.

The Yankee numbers told with time. The plan to withdraw in good order had collapsed, yet the spur became a magnet for his men, a natural place to stop running, and his lines coalesced again on their own, the companies intermingled but every man a veteran who knew what to do and did it. And the Yankees had figured out that they weren't up against a few Chimborazo nurses. They kept a bit more distance now as the two sides exchanged another round of volleys.

The mad hurrahs of another charge, the affair of other men, sounded off to the right, rising from the open fields that sloped up into the muzzles of Stuart's artillery and Kershaw's lean brigades. Heavier guns had joined the line, their belching announced their arrival on the field. The Yankees were in for a hot time of it, surely.

His men and the Federals had reached a standoff. He'd been driven back to the spur, but it didn't shame him: Numbers were numbers. He'd held the flank and was holding it still. He'd just got a bit ahead of himself.

The back-and-forth firing did less and less damage, despite the constant noise. Men were just tuckered out, too weary to steady their rifles as they fired. Waste of ammunition, waste of men. On both sides.

Colonel Perry found him. The brigade was coming up,

the Yankee cavalry had hightailed it from the courthouse. And the rest of Field's Division was extending the line on the ridge. Oates was to pull back and tie into Henagan's left flank.

When the 15th and 48th withdrew this time, the Yankees didn't follow. They'd had enough.

But Henagan's men opened fire through the trees, convinced his boys were Yankees. In a rage, Oates got that straightened out personally, running bad-legged right into the fire, waving his hat, and hollering his head off.

Back on the ridge, his weary men went right to work on battlements built of tore-down fences and piled-up dirt, clawing the earth with spoons, bayonets, and fingers. Swirl-headed from the heat, Oates undid his blouse, too blown to track down his horse and his canteen. He wanted to lie down, but would not do so. Not while the men were working.

On the south side of the ridge, men and batteries began to appear in good numbers. A sense prevailed, unspoken, that the worst of the crisis had passed.

General Stuart rode up again, merry as a drunkard with a fresh jug.

"Colonel Oates!" he cried. "Well done, Alabama! Ain't this a grand old time?"

Oates would have liked to ask the cavalryman for a drink of water. But he was too proud to do it. Nor would he drink while his men's canteens were empty. But he did say:

"This here place got a name, sir?"

"I'm told," Stuart said, "it's called Laurel Hill." The plumed cavalier's grin widened. "And laurels aplenty there are for our soldiers today."

Oates believed he'd prefer a swallow of water.

Noon
Piney Branch Church

The headquarters tents had gone up with noteworthy speed, the one thing properly managed in the past twenty-four hours. Hungry though he was, Meade found the salt pork served by his mess unappetizing. He sat and stared at the dubious meat, picking at the beans piled on its flanks, and let silence reign over his companions. They were good men, culled from his favorites: His son, young George, and Humphreys, hot as a steam engine himself at the abysmally clumsy handling of the march. Jim Biddle sat a few steps off, a man of the finest Philadelphia stock and the sort who knew the proper way to do things. Biddle all but touched knees with Ted Lyman, another fine fellow graced with a sharp eye and wit, a Harvard man trained in science by the famed Agassiz himself. Meade had met Lyman ages before, in Florida, where the young man had come bearing letters permitting him to collect starfish under the military's guardianship. Lyman was bred of Boston's best, and the two men had hit it off in the Seminole wilderness, where Meade, an aged lieutenant, had been building lighthouses on the shoals and Theodore Lyman had built a reputation. Rather against the odds, the soldier and the scholar founded a friendship. But, then, Boston or Philadelphia, breeding told. Even now, they had a great deal in common, despite disparities in wealth and temperament: Lyman, quite the *bon vivant,* seemed as uninterested in the salt pork as Meade.

It was too damned hot to eat, even under a tent fly, and a misery for the regiments plodding past. But the presence of men he trusted, drawn of those few he could trust, lowered Meade's temper, if not the temperature. He rather thought Margaret would have been proud of his self-restraint this day.

Everything had been a wretched mess. He could not help but agree with Humphreys, who was furious at Grant and his bunch for setting madcap goals for the army's march. Oh, it sounded well and good: "Move fast and leave Lee scrambling to catch up." But such blustering took no account of specimen physics, as Lyman put it. When Humphreys tried to explain that the roads were not only inadequate to support Grant's envisioned movement, but the best routes were jammed with ambulances and supply trains, Rawlins had all but called them out as cowards again. So they had marched when evening fell, and within the first few miles, the race had broken down to a crawling nightmare, precisely as poor Humphreys had predicted. And Sheridan, Grant's little Irish fraud, had badly mishandled the cavalry, so that when Warren's men finally reached Todd's Tavern—a disgusting shanty—they had found their route blocked by drowsing horsemen in multitudes, two cavalry divisions loitering without orders. On the way to the tavern, Meade and his staff had been forced to let Grant's western fellows lead, and they had nearly galloped straight into the Rebels. Then, at the tavern, Grant had gone off to sleep by a pigsty, while he had been left to sort out the errant cavalrymen, who were supposed to be far to the south, clearing the way for the infantry. Nobody knew where Sheridan, the cavalry corps' new general, could be found, so Meade had issued orders directly to the horsemen to do what they should have done five hours before. Only to have them collide with Stuart's men, who'd been lurking in the dark, at which point the cavalry accomplished precisely nothing. With dawn upon them and every man not of Grant's snoring staff exhausted, he had been driven to order up Robinson's division to brush aside the Confederate horse at last.

And Lee had won the blasted race again. Wilson's riders reached the courthouse first, but, alone and unable to hold it, they had withdrawn. Now the Confederates blocked the road to Richmond.

And things got worse, with Warren repeating the very blunder he had railed against in the Wilderness, squandering his corps' strength by committing it in bits of brigades and lone regiments against the Confederates gathering on a ridge. Warren had turned a *coup de main* into a blood-soaked debacle. And Sedgwick, when he came up, had done nothing at all.

Everyone, from the generals down to the privates, was worn to the nub. And the day was but half over.

"Lyman," Meade called, "after you've gotten the savor of your repast, have another look at things. I've got to stay near Grant."

"Yes, sir. Of course."

"Take Duane with you. I need to know if anything can be done. Without adding more wastage to the casualty rolls."

"I'd like to go up myself," Humphreys put in. "Since Grant's people don't have much use for proper staff work."

"In good time," Meade told him. "I need you here." He felt his temper rising again. Not at Humphreys, but at the great, wide world. He had been all for moving to better ground, for drawing Lee out of the Wilderness, but Grant had never moved an army of this size, and the roads were few and wretched. Nonetheless, Grant had deferred to his ever-confident sycophants, who insisted it all could be done at the snap of their fingers. Meade found Grant's determination refreshing, but the hallmark of a plan had to be realism.

The sound of horses struck Meade's ear and motion caught his eye.

Sheridan. At last. Meade's nostrils flared.

He set his plate on the sandy ground and stalked toward the horsemen.

"General Sheridan!" he snapped. "I'll have a word with you."

Gently, he told himself. Calmly. Sensibly. But it did no good.

A little man with a cannonball head and a brawler's chest, Sheridan strode up, tearing off his riding gloves.

"And I've been meaning to have a word with *you,*" he said.

"In my tent."

"Any damned where you like."

As he marched under the canvas, with its illusion of privacy, Meade thought that, if he missed any man nowadays, it was poor John Buford.

When Meade turned to face Sheridan, the two men almost collided.

As though this were his tent, not Meade's, Sheridan threw his flat-crowned hat on the desk, unsettling the papers. The cavalry chief's mouth opened, but Meade, overcome by rage, got in the first blast.

"Damn you, man, do you know what your blundering's cost this army today? *Do you know?* Where were you, off in some shebeen? You left the cavalry blocking our key route south. And doing precious little else, I might add. You held up Warren's corps, and now there may be a thousand men dead and dying, thanks to your negligence. And Lee's got the best of the ground under his feet." He drew himself up to his full height, towering over the Irishman. "Sheridan, your dispositions have been inept, an amateur exercise, and we all have paid the price. Then you stranded Wilson at Spotsylvania . . ."

Sheridan had been reddening. Now he exploded: "*You! You* dare challenge *me,* you overbred horse's ass? After you almost got Wilson captured yourself? You listen to me, you high-flown sonofabitch. If you think I'm going to let you shit on me, you can wipe your ass with a corncob and have it for dinner. *You* don't know a goddamned thing about men *or* goddamned horses. At this rate you're going to wreck the entire cavalry corps, you shit-sucker. If my men blocked anybody, it was because *you* interfered. *My* dispositions were sound. So don't piss on my plans and tell the world it's cologne water. . . ."

Frozen in astonishment, Meade gaped. Even Rawlins didn't dare . . .

He had not meant for things to go so far. Belatedly, Meade gripped his temper.

"Sheridan, I—"

"And Warren's no goddamned soldier," the little man resumed, "so don't blame his fucking incompetence on me. The problem isn't my cavalry, it's your worthless infantry, I've never seen such disgraceful acts on a battlefield, such outright cowardice. . . ."

"General Sheridan, let us—"

The Irishman looked up at Meade with eyes not short of murderous. "And as for Stuart, I'll tell you all you need to know about goddamned Stuart. You just get out of my goddamned way and I'll give you his fucking head. I could whip Jeb Stuart, if you'd let me." Sheridan snorted, a little bull, and allowed himself a loathsome, superior smile. "But since you insist on giving orders to my men without consulting me, you can take command of the cavalry corps yourself. Show us all what a fucking frolic you can get up, you bastard. *I'm* not going to issue another goddamned order, so help me God."

Meade reached out and laid a hand on the little man's shoulder. He just managed to say, "No . . . I don't mean that."

Sheridan batted Meade's paw away, took up his hat, and strode out of the tent.

It took Meade some minutes to gather himself, but in that time his own anger surged again. At the sound of horses galloping off, he left the tent, stalked by the wary expressions of his officers, and headed up the road toward the church, where Grant's staff had placed themselves under the shade of better trees than the scrub pines allotted to Meade.

Relieved to find that Sheridan had not beat him to the church—from which they had flushed a few last congregants—Meade quick-timed through Grant's lazing staff and made his way to the general in chief.

He found Grant deep in the shadows, with Rawlins and Washburne sprawled on the ground as their master puffed a cigar. Porter and Badeau hovered.

"I just had an interview with Sheridan," Meade said. Despite his intended restraint, temper burned his voice.

Grant began to smile, then blanked his expression.

"That so?"

"The man's as insubordinate as he's incompetent. After the royal mess he made of last night's march, he had the nerve to insult me to my face. Profanely, I might add. And then he started bragging that, if only *I* let him, *he* could whip Jeb Stuart. . . ."

Grant lowered the cigar. "Did Sheridan say that?"

"He did indeed. His insolence is unbounded."

"Well," Grant continued, "he generally knows what he's talking about. Let him start right out and do it."

Meade turned away from the barely suppressed smiles. Laughter trailed him as he left the headquarters.

Eight p.m.
Todd's Tavern, Federal rear guard

As the last of the wounded were carried off, the two men drank bad coffee.

"Write up Robertson for a Medal of Honor," Barlow said.

Miles tossed the dregs of his drink to the ground. "For sabering our own men?"

"For seizing the flag and rallying the the Hundred and Eighty-third Pennsylvania."

"They hardly stayed rallied." Miles looked off into the gloaming, toward the Confederate ghosts that haunted the night. "I'm ashamed."

Barlow laughed, a cawing sound that drew the attention of the nearest soldiers. "Not your fault, Nellie. In fact, I'd say you handled things rather well. The new men are the problem. Not the veterans, the trash we're getting now. Bounty jumpers and cutthroats. Draftees drooling from both sides of their mouths. They hold back, the good men are killed, and then the rest of them run."

"A few won't run anymore. Robertson can swing a saber."

"I'll see that he's promoted, he's earned his captaincy."

"Plenty of vacancies," Miles said, "after the last few days."

Around them, the soldiers had begun to calm. The Confederate plunge toward Barlow's main position had been ill-judged, and the Johnnies soon thought better of it. But the men were exhausted and less steady than usual.

Barlow's thoughts returned to the 183rd, which had broken almost immediately when struck earlier in the evening. Miles' brigade had advanced toward the Po to feel the enemy, but the Rebs had felt him instead. He had been hit on both flanks by Mahone's division and by dismounted cavalry under Hampton. The only thing that saved his left was a commissary wagon just arrived to distribute rations. Careless of the volleys ripping the air, the hooting Rebs had broken off their attack to share out the food. With help from Smyth and the Irish Brigade, Miles had managed to extricate himself. But the 183rd's collapse had been disgraceful. Only the enemy's empty bellies had prevented a disaster.

Barlow rubbed his nose and said, "The Romans were a sensible people, you know. When a cohort behaved badly, they formed up its parent legion to watch as they executed every tenth man in the bad lot. Decimation worked." He took off his cap and ran a hand over his sweat-flattened hair, feeling for nits. "We squander mercy and expect the brave to pay."

"I hear Gibbon had another deserter shot," Miles said.

Barlow's features tightened. "Right by the roadside. Draped a sign around the corpse's neck, it was quite a show."

"The Hundred and Eighty-third hasn't been a bad regiment," Miles said. "Until now, I mean. The fighting in the Wilderness . . . Frank, it did something to the men. And not just the Hundred and Eighty-third."

"Well, they're going to see worse. If I read things right." Barlow grimaced. "This coffee's wretched. Have you had anything to eat?"

"I've got to see to my brigade." But Miles paused. "You don't think the Rebs will come at us again? My men need rest. A few hours, at least."

Barlow shook his head. "Our Southron friends have had enough for tonight, I think. Thought they'd snap up a tasty morsel, but didn't expect the whole steer."

"Hancock seems worried."

"Playing rear guard doesn't suit him." Barlow pawed his head again. "It's not like him, though. Jumping at every snapped twig. When any fool can tell the fight's to the south." He slapped his hat on his head. "Go on, see to your men. And scribble some gush on Robertson, I'll endorse it."

Barlow turned away first, headed rearward, his path lit by low campfires. It had been a trying day, to put it gently.

And Miles' close call had been only one part of it. The problems had begun to unfold earlier, when Hancock bewildered him by reinstating Paul Frank in brigade command. After the man had simply fled in the Wilderness. It was unfathomable.

Then the Second Corps had been left in the rear, while Warren led the Fifth Corps into another battle as ineptly as he had done in the Wilderness. The word filtered back that every charge had been a muddled failure. Barlow didn't share the regard that others had for Warren. The general affection for Sedgwick, he understood: Uncle John Sedgwick was an affable man, the sort who pleased the commons, if no genius. But Warren seemed unsteady, somehow paltry. He might have performed splendidly at Gettysburg, but his role had not been commanding men in battle.

And Hancock, Hancock . . . Barlow had begun to suspect that his superior might not last. Nor was it just the wound. In the saddle, Hancock still looked the part of the army's *beau sabreur,* but Barlow sensed afflicted nerves in the man he had so respected.

He wondered if he might not take the corps himself, should Hancock depart. Birney and Gibbon had seniority, and corps command in the Army of the Potomac had thus far been reserved for West Point officers. Yet, Grant wanted fighters, ruthless fighters, and that meant opportunity. . . .

In the meantime, he had to get his boots off and soak his feet. Maintaining his composure while chatting with Nellie had been a trial. All day, he had yearned to scratch himself bloody and raw.

How he longed for his wife's care now! Rather than being repulsed by the sight of his feet, Belle had been pleased to bathe them. Then she would paint them with salve and wrap them in compresses. He wished with all his heart that she were present. And, damnable thing, she nearly was. Her last three letters had reached him that day, along with missives from his brothers and mother—who had sent him a copy of *The Atlantic Monthly,* laden with dreary poems and duller ramblings: Whittier and Emerson still had no sense of the world. His mother was as blithe as ever, though, and Richard sent good news on their shipping investments. But the tidings that mattered most came from his beloved. She was in Fredericksburg, a few hours away on horseback, returned to her work with the Sanitary Commission. Perhaps, if the campaign slowed . . .

He had read her letters, her loving words, in the saddle and had needed to turn to brute thoughts to battle tears.

When the war ended, he intended to take her to Europe. London first, then, inevitably, Paris, and on to Rome. Perhaps Athens after that, even Constantinople. A good, long journey would cleanse their spirits and make a clean break from all this.

His wife had concluded her letter: "Protest as you wish, dear savage, but I know you take delight in what other men dread. Do have a care, for my sake, *cher barbare.*"

Ten p.m.
The Block House

Three generals ate by the light of a single candle. Their supper was bread and hard cheese, augmented by a crock of pickled beets, the gift of a local housewife and yet another food Lee dared not eat.

"Whipped them again," Ewell said. "Dick here just plain whipped them." The corps commander was so ebullient, so overripe in his confidence this night, that it troubled Lee.

"Oh, I'd say Stuart deserves most of the credit," Anderson countered. "Just a downright wonder. I've never witnessed cavalry better handled."

Ewell made a sour face. "Well enough, Dick, well

enough. But he couldn't have held that ridge if your boys hadn't come up. In the end, it's always the infantry makes the difference."

"And artillery," Anderson said. There was a faint awkwardness in his speech, the least hint of diffidence behind the soldierly banter. Any man called upon to replace Longstreet could not but feel daunted, Lee knew. But Anderson had done well this day, pushing his men hard and gaining precious minutes on those people.

"Is Gordon up?" Lee asked Ewell. It was easier to speak than to gnaw the resistant cheese. He had always had strong teeth, but they, too, had become casualties of war.

"Been up for hours. Preening like a peacock."

"I should like to offer my compliments in person," Lee said.

"Oh, don't you worry about John Gordon," Ewell told him. "I swear, there's more mold here than cheese, things a man has to eat. No, sir, Gordon's got his division, that's the only compliment he needs." Ewell smirked. "Not that Jube Early's overjoyed about it."

"I should think," Lee said, "that General Early would have no objections. Given General Gordon's record. And General Early's own elevation to corps command."

Ewell tugged at the cheese with brown teeth, wooden leg tapping the floorboards. "Oh, you know Jube. He'll do, though."

Yes. He would do. Because he would have to do. Powell Hill had grown so ill that he could not be left in command. And Early had been the best choice, if not an ideal one, to try as a substitute. He had lost two corps commanders out of three, at least for the present. The surgeons believed that Longstreet would live, but must suffer a long convalescence. Hill's illness, the wages of sin, came and went unpredictably.

In all, more than a dozen generals had been killed or

wounded, and no end of colonels had fallen. The army could not bear such extravagant losses.

The bright spot, the one bit of solace, was General Gordon. Lee felt certain now of the man's abilities. In fact, he found it astonishing that one not formally trained to the profession could wage war with such art. And such audacity.

He had been audacious himself. At Cerro Gordo. Then in the battles before the great City of Mexico, combats that he, in his innocence, had considered fraught with gore. Now he was engaged in a war grim beyond his earlier powers of imagination, a contest of vast armies and fearsome weapons. It was a war that he had never wanted, but one to which he had committed his soul for the sake of Virginia, a war scorched with pride and one that, even in its satisfactions, clamored at his conscience in the night.

This day, though, had been pleasing. Each of his subordinates had done precisely the right thing without his urging.

"Figure Grant's had about enough, sir?" Ewell asked. "Think he'll run off like the rest of them?"

"General Grant . . . appears tenacious. If he has moved his army here, it is not without purpose. He will attack us again. After some preparation."

"And we'll whip him again," Ewell said.

"Here, here!" Anderson agreed.

"As the Lord decides," Lee said. "General Anderson, the bread, please."

"Oh, we'll whip him," Ewell insisted. "Him and old Granny Meade. These beets got sass, don't they, though?"

Negro servants ghosted in and out, passing a dead hearth, their doings so much the custom of the country that it seemed odd to Lee to notice them of a sudden. He held up his cup a few inches: water. And it was served to him.

"I believe," Lee resumed, "that we face one more trial.

Grant will put in his all." He looked at the candle's flame and into the future. "But should we disappoint his hopes and those of General Meade, those people must withdraw to Fredericksburg, if not beyond. Their losses have been so heavy I see no alternative. Then we may recuperate the army and look to—"

"*Nobody* can take the whippings we've given those blue-bellies," Ewell declared. He seemed unaware he had interrupted Lee. His voice, excited, had risen to a pitch that was almost girlish. It did not become a man of his age and position.

"If their losses have been severe," Lee said, "our own have not been welcome." He abandoned his attempt to finish his portion of cheese, adding, "This is a graceless form of war. It asks much of the men."

"Oh, they're up to it," Ewell said. He swilled down his water as if it were strong drink. "They won't shy."

"I agree," Anderson put in. "We're tougher than the Federals. In flesh and spirit."

Lee let the exchange drop. He had crossed harsh words with Marshall that very morning. The report on deserters had angered him and, caught off guard, he had taken it out on his military secretary. He had not expected so many desertions so early in the campaign. Might it not be wiser to stop shooting such men and hang them instead? The better to deter others? The rope was more fearsome than bullets.

Next, there had come a letter from President Davis, a communication so embarrassing that, after reading it twice, he had burned it himself. Posterity had to be spared such childish moonshine. The president had gone from expecting miracles to imagining that he, Jefferson Davis of Mississippi, performed them. He had written of his renewed certainty that Britain would come in with the Confederacy any time now and the blockade would be broken. The

South's problems would be solved by cotton sales, the Royal Navy, and an invasion from Canada. *And* he expected Lee's old classmate Joe Johnston to defeat Sherman's army before the month was out.

As for Johnston, Lee wished him success, but did not believe he would have an easy time of things. The matter of Great Britain was clear nonsense, though. Lincoln had sewn up the matter a year and a half before, although it had taken Lee months to see through the matter. When Lincoln issued his emancipation decree—a dictator's act— they all had expressed public outrage, while indulging in quiet glee at "Honest Abe's" folly. Such imperious behavior would further unite the South in righteous anger, they had believed, while dividing the North between the abolitionists and sensible men who saw the need for peace. They all had been blindly confident. But Lincoln had seen the future, while they clung to the past. That piece of paper had caused the North only hiccups, not lasting distress, while the decree had made it impossible for the European powers to intervene, since to do so would be to champion slavery outright. The English public, especially, would not countenance it, and the South's sympathizers in Parliament had been stymied. They had underrated Lincoln, who was canny. And far more capable, Lee feared, than the man who lived in the president's house in Richmond.

The only hope now, the last hope, was to so bloody the North's armies that the voters would turn out Lincoln in the fall, bringing in a peace candidate. Were Lincoln to be reelected, Lee envisioned only further destruction, immeasurable bitterness, and, if necessary, a war carried into the hills and lasting decades. The South would die before it would surrender.

Lee came back to the living moment, half listened to the two corps commanders teasing and praising each other, and watched a Negro servant clear the table.

What did any Northerner know of the Negro? Lee found it distasteful to hear slavery praised from the pulpit, but, practically speaking, what was the alternative for the present? To unleash millions of savages upon a civilized land? He did not need to read lurid accounts from Haiti: As a lieutenant with a new wife at Fort Monroe, he had discovered what Negro terror meant. The slave uprising in nearby Southampton County had revealed the full barbarity of the African, the instinctive outrages against chaste women and gentlefolk. No, the Negro needed a firm hand to refine him, or he would degenerate into lifelong indolence punctuated by bursts of crimson slaughter.

Of course, slavery could not persist in the modern world. But its elimination had to be gradual. Across the span of a century, the Negro might be fitted to an elementary role in American society, but it was unfair to the creature to expect more. He had long since freed his own few slaves, glad to be rid of a practical vexation, and had even paid passages to Liberia for those who wished to go. But it was too late to ship millions back to Africa.

What *was* to be done with these simple, feckless people? His father-in-law had specified that his slaves were to be freed upon his death, if Arlington's financial affairs permitted; otherwise, they would go free after five years. And the Negroes had misunderstood, expecting ladders to descend from Heaven when Mr. Custis shed his mortal coil. The plantation's books had been in dreadful shape after years of neglect and, as the new head of the family, Lee had needed to keep the servants and field hands bound for the five allotted years. He had had no choice. A few of the disappointed slaves had run away, and their apprehension had been essential to scotch the flight of the others. Upon their retrieval by slave catchers, he had required the sheriff to whip them. He had taken no pleasure in the matter, but a plantation had to have order, as did an army.

Discipline was salutary. He had refused to shield himself, though, and had stood by to watch the punishment, feeling each lash himself.

And that was the South's conundrum: Wise men understood that the institution of slavery must crumble. But hotheads had ruled the day, only playing into the hands of the worst forces in the North. Madcap fools had made this war, not soldiers. Now the soldiers must win it for the fools.

After five years, he had honored the Custis will and freed Arlington's slaves. The worst of his blacks had slipped into the maelstrom, while those who remained loyal expected gratitude. As for the plantation he had labored to save, it was lost forever now, profaned by those people to spite him. They had burned White House plantation, too, depriving his son Rooney of a home. So much of his golden world was gone forever. . . .

As if reading his thoughts, Ewell said, too loudly, "I do wish Sam Grant would send his nigger division to face my boys. We'd see about the 'dignity of the colored man,' all right. We'd set those coons to running so fast they'd be climbing trees in Maine before the morning."

"If they lived that long," Anderson said.

And now it had come to this: black men armed and uniformed, to be set upon white men with a government's blessing. The abolitionists had not seen what Nat Turner's knives and axes had wrought on the helpless.

Well, if it came to that, his men were not helpless.

For all his private complaints, he knew war suited him. As did the faith he had discovered late in life. He was not meant to be a man of business and scorned the undisguised pursuit of wealth, but he had been called upon time and again to straighten out matters reflecting on his kindred. He had dirtied his hands not by preference, but to salvage the Custis name for his dear wife. He always had done his duty, however unpleasant, by his family, by the army, and by Mary's family, and he did it with rigid probity.

The paramount aim of his life had been to restore the honor of the Lees of Virginia. After his father, once a hero and intimate of Washington's, had perished a bankrupt, and half-brother Henry, the next head of the family, descended into odium and scandal, his people had been reduced to near pariahs. Old Custis had not wished his daughter to bear the name and relented only because Mary was of age. Then, with painful irony, Custis had mishandled his own affairs. Not criminally, but incompetently. His death had left them all headaches and debts as inheritance. Dutiful yet again, Lee had taken a leave of absence to clear the estate. His life from early manhood had been naught but a succession of such obligations, and the sweetness of his childhood, of the years before the fall, at Stratford Hall or visiting the endless supply of cousins in ripe summers, all that was gone, an age as vanished as those of the Tudors and Stuarts.

He had learned what it meant to be the poor relation, disregarded in social coalitions. On top of all, he had, still a boy, nursed his ailing mother, in a household where poverty was not always genteel. It seemed he was fated to see the women he loved most dearly turn invalid, just as he must suffer other men's scandals. West Point had been his first attempt at escape.

From the day he arrived on that shelf above the Hudson, he determined to be a man of flawless deportment, of measured speech and immaculate integrity. He bound himself to every regulation and worshipped every detail of the code of honor. He did not drink or smoke, would not gamble or curse, and never did he associate with light women. Even his posture announced his rectitude, armoring him against life.

And he had come far. Perhaps, he sometimes feared, a bit too far. The night harbored demons the day might slay with reason: Would raising his sword against the flag he had once sworn to defend bring greater shame than his father's speculations? When his heart no longer beat, how would the living regard the name of Lee?

How much of his life, of his actions even now, had been decided when his father first took on a debt he could not settle? Was each man a slave to something? He had heard that George Meade, too, had suffered a family's fall, although the elder Meade's conduct had not been improper. Did Meade feel driven to mend his family's repute? Grant, for his part, was plebeian, the new sort of man, and had only his own shame to cover.

"General Lee, you look wearied," Anderson said. "Best take your rest, sir."

"Thank you, General Anderson," Lee answered. "I'm afraid I must write a few letters before I retire."

The problem with sleep was dreams.

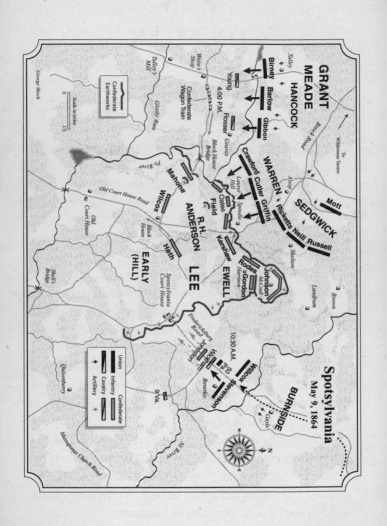

Spotsylvania
May 9, 1864

GRANT
MEADE

HANCOCK
Birney
Young
Barlow
Gibbon
Rosser

WARREN
Crawford Cutler Griffin
Oates
Field
Laurel Hill
Spindle

SEDGWICK
Mott
Ricketts Neill Russell
Shelton

Mahone
WILCOX
R. H. ANDERSON
Heth
EARLY (HILL)
LEE
Kershaw
Rodes
Gordon
Johnson
McCall
Harrison
EWELL
Landrum
Brown

Spotsylvania Court House
Old Court House Road
Old Court House
Block House

Po River
Block House Bridge
Graves
4:00 P.M.
Confederate Wagon Train
Waite's Shop
Talley
Talley's Mill
Glady Run
Grady Run

George Slack

Scale in miles
0   1/2

Confederate Earthworks

To Wilderness Tavern
Alsop
Brock Road

Fredericksburg Road
Johnston
10:30 A.M.
Wm. Johnston Ni
3d Rd.
Stevenson
Beverley
BURNSIDE
Eagle

9 Va.
Shell's Bridge

Quisenberry

Massaponax Church Road
Ni River

Union
Confederate
Infantry
Cavalry
Artillery

N
S
E
W

FOURTEEN

Major General John Sedgwick preferred to keep a man his friend, rather than make an enemy, and he knew Warren was sensitive to slights, real or imagined. So he rode to Fifth Corps headquarters himself, hoping to soothe its commander, before the wound of Meade's order cut too deep.

His passage along the lines attracted a minor cannonade.

Warren wasn't at the shack he had commandeered for a headquarters. His aide intercepted Sedgwick on the porch. A young man, Roebling looked ashen-faced and aged. He wasn't certain where his chief had gone.

Off to complain to Meade? Warren was fool enough to do it. Meade would be all right once his temper calmed, but Grant didn't care for handwringers. Warren would just make a bad situation worse.

Up along the entrenchments, the *crack-crack-crack* of skirmishing rose and fell. The intervals between bursts belonged to sharpshooters. The racket had kept up all night, making sleep a ragged affair, at best. At fifty, Sedgwick wasn't the physical specimen he had been.

You're no more tired than your men, he told himself. At least you get to ride a goddamned horse.

He said: "All right, Roebling. You know I'm not going to lord it over anybody. No matter what Meade's order says.

Tell General Warren to go on and command his own corps, as usual. I have perfect confidence he'll do what's right. He knows what to do with his corps as well as I do."

In one of his fits of spleen, Meade had sent down orders putting Sedgwick in overall command of both his Sixth Corps and Warren's men in Meade's absence. Warren had not been relieved, but put on a leash. And Warren had brought it on himself, not just by the slovenly way he'd put in his weary soldiers the day before, but by throwing a tantrum of the sort that raised Meade's ire.

As Sedgwick's staff related the tale, Meade had come forward for a firsthand look and had told Warren to cooperate with Sedgwick, after the Sixth Corps had become entangled in the Fifth Corps' mess. And Warren had picked the worst possible time to tell Meade that he was willing to be commanded, or to command, but damned well was *not* going to "cooperate" with anybody. Warren had been worn to the nub, had just seen his men savaged to no good result, and was being pressed to do more. But no excuses counted on a battlefield. G.K. was too high-strung.

"Sir . . . ," Roebling said in a careful voice, "the men are just used up. General Warren did the best he could. But this constant fighting, marching and fighting, day after day in this heat . . . then the ceaseless pressure from General Meade . . ."

"It's not from George Meade, Roebling. He's a methodical man, an engineer. Like you or General Warren. Grant's the one who keeps pushing to smash 'em up, smash 'em up. Grant, and that menagerie of his."

Sedgwick decided that he'd said enough. Didn't do to have such words repeated. Warren would have to take his medicine. But he admired Roebling's loyalty to his chief. Loyalty was crucial to the officer corps. He made a final effort to be personable:

"I heard about Fred Locke," he said to Roebling. "Friend of yours, I believe?"

Roebling lowered his gaze.

"Any chance he'll recover?" Sedgwick asked.

The aide shrugged. Then he looked up, damp-eyed, and shook his head. "His face . . . dear God, I'll see his face until the day I die, it was half shot away. . . ."

Sedgwick had a knack for soothing words. But he didn't seem to be doing so well this morning.

Warren just needed to calm down and see things through Meade's eyes. No need to get riled and flit about. Loyalty went downward as well as up the chain, and Meade was loyal in both directions. He'd saved Charlie Griffin from being relieved, and Meade would stand up for Warren, too, if G.K. didn't paint him into a corner.

It was all so hard and complicated now. Sedgwick had fought the Seminoles, moved the Cherokee, whipped the Mexicans, and chased Comanches, but all of that had been child's play to this.

"All right, Roebling. Just tell General Warren what I said. And we'll hope for a quiet day."

The day before, he'd seen dead-eyed men stagger forward into hopeless assaults. Minutes later, a smaller number of those dead-eyed men staggered back. Some of them had been his boys. Even he had got caught up in the senselessness.

Maybe Grant's approach of keeping up the pressure on Lee would work. But it seemed to Sedgwick a good way to break their own army.

Soldier on, he told himself. Wouldn't mind a pan of fried eggs, though.

Before Sedgwick could remount, Charlie Whittier, one of his aides, came on at such a gallop that he nearly collided with a wagon hauling off bodies like a medieval plague cart. Whittier was generally counted a cool one, despite his family ties to some silk-drawers poet, but today he was on the boil.

The major reined in and didn't take time to dismount, but shouted his tidings:

"Sir, it's General Neill. He's withdrawing his division from the line."

Sedgwick stiffened. "Who ordered that?"

"Nobody. Colonel McMahon checked. Neill's doing it on his own, he's gone to pieces, sir."

Sedgwick leapt to horse. Fifty years old or not, his time in the First Cavalry counted for something.

"Where's Neill now?"

"Just behind his division. He won't hear reason, sir."

"Lead the way."

Tom Neill, the hero of Salem Church and the man he had chosen to lead George Getty's division after Getty got himself shot up in the Wilderness. Neill was big and Irish in the best ways, with the grip of a bear, the finest mustache in the army, and an easy way with the men. You just never knew who would break under the strain.

After riding pell-mell along an exposed portion of the line, they found Neill and his worried staff men back in a copse of trees. Neill appeared perfectly fine, nodding as his men marched for the rear.

Sedgwick had a temper, too. He wanted to give Neill what for, and in clear language. Instead, he reined in and said, "Tom, what's the matter here?"

Neill looked at him as if only now aware that his corps commander had arrived.

"We have to withdraw," Neill said. His tone was alarmingly calm. "My men . . . they're going to be slaughtered. We have to leave." He smiled. "Look at them, aren't they fine? You can't blame me for killing Getty's men, I'm pulling them back as quickly as I can."

Neill began to weep.

Frank Wheaton rode up. He looked as baffled as anyone, but his appearance was opportune.

"Frank!" Sedgwick called. "Take command of this division. Stop this nonsense right now. Get these men turned around."

Wheaton looked relieved and instantly confident. He saluted and yanked his horse around, shouting orders to his own small retinue.

Christ, if one of Lee's bunch saw them vacating the line, the Confederates would be on top of them in a blink.

"Charlie," Sedgwick said to Major Whittier, "find Bidwell and Lew Grant. Tell them they're to reoccupy their former positions at the double-quick. Or stay in them, if they haven't left already. *Go!*"

"I won't let the men be slaughtered . . . killed like sheep . . . might as well cut their throats . . ." With tears leaving myriad tracks down his cheeks, Brigadier General Neill looked at his superior. "I did all I could, sir."

Sedgwick leaned from his saddle and gripped Neill's forearm. "You did your best, Tom. But you need some rest now. You just go back and get a little sleep, go on back to the trains."

"My men . . . Getty . . ."

"You go on back now. Get some sleep. I'm here to see to things." He turned to one of Neill's men, a trusted captain who had been a favorite of Getty's. "Take General Neill to the rear." His voice was not as gentle with the captain.

They got things straightened out before the Rebels became aware of the confusion. Sedgwick figured the sorry buggers up on the ridge were at least as worn as his own men. Still, it was a relief worthy of the ages when the last of the division's troops were back in their trenches.

His chief of staff, Marty McMahon, found him.

"General Morris has been shot, sir."

Oh, Christ. After Bill Morris had done so well in the Wilderness. Sedgwick had marked him down for a division.

"What happened? Is he alive?"

McMahon pawed sweat from his face. The morning was already torrid. His horse foamed green at the mouth, dripping on the ground.

"He's alive, but it's bad."

"Sharpshooter?"

McMahon nodded. "We ought to execute every one of those bastards we catch."

And then they execute our men, and we kill more of them, and it never stops, Sedgwick thought. All his life he'd been a soldier, but he wouldn't mind when this war came to an end.

"We're not Comanches," he said. "All right, let's have a look at Ricketts' lines."

McMahon looked doubtful. "Sir, it might be a good time for you to stay at headquarters."

"Nonsense." But Sedgwick smiled. He liked McMahon and regarded him as something between a son and a younger brother. "Who commands this corps, Marty? You or me?"

"Sometimes I do wonder about that myself."

Sedgwick laughed.

"Just promise me," McMahon went on, "that you won't expose yourself needlessly today. We're running a tad short of generals, sir."

"Tell you what," Sedgwick said. "We'll move the headquarters closer to the entrenchments, and you and I can call it a draw. Then I want an officers' call with the division commanders." He thought for a moment. "No new orders from Meade?"

"No, sir, nothing new. The corps is to remain in position, distribute ammunition, and bring up rations. Gather in the stragglers. And let the men rest." McMahon grimaced. "Although they'll have to work on the entrenchments, they're unsatisfactory. That's one thing the Johnnies do better than us."

"They have more reason," Sedgwick said. He gee-upped his horse.

Bill Morris down, too, after Getty's wounding and the loss to the corps of so many other officers. The casualties on both sides were appalling. As he rode among his men, Sedgwick's thoughts roamed across the lines to Jeb Stuart, a lovely young man. Despite the difference in their ages, they had grown close before the war. Sedgwick hoped the reckless cavalier would survive so they might meet as friends again.

The war had torn the country apart, but also severed many a worthy friendship. Thinking about Stuart left Sedgwick wistful. What was that two-dollar word that Whittier liked? "Elegiac." He supposed that captured something of how he felt, although he wasn't sure of the definition.

It was still only eight o'clock when Grant came up. He rode a sinewy pony, not the big bay horse all admired. Sedgwick sighed and mustered a dutiful smile.

"Welcome to the Sixth Corps, sir!" he said. They were just far enough out of range to permit salutes.

"How do, John?" Grant said, dismounting. He waved a hand at the surrounding hubbub. "Change from the old Army, ain't it?"

They shook hands.

"Had the same thought myself this very morning," Sedgwick said.

"I heard about Bill Morris," Grant continued. "Sorry to hear it."

Since Grant hadn't mentioned Tom Neill right off, it meant he didn't know about that problem. Sedgwick hoped to keep it that way. Neill was a good officer. A rest might fix him up.

"Morris will be a loss to the army," Sedgwick told the general in chief. "Coffee?"

"Not unless it's a sight better than the spew I get at headquarters."

"It's likely worse."

They both smiled.

Grant said: "Got this great big army, more generals than Napoleon, locomotives, telegraphs . . . and we still can't cook up a proper can of coffee."

"That's a fact."

"Now, Porter there, he'll drink any coffee you got. Man would drink pitch or tar, if you served it lukewarm." Grant turned. "Horace, go test the coffee while General Sedgwick and I do our little war dance."

Sedgwick waited. Grant stepped closer.

"How are the men?" the general in chief asked. His tone required honesty.

"They'll be all right. Once they're rested. It's been something of a shock, coming right out of winter quarters and into all this. They're not used to the pace."

"Lee's men are tired, too. Another good push or so and they're going to break."

"Lee's a stubborn man."

"He'll break. Every man has his breaking point."

Sedgwick thought of Tom Neill, of the bright Irish eyes gone mad.

He gestured toward the front line. "Trying to get up that slope head-on . . . yesterday was Injun-massacre ugly, and they weren't half dug in." He shook his head. "Remember when the Richmond papers mocked Lee, calling him the 'King of Spades'?"

"Never heard that."

"Back during the Peninsula business, after Joe Johnston

caught one. They all made fun of Lee's taste for the shovel and ax. Nobody's laughing now."

"I mean to flank him. One way, or the other."

"Better than sending men back up that ridge."

"Might have to do that, too," Grant said. "Hit him on all sides. So he can't rob Peter to pay Paul."

"He's got interior lines."

"All the more reason to hit him from every side."

Sedgwick looked at Grant. And saw a slump-shouldered, nothing-special man, the sort you passed on the street without a thought until, one day, you paused and really looked at him and he scared the devil out of you. His eyes warned of premeditated murder. Grant had not had much of a reputation in the old Army, but Sedgwick figured he just hadn't found a war big enough, not even in Mexico, for his killing ways.

"Your troops are all right, though?" Grant asked again.

"They will be."

"By tomorrow?"

Sedgwick fought down another sigh. "If need be. Although I'd—"

"Have them ready tomorrow," Grant said. "You'll hear from George Meade." He turned his head. "Horace? Had enough of that swill?"

Mounted again, Grant said, "Hot day coming on," and rode off with his staff men and his guards.

Sedgwick sat down in the shade of a tent fly and let his body sag. One of his staff men, Hyde, brought a cup of iced water.

"Found an ice cellar back a ways, sir. Thought you might like a drink."

"Wouldn't mind a drink of something stronger," Sedgwick said. "But she'll do. Hyde, sit down a minute, tell me about that ride of yours." As the boy sat, Sedgwick reached out and tugged one of his ears, as he might have done with a child. "I hear you gave the Johnnies some target practice."

"Just as soon not repeat the experience, sir."

Activity out on the road drew Sedgwick's attention. "Redlegs are swapping out guns. Who's that coming up?" He drank. The water tasted clean. The local wells would not stay that way long.

"Looks like McCartney's battery, sir."

"Well, McCartney can shoot." He drained the cup. "Guess I'd better go up for another look at things. Before Sam Grant finds something doesn't suit him."

He summoned McMahon and Whittier. They went on foot. Up on the line, all horses did was draw fire and kill men for nothing.

As usual, there was a problem. War was the oddest business, reducing intelligent men to fools every third day. The New Jersey Brigade's rifle pits had been dug so close to the Rebel lines that a man couldn't return fire, leaving them useless. Otherwise, things looked tolerably professional. Even the amateur officers were learning the arts of war. And the soldiers on the line learned even faster.

A man did what he could. The trick of leading men was to ask a great deal, but not more than they could deliver. Some of his fellow officers thought him too soft on his soldiers, but it was always the officers, not the men, who disappointed him.

As they came up to the corps' flank along the Brock Road, he found a regiment poorly positioned and blocking the fires of the battery to their rear.

"Now that's just wrong," he said. "Marty, come with me."

"General, I could handle this myself."

"Men need to see their generals. So they know we're not some fairy tale."

He was tired, though. Downright weary. When they

reached the offending troops, he let McMahon give the orders to set them in motion and clear the battery's field of fire.

As the soldiers started rearward, the Rebs opened up. Bullets made the earth cough dust and the withdrawing men broke ranks. Some ran and others dropped flat on the earth. New boys, Sedgwick figured.

Although it was just nine thirty, the heat was a torment. He hoped there was a bit of that ice left back at the headquarters. Of course, there would be none for these poor devils.

The scrambling and scattering troops were an embarrassment, though. The Johnnies were only pecking at them. When he saw a sergeant, who should have known better, flop in the dust and crawl, Sedgwick had to act.

"I'm ashamed of you," he said. "What are you dodging at?" He nudged the man with the toe of his boot. "They can't hit an elephant at that distance."

Ten thirty a.m.
Headquarters, Army of the Potomac

It's true," Lyman told Meade. "I just met McMahon bringing back the body. Sedgwick's men are crying like babies."

Ten thirty a.m.
Laurel Hill

Oates felt kin to a cottonmouth, temper ready to strike at the least provocation. His men had drawn a lucky stretch of the line, set deep enough in the trees to give shade and hide them from Yankee sharpshooters. Even so, the heat and the run-to-ground tiredness kept them testy. When he shifted a company of the 48th to better line it up with the 15th, some of the soldiers kicked about digging new rifle pits and he had gone off like a mad dog loose in a dancing class. Nearly struck a corporal, which wouldn't do. He meant, intended, determined, to carry himself with restraint befitting a colonel. But it was a trial.

Others had it worse, of course. Earlier on, some of the fellows entrenched on the open ground to the right had gone out to bring in the wounded left overnight, and the Yankees had fired on them. That got things started. Whenever a blue-belly tried to retrieve a comrade, he got the same treatment. And the wounded men of both sides lay in the sun, every so often waving an arm in a fever or giving a cry. It sickened Oates, and he told his men to keep out of it.

He was a hard man, and took an impure pride in it, but some things left him raw. He was all for killing Yankees, and no remorse ever troubled him on that count. But he never had been one for beating on a man once he went down. Not any man. You fought standing up, and if you stayed up, that sufficed. He told himself he was a fool for looking for fairness or mercy in this world, and he did not mean to put himself in a position where he'd have to ask for either. But he liked a certain justice. And it wasn't lawyering that had done that to him. Even as a boy, he'd been all fists but mostly fair, and some strange how he'd never been given to taking his born-in rage out on a weak man or stupid animal, although he'd been rough with a woman or two who demanded it. It bewildered him when the fair sex took delight in outright pain, in hard subjugation, and he shunned such creatures, unnerved. He was all for the right kind of roughhousing at the right time, but women who begged to be treated like filth dismayed him. Their unhappiness seemed a greater sin than loving somebody up could ever be. His tastes ran to a mighty give-and-take, good sweat, and nails that did not go too deep into his back.

That black-haired, black-eyed girl yesterday. Looked like she'd come at you claws and all, but in a way most satisfactory. Sort of gal who meant to be a match for the men she chose and wouldn't choose weaklings. Eager as a man, once the shutters closed. She'd been dark enough of complexion to wear some musk on her, too. He always liked a dark skin, his great vice.

A flurry of shots returned him to the moment. Why didn't some "gentleman" on one side or the other ask for a truce to bring in the poor, damned wounded? Because the gentlemen were too proud to ask first. They'd even leave their own kind lying out there.

He took pains never to show he felt such things, but every wounded man was his brother, John.

Well, every man but Lowther. He hoped his major was having a high time cavorting in Richmond and nursing his stubbed toe. While gut-shot men writhed under a frying-pan sun.

The war itself had gone drowsy to his front, and it didn't take religion to count that a blessing. It was a different story to the east, though. Boys a few miles off were having a do.

Let them take their turn. His men needed rest and he was feeling used up.

Without rhyme or reason, Yankee cannon let loose on the grove. Guessing the range, they were just passing the time, with shells to waste. Around him, men gripped the earth. Some cursed inordinately, while others prayed. Branches and a few limbs crashed down around them.

When the shelling let up, with little harm done, his canteen detail returned from the creek in the rear. The water was foul, but he drank it.

Ten thirty a.m.
The Ni River northeast of
Spotsylvania Court House

The colonel fell off his horse by the side of the road. For a worrisome moment, he lay still, as good as dead. Then he laughed and sang out, "On to Richmond!"

The enlisted man who had a good berth as the brigade commander's servant leapt to help him, propping the old man up. An aide fanned him with his kerchief. "On to Richmond . . . I'm in command here!" the colonel cried. Chin gleaming with drool, he cackled again.

"It's sunstroke!" the aide called to the passing soldiers. "It's only the sun, men. . . ."

The claim drew chuckles and murmurs from the ranks.

"Sun done him down, but whiskey done him in," Bill Wildermuth said. "I can smell him from here."

The men of Company C, 50th Pennsylvania, had lowered their estimation of their brigade commander a ways back. As they went their way down the road toward another creek that passed as a river hereabouts, Lieutenant Colonel Cutcheon galloped back from the front of the column.

"Cutcheon'll take the brigade today," Wildermuth told the men marching around him. "The old bird picked a good time to go on the bottle, far as I'm concerned."

First Sergeant Brown said: "No need to run your mouth, Bill."

But he agreed. If they were going into a fight, better to have Cutcheon giving the orders. Colonel Christ had been drinking in the saddle since the brigade was kicked to its feet at two a.m., and he hadn't even had the sense to hide it. Every man he commanded felt insulted. And powerless.

Not a week old, the campaign was wearing down every-one. They'd been rousted from a scrap of sleep that left even Brown slow to rise and formed up for what was described as a quick march forward after their stint as the army's rear guard. But their progress had been anything but swift. Within a half hour, they had been halted to allow a column of horsemen to take precedence. And they stood there for hours as endless fours of cavalrymen clopped southward.

"Must be a mass desertion," Wildermuth had declared. But the men were too tired to laugh.

As dawn neared and a fellow began to see things right, the column still streamed past, flags cased, breathing dust and horseshit, and leaving more of the same. It looked as though the whole cavalry corps were on the road. It was the sort of thing that seemed fine when sketched for the papers, with the clouds of grit removed and the smell left out. But the men of the 50th and their sister regiments had to stand there, sucking in foulness, when they could have backed off a few yards and slept a little. Then, under the sun's first glare, they had been quick-marched in the cavalry's wake, hurrying down a road carpeted with horse dung. It had not been their best morn-ing of the war.

It grew hot enough to make a darkey faint. The colonel had been a fool to drink spirits and then ride out in that sun. A fool or worse. As the column descended toward the creek, with clean dust underfoot at last, Brown looked for-ward, for once, to getting his shoes wet. He figured that every other man did, too. The regiment smelled like a horse barn. A splash of cool water would be welcome on many a count.

The first *tack-tack* of skirmishers sounded ahead, com-ing from the bald hill across the creek. Brown couldn't put a name to where they were and doubted many officers could, either. They were all just tired men going where they were told.

Apart from the heat, the day was lovely, teasing a man with spring as it slapped him with summer.

At the near edge of the creek, the brigade halted. Some of the 60th Ohio boys had been sent ahead to skirmish with Reb cavalry, and the remainder of the regiment led the column, followed by the 50th, then the rest. Cutcheon had indeed assumed command, to the men's satisfaction, but he ordered them to deploy in battle order before they crossed the stream, which drew some groans.

"Could've done it on the other side," Wildermuth said.

"Shut up, Bill," Henry Hill told him, getting out the words one second before Brown could speak them himself.

But Wildermuth was right again. The veterans knew that the road led through a ford, which would be the easiest place to cross and might even have a bed of laid-in stones. But deploying in lines of battle would send men forward through the mud, through sinkholes and ankle snappers.

They were too tired to complain much. The veterans told the new men to sling their cartridge cases over their rifles and hold them high, in case the creek was deeper than it looked, but the men who had survived previous campaigns also drew the corks or unscrewed the tops of their canteens to scoop up what water they could as they waded forward.

It made the crossing an awkward, stumbling business. If the purpose of deploying early had been to have them prepared for a Rebel surprise, it had not worked. Brown was glad to see the grayback horsemen turn and fade from the top of the hill.

The hot days had shallowed the creek, and only the

clumsiest soldiers got a dunking. After shambling up the southern bank, the men halted to form again.

Brown would have liked to strip off his filthy clothes and sit down in the current, letting the water scrape off the crust he wore. Instead, mud replaced the horseshit on his shoes. He chose to view the change as an improvement.

The skirmishing grew fevered, telling the old soldiers that the Rebs had brought up infantry behind the crest. Orders rolled down the brigade line: *Forward!* They marched at right-shoulder-shift, up through a field of young rye, and insects leapt into the air at the threat of their footfalls. Sweat flowed down Brown's temples.

The lay of the land pulled the brigade leftward, into the open ground and away from a grove. Soon, the 50th was advancing on the right of the road, with the 60th Ohio on the left side and the rest of the brigade stretching off into the fields. Brown heard a distant order and saw the 1st Michigan Sharpshooters double-quick forward, racing for the crest to aid the skirmishers.

"We're going to catch it again," Wildermuth said.

"Shut up, Bill," Brown told him.

"Yes, First Sergeant."

Corporal Doudle offered his view of matters: "Bill's still sore about that Rebel besting him back in them woods. Wasn't that a howler?"

"You shut up, too," Brown said.

Wildermuth began whistling "Dixie."

The men laughed. Plagued by poison ivy as well as ravaged feet, John Eckert the Shorter moaned, "What are you whistling that for?" *Vott are you vissling dat for?*

"Chust for nice," Wildermuth answered. "Got to be ready to make new friends, in case things turn unpleasant."

"I told you to shut up," Brown snapped. But it was all part of the company's ritual, the pattern of how they did things when every man had a right to be on edge. His role was just to tell Wildermuth to be quiet, without a deep expectation of being obeyed. "Pay attention now," he said.

To Brown's surprise, it was Henry Hill who spoke next, although his voice was muted. He marched just to the front and right of Brown and spoke largely to him.

"I don't like this. One brigade out here like this."

Brown didn't much like it, either. But it was another of those things that just plain was.

Shortly before they reached the crest, the invisible force on the opposite slope unleashed a Rebel yell.

There was no more banter.

Captain Burket repeated the order from on high to move up at the double-quick. The captain then let the two ranks of trotting men pass by and picked up at Brown's side.

"Captain Schwenk has the four left companies. Anything happens to me and Brumm, you take orders right from him."

"Yes, sir." That was fine. Schwenk, who had Company A, was as good a man as the regiment had left.

Burket ran back toward the colors, sword flashing as he pointed it toward a foe who remained unseen. The racket ahead signified a clash beyond skirmishing.

As the regiment broke the crest, Brown saw a swarm of Johnnies off to the brigade's left front, someone else's problem. The first cannon fire sounded from the rear and shells shrieked overhead, dropping behind the Rebs and accomplishing nothing.

Lieutenant Colonel Cutcheon rode along the brigade front, halting his right-flank regiments at a fence line atop the crest. Unlike the man who lay back by the roadside, Cutcheon appeared fearless. It steadied the men.

The last skirmishers dashed in. There were still no Confederates in front of the 50th.

It was a different story on the brigade's left, though. Another passel of Johnnies leapt out of a fold in the ground, as if some storybook wizard had called up spooks. They hit the 1st Michigan Sharpshooters at an angle, hard as a club.

The Sharpshooters broke, just took off at a run. As Brown and his men watched, it looked as though the brigade might crumple from the left. But the 79th New York took matters in hand, making a charge that stopped the Rebels for an exchange of volleys. The Sharpshooters stopped to rally down the slope.

More Union guns fired overhead, digging up dirt in fields behind the Rebs. Ahead, an enemy battery unlimbered its guns along a tree line.

Then it all went crazy. The sudden way combat did. The Sharpshooters no sooner got back to the line than another wave of Rebs rose out of nowhere. The Union guns north of the river dropped their range and opened again. The shells struck the 79th New York and the Sharpshooters, sparing the Johnnies entirely.

The brigade line collapsed like dominoes going down.

The Rebs wheeled a touch to the right to come at the 60th Ohio and the 50th Pennsylvania from the front, as well as the flank.

"Steady!" Brown called. He understood that panic was contagious, knew it all too well. "Steady, boys!"

Officers gathered in the road, too far away for Brown to hear a word, then Cutcheon rode back to rally the fleeing regiments. The order was given to fire on the approaching Rebs. Men used the top fence rail to steady their aim.

When the Johnnies replied, a splash of blood left Captain Burket's shoulder. He clutched himself and dropped hard to his knees.

Lieutenant Brumm ran forward.

"Doudle!" Brown shouted. "Take a man and get the captain out of here."

The corporal moved sharply toward the captain, who knelt as if frozen in prayer. Captain Schwenk ran across the firing line to reach Burket, risking his life like a lunatic. After a quick pause and a word with Brumm, Schwenk dashed back to his company again.

The men knew what to do. And canal men were stubborn, not least when angered. As Doudle and one of the Eckert boys dragged Burket off, a fair amount of profanity rose from the ranks. Burket was as well-liked as a captain could be. And he was their old harbormaster.

The Johnnies were close enough to hear the profanities and echo them. They all stood there shooting at each other, just knocking each other down, until they could barely manhandle their rifles for the sweat.

Whether at a half-heard order or not, the 60th Ohio began to give ground on their left. Not running, but inching backward. Instinctively, the 50th began to step slowly rearward, leaving the fence.

As soon as the Rebels realized what was happening, they hooted and hollered and jeered. They began to step forward. Warily at first, then ever quicker.

There weren't even all that many of them, Brown realized. The Rebs might have had the numbers to their advantage, but not by much over the whole brigade. There was no honest reason why they should win. He resented every backward step. And it wasn't only about the captain. An odd, hurt pride had flared.

But they didn't have a brigade anymore. It was just the 60th Ohio and them, with the 60th falling back more quickly now, letting the Rebs come in hard on Company A.

"Goddamn it," Brown said, and he was not given to profanity.

The Johnnies soon owned the crest. Waving their red

rags and jeering from the fence line. Hardly bothering to shoot.

Bareheaded, Captain Schwenk ran out in front of the 50th's left, saber held high. He turned his back on the Rebs, daring them to shoot him.

Schwenk had a good bass voice and it served him well. He bellowed, "Fiftieth Pennsylvania! Halt."

Astounded by the display, the men obeyed.

"Fix bayonets!" Schwenk ordered.

The men obeyed that command, too. Brown could feel their rekindled rage, swelling again like flames. Crowds of thoughts rushed by, none of them kindly.

Schwenk wheeled toward the enemy, pointed with his sword, and shouted, "Charge!"

For once, the Johnnies were taken by surprise. Bewildered. They popped off a few shots, but made no serious effort to hold the crest. Not with maddened blue-bellies flashing thirsty bayonets.

The regiment let out a cheer. Men broke ranks and ran forward, as if they were freshly rested, watered, fed, and set to a footrace.

Captain Schwenk still led from the front, sword extended, as if the blade were pulling him along. Although Schwenk wasn't his captain, Brown felt protective. Dozens of other soldiers felt it, too. They swarmed around the captain, determined to outpace him, as they vaulted over the fence or bullied right through it.

The last Rebs just broke.

Looking around in wonder, Brown saw that Cutcheon had led up the 20th Michigan from the reserve and the Michiganders had almost caught up with the 50th. More blue units were fording the creek as well.

"Pennsylvania!" someone yelled. The other men took it up.

Say one thing for the Johnnies, Brown decided, they were fleet of foot, once they got going.

The Reb artillerymen fired a few rounds over the heads of their retreating comrades, but the shells didn't do much damage. Made a wild noise, though, toppling end over end.

One brave Reb officer tried to rally the remnants of his regiment, but they had no time to form. The Pennsylvanians crashed into them. Rifle butts and bayonets, even fists, came into play. The melee was over before Brown could reach the Rebel he had singled out, but he saw Schwenk cut a man down with his sword.

Slopped with blood, Schwenk soon after halted the companies following him, letting the last sorry Johnnies slip away. Brown realized he was winded, dizzy, and suntouched enough to puke. Yet, somehow, he and the other men managed a cheer.

Ordered to reassemble back on the crest, the soldiers dragged themselves up past the dead and wounded Rebs. Brown was content to let the litter bearers earn their pay.

Lieutenant Brumm found him. "Captain's wound won't kill him," he said. "Unless the surgeons do. Won't be back for a while, though." He shook his head and looked up at the sky. Pure blue spread above a lace of smoke. "Christ, Brownie. I didn't want it to be like this."

"No good man does, sir. Captain Schwenk's waving you over."

After Brown called the company roll and found that they had come through without a man killed, he ordered his soldiers to take off their shoes and stockings and dry their feet properly. Then he had a detail collect canteens and head to the creek before its water grew unfit to drink, and he sent in a scrawled requisition for ammunition. Being first sergeant had almost begun to fit him.

When Brumm came back, he passed on orders to dig entrenchments along the crest. The men were hardly delighted at the thought of navvy labor in the heat, but most were relieved at the prospect of an end to marching and fighting for the day. For his part, Brown felt an angry discontent.

Up ahead, the road was open: The Rebs looked to be plain gone. No gambling man, he still was ready to bet they'd be ordered down that road, sooner or later. And he had a fair notion of what would be waiting for them, if it was later. Tired or not, they needed to seize their chance.

They never could seem to grab the apple dangling in their faces.

Bill Wildermuth came up beside him, blouse stripped off for work.

"You thinking what I am, First Sergeant?"

"Not sure I ever knew you to think at all, Bill."

But Wildermuth was serious. "I used to kind of like the notion that General Burnside was slow. Didn't mind getting to the barn dance late, not one little bit. I'm beginning to change my mind, though."

Four p.m.
Tally house, Union right flank

Meade stood between Grant and Hancock on the high ground above the Po. It was a battle to control his temper. Grant had come up, impatient to find a way to flank Lee, chewing his cigar and putting questions directly to Hancock that Hancock, who had just arrived, couldn't answer: *How many fords are down there along the Po? Is there good terrain behind that Reb battery yonder?* Meade longed to say, "*I* could tell you that, if you hadn't taken my cavalry away. You've left this army blind."

Instead, he said: "Duane is conducting a reconnaissance of the crossing sites."

Behind them, Hancock's last, dusty division closed on the corps.

Grant took the butt of his cigar from his mouth and flicked off a wealth of saliva. "Quicker to send down a regiment or two."

"He has other men with him," Meade said in a placating tone. "Duane's a good engineer, he won't waste time."

He sensed the swirling behind Grant's placid exterior. Still smarting from the embarrassment over Sheridan, he was learning to step carefully.

Meade waved a fly from his beard.

The various aides to the senior generals, as well as three of Hancock's division commanders, Barlow, Birney, and Gibbon, stood close enough to respond to a raised voice, but far enough off not to pry into quieter speech. Everyone understood the code, and the distances between the clusters of men were as precise in their way as the place settings at a Chestnut Street dowager's dinner.

Where the groves parted on the high ground beyond the river, a few Confederates had been observed shuffling along the road to Spotsylvania, but not enough to merit artillery fire. Wagons came along now, in a dawdling line. Meade estimated the range at a mile and a quarter, but saw no point in opening on them, either.

One of Grant's hangers-on spoke up: "Ought to put some shot on those damned wagons."

Meade turned toward the man. "And what good would that do? Scare a few niggers and old mules?"

Rawlins, who had been needling Ted Lyman, said, "Hell, I'd not only shell 'em, I'd have troops across the river by now."

Bypassing Meade, Grant told Hancock, "Why not give them a few rounds? Let your boys range their guns?"

Hancock knew the suggestion was an order. He turned to his chief of staff and told him, "Have the First Rhode Island and First New Hampshire batteries open on that train."

Morgan hopped to the task, and Meade said nothing.

In minutes, the cannon let loose. The battery officers had taken the range with impressive accuracy, and the first shells burst close to the wagons. The reaction up on the road was instant chaos, a jamboree of confusion, with teamsters steering off the road in every direction, lashing their beasts, or jumping from their wagons.

A number of the watching officers chuckled.

The Confederate battery across the river replied. Its officers were good judges of distance, too. One of the first shells struck the Rhode Island gunners. Men came apart as they flew into the air.

Hancock's other batteries joined the exchange. The earth trembled under Meade's boots.

Grant sidled up. "Might be an opening over there. Send some men across and see what's what."

Meade took the opportunity to teach Hancock a lesson about breaking the chain of command. He addressed one of Barlow's brigade commanders directly.

"Brooke, send two regiments across the river to reconnoiter. The Hundred and Forty-eighth Pennsylvania, I think. And perhaps the Hundred and Forty-fifth."

"Shall I take that battery, sir?"

The Reb guns would pull out soon enough: They were taking a beating.

"No. Just have a look and report."

It wasn't enough for Grant. Fifteen minutes later, with the Pennsylvania regiments fording the stream below or scrambling over the water on a log, the general in chief said, "Have Hancock send over a division, clear that high ground." Instead of letting Meade pass along the order, Grant turned to the Second Corps commander. "Win, can you get a division over there quick? Get hold of that high road?"

"Yes, sir."

"Tell you what," Grant said. "You get one division over there to start. But have the rest of your men ready to follow, if we find an opening. See if we can't put you on Lee's flank or in his rear. With your whole corps."

"Mott, too, sir?" Hancock asked, with eyebrows pinched.

Meade interjected: "Remember, Sam? We sent Mott's division to Wright, to tie in his left with Burnside."

Grant discarded the well-chewed end of his cigar. "Everybody but Mott," he told Hancock.

Hancock turned to Barlow, waving over the lanky New Englander, and began to repeat the order. Barlow brightened at every single word.

"You're the spearhead, Frank. *Carpe diem,* all that."

Barlow spoke up in his flinty voice, loudly enough for the generals to hear. "I'm authorized to drive anyone I find?"

Meade felt that matters were getting out of hand. He waved up Biddle, who carried his best map, and had the sketch spread on the grass.

"Look here," Meade said. "The river turns sharply from southeast to southwest behind those trees." He pointed toward Lee's lines. "To get at Lee from that direction, we have to cross the Po twice."

"It's not the Mississippi," Grant said.

"And it's late in the day," Meade added. "We only have a few hours of daylight left."

Across the Po, light skirmishing pricked the afternoon.

Grant looked at Hancock, glanced at Barlow, and returned his attention to the corps commander. "Get as far as you can. If you can't force the second river line tonight, set up for a morning assault."

Hancock nodded in a show of enthusiasm, but Meade saw concern in Win's eyes. He was glad Humphreys wasn't present: His chief of staff might have exploded in outrage. And Meade didn't want to lose the man the way he had almost lost Griffin. This was exactly the kind of off-the-cuff affair to which Grant was prone and that Humphreys despised. Humph would have demanded a proper reconnaissance and some faint semblance of an actual plan.

When Humphreys heard about Sheridan's legitimized theft of the cavalry corps, Meade had needed to grasp his chief of staff by the arm to restrain him from marching over to Grant for a showdown.

That humiliation over Sheridan had incensed Meade to the point where he had considered quitting command. But the sentiment faded. He would *not* quit, nor would he be driven to it. And, he had reminded himself, Grant had his good points, too. Lee was doubtless in shock, or something akin to it. Grant did make war, and with little regard for niceties. Better a Hun than a Hamlet.

But Grant needed an opposing mind to balance him, to counter his impulsiveness. Meade still believed he was meant to lead the Army of the Potomac.

Grant's thoughts leapt to even greater endeavors and he turned to Meade again.

"Tomorrow," the general in chief announced, "I want an attack all along the front. So Lee can't shift any forces against Hancock. Make that work, George."

Meade saw a dozen objections and stammered as he began: "The Sixth Corps . . . Sam, there's been some turmoil, remember. Wright's new to command at that level, he'll want time. . . ."

"If Wright can't fill Sedgwick's shoes," Grant said, "find

someone who can. I want an attack all along the front to-morrow."

A commotion down the slope caught everyone's eye. Barlow cantered along waving a sword as his men rushed toward the river and their destiny.

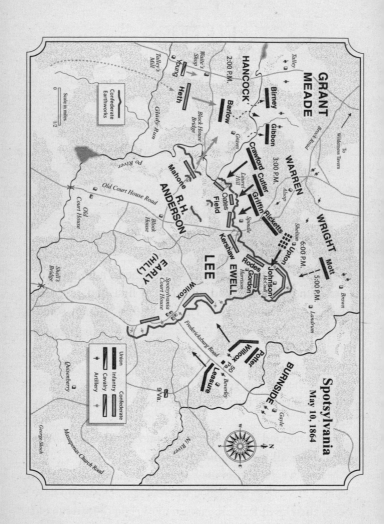

Spotsylvania
May 10, 1864

FIFTEEN

May 10, one p.m.
Headquarters, Army of the Potomac

Meade worried about Barlow and his men. Grant had made a mess of things, and the army's finest division was at risk. But Wright could not be put off any longer. His effort mattered, too.

To the southwest, the noise of skirmishing threatened worse to come for Barlow. And after Warren's failed morning attack, Meade lacked an appetite for further setbacks. Every one of Grant's schemes had come to nothing: The decisiveness Meade had admired at first had revealed itself as mere impetuosity. He intended to attempt something properly organized, an assault Ted Lyman might term "scientific." If Grant approved the change to his grand attack.

He turned to the general in chief. "Best settle matters with Wright. That business we discussed. He'll have plenty to do."

Grant nodded. He looked even untidier than usual. And tired. They all were damnably tired.

Meade waved across the yard to his chief of staff, then pointed at Wright, who stood where Sedgwick should have been, and David Russell, chosen by Wright to lead his old division after he vaulted up to command of the Sixth Corps. Wright was a handsome, imposing man who looked a general's part, while Russell was lean as an Indian and wore a narrow beard over his top buttons. David Russell, Meade knew, had graduated near the bottom at the Academy, but proved himself a good man on the battlefield.

Humphreys led them over. After routine greetings, Meade asked, "Well?"

"That young engineer you—," Wright began.

"Mackenzie," Meade said.

"Yes, sir. Mackenzie. He claims he's discovered the best point to strike their line. Up along the west side of that salient."

"Have you looked yourself? What do *you* think?"

Wright shrugged. "It's as good a place as any other."

It was not a suitable answer from a fellow engineer. Meade let it pass. Wright looked blown. And still shocked by his sudden elevation.

"And the assault force?" Meade asked.

Wright waved off a halo of flies and gestured toward his subordinate.

"General Meade," Russell responded, "we're assembling the twelve finest regiments in the corps. As a provisional brigade. It's—"

This time, it was Grant who interrupted. "Brigade ain't much."

"No, sir," Wright leapt in, "but those twelve regiments have the strength of a light division."

Meade told Grant: "I've ordered Mott to support."

"Tell me again how this dog's supposed to bite," Grant said. "Who'll have the command?"

The questioning annoyed Meade, who had explained things in detail. But he could not afford to show temperament with Grant. He had already had to resist making sharp remarks about the collapse of Grant's off-the-cuff scheme for Hancock. For which Frank Barlow stood to pay the butcher's bill.

"Upton," Wright said with a suspect grin. "This firebrand colonel I've got."

"Heard the name," Grant said. "Can't place him."

Wright grunted. "Good fighter. And the most arrogant, self-righteous shit to wear a uniform. Bread-and-water Methodist who farts scripture. Abolitionist, of course."

"And the finest brigade commander in the Sixth Corps," Meade added.

"That so?"

Russell, who had been Upton's fellow brigade commander the day before, spoke up: "Yes, sir. Upton's a bit of a character, but he's splendid in a fight. 'Barlow with a Bible,' Uncle John used to joke."

Turning again to Grant, Meade added: "Upton's been deviling everybody to try out an idea of his. May be sense in it. Rather than sending out long, thin lines and pulling up for a shooting contest, he believes an assault in column on a narrow front—an attack that stops for nothing—would punch through Lee's entrenchments. Relying on speed and thrust. And bayonets."

"Like to see that," Grant said.

"Then you approve?" Meade asked. He wanted a firm commitment in front of the others.

"Well," Grant began, with one of his slope-shouldered shrugs, "I don't see why not." He contemplated the ruins of his cigar. "You don't want a brigadier to lead it? Twelve regiments, that's a lot of cotton for one colonel."

Meade exchanged looks with Wright and Russell.

Grown sullen around Grant, Humphreys broke his silence. "This army's brigadiers have had their chance. Upton's hungry. And mean. The way those Bible-pounders tend to be. He'll bring down the wrath of Jehovah on the Rebs."

"Or the wrath of Emory Upton, anyway," Wright said. "Not sure which one might be more unpleasant."

Meade had one more matter to settle regarding Upton. "The man's ambitious," he told Grant. "He's been pestering every one of us for a star. As far as I'm concerned, he earned one last autumn, but he doesn't have the political weight." He slapped at an insect bothering his cheek. "A word from you, though . . . I'd like to authorize Generals Wright and Russell to tell him he'll make brigadier, if he breaks Lee's line."

Grant snorted. "And if he doesn't?"

Wright said: "He won't be expected back. He can try commanding cherubim and seraphim."

"Sounds like you don't like him very much."

" 'Like' is not a word that springs to mind."

The general in chief blew smoke into the afternoon heat. "Still set for five o'clock, George? No dawdlers today?"

Meade shot Humphreys a look: *Don't you say a word, I'll handle this.*

"Yes, sir," Meade said. "In accordance with your orders. At five, Warren, supported by two of Hancock's divisions, will attack the ridge again. To the Fifth Corps' left, Upton's assault on the salient will constitute the Sixth Corps' primary effort. Mott, detached from Hancock, will attack on Upton's left and exploit any break in Lee's line." Choosing his next words carefully, Meade asked, "Have you heard from General Burnside?"

Grant shook his head. "We'll get him moving. I've sent Badeau to see to things." He scratched at his ginger beard: Virginia's insects were persistent skirmishers. "If this Upton fellow's attack don't work, something else is bound to. Lee can't be strong everywhere."

Grant still had not said a word about subordinating Burnside and the Ninth Corps to the Army of the Potomac, the only reasonable solution to the confusion that was manifest. Burnside needed rigorous supervision. Lacking it, he contributed precious little. The campaign cried out for unity of command, but Grant had to find his way to his own conclusions.

As the man had finally come to his senses that morning regarding the wild-goose chase upon which he had launched Hancock the afternoon before. The Second Corps had not had time before nightfall to breach the second line of the Po, and, of course, Lee had brought up forces during the night to secure his flank. Worse, when Grant had finally taken a proper look at the map, he had grasped the point that Meade had sought to make: Hancock's corps was cut off from the army by the river, thrust into a perfect trap, its position an invitation to Lee to destroy it.

Grant had ordered Hancock to withdraw, and Win had pulled back Birney and Gibbon, leaving Barlow's division as a rear guard while the others recrossed the river. Now Barlow had to extricate himself, with the Rebs swelling around him, and Hancock had gone out personally to see to matters. For his part, Meade did not believe Lee was going to let Barlow stroll back unmolested.

Meade sighed.

Everyone looked at him.

"Problem, George?" Grant asked.

"No, sir. Thinking about something else." He waved a hand. "These damned flies."

"Sight worse crossing the Isthmus," Grant said. "This Upton. West Point?"

"Class of '61," Wright said. "As he'll be only too glad to tell you."

"And this mad dog's still a colonel?" Grant tapped the ash from his cigar. "Even without pull in Washington . . ."

"He was stuck in the artillery for two years," Russell explained. "As a captain. Before he took a regiment and got his jump." Russell, a sober sort, broke into a smile. "I don't know an officer in the corps who hasn't heard Upton's 'why I'm not a brigadier' story."

Humphreys spoke up again. "First-rate soldier, though. Brilliant work at Rappahannock Station. Knows how to take a fortified line. And to bluff. If he wasn't a damned Methodist, he'd take the drawers off all of us at poker."

Meade noted that Russell let the slight go by. Russell, too, had been a hero of Rappahannock Station.

Wright smirked and said: "Upton travels with a whole damned library. When he isn't reading the Good Book, he's crabbing through de Saxe or God knows who. Oh, General Humphreys is right, he's quite the soldier. However . . ."

Grant smiled, but this was Grant's curled little smile, an expression that made Meade wary nowadays.

"Sounds almost like you're trying to get rid of him," Grant said.

Wright looked surprised. "No, no. Nothing like that. It's just . . . I wouldn't say he's the corps' most popular officer. . . ."

Grant's smile persisted. "Wasn't all that popular myself."

Off toward Barlow's division, artillery pounded.

Two thirty p.m.
Along the Shady Grove Church Road

Brooke, can you hold?" Barlow asked.

Bullets from Rebel skirmishers hunted men in blue.

"I can hold them," the colonel shouted back. "Don't know how long, though. Prisoner claims Heth's entire division's out there."

And Mahone's division sat just across the south bank of the Po, ready to pounce. Outnumbered as much as four to one along his forward line, Barlow intended to draw blood as he withdrew.

"I need you to hold for a quarter hour, at least," Barlow told the brigade commander. "Give Smyth and Miles time to entrench at the bridgehead."

He was fighting with only two brigades up, Brooke's men and Paul Frank's lot.

As the racket increased, Brooke pulled his horse close to Barlow's. "I can do that, a quarter of an hour. Maybe longer. If Frank holds." The colonel looked doubtful about the prospect of that.

"I'm on my way to the right to have a look. Just hold them, John."

They had beaten off the Reb skirmishers handily. But great gray waves would break over them soon.

Artillery rounds shrieked overhead, Union guns firing blindly from north of the river.

Before Barlow could put the spurs to his stallion, Hancock rode up. Barlow had been furious about the botched operation the evening before, then about being left as the rear guard again. But Hancock had returned to fight beside him, after withdrawing the rest of the corps to safety. Courage canceled many another sin.

No one saluted. The Rebs were too close.

Hancock nodded to Barlow, then to Brooke. "Looks like you drew the short straw, John."

"Made sense, sir," Brooke replied. "Given our dispositions."

Barlow caught the note of criticism. Hancock had left the division spread out to cover what had been the corps' front that morning. Even entrenched, the defense was as thin as Japan paper.

Hancock turned to Barlow. "Miles and Smyth have closed at the bridgehead. And all of the guns are across, except for Arnold's." His eyes shifted back to Brooke. "The pontoons are secure, they'll be there when you need them."

"First, I'll have to get to them," Brooke said.

Barlow beat down a smile. Brooke was no toady.

And the colonel had a right to be disgruntled. Once Brooke abandoned these entrenchments and passed through the grove to his rear, there remained a half mile of open ground between his men and the paths down to the bridges. All the way, they'd be under artillery fire. Withdrawing was going to be tricky, to say the least. And Paul Frank, his weakest colonel, would have even farther to go than would John Brooke.

That morning, as the corps withdrawal began, Hancock had explained Grant's decision to leave Barlow in place as long as possible to deter Lee from shifting forces away from his left. The rationale was little consolation. The wait thereafter had been grim, until George Meade, bless him and all Philadelphia, had sent down orders to withdraw the division.

It looked as though he had waited an hour too long.

As for Hancock, Barlow was glad of his presence now, despite his taste for independent action. With an extended front to cover, he couldn't be everywhere. If Hancock just saw to the bridgehead, to Miles and Smyth, it would be an enormous help. And Hancock, regal as Henry V in the saddle, was always an inspiration to the men. Barlow had been frustrated with his superior of late, finding his hero to be a bit of a hen, but Hancock shone today with his old verve.

"Here they come!" Brooke shouted.

The three officers looked across the road and down a fallow field. Red banners waving, a motley gray mass advanced up the long incline.

The Rebs let loose with their wild squeaking and hooting. They picked up their pace.

Barlow turned to Hancock and Colonel Brooke. "I'd best see to Paul Frank. Brooke here can manage."

Hancock smiled. Voice raised to be heard, he told Brooke: "I believe, Colonel, that your division commander has just dismissed me from his forward line." And turning to Barlow: "I'll see how your micks are doing, then go on to Miles."

As Barlow kicked his horse to life, Brooke called to his men, "Hold your fire, damn it."

Brooke would give a good account of himself.

The Rebs came on fast now, screaming, thousands of footfalls beating the drum of the earth. Barlow didn't bother to look. He didn't need to.

Leading his staff through a bad bit of greenery, he had to back up and go around a thicket. He reached Frank's left just as the German's brigade opened fire on the Rebels.

Too damned soon, Barlow thought.

As he rode from the trees into another open field, a pair of Frank's officers spotted him and lashed their horses toward him as if in a race.

They didn't give him time to get a word out.

"Colonel Frank's drunk," a sweat-stained major complained.

"Drunk as an Irish priest," a captain added.

The gunfire along the road became a steady roar. Rounds snapped past the mounted men.

"General Barlow, you have to relieve him immediately," the major added.

"I'll decide what I have to do, Major," Barlow said coldly. Of course, Frank would be drunk. That was the icing on the cake, if not the cork in the bottle. His anger at Hancock surged again. Why had he reinstated the Teuton ass?

Assuming a more appropriate, if still excited, tone, the major said, "Sir, he's so drunk he can hardly stay in the saddle. The men all see it."

A wry smile crept over Barlow's features. He was tempted to think that Frank might do less harm in a drunken stupor.

The damned thing was that he couldn't muddle things further by relieving the man in the middle of a withdrawal.

"*Every* officer will be held to account," Barlow said. "At

the appropriate time. Meanwhile, I expect the regimental commanders to do their duty. For now, that duty is to defend this line. You may pass that along, Major. And look to your own responsibilities."

Barlow rode behind the embattled regiments. Frank was not in evidence.

Probably went to ground when he saw me coming, Barlow decided.

The men began to cheer. Through the smoke, Barlow saw the gray lines withdrawing, their order broken.

Well done. But only the start.

Wounded men stumbled rearward. Where were the stretcher bearers? Barlow took a hard line when it came to the medical side of things. He knew every unguent and potion in a surgeon's kit, had made it his business to know. And his surgeons had learned to wash their knives and saws at least once a fortnight.

Barlow believed in bayoneting cowards, but men with honest wounds deserved good care.

"Black," he called to his aide. "Find Colonel Frank and stay with him. You know the plan. See that he follows it. And be prepared to write a report on the idiot." Barlow thought a moment, then added, "If he questions your authority, shoot him dead."

He took off into the grove again, stopping by Brooke's brigade just as the Rebs came on a second time. Arnold's battery fired from the right, doing good service but exposed to capture.

"Maynard," he called back to a lieutenant. "Tell Arnold to find a position nearer the river. He's to keep his limbers close, he may have to run for it."

The Rebs spilled over a line of raw works he had ordered abandoned earlier. They came on shrieking, determined to reach the blue line north of the road, to reach their prey and slaughter it on the spot.

Again, Brooke's men repulsed them.

The colonel rode up to Barlow's shrinking party.

"Rebs don't seem short of men today."

"We'll leave them shorter."

"Things all right over there? With Frank?"

"As one might expect. Hold as long as you reasonably can, John. But don't lose your brigade."

More Confederate guns opened from south of the Po, off to the left. Their fires crisscrossed those of the batteries supporting Heth's attack, weaving a deadly web.

Barlow spurred his horse back toward the broad field in the rear, the expanse across which Brooke's men and most of Frank's command would have to withdraw to reach the river and safety. Faulty shells plopped in the dirt like mighty raindrops.

Thanks be to God, Barlow told himself, for the Southern gentry's distaste for manufacturing skills.

He stopped his party in the middle of the field. Short rounds burst overhead, not all Confederate. It was all a damned mess, but it looked as though Smyth had gotten his men clear. On the far left flank, Miles' skirmishers remained behind to delay an attempt at envelopment by Mahone's division.

If Rebels plunged across the Block House Bridge, Brooke and Frank would be cut off from the army.

He wanted to ride to the bridgehead to inspect the progress on the earthworks, but there was no time. Hancock would have to see to that. Better to remain with his exposed brigades. The time was approaching to pull them out in an interval between charges.

As he rode back toward Brooke's entrenchments, he saw with a start that patches of trees to the rear had taken fire. The grove was only middling thick, but with memories of the Wilderness fresh and raw, the prospect of burning woods might panic the men. Still worse, the pattern of shelling told him that Arnold's battery remained in its old position.

Bravery was one thing, folly another. He had sent Arnold clear orders to remove his guns. The situation called for an accounting, once the fight was done.

He dispatched another rider to tell the captain to withdraw immediately.

The third Rebel charge announced itself with another Rebel yell. It sounded as though the attackers had been reinforced.

Frank's brigade front would be the point of crisis now. Skirting Brooke's position, Barlow led his staff into the grove, counting on speed to get them past the stretches of fire. But burning trees blocked the way. Turning his party again, he hastened to the rear of Brooke's line. Just in time to witness a mighty charge.

This time, the Rebs came on at a full run. As men fell to Brooke's volleys, others filled their places. Red flags waved, fell, and rose again. The men in gray and homespun screamed their lungs out as they leapt over empty entrenchments and their own dead.

Before he could reach Brooke, the foremost Rebs surged over the dirt wall. Brooke's men stood their ground. The fight grew demonic.

A captain clutched his ribs and fell from his horse at Barlow's side. Barlow kept riding. Yards away, a riot of men went at each other with rifle butts and bayonets, breaking the unspoken rule that, pressed to a certain degree, men would retreat. There was a new viciousness now, an anger that thickened the air. Gore splashed from crushed skulls and guts ripped wide, from bones smashed out through flesh.

He found Brooke firing his revolver into the melee.

"Do what you can, John. Pull for the river, do what you can to keep the men together. I'll see to Frank's brigade."

Instead of trying to thread through the grove, Barlow kicked hard with his spurs and raced between the fighting and the trees. He drew his saber.

Men on foot, in blue and gray, leapt from his path.

Frank's left regiments stood their ground as well as John Brooke's boys, fighting as brutally. As he rode the line, Barlow ordered each successive regiment to withdraw fighting and move to the river. One lieutenant colonel looked over Barlow's shoulder, eyes filled with doubt. When Barlow turned, he saw the woods ablaze. The pockets of fire had become a conflagration.

And Arnold's battery *still* had not withdrawn.

More officers complained about Frank's drunken state, but Barlow had not laid eyes on the man since the morning. There was nothing he could do but give orders himself, and he gave them crisply.

Riding his horse as if he meant to kill it, he plunged through a breaking regiment. He cursed the men, but he spared them blows from his saber. They'd fought as well as any man could expect. The Confederate numbers had reached overwhelming levels.

"Form back in the trees and go to the river," he shouted.

In the burning trees.

By the time he reached Arnold's guns, he was in a fury.

"Why don't you get out of here, you fool!"

Arnold looked up, surprised. "No orders," he shouted.

"I've sent courier after courier. Save your guns, damn it. Pull back to the high ground above the river. Support the withdrawal, but no last stands." Then he added, "I'm going to need you, Arnold."

The Rhode Islander took that as a splendid compliment. He began barking orders to limber up the guns.

As Barlow cantered back over the field, he found one of the most confused spectacles he'd yet witnessed in the war. Pockets of men grappled to the death. On one side of a brawl, prisoners and the wounded hurried rearward, while on the other side, men just ran. Everywhere, blue and gray uniforms intermingled. Rebs stopped to loot haversacks, while his own retreating soldiers tore their blankets from their knapsacks, yanking them free of the straps to swing them over heads and shoulders as they dashed under flaming limbs in their flight to the rear.

The spreading fires made some Rebels hesitate to continue the pursuit. Their officers railed at them. One fired his pistol at Barlow.

Barlow galloped back to a farm track along the last high ground, beyond the reach of the flames, and made his way to the long field his men had to pass. Much of Brooke's brigade had held together, withdrawing in impressively good order, but the Reb cannoneers were merciless.

As for Paul Frank, he seemed to have disappeared from the face of the earth, along with his staff. With any luck, Barlow thought, Heth's men had grabbed him.

He turned to gauge the Reb advance and saw a lone blue regiment leveling volleys, alone and too close to the enemy, stalwart unto madness. He thought he could make out a Pennsylvania banner through the smoke.

Over the protests of his staff, Barlow kicked his horse forward.

It was the 148th Pennsylvania, Jim Beaver's regiment. The colonel sat his horse with perfect aplomb amid the chaos. His men fired by four successive ranks, a tactic Barlow recognized from his plunge into history early in the war. Marshal Turenne had used the technique to great effect two centuries before, but no one had thought to apply it to modern war.

More to Beaver than he'd realized. He'd always thought the fellow dull, if brave.

When Barlow came up, the colonel flashed his anger.

"We never got the damned order to withdraw."

"You're doing well enough, Beaver."

The Pennsylvanian growled. "Somebody had to form a rear guard. Since everybody else was off to the races."

"Good work. Slow the buggers down, but get your men back."

He turned his horse again. Most of Frank's soldiers appeared to have gone *sauve qui peut* for the river west of the bridges, but Brooke still had his brigade roughly in hand. His last men, save Beaver's, were passing the crest that dropped to the pontoons.

Reaching the river overlook, Barlow found a regiment of Smyth's Irishmen, the 116th Pennsylvania, positioned to cover the last of the withdrawal. Growing confident that he'd have some semblance of a division left at the end of the day, he made his way east to Miles' position, where entrenchments had been thrown up with remarkable speed. Two of Miles' regiments had not fully withdrawn from their forward positions, though.

Flaring, Barlow said, "Get them back, Miles. Or you'll answer for it."

Friendship was for the rear.

He paused by Miles' side long enough to look down the long field and watch a full division of Confederates advance with battle flags flying. From the higher north bank, tiers of Union artillery opened on them.

"Just get those regiments back," Barlow repeated, and he rode westward again to see if any other crises needed attention.

He soon found Captain Arnold with his little artillery column, close enough to the crossing site to make it over to safety. Arnold was weeping as if he had just learned of his mother's death.

"I lost a gun, sir," he said. "It got stuck in the trees, in the flames. We cut the others free, but I lost a gun."

"Be glad you didn't lose your whole damned battery,"

Barlow said. He had no time for the artilleryman's romanticism. Never did have, really. Guns could be replaced. He had even heard complaints about the artillery reserve clogging the roads with an excess of guns.

"It's the first piece the Second Corps has ever lost," the captain said.

"We've got more cannon than we know what to do with," Barlow told him. "Straighten up, and get your battery over that goddamned bridge."

It all went madly fast thereafter, with Nellie Miles giving the Rebs a splendid blast of musketry before scooting over the last pontoons to safety under the massed guns of the corps. Barlow was among the last to cross, and he found a number of Brooke's officers laughing like Bedlam lunatics on the other side. They tightened their expressions as Barlow approached.

"Well," he said, "what's so funny, gentlemen? Your survival, or mine?" Suddenly, he couldn't help it. He grinned, too. "Hoping you'd seen the last of me, you dogs? Go on, tell me. What's so funny?"

A brave major stepped closer, volunteering as spokesman for the rest.

"It's Colonel Beaver, sir. Of the Hundred Forty-eighth."

"I know which regiment Beaver has."

"Yes, sir. Well, you know he never touches a drop of spirits. Hasn't had a drink the entire war."

"And?"

"Well, I suppose you had to see it. To get the full flavor. Old Beaver gets himself cut off from the bridges, so he has to leave his horse and lead his men down that tangled-up bank and across that marsh a ways up. And the Rebs are shooting down at them as they're running and splashing along for all they're worth, but damn if Beaver doesn't go back to fetch some wounded officer and lug him across. The Johnnies stopped shooting, they just let him go."

"And that's comical?"

"No, sir. But . . . you really had to see it. Old Beaver drops the wounded fellow down and collapses like he's given up the ghost. And this Irish gunner, this sergeant, who's been watching the whole thing, he offers Beaver a drink of whiskey from a bottle he's got in his blouse. And Beaver looks at it, starts to wave it off, then takes it and drinks it down to the last drop. The poor mick like to fainted." The men who had witnessed the doings laughed again. "And Colonel Beaver, he gets up on his feet with a roar and starts giving orders like it's the end of the world."

"All right, carry on."

Barlow nudged his horse along, riding between his re-forming regiments, past wounded men sitting and waiting for litters or just a surge of strength. Farther up the slope, successive lines of batteries tore at the heavens.

Hancock came up, face smeared.

"Good work," he told Barlow. "Damned fine work. You can be proud."

"Seemed like a bucket of slops to me," Barlow told him.

Hancock snorted. "You want a bucket of slops? Grant's ordered Birney and Gibbon to support another assault on that fucking ridge."

"Laurel Hill."

"And I've damned well got to go over and put a good face on another fucking waste of our best men."

"Sounds like they're starting without you," Barlow said.

Hancock frowned. Then grimaced. And drew out his pocket watch. "That sonofabitch Warren. Wasn't supposed to go in until five. What the devil . . . Morgan? Do you know anything about—"

Hancock had lost interest in Barlow, and Barlow needed to get down from the saddle, stretch his legs, grant himself a long drink from his canteen, and, at some point, get his boots off and soak his feet. The itching was enough to drive a man mad.

Then he saw Paul Frank.

Three twenty p.m.
Laurel Hill

It was a damned insult. The Yankees Oates and his men faced for a third day had learned nothing. Just refused to learn. Fifth Corps blue-bellies, Warren's men, fools led by idiots, just coming on in more half-assed assaults, straight on, all of them like blind billy goats leaping out of their entrenchments, only to be butchered like sheep until the survivors flopped down like lambs under Confederate musketry and artillery so deadly it seemed unfair even to Oates, who never thought killing Yankees a bad idea.

The Federals came on so thick and stupid, one damn fool brigade or strayed-off regiment after another, that Oates and his officers reloaded soldiers' rifles for them so they could keep on firing down the slope like engines of death.

Didn't the Yankees have one sane general left?

Another pack got up, advanced, tumbled down, and fell apart. The stink was worse than anything Oates had experienced, with his men forced, even in the throes of an attack, to break from the parapet and dash back a few yards to squat, shaking, and shit brown water. To the front of the works, bodies baking for a third day reeked of burst guts, belly gas, and rot. Even a hard man lived on the verge of puking.

On top of it all, his hip pained him like the devil, even when he held still.

"Just kill 'em," Oates bellowed, angry at the Yankees for murdering themselves, for insulting the worth of all lives, blue or gray. "Kill every last one of those bastards."

Five p.m.
Headquarters, Army of the Potomac

Meade raged at the world, at all men, and, above all else, at himself. Warren had come to him hours before, earnest as smallpox, pleading to be allowed to move his portion of the grand assault up to three o'clock. G.K. had sworn that his morning efforts had fatally weakened Lee's defenses up on the ridge, that the Confederates were spread thin. Warren had positively begged, insisting, in front of Grant, that the opportunity was fleeting, that the Rebs who had faced Barlow would soon return to strengthen the line. The attack had to be moved up to three o'clock, or it would fail.

Reading Grant's mood, Meade had acquiesced. Grant promptly spoke up to support the decision. Was there ever an attack Grant would oppose? And what of his grand assault set up for five o'clock? What of Mott's supporting attack? Of Upton's ploy? And the two divisions from Hancock on their way to lend Warren a hand? All left to be put in piecemeal again. Grant discarded plans the way a rogue discarded women.

Weary, worn down, pressed from above and below, he had been unmanly, bending to Warren's fickle spirit, and doing it to please Grant. And Warren had attacked. And failed gruesomely. Again. The slope of Laurel Hill had sprouted a fresh crop of blue-clad corpses and twitching wounded. For not an inch gained.

Only Upton's small effort remained. Supported by Mott, who had yet to distinguish himself in division command. Wright and Russell had asked for a postponement of Upton's movement, given the confusion in the wake of Warren's mess, and Meade had granted that, too.

He wondered, should he call off Upton's attack? It was

bound to be another waste of men. Of good men. But Grant had made it his gospel that Lee was about to fold at any moment. It was always, "One more good blow, and Lee is bound to crack."

This had been another wretched day, the only faint positive Barlow's rescue of his own division. And Hancock did seem his old self again. Perhaps, on another day . . .

For now, there was only young Upton and horrible odds.

Six fifteen p.m.
Sixth Corps line, opposite the
west face of Lee's salient

Fornication. Blasphemy. Drunkenness. Gambling. And worse. Profane lives of philistine wealth built on the tormented Negro's bloodied back. Colonel Emory Upton knew the men he faced. They had mocked him for his piety at West Point, drawling their sarcasm, even the pace of their speech enfeebled by the monstrous god they worshipped: human bondage. Now he was about to pay them back.

Across the Sixth Corps front, the artillery did the work of Jesus Christ when he raged in the temple. Ready to assault the Moabite lines, Upton prayed a final time to serve the cause of justice and become the wrathful angel of the Lord, a glittering blade dipped in the blood of Jehovah's leprous enemies.

He knew how to make war. If the Academy taught him drill, three years of war had shown him proper practice. Joshua and Kings had become his guides: You had to fight with rigor and without compassion. The Israelites had been punished for being merciful. He would not repeat that error.

Around him, behind him, twelve regiments waited to burst from the trees and rush across a field veiled with drifts of smoke. Two hundred yards away, two hundred raw yards, waited the Midianites, the bronzed shields of Baal, the army of Pharaoh.

General Russell and General Wright were oblivious to God's hand, but surely it was not coincidence that he had been given twelve regiments this day, as many regiments as Jesus Christ, mankind's eternal Savior, had disciples. "Let there be no Judas in their number," Upton prayed.

Nor did Upton neglect mundane concerns. He studied war with a devotion second only to his Bible reading. And much had been revealed. He would not have men fight in ignorance. Ignorance lost battles, as surely as ignorance of the Lord lost souls. He had led the regimental officers forward, creeping through the trees beside the farm trail, to point out the buckle in the Rebel line where they must strike. He made each commander repeat the plan aloud, how the first block of the column would have their rifles loaded and capped, but must not stop to fire until they reached the enemy entrenchments. When crossing that field, no man must stop for anything, not for a wounded friend or even a brother. The first wave would pierce the line. The second block of regiments would split to the left and right within the enemy's works, expanding the breakthrough. The third wave would be prepared, upon entering the entrenchments, to fight straight ahead and deepen the penetration. The fourth block, the splendid Vermont Volunteers, would be his reserve. His echelons would be as the four saints inspired to set down the Gospels: Matthew, Mark, Luke, and John.

He then had made the officers explain the plan in detail to their subordinates, so that every man in the chain of command understood and the attack could continue, no matter who among them the Lord called home.

And once the assault began, every officer on the field would confine his commands to the simple word *Forward!* until they broke into the Rebel works.

The soldiers, too, had to understand their roles. They would go forward at a run to cross the field. He saw to it that knapsacks were grounded, freeing the men to fight without encumbrance, and each soldier was told that he must not cheer or yell, nor stop to fire until he reached the entrenchments. Cowards who tried to fall out must be bayoneted.

Oh, the officers had blanched at that last command—many in the corps thought him too harsh—but they did not understand these men as he did. Whether from the hills of Pennsylvania or the mountains of Vermont, from Maine's hard coast or New York's icy lakes, he knew them as a shepherd knew his flock. They came of the sturdy-minded boys he had worked beside at harvest and by whose side he had puzzled out his lessons. Together, they had sung Wesley's words of praise in country chapels, and swum together on hot afternoons when farm work allowed them respite. He knew they took the Bible's injunctions seriously, even those who had strayed from belief. They believed in justice swift and sure, and the private hardened by war saw clearly what his captain might not, that the man who faltered or ran away increased by that much the likelihood that the next bullet would strike down the braver man. He who shirked his labors in the grim vineyards of war was no more than a Cain to his brother Abel.

He finished his silent prayer: *Thy will be done.*

Around him, four thousand souls waited for his command.

The gunnery continued, further delaying an assault already delayed. He was not without concerns: The great coordinated attack of which he had been told had fallen to pieces, with the Fifth Corps attacking hours ahead of time. And Mott, whose division was to support his effort, had made no attempt to communicate, nor had Upton's courier found the man. But he would do his duty, the Lord's duty.

And should he fall, his slight sins would be washed clean in the blood of the Lamb.

As near as Upton could judge through the gauze of smoke, the artillery barrage was having little effect, with most of the guns overshooting the Rebel entrenchments. He wanted the batteries to stop, to let him go forward. Should he succeed—and he believed he would—the rest of the army would need time to exploit what had been achieved. Before Old Night forbade a Christian victory.

Would Mott be there, when needed? "Concentrate on the task at hand," he told himself, "just concentrate on the work you have been given."

It strained him to wait for the cannon to cease their work. And he felt like tension in the men around him, men who had crept forward in their multitude, quiet as serpents, after the Rebel skirmishers had been driven off to prevent them from observing his preparations and sounding a warning. But every passing minute increased the chance that his men would be detected. And that could mean a slaughter in place of success.

He believed that speed and shock had been the missing factors in the army's tactics to date. This war of fieldworks and massed fires demanded concentration at the decisive point, an unexpected blow delivered on a narrow front by a force with depth, a hammer blow descending with merciless speed. But failure now, no matter the cause, would discredit his vision and condemn the army to the old suicidal tactics.

"Speed and shock," he muttered to himself, as if it were a mesmerizing prayer. "Speed and shock."

The guns stopped.

Emory Upton raised his sword.

Would he ever see Harriet again? Captain John Kidder of the 121st New York knew what Colonel Upton would say: "If you're not meant to see her again on this earth, you will be reunited in Heaven." But Kidder longed to clutch his living wife in mortal arms.

When would the guns stop? Around him, the men of Company I knelt in the weakening light beneath the trees. Those men had kicked when Upton took over the ailing regiment a year and a half before, irate over tightened discipline and drilling in all weathers. But they had soon grown proud. Fervent believers or whiskey-loving heathens, the men might pretend to complain as they once had, but gloried in their nickname, "Upton's Regulars." And they grew vain of their colonel, too, a man hardest on himself. They had even come to enjoy his quirks and missed him when he moved up to command the brigade. He was, even the worst sort agreed, a man of integrity.

But integrity could be a dreadful thing. Kidder slapped the back of his neck, too late to kill the creature that had bitten him. It disgusted him to think that the insect might have last fed on a corpse. Nor did he wish to become a corpse, although resigned to duty. With his pick of twelve fine regiments, Colonel Upton had nonetheless placed the 121st at the right front of the attack, food for the guns. Kidder had gotten a look over the field they were to cross. Seen by a man in peace, the stretch was nothing: two hundred yards, if that. But Kidder had learned, painfully, how vast two hundred yards became in battle.

Near him, men twitched and repeated quiet prayers.

And then there was silence. As though the world had emptied.

The men understood. Veterans got to their feet. The new men aped them. The terrible call rang out:

"Forward!"

Dozens of officers repeated the command. Kidder mouthed it, too.

And just under his breath he whispered, "Harriet, I love you."

They double-quicked forward, a great animal mass. Breaking from the trees, the leading ranks sped into a true run, but held together. Kidder's throat was dry, his eyes were dry, his insides coiled tight.

"Forward!" he shouted, waving his saber and clutching his revolver in his left hand.

Puffs of smoke rose from the Rebel works. Men stumbled on the uneven ground, but few fell to the bullets. A dense blue horde filled the field.

If any cannon were aimed and loaded with canister . . .

Hundreds of tiny flames spit from the parapet, followed by more smoke. Near him, the first man from his company fell.

"Forward, forward, forward!"

Seconds had an elasticity Kidder had never known, their voids filled with both terror and exuberance. The attack gained half the distance, better than half, but the enemy line, with its bucktoothed abatis and piled dirt, seemed as far away as ever.

"Forward!"

Then, as if eternity had blinked, they were at the sharpened stakes meant to delay them. A concentrated volley tore the leading ranks, the range but a few yards. Men toppled.

Others leapt over the abatis, or squeezed between the stakes. Some hammered down the sharpened limbs with their rifle butts.

Seconds. Thin-shaved bits of seconds. The world slowed and sped by at the same time.

They hit the Rebel line. His men roared. Leaping over the parapet, thrusting with bayonets. *Now* they fired, muzzles hardly a foot from gray-clad flesh. The cries from both sides were primitive, shocking, profane.

A young Reb leapt up from a trench, waving a flag. Instead of shooting him down, a half-dozen soldiers stabbed him with their bayonets, forking him to the earth.

"Company I! Wheel right!"

Was that his voice? A Reb came for him, bayonet thirsty. Kidder began to raise his sword, then realized his folly and shot the man with his pistol. He shot another Reb, who had been about to club the company's first sergeant.

For the first time in the war, he pierced human flesh with his saber: a Confederate private, a scrawny, thin-bearded creature that passed for a man. Kidder's blade thrust through his belly and burst from his back. The look of shock on the soldier's face asked, *How could this thing happen?*

He would never forget the bewildered eyes in that dirty face. In what he later explained to himself as pity, he shot the man in the forehead, sparing him a slow and agonized death. But he never was sure his motive had not been worse.

Struggling to extract his sword, he nearly fell atop the collapsing Reb, whose carcass pulled the blade along.

Then his sword was free, christened with blood.

"Company I! Right! To the right! Forward!"

How many things could happen in mere seconds? Revolver extended, he charged a Rebel gun crew struggling to swing their Napoleon around to fire upon the soldiers still crossing the field.

"Their guns!" Kidder shouted. "Get the cannon!"

In an instant's decision, dozens of Rebels thrust their arms in the air.

Let other men see to them.

Enough of his men kept up with him to draw along soldiers from the follow-on regiments. Instead of standing to fight or raising their hands, the last Reb gunners ran.

Kidder realized they were taking away their swabs and ramrods, so the guns could not be turned on their own kind.

"Shoot the gunners!" Kidder yelled. But the melee had grown so wild, few could hear him.

The masses of surrendering Johnnies threatened to clog the attack.

"You!" Kidder called to a stunned Rebel lieutenant. "Run back across that field. Take your men with you. Or I'll kill you right here."

When he turned to look moments later, he saw hundreds of disarmed Confederates funneling out of the works, a herd of terrified gray cattle that impeded the advance of the last Union regiments.

His own men were beyond the battery now. How long had it been since they had breached the line? Three minutes? Five?

He had never seen such sustained, intimate brawling, with men delighted to bash each other's brains out, or to gut a man and grin as he clutched his intestines.

Smoke darkened the setting sun.

His revolver clicked empty, but there was no time to reload. They had to press on, to break this enemy apart and finish him off.

A thoughtful man, made for enterprise, not war, he did not think of his wife or home any longer. He was transformed. Transfigured. As were the vengeful soldiers howling around him. They lusted for Reb blood.

Kidder felt he could eat human flesh.

What happened? Lee could not understand it. The day had been going handsomely, with Grant and Meade hurling their men into one slaughter after another, losing all, gaining nothing. And suddenly his own men were streaming rearward and those people were running amok within his lines. How had this happened?

He had never liked the salient, but understood the ground could not be abandoned. Now this. The shots and cries unnerved him.

Stray bullets hissed past.

He would not allow it. He must not allow it. He nudged Traveller forward, toward the fight. He would not let those people drive him from the field.

Venable ran up and seized his bridle.

"You *cannot* go forward, sir."

With burning eyes, Lee looked down on the man.

"Don't tell me to let go, because I won't," Venable went on. "General Ewell's bringing up more men. It'll be all right."

Would it? He believed he could see Federals in the trees in the failing light. *Those people. Inside his lines.* The shame was worse than the danger. Surely, they would bring up more troops to press their advantage. They would support this success. And his army would split in two.

He glared down at Venable, who glared back. Venable had spirit.

Marshall and Taylor came up on horseback to support their comrade.

"We won't let you go forward, General," Marshall said. In his haste, he had not removed his spectacles as he took to the saddle. They hung awry.

Lee mastered himself. "Then . . . you must see to it that the ground is recovered."

"Yes, sir. Yes, sir, that's a promise."

The two of them galloped off, willing to ride down quitters who got in their way.

The sound of the fighting was terrible: The hymn of victory had become the cacophony of defeat.

And Venable still had not released the bridle.

"You *must* go back," the colonel said.

Lee shook his head. Looking into the smoke and confusion, he said, "I will not. I agreed not to go forward, but the men must not see me turn toward the rear. They must never see that."

Johnston's Tarheel Brigade came up at the double-quick. A *fast* double-quick. Men from Gordon's Division. Lord bless him. Gordon had sent him this brigade and surely had gone for another.

General Ewell, who seemed in fine command of himself this day, spurred toward the column, waving at Johnston to hurry his men along. Bullets thickened the humid evening air.

"Charge 'em, General," Ewell shouted to Johnston in his mad squeak of a voice. "Damn 'em, charge 'em."

Lee suspended his distaste for profanity and allowed himself a faint smile. Yes indeed. Damn them and charge them.

From the right front, deep in the grove that backed his broken defenses, he heard a reassuring Rebel yell. His men were coming back to themselves, unwilling to be defeated.

But surely . . . those people would follow up with an even fiercer blow? Could his men withstand that, too?

Upton was maddened. Where was Mott? Where was the promised support? His men had broken through three lines of defenses before being halted by multiple counterattacks. Now they were being driven slowly back.

Still they hung on, unwilling to be beaten so near to a triumph.

His last reserves were in. Seaver's Vermonters had become so enthused by the success of the first echelons that they had charged on their own, ignoring their officers. Few men were free of the lust for vengeance this day. And the Vermonters had carried the attack deep into the salient.

But his regiments were intermingled and difficult to command. The Rebels were being granted time to reorganize and bring up still more forces. When their destruction had been at hand, as surely as that of Sodom and Gomorrah.

He could not believe his army would throw away this chance, the opportunity the generals had longed for.

With men firing into each other's faces and beating each other to death in the rancid twilight, he galloped back across the field to the farm trail from which his regiments had debouched. The grazing wound along his ribs bled warmth.

He worried that he would end by losing twelve exemplary regiments, a victory transformed into a debacle. And all the blame would be his, not Mott's or that of the generals slurping their coffee.

He wanted a star. He wanted it as badly as he ever had wanted anything on this earth. But he did not want it badly enough to see the finest soldiers he knew be slaughtered to no purpose.

"Where's General Russell?" he shouted to the first officers he found in the safety of the trees. They'd been watching the fight, with evident amusement.

"Just there, Upton," a staff man said, gesturing over his shoulder with a thumb. "Good effort, quite a good effort."

With sweat and blood sealing his uniform to his body, Upton rode up to his division commander.

"Where's Mott?" he demanded.

"Upton, are you wounded?"

He waved off the concern. "Sir . . . we must be reinforced. Immediately. We drove them, we're three lines in. But we need fresh supports."

"General Wright sent in the Sixty-fifth New York," Russell said. "There's no one else."

Upton had not even seen the 65th, one paltry regiment.

Of a sudden, he felt faint. This was not his place. His place was with those men, with the soldiers who had trusted him.

"Listen, Upton," Russell said, "you've done admirably. Everything you said you'd do. You proved your point. I believe you sent back at least five hundred prisoners. But General Wright thinks it's too dark and too late to call up anyone, and nobody's ready." Russell exhaled a deep and troubled breath. He did not look much happier than Upton felt. "The truth is no one expected you to succeed."

Upton ignored the praise and the insult. "Sir, my men can't hold, unless they're reinforced."

"I just told you, there are no troops."

Upton thought of the thousands of men who had massed to assault Laurel Hill for the last three days, a hopeless endeavor fools had thought might succeed. Those men were needed here and now. Instead, they'd been frittered away on tactics that hadn't changed in a hundred years.

He had pursued a star, and lost. Now he had to do what his conscience demanded.

"General Russell"—his chest was heaving and hurting, and breathing had become difficult—"I request permission to withdraw my men."

The division commander didn't hesitate. "Permission granted."

Upton turned his horse about and galloped back to organize a withdrawal.

He did all he could, and the regiments—what was left of them—were saved. But many a man did not want to retreat: They had paid too high a price and had gone too far. The soldiers felt robbed, and shamelessly.

The Vermonters were the worst. At first, they bluntly refused to pull out of the salient, determined to go on killing until they were killed. It took a scribbled order from General Wright to get them to quit, with Colonel Seaver bellowing at them to do as their corps commander ordered or answer to him in the morning, as if that fate would be worse than death or dismemberment.

Among the last to withdraw, Upton had the satisfaction of hearing Rebel officers order their men to charge in pursuit, only to be flatly disobeyed: The men in gray had had fighting enough.

More men died needlessly, uselessly, as they recrossed the open field in the purple dusk. The Vermonters came back with tears rolling down their cheeks.

May 11, eight a.m.
Sixth Corps rear

Upton lay on his cot, unwilling, for the first time in the war, to rise and do his duty. He had lost a thousand men and achieved nothing. And he knew that the best, not the worst, of the men had fallen. Such veterans could not be replaced by draftees and hirelings. His assault had made his point, oh, yes. Only to weaken the army.

The sin of pride, the sin of pride . . .

He closed his eyes, letting the heat engulf him. The air was sour with the tent's flaps down, but that was as close as he could come to brimstone. He could not even steel himself to pray.

He had gambled with men's lives, as surely as the sinful gambled with money. Or the legionnaires on Golgotha had diced for the Savior's garments. He had gambled, and now he was called to account before God. It was no longer enough to reason that such was war. He had thought to perform a miracle on earth, and his pride had been humbled.

And yet . . . he had come so close. It might have been a victory to speed the end of the war. *Might* have been. . . .

The most satisfying thing in his life was his wound,

minor but painful. He relished the burning hurt as a small justice, imagining that the bullet had been a nail fit for a cross.

He looked down and saw that the bandage needed replacement, but even that could not resurrect his will.

"Emory?" a voice called. Clint Beckwith, fellow colonel, friend. A good, Christian man. Poking his head and shoulders inside the tent.

Upton could not muster the will to answer.

Beckwith stepped inside and stared down at his friend, clucking his tongue. Then he grinned and dropped a pair of shoulder straps on Upton's belly.

Each strap bore a star.

SIXTEEN

May 11, eight a.m.
Grant's headquarters

Talk to you, Sam?" Washburne asked.

Cradling a tin cup of coffee in his hands, Grant looked up from the looted chair his servant had set out for him.

"Thought you were already gone," he said. "Pull up a stump."

"Maybe someplace more private?"

Grant nodded. "Tent'll have to do, then." He splashed the remains of the coffee on the ground. "Looks like rain, you'll want to get along."

"I'd welcome a little rain," the congressman said. "This heat."

"See how you feel after you're wet through." Grant held the tent flap open.

Washburne sat down on the cot, leaving the camp chair by the desk for Grant. "Looked like you were a mile deep in thought."

"Way that colonel broke their line. Something to it." Grant stood in the center of the tent. Waiting. He was short enough not to stoop under the canvas.

Washburne braced his hands upon his knees. "It occurred to me . . . that I ought to take back more than just a verbal report for the president. Could I prevail upon you to write something? Just some words to keep Lincoln in our buggy, something he can use?"

Grant pondered the matter before speaking. "Wouldn't know what to say just now. Our doings have been mostly favorable. But I don't want to hold out false hopes."

"You were plenty hopeful a week ago."

"That was a week ago."

"Sam, I believe you owe the president words on paper. He's been behind you, solid as a rock. But he needs something he can wave at the newspapermen. Dispel the myth of Lee's invincibility, make a show of confidence. That sort of thing."

"Lee's a serious proposition. A bit more than I expected." Grant smiled wryly. "I don't suppose you want that down in writing?"

"Just give the president something helpful." Washburne put on his serious face, an expression Grant had first seen at political rallies back home in Galena. It usually appeared about halfway through a speech. "Given the casualties, we need to make sure his confidence in you remains high."

Grant decided there was no escape from doing what was asked. He wasn't worried about where he stood with Lincoln, but Washburne wanted a present to deliver. Made sense, viewed from the congressman's corner of the porch.

"Can't write directly to the president," he told his longtime supporter. "Protocol. Have to go through Stanton. Means a letter to Halleck, too. Or he'll take it as a grievance."

"Obliged, Sam. Just give me a few lines to keep up Lincoln's spirits. And the Union's."

"Requirement's getting taller by the minute. Guess I'd better get to it, before you have me writing for posterity." Resigned to his fate, he drew out the chair and took a seat at his field desk. "Have Bill fetch you some coffee. Ain't the worst. And tell him to give you a box of my best cigars to take back to Washington."

"Obliged for that, too, Sam."

When the congressman had gone from the tent, Grant took out a cigar, but put it down on the desk unlit. He stared at the blank sheet of paper, chewing his lip. Then he scratched his nose, took up the cigar, and laid it back down again. He wasn't about to lie, there'd been plenty of brag in the papers without his help. And he would not raise false hopes. He had veered too close to that mistake already. Lee was near the breaking point, he was convinced of it, but it made no sense to spout off. He knew he would defeat Robert E. Lee. But Lee would be beaten when he was beaten, not according to some politician's schedule. Not even Lincoln's.

He wished Cump Sherman were with him. Rawlins was a true friend, cut of honest cloth, but only Sherman grasped him as a soldier. No one else, not even George Meade, saw that the only way to solve a problem was to keep on trying to solve it. The fatal weakness he saw in his fellow generals was that they were all too quick to call off the dogs. You had to run the fox all the way to its den and not shy from the briars. Maneuver was a fine thing, and genius was even better, but a stubborn heart was trumps.

A drink would have been welcome, he could almost taste the gratifying burn. But that would have to wait for a good long time. His three consolations, Sherman, whiskey, and his wife, were denied him.

He shook his head above the untouched page and decided to keep things as simple as he could make them, just write something out. The president would have to be satisfied with the bait in place of the fish. And the newspapermen would write what they wanted to, anyway. As for his obligation to the Union, it wasn't to issue proclamations like McClellan. It was to win.

He wrote first to the secretary of war:

We have now entered the sixth day of very hard fighting. The result to this time is very much in our favor. Our

losses have been heavy as well as those of the enemy. I
think the loss of the enemy must be greater. We have taken
over five thousand prisoners, in battle, while he has taken
from us but a few stragglers. I propose to fight it out on
this line if it takes all summer.

Wasn't much, but it would have to do.

One p.m.
The Harrison house

Sonsofbitches fired on my ambulances," Ewell raged, clutching his hat as if he meant to strangle it. "Just trying to gather up my wounded and some of theirs, and the sons-ofbitches fired on my ambulances." Then he came to himself, ran a hand over his pate, and said, "My apologies, General Lee. I forget myself."

"Sit down, General," Lee said. "General Rodes, General Long. Sit, please. I must ask your opinions."

Still simmering, Dick Ewell clopped across the floor on his wooden leg. "Just ain't right. It just isn't right by any stretch." He dropped into a chair, as awkward as ever.

"We must regard such behavior as a tantrum," Lee said. "We have disappointed their expectations severely. Now they rage at us. They are as ill-bred children."

"Well, those children need them a lesson. Man who fires on an ambulance ought to hang," Ewell declared. He snapped at the Negro serving the table of officers: "I don't want no coffee, don't you trouble me."

Lee made his voice as firm as he could without raising its volume. "I do not believe it the policy of those people to open on ambulances. It was doubtless the action of rogues. We will speak no more of it."

Lee needed the corps commander to calm down. Grave

matters lay before them. And the absence of Stuart, two days gone on the trail of the Union cavalry, left him with less information than he desired. Judgment would have to supply the missing pieces in the puzzle of Grant's intentions.

Lee shifted the topic away from Ewell's ambulances: "General, are you confident in the restoration of your line?"

"Yes, sir. General Lee, I—"

"We will discuss the future, not the past." But Lee added, "The brief success those people enjoyed last evening would seem revealing. Gentlemen, why do you think they failed to exploit their advantage?"

"Damned fools," Ewell said.

Lee looked to Rodes, a man of great mustaches and great courage.

"Last gasp? Didn't have the men left to do any more?"

Lee nodded. "It seems to me the only sensible answer. We must not be precipitous, but I see numerous signs that General Grant is played out. At least, for this campaign."

"He's had a whupping he won't soon forget," Ewell said. "Killed himself half his army in a week."

"And what did Hotchkiss have to say?" Lee asked the corps commander. "About General Burnside's dispositions?"

Ewell grunted. "Everything's upside down. Typical for Burnside. Wagons driving off, infantry marching every which way but forward. And the Ninth Corps hasn't hardly been in the fight. It makes no sense."

"It would make sense, if General Burnside's latest order were to cover the Fredericksburg Road. For a Union withdrawal."

"What about that business on the right this morning?" Ewell asked.

"A feint, I suspect. To put us off the scent." Lee turned. "General Rodes? Your view of the matter? Will those people retreat?" Lee wanted to hear more from a man closer to the fighting line.

"Honestly, sir, I don't see how they've kept at it this long. More spunk to them than I'd credited." He swept back a heavy lock of hair. "They've got to be played out, though. Otherwise, they would've put some weight behind last night's attack. Closest they've come to success since crossing the Rapidan."

Rain pattered on the roof of the old house. It had been threatening all day. His Virginia boyhood told Lee it would be heavy, once it gripped.

"If those people intend to withdraw, as I think they may," Lee said, "their movement will start at dusk. There will be a good rain to help them cover their actions. But they'll have to move before it spoils the roads." He inspected the earnest faces around the table. "We must prepare to initiate a pursuit."

"Been thinking along the very same lines myself," Ewell said.

Lee turned to Armistead Long, his former military secretary and now brigadier of the Second Corps' artillery. "I'm concerned about your batteries, General Long. They must be ready to march, if opportunity calls. Few things sow panic in a retreating army like a sudden bombardment from the flank or rear." Lee paused, wary of interfering in details that were the province of a subordinate. But he felt compelled to add: "I speak, especially, of those guns at the head of the salient."

Long eased his collar away from his neck. "Men call it 'the Mule Shoe.' It's been a worry to me, to speak out plain. Couldn't have gotten those batteries away, if we'd been attacked and had the worst of it. One old farm road in, same bad road out. And Lord knows what the rain will do to it."

Lee tasted bile, despite the insipid contents of his stomach. "Occupying that salient has been a mistake from the start. As we saw last night. Denying one piece of high ground to those people was no excuse for ignoring the broader logic. The blame falls upon my shoulders, I knew better."

"Lucky those bluecoat fools haven't figured it out," Ewell said.

"Surely, the generals across those fields have seen the salient's weakness," Lee continued. "The fact that they have not attacked it in greater numbers . . . seems yet another sign of their broken strength. And a failing will." He turned to practical matters: "General Long, I believe you should withdraw those guns. Under cover of darkness, but without added delay."

"Makes two of us, sir. That farm road'll be a hog-wallow come morning."

"We *must* be prepared to move swiftly," Lee said, taken again with his vision of what was to come. "We must punish those people severely, before they escape us."

"Punish 'em for shooting up my ambulances," Ewell said.

Rodes put in: "Long here's talking about the batteries supporting General Johnson, at the tip of the salient. I've got good roads back where I sit. I can have the chests loaded and the teams ready to harness, but I'd as lief keep my guns on the line."

Lee looked toward Long.

"That's fine," the artilleryman said. "But the guns supporting Johnson need to pull out. Otherwise, they'll be stuck in that mud for days."

Ewell's aide, Campbell Brown, lifted a finger. Lee nodded.

"General," Brown said, "what if the Yankees don't have a mind to leave? What if they pull something like they did last night?"

"They won't!" Ewell snapped. "They're played out, I'd bet my good leg on it."

The rain began to beat the roof like fists. Lee wished, again, that Stuart had not been obliged to give chase to the Union cavalry. So much remained unknown, so very much.

But that was war.

He cleared his throat. "We are agreed, then. This army will ready itself for a forced march. If those people retreat tonight, they will overburden the roads and unmake themselves. We must stand ready to seize the opportunity."

"Ought to start thinning the lines, then," Ewell commented.

"No. Staffs will ready orders for their subordinate commands and the roads will be cleared of trains, but the infantry will remain in their entrenchments. Including the salient. Only the artillery is to be withdrawn, for the present. We must have greater assurance before abandoning our defenses. Generals Grant and Meade must tip their hand. And," he added, "I am loath to withdraw the men from what shelter they've made for themselves. Until it proves necessary." For a moment, he met no man's eyes. "I would so welcome fresh reports on those people."

"If Stuart wasn't off gallivanting, he could tell us something," Ewell said.

Lee ignored the comment. He turned to his current military secretary, who had kept his silence. "Colonel Marshall, copy down this order: General Long is to withdraw the artillery from the salient occupied by Johnson's division, in order to have it available for a countermove to the right, or as circumstances dictate."

Marshall scribbled rapidly. The man's memory was prodigious and Lee knew he need not repeat a word.

Ending the meeting, Lee said, "Gentlemen, we have beaten General Grant. If he retreats, we will break him."

The rain pounded.

One thirty p.m.
Sixth Corps left flank, opposite the Mule Shoe

It'll do, Grant thought, ignoring the downpour. Right about there. Hit them right there. With a full corps, Hancock's bunch. Other corps supporting in their sectors. Make sure Burnside pulls his weight this time. And see what Wright and Warren can do. Heaviest attack of the war, sky falling in on that salient. Just like this storm coming down. See what Lee thinks of that.

He could hardly believe a soldier of Lee's experience would bet his chips on such a flawed position. No wonder young Upton dented them. Hit the position right at the tip, and hit it hard, and it would break up like a doll's house. And that was what he intended to do, first thing in the morning. Hit that rise of ground with an entire corps, while the rest of the army kept Lee's fellows busy.

"General Grant, would you care to take shelter?" General Wright asked. "You're getting wet."

"Never saw a rusty soldier," Grant said. He raised his field glasses again, cupping his hands around their ends to keep off the rain. Rain was good. And this blow had the feel of a deluge to come, an all-night rain. Hit them in the morning, first light, when the rain would keep things murky and Lee's men would be absorbed by their discomfort. Skirmishers and sentries would be hunkered down. Percussion caps would misfire, powder would stick. Favoring the attacker who went in with bayonets.

Long space to cross, he recognized that, three-quarters of a mile at the widest point. Artillery would be the biggest threat, if the redlegs kept their powder dry. Guns loaded with canister would play Hell with anybody crossing that open ground. Have to go fast and hit hard, the way Upton had. Before Lee's people got their wits about them.

Grant smiled at the thought of Upton. He had already seen the young officer wearing his star, even though the brevet hadn't been formalized. Well, let him. He'd earned it. The rest was just Army paperwork.

Like the paperwork that had helped undo him during his time as a captain in the Territories.

The rain that had pelted began to pound. Grant sat calmly on his pony, Jeff Davis, a mount quicker in the mud than Cincinnati. He wondered what was in the minds of the men across that field. After the punishment they had taken, would the rain be enough to break their morale entirely? Was Lee contemplating retreat? For all the old man's skill, his army could take only so much.

Around Grant, officers cowered in their saddles, even those who had brought along their waterproofs. He had to fight down a good laugh. Rain left him unperturbed, as a rule, although it interfered with a good smoke. Staff men took a different attitude. He had ordered Rawlins to remain at headquarters—John's lungs didn't need any further tribulations—but as for the other gentlemen of the staff, let them feel the raw life of the infantry, if only for a half hour.

He recalled the hard ride to Chattanooga the autumn before, the icy rain and mud that never quite froze. It had worn his companions to a nub and broken horses, but his only complaint had been a sore behind.

Weather didn't trouble Grant. Men did.

Three thirty p.m.
Headquarters, Army of the Potomac

Meade was cross as a bear. And Major General Andrew Atkinson Humphreys could not blame him.

"This is an outrage," Meade declared. "*Another* outrage.

Why, there isn't sufficient time to plan, to reconnoiter. And this weather. Biddle, make yourself useful, or take yourself off." And to Humphreys again: "We don't have time to plan, to coordinate. And the corps, what are they supposed to do? Just blunder forward again? Can't the man see the plain impossibility?"

If you'd leave me alone to work on a proper plan, I might be able to do something for this army, Humphreys thought. He was vexed himself. Meade was tired, but everyone was tired. He had a right to be angry, but bombast was an indulgence they couldn't afford. Meade needed to simmer down, no matter the wrongs done to him and the army. If Humphreys could buck up at fifty-three years of age, so could the rest of them. Including George Meade.

Meade was right on every point, but that didn't make a watch tick any slower. And each subordinate element needed time to plan as well. It was essential to send them clear, written orders, as soon as possible.

Humphreys glimpsed Marsena Patrick, the provost marshal and the nastiest creature in the Union army, slipping out of the tent. Even he did not want to risk Meade's wrath.

"And taking away this army's cavalry. It's madness, madness," Meade went on. "We have no idea where Lee might be shifting his forces, what he's up to." Meade folded his arms and tapped his foot, a caricature of impatience. "I don't care if Sheridan takes Richmond and captures Jefferson Davis, he's left this army blind."

Humphreys did his best to write through the tirade. He already had sent a courier to warn Hancock to prepare for a move to the army's left, to a position between Wright's Sixth Corps and Burnside's ever-tardy lot. Even a march of a few miles was going to be wretched in the rain and the dark, and it would have to be full dark before Hancock's divisions moved, to avoid detection. Hancock's men were in for a rotten night. And a worse tomorrow.

"A grand attack!" Meade grumped. "Well, I have nothing against a grand attack. I'd love to make one, in fact. Instead of shoveling out this army piecemeal and doing every damned thing in . . . in petulant haste. But an effort of this scope needs proper planning." He turned to his son, who sat innocently by, drying off from a recent courier ride. "George, if you haven't anything to do, I'll soon find you something."

It had been a bad few days for Meade, Humphreys knew, and he was glad not to be in the man's position: Being chief of staff was bad enough. The incident with Sheridan still rankled them all, but this very morning Grant had unthinkingly insulted Meade and the entire chain of command again. Perhaps things were done that way in the western armies, but Grant's peremptory order to Nelson Miles to send out two regiments to feel the enemy on the right had skipped over Meade, Hancock, and Barlow, leaving them all sour. Grant's action may have been useful at the moment, but an army could not be run on *ad hoc* lines.

"And Burnside won't attack at four a.m.," Meade picked up again. "Not a damned chance, and everybody knows it. He won't even be awake at four a.m. And Hancock will have to make his assault alone. . . ."

"Wright and Warren will be prepared to support him," Humphreys said, without looking up from his field desk.

Momentarily driven beyond words, Meade could only sputter. Fine drops of saliva struck Humphreys' cheek.

"But that's not what Grant's order says!" Meade railed. "Burnside's supposed to *attack*. To keep Lee's forces occupied. While Hancock concentrates on that blasted salient." He bore down on Humphreys. "And even were we to take it, what good would that do?"

"It could," Humphreys said, still scribbling, "do Lee a good bit of harm."

Meade was not in a mood to be contradicted. "But how

much? Enough to justify a madcap dash at things? Say we bite off his forces in the salient. Splendid! But then what? Surely, Lee recognizes the weakness of that position—he's a damned fine engineer. He'll have reserves positioned in depth, as sure as Philadelphia sits on the Delaware. We'll bloody each other up"—Meade cleared his throat—"and have little more than casualties to show for it, mark my words." Again, he bore down, leaning so close to his chief of staff that Humphreys could smell sour breath, old coffee, and fatback. "An attack on this scale demands thorough preparation. . . ."

And I'm doing my best to prepare us, Humphreys thought. Close to losing his own temper at Meade as well as Grant, he knew he could not afford the luxury of it. He was worried about Win Hancock, who had been limping noticeably and seemed weary to the point of absentmindedness. Hancock had seemed back in form the day before, but on a headquarters visit that morning, Win had repeatedly stared into vacant space, with the deadened expression Humphreys had begun to see on too many soldiers.

Humphreys meant to do his best by all of them. But the prospects were daunting. No one was entirely sure of the point of attack Grant had fixed on: somewhere along the salient's tip, that was all anybody knew. And how were Hancock's division and brigade commanders to reconnoiter the ground? You couldn't see fifty yards in the deluge slapping the canvas, and it would be night before much could be organized. And Hancock's change of position would require hours of slogging through the mud for his men to reach their line of attack. The soldiers would get little sleep, if any, exposed to the elements. Meade was right: Even a tactical success at the tip of the salient would wind down before it reached the depth of Lee's army. Any trained engineer grasped that immediately: It was the simplest equation of force, resistance, distance, and inertia. You had to hit a shallow line, not a deep one.

Grant was thinking like a corps commander. No, like a mere division commander. He wasn't fit to be general in chief.

Humphreys was not a defeatist or a naysayer. On the contrary, he was vain of his sense of purpose. But he believed that things should be done properly. He respected the old Philadelphia tradition of "Waste not, want not." And the wastage thus far in the campaign had been horrendous.

Oh, Grant's call for a grand, coordinated attack made perfect sense, if properly done. Even the assault on that salient might play a useful part. But to have any chance of meaningful success, so broad a scheme required a full day's preparation, at the least. And it wanted a brute with a horsewhip to stand at Burnside's back and make him go forward on time. Humphreys was every bit as convinced as Meade that the Ninth Corps commander would appear late, if at all.

This had all the ingredients of a bloody mess.

Still fuming, Meade said: "I just hope Sheridan gets his damned comeuppance."

Four p.m.
Union left flank on the Fredericksburg Road

Swear I just saw Noah and his ark go drifting by," Bill Wildermuth said. "Man could float a canal boat in this ditch."

The mud was already inches deep in the trench they had inherited.

"You've been wetter," Brown told him. Men who had cursed the blazing heat now damned the chilling downpour. It struck Brown, again, how short memories of suffering and pain could be. Yes, they were drenched. But this was a hayride compared to their march from Knoxville.

"Oh, I been wetter, all right," Wildermuth went on. "Many's the day, back on the old canal. Which is where I wish I was, just at the moment. Back home I always knew there was rum for my coffee at the end of the day, and dry clothes waiting. And a fire that wasn't made out of wet green sticks."

"I could do with a glass of rum," Corporal Doudle said. Rain dripped from the sharp tip of his nose. "Never took to drinking, but I'd have me some rum right now."

Wildermuth hooted, loud even in the rain striking their torn waterproofs or pounding the canvas drawn over head and shoulders. "Well, there ain't none, not for the likes of you. Want your rum or your whiskey today, you got to be an officer. Lieutenant colonel, or better." He whistled, a gesture usually followed by a smack of the lips. The rain crushed the sound, if it was there this time. "Wonder what Colonel Christ is imbibing this splendid afternoon?" Wildermuth extended a hand, as if to measure the weight of the thumping rain. "He may be in for another bout of sunstroke."

"Shut up, Bill," Brown said. The colonel's drinking was a sore point that needed no further discussion. To the men's astonishment, he had resumed command of the brigade, relieving Cutcheon, who was preferred by all of them. Once liked and respected, Christ was regarded now as less than a dog.

But a dog who held the power of life and death over them.

"Should've made coffee when I saw those clouds," Henry Hill said. He had been promoted to corporal that morning, but had not had time to sew on his stripes before the rain burst over them. As for the stripes themselves, Brown

had known the promotion was on the way and he had cut
the corporal's chevrons from a dead man's sleeves, hoping it wouldn't mean bad luck for Henry. He had gotten
himself proper first sergeant's stripes, too.

War changed men. And not just those such as Colonel
Christ, who had fallen from grace before he fell from his
saddle. Even the year before, Brown had been reluctant to
bother corpses from either army. Now he scavenged with
the best of them—and ordered out details to strip the dead
of necessities for the company. He had taken care since his
promotion to gather in waterproofs and blankets, even some
extra tentage, and stow his prizes in the company wagon
for just such a day as this, when the new soldiers who had
discarded their equipment on the march would find themselves needy.

Brown grimaced, feeling the rain seep through the poor
seams in his cape. For just such a day as this . . . but when
he had sent back a detail to fetch the treasures from
the wagon, and after he had prepared a speech for the new
men about the importance of caring for their equipment,
Doudle and his men returned empty-handed. All of the
wagons had been ordered miles to the rear, and no one
knew why.

So now they huddled in the mud on the same ridge they
had fought for two days before, set off a few hundred yards
from the well-made entrenchments they had dug and perfected. Hartranft's boys held that position now, and the 50th
had to make do with a belly-high ditch whose parapet was
dissolving in the rain. The men weren't happy about that,
or about much of anything else. Over those two days they
had gone forward and backward, sideward, backward and
forward again, day and night, occasionally skirmishing, but
mostly just shuffling about in a manner that seemed mad
even to the officers. General Burnside's reputation, too, was
declining daily.

Men would do no end of unpleasant things, Brown had discovered, if they could be made to see some sense in doing them. Soldiers wanted to know where they were and what they were supposed to accomplish, but rare was the officer who bothered to tell them much. If the officer knew himself.

Men wanted a clear purpose. They'd die for that. But they didn't care for the thought of being killed or maimed for nothing but confusion.

It was like breaking in a new boy on a barge. If you wanted him to coil the ropes a certain way, you could order him to do it, and he might do it well enough. But if you made him see the sense of doing it just so, he'd put his heart in it. A man had a hunger to know things, to understand.

He had resolved to explain all he could to his men. But he recognized that, so far, he had done but a poor job. He couldn't well explain what he didn't know.

"Know what I'd like about now?" Isaac Eckert said to no one in particular. "A great big beefsteak. With a heap of boiled potatoes slopped over with cream."

"You ain't never et a proper beefsteak in your life," yet another Eckert, Levon, told him.

"My wife can fry up a beefsteak with the best of them," Isaac said, indignant.

"When she isn't clopping your head with the frying pan," Bill Wildermuth noted.

"You don't talk about my wife, you—"

"All of you, just shut up," Brown snapped. "Rebs would be on top of you before you know it, the ruckus you're raising."

"Nope," Wildermuth said. "You're wrong there, First Sergeant. The Rebs are too smart to come at us. Not when we're obliged to go charging at them like a herd of blind bulls and they can just take their leisure leaning over their works and potting us. No, boys, I don't expect Mr. Johnny Reb to come calling anytime soon. But I *do* expect to go calling on him, as part of an organized party of unannounced visitors. And I don't expect much of a kindly welcome."

"I would hate to go to the fighting in such rain," John Eckert the Shorter announced in his Dutchie mumble. Brown had given up on having the loaned stockings returned: Made with loving hands by Frances or not, he wasn't sure he wanted them back. Too much Eckert on them by now.

"You'll fight where you fight," Henry Hill said.

"Now that is a profound observation," Wildermuth said. "Elevation to the exalted rank of corporal has done wonders for old Henry. He's becoming downright loquacious."

"Just shut up, Bill," Doudle said.

"Yes, sir! I'll shut up. But Corporal Hill's on to something, mark my words. All the fighting so far hasn't been near miserable enough, not for the generals. They got to top themselves. Oh, we'll be in it, they won't miss a chance to charge through the mud in an outright biblical deluge. Chance like that doesn't come around every day."

"Nothing's going to happen," Doudle said. "Or the officers would be leaping all over the place."

"Oh, I didn't mean right now," Wildermuth said. "Be too easy, that would. They'll wait overnight, at least, so things get good and soggy." He turned to the huddled new recruits, cowering in their soaked uniforms. "Ever hear about the soldier who charged across a muddy field and got tramped so far down nobody ever found him?"

"Bill, shut up," Brown said. "This time, it's an order."

Wildermuth grinned through the gray curtain of rain. But he went quiet for a few minutes.

Brown wondered whether he should send Doudle back in search of the company wagon again. He didn't need the new men any sicker or more beaten down than they were. Half of them had the trots from drinking bad water, and he was getting tired of telling them to go farther off from the trench line for their business.

He decided he'd need approval from Lieutenant Brumm, given the likely distance involved. Maybe even a note of permission, in case the provost marshal rounded up Doudle and whoever went along.

Well, first he'd have to see to provisions. And dry cartridges. In the meantime, let the new men learn their lesson.

But nature liked to distribute misery fairly. The rain had found its way down his back and cold wet formed a garland around his neck. His whiskers rubbed on wet wool beneath the cape. And he was sweating. Just nothing good about it.

He gave a thought to the men on the other side. Who would be feeling every bit as miserable. There were times when the war seemed nothing but endless idiocy. Men killing each other over matters most of which weren't anyone else's business. Was this mud worth leaving Schuylkill Haven for? Leaving behind kin and sweethearts? Sometimes he felt that if he had not taken responsibility for the men around him, he'd just up and walk away.

And on other days, he swelled at the sight of a flag.

As for sweethearts, a letter from Frances had reached him the day before. It was a wonderful letter, if only because there was nothing much in it. He had to puzzle out her penmanship, a parade of great loops with tiny letters between them, but the wonderful thing was that life back home sounded just the same as always, more or less. There was a world back there, untouched by war, where folks still worried about pie bakes and church suppers. That world seemed so immeasurably fine to him now that thoughts of it left him damp-eyed. He resolved that if he returned a whole man and if Frances really would have him, he would

never speak of what he had seen here or on other battlefields. He would not soil her world with the horrors that
had become commonplace to him and the men around him.
He would not dirty her with any of it. And he would try to
forget.

As if he had jinxed himself, Brown recalled Sam
Martz's heart pulsing over the ground.

He shuddered.

Anxious to force down the memory, he almost asked
John Eckert the Shorter how his poison ivy was coming
along, but caught himself. He had given the fool boy so
much attention that murmurs had begun to spread about
him having a favorite. When the Eckert boy was a burden
to equal a hod of bricks.

He even had to be cautious with his best friend in the
company, Henry Hill. Despite Hill's promotion to corporal, it had become hard to have a private talk without arous-
ing suspicions that Henry would get better treatment than
the others. Veteran soldiers could be as jealous as young
girls were of hair ribbons. And still be willing to die for
each other, too.

Thunder cracked so loudly that even the veterans jumped.

"Christ, I nearly shit," Bill Wildermuth said.

"Be the first useful thing you done all day," Isaac Eckert told him.

"You shut up, too," Brown said.

Six thirty p.m.
Third Corps headquarters,
Army of Northern Virginia

Listening to the banter of Hill's staff over stew and cornbread, Lee felt like yesterday's man. Even young gentlemen these days cared nothing for the refinement his

generation had deemed essential. Their carefree chatter made his diction seem a relic—even, perhaps, a cause for amusement when he was not present. He had labored as a young man to perfect his public language, determined to master graceful speech to better converse with the ladies—he had valued chaste flirtations all his life—and to speak with firm precision in the company of men. His father had praised the perfection of Washington's rhetoric and bearing, although he thought Jefferson querulous. His father had spoken finely, far better than he had behaved. The result was that Lee had taught himself to exercise self-control in every utterance, and his grammar was as rigid as his posture. Once, such things had been valued. Now all his attainments did was to put those around him on guard.

His life seemed entirely of another time, as bygone as the remnants of his society would be, were this army denied victory. Oh, he knew that there were good men in the North. He had served beside them. But the grabbing hands and barking voices of the modern age, the crudity of smokestacks as tall as the Tower of Babel, and the rudeness of men delighted to jostle their betters in the street, all that was anathema. Men spoke, not always honestly, of freedom, but what he valued most in life was grace.

And dignity. Still little more than a boy, he had armored himself against the world, his careful manners a breastplate, his diction greaves and harness. He had learned to appear at ease in good society, even to be convivial within bounds, and he had friendly relations with excellent men. He knew not a single home where he was unwelcome. And yet, he had never had an intimate friend. He had guarded against that; now it was too late. Certainly, he had acquired an enviable number of sincere and pleasant friendships, but none of the sort that would allow him to confide his fears and sorrows, his doubts and waves of despair. He had never let another man that close, and even his wife was denied any glimpse of weakness.

He regretted that now. As the rain hammered the shabby roof of another unkempt farmhouse, he wished he could unburden himself, or simply complain as other men might do. He longed for someone who would understand his situation, the vicissitudes of commanding such an army, the need to appear ever-confident, to mask oneself with an unshakeable expression, to appear strong even when one's own strength was failing.

And failing his was. The change in the weather had summoned his rheumatism, the one ailment he had thought banished with the winter. He was stiff, and turbulent of bowel, and wary of his heart pains. Yet, he was responsible for the men out there in the premature darkness of a storm that wet them through and doused the meager fires that were their small comfort. Even this dilapidated house would seem a palace to them on such a night. And soon he might needs ask them to rally and march through the tempest to pursue those people and, should God will it, to put an end to things.

Or, if not to make an end, at least to purchase time, to thrust the war northward one more time, above the Rappahannock, until another year's harvest could be gotten in from central Virginia and the upper Valley, so his men might eat. With the loss of so much territory in the west and the blockade ever tighter, the South had declined from shortages of manufacturing means to a simple lack of cornmeal. The harvest was every bit as vital as gunpowder.

Let those people retreat this night, and if the Lord wills it, I will smite them mightily. And my men, my people, will be fed for another year.

Men who had dreamed of gay victories now longed to capture a commissary wagon.

The fury of the storm without conjured a stray memory. Once, before her health declined, Mary had lured him to a playhouse across the river in Washington to endure a performance of *King Lear*. He had no interest in such frivolities, but the play had moved him unexpectedly and he had left the theater unsettled, in a state that alarmed him. He had shunned the theater after that, wary of its tricks. But now, as this night broke over two facing armies, he thought again of that foolish old king, and about the poor, wronged fellow in the storm who had spouted nonsense that had the ring of law. And he thought of his men, with their empty bellies, unsheltered on this night. Perhaps there had been more to the play than he had been willing to see. . . .

What else had he been unwilling to see in his life? What did he fail to see now? Was he as stubborn as that addled king? Or, perhaps, as mad?

He caught Venable watching him. The younger man's expression was almost motherly. The aide quickly looked away, but Lee knew that those closest to him worried over his health and his meager appetite. Lee valued the lads who devoted themselves to serving him, and his feelings toward his military family went deeper than he permitted himself to reveal. Yet, not one of those men could serve him as confidant. He was alone, and had been so for years.

Across the table, Powell Hill sat, struggling to appear well. Hill was still too sick to do his duty and he knew it: He had not had the temerity to ask for his corps back. He would have it, of course, in good time, when he was well enough, but Early must do for the present. Hill only wanted to remain close to things, to still feel a part of their brotherly undertaking. Lee had no time for mysticism, but there was a bond between these men no science had explained. Only he was left apart.

"General Lee," Hill said to him, "you've hardly eaten. You must keep up your strength."

Powell Hill, who looked like a skeleton whose bones could be snapped in two with a child's strength. Who would be left to lead in the hard times ahead? If Grant proved unrelenting? He could not afford the loss of another paladin.

"That stew could almost be accused of flavor," Hill coaxed. His tone suggested the ailing corps commander might next come around the table and seek to feed him.

Lee's stomach was so torn, he could not digest cornbread.

"I supped early," he lied.

It was essential not to show weakness.

SEVENTEEN

T his is idiocy," Major General David Bell Birney declared. "Has anyone in this room actually *seen* this infamous salient?"

"Morgan did what he could," Hancock said.

"Couldn't see a damned thing," the chief of staff told the assembled division commanders. "Rain, and fog on top of that. I could barely see past our pickets."

"Idiocy," Birney repeated.

"That Sixth Corps choirboy cracked the position," Hancock noted.

"And couldn't stick it," Birney snapped. "Bloody mess, from what I hear."

"Well, it got Grant thinking," Hancock said.

"I suppose that's a triumph in itself." Wet through and at his most irascible, Birney was happy to lead the charge of complaints for his fellow division heads.

Gibbon joined in: "Sir, whatever Saint Emory of Upton or anyone else did yesterday, it's preposterous to expect us to move to a new position after dark—in this weather—then assault a position we haven't even seen. And, for what it's worth, I hear their lines are formidable over there."

A man of pointed beard and pointed manner, Birney added, "Of course they're formidable. Lee's had three days to prepare." He shook himself like a dog. Vestiges of the rain spattered the assembly. "This is an entirely new kind

of war, entirely new. Fit only for brutes. These field fortifications, the way Lee's army gets them up in minutes . . .
they'll have parapets, head logs, and rifle ports by now."
Birney made a distinctly ungentlemanly sound. "We're not
fighting an army, it's a moving fortress. . . ."

"Actually," Barlow said, speaking for the first time, "it's
nothing new. It's what the Romans did at the end of the
day's march. Any schoolboy who's read his Caesar knows
that."

"Thank you, Frank," Gibbon said. "We'll all brush up
on our Latin before the next battle."

"Look," Barlow said, "we're all agreed, that's what matters. The scheme's asinine." He looked to Hancock. The
weathered flesh around the corps commander's eyes signaled exhaustion. "Sir, we need at least a hint regarding
the defenders' situation. What's their position, their
strength? Which units are we facing? Above all, what's the
terrain like? I might as well order my brigades to march
off a cliff."

"I'm assured," Hancock said, "that we'll be provided
with all the information we need when we arrive on the
left." His tone was almost perfunctory. "Now stop whimpering, all of you. Orders are orders, and all of you damned
well know it. Barlow, you'll set off at ten. Morgan here will
join you and guide the column. We'll scare up an engineer
or two, Wright's promised to send me someone who knows
the ground. Meanwhile, the plan for the morning assault
remains unchanged: Barlow on the left, Birney on the right,
advancing simultaneously. Gibbon follows, prepared to reinforce success. Lead brigades step off at four a.m." With
grinding slowness, he looked at the face of each division
commander in turn. "Any questions?"

Attacking what, exactly? Barlow wanted to say.

"Mott?" Gibbon asked.

Morgan rolled his eyes.

Hancock said, "Used up. I only intend to use his men, if I have to."

"But he's seen the position," Birney said. "He's been over there for two days. He should be able to tell us something, give us some sense of the ground."

"I'll have him at the point of rendezvous. Another flea-ridden shanty, no doubt. Morgan here knows the way."

"The men'll be exhausted," Barlow said. "We're asking them to attack without any sleep."

The chief of staff laughed derisively. "Christ, Barlow! Since when have you given a silver-plated shit about your men getting enough sleep?"

Barlow's fellow division commanders smirked, every man gone mean against the others. Hancock joined in with a sarcastic grimace.

"Since," Barlow said, "they haven't had a proper sleep in seven days. There comes a point . . ."

"None of us has had a proper sleep," Hancock said. "Nor have the Rebels." He grunted. "Grant may not have the brain of a genius, but the man's got a constitution of cast iron. He'll wear Lee down, if nothing else. As for you, Barlow, be glad I didn't reinstate Paul Frank again."

"Last time I saw that sausage-eater," Gibbon sneered, "he could barely stand up."

"It true you went at him with that meat-ax of yours?" Morgan asked Barlow, laughing. "Poor Brown doesn't know what he's in for, taking that brigade."

Birney returned to his rich disgust. "We might as well blindfold ourselves and sing 'Pop Goes the Weasel'! It's bad enough storming entrenchments a fellow can see . . ."

"Just follow your damned orders," Hancock said. "Order of march for tonight is Barlow, Birney, and Gibbon, nose to asshole." He gave his generals a drained-to-the-bottom look. "Anything else? Or have you all got your pissant insubordination out of the way?"

"Guns?" Birney asked.

"No guns. Grant wants a surprise attack. No bombard-ment, no warning."

"Cannon would just get stuck and hold things up," Morgan said. "The Sixth Corps artillery will support, as necessary."

"Grant views this as the most important assault of the campaign," Hancock summed up.

Barlow let go a startling laugh. "What an absolute, un-mitigated delight! I really mean it, it's fresh cream on a bun. No reconnaissance. No information as to the enemy's strength. No guns. No clear notion of the objective. Hardly more than a general direction for the attack . . ." He snorted. "*That,* gentlemen, is your new kind of war."

"Just have your men on the fucking road at ten," Han-cock told him.

Eight thirty p.m.
The Mule Shoe

What the devil?" Major General Edward "Alleghany" Johnson said. He waved his cane. "You hold up there. Whoa!"

The leading limber sloshed to a stop. The second team almost crashed into the lead piece in the darkness. Gun-ners and drivers cursed. Colonel Tom Carter rode up, rais-ing a trail of quicksilver splashes, as if the rain were rising, repelled, from the earth.

"Damn, boy, why'd you hold up?" he demanded of an unseen artilleryman.

When the colonel's horse stilled, General Johnson stepped back onto the farm trail. "Colonel Carter? That you?"

"Yes, sir. Thought I'd best see to this personally."

"What the coal black devil's going on? Where are these guns off to?"

"Orders, sir. From General Long. We're to withdraw and prepare for movement."

"Nobody took the damned trouble to tell me."

General George Steuart, one of Johnson's brigade commanders, found his way into the huddle. "Ticks me off, too," he said. "No damned sense to it, drawing off those guns."

"I should've been told," Johnson muttered.

"Plumb crazy," Steuart went on. "My line's exposed enough. But there you go . . . nobody back in the rear has a lick of sense."

"Sir," the artilleryman said, "believe me, the men would rather stay right here. They've been building up those emplacements for three days, I judge them impregnable. . . ."

"Assuming they're manned," Johnson said. "Damn it, artillery's the key to this position. The whole point of exposing my division out here was to give the guns a platform."

"General Johnson, I have no choice but to obey my orders," Carter said.

"Oh, I know that, Tom, I know. But it just doesn't make any sense."

"Only thing I can figure," Steuart offered, "is that old Long must intend to replace them with fresh batteries, give these boys a rest up. Only way it plays. . . ."

Johnson nodded. That made sense. It seemed the only reasonable explanation. But why was it that the infantry never got a rest?

Each of the three officers had wearied of holding still under the downpour. Moving lessened the misery somehow.

"Well, you go on, then," Johnson told the artillery colonel. "Get your guns along, before you sink on through to China. A man can't even plant his cane in this damned

down-country quicksand. But you tell whoever's coming
up to replace these batteries they mustn't waste time, hear?"

"Yes, sir. If I see them, I'll relay the message." The colonel saluted the men whose outlines he could barely distinguish, then turned to his lead team, shouting to the driver
and outrider to haul on through the mire.

Johnson and Steuart stepped back from the slop thrown
by the vehicles.

"I don't like this one little bit," Alleghany Johnson said.

"Can't say I like any of it, at the moment," the brigade
commander agreed.

"Long *must* be planning to replace those guns. Folly to
leave those positions empty, after what the Yankees pulled
last night." He turned his head, redirecting the water that
had found its way to his neck and spine. "George, if fresh
guns don't roll up this way by midnight, you let me know."

"Yes, sir. I expect they'll be up, though. Have to be."

Johnson reset his drenched hat. "Your men all right?"

"Fair to middling. Got us some nice new tent halves off
dead Yankees. Boys rig 'em up overhead. Helps a touch."

Another gun lurched past, splashing the officers despite
the distance they had moved from the trail.

"Sonofabitch!" Johnson growled. He thrashed the mud
with his cane.

Steuart laughed, a hard man, hard-voiced, softened by
his delight in another's misery. "Not sure I'm any wetter
than I was, speaking for myself. Lord, this rain . . . at least
it keeps the Yankees tucked in quiet."

Ten thirty p.m.

The rain turned the road into such a morass that the
horses of Barlow's party had to struggle. And what was
hard for the mounts was worse for the men plodding

behind them. Marching to what would be, no doubt, a slaughter.

Barlow felt a level of compassion that had not afflicted him previously. The soldiers he commanded had performed with valor and grit for the past week, despite the grotesque mismanagement of the battles. Those who remained, by and large, were the resolute, and they deserved better than this. He rued the whittling down of his brigades and regiments in one squandered opportunity after another. Lives had to be sacrificed in war, of course, no end of them. But the generals needed to stop acting on mere whims and use their brains. If brains they had.

"So," he said to Mendell, the engineer dispatched to lead them to their assault position, "you can't tell me a thing about the ground between our assembly point and the Rebel lines?"

"It's mostly open, I think," the lieutenant colonel said. "From what I could see of it."

"And just how much was that?" Morgan, Hancock's right-hand man, put in. "Fifteen feet, or twenty?"

"After you leave the trees . . . I mean, where there are trees . . . it seems to be open ground for, say, a quarter mile. Some dips and folds. But open, I think."

"And beyond that?" Barlow asked.

"I don't know."

"Speak up, man. I can't hear you over the rain."

"I said I don't know."

"No, you damned well don't," Morgan said. "None of us do. The blind leading the blind. Fuck me to perdition."

"Sir," the engineer said, "what do you want me to do? Lie to you? Make something up? I'm no fonder of all this than you are."

"That may be," Barlow said, battered by a wind-whipped shift in the rain. "But you won't have to go forward. My men will."

"Maybe," Miles put in from behind, "it's all meant to be a map-making expedition. A 'survey in force.' To unknown lands of military wonder. . . ."

"Or a grand review in Lee's honor," John Brooke mocked. "Fine weather for it."

"Maybe the provost marshal's finally found us a decent whorehouse," Morgan said. "And we're all going to line up in turn. All twenty thousand of us."

"Hard on the girls," Brooke noted.

"Oh, shut up, Charlie!" Miles said. "You'll get me thinking about women, and that's all I need. Humping a wet saddle on my way to an early grave."

"I'll tell you, boys," Morgan said, voice theatrically thoughtful, "when I went back to Philadelphia with Hancock the last time, a friend introduced me to Mrs. Adelaide Turner's noble establishment. It was a revelation, even to my jaded and calloused spirit. My, oh, my . . . one begins to understand the fascination fallen women hold for a certain detestable class of men. . . ."

"That why you've been so grumpy, Charlie?" Miles asked. "You been clapped up all this time?"

Barlow burst out laughing, but not at the repartee. "Morgan, I've given up on any hope of a reasonable picture of the battlefield. But will you at least promise to face us in the right direction in the morning? So we don't have to march all the way through China and come up in Lee's rear?"

"Speaking of rears," Morgan said, "there was this one exquisite creature . . . a glorious wanton . . . Boys, I fear that, should I fall"—he intoned his words as if mocking every stage actor who had ever lived—"I do fear that my last thoughts will not be of my pure-hearted beloved waiting chastely by the fireside, but of that delectable— Miles, do you have any idea what some of those women actually *like* to do?"

"If you're paying them enough," Nellie Miles said, "I expect they'd like most anything. And I expect you have to pay extra, Charlie." He laughed. Grimly. "I hope you left them something in your will. Not sure you'll be visiting after tomorrow."

"I'd rather pimp a line of China whores than make this attack," Birney said. "This isn't soldiering, it's blood sacrifice."

The engineer tried to enter the circle of comrades. "I suppose I'm all for audacity in war . . . but this attack does seem extreme."

"'Audacity'?" Morgan said. "Oh, yes. *L'audace, l'audace, toujours l'audace.*"

"That's what Charlie's Philadelphia trollop kept on telling him," Miles suggested. "Charlie, she was trying to get you to move your hips a little, it all works better that way. You try it next time."

"I think the rain's easing up," Birney said. "There's that, at least."

No sooner had he spoken than a wall of water struck them.

"'Beautiful dreamer . . . ,'" Miles began to sing.

"Oh, do shut up. All of you," Barlow said. "If we expect the men to be quiet, we need to at least pretend that we're adults."

"Maybe we can just pretend to attack," Miles said.

"I told you to shut up, Nellie. All of you. Mendell, I thought this march was only three miles?"

"It is. We're over halfway there, I think."

"Christ," Barlow said.

It wasn't just the mindlessness of it all, or the rough weather. For the first time before a battle, he felt pinches of fear. Despite his wounds, he had always felt that he would not be killed, that he could not be killed, no matter how badly damaged in the flesh. Tonight, he could no longer summon that confidence.

The flashes of doubt that ambushed him had nothing to do with the common dread of pain or even of death itself. Rather, he hated the thought that he might never again see either of the two beings he most loved, Belle and his mother. He regretted that he had not had time to write since the campaign began and that Belle, so close, could not share a last embrace and a few soft words. His wife, for all her gifts, was a tender spirit, as only he knew. They were finely matched, and he felt that by dying he would let her down just awfully. And his mother, for all her failings, remained resolutely admirable and unreservedly loved. He knew, full well, with a man's nuanced understanding, how much she had risked or outright sacrificed to keep him and his brothers above water. He knew the whispers and blushed at them, but his knowledge ran far deeper than any gossip's. His mother had clung skillfully to the semblance of respectability, exploiting New England's web of obligations with a ferocity that presaged his own fierceness on the battlefield.

One of his haunting memories of his mother was a vignette that should have embarrassed him, but, oddly, didn't. It had occurred in the early, golden days at Brook Farm, when his mother was still queening it over the others. He had slipped away to fish—a skill he never quite mastered—and from a glade he had heard his mother's voice calling out the strangest pleas. He had thrust forward through the ferns to find John Dwight, the musical fellow, atop the untouchable Almira Penniman Barlow, with his mother's garments and petticoats in disarray. He had almost plunged forward to rescue her from the assault, when the tone of her begging stopped him. He had never heard such notes—or such language—issue from his mother, a dominating presence. Embarrassed and relieved he had not been observed, he turned away . . . only to be drawn back to the spectacle of his mother's weakness. He had realized quickly what the encounter entailed, he'd learned from the farm's animals and the bragging of other boys, but what struck him and stayed with him all his life was the revelation of his mother's unexpected frailty.

She had flirted aplenty after his father's departure—to the consternation of the other Brook Farm women—and her latest social dalliance had been with smelly old Hawthorne, whom Barlow refused to address as "Uncle Nathaniel." But he had always thought Dwight hardly more than a boy, and a bit silly. Now the fellow had his mother begging for a relief that passed all understanding. Instead of angering Barlow, it had made him feel that, all his days, he must protect his mother and be her defender. That glimpse of her defenselessness had been a revelation, with little or nothing to do with colliding bodies. He had learned that summer afternoon that any human could succumb to weakness.

As for his wife, men had feared her, wary of her intellect, viewing her as impossibly brash and forthright. But Arabella's enthusiasm spilled from an overflowing mind: He had known many a Harvard man far poorer in his faculties. And behind the occasional awkward display of knowledge over a dinner table, she, too, was racked with doubts and concealed weaknesses, half a Diana, and half a Trojan woman.

He would regret disappointing them with his death.

But he did not intend to shirk his duties one jot. He would fight. And he meant to fight wisely, if such a thing were possible, under the circumstances. He had heard of Upton's success—with not a little jealousy—and had queried everyone he could find on the details. What he gathered was secondhand at best, but it sounded as though Upton had solved the problem of crossing the killing space that he had pondered for months. Dense columns, rapid movement, no pauses, all violent action delayed until the enemy's line had been reached. First round fired at point-blank range, then bayonets. Or bayonets, then the first round. He had intuited some of it himself, but had gotten other aspects wrong, fixing on open-order formations when a massive phalanx was what did the trick. He pushed his tired mind to envision the correct formation for a division, the geometry that would deliver a powerful blow without stumbling over itself, the proper spacing . . . and the absolute need for surprise. . . .

He had met Upton in the war's first months, when the Regular had been a newly commissioned lieutenant of artillery, fresh from West Point, detailed to drill the 12th New York Volunteers, the regiment Barlow had joined as a private and where he had been appointed a lieutenant. Upton had impressed him with his rigor and demands, although the strictness had not pleased the other recruits, who expected a merry summer encampment full of sporting games. Barlow realized with a minor shock how much he had patterned his own leadership on that of the brusque lieutenant, and he resented the need to copy him yet again. But Upton had solved the problem.

If it had not been a fluke. . . .

Hard, hit them hard, on a narrow front, with an irresistible mass of veteran regiments. Punch through, and then keep going. Kill them before they had a chance to kill you. Barlow could see it.

The problem would be maintaining order after the collision. Loss of control in battle had become the worst of the army's bugbears, betraying every success.

He just might pull it off, though.

If there was a chance, the slightest chance, to make a

successful attack, he meant to seize it. Dense columns. Rushing across an open field. A devastating impact.

The one thing that could stop such a charge was artillery.

May 12, twelve fifteen a.m.
The Mule Shoe

Major Hunter!" Alleghany Johnson said, kicking his aide a tad harder than was necessary. "Wake your behind up, boy."

"Sir . . . yes, sir. . . ."

It was so damned dark and miserable that Johnson was almost surprised to have found the right man.

"Awake now, Bob? Enough to listen?"

"Yes, sir."

"Can't say you sound it. Listen here. There's trouble. Colonel Terry's pissing his drawers on the picket line, claims he hears the whole Yankee army rooting around in the canebrake. His men hear it, too."

"Mightn't it be the jumps? Men are awful tore down. Or the rain?"

"Fourth Virginia ain't skittish, Bob. And Terry, he don't spook. And General Steuart reports no replacement guns came up. The line's stripped bare of cannon."

"What time is it, sir?"

"Time for you to get a damned move on. Go on back, find Ewell. Knock him on his bald head if you have to, but you tell him we need those batteries back here."

"Yes, sir. Just feeling for my boots."

"Shouldn't ever take 'em off," Johnson said.

"Got the foot itch, sir."

"Show me a man doesn't. You go on off now. And don't you let Dick Ewell get to bamboozling, I need those guns."

When the major had gone, Major General Johnson

stepped outside again, defying the elements and his body's complaints, warring against the force of gravity that tugged a man earthward in the depths of one sleepless night after another.

He went up to the trench line, had a back-and-forth with a sergeant who talked thick Blue Ridge, and reassured a pup of a boy from Winchester. The lad worried about his family, caught in another Yankee visitation.

"You just keep your eyes open, son. Plenty of Yankees to whup right here. Then we'll go over and flush 'em out of the Valley, mark my words." He tapped the boy's leg with his cane. "You stay awake now, until you're relieved. Hate to have to shoot you."

After that, he listened through the rain, trying to detect the worrisome sounds Bill Terry had reported. Maybe it was just spooks and hants, after all. Enough tiredness put nerves in the best of men.

Feel better once the guns get back, he figured.

Twelve thirty a.m.
Assault position, south of the Brown house

Barlow couldn't see a blasted thing. The rain had eased to a drizzle, but the night was as black and foul as a Frenchman's morals.

"Well, this is it. Your jumping-off line," Morgan said. "General Barlow, I regret—"

"Regrets won't buy me a boiled egg," Barlow said. "How do I even know which way to point my division?"

"I can give you a compass line."

Barlow threw up his hands, but only got wet forearms for it. "Mendell, how about you? Earn your pay. At least tell me how far my men have to go."

"Something less than a mile, I should think."

"Now that . . . is supremely helpful. 'Something less than a mile.' That would fall somewhere between five feet and five thousand. . . ." Exasperated, he paused to listen to his men sloshing through the meadow, churning it to mud soup. They had been cautioned, harshly, to be as silent as possible, and there was none of the usual clanking of tin cups or other metal bits, nor complaints above a whisper. But thousands of massing men made a certain amount of noise, despite herculean efforts.

He knew he was being juvenile, but sarcasm was irresistible. "Tell me, Morgan," he began again. "And you feel free to contribute, Mendell, if you have any flashes of genius. Here's the vital question of the day: Can you even assure me that I won't have to cross a thousand-foot-deep gulch halfway across?"

Morgan played along. "No, sir. I can't. How about you, Mendell?"

The engineer remained silent.

"It was the weather," Morgan explained. "I went out as far as the skirmish line. But I just couldn't see a thing. You know how it was raining."

" 'This . . . is the excellent foppery of the world,' " Barlow said, " 'that when we are sick in fortune, often the surfeit of our own behavior, we make guilty of our disasters the sun, the moon, and the stars. . . .' "

"I'd blame Grant, myself," Morgan said.

One forty-five a.m.
The Mule Shoe

That bald-headed bastard," Alleghany Johnson roared.

"Sir," Major Hunter explained, "General Ewell said the order to withdraw the guns came straight from General Lee, it wasn't Long's doing. General Lee has firm information that Grant's moving Meade and Burnside to the far right, probably to withdraw up the Fredericksburg Road."

"Well, I guess half of them got lost," the general said. "Just had a Louisiana boy up here telling me the entire Union army's about to land on him. And Colonel Terry, he's ready to crack the Book with Seven Seals."

"Should I wake the men, sir?"

Johnson considered it, looked at his watch, regretted its fickleness, and said, "No, not yet. They're tuckered out. Let them sleep a tad longer. Dick Ewell really told you he wouldn't send me a single goddamned battery?"

"He didn't put it quite that way."

"But that was the gist of it?"

"Yes, sir. That was the sense of things."

"We'll damned well see about that. Crawley, get my horse."

Two thirty a.m.
The Brown house

Barlow, you're mad," Hancock said. "If you do that, the guns in that salient will knock down your men like pins."

"Really, Frank," John Gibbon said. "They'd be annihilated by canister, they wouldn't get halfway across the field."

"The field nobody's seen?" Barlow was all the crankier for having had an hour of brute sleep on the floor of the house.

Teddy Lyman came in, cape shiny with rain. Most of the gathered generals ignored Meade's aide, but Barlow nodded. Lyman had another officer with him whose face Barlow couldn't quite place. The two kept a respectful distance, huddling by the telegraph men who were setting up a station in the corner. To report back to Meade and Grant on the coming assault.

So damned tired. . . .

"When you don't know what's in front of you," Hancock said, "it's all the more reason to stick with the tried and true. Frank, I'll have to forbid—"

Barlow exploded. "Then relieve me! Right here. On the spot. If I'm to lead this assault, I'm damned well going to do it the way I think best. And I propose to have men enough when I reach their works to charge through Hell itself. As for their artillery, I intend to capture every gun they mass on my front." He glared at Hancock. "With all respect due to rank, sir, sticking with the 'tried and true' is poppycock. The only time this army's had any success on these fields was Upton's little adventure. Which I intend to repeat with a full division."

"The Johnnies will be on to that trick now. Every gun on that ridge will be loaded with canister," Gibbon said, as surly of voice as any of them that night.

"My division's out in front, not yours," Barlow shot back. "Damn it, I'm not going to lead my men like sheep to the slaughter again. They're going to have a fighting chance." He looked, murder-eyed, at Gibbon. "And I'll be at their front, not smoking a pipe in the trains."

The room was on the verge of erupting in its own civil war.

Hancock shook his head in grand disgust. "All right, Frank. All right, then. But make a wet shit of this, and I'll have your head. *And* your division."

"If I fail, my head won't be your problem."

"Sounds rather melodramatic," Birney observed. "Thought you didn't go in for that sort of thing."

"A man adjusts his tenor to his company," Barlow told him. He quite liked Birney the rest of the time, but hated him at the moment. Just then, he hated everything and everybody.

"All right, then," Hancock said, straining to conjure his

bluff, customary voice. "Jump off at precisely four a.m. Let's set our watches, gentlemen. I have . . . two forty-seven."

"Two forty-seven," a number of voices confirmed.

"To your commands, then," Hancock said. "And shove the goddamned graybacks down the shithole."

As the assembly began to break up, Lyman raised his high-pitched voice.

"General Hancock . . . Colonel Merriam's seen the ground to your front, I thought he might describe it."

Bless old Teddy. Harvard was good for something. And yes, that was Wally Merriam, of the 16th Massachusetts, from Mott's bunch.

Too tired to recognize a man he'd known for years. And he was about to lead seven thousand men in a blind attack.

"Well," Hancock said, "what have you got to impart to us, Merriam? These men are in a hurry."

Merriam was the classic Yankee sort, stingy with words. Instead of beginning with pleasantries or good wishes, he strode over to the fireplace, where damp wood smoked, and picked out a charred stick. He began to sketch on a filthy wall.

It wasn't a work of art for the ages, but there was enough detail for Barlow and the others to begin to grasp the general situation. The best news was that the salient didn't have an especially broad tip, so there was a limit to the number of guns that could be massed for converging fires. Still, the corps had to traverse up to three-quarters of a mile of rolling ground, then climb over abatis under fire to reach the Rebel entrenchments. It was a deadly, daunting space, almost as far across as the fields at Gettysburg, and no matter how quiet the men sought to be, the Johnnies were bound to hear them coming too soon. Whatever the number of guns that had been squeezed into the salient's apex, their double-shotted canister at close range would be simply murderous.

Was he making a terrible mistake?

Bet all, or fold, he told himself.

He felt mildly better for Merriam's description. If he had to die, he preferred not to die a fool's death in total ignorance.

"All right, gentlemen," Hancock said. "I hope to see you all at day's end, let's go."

"I'll be glad to make it to breakfast," Birney muttered.

Before returning to his men, Barlow took Lyman aside.

"Good stroke, Lyman," he said. "You academic sorts aren't totally useless."

"I seem to remember a certain valedictorian . . ."

"We all have our sins to repent." He worked his wedding band off his finger, drew out his folding wallet, inserted the ring, and handed the packet to Lyman. "And this," he added, fishing out the carefully wrapped image of Belle he kept in a breast pocket. "Do see that Arabella gets these, if I make a mess of things. I'd like to send her my watch, but seem to have need of it."

"Barlow, this isn't like you."

"Not quite certain what I'm like these days. Now don't go off whoring with the funds in there."

Insufferably happy in his marriage to a bride almost as rich as he was himself, Lyman turned a warm and mottled pink.

"Oh, I know, I know," Barlow said. "I'm socially impossible. Might do for Boston, but not for Beacon Hill. Isn't that what you said about me?" Barlow smiled, but there was unexpected sweetness, rather than malice, in it. "Only teasing, for Heaven's sake. But do remember what I told you, I wasn't joking. Back when you asked about seeking a command. Stick to staff work, Teddy, you were born for it. But you couldn't get an Irishman to follow you into a bar that was ladling out free whiskey. You tell Belle my last thoughts were of her and that I had no time to write. And good luck with your starfish."

He slapped on his hat and went into the rain.

Two thirty a.m.
Lee's headquarters

Roused from his slumbers and already dressed correctly, Lee struggled to make sense of the conflicting reports.

"Look at our dilemma, gentlemen," he said to his drowsy aides. "Here we have a perfect lesson in how difficult it is to be truly certain of information and determine what course is best. I have here a dispatch from General Early claiming, of a sudden, that those people are moving around our left. And this is from General Johnson, endorsed by General Ewell. *He* insists that Meade has moved to the right and is massing in his front. He begs that the withdrawn guns be returned to the salient." Lee's bowels quaked. "Which of these reports am I to believe?"

Taylor said: "General Johnson does appear convinced, sir."

"But so does General Early. He's not a man to see phantoms."

"General," Taylor said, "we've had no further reports suggesting a Union retreat. Nothing trustworthy. Only word of various movements of unclear purpose. And that was yesterday. The artillery was withdrawn with a pursuit in mind and—"

"And my conclusion may have been premature," Lee said. He looked around the tent. In the lantern's light, the faces of Taylor, Venable, and Marshall appeared as grim as a deathwatch. "You all believe the

guns should be returned to General Johnson's portion
of the line?"

"Yes, sir," Venable said. The others nodded.

"So do I," Lee said. "We must make haste."

Three fifteen a.m.
Barlow's division

Barlow huddled under the canvas his brigade commanders and aides held over their heads, shielding the lantern's
light from the enemy's view. On the chance in a thousand
it could be seen through the murk. The rain had softened
to a light blow and pattered on the cloth, dripping from the
edges. Fog rolled over the fields and through the groves
as if God were smoking a meerschaum. Beyond the lantern's cast, the air was Hades black.

Drawing in the mud with a stick, Barlow said, "Make
your peace with God, gentlemen. I have a hot place picked
out for some of you today." The attempt at humor fell flat.
A pall worse than the weather hung over them all. Barlow
ached to display his usual confidence, but every time he
spoke a false tone spoiled his voice.

"It isn't much to go on, but the salient's here, shaped like
this. Pay attention to the tip. We'll aim to hit just off its
center, slightly to the left, just about . . . here. Of course,
there's no telling where we'll actually end up . . . but as
soon as you catch a glimpse, the vaguest outline, of the position, that's where I want you to do your best to hit them.
Now . . . we're here. When we move out, we're going
straight ahead. Nothing fancy, no nonsense. I'm told this
ground is open and what trees there were near the works
were cut down for abatis. Be prepared for plenty of abatis."

"If they used poplar," Nellie Miles said, "it'll snap off."

"Not when it's wet," Brooke said.

Paul Frank's replacement, Hiram Brown, added, "Rain's been so heavy, the stakes may not have much purchase. Might be able to pull them right out of the ground."

"Fine, but let's not count on it," Barlow told him. "What's essential is that you all keep your men closed up. Keep them moving fast, as fast as you can without losing all sense of order. If this mist holds, they won't be able to see us until we're a hundred yards off, or even closer."

"They'll hear us."

"Can't aim at a sound with very much confidence," Brooke observed.

"Exactly," Barlow said. "They'll have to hold their fire, until we're close enough to make a dash for it. Even if they've laid guns to rake the fields, they'll be hesitant to open until they think they've spotted something of value. They'll be worried about the time they need to reload."

"And then the lovely point, sir, would be to keep on a-going," Smyth said.

"Right. No matter what damage the guns do—and it won't be pleasant, gentlemen—just keep whipping the men forward. Get over the abatis, get in among the Rebs. It's the only chance. And once we're in those trenches, I do expect scalps by the wagonload."

"Literally?" Brooke said. "We never quite know with you."

"Corpses and prisoners have to do, I suppose. That's it, then. Miles, you're up on the left, followed by Smyth and the Irish Brigade. Brooke's up on the right, followed by Brown. Ten paces between brigades, five between regiments. No one fires until we reach the entrenchments. No one stops, no one fires. Only bayonets, when we hit their skirmish lines."

"Their skirmishers will fire. That'll warn them we're coming."

"A few stray shots are one thing, regimental volleys are

another. Just don't let anything stop this attack, or delay it, or break it up in any way. Hit them hard." He tried to smile. "I do expect an interesting morning. All right, go and explain things to your regimental officers. And be ready to step off precisely at four."

His subordinates began to break up the party, muttering about the inability to maneuver when packed so tight and the prospects of canister on the prescribed formation. But it didn't rise above the normal level of complaints; sour remarks were almost a form of prayer for men at war.

"Hold on," Barlow said. "All of you. Black, don't douse the lantern yet. Hold it up, so we can see one another's faces."

Surprised, the aide did as ordered.

"Gentlemen . . . ," Barlow began, "if I have offended any man in this command . . . if I have done so unjustly . . . you have my apology. You are, each of you, fine officers. I am proud to have commanded this division. There is no better in the army. And . . ." He strained for words, ever a reluctant public speaker. "And I wish each of you well."

"Really, sir," Nellie Miles said, "we're not dead yet."

Three forty a.m.
Artillery park, Early's rear

Carter, for God's sake, get up!"

The artilleryman jumped at the hand shaking his shoulder, at the bite in the voice. He had dreamed of being captured in a woodland, and for a moment, it seemed all too real.

Coming partway back to sanity, he reached for the top of his field desk, hand feeling for a box of lucifers.

He struck a match and found General Long standing over him. Long was drenched with rain: He had come out without bothering to put on his uniform blouse or even a shirt.

Carter touched the match to the stump of a candle.

"You have to get those guns back up to the salient," Long cried, almost childish in his anxiety. "Here. Read this. It's from Lee. Christ almighty. It sounds like the blue-bellies may be up to something, after all. You've got to get those guns back into position."

The one thing Carter had learned, painfully, was to get something down on paper in a crisis, since recriminations always followed. He checked the time on his pocket watch, then put a pencil to the order and wrote, "Received at twenty minutes to daybreak. Men asleep. Artillery will be in place as soon as possible."

As he pulled on his boots, he began to shout orders through the tent's walls.

If the Yankees were coming, they were going to come damned soon.

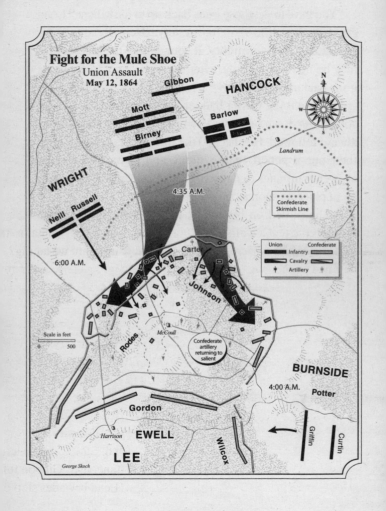

Fight for the Mule Shoe
Union Assault
May 12, 1864

HANCOCK

Gibbon

Mott

Barlow

Birney

Landrum

WRIGHT

Neill   Russell

4:35 A.M.

6:00 A.M.

· · · · · ·
**Confederate
Skirmish Line**

Union	Confederate
Infantry	
Cavalry	
Artillery	

Carter

Johnson

McCoull

Rodes

Confederate
artillery returning to
salient

BURNSIDE

4:00 A.M.   Potter

Scale in feet

0   500

Gordon

Harrison

EWELL

LEE

Wilcox

Griffin   Curtin

George Skoch

EIGHTEEN

"General Barlow!" some idiot called out. "Where's General Barlow?"

Barlow turned to his aide. "Black, shut that fool up. Cut his throat if you have to."

For all the precautions taken to keep thousands of soldiers quiet, one barking moron could ruin their hope of surprise.

The rain had gentled to a drizzle, hardly more than a mist. Ground fog hugged the landscape. A horse nickered and was instantly quieted. But the blundering ass crashing through the ranks of soldiers kept calling Barlow's name.

Black collared the noisemaker and dragged him through the darkness.

"Courier, sir," the aide said. "From General Hancock."

Calling off the attack? Earlier, Barlow would have welcomed such news. Now, every man was primed to advance and be damned.

"Sir," the courier began, "urgent message. Urgent, sir. The attack is delayed until four thirty. General Hancock feels it's still too dark. With the rain and what all." The man handed Barlow written confirmation, but it wasn't worth the risk of striking a match. And there was no time.

"Get runners out immediately," Barlow told his aide. "Attack's delayed a half hour. Hurry, man!"

Hancock had cut it damned close. If even one man in the corps failed to get the word . . . and wasn't this supposed to be a grand attack? Someone had spoken of Burnside bringing in the Ninth Corps on the left. Would that alert the Johnnies in Hancock's front? And guarantee a slaughter as his men advanced?

The wet on Barlow's back was sweat, not seeping rain.

With the attack expected to begin in minutes, every heart in the division would be battering at its ribs, a captive shaking the bars of a prison cell. The tension had neared the unbearable, with his officers and men exhausted yet ghastly alert, waiting to plunge forward and take their chances.

Summoned back to the headquarters shack not twenty minutes before, Barlow had argued for a delay himself, certain the darkness would linger past the dawn in the rain and fog. The troops could advance in faint light, but their order would collapse if they couldn't see anything. Near catatonic with lack of sleep, Hancock had seemed deaf to Barlow's reasoning, unable to bear the weight of more decisions.

So he had steeled himself to go forward as planned. And he was ready *now.* It made every kind of sense to delay, but he no longer wanted to wait. The rational man within had been locked away, replaced by a monstrous, impassioned, explosive creature.

He smiled to himself: *We rush toward death. It's certain madness. Exhilarating madness. If Emerson wanted to experience transcendence, this was where the old charlatan needed to be.*

He told himself to be glad that Hancock had taken his advice. He could not see beyond the outline of the nearest troops, and to go forward at present begged for a tragedy. But things had gone too far in the soul's dark places. The mood among the men was such that a snapping twig might have unleashed a riot.

He waited out the minutes, dreading that somewhere along the line a cheer would go up, or guns would open, or Burnside would be punctual for once, or that one of his own units would blunder forward punctually at four.

The drizzle all but stopped, leaving a racket of droplets falling from leaf to leaf in nearby trees. The fog writhed.

Four o'clock came and went, with no hint of battle.

Thirty minutes more. Of waiting. In the loneliest darkness Barlow had ever known.

His feet itched monstrously.

Four twenty a.m.
Base of the Mule Shoe

Whip them, damn it!" Carter shouted.

"We've *been* whipping them," his younger brother, Billy, hollered back. "They haven't got the strength."

The colonel knew his brother, a captain, was right. The artillery horses had been poorly fed for so long they were merely nags. Now they were expected to pull guns through the bog that passed for a trail to the salient's tip.

Whip a horse to death so it falls in harness, and that only slows things more, Tom Carter realized. He leapt from his horse, landing with a plop that shot mud up to his crotch, and joined the gunners pushing the limber's left wheel out of a hole.

He had hurried Page's battalion forward, with his brother's battery leading. If any man could get there in time, it was his younger brother. Carter grasped the risks, but saw no choice beyond duty.

Their mother would never forgive him if anything happened to Billy. But, then, he wasn't sure he'd ever forgive himself.

"Heave!"

The limber lurched back onto firmer ground. Sodden men jumped out of the path of the gun.

The following caisson got a rushing start and bounded through. Fortunately, without breaking a wheel.

Between teams, soldiers who had rushed up to help tossed sticks and brush into the road's worst cavities, dozens of men guessing what things needed doing and working by the light of a single lantern.

The guns were rolling, though. Toward their old positions facing the enemy.

Four thirty-five a.m.

Hancock had come forward, gathering his generals near the front of Barlow's division, to deliver the order to start the assault in person.

And they waited.

The landscape remained shrouded, gripped by fog the color of soiled cotton.

As the generals stood about the corps commander, bearing the unbearable, nearby troops cursed or prayed or emptied their bladders a last time where they stood. But it was all done so quietly you could hear them draw breath by the hundreds.

The faintest possible paleness appeared in the fog. As if someone held a candle behind a drapery.

The India-ink night thinned.

"To your commands," Hancock said. "Advance immediately. God bless you all."

Four forty a.m.
Skirmish line, 4th Virginia Infantry

Couldn't see one damn thing. Fog to the front, stray rain-drops still coming down. The morning was ugly as a preacher's wife.

Ezekial Goodman just wanted to stay awake till he was called back to the line. He was wearier than a farmer rushed at harvest. With his feet deep in slop as miserable as any he'd ever had the pleasure to meet, worse than a pigsty hadn't been mucked for years. Different country hereabouts. Poor soil, not fit for growing much more than this crop of mud. Far cry from Rockbridge County, where the bottomland was glad to grow just about anything. July corn up taller than a big man. Wheat waving high on the hillside, taunting the scythe, "Come and git me, afore a hard rain comes." Wild raspberries, late June on, if you knew the good patches. And the pretty-as-your-best-friend's-wicked-sister mountains to shade the morning and please the eye. When he got home, he wasn't going anywhere, 'least no farther than Lexington. No need to go back to Pennsylvania, ever. Stonewall Brigade had planted too many men up there. And Maryland? Maybe your'n, but not *my* Maryland. Keep it for the crows. Even right here in Virginia, east of the Blue Ridge was almost a foreign country. The Valley was a special place, Eden with apples it weren't a sin to eat. Many a man would never see it again, his mortal remains left to rot some-where between Beaver Dam Creek and Gettysburg. But Ezekial Goodman was going to make it home. He had a feeling about that.

Somebody had to live on, didn't they? Not many of the first-joined-up fellows were left to complain about the weather this morning. Hardly more than a handful remembered Jackson now, the meanest man a soldier ever did love.

Weren't making them like Jackson anymore, not by a mile. Colonel Terry, he was all right, though. Out on picket with his men, not one of your fine-tent officers.

Goodman wrapped the looted canvas more tightly over his shoulders. Wasn't no ways cold, but he felt a chill. Would've given an acre of good land, and maybe two, for a warm, dry place to rest his bones for an hour.

"Zeke?" Cy Benway asked. "You hear something?"

"Been hearing things all night."

"Something different."

Goodman listened. He was so tired even listening was an effort.

"Like leaves rustling," Cyrus added.

"Plenty of trees yonder."

"But the wind's down."

Goodman peered into the mist, which had grown paler by a shade.

"I don't—"

Then he heard it, too. Sudden, huge, and close. Like the rustling of leaves on every tree in Rockbridge County at once.

He opened his mouth to holler, "They're coming," but the sight before him stunned him into silence: Bursting out of the fog, an apple-toss off, the entire Yankee army had appeared.

Just like that.

"They're coming!" he shouted. Or thought he did, hoped he did. His mouth was dry as ashes.

He raised his rifle as Cyrus raised his own.

"Christ almighty!"

Goodman took quick aim. The Yankees were almost on top of them, bayonets leveled. He pulled the trigger.

The rifle misfired.

In the second it took to decide to run or surrender, the Yankees swept over the rifle pit. With vengeance in their hearts.

Four forty-five a.m.

Captain William Carter led his number one piece forward until entrenchments blocked the horses. Helped by soldiers recently awakened, his boys manhandled the gun toward the nearest emplacement, careful of men asleep in the traverses, while others scrambled to haul up the ammunition chest.

Men slipped and fell. A chest tumbled. The gun's wheels grew stubborn.

"Keep that swab out of the mud!" the first sergeant called.

A lieutenant yelled that a caisson was stuck and blocking the way for the column.

Leaving the lead section to the first sergeant, Carter remounted to hurry the trailing guns along and direct them into position. Around him, conditions seemed queer as all get-out, with some soldiers up and looking to their breakfasts, while others slept the sleep of the just or the dead. He had to wonder whether the alarm that had called out his battery had been a fuss over nothing. They'd lost their first chance at real sleep in a week.

Here and there, dutiful officers barked orders, but the overall feel was of lethargy and the stone-heavy drowse that had gripped the entire army. Carter felt as though his gunners were the only fully alert men in the works.

Time, they just needed time, another few minutes. . . .

As he pointed the way forward for his second section of guns, the captain heard shots.

Four forty-five a.m.

Through a pearly haze, Barlow watched his skirmish line sweep over the rifle pits. The discipline of his men regarding noise was remarkable, each man aware that his life truly did depend on it. A few of the Johnnies got off shots, but his men went through them with bayonets and clubbed muskets. Serpents of mist wound over the earth, clinging to it, and watching the brief struggle at the rifle pits was like spying on ghosts at war.

Riding in the interval between his two leading brigades, he saw his ranks growing ragged, with the packed-together men sacrificing order to move more swiftly than a regular quickstep. With their rifles still at right-should-shift, the brigades followed hard on their skirmishers, who had gained a low ridge topped with a fringe of trees. His skirmishers were mere silhouettes in the gray glow.

Some of the men in the front ranks broke into a double-quick. New men, Barlow realized, imagining that the low ridge would be where the Rebels waited. Veterans called them to order, calling as softly as they could, and most of the befuddled soldiers took their places again.

The man-shadows of the skirmish line disappeared down the far slope, eaten by mist.

His soldiers in their thousands made a peculiar rustle, almost like the sea heard from a shuttered room. The first few prisoners, astonished men, passed by, herded to the rear. On the right, more shots snapped off from Birney's front, but a grove blocked Barlow's sight of the action. His men hastened up the final steps of the slope, churning a derelict meadow to mud underfoot.

It was just light enough to begin to see the patterns on their flags.

Atop the gentle ridge, the view was horrid. The mist had

thinned, and the last true fog had retreated to a ravine to the front. Every man in the first few ranks saw the raw-dirt line of Confederate entrenchments, barely two hundred yards away, glowering above the sinking fog. Abatis bristled and, here and there, the crossed stakes of *chevaux-de-frise* doubled the obstacles.

In an unspoken compact, his men paused to straighten their ranks, as if good order guaranteed protection. Against the inevitable firestorm about to start.

But to Barlow's astonishment, the Rebel guns didn't open.

It was sheer folly. The time for the batteries to do their work was *now*.

Unless they had a surprise waiting. . . .

He waved his saber and the officers who saw him called, quietly, for the advance to resume. After the shock of seeing the Reb entrenchments, the men quickened their pace again, burgeoning forward, the front ranks dropping toward the fogbound ravine.

Hopefully, it's not a thousand feet deep, he told himself, still not free of the long night's doubts and acrimony.

Why didn't the Johnnies fire? Surely, they must have seen his men by now? You couldn't mistake the advance of an entire corps.

As his skirmishers emerged from the fog on the far side of the ravine, his lead regiments dipped into the earthbound cloud.

A Confederate gun fired. The ball soared overhead. The cannon had not been properly laid. It made no sense.

Or was it merely a signal? The beginning of the slaughter?

It was certainly a signal to his men. They dropped their rifles from their shoulders to the charge alignment and began to run. Forward.

And they cheered. Barlow had ordered them to wait

until they reached the line of works, but it no longer mattered. They were too close for even strong volleys to stop them.

Their ranks disordered, a thick wave of his men rushed up the far slope, howling spooks still gripped by shreds of fog.

Why didn't the Rebs open up? It was the perfect moment to let go a battalion's worth of canister.

He kicked his horse forward, feeling his staff close around him.

"Why the Hell aren't they shooting?" a lieutenant asked. "Are they gone?"

No man had an answer.

Just short of the ravine and barely a hundred yards from the Rebel works, Barlow held up his party. He didn't want to lose control, had to see how things developed. But he longed to spur right into the fight, to leap the abatis and go in with his saber.

And behave like an ass, he mocked himself.

Was there a chance that the Rebs had abandoned the line? If so, they'd left a large rear guard: He could see heads bobbing behind the defensive berm. And rifles. Yet, his soldiers were already climbing over the stakes, tugging at them and hammering them down, unmolested by Johnnies ten yards away. The obstacle was no obstacle at all.

Rifles cracked and a few men tumbled. But the firing summed to nothing, when it should have caused sheer butchery.

More Johnnies crowded the line, rushing up, leveling their rifles to no effect.

Barlow began to laugh.

"Their powder," he said to the staff men at his side. "Their powder's wet. The sorry bastards. They're all misfiring, the lot of them."

His soldiers went over the dirt wall in a blue mass, bayonets thrusting and rifle butts swinging. The report of shots and points of light in the haze announced that his men had kept their powder dry.

The slope was a disordered mass of frenzied men in blue. Shouting. All of them anxious to get in on the kill.

To the right, he could see Birney's men again. Swarming forward as well. Racing his men into the salient.

"I'll be damned," Barlow said.

Four fifty-five a.m.

Damn them all," Alleghany Johnson bellowed. "Shoot, goddamn it, fire!" He waved his cane as he walked behind the trenches, uninterested in safety, concerned only with stopping the waves of blue from swamping his line.

How had it happened? He'd sent out circulars, warning his brigades to be prepared.

Now this.

There were no Rebel yells now, only curses.

"Well, shoot 'em, goddamn it!" he ordered a line of his men working their rifles.

"Powder's wet. Won't fire."

"Try new caps, damn it."

"Done tried."

Only seconds left to save the position. He could even make out the badges on the attackers' caps: Hancock's boys. Win, his old friend. His mortal enemy.

"Fix bayonets!" he shouted, waving his cane at the swelling blue tide, as if he meant to thrash it back across the Rappahannock.

But his men had rushed up to the line, and many had not bothered to grab their bayonets.

Screaming in a fury that chilled even Johnson, the Yankees flowed over the wall of dirt, leaping down into the trench bayonets first. Some of the blue-bellies impaled themselves on Confederate rifle barrels, no need of bayonets, while others landed atop one another. But his men were under them all, literally crushed by the attack's weight.

His men swung their rifles at heads or pounded the butts into blue-clad chests and bellies, desperate as men attacked by rabid animals. Some Yankees paused at the lip of the trench to fire down into it. A boy in a ragged calico shirt leapt up on the wall, waving the flag of a Virginia regiment. The Yankees skewered him. And took the flag.

The Yankees were all around them now, and some of his men were running. A Yankee came at Johnson, bayonet lowered, demanding that he surrender.

Johnson swept his cane across the man's face, then seized his rifle and shot the Yankee dead, muzzle to gut. The man's blouse caught fire where the round went in.

Cane in one hand, rifle in the other, the general fell back. The survivors of his staff had rallied to him now.

Mortified, he saw dozens of his men raise their hands in surrender.

His staff fought through the melee as far as they could, with the general shouting commands and sending runners off with desperate orders, men unlikely to reach their destinations.

A pocket of fog saved him for a time. He saw twinkles of light on every side, and bullets scorched by like wasps from a bothered nest. Phantasms dashed through clouds of mist and gunsmoke.

He turned to his adjutant.

"Bob, you get on back to Ewell. Any way you can, boy. Tell him we need every man this damned army can spare, hear?"

"Yes, sir."

They parted in the muck of a patch used as a field latrine. Eyes connecting a last time, unwilling for that last second to go their separate ways, the grip of the moment broken only when Johnson tapped the major—a mite hard—with his cane.

"Git!"

Johnson hoped Hunter would live to a ripe old age. But, right now, he wasn't sure his division would survive. Or the rest of the army.

Blundering out of the curtain of mist, he found himself in the midst of a blue horde. In their thousands, the Yankees were rushing deep into the salient, the only Confederates in evidence a swarm of disarmed men being herded rearward. The firing had all but stopped as resistance collapsed.

"Oh, Hell," the general said.

Alleghany Johnson raised his cane, ready to lead the remnants of his staff in a final charge, but dozens of Yankees deigned to pause and lower their muzzles and bayonets in the direction of his little band. And they took special note of Johnson.

When he turned, he found Yankees crowding behind him, too.

Nervous as a fifteen-year-old bride, a pimple-plagued lieutenant stepped from the blue ranks. He attempted a strut, but only made a goose of himself.

A goose with a hundred bayonets to back him.

"Sir," the lieutenant cried in a too-loud, cracking voice, "I am prepared to accept your surrender."

The boy was so earnest, Johnson almost laughed. Not that there was a great deal else to laugh about.

Instead of laughter, tears betrayed him. Mutinous, uncontrollable, shameful tears.

He lowered his cane.

"Oh, Hell," he said.

Four fifty-five a.m.

Stop firing that gun, or we'll kill every goddamned one of you," the Yankee sergeant yelled.

Their own infantry had disappeared. Federals were all around them. And streaming past in multitudes.

"Stand down!" Captain Carter shouted. "Get away from the gun!"

The Yankees closed tighter around them, rifles still leveled to fire. Rare was the blue-belly who didn't wear a murderer's look.

Carter had gotten his number one piece into action. Just long enough to fire a single round and reload. His other guns were short of their emplacements or mired on the trail. It was the worst day of his life, and he feared it would be his last.

As swiftly as he could, Carter scanned the Yankees for an officer. Settling for the sergeant with blue stripes, he said, "Don't shoot my men. We surrender. We all surrender."

"Goddamned right you do," the sergeant said. He detailed a few soldiers to push his prisoners toward the Yankee lines. First, though, the sergeant helped himself to Carter's artillery sword and pistol belt, tossing them to a private with the admonition, "You see that these don't go astray, or I'll beat you like a whore in the street, Mehaffey."

Driven over the wall, away from their lost guns, Carter and his men met a spectacle even more humiliating. Between drifts of white mist and gray smoke, many hundreds, perhaps thousands, of disarmed Confederates swarmed northward, cursed to damnation and prodded to run by their captors. So many had been taken prisoner that they disrupted the advancing Union formations.

"I'm just glad Jackson ain't here to see this day," a sergeant said.

Five a.m.

Barlow had done his duty by Hancock, sending off a scrawled dispatch so the corps commander could do his duty in turn and send a telegraphic message to the army's headquarters.

What stunned Barlow most was the swiftness of the action. He had not been able to keep up with his own men and still direct the following brigades to their proper places. The corps had made a brilliant, unexpectedly brilliant, start. But it was only a start, and he worried about preserving cohesion sufficiently well to keep his men driving forward. With the artillery threat behind them, the risk now was a collapse of unit discipline amid the chaos.

He rode through a gap in the abatis and leapt from his horse onto a berm, tossing the reins to an orderly. When he looked down into the trench, he found a snake den of tangled bodies, most of them gashed bloody, many gut-ripped, and almost all in gray or some rough approximation of a uniform. Trapped under corpses, wounded men struggled to free themselves. The stronger cried for help.

A long, filthy hand clutched the air, searching for a grip.

His staff surrounded Barlow, pistols ready. The ditch was too wide to leap, and he thought it tasteless to scramble over the casualties. He walked the berm until he found a traverse wall, then made his way into the smoke and confusion. He found himself in a queer, twilit world, with the noise of the heaviest fighting hundreds of yards on ahead, but little quarrels of fists or clubbed muskets still erupting in the assault's rear.

As word spread that he had come forward, soldiers and officers brought him flags, over a dozen in the first few minutes, ready to lay them at his feet, as though he were Caesar himself. He ordered them sent to the rear.

Some of his soldiers had paused to loot the meager Reb possessions, a practice Barlow despised. But he hadn't time for it now.

His party was nearly trampled by another mass of Confederate prisoners, shock-faced, bitter-eyed, bleeding, gap-toothed men, in wet rags, skeletal, but bearded like the Patriarchs, some weeping, some defiant, their wild pride humbled, even as they sought to hold their heads high. The better of them stared at him as though, left to their own devices, they would tear away his flesh with their bare hands.

He jostled his way through men already separated from their units and pushed through briars and military wreckage, discovering corpses in unexpected places, their bodies contorted, some comically. Wounded men from both sides sat dumbfounded, or staggered, or crawled. One Reb pulled himself along, leaving a trail of intestines behind his bare feet.

As he came up behind the crowded regiments alternately pressing and chasing the Johnnies toward the heart of Lee's army, Barlow collared every officer he spotted and ordered them to get their men under control and keep them under control, to maintain their organizations and drive on. But he sensed that his inflamed men were growing uncontrollable, that their bloodlust trumped discipline now. He felt it in himself. Men of every rank had the taste of raw flesh in their mouths: This was revenge for the terrible week behind them, and for every humiliation and loss suffered over the past three years. His men would fight on with fury, but responding to orders was another matter.

The fog grew thicker again, while the rain spit on and off. He couldn't see far enough ahead to give detailed commands, but his division had an intelligence of its own, grinding into the Rebels. His men stormed past a second line of entrenchments, a supporting line that had done the

Johnnies no good. More prisoners moped rearward. Just ahead, the noise of the fighting grew uncanny, a summation of rage and terror expressed in voices, with remarkably few shots.

Today, men preferred the bayonet.

He found John Brooke. The brigade commander's face was streaked with powder, and the eyes of this coolest of officers blazed wildly.

"We're driving them . . . damned well crushing them." The hate released in each word startled even Barlow.

"John, you've got to get your men into some order. Lee's bound to counterattack. Control your men, for Christ's sake."

Brooke shook his head. Eyes utterly mad. As if even his commander might be an enemy. "All tangled up. My men, Birney's. Damned mess. But we're cutting the bastards to ribbons."

"Brooke, you *must* control your men."

The tone seemed to penetrate. At least partway.

"I'm doing my best, sir. But the men . . . I've never seen anything like it. It's all I can do to stop them from killing prisoners."

"Listen to me! Push on. Yes. Drive on. But think, man! Be ready for a counterblow. Lee isn't going to simply fold up and run."

"Counterblow," Brooke said.

He snapped to, suddenly alert, aware. "Yes, sir. Certainly. But I can't work miracles. Brown's new to command, he's got regiments coming in all over the place, crowding my men. It's not an army up ahead, it's a bloody mob."

"It's your job," Barlow told him, "to make it an army again."

Barlow turned away. Just in time to see a not quite familiar regimental flag cutting through the mist.

Gibbon's men. Committed far too soon. They were only going to worsen the confusion.

There were still more prisoners, though. The advancing, still unbloodied Federals jeered at them.

As he strode through the wreckage, human and matériel, Barlow saw, hardly ten yards off, a kneeling Johnny begging for his life, surrounded by taunting men in blue. The man bent to kiss their boots and they clubbed him to death. Laughing.

He would have had those men court-martialed, lashed, and imprisoned. Any other day but this.

There was no time.

He scrawled another brief note to Hancock and sent it back with a runner. It was difficult to see much of anything, even to keep a proper sense of direction. In the wake of an advancing blue line, he found himself amid a donnybrook of clubbed muskets and angry Rebel resistance. Jim Beaver's Pennsylvania boys were beating the daylights out of a brave and hopeless bunch of Johnnies.

Beaver tapped him from behind, almost getting a taste of saber.

"Sir, it's a splendid day! I do like going forward better than playing rear guard."

"You have your men under control?"

Beaver gestured toward the fray. "It's a struggle. But yes, I think."

"Be certain." There was more firing now and the smoke had grown choking thick. "Lee's going to counterattack us, as sure as fish drink tea in Boston Harbor. And I don't want to be rolled up and shoved back to where we started."

"Sir, we captured General Steuart." Beaver grinned. "*George* Steuart. When he introduced himself to surrender, all snoot in the air, I thought he meant Jeb Stuart. I was ready to piss my pants and dance a jig."

Barlow couldn't help smiling at the image. Pissed pants,

maybe. But he really couldn't envision the sober Beaver dancing a jig.

"I sent him back to General Hancock, I believe they knew each other."

"Everybody knew Win Hancock," Barlow said. "He was probably on a first-name basis with Jesus and the Disciples."

That went a bit too far for the straitlaced Beaver. His expression made a prune seem like a fresh-faced girl in May.

"Get back to your men, Beaver. And remember what I said. Those buggers will be coming, as quick as they can."

Five fifteen a.m.
Grant's headquarters

Grant sat outside the headquarters tent, wrapped in a greatcoat against the rain's rear guard. Couldn't hear much. No artillery, that was the likely reason. Sound of guns carried, rifles not so much. Wind wrong, anyway.

He took an easy breakfast, a cucumber split and splashed with a pucker of vinegar. Around him, men drank coffee in the smoke of a poor fire, unwilling to take shelter while the general in chief remained outside. Everyone was impatient for news, skittish. John Rawlins looked starved in body and soul, and his cough was back. Grant had a mind to tell his chief of staff to go on in the tent, but didn't want to shame him. Anyway, the rain had soaked the canvas to a sagging weight, and there was probably as much risk within as without.

A courier ran up, waving a piece of paper.

"From General Hancock!" he shouted.

Telegraphic message. Rawlins intercepted it. After scanning it quickly, he announced, "Hancock's men have the works! Hundreds of prisoners . . ." Rawlins stared at the

paper, making out another scrawl. "He's in their *second*
line of works."

The staff men cheered, slapped each other's backs, and
spilled a good bit of coffee.

When Rawlins looked over to him, Grant just nodded.
And took a bite of cucumber. He didn't know where Bill
got his special vinegar, but it bit all the way down to a man's
knees. Kept his drain open, too.

Another courier arrived.

"Over two thousand prisoners!" Rawlins shouted. He
looked around the assembly, so excited he appeared downright astonished. "He's captured two generals."

"Who?" Grant asked.

"E. Johnson and G. Steuart, it says."

Grant nodded. Cucumber was all up. He flicked his hand
dry.

The dispatches came in an avalanche after that: The
Confederates were broken. Barlow and Birney continued
to advance. Hancock was sending in Gibbon and Mott to
maintain the attack's momentum.

There was even a message from Cy Comstock, who had
been sent over to put some backbone into Burnside. The
Ninth Corps, too, was attacking. And almost on time.

A fresh message estimated three thousand prisoners.
Dozens of flags had been captured. At least sixteen guns.

Hancock was a quarter mile past Lee's second line of
works.

"By God, they're done, they're whipped!" Rawlins hollered. "Hancock'll drive them to Hell." His face looked almost mad, his eyes fevered.

Grant let his friend and all the rest take their pleasure
in the goings-on. Smoke from the damp firewood was a
bother to him. And the rain was picking up again.

Rawlins strutted up and stood before him.

"Well, General! Isn't this just grand? *Over* three thousand prisoners. Lee's done for."

"Kind of news I like to hear," Grant said, willing to please his friend. "Hancock's doing well." Damned smoke burned his eyes right through. He added, "Ain't finished, though."

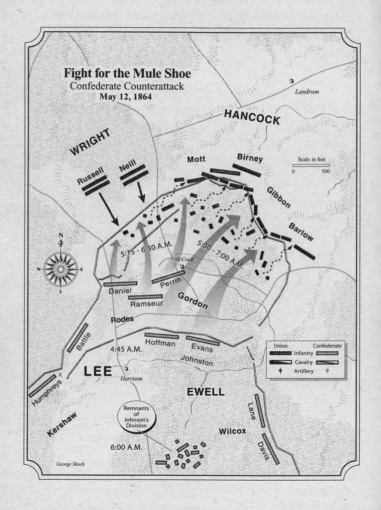

Fight for the Mule Shoe
Confederate Counterattack
May 12, 1864

NINETEEN

*May 12, four forty-five a.m.
Gordon's headquarters, base of the salient,
Spotsylvania*

Gordon was up and dressed, but still waiting for a cup of the glorious coffee looted in the Wilderness. In all the chronicles of war, not the Sabine women, not Helen herself, had been so cherished a capture as the sacks of beans the Yankees had forsaken. The prisoners he had gathered in meant laurels for the ages, but the value of the coffee beans was immediate.

Light rain spit through the trees.

He turned to Bob Johnston, commander of his North Carolina Brigade, four days back a peer, now his subordinate. The brigadier had left his reserve position in search of news, but Gordon had none to offer. Everyone waited for what the Yankees would do or what Lee would decide to do himself.

"I do believe," Gordon said, "that the side that figures out how to boil up coffee quicker is bound to be the side that wins this war."

"I don't know," Johnston said, "if I'd be inclined to stake the war on it. Yankees tend to figure out things like that. Probably come up with some infernal contraption."

"'Rude mechanicals,'" Gordon said. He smelled the morning coffee now, rich as sin in the silken harem of Darius. "Men up?"

Johnston nodded. "Not that they like it much. Can't really sleep in this, but they don't mind trying."

"Hear that?" Gordon said suddenly.

"Hear what?"

"Thought I heard something." He wiped the morning crust from his eyes. "Wouldn't object to a longer visit from Morpheus myself."

"Heard from Fanny?" Bob Johnston asked.

"Not for days. Yankee cavalry between here and Richmond."

"Hell with 'em. Stuart'll give 'em a licking they won't forget."

"Any news from your folks?"

"Crops are poor, people are poorer," the young brigadier said. "If I was back lawyering, doubt I'd have a client come by a week. Folks too poor to have their wills done proper."

Gordon laid a hand on his comrade's shoulder. The gesture was meant to be kind and reassuring, but it was too early in the day for rich feelings.

"Be different after the war. Everything's going to be different," Gordon said.

"That's what worries me."

Gordon cocked his head. "Tom Jones! Where's that glorious nectar of Olympus, son?"

"Sir, you know you don't like it cooked up weak."

"I do not desire Stygian mud, either, son. Why don't—"

One of Johnston's lieutenants rode up, reckless in the fog.

"General Johnston! General Gordon!"

"Here now, boy. What's the to-do?"

The rider dismounted, flustered, without a hat. "General, I think there's something wrong. Down in the woods. Where Alleghany Johnson's men are."

"And what, exactly, do you believe is wrong?" Bob Johnston asked. He had summoned his no-nonsense courtroom voice.

"Hard to tell, sir. Can't say exactly. But something's gone all queer."

"'A dagger of the mind . . . ,'" Gordon said.

Bob Johnston's voice shifted to annoyance. "Damn it, Bartlett, an army runs on facts, not fantasies. If anything that mattered was going on, we'd surely hear something."

"Sir, there was firing, bunch of it. Then it calmed down and—"

"No doubt, our usual morning skirmishing." Then the brigadier softened. "It's all right, Bartlett. We're all tired."

Gordon tensed. "Bob, I *do* hear something."

Another rider appeared, trailed by a private who came up at a run—a man well-known to be fleet of foot and a popular courier from Gordon's old brigade.

The rider saluted without dismounting and called, "Sir, the lines have been breached. All over the Mule Shoe, the salient."

His breath a gale, the soldier on foot added, "Yankees are everywhere."

Gordon's cup of coffee went forgotten. He shouted for his horse and for his officers. "Bob, ride with me. We need to get in the fight."

"Shouldn't we see what General Ewell—"

"No time. Wasted too much time already."

Johnston commandeered the lieutenant's horse. Gordon's aide led up the division commander's wet black mount and his own dapple gray.

Leaping into the saddle, Gordon patted the animal and whispered, "Don't you misstep now. You must be as Bucephalus."

Bob Johnston overheard. "Lord almighty, John! You think your horse speaks Latin?"

"Greek," Gordon told him. He kicked with his spurs.

They rode with rain biting their faces. It wasn't far to Johnston's Brigade. His regimental colonels had already formed up the men: The sound of fighting was clear now, and all too close. Gordon sent a rider to tell Clem Evans and John Hoffman to organize their brigades for battle by the Harrison house, but suspected that at least some of their troops were already heavily engaged. The afternoon before, they'd been positioned as reserves for the corps and the salient.

"Let's go, Bob," Gordon said. "Get them moving."

Johnston ordered his nearest regiment, the 5th North Carolina, to lead the column into the depths of the Mule Shoe. The morning remained dark, and fog wreathed the trees. A man could not see twenty yards ahead. Gordon tried to judge the shape of the battle by the noise, but the weather played tricks with sound as well as sight. All he could do was to press on and seek the enemy.

Only a few lengths back from the head of the column, he and Johnston rode beside the soldiers. The first smoke of battle reinforced the fog.

"Sounds like they're more to the right," Johnston said.

As he spoke, rifle fire erupted just to the column's front. Men fell. Others halted to fire into the mist. The men to the rear bunched up, in need of orders.

The Yankees called out, impolitely, for them to surrender.

Johnston said: "I'll show those damned—"

Droplets of the brigadier's blood sprayed Gordon's cheek and eye. He caught Johnston, who struggled to right himself after nearly falling from his horse. There was just light enough to see he'd been shot in the head.

"Get him to the rear!" Gordon shouted. He held Johnston's reins until an aide rushed up. Then he called to the commander of the leading regiment, "Colonel Garrett! Take command, you have the brigade."

The firing had grown wild, mad. Garrett rode up and saluted Gordon, only to recoil from a bullet's impact.

The colonel jerked at a second wound and tumbled to the ground.

Who was the brigade's senior officer now? Toon? He'd been sick as a dog for days, but Gordon had glimpsed him minutes before, gamely leading his 20th North Carolina. After ordering the 5th to deploy on line—an action the veterans had begun to take on their own—he rode back and found Toon rushing forward for orders.

"Tom, can you command this brigade? You well enough?"

"Well enough to kill some goddamned Yankees."

In the bad light, Toon looked as pale as a widow's cadaver.

"All right. You listen here. We're going to pull the brigade back a hundred yards. Yankees can't see any better than we can, they'll spend a few minutes feeling their way forward, now they've been stung. And we're going to form a skirmish line back there. Right across the salient. As far as we can reach. Don't look at me like I'm crazy, just listen now. Only chance is to bluff them. So you're going to form this brigade into a skirmish line and then you're going to charge straight forward with a howl to rattle the devil. You understand me?"

"Yes, sir, but—"

"Tom, I know. We're going to lose this brigade. But we're going to save the army. You buy me a quarter hour, and you damned well might save the Confederacy."

Toon saluted. And turned his horse to the challenge.

Between them, they got the brigade spread out on line, specters in the fog. Gordon figured that each of the soldiers faced dozens of Yankees. But he'd already sensed that the Yankees were more than a touch confused, stumbling about, overconfident, unsuspecting.

And he knew, for damned sure, that what he was doing defied every Army manual and even common sense. If he failed, the West Point officers would laugh over his grave. But he did not see what else could be done, and his belly told him to go ahead and do it.

Wasn't much of a line, and he could hardly imagine what the spread-out soldiers felt. But when he nodded to Toon and the colonel gave the order, they went to their fates with a Rebel yell that would have put to shame a legion of demons.

Gordon turned his own horse to rally his other brigades, still trying to figure out just where the Yankees were, how deeply they'd penetrated elsewhere in the salient. As he rode rearward, a bullet ripped through his coat, to Tom Jones' alarm, but Gordon made light of it: This was a day that could not accommodate fear.

Nearing the Harrison house and reading the world by the first hint of real light, he encountered General Ewell, who waved to him with a lunatic's enthusiasm.

The corps commander spouted gibberish in his high-pitched voice, confusing all around him. He appeared to have outrun, or just lost, his staff, and he asked Gordon for an officer. Gordon left him an aide and moved on. Before Ewell could give him an order he didn't want.

If today would be his last day on earth, he wasn't going to be the plaything of the gods in the form of Dick Ewell.

"Clem!" he called to Colonel Evans, who had taken his old brigade. Evans steered his horse closer. "How many regiments have you got?"

"Only three. The others are already in, supporting Daniel."

"Then three will have to do. Three hundred Spartans blocked the might of Persia." Gordon did not add: "And they died for it."

John Hoffman left his forming men and joined them.

"Had to pull back from the fight to get 'em organized. But they're ready. Rounded up a few of Alleghany Johnson's boys and folded them in, too. Just a handful, but they're riled."

Both of the brigade commanders snapped their attention away from Gordon.

He whipped about, expecting to see Yankees. But it was Lee, with a few members of his staff and young Bob Hunter, Alleghany Johnson's aide. It was light enough for Lee to see the formed-up regiments, and for the men waiting silently to see him.

The air sparked like an electrical experiment.

Lee stopped Traveller and, facing the soldiers, took off his hat and held it over his heart. Stray shots nicked the air, but the old man was imperturbable.

They won't have to cast a statue of him, Gordon thought. He's already a statue.

Gordon ordered his brigade commanders back to their men. Every officer who had a horse was to remain mounted today. The men must be properly led, visibly led, no matter the cost.

But as Gordon cantered to the center of his line, where Lee waited in silence, the army commander pulled Traveller around to face the Yankees.

In that moment, Gordon seemed to see down to the man's depths. And what he saw was human, desperate, and dreadful.

He galloped up to Lee, reined in, and seized Traveller's bridle.

"General Gordon," Lee said. As if waking from a trance.

Gordon needed to turn the situation to his advantage. He raised his voice to its grandest oratorical level and announced, "General Lee! You shall not lead my men in a charge!" He swept his hand wide. "Another is here for that purpose!" He dared to look away from Lee, sweeping his eyes over the breathless ranks. "These men behind you are Georgians and Virginians. They have never failed you on any field. And they will not fail you today!" Gordon levered his ramrod spine a few inches from the saddle. "Will you, boys?"

The response was a sprinkle of cries that became a roar: *"No! We won't fail you . . . we won't fail him . . . danged if we will . . . no, no . . ."*

Gordon sensed he needed to drive the challenge home. Before Lee lost them everything by throwing away his life. He had heard the rumors of Lee's near suicidal behavior in the Wilderness and sensed the old man's desperation now.

He'd rather die than lose, Gordon understood.

As the soldiers' cries faded and the sound of battle swelled, Gordon called up the deep reserves of his voice and lungs, speaking to Lee, but really to his soldiers:

"You *must* go to the rear, sir!"

At that, the soldiers broke ranks, rushing to surround Lee, shouting, "Lee to the rear! Lee to the rear!" They pressed against him, grasping his bridle, pushing against the horse's flanks the way a fool boy might press the rump of a mule, ready, if need be, to lift horse and rider and bear them to the rear.

Lee's eyes clouded. When they met Gordon's calculated gaze, the old man looked away, raising his face to the sky, determined that only the Lord would see him so moved.

A sergeant tugged the horse around and Lee did not resist.

"To your posts!" Gordon shouted. He could tell with certainty that the Yankees were almost upon them. Cantering along the line, he ordered, "No yelling, boys. Not until we hit them. We're going to give those blue-bellies a taste of Georgia and Virginia for their breakfast!"

The instant he saw that the ranks were ready, Gordon

spurred his horse to Clem Evans' color party and seized the red battle flag in his right hand.

His horse pranced as he held the banner high.

"Virginia! Georgia! Forward!"

Six a.m.

As Barlow struggled to reorganize his division, a fresh Union brigade drove into the rear of his men, confusing things further and throwing away the value of the new troops. He went after them in a white rage and found Lewis Grant pushing his Vermonters forward.

"Grant, what the devil is this? What are you doing?"

"Doing as ordered," the bearded brigadier said. His voice was annoyingly calm.

"For God's sake, *whose* orders? What's a Sixth Corps brigade doing over here?"

"General Hancock's orders. General Wright sent us over to reinforce you."

"Does it look like I need reinforcement? There must be twenty thousand men squeezed into this . . . this hellhole."

The Vermonter refused to be riled. "Followed my orders. To the letter. Didn't expect such a mess."

Barlow wanted to give him the flat of his saber. Instead, he snapped, "Well, make yourself useful, if you can. I'll take this up with Hancock."

The attack needed reinforcements, all right, but on the flanks, to firm up and expand the shrinking breakthrough. After the first shock, the Rebs had recovered with spirit, launching one screaming attack after another. And they paid for it, the carnage was unspeakable. But his men were little more than a confused mob, if still a bloodthirsty one. In the grimmest close-quarters combat Barlow had witnessed, his soldiers, intermingled with Birney's and

Gibbon's—and now the Vermont Brigade—fought with rifles, bayonets, swords, pistols, fists, and fallen limbs as they and the Johnnies literally pulped each other. Lacking cohesion, his men had been forced to give ground in fits and starts. Now some portions of his line—of the brawl that passed for a line—had been driven back to the main Rebel entrenchments.

Careless of the combat raging around him, he strode back to the spot where he'd left his aide to receive messages. Yanking him along, he told the captain, "I'm going back to try to talk sense to Hancock. We're throwing it all away."

"Sir, General Hancock's very pleased, I told you—"

"I know what you told me. 'Compliments, splendid work.' Hancock hasn't a clue what it's like in here."

"Sir . . ."

Barlow smiled. Bitterly. "I know, John. I'm to be recommended for major general. And Brooke and Miles will have their stars." With bullets flirting around them, he looked into the aide's laughably earnest face. "And you don't want me to ruin it for myself. But Hancock shouldn't be passing out cakes till we're done with the meat."

He found the orderly minding his horse tucked into a swale beyond the salient. The animal bled slightly from its hindquarters, grazed by a bullet.

"Sir," the orderly began, "there was nothing I could—"

"I'm not a fool, man. I can see what happened."

He swung up into the saddle, landing hard. Only when seated did it strike him how utterly drained he was. And he had far less reason for it, he knew, than the men in the scrambled fighting, clubbing each other's brains out.

He galloped across the field, through human wreckage, hundreds of wounded men stumbling along between the last trickles of captives in gray rags. That phenomenon, too, had turned around: Brown, the brigade commander he had put in Paul Frank's stead the day before, had been reported captured along with dozens of his men.

Shortest term of command on the books, Barlow thought wryly. There was no pity or compassion in him now. He just didn't want another potential victory squandered by flaccid generalship. Nothing else mattered. And Hancock, of all people, had let him down.

Galloping over the intervening ridge, he spurred his horse with a cruelty he had long reserved for men. For men who failed him.

At last, he saw the meadow where they had formed in the light of day. Batteries waited in perfect order and staff men walked their horses, as if in search of a stirrup cup before setting off on a hunt.

He spotted Hancock, standing on the porch of the wretched shanty, chatting with his chief of staff.

Barlow spurred the horse again, only to rein in next to the porch, close enough to splash mud.

"Hancock!" he cried. "For God's sake, don't send any more troops in here! You're only making things worse, it's goddamned chaos."

The corps commander paled.

Morgan, who had stiffened, said, "It's *General* Hancock."

Barlow looked, fiercely, at his superior. And saw anger, but also unsettling weakness, in the corps commander's face. Hancock's exhaustion was evident, worsened by the elation that had soared too high and now had to crash down. The older man unthinkingly rubbed his thigh, the Gettysburg wound.

"My apologies, *General* Hancock. I can only plead urgency."

Hancock nodded.

"I sent you Lewis Grant." He said it in the tone of a truant boy making an excuse.

"He just plowed into the rear of my division. It's an utter mess."

The corps commander nodded a second time.

"Sir, we needed—need—help on the left, we need to shore it up. Burnside hasn't tied in with us, his men have disappeared, there's a gap on my flank. It's an invitation to Lee to give us a hammering."

"I've asked Meade . . . Grant . . . about Burnside . . ." Hancock rubbed his thigh forcefully, something he never did in front of others, if aware of it. Barlow had seen him do it only once before.

"Can you hold, though?" Morgan asked.

"I *intend* to hold. Every inch I can. But we've already been driven back hundreds of yards."

"Just don't let them retake the main entrenchments," the chief of staff said.

"They'd have to kill me," Barlow said. And he spurred back to his division.

Six a.m.
The Mule Shoe

It was light enough to see more of the fighting between the clots of smoke, and what Gordon saw left him desperate. His men had shoved a body of Federals back to the edge of the salient, where the to-and-fro was merciless. He had long since emptied his revolver, but found no time to reload it. He had to rush from one dissolving regiment to another, appointing replacements on the spot for fallen officers and holding broken companies together by force of will. A man could have leapt from body to body to make his way, and the wounds Gordon saw were ghastly, inflicted by blades and blunt objects. Even the badly injured, heretofore allies in suffering, crawled to kill one another. One dead Yankee's face looked chewed away.

His men had performed a miracle, but not an eternal one. His bleeding line was all that stood between the Federals and a renewed breakthrough to the army's heart. He had sent every runner he could spare to beg reinforcements, but had not had a response. And the fighting was so confused, so ruptured, that he could not be sure a single courier had made it to the rear.

Now that there was light enough to spot targets, the Yankee artillery had opened, pounding the salient's flanks. Hoffman's men had broken right through the entrenchments and spilled out into the field, only to be driven back by all too accurate shelling. They could advance no additional step, while the Yankees held on a bayonet thrust away.

On foot now, Clem Evans found him. The Georgia Brigade had made Gordon proud, but he knew it was in tatters.

"General Gordon . . . men . . . in a bad way . . ." Clem was out of breath and choking on smoke. "Sixty-first . . . lost the flag . . . men captured . . ."

"Fortunes of war," Gordon said with pretended confidence. "The remainder of the regiment will hold that line. Even if only a single man remains." He raised his chin, his sweat-clotted beard. "Horatius on the bridge, Clem. A single man saved Rome."

"Sir . . . the brigade's coming apart."

"Nonsense," Gordon assured him. "You're holding them. The Yankees are already beaten, they just haven't realized it."

Lies. War was the realm of lies.

The colonel looked exasperated, unable to understand why Gordon could not see what was all too evident: They'd done their best, but now could do no more.

Gordon grasped the other man's upper arm. "You've done splendidly, Clem. Now it's time to do a little more."

"The Sixty-first . . ."

"They'll hold," Gordon said.

"They're *gone,* sir."

"They'll hold," Gordon told him. His tone warned there could be no contradiction. "You hold that line, Clem. This is the hour of glory. See to your men."

Lies . . .

In an interval between Yankee bombardments, Gordon listened to the combat raging around him. It was unlike any battle noise he had ever heard: This wasn't the sound of modern armies shooting each other down. It was the sound of medieval warriors hacking each other to death.

It pained him to think of the fate of the 61st Georgia's men and the shame of the loss of the flag. But he would give every man under his command, every flag and his own life, to hold this muddy prize.

It wasn't anybody's hour of glory. That, too, had been a lie. It was the hour of men reduced to beasts.

The Yankee cannon thundered again, evenly sequenced, by section and battery, and explosions gnawed the earth to Gordon's right. Those gunners had the luxury of good order, of time, of bottomless reserves of ammunition. They lived in an utterly different world a mere thousand yards away. The Federals had superb artillery, a great deal of it. They had a great deal of everything. And he had these men, outnumbered and running out of their soggy cartridges, men who were fighting because nothing else was left to them.

He called through the mist to his aide, hoping the boy remained whole. He wanted to ask him to reload his pistol. Gordon still didn't feel he dared turn from the fight for the time required to fill the chambers. But he did not intend to meet his foe unarmed, in abject surrender.

It was time to see to Hoffman's Brigade again. If Hoffman was still there. The fighting snarled with fresh musketry, hard on his flank.

Horatius at the bridge, Leonidas at the pass . . . what would they say of his division's stand?

Was Lee withdrawing the army? Leaving him and his men as a rear guard? Had he been forgotten?

Well, he would fight. And Fanny could mourn him.

Jones appeared, miraculously unscathed, though dirtied with smoke and powder. Gordon held out his pistol, not Ulysses, after all, but Hector.

A bleeding courier found him.

"General Gordon, sir! General Ewell says that, if you can hold for fifteen more minutes, you'll have all the help you need. . . ."

Eight a.m.
The Harrison house

Lee had looked into the abyss and found only despair. Now there was hope again, if only a sliver of it. And Gordon had delivered it. For all the ineffable bravery Lee had encountered that morning, he owed a debt to Gordon no promotion could repay. According to camp talk, Gordon had saved Ewell's corps that first day in the Wilderness. Today, he had saved them all.

If saved they were.

Lee had needed to sit down, out of the rain, for a time. To gather himself. He had not behaved at all to his own liking. Unbalanced by events, he had forsaken control of himself and of the army. If not for Gordon . . .

In the damp, drear room, members of his staff went about things carefully, deflecting trivial queries from Lee's ears and deciding lesser issues among themselves. They knew him. And he knew that he had frightened them again. With his foolish bravado that morning.

Gordon had put his folly to good use, thanks be to God. But Lee had been as if possessed, for the third time in a week, almost relieved at the prospect of his own death. His selfishness astonished him, the alacrity with which he had been ready to cheapen duty to a gesture.

Outside, some hundreds of yards away, the fighting remained undecided, but unmistakably grim. He had taken every possible measure to hurry reinforcements into the cauldron, committing his army piecemeal because there was no choice. And Gordon had held just long enough for the others to arrive at the double-quick, rushing from every division left to the army. Many, too many, had fallen. But there was hope again, a candle in the dark hallways of nightmare.

Hope, but not of a victory. Merely of the army's survival this day. He worried that the age of resounding victories might be past, that only this grinding down of lives remained. As gutted regiments gripped those people at the salient's edges, he had put the men from broken units to work constructing a more defensible line across the base of the salient. But it would take many hours to finish the task. Meanwhile, the Federals had to be held off, no matter the cost.

He felt more alone than ever, bereft not only of friends but of reliable subordinates. For all Gordon's dash and brilliance, the man was a newly made division commander and could not be advanced without more experience. Of the corps commanders left him, Anderson struggled in place of the wounded Longstreet. Hill remained sick, with Early still untested in his place. And Ewell . . . that morning, the man had made a spectacle of himself, profane, foolish, and weak, railing at the men instead of leading them. Lee had been forced to admonish him publicly, something he was always loath to do. Richard Ewell had served the Confederacy handsomely, at great sacrifice, even that of a limb, but Lee feared he was unfit to remain in command. Perhaps Ewell needed no more than a respite, but things could not go on as they were now. Lee intended to find an excuse to move Ewell aside that would not shame the man.

If the army still existed at day's end.

His soldiers were holding, but holding was not enough. He needed to find an opening for a counterattack, if only a limited one, to relieve the pressure on the salient and muddle the purpose of the men opposing him. It would take some hours to reorganize the remainder of his lines and draw off a few brigades to build an attack force. But he *had* to stymie those people, to reassert his will and break their hopes.

Burnside? Was he the weak link? Could a few determined brigades cripple his corps? Or at least befuddle the man and leave him useless?

He needed time, it was all a question of time now. But how much remained to this army? To his cause? His life? It embarrassed him anew to recall his loss of self-possession. He had *wanted* to go forward, to make a swift end of things, to turn his back on the responsibilities that pursued him day and night like very devils.

He must never do that again. Such a death would have bought him cheap renown, but would have been unmanly and indecent. He had learned long ago that dying was not hard. The harder course was to defy the odds, to endure life's torments stoically. To seek death was a coward's act, no matter how others perceived it. And he did not mean to end his life as a coward.

Other men might have judged him brave, but the Lord would have known his heart.

He told himself he must grasp control again. To plan a counterblow. To claw his way back to equilibrium with those people. To survive this day and as many more as the Lord allowed.

It was all so difficult now. The put-upon flesh was unwilling, the heart enmeshed in fears that had no words.

Lee rose from his chair at his own command, stiff with the latest visitation of rheumatism. He stepped out onto the porch, which was fouled by tobacco spew and smelled of urine. The rain had shown its temper again and his soldiers shoveled mud, not soil, as they labored in the new trenches. To the north, in the mist, the clash of arms continued unabated.

He had lost an entire division, Johnson's, including the bulk of the Stonewall Brigade. His miscalculation as to Grant's intentions had cost the army dearly, and he pledged he would never underestimate the man's tenacity, his brute confidence, again. Had he only had the sense to leave those batteries in place, had he not succumbed to wishful thinking, imagining that Grant would retreat when he himself would not have considered quitting in Grant's position . . .

Grant appeared to be inured to slaughter, a quality Lee had regarded as his own unremarked strength. He had learned a lesson at the cost of many other men's lives, an obvious lesson to which his pride had blinded him: Grant cared little for casualties, if he believed he could win.

Lee saw that he had to wield his army more guardedly now.

If the army survived this terrible day. The number of killed, wounded, and captured generals and colonels was already so great he could not bear to name them. Short of complete disaster, he did not know how this day could become any worse.

Venable strode up through the mud. A neat man by nature, careful of his dress, he was slopped breast-high with filth. But it was his eyes that troubled Lee.

Bent under the rain, the aide straightened his posture as

he neared. He stopped short of the porch and its imperfect shelter, and saluted.

His eyes, his eyes . . .

"What is it, Colonel Venable?" At least, Lee thought, I am in command of my speech again.

"A courier, sir. From Richmond."

Venable's eyes.

Was it his wife? Defeat in the Valley? Bad news from Georgia?

"General Stuart . . . was wounded. Yesterday. In a cavalry action."

Not Stuart, too . . .

"How badly?" Lee asked. Demanding of his voice that it not tremble.

"It's believed," Venable said, forcing out the words, "that the wound is mortal."

Eight thirty a.m.
Headquarters, Army of the Potomac

Don't let up," Grant said. "Keep at them. Dog them."

He had walked down to Meade's headquarters in the rain, worried that Meade and his generals would talk themselves into calling off the attack, now that it seemed deadlocked. But the worry had been groundless. Meade's fire was up, and Humphreys came just short of jumping on a horse himself and charging into the fuss.

There were problems, though.

Humphreys spoke what Meade would not: "General Grant, Burnside has to pull his share. His divisions went in, all right. And came right back out. Hancock and Wright are battling it out, but Burnside . . ."

Over the past week, Grant had grown well aware of the Ninth Corps commander's wanting a certain fortitude. The morning's attack had driven the lesson home again, and he had already decided that the lines of command he had set up just didn't work. The Ninth Corps would have to be folded into the Army of the Potomac. If Burnside didn't like it, he could resign.

Wouldn't do to make such a change with fighting under way, though. And he could hear Washburne's voice in his head, cautioning him not to humiliate a man who, if not powerful on the battlefield, had powerful friends in Washington. No, placing Burnside under Meade required a calmer moment. And cooler tempers. Mustn't look like a punishment. Had to be presented as a practical matter.

"I'll see that Burnside goes in again," Grant said. "How about Warren? He in? I wanted him in. An hour ago."

"He'll go in," Meade said. "He's kicking a bit. Doesn't want to attack those same entrenchments again." Meade made a face so woefully serious, it tickled Grant. "And, frankly, Sam, I see his point. But he'll go in."

"His corps is shot," Humphreys said. "The men are demoralized. They've been going at that ridge for the last four days. Another off-the-cuff assault . . ."

Grant could not completely suppress his smile. He knew that Humphreys, a good, blunt man, wanted to say, "It's all because your damned attacks weren't half as planned as a carouse in a Mexican whorehouse."

Truth was that Meade and Humphreys had been partly right. The morning's attack could have used more planning. But that would have given Lee more time to get ready, too. Man just had to take his chances where he thought best. Sometimes the cards ran your way, sometimes they didn't. But you couldn't win if you kept backing up from the table.

And he had been right that an attack by a full corps would crack that salient. In his experience, no man had it all figured out. You just had to figure a tad better than your enemy.

As for the august Robert E. Lee, Grant reckoned he had not had his pleasantest morning of the war. His army had suffered a grievous hurt. Pride, too, most likely.

Turning to Meade, Grant said: "I'll move Burnside. But I want supporting attacks across the front, not just from the Ninth Corps. I expect Warren to attack within the hour, keep Lee from raising the bid against Hancock and Wright." He thought for a moment, then spoke to Humphreys: "You and Warren go back a time, ain't that right?"

"We're old friends," Humphreys said.

"With General Meade's permission, maybe you could go on down to the Fifth Corps? See that General Warren gets the gist of things?"

Humphreys appeared surprised, almost taken aback. But not unwilling. Man could smell blood, Grant knew the sort. He'd make it plain to Warren that he could either attack or lose his corps.

"Listen here," Grant said, speaking now to all the nearby officers. "Fine fighting this morning. Way this army's meant to fight. Nearly broke Lee. Still might." He patted his pockets for a cigar and found them empty. "Meantime, this army is not to give back another inch of ground up in that salient."

Ten a.m.
Laurel Hill

The rain had eased again, but the mire in the trench line rooted the men in place. Sometimes the suck of it threw off a man's aim, as he wiggled about to get a dead-on shot. And all the while the Yankees just plodded up through the

mud and the shattered trees, moving awkwardly, almost
as if clowning, as if they downright wanted to get themselves killed.

Oates was out of temper. His men were sick, the food
was bad, what there was of it, and they were all soaked
through. The Yankees could have just stayed in their lines
and stuffed themselves full of salt pork. But no, they had
to come on, blockheaded, goddamned fools, up that same
slope, past their own gone-green dead, corpses that, struck
by a bullet, flopped about as the gas burst from death-
fattened bellies. The Yankees just came on, butt-stupid
Fifth Corps boys, and his men shot them down easy as
hunting possums. Except that possums took their killing
one at a time, and the Yankees came on by the thousands.

He hated the mud, hated the stink, hated the shit water
staining his own drawers and the sudden bites in his belly,
like a sharp-toothed animal in there, and the dizziness that
only made him so angry he could almost kill the man next
to him for spitting.

Wasn't just far from Alabama. He was far from himself.
Far from what he once thought he knew of human beings.
Dirty-ass animals, every one of them, dirtier than dogs
bloated by worms, that was all they were. And the life in
which he had reveled, the animal joys that had been his
heart's delight, the cries of women and his own near howls
when they brought him out of himself, all of it was drown-
ing in this filth, in this disregard of everything a fool might
have called "good." In this great insult to a God who didn't
have the decency to exist, after all those lies he spawned,
in this bottomless human filth worse than any mud, worse
even than mud mixed with dripping shit from men too
weary, sick, or excited to leave the firing line or who didn't
even know anymore when they soiled themselves.

The Yankees came on, and his men just shot them down.
He wanted to reach down and scoop up the vile mud and

hurl it at them, to try to shock sense into them. It was an insult to all godless creation, an ingratitude so loathsome it made Oates feel like a madman in need of a locked cell and buckled restraints.

The cheapness with which those blue-bellies squandered their lives riled the deepest parts of him, hidden places that had no decent purpose, that were best left undisturbed from birth to death. He was done damning their generals. Now he damned the men who lacked the sense to just fall down and play dead or find a nice fat body to lie behind, the sense to save the only damned thing they really possessed, their lives.

His men fired as rapidly as they could. Many of the cartridges were damp or soaked right through and could not be used. Rifles jammed, requiring urgent labor. Even so, the toll of men in blue was downright frightful.

When they just would not stop their obscene, idiot attack up through the stumps where a grove had been, Oates leapt up on a sharpshooter's bench, raised himself to his full height above the parapet, head, torso, arms, and one balled fist exposed to whatever the Yankees could bring to bear, and he shouted in a voice so naked it shocked him at least as much as it startled his men:

"Learn your lesson, damn you! Learn your lesson!"

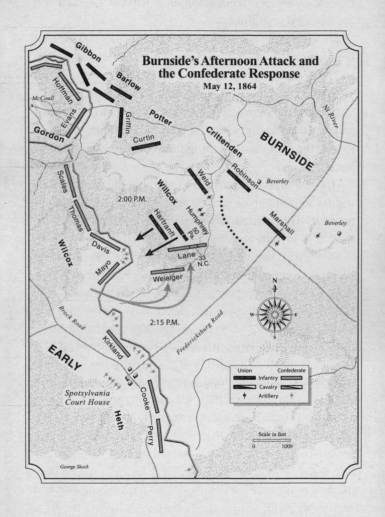

**Burnside's Afternoon Attack and
the Confederate Response**
May 12, 1864

Gibbon

Hofman

Barlow

McCoull

Evans

Gordon

Griffin

Potter

Curtin

Crittenden

BURNSIDE

Ni River

Scales

Willcox

Weld

Robinson

Beverley

2:00 P.M.

Thomas

Davis

Hartranft

Humphrey

50
Pa.

Marshall

Beverley

Willcox

Mayo

Lane

33
N.C.

Weisiger

2:15 P.M.

Brock Road

EARLY

Kirkland

Cooke

Fredericksburg Road

N

Spotsylvania
Court House

Heth

Perry

Union	Confederate
Infantry	
Cavalry	
Artillery	

Scale in feet

0   1000

George Skoch

TWENTY

May 12, two p.m.
On the eastern flank of the salient

Despite the rain, Brown had slept a few hours and dreamed. He had been escorting Frances to the Methodist church. Only they weren't in Schuylkill Haven. It was Knoxville and sharply cold. Concerned, he told her over and over that she needed a coat or a shawl. He had his greatcoat, but he couldn't give it to her, though he didn't know why. Then she was gone and he was shut in a room he could not leave, nauseated by piles of rotting apples riddled with huge worms. Later, he had a more private dream, an embarrassment and a pleasure.

Now he stood at the rear of Company C, waiting for the order to advance. The rain had retreated, but looked apt to come on again. Meantime, a breeze swept old wet from the trees speckling the slope. The sodden men in his charge waited in two lines, facing west, peering into the smoke on the next ridge. That was where the Johnnies waited, but to the company's front, their lines were hidden. The 50th Pennsylvania had drawn a position in the attack that would take them down across an open field and into woods that climbed to the waiting enemy. It was hard to say whether it was worse not seeing the Rebels than having them in plain sight.

Brown told himself it might not be too bad this time. The 50th and the rump of the Second Brigade had been assigned to the second helping of troops, following Colonel

Hartranft's men. And Colonel Christ was gone, at last, replaced that morning by Colonel Humphrey of the 2nd Michigan, a fellow who seemed all right. No, it might not be too bad, Brown thought. Hartranft's boys would get the worst of it, the first lines always did. With any luck, the 50th would get into the Reb ditches without many casualties. . . .

That was only a fantasy, Brown knew. But a man had to fool himself sometimes, if he meant to keep going. Rumors had been chasing each other all day, every one of them ugly. And the fighting up to the right was just plain queer. Battles, even rough ones, hit lulls of minor skirmishing while both sides squirmed around searching for an advantage. But this day produced steady noise. Up there, on that high ground, in that smoke, men were killing each other with a fury, and no one was quitting.

Lieutenant Brumm had command of the company now. He walked back to Brown and stood close to him.

"What do you think, Brownie?"

"Waste of breath to tell, sir. Just waiting."

Brumm thought about that and smiled. "You're probably thinking about the same thing I am."

Brown smiled, too, although he didn't mean to. "That we ought to get started and get this over with?"

"Something like that."

Smoke filled the low ground before them. Their fate waited beyond it.

Both men grew serious again. Wet and unhappy, and duty-bound to behave as if they were fearless. And no man, no sane man, was fearless.

"Going to be hard to keep our alignment, once we reach those trees," Brumm said. "I'll be counting on you, First Sergeant."

"Do what I can, sir."

"Oh, I know that."

What was there to talk about, really, when a man couldn't know if he was to live or die? Yet, men felt the need to talk. Maybe as a way of proving they were still among the living.

From the low ridge behind them, Union batteries opened. The shots screamed overhead. Brown could not see where they landed.

"Soon now," Brumm remarked. "Soon enough now. What do you make it, Brownie? Five hundred yards?"

"Maybe six," Brown said. "Hard to tell, with the trees and all that smoke." He wanted, badly, for things to have a reason. "I figure the point of our going in is to make the Rebs ease off elsewheres."

"Or get in their rear." Brumm liked to add his baritone to Doudle's tenor around a campfire. Now his voice cracked. "That's likely what the generals have in mind. They like their fancy plans." He smiled a last time, the sort of smile that had nothing to do with good humor. "Best take my position. Got to say it out loud, though: I miss Captain Burket."

"You're doing fine, sir," Brown told the lieutenant. He, too, smiled, amused at the way things went. "Myself, I miss First Sergeant Hill every single day."

"Good man, Hill."

Brown gestured toward their waiting men. "All good men. Pretty much."

"Pretty much," Brumm agreed. "See you on the other side, First Sergeant."

Under the shield of the barrage, Hartranft's men went forward. Brown knew the 17th Michigan, a good pack of boys, led to the 50th's front. The Michiganders were offset, though, enough to leave the 50th exposed as the left flank of the division's attack. The only comfort was that the left had been quiet all that day.

After the lead brigade had advanced a hundred yards,

the order followed for the next lines to advance. The 50th stepped off.

Ahead, the guns tore into Hartranft's lines. The men down in the swale double-quicked into the smoke and disappeared.

"Going to be a lively afternoon, yes, sirree!" Bill Wildermuth declared.

"Shut up, Bill," Corporal Hill said.

As they marched down the slope, it struck Brown that they were trampling a field of new rye, its furrows at odds with each other, as if put in by a wife in her husband's absence. It was the smallest part of the war, a thing no man among them would remember, but no doubt the destruction would be a cause for sorrow in some run-down homestead. It was a poor place, this stretch of Virginia, as unlike the perfectly kept Dutch farms out Long Run as any farms could be. Home was so much the better place that Brown felt like a bully trampling those shoots.

Ahead, the trees loomed. Smoke prowled between their trunks.

Hartranft's men were in the fight: Brown could hear the firing and shouting, but couldn't see much.

The Reb artillery shifted its efforts to the second wave, but the lines of fire spared Company C.

"Keep your alignment in those trees," Brown called. "Veterans, keep the new men in line."

Of course, they were all veterans now. The Wilderness had been worth a dozen other battles for breaking men in. He was glad that scrap was behind them.

On the regiment's right flank, Captain Schwenk's company veered off into the open ground. Lieutenant Brumm told Company C to keep up the pace and maintain its order.

Leaf trees gave way to scrub pines: The woodland was the sort of place where kids played hide-and-seek.

"Just get on through there," Brown called, "get on through."

The branches splashed the men and scratched their faces. But at least the pines weren't useful trees for sharpshooters.

Someone called, "Charge!"

All of the company officers repeated the command, but Brown doubted a one of them knew where they were going. A man couldn't see beyond the next few trees. They were climbing the far slope, though.

The noise of battle closed around them, water swamping a barge. Couldn't see a single Johnny. Only smoke and trees, and his men slipping on wet roots.

Quitters from Hartranft's assault filtered back through the pines, almost getting themselves shot by men from the 50th.

"They were ready for us," one soldier called, by way of an excuse.

"Guess you weren't ready for them, though," a Pennsylvanian answered.

"Watch what's in front of you," Brown snapped.

Bullets tore at the fog. But he had yet to see a man from the company fall.

"Come on!" Brumm shouted, determined to give the slowing attack fresh life. "Charge! Company C! Charge!"

The bushy pines had disordered the entire regiment, but the men remained game and responded to the command by rushing ahead.

Then the Rebs were right there, in front of them, their entrenchments tracing a jagged course through the trees. Blue-clad bodies decorated the raw dirt to their front.

Brown's men howled. The regiment howled. The Johnnies let go a volley and a shriek.

Then it happened. Before they could close on the parapet. A Rebel yell and firing exploded to their left rear. It all went so fast that Brown couldn't give an order, not at first. Rebs came swarming through them from somewhere deep in their flank, shooting on the run, clubbing men with muskets, and calling for them to surrender.

Brown turned in time to see Levi Eckert fall, clutching his leg. Frank Sharon took a bayonet through the neck. Brown parried a tall, red-bearded Reb, and John Eckert the Shorter shot the man in the spine from five feet away.

Brown nodded to the boy. He'd earned the pair of stockings.

Lieutenant Brumm shouted for his men to rally, and Brown repeated the call. But the Rebs were just everywhere.

Captain Schwenk reappeared, leading his company in a charge back down through the tumult, shocking the Rebs in turn. Men went at each other close as stink, sparks from their muzzles setting the garments of gut-shot soldiers afire. Isaac Eckert and Henry Hill were fighting back-to-back. Brown moved to join them, calling for other men to rally to them. As Brown neared his comrades, he shouted to get the attention of a Reb who was troubling Isaac. For one fatal instant, the Johnny glanced toward him. Isaac swept his rifle's stock up into the man's jaw, a perfect motion that snapped the Rebel's neck. One thing no man could take away from Isaac: He fought mean.

The three of them did the best they could to grab other soldiers and put up a fight, but below and behind them, surrounded men of the 50th began to drop their rifles and surrender. Cornered by half a dozen Rebs, Corporal Doudle raised his hands.

"I ain't giving up to no damned Johnny," Isaac declared.

Bill Guertler and Dave Raudenbush raised their hands, too.

"Rally to Brumm," Brown ordered.

"Where the Hell is he?"

"Over there," Henry Hill said.

Brumm and Sergeant Levan were wrestling a brace of Johnnies for the regiment's flag. Down the slope, Captain Schwenk was struggling to form a firing line, and failing.

Brown saw a gang of Rebels push John Eckert the Shorter into captivity, too distant for a rescue attempt to make sense.

The men who hadn't surrendered were falling back. Some began to run. Then more of them ran.

"Come on," Brown said to Henry, Isaac, and the handful of others they had gathered in. "We're going straight down this hill, and straight through anything that gets in our way."

As they charged back toward their own too-distant lines, more soldiers joined them. Some fell to Reb bullets, but most pressed on. From all sides, Reb voices called on them to surrender.

Their course intersected that of Lieutenant Brumm. He had the regiment's flag, with Jim Levan swinging his rifle to clear a path. Brown dashed toward them and the other men followed, just because they wanted to be led: Somewhere. Anywhere. Away from the Rebs.

They had a last brawl with a pack of Johnnies who had strayed from their regiment. After a go-to with rifle butts and bayonets—and some fists—they were able to take two prisoners of their own along. But it didn't make up, couldn't make up, for the dozens of men from back home forced to surrender.

"Run, damn you," Brown told the two sorry Rebs they herded along. Thin as famine itself, one of the men wore torn Union pantaloons, while the other Johnny was barefoot.

A few shots trailed them into the trampled rye field.

Out of breath, the men wheezed as they trotted up toward their busy guns, slowing as the slope punished them and the Rebel fire slackened. To their bewilderment, dead and wounded Rebels littered the ground where the 50th had waited to attack just minutes before.

"What the devil happened?" somebody asked.

The shoeless Reb said: "We done just crossed each other up, that's what. Wasn't after you-all, but them guns yonder. Couldn't get 'em, and met y'all coming back, and howdy-do."

"Who you with, Johnny?"

"Reckon I'm with you-all now, 'less I have a choice." He spit out an object that might have been a tooth. "Marched with the Thirty-third North Carolina nigh on three years, though."

"Just keep moving, everybody," Brown said. "Form up, once we get behind the guns."

"Sergeants," the Johnny said in disgust. "I reckon they're just the same old yard dogs ever'where."

Bill Wildermuth appeared, pale but unharmed. Brown felt the joy of a child.

The men teased Wildermuth. Lovingly.

"They got Doudle," Wildermuth told them. "And John Eckert. Heimie . . ."

"Saw that," Isaac Eckert said. "Made a man sick." They funneled through the space between two batteries and a sequence of fires interrupted Isaac's speech. In the ringing quiet that followed, he added, "Old Doudle always did have a dread of Andersonville."

The two Rebs remained quiet after that.

Lieutenant Brumm stabbed the regiment's flag into the earth and ordered a private to hold it upright. "Company C," he called. "To me! Fiftieth Pennsylvania!"

Captain Schwenk showed up, too. He seemed to be the senior officer left. Many, many men were missing now. For a time, they waited, hoping that more survivors would make their way back across the field, and a trickle did come in. Then it stopped. Brown guessed the regiment had lost at least a hundred men. A good sight more, if you counted the wounded still on their feet but who would be leaving the ranks. He dreaded calling the roll.

They had accomplished just plain nothing. Again.

It began to rain.

Eleven p.m.
Grant's tent

Bill said: "If'n you ain't going nowheres no more, them boots wants oiling up."

At the end of a rough-hewn day, Grant slumped and told his servant, "I suspect there's a general or two wouldn't mind seeing me confined to quarters about now." He nodded toward the boots, which Bill had just helped him remove. "Smell like week-old fish, too."

"Nothing I can do 'bout that, Genr'l. You gots the feet the Lord give you."

The rain hit the canvas hard, but could not drown the sounds of combat from the distant salient. It was a soldiers' fight now, relentless, and had been that way since the morning. The men had struggled at close quarters for over eighteen hours, with no hint of an end to the intimate killing. Grant tried not to think about it. He had no more wish to see it in his mind than he did in the flesh. After evading a close look at the savagery all that day, he hoped to avoid dragging it with him into sleep. It did no good to dwell on the horrors, when horrors had to be. A man did what was necessary, after which you had to let things run. The battle belonged to the men out in the rain now. Tomorrow was his affair. If the rain eased, he meant to attack.

The day had started grandly, but Lee had spunk. Give him that. And his scarecrow soldiers had heart. What had surprised Grant was the determination of his own men to stick to it, going at it hand to hand in the mud. The Army of the Potomac had more grit than folks credited.

The generals were another matter. Burnside had pissed in his hat again. And Warren's men had achieved just about nothing. Wright needed time. Hancock puzzled him. Win seemed not to have bothered thinking beyond his first jump at checkers. As if he had lacked faith in his own success. He was still the best of the corps commanders, especially now that Sedgwick was gone, but Win seemed burdened by common things he would have carried lightly in the old days.

They were tired. Grant understood that. But Lee's men were worn down, too. And the first side to give up would lose, no fact shone with greater clarity. The past week had taught Grant that the Army of the Potomac could fight. Now he wasn't sure that it could think. For all his temper, Meade was steady enough. A thorough soldier, he did what he was told. But George Meade thought things through too finely, until the dangers got to him. Like too many generals, he saw spooks. And some of those spooks were real, but others weren't. As Meade's chief of staff, Humphreys was four aces. But even he wanted to see everybody else's hand before he bet.

Well, a man had to play the cards he drew. And the hand he held would serve. Game might run on for a time, though.

Bill had the mud-crusted boots in hand, but dawdled. Fussing. Which meant he had something itching him.

"Know what I'd like?" Grant asked. His expression was pure mischief. "Any idea what I'd appreciate right about now? What would truly do me good?"

Bill applied a grave expression to his blue black face. "Ain't going to be none of that, Genr'l. Mr. Rawlins, he'd chop me up and feed me to the hogs."

"Now, Bill . . . John Rawlins is the gentlest creature to walk on God's green earth."

"That some other Rawlins, maybe, not the one I'm fearing. He love you like a dog, but he guard you like a wolf."

True enough. If ere a man had befriended him sincerely in this life, it was John Rawlins. With Pete Longstreet next in line. Pete had been wounded in the Wilderness. Badly, if the reports were true. Grant worried over him. As he did over Rawlins' cough.

He had been teasing Bill, nothing more. He understood that indulgences of any sort did not lie in his near future. But it was one of his few allowable pleasures to see Bill flustered.

"Well, then," Grant said, "I suppose I'll have to settle for hearing what's on your mind. And don't tell me there's nothing. You're just about spilling over."

Bill inspected the seams of the battered boots. "Oh, just got to thinking as how it's a shame those U.S. Colored Troops ain't in all that fighting. Now it's dark and all."

"You want them to do their part? That it? For the 'dignity of the Negro'? And everything else I keep reading about in newspapers that want me to turn left today and right tomorrow, then go forward and back at once?"

"Wasn't thinking nothing so high up, now. Not my place. Just chewing on how the Rebs couldn't even see them boys for all the dark and rain. Be just about invisible. Not like all those poor white fellers. No, suh, the U.S. Colored Troops would be behind those Rebels even before they was in front of them. Scare the drawers off 'em, too."

Grant considered the man before him. "Really troubles you? That I haven't sent them in? Somebody has to guard the trains, that's honest work."

Bill frumped his chin. "Not my place to be troubled. Just thinking about those bone-weary white men up there, all moony-pale and shiny, getting theyselves killed . . ."

"Not sure they're all that shiny at the moment." Grant sighed. Picturing things he did not want to imagine. "Bill, it's politics. War is nothing but politics played for keeps. The abolitionists up north, they want the Negro in uniform. And I have no objection to that. But while those high-and-mighty thinkers and editors and 'consciences of the nation' are willing to accept any number of white corpses and cripples, they'd howl if General Ferrero's division suffered the kind of casualties, say, Barlow's or Griffin's have. In the South, the Negro's a slave. In New England, he's a pet."

"Wasn't pettin' going on last summer in that New York City."

"That was the Irish. The only power they have is in their fists."

"Power 'nough."

"To Boston society, you're a cause. To the Irish, you're competition."

"Don't mind my astin' it, Genr'l, you afraid coloreds can't be got to fight?"

Grant weighed his answer. "They're still green. One step at a time, Bill. Let them get a sense of things."

"Maybe they got them a sense of things already. Maybe they got them a powerful sense of things. 'Course, it's none of old Bill's business, but I 'spect they didn't volunteer to be no house niggers on display for high-toned visitors. They might not fight like the veteran man, but you give those black boys a chance . . ."

Fort Pillow, Grant thought. *Fort Wagner. The hatred.*

"Bill, I'm not sure white men want black men fighting beside them."

"Then maybe things ain't got bad enough."

Grant's lips twisted until they settled between a smile and a grimace. "Oh, they're bad enough. Marse Robert's a tough nut." His eyes met those of his servant. "What do you think of Lee, Bill? And don't give me any of that 'not my place to say' nonsense. Tell me what you make of Robert E. Lee. That's an order."

Bill let profound thought—largely feigned, Grant suspected—play over his face for a carefully judged period. Then he said, "Well, now . . . that man . . . he tougher than a one-eyed, grizzly old tomcat, and just as mean."

Grant laughed. "I suspect he'd be complimented by that. Although it may not be precisely the image he has of himself." His expression tightened slightly. "If he's a one-eyed old tomcat, what am I?"

Again, Bill displayed a counterfeit of thought. Grant knew the man had anticipated the second question before answering the first and had the answer ready. But Bill was a proud thespian by nature and needed to act his play at his own pace.

"Well, now . . . I s'pose you're a one-*eared* old tom. That's what I s'pose."

Grant thought about that for a time, then laughed out loud. "Meaning that I might see more than Lee, but don't hear so well. Or"—Grant smiled—"that I don't always listen."

"Oh, now," Bill told him, "that was just my way of saying. Old Bill just meant as you got two good eyes in your head. And Mr. Lee, he can't see what's looking him straight in the face."

Midnight
Spotsylvania Court House

It wasn't so bad. Corporal John Doudle had dreaded capture above all things. The whispered name "Andersonville" had made him shake like a child affrighted by spooks. And now, sitting in the mud, surrounded by those captured at his side, hungry, robbed, and pelted by more rain, he almost felt relieved that the wait was over. A man was an awfully funny thing, he decided.

The Rebs had stolen their money, rings, watches, belts, anything that seemed of the slightest value. Then they cursed the captives for not bearing food, for leaving behind their haversacks when they attacked.

Cackling, one Johnny had assured them, "You'll larn how a empty belly feels."

He had heard that Confederates could be decent sorts, accepting that a captured man faced misfortune enough. But good behavior was just one more made-up story. The Rebs who had driven him and his fellow prisoners to the rear had threatened to beat or even kill them every few steps. The captives were cursed aplenty, in language that seemed, at times, almost a foreign tongue. But the tone always made the meanings clear enough. The worst of their guards looked barely human, men left to the wilds, savage-eyed. One starved-looking Johnny had been such a paragon of filth that the lice in his hair were visible from a rifle length away.

Now Doudle sat, wet through, in the midst of hundreds of captives, some wounded and others sick, all of them wretched. Nearest him were the members of Company C who had surrendered at his side, the dumber of the two John Eckerts—moaning now and then like a wounded ox—Dave Raudenbush Raudenbusch and Eli Berger, Bill Haines and Billy Guertler, a few others. It had been a black day for Schuylkill Haven, but, as Doudle had pointed out to them all, at least they were alive.

"*Still* alive," Gerry Kerrigan corrected him.

Hunched shadows bearing arms, the guards teased their charges with tales of prison camps, of scurvy, death from the trots, swamp fever, hunger, and human flesh devoured, of madness.

"Y'all want to free the niggers? Let's see if them niggers free you."

Around Doudle, more than one fellow captive wept.

Doudle had borne enough. Instead of fear, he felt a burst of courage. Blessed with a church choir tenor, he sang out as loud as he could. First, he gave the Rebs a verse of "The Battle Cry of Freedom," expecting at least a few other men to join in. No one did, which only angered him further. He pierced the rain with a threat to "Hang Jeff Davis from a sour apple tree . . ."

Unable to spot the source, guards tore through the mass of prisoners, wielding their rifle butts and demanding to know who was singing, threatening to kill the offender and everyone near him.

"John, shut your mouth," Eli Berger hissed. "Before you make things worse."

The other Company C boys shared the sentiment.

May 13, nine thirty a.m.
Barlow's headquarters

Still the valedictorian, I see," Lyman said by way of greeting.

Barlow looked up from the field desk set out in the open air. "Whatever are you talking about?"

"Your success yesterday. You're the toast of the town. Or of army headquarters, anyway."

Barlow leaned back in his chair. Fugitive sun paled his face. "My success? Good Lord, Lyman. We bought a worthless patch of ground. At the price of a thousand men for every acre. And the best men, not the shirkers." Appearing at least a decade older than his twenty-nine years, he added, "*My* success. It was nothing but a damned fluke.

They'd withdrawn their guns, we had impossible luck. And we *still* made a mess of it."

"Really, Barlow . . . this isn't like you at all."

"That's the second time you've told me that in two days." He yawned. "Christ, I'm tired."

Lyman reached inside his tunic. Tailored by Huntington's, it was in tatters now. "Here. You'll want these." He held out Barlow's wallet and the wrapped picture of his wife.

Nodding a perfunctory thanks, Barlow took the items.

The headquarters crackled around them, but the air between the two former classmates was dead. Lyman felt compelled to lift Barlow's spirits.

"You've been recommended for promotion to major general, you know."

Barlow laughed a single hard note, a human gunshot. "And I'll damned well take it, should it go through. I'll grab it." He looked up sharply, meeting Lyman's eyes. "That's the thing of it, Teddy. I'll take the promotion. We'll have champagne, you and I, something decent. We'll invite Chandler and the rest. I'll be terribly vain about it all, proud as a slut with new garters. Of course, I shan't let it show too much. Wouldn't do for a Harvard man to reveal too great an appetite for accolades. Let others praise Caesar. I'll quietly accept it as my due." He stood up, one tall man looking down slightly on another. "You know who I was thinking about? Just this morning? Your cousin, little Bob Shaw."

"Cousin by marriage," Lyman said. "Twice, though."

"Poor Bob." Barlow's mouth twisted into a shape a man who didn't know him might take for a smile. "I tutored him, you know. Old blood or not, he wasn't the brightest fellow. And his mother, that witch. Bullied me into trying to teach him enough to squeeze into Harvard. And you know why I agreed? Because the formidable Mrs. Shaw could have ruined my mother with a single word. So I tried to convince Bob that two plus two actually makes four more often than not. Fool's errand." He snorted. "Rather like yesterday."

"He didn't graduate," Lyman said. "There was talk."

Barlow raised a shoulder, dismissive. "There was no scandal, that's nonsense. Bob didn't have the substance for a scandal. He just gave up, quit. When he could have got through by simply hanging on. Come now, Teddy. Would Harvard fail a Shaw? He could've been a drooling moron deep in the opium trade and the magi would've let him have a degree." He shook his head. "He was so weak. That's the thing, Teddy. Beyond the social armor, he was so weak. His mother—"

"I know the story, Frank."

"His mother," Barlow resumed, "killed him. The last thing Bob wanted was command of a regiment of darkies. But Mother insisted. Cared more for her abolitionist principles than for her flesh-and-blood son. And he didn't dare disappoint her a second time. The poor bastard's sense of duty wasn't to the Union or the darkies, but to *her*. Bob was no more meant to command a regiment than you are. No. Let me be fair. You'd make a far better regimental colonel. The combination of stupidity and a misplaced sense of duty never ends well."

It was Lyman's turn to don a complex smile, to mutter a laugh. "You know what he wrote me? When I was still abroad, wondering what to do?"

"And he was still alive, presumably?"

"I asked him about the most useful way I might serve." Lyman felt the cut of his smile deepen. "He suggested I apply for a post as chaplain to his regiment—the old regiment—if I felt absolutely compelled to wear a uniform." He dropped his eyes away from Barlow's. "I was insulted, of course. You, at least, could see me as a staff man."

Barlow's concern grew genuine. "Teddy, did you so resent me? Coming top of the class?"

"Rather. But I didn't really try until my final year, you know."

"I remember your commencement speech. That dig at the abolitionists. And here we are."

A sour memory puckered Lyman's face. "My family viewed the Republican sort as busybodies. Troublemakers. And their predecessors were hardly better. Silk-stocking Democrats to a man, it's simply who we were. Solidly for the Union, of course. But uninterested in glorifying the Negro." He waved off a fly. "Frankly, Mrs. Shaw was an embarrassment, the sort who belonged in Concord with the enthusiasts." He sighed. "I've come around, of course. To a degree. Slavery does seem impossible. And now . . ." He glanced southward, toward the enemy. "We can't go back." Quickly, he added, "*Our* society will go on, that's beyond question. Sounder values."

Barlow laughed so loudly that everyone in the grove stopped work and turned to look. "Spoken like the true heir, Teddy. How far back does your family go? Since they first begged corn from the Indians? Seven generations?"

"Eight, actually. You know, I shall never so much as whisper it back home, but I do agree. Bob was the one among us who shouldn't have been a soldier."

"Wrong. He just shouldn't have been made a colonel. Captain in charge of a company would've been about right. He could've brought that off. God, Teddy, how many of the old boys are dead, the old crowd?"

"Ten, I think."

"Your fellow Porcs?"

"Three."

Barlow ran a palm over his scalp. "Glad you came back? From your European sojourn? In time to see all this? Ever wish you would've stayed in Europe?"

"I stayed too long as it was. I should've come back sooner, of course. My duty. But Mimi, the child . . ."

Barlow waved that away. "You needn't make excuses. Not to me, for God's sake. But you didn't answer my question. Do you ever wish you'd stayed in Europe? And avoided this . . . this idiocy? Tell me the truth, Teddy."

"I think not. Really, Barlow, you're not the only one who takes an interest, you know. In war, I mean. Scientifically speaking, it's a remarkable phenomenon. One should be afraid . . . but, somehow, it's so cussed fascinating. . . ."

"More than starfish?"

"Different. I mean, one does learn a great deal about oneself. In Europe . . . in Brussels, to be specific . . . I had the most dreadful nightmares. Wild imaginings about the war, insufferable dreams. I *was* afraid, I daresay. Of war as I painted it to myself."

"And now you aren't?"

"Oh, I'd rather not be shot at. But . . . isn't it odd how war can be such a combination of the spectacular and the utterly mundane? At the same time?"

"Teddy . . . I'd like you to do something for me. For yourself, actually. Do you have to go back to headquarters immediately? Can someone else hold Meade's hand for a few more minutes?"

"I could fudge it a bit. What—"

Barlow tossed a paw toward the salient. The low ridge was just visible. The rain had faded at dawn, but the mud it left had prevented a renewed offensive and more clouds rolled toward them from the west. Wreckage steamed in the heat.

"Ride over there, Teddy. To the first line of entrenchments. It's perfectly safe. Lee's retired to a much stronger line a half mile back. Leaving us the proud possessors of a charnel house made of mud pies. Do have a look, you'll find it awfully interesting. From the scientific perspective."

"Actually, I'd been planning to inspect the ground," Lyman said, "so I can describe it to General Meade. That's why I rode over. And I wanted to return your things, of course." Lyman squared his hat upon his head. "Don't suppose you'd care to come along? For old times' sake?"

Barlow's eyes were stones.

"I had a good look," he said.

Ten a.m.
The Bloody Angle

The Union dead were horrible. The Confederate dead were worse. Inside the trenches, bodies had piled up five or six deep, as corpses might have been heaped in medieval plague pits. Here and there, a wounded man strained with his last strength to work his way out from under the crush of the dead. Fingers curled. A foot twitched. The faces that remained whole had the look of the terrified dead in paintings of the damned by German masters, but none of those artists, not Cranach or even Grünewald, had dared twist limbs so madly or reveal the truth of what lurked beneath the human canvas of skin. Open mouths and open eyes stared heavenward, caught in agony. When a wounded man moaned from the depths of the filth and flesh, it was as though one of the dead had spoken.

Rain clouds darkened the earth anew.

Busy with the blue-clad dead and clearing the last few wounded of their own, the troops on burial detail ignored the Rebel wounded and simply shoveled mud over the trenches. The Union dead got shallow but private graves, with markers splintered from ammunition boxes.

A few yards off, a soldier raised a shovel high and swung its edge down fiercely. Thrice. Lyman chose not to inquire.

All over the field, officers hunted fallen comrades amid

the disfigured and dismembered corpses, with many a man reduced to shreds of meat, unidentifiable. More than a few soldiers wandered about, eyes dead to the world through which they stumbled. Bedlam mad, a sergeant stood amid a slew of bodies and preached to anyone who would hear, shouting imprecations at earth and sky. He went ignored: Language had lost all power to dismay.

Beyond the trench line, the dead of both armies reached into the shattered grove, literally as far as the eye could see.

A vision stopped Lyman. Perfectly composed, the face of a Botticelli youth lay turned to the heavens, eyes closed as in prayer, the handsome features framed by golden locks.

There was nothing below the neck but a cutlet of shoulder.

Lieutenant Colonel Theodore Lyman III, of Brookline, heir to a splendid fortune and related safely to the Eliots, Parkmans, Shaws, and a half dozen other unassailable families, had been keeping a diary in fine detail, determined to leave an objective—indeed, a scientific—record of the war. But he did not think he would write down what he saw here. Decency took precedence over integrity. He could not present such a world as this to his wife or infant daughter.

As he rode back to resume his regular duties, Lyman thought it unfortunate that men could not regenerate limbs like starfish.

PART IV

MARCHING TO HELL

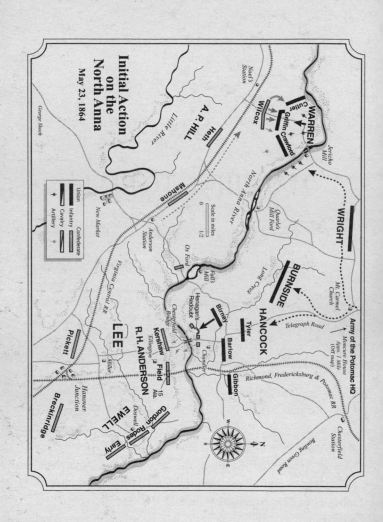

Initial Action
on the
North Anna
May 23, 1864

George Skoch

A. P. HILL

Heth

Little River

Mahone

New Market

Anderson Station

Virginia Central RR

Noel's Station

Wilcox

Cutler

WARREN

Griffin Crawford

North Anna River

Jericho Mill

Quarles Mill Ford

Scale in miles
0   1/2

Ox Ford

Falls Mill

WRIGHT

Quarles' Mill Ford

BURNSIDE

Long Creek

Mt. Carmel Church

Heragan's Redoubt

Chesterfield Bridge

Chandler

HANCOCK

Birney

Tyler

Barlow

Gibbon

Telegraph Road

Army of the Potomac HQ
Moncure House
Appx. 1 Mile
(Off map)

LEE

R. H. ANDERSON

Kershaw Field
Ellington   15
            Ala.

Pickett

Miller

Hanover Junction

Doswell

Gordon Rodes Early

EWELL

Breckinridge

Richmond, Fredericksburg & Potomac RR

Chesterfield Station

Bowling Green Road

N S E W

Union
Confederate
Infantry
Cavalry
Artillery

TWENTY-ONE

Lee considered the buttermilk. He had been ill again, and no morsel had sparked his appetite for days. Then his host, Parson Fox, reappeared on the porch. Deserted by his servants, the good man delivered an offering of bread and buttermilk. Almost the shade of Mary's beloved yellow roses at Arlington House, the beverage tempted Lee.

He told himself that those people—pawing toward the redoubt across the river—would not attempt to force a crossing for hours, if at all. Surely, their reverses at Spotsylvania had dimmed their ardor for headlong adventures. He judged it likeliest that the activity was but a demonstration to veil a movement on Hanover Junction from the east. His son's cavalry reported few Federals to the west, above Jericho Mill, not even sufficient numbers for a feint. So the left flank was secure, and if the right was still in question, Lee had reason to feel confident. His army had concentrated handsomely, while Grant and Meade were extended along the roads north of the river, according to Hampton's scouts. He had time to prepare to repel a crossing, once the Federals revealed their true line of advance. A few moments might be spared for needed refreshment.

Surrounded by his staff on the high porch, by men whose spirits mixed courage and consternation, men whose wits had dulled as the month advanced, Lee sat, relieved not to be on horseback for a time, but annoyed by the carriage Venable held ready in case he could no longer keep the saddle. He knew himself and recognized that his body's betrayals put him out of sorts, so he cautioned himself not to take it out on those who meant him well. But that carriage, with its torn seats and a hood like an old woman's bonnet, was almost an insult.

Things that once had been managed with ease had grown frustratingly difficult as he faced these newly ruthless men in the uniform he had worn for so many years. He had parried them for twelve days at Spotsylvania, disappointing their every effort, despite the near calamity of the Mule Shoe and the appalling drain of casualties. By right of war, Grant and Meade had to quit the field. And they had done so, but only to move around his flank again, to march deeper into Virginia, forcing his weary army to outrace them at killing speed, his only advantages knowledge of the roads and interior lines. And the good hearts of his soldiers, he must not forget them. Now he was twenty-five miles closer to Richmond and pinned along this river by the need to keep open the rail link to the Valley.

Lee felt Richmond breathing at his back.

He knew from prisoners taken that Grant had robbed the defenses of Washington itself to replace his immense losses, impressing garrison artillery regiments into the infantry. But his own losses neared the unbearable, and he had begged President Davis to send what troops he could from Richmond's defenses or the Carolinas, before courage succumbed to lowly mathematics.

Not all of the news had been bad, the Lord be thanked. After suffering through long days and nights of rain at Spotsylvania, his men had rallied to beat back a last grand attack and had done the work handsomely. Word arrived that Union armies had been defeated badly in the Valley and frustrated in the west, while Butler had been checked along the James. Beyond Virginia, only Sherman remained a threat. But the decision, Lee knew, would come here, between his weary men and the invaders chewing southward in their hordes.

On the wrong side of the scale, he had lost so many of his finest officers—not least, Stuart—that he had to worry about the reliability of this brigade and that division, even of entire corps. Hill had returned to command, but still looked ghastly, and Ewell verged on the unfit, unsteady of judgment and newly stricken with dysentery. After a fine beginning at the head of Longstreet's corps, Anderson had proved lackluster. More than ever, Lee felt the need to control not just the army, but the actions of each corps with his own hand.

On top of it all, Mary was ailing again, and there was nothing he could do. He could not leave the army for even a day, and all the while his own health threatened constantly to unman him. If a grave indisposition came to pass, what would happen to his men, let alone his wife? He feared the battered army could not resist those people without him to lead it.

The swelling heat made all things worse, including the stench of his body and those around him. They had left the reeking fields of Spotsylvania days behind, but he still could smell the death on his clothes and person. He had written home for cotton undergarments for the summer, but received no answer. He longed to bathe.

Instead, there would be more fighting, perhaps on the morrow. He needed to know where those people would concentrate. He was nearly certain it would be downriver, closer to the confluence with the Pamunkey. But he was not certain enough. The cavalry had been ordered to maintain its vigil. Grant and Meade must not surprise him again.

How he longed for Stuart, with his dash and sure reports! Why could his brilliant cavalier not rise from the dead, a second Lazarus?

Lee caught himself: Such impertinence before the Lord came too near to blasphemy. If the Lord of Hosts had seen fit to call Stuart to his celestial ranks, his will be done.

Times there were when the Lord God's will fell hard upon his children.

As he sat in the shade above a brown river on a sparkling day, Lee strained to divine his opponents' intentions and longed for Divine Grace. It might do well, he told himself, to ask Parson Fox to pray with him before he departed to inspect the ground. But first there was the temptation of the buttermilk. The occasional sips he had braved in the past few weeks had done him no harm. On the contrary, they seemed to have aided his digestion: Perhaps his stomach's chemistry had changed? And he wanted sustenance.

With his host hovering in anticipation, Lee reached for the beckoning liquid and began to drink it down.

The sky tore open. A round of solid shot smashed through the frame of the porch door, a body's length from Lee. Within the house, splintering wood and crashing china triggered screams of terror, but, blessedly, not of pain. Lee had long ago learned to tell the difference.

His party's waiting horses had grown unruly, whinnying for their masters and kicking at orderlies.

Lee drained the glass, rose, and brushed the dust from his coat. He told his pale host, "My apologies, sir. Our presence has inconvenienced you." About to step off to remount, he added, "Your buttermilk was delicious."

Two forty-five p.m.
The Moncure house: Headquarters,
Army of the Potomac

From Warren," Humphreys said to Meade. Gruff of voice, he could not completely subdue a tone of excitement. "He's at Jericho Mill. Listen to this: 'The enemy made no show of resistance at this point. My infantry are fording. I do not believe the enemy intends holding the North Anna.'" He looked up from the paper and met Meade's eyes. "He's across the river."

"Bless him," Meade said.

Humphreys sensed relief from all the staff. Warren had performed disappointingly at the Wilderness and Spotsylvania, but today he had outpaced Hancock, who was just coming up and passing Carmel Church.

"Shall I send this up to Grant?" Humphreys asked.

Meade held out his hand. "Let me endorse it. Send an order to Warren. He's to pass his entire corps over the river and entrench."

Humphreys cocked his head, just askance.

Meade's face sharpened. Humphreys read the expression: *I still command this army.*

"I see no conflict with Grant's intentions," Meade said. "Quite the contrary. Meanwhile, I want Warren across that damned river. With everything he's got. And digging. Lee's bound to counterattack. The moment he learns what's happened."

"Grant's people don't think Lee will contest the river line."

Meade nodded. "And two days ago they insisted he'd fight to the death for it." He bit off a growl. "We'll see, Humph, we'll just see. Until then, I want Warren across the river and digging in as fast as his men can dig. I'll find out what Grant has in mind for Wright and Burnside, given developments."

"Warren's trains are backed up. At Carmel Church."

"Remind him. That road belongs to Hancock. But make it clear he's to get across the river with all his fighting strength. And he's not to waste any time. The last thing I want is Warren dawdling for commissary wagons." Thoughts moved across Meade's face like clouds sweeping over a field. "Do his engineers have their bridging up? He'll need to get artillery across. A lot of it. Soon."

"George, the Fifth Corps has the best engineers in the Army."

Meade nodded. "My old corps. Just get the order off to Warren, I'll parley with Grant."

Humphreys turned to the task. It was good to see Meade in form again. A decisive man by nature, he had been hobbled by Grant's constant presence. But an argument Meade had lost two days before seemed only to have renewed his fighting spirit. Meade had proposed—soundly, in Humphreys' view—that it made the most sense for the army to swing east and race Lee to the Chickahominy, to dash for the gates of Richmond. If the army moved east, there would be but one river to cross, the Pamunkey, and not all four of the rivers that fed into it. Hanover Junction, the key rail crossing, would fall of itself.

Instead, Grant had chosen to head for the North Anna, unwilling to hear counterarguments, almost as if he meant to belittle Meade. Tempers were short all around after the last botch at Spotsylvania, a hopeless assault Grant demanded. Grant and his chorus of staff men—who seemed to do little real work—insisted that Lee would defend the North Anna to protect the junction. And the army must follow Lee, wherever he went. Meade had wanted to force Lee to do the following.

Subduing his temper admirably, in Humphreys' opinion, Meade had then applied himself to his allotted task, getting the army across the North Anna River. The march from Spotsylvania had been fitful, confused by wretched maps that put roads and waterways miles out of place, but today the army had sparked back to life, scenting a conclusion to the wanton gore as its soldiers followed the dusty tracks that passed for thoroughfares deeper into Virginia.

Humphreys handed the dispatch to a courier. "For General Warren. Urgent."

Cavalry had reported a small redoubt on the north bank, guarding the Chesterfield Bridge, along Hancock's route down the Telegraph Road. There seemed to be some minor entrenchments on the south bank as well. But it had more the feeling of a rearguard effort than of a determined defense. And now Warren was across, a few miles upriver. Humphreys was glad of it, but it just didn't seem like Robert E. Lee not to fight while he had the advantage.

Was Lee even there? Or was he retreating and licking his wounds, studying a defense of Richmond? What Humphreys saw before him and what he knew of Lee did not match up.

Meade was correct, of course: For now, Warren had to get his entire corps onto the south bank. And the Sixth Corps had to follow before any trains crossed, excepting a reserve of ammunition. In case Lee had set a grand ambush. Rations and niceties could wait.

What was Lee up to? Why had he let Warren cross?

Since Sheridan had recast the army's cavalry for his personal use, reconnaissance had collapsed. While that foulmouthed little mick went gallivanting. Humphreys needed hard information, but Sheridan only gave men a hard time.

Teddy Lyman came in, gleaming with sweat and uniformed in dust.

"Infernal roads," he said. "Half don't go anywhere near where they're supposed to."

"We've noticed," Humphreys told him. "Where have you been, Lyman?"

"At Warren's ford," the New Englander told him. "Map was utterly useless, had to get directions from a blackamoor. And *he* spoke some gibberish *patois*. Quite the spectacle, though. At the ford, I mean. When I left, Warren had a full division across, Charlie Griffin's boys, with Crawford's lot hard on their heels. The engineers got up a splendid bridge, really quite impressive. Frightfully quick, too. Despite Roebling's meddling. Fancies himself quite the expert. German heritage, I suppose."

Humphreys drew in his eyebrows. "No sign of Lee's army?"

Lyman thought about it. "There may have been half a dozen irregulars, local men. I believe I heard somebody say."

Humphreys could not understand it. Why would Lee let them cross that river unchallenged?

Three p.m.
Along the Virginia Central Railroad,
east of Anderson Tavern

Lee slumped in the carriage. He wished to sit erectly, that at least. But his body betrayed him. Dizzy and sick, he had needed to dismount along the road and blunder toward the trees, undoing his trousers as he went, afraid that he would not remain in control of himself long enough to avoid shame. Venable had helped him back up from the stump, assisting him in matters as distasteful as they were embarrassing.

"You mustn't tell them," Lee had insisted. "They must not think me incapable."

Venable murmured something in response.

Now Lee rode in the carriage, with tufts of horsehair bursting through rents in the cushions and a general air of poverty befitting a Methodist circuit rider. He disliked displaying himself in such an unmanly condition, but had to ride west, toward Hill's corps, to look into the rumor that those people had forced the river. *The heat, the heat.* His stomach attacked him with razors, bending his body forward. Soon . . . too soon . . . he would need to dismount again.

Blue sky ahead. This heat, the blue sky. A fanged animal roamed his bowels. The army needed him. He must not waver . . . not waver . . .

The carriage approached a knot of soldiers, *his* soldiers. Lee straightened his back, an act of immense will. The soldiers removed their hats—straw or ragged felt, chewed around the brims, with here and there a crushed regulation cap—and voices as bare as the fields they had abandoned cried out well-meant words, good wishes, devotion. Lee maintained his solemn expression, unable to so much as raise a hand.

He could not go on. He must go on. Those people . . .

A horseman met the buggy and Lee's retinue: a dispatch. Marshall seized it.

The world had grown unsteady. The sky quivered. He needed a private place. A cool place. To hide the body's shame. To lie down. To rest. To gather strength again.

You must remain clear of mind, he told himself.

Sweat burst forth, not only from his wool-sheathed torso, but from his limbs and even the backs of his hands. His body was hot and the sweat was cold and everything was confused.

Just to lie down . . .

Fangs in his belly . . .

Marshall? What did he want?

"From Rooney Lee, sir. No major Union elements on our

left. Only some minor doings at Jericho Mill, a few Yankees crossed at the ford."

Lee felt his military secretary watching him. Venable, too, had come up. Venable and this vile carriage . . .

"A reconnoitering party," Lee said, perhaps with too much emphasis. Almost with temper. "Those people will not cross there . . . not to their advantage . . . at most, a ruse. . . ."

"General Lee," Marshall said, "*if* they have men across the river, even a few, General Hill must move against them. Before they can consolidate their—"

"They will *not* cross higher up," Lee snapped.

The world hushed at the outburst.

"Sir . . . ," Venable said in a voice meant to soothe a child, "this is the turn to Ox Ford, the old coach road. Do you still wish to visit the ford? I could go myself. There's really no need. . . ."

Why was there such doubt in Venable's voice? Was it too hot for the pup? Of course Lee wished to inspect it. He needed to inspect the entire line.

Volcanic again, Lee's bowels threatened to burst.

"The trees. *Stop there*. Those trees."

He was not certain how long it took his party to reach Ox Ford, but the road was sunken, shaded, and cool for much of the way. At the bluff overlooking the river, he managed to dismount and walk, slowly, to the picket line. It was a fine position, high above the coursing water, with an overgrown island in midstream and lower, open ground on the opposite bank. The bluff could not be easily taken, if it could be taken at all.

There was no sign of those people.

He gestured for his field glasses. Holding them as steadily as he could, he scanned distant fields and groves. And saw nothing of import.

There were other fords, of course, at Quarles's Mill and

then Jericho Mill, farther up the river. He did not believe Grant and Meade would move their army so far west, but he needed to see the ground with his own eyes.

The way was long, though. And the heat . . . was killing. . . .

He craved rest, the chance to lie down and close his eyes. To gather strength for the battle, whenever it might come. The army *needed* him. They would not fight today, but, perhaps, tomorrow . . . or the day after. . . .

It made no sense for those people to cross higher up. No sense at all. Would it not be wiser to rest? Than to press on and risk debility?

What had Jackson said? Let us cross over the river. Not this river. Morbid thought. Rest under the shade of the trees. No. A cool room. Even a tent. Privacy. He dreaded soiling himself before the men. Not all his years in the army, in two armies, had hardened him against such a common disgrace.

He turned so quickly he almost lost his balance. His guts were in full revolt. But he would not let the men see him disabled. He thrust the field glasses into the nearest hands.

"The carriage."

His aides closed around him.

"Away from here . . ."

"Yes, sir."

Seated in the buggy again, forcing himself to sit as though he were in as full a command of his person as he was of the army, he beckoned Marshall to him.

"A courier," Lee said. "Hill's man. *Now.*"

Hill had been worried . . . worried . . . just returned to command and jumpy, unsettled. Seeing phantoms. In the heat. Under this blue sky. God's blue. Not Union blue. Not the old blue . . . with which he had not kept faith . . . blue sky through myriad leaves, somnolent in the dead middle of the day. Where were they going? What road was this?

Where was Jackson? Longstreet? Stuart? They had left him behind. . . .

Not Longstreet. Peter had not deserted him. Longstreet would recover from his wound. Perhaps then . . .

Stuart! The man had never brought him a false report. Now Rooney. His son. His beloved son. But no Stuart. White House plantation burned. Act of spite. Two years ago now. Was it that long? Why could they not behave as gentlemen? Rooney doing his best. Must not shame the family. Lees of Virginia . . . his father's shame, his brother's . . . all he had done to make the name glisten again . . .

The rider from Hill's headquarters waited beside Marshall.

"Go back," Lee said, enunciating carefully, "and tell General Hill to leave his men in camp. They must have rest. The Union actions above him are merely a feint, the regiments on picket can address them. The enemy is preparing to cross below, toward Hanover Junction."

Three thirty p.m.
South bank of the North Anna,
Jericho Mill Ford

Brigadier General Charles Griffin rode along his line, watching his men entrench. Blouses off, they tore at the clay with spades or swung axes at nearby trees to bank up logs and uncover fields of fire. Crawford's division had begun to fill in on his left, closing the gap all the way back to the river, while Cutler's division was just a few hours behind, assigned to extend the right. And Wainwright, that redleg bastard—more power to him—had the corps artillery rattling up at a gallop.

If the damn fool Rebs didn't come on soon, they'd miss

their chance and pay for it. But the fields to the front remained empty. There'd been a fuss with skirmishers, but nothing after that. Either the buggers were in retreat, or their generals were taking a Mexican *siesta*.

Griffin's division had been hard used since the first day in the Wilderness, and the pointless assaults at Laurel Hill had cost him many of his finest soldiers. But, as an old trooper, he was a fair judge of men, and he sensed now that the boys still in the ranks had not had their spirits broken, just banged up a bit. They wanted to get their own back, that was all, to have a chance to do to the Johnnies what had been done to them.

And it looked to Charlie Griffin as if the chance might come very soon.

He paused behind the raw dirt line thrown up by Sweitzer's men. When their general didn't spur off in a billow of dust, the men eased up on their work and turned toward him, wiping sweat from their faces with the filthy sleeves of filthy undergarments. Waiting.

"Damn right," Griffin barked. "Dig in deep, you sorry sonsofbitches. Those grayback cocksuckers are like to be along, and we're going to let them do the charging this time. Then we'll see who's fucked for beans come suppertime." These men were mean, hardened, and beautifully vengeful. Not about to run away for two shits and a whistle. They wanted their fair turn at doing the damage. "Well, stop playing with your willies and dig, goddamn it."

Several of the men began to cheer him.

"You sorry sonsofbitches," Griffin told them. "What the Hell are you cheering for? Get back to work, you buggers."

His boys. God bless them.

Four p.m.
Headquarters, Third Corps,
Army of Northern Virginia, Anderson's Station

Powell Hill told Wilcox: "Cad, I feel like I've been handed a shit-bucket. And the bucket's just about full. Here I've got this report of Federals up at Jericho Mill. And over here I have a message from General Lee saying it isn't to worry me, there's nothing to it, let the men rest. I have one message from young Rooney Lee telling me there's nobody out there to speak of, and another telling me there's Yankees across the river, but not how many, and no time of day written down on either one."

"Well," Cadmus Wilcox said, "the boys I sent out for a look ought to come in soon. Orr didn't think he was up against any major force. Just big enough to make him wary of taking them on with one cut-to-the-bone regiment. Figured I ought to send out men I could trust, get a proper report."

Hill punched a bony fist into his left palm. Not fiercely, but repeatedly. "I swear, I've got half a mind to dig up Stuart's body and see if I can't breathe life into his carcass. I've never felt so blind during a campaign." As he spoke, Hill realized the claim was not true. He had been even less well-informed at Gettysburg, on that first morning. And Stuart had been alive then. Off on a lark to get his name in the papers.

Wilcox didn't say a word, just looked at Hill with that slightly cross-eyed stare of his.

Hill went on: "Word is the old man's feeling poorly."

That, too, Hill realized, might have been left unsaid. Given his own recent absence from command. It just seemed a day when nothing would go right, when none of the numbers added up to the proper sum.

"Any idea," Wilcox asked, "what Lee means to do?"

Hill shrugged. "Fight. Beyond that, I'm not sure he knows himself. That peckerwood Grant . . ."

"Man got spunk, say that much," Wilcox remarked.

"Damned butcher."

The division commander sucked in a cheek. "Wouldn't pretend to admire the gentleman . . . but we do seem a tad closer to Richmond than when we started out."

Hill spit. "McClellan got closer. And look how that ended up."

"I reckon. But I'm not convinced to a certainty we're dealing with Georgie McClellan."

Looking up sharply, meeting his subordinate's close-set, not-quite-right eyes, Hill said: "You think he can whip us?"

"Didn't say that. Stubborn feller, though."

Hill thought: There is no man upon this earth as stubborn as Robert E. Lee.

"Wouldn't mind hearing from one of those gussied-up, Charleston staff boys of yours," Hill told his subordinate.

"Getting them a good look, I expect."

Hill's mood was as changeable as that of an ill-trained horse. "Probably nothing, after all. Lee's like to be right."

One of Wilcox's aides, Major Browning, galloped into camp, horse lathered and heaving.

"Young buck of yours is reckless with a horse," Hill commented.

"Not as a rule," Wilcox said. "And he's from Raleigh, not Charleston."

Browning swung out of the saddle. With too much flair for Hill's mood. Mustachioed like his division commander and looking a bright paragon of health, he strutted up to the generals, saluting and then sweeping his cap from his jet black hair. Hill decided he did not like the lad.

"Well, Browning?"

"Yankees, all right," the major said. "Passel of them. Digging in."

"How many?" Hill asked.

"Got as close as we could, didn't want—"

"How many?"

The staff man recoiled at the corps commander's tone. "At least a brigade. Could be two."

"And that's all?"

"All we could see, sir."

"Artillery?"

"Didn't see any."

Hill turned to Wilcox. "Get your division moving. Run those bastards back across that river. No. Cut them off from the river. And kill every man who won't surrender when asked." He snorted. "Looks like the old man was right. Yankees dangling some bait, get us looking the wrong way. We'll make 'em pay for it." He bore down on Wilcox. "How fast can you get up there with all your men?"

Seven p.m.
The heights south of Jericho Mill

Colonel Charles Wainwright, chief of the Fifth Corps' artillery, watched with immeasurable pride as Charlie Mink's battery rolled forward through the shambles of Cutler's division. The New York gunners trotted up as neatly as if on parade, parting the mass of fleeing soldiers to unlimber on the knoll the just arrived troops had abandoned.

In moments, Mink's boys were blowing canister into the screeching, hallooing Rebs, stunning them into confusion.

Wainwright wasted no time: He sent riders to Walcott and Matthewson to bring up their batteries on line with Mink's roaring guns.

Even before the reinforcing pieces went into action, the

Confederates halted in the open field. Unready to retreat, they concentrated their fire on Mink's gun crews, dropping men rapidly. But the best of Cutler's lot had thought better of their flight and rallied around the battery, with infantrymen leaping to serve the guns.

When they saw Walcott's battery crest the hillock, the Confederate officers goaded their men to go forward again, to rush the knoll before the additional pieces could open up. But the effort was futile. Walcott's sections, then Matthewson's, shredded what remained of the Reb formation.

Just in time to finish them off, Bartlett's fresh brigade burst out of the trees, extending Sweitzer's embattled flank and hitting the bewildered Johnnies at a right angle.

Wainwright had the splendid pleasure and downright joy of watching Lee's veteran infantry break and run.

His boys would never receive due credit, of course. The artillery never did. But *he* knew that his men had broken the Reb attack that threatened to slash all the way to the river, cutting off Griffin's and Crawford's divisions in another damned debacle.

As for those two divisions, they had held their ground. Sweitzer's brigade had been threatened by the collapse of Cutler's mob, but Charlie Griffin had simply refused his flank and kept on fighting. Now, to Griffin's front, other Confederate regiments turned and ran. Without, Wainwright had to admit, falling subject to the effects of artillery.

The Johnnies just didn't seem to have their old spark.

Or numbers. Wainwright galloped over to the knoll, full of advice and orders to prepare to receive a renewed Rebel attack. But nothing materialized on the right flank, the one vulnerable point. Instead, the Johnnies made a last half-hearted effort to break into Charlie Griffin's lines. The old buzzard saw them off sharply.

Had they been mad? Attacking a corps with what appeared to be no more than a single ill-led division?

In the softening light, Wainwright watched through his field glasses as a last, weak assault crumbled, its survivors running pell-mell for their lives.

Before the victorious batteries, Johnnies lay dead in heaps, while their wounded crawled and pleaded.

Ragged prisoners shambled in, mocked by gloating soldiers who, a half hour past, had been on the run themselves.

On his way to inspect the batteries he had positioned across the field behind Crawford's division, Wainwright met a grinning Charlie Griffin riding along, trailed by his division flag and a gaggle of prancing staff officers.

Griffin reined up just long enough to say, "Damned fine work there, Wainwright. You're not completely worthless." He swept an arm toward the Confederates, who had disappeared into groves and gullies and distance. "Who's fucked for beans now?"

Nine p.m.
Headquarters, Army of Northern Virginia,
near the Miller house

We cannot abandon Hanover Junction," Lee said from his throne on the upthrust root of an oak tree of biblical age. Looking around at his gathered generals, he waited for someone to brave a suggestion as to a course of action. Ewell, Anderson, and their flocks of subordinates stood about the map spread over the ground. In the lantern light in the purple dusk, the faces were those of weary, uneasy men.

The day had turned against them. His son's reports had been faulty, and Hampton's were little better. Hill had squandered his opportunity, sending one division into the maw of a Union corps. And moments before the lighting of the lanterns, word had followed that the artillery fire off to the north had heralded an assault on the redoubt defended by Henagan's men. Those people—Birney's division of Hancock's corps—had stormed forward under a brief and isolated shield of rain, and Henagan had failed to hold the northern end of the Chesterfield Bridge. Compounding the effects of the reverse, Lee did not believe the south bank could be held at that site, nor did his engineers.

He chastised himself for being sick, for giving in to his body's complaints, and for his errors of judgment. He had misled Hill, even before the corps commander misled himself. Now, as soldiers' fires dotted the meadow in the gloaming, he forced himself to sit erectly on the bench nature provided, to keep his features steadfast and his voice infused with confidence. He *refused* to be ill. As he refused to be beaten.

He had sent a message to Powell Hill to remain with his corps and position it advantageously, but the true reason for the order was that he did not want to lose his composure with the man. Whatever he had believed the situation to be, Hill had owed it to his troops to ride to the sound of the guns, to reinforce the attack when it became clear those people had crossed more than a brigade or two. If only Hill had struck with his entire corps . . .

Regrets never won a single battle, Lee reminded himself.

"Well, gentlemen?" he said. "Do we retire behind the South Anna? I dread it. The rail line *must* remain open."

"Fight 'em along the railroad," Anderson offered. "Embankment makes a good line."

As night settled over the landscape of men, horses, and mules, of lush spring and rising damp, Lee said: "No, General Anderson. Warren could turn General Hill's left too easily that way."

"I'm with you, sir," Ewell put in. "Got to hold Hanover Junction. Just got to. Can't do that, we might as well head straight for the Chickahominy. Or Richmond."

"But *how,* General Ewell? Hancock will cross the river in the morning. Warren is already on our left, on solid ground and entrenched. Our position . . . our present position . . . appears untenable."

His belly bit him again, but he kept his features steady.

The generals fell silent. A few miles to the north, the Union guns bombarded positions Lee had ordered abandoned. That spendthrift shelling was seconded by artillery off to the west, where Hill had failed and, if reports were to be believed, once proud brigades had broken and fled the field.

The pestering insects grew louder than the men surrounding Lee.

"Sir, if I may?" The speaker was Colonel Martin Smith, his senior engineer, a man who possessed a genius for plotting fieldworks. Lee knew that whatever the colonel had to say would be reliable, for good or ill, and his words would be spoken temperately. The colonel had waited to offer his views until the generals had talked themselves out, so no man's pride was threatened. Smith preferred making fortifications to making enemies.

A Northerner by birth, Smith had married south. Lee knew his type full well: the insecure man who feared putting a foot wrong, a gifted man who let fools step ahead of him.

Lee nodded: *Go ahead.*

In a tone ill-suited to the hour, the ailing Ewell said, "Well, the floor recognizes Colonel Smith, our favorite Yankee. Do tell, Colonel, do tell."

Ignoring Ewell, Smith knelt at the head of the map, across from Lee and careful not to block the cast of the lanterns, whose glass was under mad assault by moths.

"Sir, I rode across the army's front today. And beyond it. There's a natural line of defense, we'd just have to cut some trees in front of the batteries." He traced a finger along the map. "That old stage road to Ox Ford? It follows the line of a ridge that's better than any ground we've held since Mine Run. It rises from the rail line . . . just over here." He tapped the current position of Hill's Corps. "Then it slants northeast to the river, to Ox Ford. The high ground up there's a natural bulwark, absolutely commanding."

Guts in turmoil, Lee nodded. "I saw that ground myself. Go on."

"The bluff follows the river east for a half mile, then drops off toward the Chesterfield Bridge. But a spur runs southeast, back toward the rail line." He retraced the entire position, west to east.

"That's another damned salient," Ewell burst out. His voice squeaked, as it often did when the man grew excited. "Had enough of that at Spotsylvania."

Annoyed by the man, by his unthinking language and brashness, Lee felt the impulse to give him a public dressing-down. But Ewell was ill and this was no time for a rupture.

Lee signaled for Smith to resume.

Speaking even more carefully, the engineer said, "Of course, it *appears* to be something of a salient. General Ewell's correct, in that sense."

"Damned right I am."

"But there are other factors in play that render the position advantageous. This 'salient' has no vulnerable apex, no tip, but a half-mile wall of natural battlements towering over the river." The engineer sought Lee's eyes across the map. "A direct assault by the Federals at Ox Ford would be disastrous for them. And the legs of the position, stretching back to the railroad on both flanks, follow splendid terrain that begs fortification. Beyond, the rail embankment provides a base, extending our flanks."

Lee grasped the brilliance. "It splits their army in two! Should they rush forward. I see it, Colonel, I see it." Lee almost smiled. "We must conceal ourselves, our strength. And lure them to divide the wings of their army."

"Precisely, sir," Smith agreed. "It's Napoleon's 'strategy of the central position.'"

"Napoleon!" Ewell snorted. "Hah!"

Lee concentrated on his engineer. "Once they're across the river . . . by the time they discover what we're about . . . for one of their flanks to reinforce the other, those people will have to make *two* river crossings. And march several miles."

As more officers caught the vision, they crowded around the map. For a few bright minutes, Lee soared above all illness.

"If," he went on, "they reinforce Warren, passing another corps over the river on our left . . . a third corps would have to remain . . . at least two divisions of a corps . . . on the north bank to bind the wings of their army together. Any such force would be fixed in place and useless." Lee pointed at the tattered map. "That would leave a single corps exposed on our right, south of the river."

A major could not contain himself. "Hancock! We could trap Hancock!"

Porter Alexander put in, "Artillery can control the Chesterfield Bridge, keep off reinforcements."

"Or keep Hancock from getting away," Early said with bloodlust in his voice.

Anderson, whose corps held the center, added: "He'll be caught up in a vise. Whether he swings west, or heads straight south, don't hardly matter, once he's crossed that river. Either way, he comes up against entrenchments to his front. While we envelop him."

"Exactly!" Even Venable, a creature of worry this day, had grown excited.

"Gentlemen . . ." Lee considered rising, then decided the wiser course was to remain seated. "We must thank Colonel Smith for his diligence. I believe we see a way. Should matters develop as hoped . . . should it be the Lord's will . . . we may destroy the finest corps in the Union army tomorrow."

Eleven thirty p.m.
Grant's headquarters

Standing in the hallway, Grant said: "Well done, George. Compliments to Warren. Sixth Corps up?"

"Wright crosses at first light, over Warren's bridges." Cheap candles sputtered. "We'll have two corps over the river on our right well before noon. Really, it's going splendidly." Meade did not add, "For once."

Beyond the two men, who spoke privately, Grant's intimate staff had given up work for the evening and filled a shabby parlor. The westerners bantered over pipes and cigars, draining mugs of coffee. Grant's Red Indian, Parker, seemed to be the butt of ribald teasing about a woman.

"Hancock still not across?" Grant asked, tone sharpening.

"He's got the north end of the Chesterfield Bridge. Rebs tried to burn it. Birney drove them off."

"He had that bridge hours back. Why didn't he cross?"

"Guns across the river. And entrenchments. No good sense of how many Rebs are over there, in those trees. Win wants to have his entire corps up when he crosses. No sense going in piecemeal." He did not add, "Again."

"Missed opportunity, seems to me," Grant said.

"He's concerned about needless losses, the Confederates—"

"Missed opportunity," Grant repeated. "Just get him across in the morning. Lee's about beat. Can't let up on him now."

"Lee may not—"

"He's just about beat. Prisoners we bring in look like scarecrows. And those Negroes you sent up. Bill figures them for honest. Talked to 'em myself. Said Gordon's Division was on their master's land, but marching off south. Don't want Lee to slip away. If he isn't already gone."

"Hancock will cross in the morning, Sam. At the railroad bridge as well."

"Not like Hancock to get the slows."

"Every man in the army's exhausted. Win's a good judge of how hard he can push."

"Lee's men are worn out, too. Worse than ours, I'd reckon. Smash 'em up one more time, and put an end to things."

Meade found Grant unreasonable. Hancock had done the best he could by day's end, and Birney had performed brilliantly at the redoubt. But as for pushing across the river with twilight coming on . . . no one knew what was on the other side. And what the Negroes had to say was of interest, but they were Negroes, after all, and given to tale telling. He was sorry now that he had passed them on to Grant, after Hancock sent them up. He had thought Grant would be pleased at their news, however doubtful, but forgot Grant's impetuosity.

They were all so wickedly tired. Was anyone thinking clearly? The army had been either fighting or marching for three solid weeks. Privates and generals alike resembled ambulatory corpses.

Except for Grant, who seemed as robust as a bear.

"Regret our disagreement about the Pamunkey took a hard turn," Grant told his subordinate. "Figured Lee was going along this way, think I've got a sense of him. Now we just have to bag him."

Easier said than done, Meade thought. "Well, I'm glad to be proven wrong, if it means we can break Lee. I'd like to see an end to this."

"Something else to tell you," Grant said. "Order goes out tomorrow. Under my hand. Putting the Ninth Corps directly under the Army of the Potomac. Arrangement hasn't been working, it's all cockeyed."

"Sam, I . . . really, I *thank* you." Meade was surprised and flustered. And grateful. Even though the action was overdue. "I do think it's for the best, you know. It's going to improve coordination immeasurably. I'll treat General Burnside with tact, of course."

"Just keep it quiet until the order's issued. Oh, tell Humphreys, he needs to know. Nobody else. Don't want Burnside to hear it first as a rumor, get his back up. He'll put a good face on it, but he's going to feel raw." Grant yawned. He didn't cover his mouth. There were gaps in his back teeth. "Has his hands full. Getting his corps to Ox Ford. That's why I'm holding off until tomorrow. Let him take care of his business, see if he can get his men across the river. Before he gets his dose of salts."

"The heights are formidable. Along that stretch."

"Hardly Chickasaw Bluffs." Grant searched his pockets for a cigar and discovered a lone specimen. He looked at Meade. "Offer you one, but this here runt seems to be all I've got on my person. We'll see what Burnside has to say, come morning. Rebs may all be gone, wouldn't be surprised. Lee knows he's licked. Anything else?"

Meade had meant to complain about the lack of adequate cavalry to reconnoiter ahead of the army, but Grant's promised action on the Ninth Corps made him feel a complaint would be ungracious. Damn Sheridan, though. Damn the man. . . .

"Nothing pressing."

"Well," Grant said, "just get Hancock across that river

first thing. If Warren can brush away a Reb rear guard, I figure Win can. Then we'll see if we can't catch Bobby Lee."

Midnight
Right wing of the Army of Northern Virginia

Damnable. That was all the whole business was, plain damnable. Worn as a hard-whipped nigger and jacketed in filth, louse-bitten and flea-bitten, raw-crotched and all but moldering, Oates never had believed he would sink so low that he'd fall to thinking first not of fine woman-flesh, but of a bathtub like Colonel Toney's back home, with a stream of hop-to-it house niggers to carry up all the hot water a man could want. If he had taken proud care of his uniform in days past, he still would not have accused himself of being an overly tidy man, no, there never had been one hint of highborn fussiness about him, but, by God, for a man to smell himself stinking twice worse than the lowest riverbank hoor run out of Natchez, to scratch himself bloody and curse himself breathless and still go on feeding half the insect population of Virginia with his person, it was just a damned shame. And his men were worse by a drunken grocer's measure.

Did anybody on high know what they were doing? Even Evander Law, back in command of the brigade, could not make sense of things and just repeated, "Do like I said. Picking sores don't help. You do like I told you, the mighty on high have spoken."

And he had done it, was doing it, dragging his men along by force of will, men who had been promised one day of rest at last, maybe even a quick hussy's wash, only to be rousted early and marched back to the ground above the river, looking at that railroad bridge and just knowing it was meant to carry trouble, just looking at it a time, exhausted already, then stripping down and digging entrenchments as ordered, to keep off Yankees still not visible, and they had dug like rabid corpses, if rabid corpses could dig, because the one damned thing they had learned that was of any use was that digging hard meant living, and even rabid corpses wanted to live, he expected.

The Yankees had come, all right. In the afternoon. Poking around, like kids fussing at a snake hole with long sticks, but they hadn't gotten up to much, no doubt worn hard themselves, and even their cannon seemed lazy when they fired. The heat and the waiting were a trial in themselves, though, and then a narrow squall swept down upon them, bringing not only rain that stank of bad soil, but an eruption of battle sounds just up the river, where another bridge had been defended by a mud fort too small to be anything but a temptation to an enemy. He imagined he heard cheers, maybe didn't, but in his mind they were not the sound of his people, his blood, no, they were hideous in their joy, even if unreal, the product of an exhausted delirium, and then the cannon directly across the river got in a temper and plowed shells into the general area of his men's entrenchment, and two of his boys, cousins from the backcountry, from dead clay country all chiggers and cottonmouths, maybe a rattler or two, those black-toothed, toothless, happy-to-stink-like-dogshit sonsofbitches just started pounding each other with their never-once-washed fists, and they could fight, those two, probably nary a thing to do but fight back in those weed-starving wastes that spawned them, unless a man fucked whatever four-legged half-female thing he could corner in the never-completed, falling-down barn he was doomed to inherit, taking his furtive pleasure with beasts until he found himself a gal distasteful as his own flesh, a gal from identical, poorer-than-poor-white fields, for no town slut nor even a tinker's wife would accept his seed for money, not even a gold piece, and those two damned roughs, fine Yankee killers, give them that, tumbled out of the ditch they had dug, slamming into one another's meat and splashing blood to the sky, with those Yankee shells bursting reliably on every side, well-fused shells, not like the monkeyed-up rounds his forlorn excuse for a stillborn, goddamned, I'll-fight-for-it-damn-you nation sent to its own ramrod-buggered artillerymen, no, fine shells these were, just pounding God's own earth, or somebody's, since God, if he existed—which Oates would not believe—was unlike to be bothered with such a forlorn place and men grown unrecognizable as a species, and Oates leapt out after them, bigger than either man or boy, call them as you will, bigger than both of them put together, putting on his black-bearded devil face, and he collared one, hurled him back in the trench, then heaved the other after him, catching him in flight with an artful kick. They had been fighting over the color of a dress each said he would buy for a woman they had created from nothing but untutored, cow-fuck thoughts.

And for whatever monstrous reason, nature itself had turned on him, not with the rain, which was no better or worse than everything else in this no-God, godforsaken life, but with a trick of memory, the violent cousinship of those two conjuring a dreadful matter, the worst memory of Oates' life, his grave shame, his greatest shame, the one memory still more painful than that of leaving his younger brother behind, dying on that slope in Pennsylvania, and he wrestled it down, tightening his fists as if he could strangle the past, going at the memory the way a man goes at a bear that means to kill him.

John!

Battling the memory of his shame, immense and beyond all remedy, he had said, roughly, loudly, to all present:

"Only good day I've had this here month was when the Yankees up and left Spotsylvania. Wasn't that a time?"

"Surely, Cunnel," a crust-faced, pustule-badged sergeant said. "That there was a time." He glanced toward the railroad bridge. "Wouldn't mind another such."

When the Yankees, after a last fool's assault, or attempt at one—for they soon quit—had drawn off in the night, leaving behind not only their dead to be plundered, but treasures they merely declined to carry off, too lazy to husband what was theirs, how could such men ever beat his boys, how had they tricked them to drive them here, so much closer to Richmond? But none of that, choose the sweet memory bubbling like molasses in a pot, the picturesque orgy of his men unleashed, for a precious half hour, from the trench that had confined them for ten days—or was it more?—and they had begun by stripping haversacks from rotting Yankee bodies to their front, their stink no worse, or hardly worse, than the living men who robbed them, and motive skeletons gnawed rancid bacon, its scent grown indistinguishable from the putrid meat of man that had shielded it from the sun but not the maggots, what a feast they had! And in the abandoned lines themselves, full knapsacks waited, and barrels of crackers not half-devoured, and, in one leather bag, a fancy set of woman's underwear, which no man could explain, but a gleeful soldier pulled on the frillies, prancing for all to see, until Oates told him, Stop that nonsense, boy, gather up some eats, then take up all the cartridges you can find, that's good Yankee powder. And men who had gorged on rotten food with alacrity and joy shit themselves half-dead, then ate the rest of the provisions they had looted, such was the way of things.

The Yankees never did come over that bridge all the just-gone evening, but only fired their cannon wastefully, spitefully, not so much as marking one of his men, barely sprinkling them with dirt, for they had learned to dig and dig, indeed, and Oates judged they could have held that position and that bridge and done a plenty of killing, but in the first dark the unaccountable order had come down to withdraw from the fortress they had made of the hillside, to just quit that fine ground, and they had followed another regiment back to a railroad embankment, every man on the verge of fall-flat sleep at every step, only to be told: You come too far, go on back, maybe a third of the way, staff man there to guide you, sure enough, how did you miss him? And with midnight coming on, his still damp, filthy, rain-can't-wash-this-off, weary-beyond-all-saying men had been told to dig new entrenchments, because, first light, the Yankees were expected to cross the river they had just abandoned, and day must not find the Army of Northern Virginia unprepared. Oates half expected a mutiny, but the men were too tired for that, emotions duller than their work-numbed limbs. He asked about rations and was told, "Tomorrow."

So his men dug, and chopped, and built in the darkness, men reduced to wires where fine muscles once had been, swinging axes fearsomely in the black Virginia night, while, to the north, the Yankees kept on pounding the emptied entrenchments, as if they meant to sink Virginia like a goddamned ship.

He bit the inside meat of his cheeks until he tasted blood. Forcing himself to stay awake with his men. He might have murdered a child for a cup of coffee.

And the memory attacked in the darkness, in Hell's own darkness, brimstone black. The shame of Cain, redoubled because of the terrible innocence exploited, violated, savaged, fell upon him again, and he wished to flee, but there was no place to hide, not from this guilt. That gut-cutting, heart-stabbing remembrance was the only thing that might, one day, drive him to violate the oath he had taken for his mother's sake never to touch a drop of liquor of any kind. The memory was that bad, though he could not even recall what he had done on that hot and dreadful day— thought now that it had to do with the hogs, or maybe a gate left unlatched—but the doing of it had set his father off like nothing before. He had been nine, ten, John younger by a speck of years, and his father had not slapped him nor wielded his belt, not this time. The big man had gone at him with his fists, knocking him down, demanding that he get back up, and knocking him down again, drawing blood and setting teeth a-wobble. Unsatisfied, his father took up a plank and slammed it across his broadening boy's shoulders, twice, and when he would not, or could not, rise again, kicked him and cursed him mightily. For the first and last time in his uncertain life he begged his father to stop, broken to crying out, uselessly, for his mother, who loved him but would not interfere in this male domain, not even had he been beaten unto death. He cried and pleaded, hurt beyond shame, but his father just brought that board down on him a third time.

"It weren't me!" he cried at last. "It was John, it was him that done it!"

And his father, heaving breath like a rutting bull, had growled, just once, and said, "Get up, you pisser," yanking him to his feet, which he could barely keep.

Through a not-yet-closed, blood-filmed eye, he had seen John standing maybe ten feet off, just standing there like the damnedest fool in creation.

His fathered beckoned his younger son to approach. John did as commanded. And his father asked, "That true, boy? You the one done it?"

John had looked not at his father then, nor at the board raised half-high, but at Oates. And his brother's expression had been not of anger seething, nor even of disappointment, but a nearly blank, ravishingly gentle look that might have been last seen on the face of Jesus Christ himself up on the cross, a look that just said, *Well, the world is just this way, and I can't help it no more than you can, neither.*

And John said, "Yes, sir. I done it."

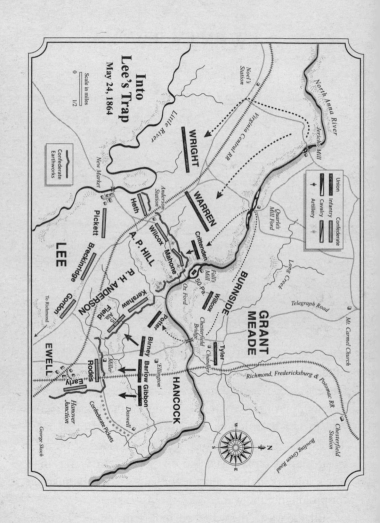

TWENTY-TWO

May 24, nine thirty a.m.
Ellington House, on the North Anna River

A piratical-looking darkey claimed that Lee had sat on the porch of the once proud house the day before. The notion pleased Hancock. Lee had quit the river line, instead of fighting. That wasn't the Lee of old. The match truly might be moving to a close.

The first men over had ravaged the house, which had been a goodly place. The owner had fled in haste and, squandering not a moment, soldiers had torn up floorboards, hurled china and pictures about, smashed a rosewood piano, and tossed books from a library into the hallway and beyond. Riding up, Hancock had encountered two delighted stragglers, one cuddling a ham, the other fumbling as he balanced an ambitious stack of books. Once, Hancock would have had such looters arrested, to say nothing of those who had wrecked the house for the raw joy of destruction. But things were different now. This was war to the death. The South needed to be punished until it broke. And the civilians were worse than Lee's soldiers in their appetite for hatred, their enthusiasm for prolonging the war.

Still, the waste, the waste. All of it. This house. The lives. A country put to the rack, tortured for a dozen and more political heresies. Behind his bold exterior, another Hancock kept minute accounts. Even now, as he justified it, waste troubled him. He deplored the loss of even little things, of a shirt or a collar stud. The Army, he thought, really should have made him a quartermaster.

"Here," he said to Colonel Morgan. "Send this to George Meade. It'll keep Grant off his back for an hour or two."

The chief of staff took the message and carried it out to the knot of couriers gathered in the shade. The day was already stinking hot, and humid from the past evening's burst of rain. Hancock had indulged in a cup of iced water, then a second and third, after his headquarters cavalry broke into the plantation's icehouse. He had reveled in the treat like a child given candy. Simple things were enormous pleasures now.

He had even run out of clean shirts, his cherished indulgence.

Morgan came back in. "Goddamn it, there's no discipline anymore. I had to chase off two sonsofbitches breaking windows for the Hell of it. And they wanted to know who *I* was."

Hancock snorted. "I'm not far shy of breaking windows myself."

The colonel looked at him.

"I know, I know," Hancock said. "Everything's going fine. Birney's across, Gibbon's crossing, Barlow's on the way." He smiled. "Thought he was going to chase me with that great butcher's knife of his, when I detached Miles."

Morgan cocked an eyebrow: *And?*

"It's not the damned leg, Charlie," Hancock told him. "That's all right today." He shook his head, wishing for still more iced water. "Sometimes I think a man can only take so much of this. Before the killing starts to seem pure murder." He laughed. "Bugger a monkey, you know I used to think there was glory in it?" He laughed again, the bitterness level rising. " 'Hancock the Superb'! That's me, you know. Proud as a pissing peacock." He lifted a heavy arm and gestured southward. "Now I just want to beat them all to death, crush skulls with a rock."

Morgan appeared bewildered by the outburst, a display hardly characteristic of their relationship.

Hancock's smile faded from bitter to sour. "I know I'm contradicting myself. Man is a contradictory beast, Charlie. Delighted to kill, and repulsed by it. Proud, but ashamed." He cocked an eyebrow and ran a hand over his roughly shaven chin. "How are we supposed to master our enemies, when we can't even master ourselves? Or at least be honest about what beasts we are?" He gestured at the wreckage of the parlor, the toppled piano. "You know, this doesn't even make me angry? Year ago, I would have been in a fury. But I just can't be self-righteous anymore. Why should we give a shit-pot damn about property, when men are dying by the tens of thousands? What are *they* worth? Weigh a man against a Chesterfield sofa, and war tips the scales in favor of the furniture. Whole damned war was cried up over property—in the case of our gray-backed brethren, a few million coons. So why should we spare a parlor? If we're going to take revenge, why not on property? And spare the lives of those poor bastards out there? Christ, if I were in their shoes, I'd be smashing things up myself." He snorted. "Wife would take a stick to me, though, if she saw a mess like this. She'd know the price of everything in this house."

"Sleep all right, sir?"

"Like a baby just off the tit. It isn't lack of sleep. Charlie, I feel like a prisoner serving a sentence, not that august general in the newspapers. Not sure I even know that fellow." He turned up one side of his mouth. "Of course, a prisoner knows how long his sentence will run. Us? We'll just keep on killing. Until the war just stops like a wind-up toy." His bitter smile returned. "That day may break Frank Barlow's heart, but it surely won't break mine."

"Yes, sir."

Hancock snorted again. "I suppose I should shut my damned mouth and command my corps. At least pretend I'm still a fervent believer in our glorious cause." He leaned in toward his chief of staff and his voice grew earnest. "Charlie, what do the captains think these days? What are *they* saying? Or the privates? Do *you* have any idea? I used to think I knew my men. But now . . ."

"There's a sentiment in the army," Morgan said, "that Lee's really whipped this time. Might be something to it. Look how easily we got across this morning." A cannon boomed, then another, from the south. The firing had been intermittent since daybreak, annoying but hardly menacing. The chief of staff glanced toward the distant guns. "Not exactly the barrage at Gettysburg. Lee can barely field a proper rear guard."

Hancock narrowed his eyes. "You really believe that?"

"I *want* to believe it. For now, I'm content with what Birney and Gibbon report. Nothing but skirmishers, a few goddamned sharpshooters, and a rifle pit here and there."

In the depths of the house, a soldier began to sing "The Rose of Tralee." He sounded as though he had found the absent householder's hidden whiskey.

"All right," Hancock said. "That's enough. Get the provost's boys to clear them all out and clean up this Irishman's breakfast. We'll keep our headquarters here. Until we find out if Bobby Lee's really bolted."

"Anything else, sir?"

"Message get off to Burnside? About tying in?"

"Sent it myself."

"Good. Otherwise . . . just keep them all moving forward. But no recklessness. I don't want things to spin out of hand before I've got the whole corps this side of the river."

"Barlow's just waiting for Gibbon to clear his bridge. There's a second bridge going in down there as well."

"Well, I'm going to sit on my ass for a few minutes. Try to make sense of the things I'm paid to look after." He glanced at the wanton devastation again. "Help me right that sofa? I wonder, if our noble American public could see us now, just how superb they'd think me? Wouldn't it be a tickle, if *Harper's* published an engraving of something like this? 'Another Triumph of Our Gallant Troops!' " He smiled, genuinely this time. "I hope my tender sentiments haven't disconcerted you. Take that end."

The chief of staff bent to the labor and they heaved. The sofa landed upright. Someone had taken a blade to the upholstery.

Not so long before, Hancock would have manhandled the piece of furniture himself. But between his wounds and his waistline, it seemed wiser to ask for help. Didn't shame him, just stuck in his craw a bit.

"Well, I won't subject you to any further reveries," he promised the chief of staff. "All of that's just pissing in the wind."

"It's the goddamned iced water," Morgan told him. "Addles the brain. It's enough to cause convulsions, in this heat. Next time you want a drink, sir, I'll have them serve it hot and stir in salts. Give you the shits instead. Lesser of two evils, compared to philosophy."

He was a wonderfully hard man, Morgan, a fighting chief of staff.

"Before you go," Hancock said, "tell me one thing honestly, Charlie. What in the name of Christ are *you* going to do when this blissful little war of ours is over?"

Morgan didn't hesitate. "Diddle every willing woman in Pennsylvania, Delaware, and New Jersey. Then head west."

Ten a.m.
Headquarters, Third Corps,
Army of Northern Virginia

General Hill, *why* did you let those people cross here?"
Lee's voice carried so much venom it confounded him. But
his loss of self-control only angered him further. "Why
didn't you throw your whole force on them? And drive them
back? As Jackson would have done?"

Red-faced and silent, Hill offered no excuses. But he
fidgeted. Straining to master a hot temper of his own. Lee
understood, and the corps commander's forbearance
kindled his anger again.

"And your lines, sir!" Lee renewed his tirade. "Generals Anderson and Ewell have followed my orders to the letter. Your entrenchments are slovenly, your guns ill sited!
What can I expect of you?"

Maintaining control of his voice as best he could, Hill
said, "You may expect, General Lee, that I will hold this
line against any force Meade and Grant can send against
me."

"Easily said. But you could not hold that ford against a
detachment of . . . of brigands."

Hill did not reply, but looked to the side. Lee thought
the man's eyes glistened. Whether from rage contained or
humiliation.

Lee knew with every word he was being unfair. Hill's
lines were every bit as well developed as those of Ewell or
Anderson. Better, perhaps. And if Hill had performed disappointingly the day before, had he not told the corps
commander to keep his men in camp?

Reason is the weakest human faculty.

Bowels in torment, Lee added, "I will not tolerate failure today, sir. You may face two Federal corps, perhaps

part of a third. And if you do not hold them, you will not return to this army."

After a delay of several seconds, of lengthy seconds, Hill blinked his eyelids fiercely and nodded.

"I will hold this line, General Lee."

A lightning bolt of pain tore through Lee's abdomen. He flinched, but remained erect.

"Do not disappoint me," he said, and turned away.

Every step back toward the carriage required a struggle. To stay upright, to remain master of his innards, to restrain himself from shouting out his fury at all his misfortunes. He had begun the morning determined that his health was on the mend and had forced himself to breakfast with Ewell and Anderson, then to conduct a long inspection of their lines. But his progress had been interrupted by the frequent stops required by his debility. Now he felt himself on the verge of collapse, the heat weighing on him like a physical burden.

Venable walked beside him, ready to assist, should Lee need help.

"Let us not make a spectacle," Lee snapped.

"Yes, sir." Venable hesitated, then went on. "If you need to use the privy, I know where it is."

"*Not here.* We will drive some distance away."

The aide's doubt was palpable.

Lee *ordered* himself not to be sick. Not today. He must not be ill. With a great victory not only possible, but probable. He got himself into the carriage, but felt an appalling wetness when he sat.

Soldiers watched him, seeing only what they chose to see, needed to see. Robert E. Lee. Their idol, their hero, their father by proxy. A father who sent them to their deaths in myriads.

Tears crowded Lee's eyes now. Not at the thought of soldiers lost, or of the losses to come, but because his belly urged him to cast himself down and ball up like an infant. Sweat sheathed him.

He gestured for Walter Taylor to ride close to the side of the carriage. Not Venable, who understood too much.

The dust-caked officer edged as close to the buggy's wheels as his horse dared go.

Did all of them know how sick he was? Able to control neither bowels nor temper? His head had to remain clear, that was the thing. He had to be able to *think*. That would be enough.

The blue sky quivered.

"Back," Lee said. "The shortest way."

Taylor understood, but still said, "To headquarters, sir?"

"Where else?" Lee snapped. His tone carried the force of the profanities he never uttered.

The ride was interminable, with desultory artillery fire and the *pop-pop* of skirmishing in the distance. Lee closed his eyes and clutched himself, hoping his visage might pass for one deep in thought.

He prayed. Nakedly, selfishly. To be allowed this day, to be granted a modicum of good health and clarity of mind, until he had completed the task at hand.

He meant to tell his party to stop, but realized it was too late.

At last, Venable and Taylor helped him down and kept him upright until he reached his tent. Released by one man but not the other, he staggered and almost fell. The heat in the tent seemed colossal. Yet, it was a private place. A hot, private place. It smelled, stank.

"Leave me," he said.

He caught their doubtful expressions.

"Leave me."

One following the other, his self-appointed guardians went out. Did they believe they were his masters now?

He felt shame. He had done wrong. What had he done wrong?

He needed the slops bucket. Undoing himself as best he could, he strained to lower himself and maintain his balance. Needs but half-satisfied, he lost his equilibrium and sat down hard, upsetting the bucket as he collapsed to the ground.

Eleven a.m.
Ox Ford

No good, no good. Why was he always given the nasty work? Look at that, look at that. Cliffs must be two hundred feet tall, if an inch. Cross the river? Here? They'd cut his men down like a scythe. Then what, then what? Even those who got across could not get up that bluff. The guns, the guns. Rebels knew. Of course they knew. How did they know? He couldn't say. But they always seemed to know. Where he was, what he was to do. As if they had been told it all by his enemies.

Major General Ambrose Burnside tried not to make enemies. Did a good job, too. Overall, overall. Always exceptions. Beastly Meade. What if the rumors were true? Meade his junior on the Army rolls. Wouldn't want the job, of course. Thankless, thankless. He had done all he could do at Fredericksburg, and did it help him? No, no. Criticism, mockery. Now this. Get across the river? Not here, not here. Look at those bluffs. Rebs thick as lice on a Chinaman. Up there, up there. Nothing to be done.

Had to do something. What, what?

"Really, this is impossible," he said, lowering his field glasses. "What's the news, what's the news?"

His nearest aide said, "We're across at Quarles's Mill.

A few men, at least. Detachment from Warren's already up there."

"Why didn't you tell me? Why wasn't I told?"

"Dispatch just came in, sir. Didn't want to disturb you, you looked deep in thought."

"Indeed, indeed. Strategy! Think things through. Never act rashly, Major, never rashly. No good ever comes of it."

"Hancock wants to know why we haven't tied in with him," the major added.

Burnside felt a quizzical expression overtake his face. "Why haven't we?"

"Confederates, sir."

"Nonsense. Headquarters says they're all gone."

"Well, sir, there seems to be a plenty of them up there on those bluffs."

"Rear guard. Grant himself believes Lee's fled the field, simply fled."

Grant, Grant. Would he really subordinate the Ninth Corps to that impossible grampus Meade? The shame of it. Mustn't be rash, though. No need to make enemies. Count on Washington. Safe as a babe in the cradle on that flank. How many years was Meade behind him on the Army rolls?

"Must do something," he told the small assembly gathered about him. "Inactivity will not be excused. General Grant expects our corps to shine."

True? Doubtful, very doubtful. Anyway, he had to show Grant he was a horse that could run. Warren across the river, and Wright. Now Hancock. And here he was, facing a bluff more forbidding than anything he had faced at Fredericksburg. And that had been bad, impossibly bad. Were they making a fool of him? Was it a plot? Why did he always draw the wretched ground?

"Must do something," he repeated.

"Sir, we might begin crossing at Quarles's Mill, upstream. Now that we're tied in with Warren. We could get a division over, maybe turn the Rebs out of their position." The aide gestured toward the forbidding heights.

"What division? Whose division?"

"Ledlie's well positioned."

"Ledlie? Oh, Ledlie. At Quarles's Mill?"

"Or a division could follow Hancock. Down the Telegraph Road. Turn the Rebs from the left."

Follow Hancock? Why was he always behind Hancock? Or behind somebody, anybody? Were they all conspiring against him? Well, he could conspire, too. They wouldn't dare relieve him. Not until the election, that much was clear.

But reassigned? How would that look? He had expected better of Grant, elementary courtesy, a modicum of respect for a man of experience. Grant, a sullied upstart with a wastrel past. Lincoln had made the grubby fellow a king, a veritable emperor of the armies. Letting him lord it over upright men, men of position, sensible men.

Was subordinating the Ninth Corps to the Army of the Potomac to be the start of his humiliation, his degradation? Ghastly to think the rumor might be true. And what about Ledlie? Dubious creature, new to division command. Man of connections, though. Powerful backing from his political faction. Risk it, should he risk it?

"Do something," he said.

"Sir . . . there's an island down in that creek. Just below the bluffs. We might outpost it. See how the Johnnies react."

Excellent idea! He had not seen the island. No matter, no matter. Outpost it! Show them all that Ambrose Burnside would not be cowed by a few obstinate Confederates.

More than a few of them up on that high ground, though.

No matter, no matter.

"In your best judgment," Burnside asked his foremost engineer, "how many men will this isle accommodate?"

The engineer shrugged. "Haven't seen it myself. Suppose I ought to go down there."

The officer who had raised the matter said, "Start with a regiment. See what happens."

Indeed, indeed. They couldn't claim he was sitting idle then.

"Who's closest? I want a regiment on that island."

Noon
Headquarters, Army of the Potomac and
the general in chief, Carmel Church

Meade exploded. In front of dozens of staff men and hangers-on, he spoke directly to Grant: "Sir, I consider that dispatch an insult to the army I command, and to me personally. General Sherman knows nothing of this army or its accomplishments." He stepped toward the general in chief as if to do him violence, but brought himself up short. He did not lower his voice or soften its tone, though. "The Army of the Potomac does *not* require General Grant's inspiration—or anybody else's inspiration—to make it fight. General Sherman's armed rabble might suffice for Georgia, but the man has never faced Robert E. Lee."

When the raw concussion of the outburst had faded, leaving an enormous silence, Grant found his way to a dubious smile and said, "Sherman does have a knack for pulling the trigger before he's measured his target. It's just his way, General Meade. Let's go a volley, then regrets it later." His smile deepened. "Like your General Griffin."

Meade straightened his back and lifted his chin. "Sir, that is an official dispatch. It will enter the department's records." He turned to face the man who had read it aloud. Dana wasn't sorry one bit: He looked like a gloating undertaker. "And it was dispiriting that it should be read publicly."

"Well, now," Grant said, "I can't rightly speak for Mr. Dana there. But as the assistant secretary of war, I reckon he outranks us and can do about as he pleases. Probably didn't even know what was in that dispatch before he got started. Did you, Charlie?"

Dana's grin tightened into a smirk.

"I demand an apology," Meade said. "A *formal* apology. From Sherman, at the very least. This army has performed with . . . with sacrificial bravery. And has suffered unprecedented casualties as a result."

"Well, we'll have to see." And just like that, Grant dismissed the matter, turning to the just arrived Captain Wadsworth to ask, with clear delight, "How soon did you say Sheridan would get here?"

Meade left the church, exchanging its dead heat for the vivid sun. He tried to march off nobly, but felt he must look like a skulker.

How dare they? How dare Grant? Not twelve hours before, Meade had hoped their relationship, strained though it had become, was on the mend, given Grant's promise to resubordinate the Ninth Corps. Now this. It was intolerable, insufferable. Obviously, Sherman—rumored to be half-mad, at the very least—had not laid eyes on the army's casualty rolls: ". . . if Grant could inspire the Army of the Potomac to do a proper degree of fighting . . ." What had the Wilderness been? A cotillion? And the nearly two weeks of slaughter at Spotsylvania? Did that count for nothing? While Sherman engaged in *faux* maneuvers, a mere ballet, with old Joe Johnston? That redheaded ass might as well have drained his kidneys on the graves of the men who had fallen between the Rapidan and the North Anna.

And Sheridan! When young Wadsworth rode in and announced the vile little Irishman's impending return to the army, after his extended absence on his vainglorious cavalcade, Grant had perked up like a hound at his master's footsteps. Grant, who rarely engaged in profanity! What did he see in the filth spewed by that beastly little cretin, a man born to dig ditches and strutting about like some saloon Napoleon?

When the newspapers that reached the camp weren't full of praise for Grant, they printed flamboyant nonsense about Sheridan. It was as if the Army of the Potomac had nothing to its credit worth the ink. Oh, Hancock might get a mention here and there. But everything else was Grant and Sheridan, Sheridan and Grant. The situation was infamous.

If it would not have been unmanly to do so in midcampaign, he would have offered Grant his resignation. He had *wanted* to like Grant, done all he could to get along with the fellow. Now he wondered if he should not have resisted more firmly as Grant slaughtered a third of the army in his impulsive assaults. Had he betrayed the men whose command he cherished? Had he allowed himself to become a mere dogsbody?

Grant's front-porch demeanor masked an astounding capacity for cruelty. Meade had noted—many had—the man's distaste for the wounded or even for beef left pink by the headquarters cook, but the modest speech and slumping shoulders masked the iron willfulness of a Caesar.

Did Grant recognize its full extent himself? There were times when the man seemed a husk, emptied of substance. Judged plain at a first encounter, he masked wrath in homespun whispers and grew more indecipherable by the day.

And still Meade wished they might forge a cordial partnership. Even be friends.

What could Grant see in a snake like Sheridan?

Trembling with fury and wounded in spirit, even vaguely fearful, Meade paused in a stand of scrub pines that had been abused by passing soldiers. Amid the reeking evidence of man, he stood until he composed himself.

As he walked back toward the church, where shutters laid over pews served as headquarters desks, Humphreys intercepted him.

"George? I thought you might like to know . . . Hancock still reports nothing but skirmishing parties and stragglers to his front. And Warren's probing forward. It looks as though we may have got off on the cheap."

"Burnside?"

Humphreys' expression grew quizzical. "Can't make sense of the man. Writes those florid dispatches to Grant, all equivocation and obfuscation. I used to think he was being clever, now I'm convinced he doesn't know his own mind." The chief of staff tossed his hands in the air. "I *think* he's across the river at Quarles's Mill. But most of his force seems to be stuck at Ox Ford."

"I told Grant the site was impossible," Meade said.

Humphreys paused, then said, "I'm beginning to think you can't tell Sam Grant anything."

Still seething, Meade said, "I don't care if Lee's halfway to Richmond by now. I *still* believe we should have crossed the Pamunkey. You're an engineer, Humph. You know that I was right."

After delaying his reply by a few breaths, Humphreys said, "George, you're a better man than any of them. But you have to act like one."

Two p.m.
Ox Ford

First Sergeant Charles Brown said, "Just keep your heads down, damn it."

The remnants of the 50th Pennsylvania clung to the

earth, doing their best to hide in the island's foliage. Two men had already been wounded from Company C, and Brown did not intend to lose any others, if he could help it. He only prayed that no idiot with shoulder straps was going to order an assault across the second channel and up those impossible banks.

The men had lain in the mud for over an hour as sharpshooters, perched high above them, aimed at disturbed leaves or moving branches. The only advantage Brown saw in the position was that the Johnnies could not tilt their artillery muzzles low enough to rake the island with canister.

"Now ain't this one great, big *verfluchte Dummheit*?" Isaac Eckert asked all within hearing. "I suppose they sent us out here 'chust for nice.' Any man can see the sense of it, *sag' mal.*"

"Next time you see him, ask General Burnside," Brown told him.

"I'm growing so minded, First Sergeant. Just give me permission to go on back right now."

Brown laughed despite himself. He was almost starting to like Isaac, who had slipped into Bill Wildermuth's old role.

"I've noticed," Brown said, "you get to talking Dutchie when you're scared."

Isaac guffawed. "That was true, First Sergeant, you wouldn't hear anything else but Dutch come out my mouth."

Somebody crashed through the bushes. Lieutenant Brumm dropped beside him.

"Any news, sir?"

"Nothing. I don't know if they've forgotten us, or if we're part of some grand scheme I haven't the sense to figure. All Captain Schwenk knows is that he was ordered to take the regiment out here and wait."

"Like I been saying," Isaac put in. The two men ignored him.

Brown lowered his voice so that only Brumm could hear. "Think they're going to order us up that bluff?"

Brumm, whose face wore an ugly rash, said, "Brownie, I don't know any more than you do. And poor Schwenk's still figuring out how to run a regiment. Or what's left of one. All I can think is we're here to hold the Rebs' attention. While a crossing goes on someplace else."

Isaac Eckert, who had inched closer when the voices dropped, said, "Wouldn't mind letting somebody else take a turn at holding Lee's attention. Seems we've been doing a fair amount of that."

A flurry of shots probed the greenery.

"Stay down!" Brown called again. "Piss your pants, but nobody moves an inch." In a lower tone, he told Brumm, "If they order us forward, let me slip ahead and size things up. You know how rivers cut under the banks at spots like this. Hard to get up, even when no one's trying his best to kill you."

Brumm said: "No. I can't afford to lose you." Another swarm of shots bit through the leaves above them, around them, behind them. No man cried out, a small blessing.

Close enough for Brown to smell him, Brumm mused, "I do miss Henry. He's the man I would've sent. Not that I would've cared to risk him, either. Just always thought he had some kind of magic charm, doing all he did and never getting so much as a nick. That stunt you two pulled back there in the Wilderness."

Brown said nothing.

Brumm went on: "I suppose you miss him. You seemed close."

"Yeah."

"Good man, Hill."

"I'm glad he's out of this," Brown said. "I suppose they'll send him back, when he's healed up. But maybe the worst will be over by then."

"With leg wounds, you never know."

"He'll be back. He's that way."

"Well, he'll have a sergeant's stripes, when he does."

"He won't want them."

"I don't care. He'll wear them, because I'll make him. Just like I made him put on those corporal's stripes." Smiling, Brumm patted Brown's shoulder. "Remember how *you* didn't—"

One shot and a small thud. Brumm groaned, rolled sideward.

"Sonofabitch," the lieutenant muttered.

Brown scrambled over the endless inches to where the company commander lay on his back, rolling from side to side and clutching himself near the collarbone.

"Jesus," Brumm said. *"Jesus . . ."*

"Isaac! Pick a man and get the lieutenant out of here."

"They'll shoot us down, second we try to move."

"He's bleeding a river. Get moving."

"I'm all right," Brumm insisted. "I can . . . get back on my own." His face wore a constant grimace of pain. There was too much blood.

Brown felt along the pierced wet cloth.

The lieutenant jerked and cried out. Brumm was a hard one, tough as they came, and Brown could only figure the wound hurt like blazes. You just never knew. A man might not feel a blown-off leg, but suffer agony over a grazed elbow.

More bullets punched into their muddy jungle.

Brown and Isaac Eckert tugged the lieutenant forward to a sitting position, then got him to his knees. In a burst of movement, Isaac hauled Brumm to his feet and thrashed off with him, asking no other assistance.

"Don't count on me rushing back, First Sergeant," he called over his shoulder.

"The rest of you just stay down!" Brown roared. "It's not a damned minstrel show."

He regretted his increasingly frequent use of profanity. Frances didn't approve of undignified speech.

But Frances wasn't here, and these men were.

He was going to miss Brumm. He missed so many men now. He wondered how Doudle was doing in captivity, if he really had been sent to Andersonville. But Henry . . . he missed Henry Hill above all others, hoping, nonetheless, that his wound would be just bad enough to keep him out of the war for the duration. Which rumor held might end in weeks, even days. As bad as things had been, most of the soldiers Brown encountered agreed that the Rebs had gotten the worst of it.

Which was little consolation at the moment. If the regiment was ordered to assault across the second channel and go up that bluff, it was going to be the Wilderness and Spotsylvania both tossed in one sack for the men engaged.

He truly was glad that Henry wasn't present.

After all the wild ordeals they had gone through together, Henry's wounding had been empty of drama, almost trivial. Near the end of the last assault at Spotsylvania, the 50th had been ordered forward to make a charge. But before they stepped off for the assault, the order had come to halt in place. The day's attacks were over. Just then, Henry had staggered, as if he had stumbled over a hidden rock. Jigging a few steps forward from the line, he seemed unable to control one of his legs. He didn't utter a sound.

In moments, Henry had mastered himself, turned around, and started back, using his rifle as a crutch, with blood shining through the fingers he pressed to his thigh. Brown had rushed forward to help him, but stopped short. Other men, lower in rank, had stepped up to assist Henry to the rear, and Brown had greater duties to perform. They had not had time to exchange a word, and by the time the 50th returned to what passed for a camp, Henry had been taken off in an ambulance wagon. He had just put on his corporal's chevrons that morning.

Brown hoped, assumed, that his friend would keep his leg. He wanted him out of the war, not destroyed as a man.

Gathering himself, Brown rose to a crouch and dashed along the company line, chased by zipping bullets and the thud of rounds hitting wood. It wasn't a very long line these days.

He dropped beside Bill Hiney, who had been promoted from sergeant to lieutenant the year before, moved to another company, then come back again.

"Brumm's been shot," Brown told him. Anticipating the question in Hiney's eyes, he added, "Collarbone, I think. Should be all right. Just bleeding like the dickens. Sent him back. With Isaac."

"If they don't get shot crossing back over the damned creek," Hiney said.

"You have the company now, sir."

"Brownie, can't you just call me 'Bill'? At least, when it's just the two of us?"

"Don't want to get in the habit."

Hiney shook his head. "Christ, I didn't want this."

"That's what everybody says," Brown told him.

Three thirty p.m.
Confederate lines

Give it to them! Pour it on!" Oates shouted.

And his men surely did. Yankees came on across a bare-ass field, cocksure, maybe even brave enough, overrunning his advanced rifle pits and those to left or right. The blue-bellies were out to do business, but seemed surprised when the 15th Alabama and the regiments to its flanks popped up from their entrenchments, the ditches a tad too much like stretched-long graves for Oates' predilection but good for keeping a dead-tired man alive when somebody lacking a ditch of his own had a mind to kill him.

Sun was Alabama hot, and they'd been allotted a stretch that lacked a well. Mouths so dry it felt like a man's whiskers were growing in, not outward.

The Yankees yelled and hollered, angry as chained dogs taunted by boys, cursing proud enough to be heard all the way to Montgomery, but they paused out there, thinking hard on what they'd come up against, firing steadily enough, even as their ranks broke into little groups, some of the men smart enough to kneel to fire, steadying those long, heavy barrels while making themselves as small as they could get.

"You're shooting like damned girls," Oates berated his soldiers, angry again for not much of a reason, if any reason at all. He was angry near all the time now. "Load faster, shoot truer. Damn it, Carter, you need me to load that shooting stick for you?"

His men were just worn out. But somehow they had reared up for the fight again. Never ceased to be a source of wonder how a man too tired to eat could rouse himself like a horned devil when the chance for killing came.

Yankees weren't quitting, but they surely were not getting the best of it, either. Dropping here and there. But they were veterans, those bluecoat sonsofbitches, see that much in how they handled themselves. Kept off at a fair range, not ready to be slaughtered outright, if they could help it. Waiting for some general to decide something or other.

Numbers were a good sight less than even, much in the Southron favor, it seemed to Oates. Yankee officers seemed uncertain, strutting around to confer behind their men, as if they had stumbled on something unexpected and were struggling to figure out whether it was a yellow dog or a rhinoceros. Fool could see that any one of the generals Oates and his fellow colonels answered to, any one of them with gumption, could order a counterattack to sweep from one flank right to the other. Scoop those suckers right up, killed, crippled, or captured, made no never mind.

"Passive." That was the word. For all the spilled-out bellies and brains, it seemed to Oates that things above the stand-up-and-shoot level had gone passive. As if the gold-braid generals had decided to have them a few rounds of poker and let things hang.

This here was a golden opportunity. And opportunities didn't last forever.

Oates noted that Major Lowther, who finally had seen fit to return to the regiment, kept himself low, clutching his hat to his head as if he could squeeze himself shorter. Man was worthless as a tramped-on turd, and harder to get rid of than the itch.

Billy Strickland came up on him, speaking a shared thought.

"Sir, why don't we just go on out there and get them? Bag 'em all, and call it a good day's hunting?"

"No damned orders," Oates said.

Five p.m.
Headquarters, Army of Northern Virginia

We must strike them a blow!" Lee cried out. Or believed he did. "Never let them pass us again. Strike them a blow!"

The tent was hot and fetid, the air funereal. The stink was worse than the slave quarters on an ill-managed plantation. What time was it? There was still time. There had to be. He had to rise. Couldn't. Try again.

He could not even raise his shoulders from the soiled cot.

"Strike them a blow!" he commanded.

Had Marshall come in? Where was Marshall? Taylor? Venable . . . Venable had made him sick with his attentions . . . terrible . . .

When he opened his eyes, they would not focus. When he closed them, the universe swirled, threatening to spin him into oblivion.

His body felt raw, as if scalded. He had begun to vomit, adding to his afflictions.

Doctors. No help. Not one of them.

Had to strike them a blow . . .

There was still time, he was certain.

If Longstreet . . .

In a lucid moment, he remembered someone begging him to give the order to attack, telling him those people were in disarray, vulnerable, unsuspecting. But even in his sickness, he had known that he dared not trust his army to Ewell, who was ill himself, or to Anderson, who lacked sufficient experience, or to Hill . . . who had let those people cross the river.

Only he could lead the army now. No one else. His army . . .

A face, two faces split from one, hovered over him. He closed his eyes to make them go away. So terrible they were, dreadful, a man split in two.

He knew that face. Did he not? Those faces . . .

"Did you call out, sir? General Lee, will you order the attack? We're running out of time, sir."

Lee tried to understand the words. He had heard them, heard each one distinctly, but they did not fit together.

"We must strike them a blow," he said. But he could not hear his voice.

Six p.m.
North of Hanover Junction

Barlow scribbled in the saddle:

> *Major General Hancock,*
> *The enemy is <u>not</u> withdrawing. He has entrenched. Re-*
> *sistance is sturdy. Prisoners report that Ewell's entire*
> *corps waits in our path. I do not think it wise to press*
> *the attack, unless to relieve pressure on Gibbon, and pre-*
> *fer to entrench at our forward-most positions.*
> > *Your obedient servant,*
> > > *F. C. Barlow*
> > > *Brigadier General*

"Black, take this to Hancock yourself. Wait for an answer. And I don't need a written order, if he's pressed."

The aide saluted, turned his mount, and applied the
spurs.

Ahead, the firing ebbed and flowed, stalemated for the
present. What on earth had possessed Meade or Grant or
any man to imagine the path to Richmond lay wide open?
Had they learned nothing over the past weeks? Of course
Lee was going to fight.

Bitten by the heat, he nudged his horse toward the cool-
ness of a stand of poplars. His retinue followed. After the
hard light of the slanting sun, the interior of the grove
seemed almost black. The heat was bad, but worse was
Hancock's insistence on forever using him as the corps reserve, only to strip away his brigades, one after the other.
First it had been Miles. Then Brooke. And now he had a
Confederate corps to his front, Ewell's men. The latest
batch of prisoners flushed from the skirmish line—
deserters, he suspected—were only too glad to blabber

about reinforcements Lee had received. One verminous creature had spoken of the arrival of Pickett from the south and Breckinridge from the Valley of Virginia. Even if only a quarter of what those scarecrows said was true, it meant Lee intended anything but retreat.

In fact, Barlow considered, it rather looked like they'd marched into a trap.

His feet itched terribly.

General Hancock says entrench, and do it fast," Black reported to Barlow. The aide had ridden madly and his horse was blown. "He believes Lee may attack at any time."

"I've already given the order," Barlow told him.

Seven p.m.
The Telegraph Road

Hancock stood on a low ridge, just steps from the road, peering through the dust-addled light with his field glasses. Nothing worth seeing. But enough to hear to keep him alert and short-tempered. Sporadic fighting, most of it out of view, annoyed the evening, and oncoming clouds threatened rain, which meant more mud and misery for the troops. Instead of easy progress, his corps had run into resistance across its front. Resistance and, he worried, serious peril.

Litter bearers lugged their burdens northward. Sweat-drenched and somber, the now silent bandsmen and medical orderlies stepped aside to clear the road as troops or guns rushed up, then resumed their journeys through the dust. Morgan had needed to send the ambulances rearward as shelling increased. The Chesterfield Bridge was under constant fire now, another surprising development. The only consolation was that Burnside had at last tied in to his flank, so Lee wasn't going to come strolling in between them.

Another cluster of wounded men plodded rearward. A blinded fellow held to a corporal's shoulder, while the corporal cradled an arm that jutted bone. The sightless fellow swung his head wildly at noises, new to the state that would define his lifetime. The corporal stared ahead with a grim expression. A laborer by the looks of him, his days, too, would be forever altered. But it wasn't the casualties—their number still minor by the measure of the campaign—that alarmed Hancock. It was the reports arriving every few minutes now, warning of Rebs where Rebs weren't supposed to be.

On impulse, Hancock handed off his field glasses and walked over to offer a few bluff words to wounded men trailing their comrades. One young man, still scrawny of beard, trembled fiercely on his litter, thumping his head back onto the canvas and grunting from his depths. His features had already set in a grotesque rictus. Reaching to pat the lad's upper arm, Hancock was startled when the boy convulsed, jackknifing upward to spew a gut full of blood on the general's sleeve.

The boy tumbled from the litter. His eyes remained open after he slapped the dust, but the only light in them came from the dropping sun.

Blood seeped through layers of cloth to Hancock's skin. He caught himself before a curse burst out.

He had blundered into a snakepit. He could only be thankful he had not behaved too recklessly as he'd edged his men forward that day. At first, it had indeed appeared that he faced only a rear guard, if one with spirit. Miles had advanced handsomely, and Smyth had quite distinguished himself in driving in the Confederates he encountered. But the next scrawled reports told of stiffening resistance, of enemy numbers larger than headquarters claims had led any man to expect. Now even Barlow thought it foolhardy to continue attacking.

Lines had to be corrected, though. A few brigades, including one of Barlow's, would have to press ahead to better ground. But where the advanced positions were defensible, the men already had orders to dig hard and deep.

All too aware of the corps' present disarray, Hancock feared that the enemy—at least a full corps and quite possibly a second—would strike before his divisions could prepare to receive an attack. Division flanks remained loose, and the reinforcing artillery was not up. If Lee's devils came on now . . .

He decided to go farther forward and inspect matters himself. It was a risk, of course—Sedgwick's death was still fresh in everymind—but he needed the reassurance that could only come from seeing entrenchments deepen. He waved to the orderly holding his horse.

It bewildered him that Lee had not swooped down on him. The emerging picture he had of the Reb positions suggested they'd had him flanked all afternoon. Had Lee hit him earlier, hit him hard, it might have been a debacle as bad as that first grim day at Gettysburg, with Reynolds dead and Howard hanging on by one of his Bible verses. For hours, they had even had the chance to cut off the bulk of his troops from their river crossings.

It prickled his flesh to think of what might have been. And what might still be.

Why on earth had they waited? Why were they waiting now?

Heaving his stiff leg across the saddle, he knew full well he was putting off another burdensome task.

He needed to write to Meade. To fill in more of the situation that lay before the army. But that would be a trick, alerting Meade and the rest of them to the apparent scale of the Confederate presence, without appearing to be afraid of his shadow. Meade would understand him, but Grant was another matter, and Grant read every dispatch. With Grant, a man had to put up a front of immaculate and un-impeachable confidence. Anything less marked a man as undependable, as surely as the "D" branded into a desert-er's cheek marked him as dishonorable.

Yet, confidence was one thing, folly another.

His thoughts had grown teeth: Why didn't the Johnnies come on with their yells and howls? Were they beaten down, after all? Had Robert E. Lee grown timid? That was a prospect Hancock found hard to credit.

The long day's shadows stretched eastward, trailing from the groves like the trains of widows. New widows aplenty there would be, if Lee made use of the last few hours of light.

Hancock caught himself and suddenly felt ashamed. Where was his old spirit? He straightened in the saddle, feeling only a wince of pain from his thigh. To Hell with them all! Grant could kiss his ass if he didn't like the way he handled his corps. And if Lee was such a blundering ass that he failed to attack by dark, he'd get a fine surprise if he tried in the morning. Just let him wait and try it then. That high-flown sonofabitch would be in for a fight.

Seven p.m.
Confederate reserve position
on the Virginia Central line

Gordon was out of coffee, out of speeches, and out of tem-per. What was Lee waiting for? There were rumors that Lee was ill, but surely he was well enough to give a sim-ple order to attack? Gordon had watched, first with cha-grin, then with building rage, as the Yankees snuffled forward like witless hogs, begging to be trussed and slaughtered squealing. But the order hadn't come. His division had waited in reserve, along with Breckinridge's men and a stack of additional brigades, as the Yankees blundered into skirmishers, then rifle pits, then the Confederate line itself, baffled as dunces called up to the chalkboard. And still the order to attack hadn't come. The Yankees sent more regiments forward, followed by full brigades, all spread out in delectable disarray, as the afternoon advanced into evening, but the order to strike them did not come then, either. Now, belatedly, infuriatingly, the Federals had begun to grasp that they weren't on a frolic, after all, and had begun to dig their own entrenchments, clawing at the soil with a haste that would have been comical had so great an opportunity not been slipping away. And still the word to attack did not come down.

There was still time. Not much, but enough to do them real damage. If the order came soon. Gordon had repeatedly ridden forward to scout matters for himself, even dismounting and scurrying out to Law's rifle pits. He had seen an opportunity even grander than the one he'd discovered on the morning of that second day in the Wilderness. But now this spectacular chance, this gift from the heavens and Ulysses S. Grant, looked about to be thrown away. The Yankees had been as befuddled and vulnerable as the Persians in the lapping surf at Marathon. But Lee had been no Miltiades this day.

The comparison soured. What was the use of his classical pretensions? Asinine, all of them. The last three weeks had made that clear enough. His rhetoric had roused men falsely, coaxing them to their deaths to swell his vanity. If anything, he had been a vulgar Siren, his song as fatal as it was alluring. What had he to offer men from the Greeks, when the truth was that he could not read their alphabet? What did he really know of the Romans, beyond schoolboy Latin and a few legal terms?

As for legal affairs, that very morning a letter had caught up with him, another missive from a judge threatening action over a defaulted loan. What did such nonsense matter in these hours? Must so much be made of a sum so small it barely reached one thousand dollars? Amid a war such as this? The way men clutched money seemed absurd to Gordon. Women were for clutching, money for spending. And he had spent what came his way. Now it was gone, and creditors had to wait.

Worse, the coffee had run out, the last beans from those treasure sacks seized back in the Wilderness. His officers had not rationed it, but consumed it with abandon. Money was to be spent, and coffee was to be boiled and drunk down hot. They were spendthrift people, his kind, and he was not last among them. For such as they were, the day sufficed, and tomorrow could only dawn brighter in the mind, if the mind had to be bothered with tomorrow. It was their glory and their weakness, this passion for delights to be seized right now. How far into the future had they peered when they began this war, cocky as roosters? How many of them had looked beyond the chance to wear a dashing uniform and add a rank to their visiting cards? How many had foreseen the carnage? Not one. The intoxication of the moment had been all that mattered to them. They had not even counted their iron foundries.

They were a backward-looking people, he saw that now. Instead of thinking through the complex demands of modern war, they had celebrated battles fought by their grandfathers. Or the grandfathers of their grandfathers. They had decorated the past the way a plantation mistress did up her mantels at Christmas, covering cracks and stains with branches and boughs already dead, but charming in their scented illusion of life. What was his love—no, his tawdry exploitation—of the classics, if not a means of clinging to the past, of robbing the achievements of long-dead men, all for the sake of a gimcrack, threadbare elegance? It was an affectation so cheap and false it was vile.

Was there a single thing about his people that was true, or solid, or worthy in itself? Beyond this spiteful sacrifice of blood, ennobled only by their stubborn pride? The Yankees were right that the war was born of slavery: the enslavement of his people by the past, their Negro chattels only one manifestation. His men were dying for a graveyard romance.

The Yankees were men of the future. He would not say such a thing to any peer, nor to the rapscallions who fought under his command. But Gordon saw it as clearly as a veteran knew a death wound.

He and Fanny would have a future, though. He would fight to the end, even die if death was ordained, but should the Lord let him survive the war, this folly's end was not going to be *his* end. The present day might stink of death, but tomorrow smelled of industry, power, and money, of government by the clever and fortunes for the astute. He had no intention of betraying his heritage. But he sensed it was more malleable than men knew, than men wanted to know. The South would not be finished by this war, but it would be changed. And the men who understood how to change while praising continuity would be the masters of all that rose from the wreckage.

As for his fellow Southerners, he was astounded by their courage and ever more appalled by their neglectfulness. What could you make of a people who failed to grasp such an opportunity as the one lingering before them even now? John Brown Gordon had never felt as pessimistic about his infant nation as on this sweltering, waiting-for-the-rain evening, nor had he ever felt more lust for a fight. If the war was to be lost, he did not want it lost from inattention.

He wanted to cry aloud, "For God's sake, let us attack!"

A courier galloped up in the softening light, exciting a last burst of hope, but the man only asked for directions to the supply trains.

Eight p.m.
Headquarters, Army of Northern Virginia

The doctor left Lee's tent with a worried look. After he passed the three aides without a word, Walter Taylor said, "We should all go in together. And tell him."

Marshall looked doubtful.

"No," Venable told his comrades. "Only one of us. And I'm the logical choice."

"It would be stronger coming from the three of us."

"No. It would look like we conspired." Venable held his hands upturned in front of him, weighing the air. "We can't have him feeling cornered. Or betrayed. And I'm on his bad side already. Over that damned buggy."

"He needed it," Marshall put in.

"He's not interested in what he needs. He hates to need anything. Or anybody. You know that, for God's sake." With time racing by, Venable added, "Walt, he trusts you and likes you. Better than anyone else. We can't afford to damage that." He turned to Marshall. "And Charlie here. Comes to getting out orders, he knows what the old man wants before the old man knows it himself. He needs the two of you, needs to trust you both. If any of us is going to be cast out, it has to be me."

His two friends opened their mouths to protest, but Venable shushed them.

"Take yourselves off. I'll handle this."

He turned his back on his friends and walked to Lee's tent. He didn't need to open the flap to scent the old man's sickness.

As he stepped inside, a grasshopper leapt away, landing on Lee's boots. They were still covered with mud and, perhaps, worse. Venable decided to have a word with Lee's body servant. Afterward.

Lee lay on his cot in tawny light, covered to the armpits with a blanket. Sweat jeweled the old man's exposed skin, spotting his forehead with diamonds. His eyes were closed, almost clenched. Like his fists.

"General Lee?" Venable said.

The eyelids did not flutter, the head did not turn.

"General Lee, can you hear me?"

Nothing but a brief tic at one corner of his mouth.

Venable reached down and did something he suspected no man had done for many a year: He gripped Lee's shoulder and shook it. With some force.

The old man's eyes popped open. Venable saw fear.

"General Lee, you are not fit to command this army. You must send to Richmond for General Beauregard."

The old man's eyes found Venable. The aide watched as the familiar gaze moved from alarm, to doubt, to resolve.

"No," Lee said.

Eleven p.m.
Headquarters, Army of the Potomac,
Quarles's Mill

Rawlins coughed. The hacking announced his arrival like a trumpet. As Humphreys watched, Grant's chief of staff drew off his waterproof and tossed it to an orderly. His eyes burned.

Rain battered the roof of the old house.

"All of you," Humphreys said, "clear out."

When the shabby parlor had emptied, he signaled to a guard to shut the door.

Rawlins looked feverish. There was no doubt in Humphreys' mind: The man was a consumptive, rotting away.

"I would've come to you," he said.

Rawlins shook his head. "Better this way."

Humphreys looked down, then up again. "John, things can't go on like this."

"I know."

"Meade's a tough old bird. But he has his pride. Shaming him in front of his own staff . . ."

"Dana isn't worth a pound of horseshit."

Humphreys refrained from pointing out that only weeks before, Rawlins had set the precedent for embarrassing Meade in front of his subordinates. Rawlins and the better of Grant's paladins had grown quieter, though, as the casualties mounted and Lee didn't up and quit. But even beyond that, Humphreys had come to see the value of Grant's right-hand man. At first, he had thought Rawlins a boisterous ass, but under the press of relentless campaigning, he had discovered that the small-town lawyer was the only man who could really challenge Grant, who could temper the general in chief's worst impulses, and who could keep Grant on the straight and narrow. Grant's great strength—his determination to see things through, no matter the cost—was also his weakness. Only Rawlins could whisper contrary advice and not be rebuffed, once Grant had been captivated by an idea.

"Well, do what you can. Please. Meade's as dutiful an officer as I've ever served under. But humiliating him hardly brings out his best qualities."

"Meade's a good man," Rawlins agreed. Nearing another cough, he cleared his throat. "Grant knows that. Otherwise, he'd be back in Philadelphia."

"Sheridan—"

Rawlins held up a hand: *Stop.* "Nothing I can do about Sheridan. Maybe have a word with Dana, he's a burr under everybody's saddle. But Grant likes Sheridan just the way he is. And he did finish Stuart, just the way he promised."

"The man's an insufferable egotist."

Rawlins half closed one eye and the other shone. "You're wrong there. He's plenty sufferable. To Grant, anyway. Phil entertains him, that's the thing. Grant likes a good story, a joke, a laugh." Rawlins stepped closer. Humphreys thought he saw dried blood in the man's beard, below his lip. "That's the thing of it, see. Grant *values* George Meade. Values him highly. But he doesn't *like* him. Not that he dislikes him particularly, either. They're just different animals. Talk military matters, and they understand each other. More often than not, anyway. But when it comes to sitting under a tree and talking friendly, Meade and Grant don't even speak the same language." Rawlins thought about what he had just said, then added, "Sometimes, even I can't figure what Grant's got in his head."

Humphreys could see it all. Meade was diligent, experienced, and masterful. He was courageous and, left to himself, decisive. But he wasn't especially likable, nor was he an easy man. Meade wasn't the hearty or obliging sort. Friendly to a chosen few, he held the rest of humanity beyond an invisible picket line. Humphreys could not imagine a friendship between young Lyman and Grant, but the Harvard man and Meade got on just swimmingly. On the other hand, Meade despised Grant's raw-mannered western men. And Meade's pride was nicked as easily as the finish on a costly lacquered cabinet.

Humphreys, too, often felt impatient with Meade. But he recognized that Meade had persevered under crippling restrictions for those long months after Gettysburg, only to see Grant brought east and given the free hand he never had been permitted. It was easy enough for a Plug Ugly like Sheridan to mock Meade's patrician ways or to taunt him into foolish displays of temper, but there wasn't a more honest man in the Union than George Meade. On the other hand, honesty sprang from innocence, and Meade never grasped the devious nature of others. He was all rectitude and no reckoning. From what Humphreys heard, Meade's father had been the same way, trusting that a good act would be appreciated, only to be fatefully disappointed.

Meade needed a protector. And Humphreys felt the lot had fallen to him.

"I suppose we ought to sit down, talk this out properly," he said. "Shall I send for coffee?"

"No need to sit. And I've drunk enough coffee to piss me a river." Rawlins pointed across the room to where a door laid atop provision barrels served as Humphreys' desk. "Show me where we are on that map of yours. I don't like what I've been hearing. And Grant's just lighting one cigar off the other."

Humphreys led the way. "Bobby Lee's played another one of his tricks. Situation's unclear in front of Warren, but it looks like Hancock's walked into a trap." He shifted a lantern closer to the map and traced what he knew of the enemy lines with the dull end of a pencil. "There's a heavy concentration in front of Hancock. From the rail junction back to the river, their lines are shaped like a jackknife three-quarters unclasped."

Arms folded, Rawlins leaned in over the map. "And ready to snap shut."

"Exactly. What makes no sense is Lee waiting to spring the trap." Humphreys pointed a finger toward the roof, which sounded as if it could barely resist the rain. "And I don't think he's going to attack in this." For a bad moment, he imagined the tragedy that almost had come to pass. "Lee had a magnificent opportunity. And he just didn't take it. I, for one, can't fathom it. It's just not the way he does things. And if he decides to attack tomorrow, after all, he's going to pay a price he won't much fancy. Win's entrenching, as fast as his men can dig."

"Mud soup," Rawlins said. He stifled another cough. Humphreys smelled odorous breath, a scent of mortality.

"If I'm correct about what I think I see," Humphreys continued, "Warren and Wright will come up against a well-prepared defense on our right, as well."

"Burnside's already had a bad time of it. This afternoon," Rawlins noted. "Far as I'm concerned, putting the Ninth Corps under you has been long overdue. Should've done it at least a damned day earlier, saved some lives." He turned his face from the map to Humphreys. "You heard about Ledlie, I reckon?"

"Drunk. Falling off his horse during the attack. Meade's furious. Young Chandler was a favorite in the army. And quite the darling of Boston's high society."

"Meade ought to relieve the man. Court-martial the sonofabitch. The order's been published, he has the authority."

Humphreys shook his head. "He'd like to. But if his first order to Ninth Corps cuts out one of Burnside's boys, he starts off on the wrong damned foot. Bad blood. On top of the spilled blood."

Rawlins cleared his throat again. The smell wafted to Humphreys' nostrils, but his features remained immobile.

"Well, that's Meade's business now," Rawlins said. "God knows, there were plenty of people out west I would've liked to get rid of and couldn't, for one reason or another. But my advice is still to cashier this Ledlie sonofabitch." He paused for a moment, then added, "There's nothing worse than a drunkard on a battlefield."

Humphreys turned back to the map and gestured toward the newly revealed Confederate positions. "How much of this does Grant see?"

"More than he wants to. He thought he had Lee bagged."

"At best, we're in a standoff." He met Rawlins' eyes. "John, we can't afford more assaults like those at Spotsylvania. Not unless we *know* there's a chance of success. We should start planning to pull back, methodically, but damned quick. As long as we're south of that river, the army's paralyzed."

Rawlins recoiled. "Grant hates to turn back. Ever. Trait of his. Hates to retrace his route on horseback, hates to leave a position. Unless it's to go forward."

"Then put it to him that we'd be going forward. We could still get across the Pamunkey. Turn the tables on Lee."

"He won't go for it. Not yet." A note of exasperation sharpened Rawlins' voice. "Look, Meade was right. *I* give you that. But Grant can't admit it, not outright. It's just not the way he is. He's going to need at least another day to chew the cud before he spits it out. Meanwhile, I'll try to discourage any unreasonable attacks. That's a promise, for what it's worth. But he's going to have to reach his own conclusions about the situation." Rawlins patted his mouth for spittle. Or blood. The gesture seemed unconscious, the man was excited. "Don't underestimate Grant. Put a problem in front of him, and he's like a dog with a great big ham bone. He'll just gnaw it and gnaw it, until it snaps in two. Vicksburg took him, what, eight months? Nine? But he took it, by damn. And I'll tell you what he's going to do tomorrow. He'll grasp about for alternatives to pulling back across the North Anna, any way to go forward instead of backward."

Humphreys grimaced. "Warren will argue for passing Lee on the right. Where he's been successful."

"Might be a good idea."

"We'd be cut off from our supply lines."

"Might appeal to Grant. Remind him of Vicksburg. Worked then."

"Lee's not Pemberton. Or Johnston."

Humphreys recalled Meade hours earlier, as the outline

of the Confederate positions before Hancock grew apparent. He had spit out, "Second Bull Run! Damn it, Humph, Lee's pulled the wool over our eyes! Just the way he did to that horse's ass Pope. But I won't oblige him further, so help me God."

"Well," Rawlins resumed, "Grant's convinced that Lee's on his last legs. Why else wouldn't he attack, when he had a chance like the one he had today? And like I said, Grant only knows how to go forward. Won't be pleased that Meade was right about the Pamunkey, either. Sam may be on the quiet side, but his pride's a powerful thing. If George Meade's proud, Sam's prouder. The horses just show different."

"That's where you and I come in. Keep them working as partners, rather than rivals."

Rawlins seemed to drift away for a moment. Instead of agreeing, he said, "Show me how you'd do it. Cross the Pamunkey, I mean."

"Will the cavalry be available? Can I assume that?"

"I believe so."

"Well, the first thing to do is to withdraw the army. Without getting caught by Lee. We'd have to—"

"Jump over that part. What happens next?"

Humphreys detailed the way the cavalry should be used to screen ahead and secure the crossing sites. Then he described how the network of roads could be used to best effect, moving all the corps rapidly, but with minimal confusion.

"If we plan this thoroughly, do it right . . . we could throw Lee's army off balance."

"What happens once we're over the Pamunkey? Where do we end up?"

"Lee may have an opinion about that. But, if we're quick, we can catch him out in the open, with no time to entrench. That's the chance Grant's been looking for."

"Lee's quicker than us," Rawlins said. "I've learned that much."

"That's why we need to plan things properly. Proceed in a disciplined manner."

"Where do you think we could catch him out? Presumably, north of Richmond. . . ."

Humphreys looked hard at the map, studying the roads that led to the Chickahominy, then to the Confederate capital. He knew some of that ground firsthand. As did Meade. And many another officer and man who had served in the Peninsula Campaign.

Whatever faults he might possess, Grant was not George McClellan.

"So where do we catch him?" Rawlins demanded, returning to his customary bristling tone. "Or where does he catch us?"

Determined to give a serious answer, Humphreys traced his index finger over one road after another, reminding himself that human feet, not just colored pencils, had to cover those distances.

His fingertip touched Cold Harbor and moved on.

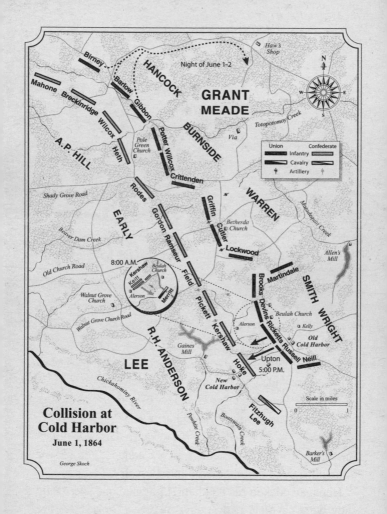

Birney

Mahone

Breckinridge

Wilcox

A.P. HILL

Heth

HANCOCK

Barlow

Gibbon

Pole Green Church

Porter Willcox

BURNSIDE

Crittenden

Night of June 1–2

GRANT
MEADE

Totopotomoy Creek

Via

Union   Confederate

Infantry
Cavalry
Artillery

Shady Grove Road

Beaver Dam Creek

EARLY

Rodes

Gordon Ramseur

Field

Griffin

Cutler

WARREN

Bethesda Church

Lockwood

Maechunkin Creek

Allen's Mill

Old Church Road

8:00 A.M.

Kershaw

Kent

Beulah Church

Alerson

Merritt

Martindale

Brooks Devins Ricketts Russell

SMITH

WRIGHT

Beulah Church

Walnut Grove Church

Pickett

Kershaw

Alerson

Kelly

Old Cold Harbor

Walnut Grove Church Road

R.H. ANDERSON

Gaines' Mill

Hoke

Upton

5:00 P.M.

Neill

LEE

Chickahominy River

New
Cold Harbor

Fitzhugh
Lee

Scale in miles

0   1

Pontlice Creek

Boatswain Creek

Barker's Mill

Collision at
Cold Harbor

June 1, 1864

George Skoch

TWENTY-THREE

June 1, morning
Cold Harbor

Pride. He would allow no man to sully his honor or infringe upon his rights. What hath a man, but his good name? He was entitled to command, not merely by virtue of the seniority of his commission, but by his merits and services to the South over many years. And *he* would not submit to the hollow arrogance of these men whose failings had brought the Northern Vandal to the gates of Richmond, men who no longer rose to the chivalric grandeur expected of South Carolinians. Indeed, these ragtag colonels and unkempt lieutenant colonels crowding around him seemed possessed by that most dishonorable of conditions that could afflict a gentleman: fear.

Colonel Lawrence Massillon Keitt said: "My men will brush them aside."

His new subordinates exchanged glances and muttered. Their arguments had not moved him.

Turning to Colonel Henagan, a lowly sheriff back home, the former United States congressman added, "You've said yourself they're merely dismounted cavalry."

Henagan cocked his head and tightened one eye. "Said they were cavalry. Didn't say 'merely.' Those boys are armed with repeating rifles, shoot just about all day without reloading."

"You indulge in hyperbole, sir."

"I'm indulging in not wanting my men shot up no more

than necessary." Even as he spoke, Henagan's features reflected the realization that, beyond his depleted regiment, the brigade was no longer his: He had been permitted to lead it only until Keitt's arrival the day before. "Ain't a job for just one brigade, neither."

Towering over the colonel in the fouled and ragged uniform, Keitt said, "You underestimate the valor of the men of your own state."

If the regiment he had raised himself had not been privileged to join the field actions of the contending armies until now, still it had done noble work at Battery Wagner and in other coastal defenses. And the 20th South Carolina's precision drill put to shame these barefoot vagabonds. War was no excuse for shabbiness so degraded it neared the lascivious.

It was clear to Keitt why President Davis had looked with favor upon his assignment to this brigade: It wanted leadership.

Dirty uniforms rustled around him. Keitt found the very smell of these men jarring: worse than any slave he had ever owned. And some of these officers were not unknown to Charleston society. . . .

"Let us rejoin the march," Keitt concluded. "The men must see who commands them." Riding gloves in hand, he saluted his new subordinates with a gesture practiced many a time in the looking glass. "To horse, gentlemen!"

Henagan didn't move. Keitt had heard that the man had been roughly handled at the North Anna.

"At least, Colonel," Henagan said, "don't ride that big gray horse of Kershaw's on into the fight. Or you won't stay on it long."

Keitt regarded the advice as a flagrant insult, but let it pass. First, he had Yankees to address. And he did not doubt for a moment that his fresh regiment—larger than the re-

mainder of the brigade—could vanquish a mob of Northern muleteers.

Nature herself seemed to recognize his prowess. Choirs
of birds lauded him on his way past plodding men who eyed
him with curiosity, almost suspicion. Serflike, these
soldiers had grown unaccustomed to manly vigor, their
officers reduced to poor-white fecklessness. But the sun
shone, butter smooth, and the air in the groves was fresh,
as welcome as a card for a holiday ball. Beyond the tunnel
of dust raised by the column, the morning light possessed
the brilliance of diamonds.

As he reached the rear ranks of his own regiment, which
led the brigade's march, Keitt felt a rush of pride. *His* men
looked like proper soldiers and didn't straggle like niggers
sent to a far field.

Oh, if Susie could but see him now! That woman . . . he
loved her with a passion exceeded only by his love of freedom, of his state, of his glorious new country and lifelong
cause. For her, he had abandoned his ideals, sacrificing a
splendid career in politics to indulge her dedication to
music and art, taking her, as the price of her much-
delayed agreement to wed, to Europe, to realms at times
congenial but never as true and fair as South Carolina. As
secession loomed, however, he had turned homeward, defying Susie's threats to remain abroad with their two infants.
Ultimately, she had accompanied him back to Charleston
and on to Orangeburg, but did not pretend to be happy at
the change.

She had accepted her own smaller duty in time, though,
supporting his aspiration to the vice presidency, an ambition frustrated by a low cabal. How he missed that
compelling woman now! The intimacies of body and soul!
Her dark-eyed wit, her white and giving flesh . . .

He reached the head of the column, smiling at his aides

and the rough-clad guides. "Isn't this splendid?" he said, his words more a declaration than a question.

Ahead, skirmishers niggled.

The South would win. On this day and forever. He and his kind would never accept defeat. Northern tyranny, the monstrous Yankee lust to destroy the birthright freedoms of his people, would never again annoy one Southern hearth. If others lost heart, *his* heart was strong enough to bear their burdens.

How could any man have imagined that the Union might be preserved? He had been willing to fight, in any way, in any venue, for his God-given rights, for freedom. When his friend Brooks had given old Sumner the caning he had coming, Keitt had stood in the aisle of the House chamber, pocket pistol leveled at any abolitionist scum inclined to rush to Sumner's aid. For that and much else, his constituents reelected him. And later, when a black Republican puppy had called him a "Negro-driver," he had taken his fists to Grow right there on the House floor, the act flawed only by the lucky punch Grow, a smaller man, had landed.

None dared claim to have more boldly represented the Southern cause in the benighted halls of that perfidious Congress. Had not his famed oration of 1857 made the clearest case for the moral necessity and wisdom of slavery put by any man of his generation? The men of the North ignored the force of reason as willfully as they did the lessons of history. Slavery an evil? It was a primordial fact, rooted in the origin of things. Yankees made much of their admiration for the glories of Greece and Rome, but was not slavery the basis, the lifeblood, of those civilizations? If pallid abolitionists misrepresented the classics, he, Lawrence Keitt, had studied them with reverence and in detail. Had not Homer and even great Plato accepted slavery as a natural part of the human condition? Had not the census of Demetrius of Phalerus counted four hundred thousand slaves in Athens, the very birthplace of democracy? And what of the Hebrews, whose enslavement of others had been ordained by God? Only the godless North could construe slavery as an evil. It was an institution as inevitable as marriage and every bit as sanctioned by holy writ.

How could any white man placed in contact with the Negro imagine the primitive African as his brother? Suffering? Who suffered more indignities, the starving Northern laborer who quaked at inconstant markets, or the valued and cared-for Negro slave, whose lodging and feed were reliably provided? What would become of the African if he were turned out to make his way in the world? What awaited the poor devil but a life of beggary, crime, and vice, of indolence and outrage? Educate him? A hundred years hence the poor beast would still sup on charity, or not at all. Slavery was as much a part of the natural order as these songbirds celebrating infant June.

Now the degenerate Yankees, unable to find reserves of courage in their white population, had stooped to arming the apes.

A guide signaled for the column to veer left.

"Ain't far now," the ragamuffin said.

Yankees been busy," Henagan said. "Plenty of 'em, too." He swept the Union line with his field glasses. "Still no infantry, though. Not as I can see."

The other regimental commanders appeared to accept Henagan as their spokesman, but kept a careful distance, for all that. The sun mottling the tree line touched weary faces.

Keitt wanted to ask his subordinate how he knew there were no infantry over there and what evidence there was of "plenty" of the enemy. He saw only quick blue smudges behind crude earthworks. But he did not want to appear unknowing.

"Colonel Keitt," Henagan resumed, "I was you, I'd wait for the rest of the division to come up. See what Genr'l Kershaw has to say, he'll be along soon enough. Yankees may be slow at learning, but they've picked up some."

You're *not* me, Keitt thought. He said: "The honor has fallen to us to retake that crossroads. Honor delayed is honor diminished."

Henagan looked dismayed to the point of faltering: It was clear the man lacked the character to lead. The other regimental commanders seemed doubtful as well. This Army of Northern Virginia needed bucking up.

"Well," Henagan said, "I reckon I'm more concerned with taking the crossroads than with the honor of it. The plain fact that those Yankee cavalry are still here, that they've been rooting and digging all night to get all nice and ready for us, tells a man they're minded to hang on to that crossroads themselves. Just waiting for their infantry to come up."

"Then we must strike them promptly."

"Had yourself a look at those entrenchments?"

Keitt corrected his posture from fine to perfect. "I have. And I find them no more than a hodgepodge." He turned to fully face the jumped-up sheriff. "Battery Wagner had *proper* fortifications. There's a difference between a Vauban and a vulgar ditchdigger."

Henagan's lips moved, but no sound came out. Keitt wondered what the man lacked the courage to say.

"If those cowardly mule drivers are, indeed, waiting on their infantry," Keitt added, "better to see to them now."

Henagan began to shake his head, but caught himself in the act. "Sir, I'm asking you. Consider this a formal request, if that's what it takes. At least wait for Bryan's Brigade to get itself organized right. If nothing else, wait for

Bryan. I know you were one of them Fire-Eaters in Congress, but this ain't—"

"If you feel . . . trepidation, Colonel Henagan, dismiss your concerns. My Twentieth South Carolina will take the *place d'honneur* on the right front. Your soldiers may follow behind." He smiled, determined to encourage all the poor devils around him, men distinctly wanting in morale. "The Yankees haven't seen anything like my men. They'll think they're facing Prussian grenadiers."

Henagan was impossible to console. He just said, "No, I reckon the Yankees ain't seen anything like that."

Along the line of the 20th South Carolina, sergeants adjusted the alignment of belts and cartridge boxes, straightened caps, and saw that collars were buttoned. Keitt could not have been prouder of his men. They would fill two-thirds of the brigade front as they advanced, weapons straightened at right shoulder shift and each man raising a knee exactly eight inches at every forward step.

He nodded at his adjutant, who ordered, "Uncase the colors!"

Henagan, on foot, peered up at him. The man was becoming an insufferable nag: No wonder a drunken ne'er-do-well had been able to push this army back against Richmond.

"Sir, we could swing around through the woods. Take 'em in the flank. Ain't no need to march out across that field."

"The shortest way to the enemy is the best way to the enemy," Keitt told him. He kept his tone civil, but his supply of patience had neared depletion.

Henagan looked at the ground and back up past Keitt's gleaming, just dusted boots. "Dismount, at least. Go forward on foot."

"You may walk, if you wish, Colonel Henagan. I'm sure I have no objection."

Henagan saluted and turned away.

Keitt unsheathed his sword. Raised skyward, it caught the sun.

"South Carolina! Brigade! Forward!"

The command echoed down the line.

Instead of a supplementary command, Keitt lowered his blade to the horizontal, pointing it at the Yankees, and spurred forward. Barked orders moved the long line from the trees and across the road along which they had formed. As soon as they reached the edge of the open field, the men of his own regiment snapped into place beside their comrades, rectifying their own alignment and leaving hardly anything for the noncommissioned officers to do. In the sunlight, the lines—which he had ordered be kept compact—were fit to dazzle the world. Finer, he told himself, than the British Regulars he had seen on parade before the queen.

He had not deployed skirmishers to herald his attack. He believed them to be undisciplined and unnecessary, fit only for march security. Shock would be the order of the day.

Henagan had whined about that, too. Receiving the order, the man had all but cringed.

From his perch in the saddle, Keitt twisted his erect spine to look past his own men to the remainder of the brigade. Deployed on the flank and coming along behind, the soldiers loped like cracker-barrel militia.

He would see to that, in time.

Masses of spring insects leapt from the grass, fleeing before the footfalls of his men. The Yankees, he imagined, would flee just so.

The early sun grew warm, but the effect was not unpleasant. For one delightful moment, it seemed to embrace him.

Again, he raised his saber high, letting it glitter before he employed it to point the way again. When the weight of the blade began to tell, he settled it against his shoulder.

He had expected cannon, if only horse artillery, to contest his brigade's advance. He had read of the destructive fire of the guns, how they opened first, long before the plank-on-plank clapping sound of rifle fire might be heard. But no artillery fire sought his troops, no cannon disturbed the excellence of the morning.

Anyway, paltry fieldpieces would be nothing to the great guns defending the approaches to Charleston Bay.

He spotted more of them now, the Yankees. Keeping low behind their sordid dirt piles, their logs and stacked fence rails, they appeared quickened, perhaps by dread.

Susie! For all their squabbles and differences, the confusions of their passion, she would be burstingly proud of him this day. The former Miss Susanna Sparks had been a more formidable conquest than this Mongol horde of Yankees was apt to be.

He raised the hand that held his reins to brush sweat from his eyes. Confused, his horse shied mildly, then eased again.

He could not hear the birds now, but the brigade had long since left the trees behind. Thousands of footfalls sounded at his back, tapping the padded earth, swishing through a field that had gone to weed.

He could not resist another look at his lines.

They were perfect, immaculate. His men had not marched more grandly before the belles of Charleston.

He saw the first Yankee faces now, bobbing here and there above blue jackets. He could almost make out their features.

The heat seemed to have increased by twenty degrees in twenty yards. Sweat gripped him. He wanted to tug his collar away from his neck, but the act would have been unseemly.

Why didn't the Yankees open fire? They were infernally close. And yes: He saw cannon, their black muzzles gaping.

He raised his sword and turned, ready to shout, "Charge!"

The Yankee artillery opened. The range could not have been two hundred yards.

Canister turned men into clouds of blood. His ranks gaped. Soldiers rushed forward to fill in the holes, only to be blasted in their turn, converted into lightning streaks of blood.

He could not make his voice heard, could not speak, did not know if he had spoken. He felt caught in a world that sped by and held still at the same time. He meant to raise his sword, but his arm refused.

Bewilderingly, a band played "Yankee Doodle."

Turning back toward his foe's entrenchments, he saw a narrow, brilliant line of flames.

Keitt struck the ground before he knew he'd been shot.

Charge, damn it! Charge, boys!" Henagan shouted. He did not want the slaughter to be for nothing.

That damned shit-for-chivalry Keitt. Yankees had led him on the way a hoor teased a drunken farm-boy. Men dragged him off with his eyes rolled back in his head, gut-shot, lung-shot, just shot to Hell, but alive thanks to, maybe, his sheer, arrogant bigness. But not alive for long, Henagan figured.

Damned fool.

He tried to rally his boys and the others, but the Yankees were sweeping the field with their cannon and repeating rifles, dropping men by the dozen, right and left. He had never experienced such a volume of fire.

The only thing saving anybody now was the thick pall of yellow smoke that covered the Yankee line, leaving them to shoot blind and hope they hit something.

Didn't stop them from shooting, though.

Taunting their attackers, the Yankee band struck up "Dixie." Henagan would have like to cut the throat of every last musician.

Unlikely he was going to get the chance, though. The attack had gone into a stupor, with Keitt's new men bewildered by the gore, by the raw noise, paralyzed like a boy shot in the spine.

A section of Yankee artillery gave his own regiment another one-two of canister, shredding men like china dolls bashed on a wall.

It was enough, enough. Fool charge, led by an idiot. He was about to order his men and Keitt's pack rearward on his own responsibility when a runner found him.

"General Kershaw says y'all are to pull on back. He says there ain't no use to it."

Henagan wasted no time. "Back to the trees!" he shouted to his own men as he dashed to recall the survivors of Keitt's regiment. "Withdraw to the trees. And start digging."

Three thirty p.m.
Headquarters, Army of the Potomac,
at Via's Farm

I suppose," Meade said to Humphreys, "I'll have to be gracious to Sheridan."

Briefly free of the crowding and insistent grime of their headquarters, the two men watched from a shade tree as a column of soldiers marched away from the war. Volunteers whose enlistments were up, those troops were the only jolly men in the army.

"Quite a feat," Humphreys responded. "I'll credit the bullet-headed little Fenian with that much. Holding off

Lee's infantry with those Camptown jockeys of his." He waved off a veil of flies. "Maybe Grant's right. That Lee's on his last legs."

"Generals on their last legs don't attack."

"Lee might. Desperation. Or a bluff."

"We'll see, Humph. *If* Wright pitches into them before the end of the century." Instinctively, he felt for his watch, but dropped his hand away. He knew what time it was. And for all the intermittent blasting of cannon and the crackle of skirmishing, there was no hint of a major assault. Nor would there be for another painful hour and a half. Wright's men had reached Cold Harbor dead on their feet, and Smith's corps was just closing, after one of Grant's prized stock of aides had sent it off in the utterly wrong direction the night before.

"Babcock, wasn't it?" Meade asked.

"What?"

"Grant's man. The one who took Baldy Smith on a wild-goose chase."

"Yes. Babcock. He's hardly the worst, though."

"Order out to the chief surgeon?"

Humphreys nodded. "He'll do all he can."

A band struck up to serenade the departing veterans: "The Girl I Left Behind Me."

Meade's voice came just short of a growl. "I *still* can't believe the man. Steaming his corps down the James and up the York, leaving all of his medical supplies behind."

"And his ammunition reserve," Humphreys added. "I suppose he saw us as the Horn of Plenty."

Meade grunted. "He'll want rations, too, I suppose."

"He's already asked for them."

"Yes," Meade said. "And neatly done. Grant's bunch couldn't plan a picnic. Had *you* been in charge of his movement, this wouldn't have happened. The man would've had his wagons *and* marched on time last night."

"Well, we've got him and his pack now. As of noon today." Humphreys took out his pipe and began to fix it with fresh tobacco. "God knows, we can use them. When we're stripping garrison artillery regiments to rebuild this army's strength. . . ."

It was Meade's turn to fan away the Virginia gnats, which took sharp little bites out of a man. And his legs were tormented by fleabites gotten during a too-brief sleep. "Let's just hope they can fight."

"Eighteenth Corps?"

"No. Our tender redleg converts to the infantry. But, for that matter, yes. The Eighteenth Corps, too. We'll see if serving under Butler hasn't ruined them."

"Well, we know they don't like marching," Humphreys said. With a thin smile.

One of the telegraph orderlies approached and paused at a careful distance. Humphreys gestured for the man to come closer.

The corporal saluted. "Telegraph line's in to General Wright's headquarters, sir. You wanted to know."

Humphreys nodded. "Fine, Halloran. I'll be in shortly."

The corporal, new to the headquarters, saluted again and did his best to perform a crisp about-face.

"I don't know how you do it, Humph," Meade said, watching the young man go.

"What?"

"Remember all their names. Lord knows, I try."

"You've got other things on your mind."

Meade snorted. "And you don't?"

"I suppose I really should go in. Nudge Wright a bit. See if there's an acknowledgment from Hancock. Christ, George, I could sleep like Rip Van Winkle."

A smile, untainted, crossed Meade's face. "I'd outsleep you by a decade. Clean sheets, though. I'd like clean sheets." He scratched at a bite on his cheek. "Isn't it remarkable, though? We live in an age of wonders, Humph. Telegraph lines to every corps headquarters. . . ."

"Not to Smith yet."

"In principle, though. Think of it for a moment. Telegraphic communications right on the battlefield. Troops moved by steam on land and sea . . . and the weaponry, rifled guns, repeating carbines . . . war's changing. No, it's already changed. Sometimes I feel I'm being left behind."

"You forgot the damned entrenchments. *That's* the face of modern war, men digging their own graves and waiting to die in them." The chief of staff's expression reinforced the gripe in his voice. "Christ, I'll be glad to get off the Totopotomoy. Another squandered chance, thanks to Slapdash Sam."

"Barlow took a bite out of them."

"A bite's not enough." Humphreys shook his head. "At least, the ground at Cold Harbor looks a bit better, we should be able to get at them for once."

"*If* we hit them before Lee has time to turn it into a fortress." Meade's face grew as somber as the day was hot. "I can't abide this slaughter, Humph, just banging up against entrenchments the men know can't be taken."

"Tell Grant."

"I have."

"And?"

"You know."

Humphreys nodded. "And we'll both obey our orders to the end. We're trained like show horses."

"Well," Meade mused, "Grant was a champion horseman at West Point." He shook his head, part weariness, part despair. "One hopes he knows what he's doing, after all."

"Lincoln believes in him. Grant's got the man charmed. Two westerners. Speak the same language, I suppose."

Meade sighed and could not resist saying, "I wish he'd

believed just half as much in me. What you and I could have done together, Humph . . ."

The final increment of departing troops left a billow of dust. Another contingent of infantrymen turned into the road, marching in the opposite direction. These men, in distinctly different spirits, headed toward the war.

Humphreys shook his head. "You're right, though. War's changed. And I suppose it's only going to get deadlier. Story of mankind's history." His smile twisted, as if screwed from within. "Give us time enough, and we'll figure out a way to kill every last man and dog upon this earth."

"Oh, come now. It's not as bad as all that."

"You're more of an optimist than I am," Humphreys said.

Meade laughed. He could not remember the last time he had laughed like that. "Great God, Humph! I believe that's the first time any man's ever said those words to me. I'll have to write Margaret and tell her."

Humphreys shared a smile, but didn't quite laugh. "All right, George. Too much thinking, not enough doing. I'll go back in, push Wright and pull on Hancock."

"Warren?"

Humphreys shrugged. "Back to his old tricks. More promises than activity. Complains that his men are tired. We're *all* tired, for Christ's sake. And Burnside's always got an excuse. He's like a tardy schoolboy."

Meade shifted the subject back to the day's priority. "I wouldn't mind a bit, if Wright—or even Baldy—gave Lee's men a whipping. Not a good day when only Sheridan shines."

"Well, shine he did. He's a curious man, our little mick."

Meade swept a drift of dust away from his face. "What I've noticed about Sheridan . . . is that he's quite the she-been scrapper, all right. He *likes* to scrap, that's the thing. But ask the man to do what cavalry should, screen the army

or conduct reconnaissance, and he's Burnside on a horse."
He frumped his chin, pulling thoughts into words. "I'll be
fair to the man, though: He's splendid when he's doing what
he wants to do. And worthless at anything else."

The gnats swarmed the two men again. Virginia hardly
seemed worth such a terrible struggle. "Make sure Hancock's on the road by dark," Meade said. "If Wright makes
any progress, Grant will want a general assault in the morning."

"And if Wright *doesn't* make progress, Grant will want
an assault in the morning." Humphreys shook his head,
swatting at the flies and turning to go. "I *want* to believe
he's right. After we've lost nearly half the men we had back
on the Rapidan." He raised his eyes. "What you said about
our friend Sheridan? Apply it to Grant, too. He's all for doing what he wants to do. And the rest of the world can go
hang."

From the miasma of dust along the road, a man emerged
astride a grand brown horse. A small retinue trailed him,
edging past the soldiers plodding south.

"Speak of the devil," Humphreys said.

Four p.m.
Via's Farm

None of them understood it. And explaining wouldn't do.
They wouldn't know what to make of it. But some things
just had to be.

He dismounted and, limping slightly, approached Meade
and Humphreys. The injury he'd taken from his New Orleans tumble had come back to nag him, right out of the
blue. The way an attack ought to come. You needed to hit
the enemy the way pain struck a man, without warning and
without mercy.

"Don't hear the guns," he said. There was desultory artillery fire in the distance, as well as the intermittent snap of rifles, but the two men understood him.

"Soon," Meade said. "Wright and Smith don't step off until five."

Grant nodded. "Late."

"The men were exhausted. Smith's last division still hasn't closed."

Grant sensed that Meade would have liked to point out Orr Babcock's role in the mess of a march the night before. But he knew Meade would restrain himself just short of mentioning it. Meade bucked sometimes, but never enough to embarrass a good rider. Unlike that damned black stallion in New Orleans. He could still hear the slice of horseshoes on wet cobbles in that instant before the beast tumbled sideward. With him still in the saddle.

"Smith's only got the ammunition his men are carrying," Humphreys put in. "No medical supplies, either. Or rations."

"Give him what he needs," Grant said. "Rather see the men first and supplies after, than the other way round."

Meade and Humphreys. Excellent officers, good men. But they could not see beyond the coming fight. Meade knew exactly what the book said a man should do, and Humphreys could have written the book. But the book didn't work anymore. Books tried to help a fellow win a battle, but what mattered now was to win campaigns entire.

The scale of war was bigger now. Big as the country.

"Things all right with Hancock?" Grant asked.

"Yes, Sam, they are," Meade said. "He'll begin to withdraw as soon as darkness falls. Skirmishers will remain to keep Lee occupied. Captain Paine from the staff will guide the march."

"Hit Lee hard," Grant said. "And early. Wright and Smith

can start things up today, keep the Rebs off balance. But we're going to have to finish the job in the morning."

Meade nodded. "We're agreed on that. The last thing any man in this army wants to do is give Lee time to entrench again. The casualty lists . . ."

Men who had never been poor as dirt didn't understand the hard-figured cost of things. Meade and Humphreys were fine, fine men. But they did not understand, even now, how much killing this would take.

He figured things were just about up with Lee. Put up a devil of a fight, give the man that, but the Reb attacks across the past few days had been easily broken. Feeble. Lee's boys had to be about bled out. Take more blood to finish them off, though. And you couldn't shy from it.

Just had to make up your mind to do a thing. All the fine generals fought to win battles, trying again and again, while the war dragged on. Even Sherman had had a touch of that, thinking in terms of winning the next battle, all clean and proper. Cump was about over that now.

You just could not relent, no matter the cost. If you did, the lives already spent were wasted. The way the Union was going to win this war was to outspend the Confederacy on every account, in men and blood, war supplies and gold, and to apply a strategy that didn't look just at Virginia or Tennessee or the Mississippi Valley, but at all of it at once, from Georgia to Indian territory. You had to step back and look at how the whole country fit together and not worry too much over any one little piece of it. You had to see farther and think bigger than your enemy. And you had to close your heart to suffering now to save yourself greater misery tomorrow.

He had been trained as all these fine officers had, by West Point, Mexico, and the frontier Army. They had been taught how to build bridges and harbor fortifications, how to fight brown men forced to fight by others, and how to keep a knee square on the back of broken Indians. But this war wanted more, a great deal more.

Meade, Humphreys, Hancock . . . good men and fine. Skilled officers. And skill mattered. But nothing mattered as much as strength of will. The man who couldn't fight to the last of his soldiers just wouldn't do anymore.

Lee had that strength, the necessary hardness. But Grant knew the man didn't see the country whole. *He* hadn't trapped Lee in Virginia. Virginia had trapped Lee. *Lee* had trapped Lee. And this was where the idol would be broken.

You had to swing the hammer, and not worry about whose fingers might be crushed.

Lincoln understood. Didn't like all the pieces, but he saw the puzzle whole. Maybe it had to do with the western rivers, the way they captured the spirit. Maybe it all had started with him as a boy, taking his father's tanned hides down the Ohio to the Mississippi and on down south, getting schooled in the bigness, the immensity, of the living land, with its muddy veins and arteries. Maybe all this was a child's dream made real with the blood of millions.

Didn't matter if it was. All that mattered was winning.

To the south, artillery opened *en masse*. Wright's guns. And, he hoped, Baldy Smith's batteries, too.

He lit a cigar to keep off the flies and said, "Wouldn't mind a cup of your mud coffee, George." He creased his mouth in a smile to put his hosts at ease.

No, they didn't understand. Lincoln did. And Sherman, more and more. But the only other person who saw it was Bill.

"Yassuh," his servant had said to him, "you jes' like a dog has got him a big ole ham bone. Eat up all the meat to once, then chaw that bone in two. Even if it cut that ole hound's mouth all up and bleeding. Just ain't got no give-up, no suh-ree. I pities the man try to take that bone away."

Lee was a bone that had to be chawed in two.

Four forty-five p.m.
Cold Harbor

The mulberry trees had been picked clean, as if by biblical locusts, and the dead had all been buried in shallow pits. His brigade had relieved the cavalrymen at noon, arriving so weary that many a soldier could barely keep his feet, but Brigadier General Emory Upton adhered to his hard-learned standards: The dead Confederates from the morning's fighting had to be put in the earth, not to honor them—he would not honor men who fought for slavery—but to keep his own men in health. Discipline, sanitation, and faith were his bedrocks, and he would not have his men lie down among corpses.

There would be more corpses, many more. The artillery had already begun its work, firing at targets hidden by a veil of scrub pines. His trusted 121st New York had deployed a heavy skirmishing party to clear the Rebs from their forward rifle pits, but the main Confederate line lay across a field and beyond a grove. His skirmishers reported trees felled as obstacles in front of a trench line that had already been given head logs. The enemy had learned to fortify with speed.

He rode back into the low ground where his first line stood ready. The soldiers looked dusty and worn, impatient, nervous, and eager. Beneath the grit, their uniforms were new. They had not seen the elephant.

His shriveled brigade had been reinforced by a garrison artillery regiment, the 2nd Connecticut Heavies, who had been converted into infantrymen with the suddenness of Saul transformed into Paul on the road to Damascus. Those fifteen hundred new, untested men had more than doubled his brigade's strength on the road not to Damascus, but to Richmond. And their colonel, a profane but earnest man,

Elisha Kellogg, had volunteered his men to lead this attack. Upton had been glad of it. If the artillerymen wished to disprove the jeers that they were bandbox soldiers, that was meet and good. Their turn had come to suffer battle and put their trust in the Lord. And his ever-fewer veterans would be spared the worst of the fighting for one day.

The dead were buried, but the flies still sensed their presence and plagued the living. It would be a relief to go forward. It always was. Even when an attack appeared unlikely to succeed, all things became clear and purposeful once the first line stepped toward the enemy.

He had arranged his men in the same formation he had used three weeks before at Spotsylvania, four lines that would advance briskly, with the same instructions not to fire until they had breached the enemy's entrenchments. He would not have the element of surprise today, but punching rapidly into the defense seemed the only hope.

The enemy knew they were coming. It was going to be bloody.

Colonel Kellogg harangued his men, shouting to be heard over the guns, encouraging them to prove their worth in battle. Upton waited for the man to invoke the Lord and ask his blessing, but the call never came. He did not interrupt, though. Kellogg had the loyalty of his men, and Upton had learned the value of worldly emotions.

He would pray for all of them.

Follow after me: for the LORD hath delivered your enemies the Moabites into your hands . . .

His horse knew him and fidgeted, ready to go forward. Upton sometimes felt mortal tremors, the rebellion of the flesh, but his mind was ever at ease in the face of death. He knew this was a holy war, against Moabites and worse, against human beasts that had enslaved God's children. Their ruler was Pharaoh, their priests were the priests of

Baal. He who fell in battle against such enemies would be lifted high upon the wings of angels.

And they slew of Moab at that time about ten thousand men, all lusty, and all men of valour; and there escaped not a man.

Lord, let it be thus. Let it be for the righteous as it was in the days of Joshua, of Judges and Kings.

And Judah went up; and the LORD delivered the Canaanites and the Perizzites into their hand; and they slew of them in Bezek ten thousand men . . .

Lord, let it be so.

For thou shalt drive out the Canaanites, though they have iron chariots, and though they be *strong.*

Lord, grant us victory, in thy name.

He looked over the dust-caked, unknowing multitude, three ranks of former artillerymen and the last rank composed of his veterans. And he prayed that the Lord would have mercy on those who perished, especially on those deficient in their faith, for all would do the work of the Lord this day.

He thought, as he often did, of the Negroes he had known at Oberlin College, before he had been selected for West Point. If their skin had been dark, their faith had been bright as silver. The thought of such men enslaved and bodily chastised, abandoned to conditions worse than the Babylonian captivity, made Emory Upton wish he could call down fire upon every Southron head, and on the beasts of their fields, on their orchards and vineyards.

The South was not the mere Babylon of old. It was a Babylon of leprous souls.

The cannon stopped.

The silence swelled.

A crow cawed.

Colonel Kellogg looked to Upton, who nodded.

The colonel dismounted and strode to the front of his

troops. Raising his sword, he called, "Forward! Guide center! March!"

Upton rode forward with them.

Well, it had been a good life. If it ended here, it did. Nothing to be done about it. No choice. He had to set the example for his men, who were going to fight at last.

As he strode forward at the head of his regiment, Elisha S. Kellogg felt sweat trickle down his back. He knew it was not only from the heat.

This barren place. Well, he had known others as bad. Young, he had sailed the seas on British merchantmen. He had chased the gleam of gold in the fevered beauty of California. And when the gold refused to leap into his hands, he had built a solid life up in Connecticut.

He had regrets. And faults. He knew he blustered at times, but such was his nature. A man learned to live with his foibles, even to be amused at his own helplessness. And if he had, at times, been hard on his troops, determined to keep them soldierly in their long, dreary months in garrison at Washington, manning guns they had never fired in anger, well, he believed they had forgiven him, even that they respected him.

Almost a nervous tic, he glanced rearward. And there they were. Marching handsomely enough to please that fox-faced babe of a brigadier general with Bible verses on his lips and murder in his eyes. The veteran regimental commanders had warned Kellogg never to swear or take the Lord's name in vain in Upton's presence. It was a hard sentence for a man who had strayed along the docks in San Francisco. Keeping off the Lord wasn't hard, but cleansing his speech of the virile joy of obscenity—sailor's delight—required vigilance.

As his men tramped forward, three thousand feet marching over a fallow field, Kellogg did not call on the Lord to spare him or his soldiers. He had lived as he had lived, and he would die, if need be, as he died. And that was that.

Wouldn't mind living, though.

He'd heard the dreadful tales of these frontal attacks. Arriving at Spotsylvania just in time to march southward under Upton's unforgiving eye, his soldiers had been shocked by the look of those they joined—not only by their ragged filth, but by the dead eyes they brought to bear on a man.

He stepped between abandoned rifle pits. The veteran skirmishers filtered back through his ranks. They did not pause to tease his soldiers now.

He lifted his sword and felt the suck of rich sweat in his armpit. His regiment's colors trailed him, limp in the still air.

His men looked fine, though.

He had been told that other brigades would advance on either flank, but he saw no one, not even a flag. He realized what that absence meant and shuddered, but kept his shoulders squared.

Trees ahead, a pine thicket. Good for nothing but breaking their marching order.

He turned his head sharply, to one side and then the other. Hunting the swarm of insects they had roused. Only when a soldier fell did he understand: The air was full of bullets. *That* was how they sounded.

He turned to face his men. Marching with his back to the enemy, he saw one fellow break from the ranks to run rearward.

"Steady, men! Follow your colonel!"

He wheeled to face the enemy again. Before he tripped and made a fool of himself. Dignity mattered in a man's life. He had never understood those for whom it was of no consequence. Every man did foolish things, but a good man lived his life upright.

Ah, not all of the foolish things were things he wished undone. . . .

He brushed past a pine tree. And saw a living Rebel. Aiming and firing, then trotting rearward. The trees hardly made up a forest or even a grove, but they hid whatever waited behind their greenery.

That henna-haired darling in green velvet on the Barbary Coast . . .

Won't find one like that a second time.

He stiffened his arm, pointing his sword like the needle of a compass. For the last course a man sailed.

Why was he being so morbid?

He knew why.

The fox-faced brigadier would have no complaints about his men this day. Again, he looked rearward. His men struggled to keep their ranks amid the starved-looking pines. Upton, on horseback, followed behind the first battalion, staying ahead of the second. Even at forty yards, the man looked savage.

Their course sloped downward, easily, into a dry swale. More firing now, from men who could not be seen. Soldiers fell, some with a small cry, others as silently as if in an opium trance. The colors dipped, but an eager sergeant caught them.

Good, good.

One of his men had surprised him by bringing him a cap half-filled with mulberries. They had tasted all the better for the kindness. He had not always been a gentle commander. But he was a man whose heart was touched by the oddest things, sentimental in ways he could never share.

When he told her good-bye that last time, the night before he sailed from San Francisco, she had refused his money. Of small gestures were the sweetest memories made.

Why think of her now, and not of his orderly later life, his upstanding years?

He knew why. Oh, he knew.

He was a large, strong man, but the damned sword seemed as heavy as China-trade ballast. Still, he held it extended.

A compass needle, pointing God knew where.

They climbed the far side of the swale. Confederate cannon, still unseen, opened fire, but overshot. All those long months of manning big guns, and now the cannonballs were coming toward them.

He could be an awfully clumsy fellow in dealing with other men, awkward, but quick he was at seeing the humor in life, the jokes fate played.

He glimpsed open space beyond a last row of pines.

Was that where they were? Waiting?

"Come on, men, come on! That's it, boys! Onward, Connecticut!"

His throat was so dry his words seemed to cut its flesh.

It wasn't a field that awaited them. Pushing through the last pines, he saw a midget's forest of stumps, their tops pale and glinting with sap.

Across the new-made clearing, the harvested trees had been woven into an obstacle. Behind rose a rampart of raw dirt and fence rails, topped with freshly cut logs. The Rebels were not even visible. He saw only their rifle barrels, thrust through narrow gaps. To the left, the muzzles of cannon peeked from hastily made emplacements. A red flag hung slack in the trees.

The earth exploded. Rifles flared. Artillery flashed blindingly, then gauzed itself with smoke. All around, his men recoiled, struck, shocked, wavering.

He lifted his sword so its point aimed at the heavens.

"Come on, boys, come on, *come on!* Forward the Heavies! Come on!"

He dared not look about him. Then he looked anyway. Yes, some men had lost heart. But most stayed with him.

The enemy rifles had disappeared, drawing back like serpents' tongues. Now they thrust through the openings again.

"Down!" he shouted on instinct. "Get down!"

The men who heard him dropped. Others followed their example, just as another dragon's breath of flame shot from the line.

"Re-form! Re-form! On your feet, re-form!"

The cries of the wounded, of his shattered men, cut through the gale of noise.

But men rose. Still plenty of them. They dutifully sought to form ranks.

As he looked about, he saw—to his astonishment—that Upton remained mounted, showing himself above a stand of dwarf pines, a pistol shot away.

Waving his sword like a signal flag, Kellogg began to run forward, toward the mesh of felled trees, toward the fortress the Johnnies had forged from the wretchedness of Virginia.

"Come on, boys! *Charge!*"

They ran forward. Shouting. Their force felt irresistible.

He dashed between the stumps, waving his sword. Bursting with passion, he pulled off his hat to wave it, too. He felt as if he could tug the whole army behind him.

God love the bad women, for the awful truth was that they'd been the joy of his life.

He did not think once of the innocent face he had left behind in Connecticut.

"Come on!"

There were years in every second. . . .

The Rebs fired freely now, as swiftly as they could load. His men dropped like bottles in a barroom brawl.

A man could be an awfully fragile thing. . . .

He slashed at the tangled branches keeping him and his soldiers from the hateful entrenchments. Furious. Determined to accomplish something worthy.

"Come on!"

To his right, a pair of his men made it all the way to the entrenchments, smashing their rifle butts at the protruding muzzles.

"That's the way!" Kellogg shouted.

But when he looked rearward, wanting to lead a mass of soldiers over those piled logs, he saw little more than men falling, arms flying outward, while others crumpled in on themselves to drop headfirst and lie still. The hewn grove showed as many bodies as stumps.

Yet, amazingly, wonderfully, living men in dark blue coats surged forward, toward the ramparts.

He knew, though. They were no longer enough. His second line seemed to have gone to ground. He did not have enough men, of these good men, to break the Rebel line. They would have to regroup and charge again.

Lowering his sword, he waved his hat.

"Fall back! Regroup! Fall—"

Someone punched him terribly in the jaw. He had never been hit so hard, not even in his wild sailing days.

Just as he realized, an instant later, that it had not been a fist that staggered him, another bullet struck him, and another.

Upton spurred his horse forward, shouting, "Lie down, lie down! Don't return fire. Lie down!"

He was angry enough to feel the lure of profanity. Eustis' brigade had not even attempted to come forward until too late. And Truex, from Ricketts' division on the right, had gotten off to a tardy start, then disappeared into a ravine, as if the earth had swallowed him. His single brigade opposed a Rebel division, well dug in.

Didn't anyone in the army have *any* sense? Couldn't anyone *think*?

The Heavies were brave enough, though. He had seen Kellogg fall just short of the Rebel entrenchments. The other field officers from the new regiment had dropped at the head of their troops. It was now a captain's fight.

"Lie *down*!" He almost added, "Damn it."

He heard double *thwaps* in the instant before his horse buckled. Flinging himself from the animal's back before it could trap his leg, he landed hard and felt his lungs empty of air. Gasping, he rose and ran from the shuddering, kicking animal to continue trying to save what men he could. The last of his aides had disappeared, sent back to demand assistance, support, anything that might save the attack from failure.

Black specks flashed by. The Rebs were sporting with him. In a rage, he threw himself to the ground among the soldiers. Unable even to command his brigade.

He knew that if he fell, the attack would collapse completely. And he wanted, at the very least, to hold on to the ground their blood had already earned. Surely General Russell, or Wright himself, would act like a leader, not an ignoramus?

Even as he lay there, amid wounded, frightened, and slaughtered men, he could not stop thinking through the problems of modern war. There *had* to be a way to pierce entrenchments. At Spotsylvania, surprise and compact mass had done the trick. But there had to be a more reliable answer. And he believed he would be the man to find it.

He did not pray. He would not insult the Lord by begging in time of danger. He *trusted* in the Lord.

Minutes passed. And more minutes. The light began to soften. Now and then, a soldier called out in the short, surprised cry of a man struck by a bullet.

Upton refused to give up. At the very least, these men would hold this ground. It would *not* be another Spotsylvania, where his success had been wasted. And it galled him to think that the first experience these new soldiers had of combat might be failure. He needed them to be confident, if they were to replace his butchered veterans.

They had not performed badly. On the contrary. The march from Spotsylvania had been a torment for the pampered artillerymen, their feet unused to distances greater than the parade ground to a parapet. And they had been teased and chastised for their struggle to keep up. He had been merciless, because that had been the requirement. But now they had fought bravely, done their best, and he hated the thought of their lives and efforts wasted.

"Stay down!" he said. "Don't fire back!" If there was a chance, any chance, to push forward one more time, he wanted their rifles loaded when they reached the entrenchments. And firing now, into earthen walls and ramparts of logs, gained them nothing, merely drawing the attention of sharpshooters.

Sensing that he was still obeyed, he rose and rushed back to the pines, pursued by bullets. Russell had to do something, drive Eustis to try again, anything. He did not want to order his men—these men—to retreat into failure.

The third rank had taken shelter in the swale amid the pine grove. His veterans waited behind them, the last rank, perhaps a last hope. But he hated to order *those* men to carry the works.

He found one of his aides, lightly wounded but unwilling to quit the field.

"What word?" Upton demanded.

"You're bleeding, sir. Are you—"

"My horse went down. What word from General Russell?"

"General Russell's been wounded. No further orders."

"Badly?"

"I don't think so. He's still on the field. But everything's confused."

"Everything's always confused."

Something shifted. It took him a moment to reorder his thoughts, to grasp the meaning.

Hurrahs. *Union* hurrahs. Not Rebel screeching. Amid a great burst of firing. *Behind* the Rebel lines, if his ears were worth anything. *In* the Reb lines, and just to the right.

Truex. Had his brigade reemerged from the underworld?

Upton grabbed the aide by the upper arm. "Find General Russell. Tell him we're attacking. With everything. Tell him we're in their lines." He thought for just an instant. "First go to the Hundred and Twenty-first New York. They're to advance on our right flank. The other regiments are to remain in reserve until I call for them. Then find Russell. Tell him to put in everything he can."

The aide stared at him in disbelief.

"Just do as I say," Upton commanded. *"Go!"*

Upton took off himself, drawing his sword again. He had always envied Wellington's decisive command at Waterloo. Now he had his own chance to adopt it:

"Up, men, and at 'em! We're in their lines, we've broken their lines. Come on, boys, up and at 'em!"

A few men rose, then more.

There was no time to order their ranks. Seconds mattered.

Smoke drabbed the weakening daylight. But Upton saw U.S. colors behind the parapet.

"Come on, boys! It's our turn now! Come on, let's go!"

Men sensed things. He could not say how. His faith was of the practical, orderly, impatient-with-mysteries sort. Yet, he'd noted a magic in masses of men, an abrupt heightening of awareness, as if a greater mind had taken over. And these men, his men, grasped that their lot had changed.

They rose up and followed him, outpaced him. It was their turn now, and they knew it.

They began to hurrah.

The Reb fire from the entrenchments still killed, but had only a shadow of its former power. The Heavies crashed into the barrier of felled timbers and branches, clawing and climbing, some of them shouting obscenities ripe with hatred.

"Get inside! Get inside and fire. Then use your bayonets!"

The first of his men were at—and over—the rampart, shouting and shooting. The 2nd Connecticut's flag came up beside Upton.

"Plant the colors on that wall!"

An artillery section blasted the men following him with canister, turning their flesh into rags of meat. But others came on, undeterred.

The Johnnies were about to get a lesson.

"You! Captain! Get your men inside and wheel left. Silence those guns!"

Climbing over the berm himself, he saw that Truex's men were deep in the trees, sweeping leftward, southward.

"Wheel left!" Upton shouted, waving his sword. "Don't stop! Wheel left! Charge!"

Some Johnnies were fighting hand to hand, no cowards. Others, wiser, withdrew, firing as they went. A few just plain ran.

Then more ran.

His rechristened artillerymen became furies. What they lacked in skill, they made up for in brutality, crowding around resisting Rebels to club and bayonet them beyond all need. One long-bearded, withered-looking Reb fought madly, holding his rifle by the barrel and swinging it, catching a sergeant on the side of the head. A second later, a soldier pressed a muzzle to the Johnny's ribs and fired, blowing the man backward.

"Don't stop! Push on! Wheel left! Come on!"

The Confederate line collapsed like a row of dominoes.

His men howled, driving all before them, seizing guns and hurtling over secondary trenches. Deep in the grove, Truex's men thrust on.

Men wrestled for flags amid drifts of smoke.

A lean company of Johnnies tried to organize a volley, but barely half had loaded and fired before the Heavies crashed into them. Deprived of his rifle, a Reb charged into the melee, wielding a log as a lance.

Why wasn't the rest of the division, of the corps, supporting their success?

They had pushed so far down the line of entrenchments so quickly that Upton knew his men were overextended. And he also knew what would be coming soon: a Confederate counterattack. Lee and his paladins would not let this success go uncontested.

The only question was how near the Reb reinforcements might be.

His New York veterans were fighting on the flank, not wildly, but methodically. His other veterans remained to the rear, spared, holding the ground bought with blood in the earlier evening. He wanted them there, a surprise for the Rebels, if a surprise was needed.

He remained with the Heavies, who were going to need leadership when the Rebs came screaming through the trees with the last sun at their backs.

Knots of tattered prisoners scurried rearward, outraged at their predicament, shocked, but bending forward as if from a heavy rain, determined not to catch a bullet now that they were formally out of the war.

He looked around for officers from the 2nd Connecticut.

They had to regroup, get the men into some form of order that could respond to commands.

Slow and brilliant, the final shafts of sunlight stabbed through the trees. The denser patches of the grove had already succumbed to the twilight. In gilded smoke, men gasped for breath, eyes vivid and astonished to be alive.

"Company commanders! Form your men! Form up!"

Some soldiers responded purposefully. Others just meandered.

"Any man separated from his unit, join the nearest company. Officers, pass on the word. Gather ammunition from the dead. Wounded men, turn over your ammunition." He strode among the trees, ignoring harassing shots from defiant Rebels. "They're going to counterattack. Every man, get ready."

He heard an irritated voice say, "We whipped them, fair and square." As if there were rules the enemy must obey.

"Prepare for a counterattack!" Upton shouted.

Some of the new men appeared dazed, while others had lost their rifles but tagged along anyway. Most still seemed capable, if no longer eager. Upton understood that, too, the sudden deflation of energy as an attack runs out of push.

He seized upon a sergeant who seemed to have his men in decent order. "You, Sergeant. Take these soldiers back to the main entrenchments. And don't let any of these other men pass by." He stepped closer, raising his voice instead of lowering it. Needing each of the nearby men to hear him. "Shoot or bayonet the coward who runs."

It was a bluff. He doubted these men would shoot their own comrades, let alone give them the bayonet. But he also knew that men, especially those new to battle, could stand only so much. And he would need to push them to the extreme.

The firing had dropped to a grudging give-and-take. Deeper in, Truex was still advancing, by the sound of it.

The prospect made Upton long to renew the attack. But that would be a fool's choice. When the Rebs hit Truex, he'd be spread too thin to hold.

Fight for every inch, he thought. Swing back, if need be, to the primary trench line they had conquered, but not a step beyond it. Hold that ground.

If you held until full night, you probably could hold until morning. And in the morning, surely, reinforcements would be up.

The luminous twilight darkened.

He sensed them even before he heard them raise their Rebel yell. Bounding through the forest, predators hungry for a kill. Veterans coming on against these tired men of his, their spirits half-disarmed by their success.

The howling began. It was always startling, even unnerving, to men who had heard it for years. A thousand unsure soldiers tensed around him.

"Here they come!" he shouted. "Men of Connecticut! We *must* hold this line!"

The surviving company officers appeared solid. That was good. On their own, they were cautioning men to hold their fire until they had a good target, to let the Rebs come close.

A shot-through man pawed at Upton's boot, begging, "Don't *lee*-me here, don't *lee*-me here . . ."

Upton walked on.

They held. Bless them, they held. They had not maintained their forward-most position, but the best of them wouldn't quit the Rebel line and they still owned a stretch of it. Most of the other Heavies had halted in the field of stumps, on the left and just to the rear, asserting a ragged line of their own, many a man lying flat, but at least not running, while their comrades fought on in the near dark.

He had needed to call up one more veteran regiment,

but his brigade still had some depth. In case the Johnnies brought on reinforcements and risked a night attack.

Much of the Reb order had broken on Truex's men,
driving them back, but growing confused in the process.
A line-turned-mob had struck Upton's soldiers hard,
forcing them back amid fighting that was often hand to
hand—or fist to fist. He had seen a Johnny thrust a rifle
muzzle under the chin of an artilleryman, literally blowing the man's brains out when he pulled the trigger, but
fatally misjudging his own action: The rifle's recoil had
slammed the butt down upon the Rebel's knee, making
him stagger in pain for the pair of seconds necessary for
one of Upton's men to catch him in the face with the tip of
a gun stock, bashing him down and then bending to crush
his skull.

But Upton sensed that the Heavies were nearly used
up. The men holding in the shelter of the trench still
fired into the smoke-bruised glow that was giving way to
night, but more and more of those scattered among the
stumps and trees just lay there, letting other men decide
the battle.

If the Rebs, who had stopped a mere fifty yards away,
caught their breath and came on again, these men were going to run . . . or quit and surrender. It was just the way men
were, taking so much, but no more. God had made them
so, for his own purposes.

You couldn't let them lie there cuddling their fears, that
was the thing. They had to be active, too busy to think,
whatever the action you squeezed from them might be.

"You!" Upton snapped at a soldier tucked behind a
stump. "Load your rifle and give it to me. Now!" Other soldiers had alerted, lifting their faces a few inches from the
earth in expectation, though they knew not of what. "You,
too. And you. All of you. Load your rifles and pass them

here to me. And keep reloading. We're going to hold this line, we're not going one step back."

Ill-aimed bullets hissed through the settling night. A slash of moon above the groves and random firing lit the world enough for men to see each other's forms and blue ivory faces.

A soldier held up a rifle. Upton took it.

He steadied his elbow on a stump and fired toward the opposing muzzle flashes. For a second time, he nearly pronounced a profane word. He had not fired a rifle in many months and had forgotten to pull the stock tight against his shoulder. The kick hurt.

He passed back the rifle and chose from the others extended toward him.

"Don't point it *at* me!" He took the proffered arm.

Shifting deeper into the pack of men strewn over the ground, he chose a surviving tree for his position. It wasn't much of a tree, but it concealed his silhouette from the enemy. He was not afraid of being shot, but knew that if he was hit, these men would flee.

Again, he fired toward the shadowy Johnnies. They were almost close enough to duel with rocks. But they had stopped. That was the thing that mattered. As long as they didn't rally for one more charge.

He fired. Took another rifle and fired that. And he kept firing, shoulder hurting like the dickens. A man forgot so much of what his soldiers felt. . . .

Around him, first one man, then more of the Heavies, fired in the direction of the enemy. Upton knew it would be pure chance if any shot hit a Reb, but that didn't matter. What mattered was the belief of these men that they were fighting back.

It was always belief that mattered.

The sword of the Lord, and of Gideon.

Each muzzle flash was a tiny hint of hellfire.

And he smote them hip and thigh with a great slaughter . . .

With enough men firing now to warn off the Rebs, Upton shouted, "This ground belongs to us. Every man not firing, start digging in."

That was a command the men were glad to follow. They scraped with bayonets and their bare hands.

Upton chose a soldier who seemed reliable, waited until the fellow got off a last shot, and tapped him on the shoulder. "Go to the rear. Find any officer at the rank of major or higher. And tell him General Upton"—he almost said "needs," but caught himself—"wants ammunition brought forward immediately. Tell him we're holding a lodgment in the Rebel entrenchments." He considered. "If you can't remember those words, just tell him we've taken a good bite out of the Rebel line and mean to keep it." He gripped the man's arm. "Understand?"

"Yes, sir. Sure do."

Upton looked at him hard, at the pale eyes in the night, trying to judge whether this man would do as told, or run away the moment he had the chance.

"Don't know if I'll find my way any good," the man volunteered. "Coming back, I mean. It's dark, General."

"Just come toward the firing. Now *go.*"

The soldier scuttled off, clutching his rifle.

A few dozen voices raised a Rebel yell. Blurs rushed off to the right, toward the stretch of entrenchments his men still held. Rifles blazed from the ditch. The foray disintegrated.

If they didn't come on in force, these men would hold. He moved along until he found a captain.

"Name?"

"Archibald, sir." Or that was what Upton believed he had heard. The name didn't matter, really. What mattered was that the man had spoken his name and assumed Upton had heard it.

"I'm putting you in command of this stretch of the line. See that these men dig proper entrenchments. If I can, I'll have spades brought forward, but they'll construct a proper line if they have to use their fingernails and teeth. Do you understand me?"

"Yes, sir."

"Organize a rotation of the men, one-third firing, one-third digging, one-third resting in place, but ready to repel a rush by the enemy. Do you understand?"

"Yes, sir."

"Captain, you will *not* quit this line. If you withdraw one step, I will have you shot. Do you understand that?"

"General, you don't have to threat—"

"Did you understand me, Captain?"

"Yes, sir."

"Execute my orders."

Upton turned from the man and strode rearward into the grove. He did what he could not to step on or kick the wounded. The dead mattered less. Men's souls, not their bodies, had value. The dead were saved or damned, as their lives and the Lord determined.

He had to speak with Russell, if the man's wound had not driven him to the rear. He needed to be reinforced. The men needed ammunition. The worst of the wounded had to be gathered in. And he could not count on the soldier he had sent rearward. The need for certainty demanded he do this himself, now that things had settled down into harassing fire.

First, he prowled the pine grove until he found his horse. A black shape in the blue night, the creature was still alive and breathing monstrously. Its kicks had grown feeble, warding off great pain.

Whether from sight, or smell, or the sense that animals possessed, the horse alerted to his approach and raised its head slightly in greeting. Huge eyes gleamed like wet china.

Upton shot the horse with his revolver.

TWENTY-FOUR

June 2, noon
Ninth Corps line, Union right

I don't need a commission," Brown told the captain. "The men need rations."

Steam wisped off their uniforms. It had rained at dawn. Before the sun dried their rags, the Rebs had probed them again. Then it rained again, just long enough to drench everybody, and the sun came back to boil them in wet wool.

"They'll fight, sir," he continued. "They'll march. They'll dig all the way to China." Brown wanted to shake the captain's arm, to be sure the man was fully awake. "But they need to be *fed*."

Captain Schwenk looked to the side before meeting Brown's eyes anew. "I'm trying, Sergeant Brown. Nobody in this division seems to be responsible for anything anymore."

Schwenk was a good man, Brown knew. Best officer in the regiment. Certainly, the best one still alive. So many officers had been killed or wounded that Schwenk was the senior man left, filling the colonel's position.

The strain showed. Normally a solid man, the captain looked starved himself, eyes sunk so deep in his skull that crevices showed between his eyelids and brow. Virginia grit and powder burns had painted his face for a minstrel show, mirroring the faces of his men.

A fly settled on the captain's cheek. Schwenk seemed unaware.

Brown didn't want to add to the captain's burdens. He knew Schwenk was doing his best. No man was better suited to lead the regiment. And yet he could not stop himself from adding, "It's been two full days, sir. I told the men we'd be on half-rations, not no rations."

"I'll see that the men are fed today. That's a promise." Schwenk shook his head hard, waking himself again. "Christ, what I wouldn't give for a pan of eggs. And some scrapple."

Brown did not want to think about that. But he did. His mouth tried to water, but couldn't. The liquid in his canteen was so foul, he sipped only enough to stay on his feet.

"I *promise* you the men will be fed today," Schwenk repeated.

Brown accepted that. He had gotten what he had to say off his chest. And he didn't want to become the sort who confused complaints with doing. He asked: "Any word on Lieutenant Hiney's leg, sir?"

"Won't have to come off. So they tell me."

"Corporal Cake?" Brown lifted his cap and passed his fingers through clots of hair, yearning to be free of lice.

"Won't be dancing for a time, but he'll be all right. Queer business, one bullet, two men. And both in the leg."

Skirmishing erupted again. Neither man bothered to look in its direction.

"Wasn't even much of a fight," Brown said. "Just more grinding down. We brush up against the Rebs, they brush up against us. Nobody makes any headway, but the company's a little smaller."

"And the regiment," Schwenk put in.

"Then we march off again, and they march off just as quick," Brown continued. "And it just keeps going along."

Schwenk told him: "It's called 'maneuvering,' Sergeant." His tone had grown uncharacteristically bitter. "It's what generals do between one mistake and the next."

Lusting for sleep, Brown said, "Guess I'd better get the men ready to march." He didn't like the dead sound of his voice, but didn't know how to make it sound right, either. "Know where we're going, sir?"

"Pulling back by that church, for a start. Then south again, I suppose. General Burnside may not know himself, way things seem."

"Wouldn't mind not smelling corpses for a while." Brown tried to smile, but failed. Some days before, in the course of a brief, grabbed sleep, he had dreamed of returning home to Frances. He carried the death-stink with him. She ran from him, screaming.

"Just bear in mind what I told you," Schwenk said, returning to the start of their conversation, "and I'm not going to have any arguing. I intend to push you for lieutenant. As soon as I can put one clean hand to a clean piece of paper." His mouth took on a lemon-bite twist. "I wish it could be a captaincy. Given the captains who've managed to survive."

"I could go on fine like this," Brown offered. Although he wasn't sure that anything would ever be fine again. "Just the way you do, sir. Rank doesn't matter."

"It damned well *does* matter. *Listen to me*. Lieutenant Brumm wanted you to have the company. *Ahead* of Lieutenant Hiney. Yesterday, Hiney begged me to put you in charge and keep you there." He reached inside his blouse to scratch himself. "Anyway, you're the senior man now. What do you want? Some green, parade-ground Napoleon to take your company? Some on-the-teat brat commissioned by the governor? And kill everybody who's left? If I can't get you an officer's rank, that's exactly what's going to happen."

Schwenk's voice had broken discipline, revealing nerves and strain. It pierced Brown. They had both seen so much death in so short a time.

Now and then he thought he was going mad enough for manacles. The rest of the time he just felt hungry and tired. Fear was a luxury up there with feather pillows.

He fingered his hair again, then scratched his scalp. Wishing he had the learning to speak words of comfort to the good man standing before him. Schwenk's responsibilities dwarfed his own. He'd been acting like some private, whining like a woman.

"Well, I suppose if they're dumb enough to make me a lieutenant . . ."

"I'm more concerned that they're dumb enough *not* to," Schwenk told him. "Anyway, the war might be over long before it goes through. So don't buy yourself a new uniform just yet."

"Fine with me, sir."

"It's settled, then." Schwenk clawed at his armpit. "Know what paradise would be to me right now? A bath and a plate of sausage." He grinned, showing unclean teeth. "I joined up believing war exalts a man. But it only humbles us."

"No, sir," Brown said. "It shames us."

Three p.m.
Cold Harbor, Union left

Thank God they've postponed it," Gibbon said, steadying his horse. "My men are blown. I've been on hellish marches, but last night . . ."

"Night marches are most appealing on a map," Barlow said. "Paine ought to be whipped. In front of every soldier he misled."

"How far out of the way do you think he took us?"

Barlow shrugged. "Five miles, at the very least. Of choking dust, then rain to glue it on. I'm almost beginning to sympathize with my stragglers."

"I doubt that."

Barlow wanted to dismount, strip off his boots and stockings, and order up a bucket to soak his feet. Without the slightest change of expression, he said, "What we escaped today comes in spades tomorrow. Your front any more promising than mine?"

Gibbon wiped the sweat from his mustache. His horse dropped a steaming pile. "There's only one point where I've got any hope of punching through. And that's one chance in a hundred."

Barlow offered his wry smile-for-all-purposes. "You're more hopeful than I am, then. Have a look at that hill out there. I wouldn't want to attack it this afternoon, and I certainly don't fancy going there in the morning, after they've had all night to decorate. Get out your field glasses and take a good, long look."

"I've seen it."

"Perfect artillery position, absolutely commanding. Nothing comparable over here, of course. Too much to ask of anyone to perform a reconnaissance of the positions we're ordered to occupy. Might take the sport out of it. Better to roll the dice." He breathed deeply, trying to enliven himself, but only filled his lungs with the fragrance of horse droppings. "I've had Miles out skirmishing. He reports they've already built themselves a regular line of works. With half a mile of open space in front. I won't call it an invitation to butchery, since proper butchery serves a useful purpose."

Underscoring his point, a section of enemy guns fired over the line his soldiers were busy hacking into the earth.

"Careful of the sarcasm, Frank. You're getting a reputation."

"Oh, I can still kill ragged men as well as any general. Nothing to worry about."

"Anyone on your left?" Gibbon asked. "Any danger of being flanked?"

"I hardly know. I've got a mile-wide gap between my left and the Chickahominy. Cavalry were supposed to cover it, according to the high priests in the temple." The cut of his smile deepened. "Know what the mighty powers sent down? One regiment, on jades. They scampered off as soon as somebody shot at them."

"Christ," Gibbon said.

"Not certain he bears on the problem. Although there's a certain sacrificial element."

"At least we didn't have to go straight into the attack. I suppose I'm a brainless old soldier to you, but I'm pleased with the mercies I get." Gibbon's weather-worn face grew grimmer. "I'm not certain I could have gotten the men to go forward today. Not far, anyway. They really are dead on their feet, the sorry bastards."

"They'll be dead on their bellies and backs tomorrow," Barlow assured him. "The time to attack was this morning. We didn't get here in time, and the opportunity was lost. Late is *not* better than never." He shook his head. "I can't believe old Meade doesn't see the senselessness of this 'grand assault across the entire front.' When the Rebs will be ready and waiting, for all that's holy. The only hope, and a slight one, would be a narrow attack in deep echelon on *one* decisive point. Not this all-in-and-hope-something-good-happens nonsense. Meade *has* to see it."

"Meade does, Grant doesn't."

"Small consolation. Gibbon, I don't care to make this attack. It's damnable folly. Oh, I'll do it, of course. And you will, too. Along with the rest of this army, more or less. Come four thirty a.m., we'll behave like little gods, deaf to the lamentations of mere mortals. Because not one of us has the spine to do otherwise."

"And God damn us all."

"Redundant." He sighed, but even that had a cutting edge. "I shall speak with Hancock. One last try. Ease the suppurating conscience."

"He's unwell."

"Better than being dead out in that field. He needs to persuade Meade to call it off."

"Frank, I told you. It's not Meade, it's Grant. You don't think for one minute that Humphreys would concoct something like this? It's slops."

"Hancock to Meade, Meade to Grant."

"Grant doesn't care to know. Have you ever seen him at the front? Even once? From what I hear, he sits back there reading telegraphic messages, writing to Washington, and letting his staff kiss his feet. You're wasting your time."

"Preferable to wasting my division." He wouldn't have minded if somebody with a great wet tongue had kissed *his* feet, at the moment.

Humphreys shook his head. Wearily. "You do surprise me. A month ago, you would've charged through an ocean of blood, sacrificed ten thousand men, and called it a good day's work."

"Was it a month? Or a hundred years?" Watching Gibbon wave off a halo of flies, he let his smile widen. "You know, Gibbon, this *is* an interesting phenomenon. I'll have to ask Teddy Lyman about it."

"What are you on about now?"

"A living study in the degradation of a classic human type, *Homo bellicus.*"

Gibbon took the bait and looked at him quizzically.

"We've fallen so low," Barlow said, "that the flies prefer you to a pile of fresh horseshit."

Four p.m.
Gaines' Mill

Lee dismounted from Traveller, landing flat-footed enough to jar his spine. It reminded him of his frailty.

He passed the horse's reins to an orderly. The corporal's uniform was beggarly, but his eyes were eager. Lee patted Traveller's neck and thanked the man.

He was better, much better. Perhaps he had grown too confident, though. He had ridden as far as Mechanicsville before locating Breckinridge that morning. Normally a reliable young man, Major McClellan had guided the soldiers from the Valley astray. Nor had he communicated the terrible need for haste.

Chastisement would come later, within measure.

His body obeyed him again, but not without effort. Riding his new lines, he had inspected the ground his army occupied, then gone on to the southern stretch that waited for more soldiers to arrive. It had been a draining effort in the heat, and he had been plagued by fears he dared not reveal, expecting those people to attack before he could get enough men in place to repel them. Here, within the sound of Richmond's bells.

Two years before, he had fought upon this very ground, with what he had deemed success. But now those people had returned, after all those bloody months. Over the last, terrible weeks, he had parried Grant again and again. Yet, here they were, facing off on fields picketed with bones and rotting leather from battles past. He had observed soldiers playing toss with a skull, and had admonished them.

Jackson had been with him then, in their first great campaign together. And Stuart had fairly danced around McClellan. So many good men had served him well, only to fall away.

If he could not resurrect Tom Jackson before Judgment Day, Lee mused, he would at least have welcomed McClellan's return to command. How much better to face a cautious general captive to his fears than these remorseless men and, above all, Grant, who seemed to advance as relentlessly as the plague.

He did not know what he could have done differently. He did not know what else he could do now, beyond what he was doing. The army had not let him down, but, privately, he wondered if he had not let down the men lost from its ranks. And those still with him.

But this day Grant had not attacked, which was a welcome blessing. He now had enough men on the field—men who had trudged southward yet again—to make an assault on his lines so costly that even Grant would feel it.

If they did not come tonight, they would come in the morning. Those people were running out of room, nearing the impossible obstacle of the James. Grant would fight because he had to fight.

Deserters claimed that Union morale was poor. Lee yearned to believe it. Yet, deserters were contemptible men, no matter the army they fled, and he was ever wary of their claims.

Still, if it was true, if the Army of the Potomac was nearing collapse . . .

He dared not ask the Lord God for a miracle. But he would have been thankful, had the good Lord delivered one.

On his worst days, he foresaw losing the war, a thing once unimaginable. Angered by events yet to transpire, he raged and thought he would take his men to the hills to fight as partisans, anything to avoid the gross indignity of surrender. In calmer, wiser moments, though, he knew he would not carry out the fantasy. He was too old for the life of a guerrilla. Too old, perhaps, for the weight he already bore.

Correcting his bearing at every step, he approached the headquarters tent, miffed that no one had emerged to greet him and annoyed by the thought he might need to return to the carriage tomorrow.

Today had been crucial, though. This was the day he had needed to be on horseback. Hancock had stolen a march on him and Lee still could not understand why an attack had not swept over his entrenchments early that morning, before his line was extended and prepared.

Was it possible that Union morale truly was that bad? Might there have been a mutiny?

He warned himself not to luxuriate in daydreams, but to deal with the facts at hand.

Belatedly, Marshall emerged from the tent. The two men almost collided.

"Your pardon, sir," the military secretary said, adjusting his glasses. "I was finishing an order."

"What time is it now, Colonel Marshall? My watch has grown unreliable again."

"We do have to get you a better timepiece, sir. We—"

"A matter of sentiment. What time is it?"

"Five minutes past four."

Lee's features tightened, but his voice remained controlled. "I hear no guns."

"It's a good distance away."

"No, Colonel Marshall. We would hear the guns." A first note of agitation infected his tone. Early was fiery, but new to corps command. With Ewell sent off to Richmond as an invalid. "General Early *must* make this attack while there is time."

"Getting Early to attack isn't a problem."

"A chance such as this may not come to us again. With General Burnside leaving Warren uncovered. If General Early catches Burnside in midwithdrawal . . ."

Addled by his own concerns, a young officer thrust past

them. When he recognized the men he had rudely handled, his apologies threatened to run out the decade.

"Haste *becomes* a soldier on such a day," Lee told him. "Go on now, Lieutenant."

When the boy had disappeared into the tent's shadows, Marshall said, "Two Union corps *hors de combat* would certainly put a damper on their purposes."

"I count on General Burnside's unique qualities," Lee said, almost merry for that moment. "I trust he will not disappoint me."

"Never has before," Marshall noted.

Lee felt a sudden need to attend to personal matters. His recovery was still incomplete.

From the north, the sound of cannon rolled down the barren landscape.

"Little late, not much," Marshall said.

Lee began to turn away, but halted to ask, "Which division has General Early detailed against Warren's flank? Has he informed us?"

Marshall shook his head, but added, "Figuring from this morning's dispositions, it must be Gordon's."

Four thirty p.m.
Ninth Corps headquarters, Bethesda Church

The chicken was splendid! Simply splendid! No other way to describe it. Careful of his uniform, Major General Ambrose Burnside held the dripping breast gingerly, bending his bulk to take another bite.

Best part of the day, this chicken. Best part of the day. No question, no question. Warren. Rude man, distinctly unpleasant. What did Meade mean, telling him to "cooperate" with Warren? Bad enough being subordinated to Meade, that was bad enough. He was so far ahead of

Warren on the Army rolls it was contemptible of George Meade not to place him over both corps and give him command of the right wing of the army. Meade could do that, at least. But no: All of them were forever playing favorites, playing favorites.

Delicate maneuver, a withdrawal in the face of the enemy. All the books said so, every one of them. Bit like breaking things off with a mistress. It asked maturity, skill. Warren was all thunder and no lightning, as far as Ambrose Burnside was concerned. Cooperate? Damned if he'd subject himself to *that* humiliation. Warren could take his bird beak and peck for himself.

"Awfully good chicken," he said, still chewing, "awfully. Compliments, my compliments. Simply splendid."

"Plenty more, General," a grinning aide declared. "Virginia chickens been volunteering for the good old Union."

Burnside swallowed and said, "I'm sure the men are availing themselves of the bounty."

"They're eating like pigs," his commissary chief put in. "If there's one hungry mouth in this whole corps, shame on him."

Burnside tossed away the bones and rested in the shade, gathering strength to assault another chicken breast. Bottle of chilled champagne would have capped the fare, just one good bottle. Hadn't had a decent drop since crossing the Rapidan. Deprivations of war, dreadful business. Had to get in with Sheridan, that was the thing. Rumor had it the man kept a good supply, enough to waste on newspapermen. Befriend the fellow, worth the bit of effort. Word had it Sheridan disliked Meade, so they had that in common.

Fortifying his constitution with a heel of bread—fine napkin it made, too, soaking the juice off a man's chin—he surveyed the chicken parts piled on tin plates, selecting his target with a marksman's eye. The commissary's remark had troubled him, though. Couldn't have the men indulging too recklessly. This wasn't about killing chickens, after all, but war, cruel war! Soldiers needed a certain rigor, discipline. That was the thing, discipline! He tried to remember a French phrase he had read, something from de Saxe, but it eluded him.

He grasped at the breast he had chosen. It lay just beyond his reach. About to roll forward onto a knee, he heard the *clap-clap-clap* of rifle volleys, followed by the thumps of a number of cannon.

"What's that, what's that?" he demanded.

No one had an answer. And a captain snatched the chicken breast upon which he had settled.

"Find out, find out!" he snapped. "Can't have this. Surprises, always surprises! Why ain't I told anything?"

As if in response, a horseman galloped up to the headquarters tents and was redirected to the officers clustered under the oak. The man stayed on horseback and came on as if he meant to charge right through their picnic.

"Gather up the chicken," Burnside ordered.

The courier flung himself out of the saddle as smoothly as a trick rider in a circus. Nor did he observe the proper formalities, but aimed his eyes and words directly at Burnside, ignoring the staff and the proper chain of command.

Burnside made a note of that.

"Sir, General Crittenden says 'least a corps of Rebs coming down that 'ere Shady Grove Road, a-coming on with all but a brass band. General Crittenden's got his line stretched out a little ways north of here, but he says you better bring Potter and Wilcox up, 'cause there's a serious to-do a-coming on." Belatedly, the man saluted.

"*I* shall be the judge of whether my other divisions move or not," Burnside told the man.

"Yes, sir. I just—"

"You are dismissed, my good man."

"Yes, sir."

Burnside heaved himself to his feet. He was angry. First good meal he'd had in days, and the Rebs had managed to spoil it. They needed a lesson, a lesson.

He turned to his chief of staff. "Send to Wilcox and Potter. They're to move north at once and reinforce Crittenden. No shilly-shallying. Bring up my horse."

He was sure the chicken would be gone by the time he returned, dead certain. It was simply infuriating, no less than maddening. For the first time in as long as he could remember, Ambrose Burnside felt a young man's vigor swelling in his breast. And rage born of righteous anger.

After two attempts to swing into the saddle, he succeeded and spurred his mount straight to a gallop. He and his trailing staff had not gone far when they encountered fleeing soldiers. Many had discarded their weapons in their panic. Burnside gave his horse another kick.

The sounds of battle swelled to a roar, but he felt no trepidation. The vengefulness he reserved for political squabbles had swung against the ill-mannered Confederates, and he saw with astonishing clarity what must be done. He even grasped that he had been attacked because he was perceived as the army's weak point.

The Rebels were going to learn differently.

He had forgotten his hat, just left it on the ground under the tree. Bound to be stolen by some Irish scoundrel. Good hat, too. Expensive. The thought served only to stimulate his ardor.

Round shot ripped through the trees. Rifle fire crackled. Not all of his men were running, no. Ahead, he saw a blue line in good order, stretching across the road.

Fresh rain spattered.

Ambrose Burnside was about to frustrate Robert E. Lee and give his best performance of the war.

He even forgot the chicken.

Four forty-five p.m.
West of Bethesda Church

A thing of beauty is a joy forever,'" Gordon recited. It was a favorite refrain of Fanny's. Fanny, who was in Richmond, so close but as good as separated from his embrace by oceans.

The beautiful thing was the spectacle before him. Yankees ran pell-mell, their skirmish line surprised and their forward positions shattered. Disarmed and made prisoners, men in blue and others in Zouave dress shambled by, now and then glancing furtively at Gordon as he trotted forward. The Yankees who tried to form up were cut down, shot or clubbed, as his magnificent ragamuffins swarmed over them. Even those Georgians newly arrived and untested fought like lions. Their unsullied uniforms stood out at a distance, the gray so dark they almost looked like Yankees. Hollering their heads off, they slaughtered any Yankee who made a stand.

His men thrust forward so quickly he almost had to spur his horse to a canter. Even the rain was battling the Yankees, blowing into their faces.

Taking off his hat and sweeping it in a forward arc, Gordon cried, "Lord, boys, cavalry couldn't keep up with the likes of you!"

The soldiers nearby cheered him and charged on all the more fiercely.

He spotted Clem Evans leading his old brigade, merry as a drunkard in a distillery, driving his men through the rifle pits.

Colonel Terry had sent back word that things were going pudding-fine on the flank as well, where Gordon had placed a brigade to envelop the Yankees and slam into their rear. The message had barely reached him before he saw

Terry's bag-of-bones devils with his own eyes, racing down an open field at a right angle to his main advance, chasing Yankees like hellions at a fox hunt. The bewildered Yankees had to fight on two sides, those that had any fight left in them. Soon it would be three, if Clem Evans kept punching deep on the right flank.

He had expected to hit the seam between two Yankee corps, and that alone would have been a handsome thing. But there had been no seam, just a flank hanging out like drawers on mammy's clothesline.

More Yankees raised their hands. Other ran like jack-rabbits from a wildfire. And they still had not gotten a single piece of artillery into play.

"Don't slow down, boys," he called to a pair of soldiers who'd paused to root through a rucksack. "Fun's just beginning."

He almost added a phrase about his "brave Myrmidons," but shut his jaw before the words escaped. He was done with all that now. Done with all the fancy talk, with everything but the killing.

His men collided with the remnants of a Union regiment and swept right through it, leaving blue-clad figures on the ground, writhing or stone still, while others stumbled westward into captivity.

Another glorious Rebel yell resounded. Caught up in the rapture, Gordon bellowed, "That's the way, boys! We're going to that church yonder, and not for a hymn sing. You keep on going!"

A thing of beauty. . . .

Five p.m.
Fifth Corps right flank, west of Bethesda Church

Fucked for beans," Charlie Griffin muttered. But he damned well wasn't going to shout it out loud. Things were bad enough.

And the damned rain, too.

His men were running like he'd never seen them run before, pouring back from the skirmish line and their forward positions. And those were Rome Ayres' men. On the right, Bartlett's brigade had just plain collapsed, as if the burst of rain had melted their lines. From the saddle, Griffin could see the Johnnies pursuing the skedaddlers, descending from the flank and front, a screaming, squalling mob of scarecrows from Hell.

That sonofabitch Burnside had just pulled out, with no word of warning. And not one soul in the brick-brained Army of the Potomac had seen fit to tell Charlie Griffin his flank was open.

"You!" Griffin shouted. "Captain! Rally your men in those entrenchments. And hold your ground, or I'll horsewhip you myself!"

As he watched, a color-bearer was shot through the throat. Blood erupted from his neck and the white bone of his spine showed as he fell. Other hands took up the banner.

First Bartlett, now Ayres. He'd ordered up his reserve, Sweitzer's brigade, to occupy the old trench on the farm west of the church, warning the colonel to refuse his right. He intended to re-form the division on that line, his last, grim chance.

A slash of rain cut across his face.

Great buggering Jesus! Ayres' Regulars were streaming back: He knew their flags at a glance, even soaked and drooping. It had been hard enough to see the remains of

Bartlett's toughest regiments, the 83rd Pennsylvania and 20th Maine, fleeing like girls in petticoats chased by a snake. Now this.

Ignoring the bullets flying his way—downright insulted by them—Griffin drove his horse out into the field, cursing like a clapped-up sailor and waving his fist, to Hell with swords and niceties.

"You quim-tickling sonsofbitches, you call yourselves Regulars? You're not men enough to piss out a lucifer match. The goddamned Rebs are *that* way. Come on, I'll show you!"

It was an art, Griffin knew. You shamed the Regulars, but encouraged the Volunteers.

"I can do more with two fists than you fucking ladies can do with a goddamned brigade."

The Regulars, most of them, stopped.

"Form up, goddamn you," Griffin told them. "If you've got a dripping cunt's worth of pride left in you, form on your flags and follow me."

The men fell into ranks with remarkable speed. All they damned well needed was clear leadership.

The Rebs were almost on top of them, spit-close. The Regulars bit off cartridges, shielding the powder from the rain.

"Come on, damn it. Those are cartridges, not tits. You don't have to suck 'em."

A shot clipped a lock from his horse's mane.

"Regulars! After me!" Griffin barked. He drew his sword for effect.

A bearded sergeant, farm-boy big and slum-lad mean, stepped from the ranks and raised a broken-nosed face.

"Get out of here, old man. You're in the way."

His men cheered the sergeant and called for Griffin to get back to their rear. Another man shouted, "Git yerself kilt, we'll have nobody fer to learn us our vocabularies."

The men laughed and cheered and went forward.

It was rain in his eyes, Griffin told himself.

The last time he saw the bearded sergeant, the man was racing ahead and shouting, "Knock the bastards down, then give 'em the bayonet!"

Not enough to stop the onslaught, Griffin knew, but they'd buy time to ready a line. Chased by bullets, he turned his horse to the crisis on the right. Rome Ayres caught up with him.

"You shouldn't be this far forward. I can lead my own brigade." Ayres touched the brim of his hat.

"Then fucking well *lead* it, Rome. The Rebs are going through you like cholera shits."

"I don't know where they came from. I heard a few shots. Before I knew it, the Zouaves were bolting."

"Dressing up like a fancy-boy never helped one peckerwood. Form over there, on Sweitzer's left, and don't give a goddamned inch."

Here and there, rump regiments were fighting their way back, not running anymore. Terrified strays still headed rearward, but not so many now.

Thank God or the devil, and take your choice, Griffin thought.

A battery came jouncing and jangling over the fields at last, approaching the new line without slowing down, as if it intended to run over his men. To the front of the guns—well to the front—Griffin recognized Wainwright, a cranky cuss with a mouth on him and his own opinion on everything since Genesis, but, for Griffin's money, the finest gunner ever to straddle a caisson.

The two men met by the trench line. There were no salutes.

"Wainwright, where've you been, you sonofabitch? Pissing in the powder again? Off on the grand tour?"

"Roads were blocked up with infantry, General. Headed

in the wrong direction. I've seen horse races slower than those girls of yours."

"Just put your syphilitic sonsofbitches to work, Wainwright."

"Infantry must've got to the whorehouse first. Where do you want my batteries?"

"Put one in that field. The rest wherever you can lay on canister."

A trace of bullets ripped the air between them. Both men grinned.

"With your permission?" Wainwright tipped his cap and bowed from the saddle, dripping wet.

"Any redleg worth a bucket of turds would've opened by now," Griffin told him.

As he spoke, a covered battery boomed in sequence, sending explosive shells in perfect arcs over his troops toward the Rebs.

Sweet Jesus, Griffin thought, if I loved those redlegs any more than I do right now, I'd have to bend them over a gun carriage and bugger every one of them.

Banishing his smile, he turned to a knot of Michigan Volunteers who had paused to fire back at their tormentors.

"Good boys!" Griffin told them. "Brass balls and iron peckers, every one of you. Pour it into the sorry sonsofbitches."

A second battery began firing over his withdrawing soldiers. Within the minute, a third roared into action. They had the range of the Rebels from the first shot.

Even before the artillery entered the fight, the attack had become disordered, broken up by its rapid advance, with the Johnnies coming on boldly still, but without the deadly power of men well organized.

"Back to the diggings now," Griffin told the men fighting around him. "Get back to that trench and we'll give the bastards the bloody red fucking they're begging for."

A frock-coated man raised his hand in remonstrance.

"You, too, Chaplain," the general called. "Get back behind that goddamned trench and pray like a broke-jawed cocksucker."

As he spurred his horse toward his stiffening line, Griffin glanced back at the Rebs, who had more spunk than prospects now. Shells exploded in their midst, dismembering those near the impacts. Wounded men jerked like fish tipped into a boat. To the rear of the Johnnies, an officer rode a black stallion, as careless of the rain of shells as he was of the rain from the heavens. His posture was as rigid as a knight in a picture book and everything about him spoke of fearlessness.

But Griffin knew no man was free of fear. They only feared different things.

"Fucked for beans yourself," Griffin told the horseman.

Six p.m.

Upon finishing a novel by Ann Radcliffe, of whom Gordon did not entirely approve, Fanny had asked him if he would like to be granted immortal life.

"Only if it was shared with you, pet," he had replied. His response had been immediate and, he thought, artful.

Lovely in the lamplight, Fanny had drawn in her brows. "I don't know, John. Really, it sounds grand at first, but when you think about it . . . isn't it the brevity of our lives . . . the finite term . . . that gives them their poetry, their poignancy?" She smiled. "Would you really love me so much, or the same way, if you knew I'd be here forever?"

He had not risked a second clever ploy. When his wife was of a serious mind, she expected earnest answers. And he had not found a good one in the course of an otherwise sweet and peaceful evening.

Four years ago? It seemed at least a lifetime.

He had an answer for her now, at least a part of one. There was no beauty, no "poignancy," in lives cut short in grim ways once unthinkable. There was no poetry, either. Just this wanton slaughter, this enticing, seductive butchery, irresistible and revolting. He had, again, found himself caught up in the near delirium of a successful attack, experienced enough to keep his wits and give sharp orders, but intoxicated all the same. He had believed, for twenty minutes, almost for a half hour, that he finally had scored the victory he had hoped for since the fighting in the Wilderness. His men had brought in prisoners by the hundreds, had torn through the Yankees like wind through an arrangement of paper dolls. Only to find, once again, a new line behind the broken line, massed cannon, and a supply of human meat greater than the number of bullets his men could bring to bear. The attack had climaxed with the bravest men briefly piercing the new Yankee line, only to disappear, swallowed by a great, blue maw.

Now his blown soldiers manned worthless rifle pits seized from their enemies. And those enemies were still there, merely pushed back some hundreds of yards at a cost of equal hundreds of precious lives.

Had they reached a point, Gordon wondered, at which neither army could defeat the other decisively on a battlefield? A point at which they could only bleed each other white, a stage of the war where even idiocies—such as an unguarded flank—could soon be redeemed by men who had fought so long they would not panic, but simply do what had to be done to restore the equilibrium? If that was so, the South was lost. Because the South would run out of men long before the North felt more than a pinch.

Unless they discovered a way to kill Yankees in masses.

Clem Evans found him in the dark.

"Miss the tall trees of home on a night like this," he said. "Stay right dry under one of our Georgia pines."

"I don't mind the rain," Gordon told him. "Breaks the heat a touch."

"That's a fact."

"You did good work today, Clem. Everybody did."

"Tried my damnedest. New men come as a surprise, that Twelfth Georgia. Went at those blue-bellies like bobcats loose in a sheep pen."

"I saw."

"Damn it, John . . . I just don't know how we could've done any more."

"I know."

"Makes a man sick sometimes. I mean, how many damned Yankees do we have to kill?"

"A lot."

"Well, it makes a man sick."

"The killing? Or the failing?"

Face half-hidden by his rain-drenched hat, Evans told him, "Both, I reckon."

"Clem, we are damned beyond hope of redemption."

Gordon shocked himself when he heard his own words. They hung in the air between the two men. He had not meant to say them, had not known that he had even thought them. The words had just appeared. Like the automatic writing Fanny's cousins practiced.

He tried to make light of it, adding, "Just the doctrine of original sin, Clem. We're all damned, but for the mercy of Jesus Christ."

But the words were out there.

Eleven p.m.
Grant's headquarters

Meade's heart isn't in this attack," Grant said.

"Is yours?" Rawlins asked him.

Grant shrugged. "Has to be."

"Why?" Rawlins glanced about, as if he might glimpse eavesdroppers through the canvas. He heard Bill puttering in the rain.

"You read the letter from Washburne. One more reason."

"Washburne isn't here. He doesn't know."

"He knows. He knows what matters. Lincoln. Baltimore. The convention."

"It's five days off. You could bluff that long."

"Lincoln needs a victory. Clear one."

"And what are the chances of that, Sam? Even Hancock doesn't want to attack. Not here. His division commanders are against it. And I wouldn't class Barlow and Gibbon as tender flowers."

Grant smiled, but not much. "They'll do all right. You're beginning to sound like George Meade."

Rawlins smiled, too. And not much, either. Then he coughed. Between coughs, he said, "You always wanted me to tell you what I think, Sam."

"You need to look after yourself. Get some sleep. Maybe go back to Washington for a few weeks."

"No."

"I think I can behave myself. If that's your worry."

"No. No, it just wouldn't look right."

Grant took out a fresh cigar, then returned it to his pocket. Out of concern, Rawlins knew, for his lungs. He didn't want to be pitied.

"Go ahead, Sam. You think better with a cigar."

"Don't care to. Like to be the death of me, anyway."

"Lee's had plenty of time to entrench. Every report says his line appears formidable."

Grant's voice sharpened. "Broke his line at Spotsylvania. Twice. Almost broke him in the Wilderness. He's weaker now. Wouldn't have the push to plug the hole." He reached for the cigar again, but stopped his hand short. "Must've lost half his men. And all the deserters coming over. That army's ready to break, feel it in my bones. And Lee. You heard Sharpe. Lee's been sick as a sheep taken with the blight."

"We've had losses, too."

Grant nodded. "All the more reason to finish this here and now. The attack goes in at four thirty." He leaned closer. The lamplight showed deepening lines around his eyes, fair skin ravaged. "What can I do, John? Move south again and try to cross the James? With Lee set to pounce when he's got me halfway over? And go where? Petersburg? Just leave here without a fight, when we're nearly in sight of Richmond? What would the newspapers say?"

"You never cared about newspapers before."

"And wouldn't it boost Confederate morale? If we tried to slink off?"

"What about *this* army's morale? An attack across the whole front, everybody committed . . . what if it fails, Sam? What if Meade and Humphreys and Hancock are right? Good Lord, I'm told that soldiers down in the Sixth Corps are sewing their names to the backs of their jackets, so their bodies can be identified. I've never seen Meade so dejected, he's like a sleepwalker."

"Meade'll be all right." Grant breathed deep. Rawlins knew that sound. Somewhere between a sigh and exasperation. "Failed at Vicksburg. More than once. Whipped 'em in the end, though. Do the same here." Grant looked down at his outstretched fingers. The gesture was pensive, almost delicate. "Stakes are high, John. Couldn't be higher. Break

Lee tomorrow, the war ends. On Richmond's doorstep. Save more lives in the long run than any attack could cost."

"I understand that, I see it. But . . . Sam . . . I have to ask you something. As a friend. Has all this come down to a personal feud? Between you and Lee? Just two scrapping boys who won't back down while the other boys are watching?"

Grant took out the cigar.

"That's what war is," he said.

Midnight
Confederate center

Tell it. Just tell it to me, Oates thought. *You tell me just how it is that we keep whipping those blue-belly bastards, just cutting them down like hay in a fat field, and here we are with our rumps up against Richmond. Just tell me how that happens.*

General Law resettled his tattered waterproof and said, "I'll get a gun up there."

Oates felt the man calculating, but on the slow side. Tired. Old-dog weary. Every one of them. His soldiers up on the new line had it the worst, sleepless and sour and just plain burnt, but determined to live through the coming day and working with the spades and picks brought up, digging down through an inch of mud and five feet of worthless dirt a poor-white wouldn't farm, not even a set-free coon, a stretch of earth not worth the pissing on, but now worth dying for.

Law asked: "Rather have two pieces up there? Fairly sure I could rustle up a section."

"No, sir. Just one. Don't have no more room than that. But tell them to bring all the canister they can scare up. They'll be able to fire front or, Lord a-pity those blue-belly sonsofbitches, put out enfilading fire to sweep right down the whole front of my regiment. Nary man nor beast going to live through that." Oates swept rain from his beard, feeling the waterlogged weight of it, like a playful woman tugging slow and steady. "Any hope of food, General? Men been marching, working. Don't want 'em giving out."

But he knew they would not give out. When the Yankees came, they would rise to the work, maybe even fight on a time after they were dead, killing bluecoat bastards from pure habituation, the way a man's arms and legs kept moving after his head got blown off.

"Commissary wagons aren't up."

And even if they were, Oates suspected, they'd be empty by the time they reached Law's Brigade and the 15th Alabama. The great sow of this army didn't have a tit to spare for the men who actually got down to the fighting. And the Yankees over there stuffing themselves full of side meat, no doubt. While his boys would've looked upon a quarter plate of half-cooked beans as the equal to a beef roast bright with gravy. His own belly didn't just pester him, it hurt.

"Roads are being kept free for troops and ammunition," Law added, Methuselah-voiced, aged beyond the biblical span by this turned-blunt-and-senseless war that had become all dumb muscle and no brain, just I-fight-you-and-you-fight-me because nobody could think of anything smarter and, Christ almighty, the newspapers still told of glorious victories and heroic struggles that Oates surely couldn't recognize, all of them dressing up an old whore as a princess.

"Anything else?" Law asked. Law was a good man, given back the liberty of command until that black fool Longstreet returned some not-yet day to renew his call for a court-martial because Old Pete couldn't shoulder the blame himself for the mess at Knoxville. What kind of army was it in which the generals cared more about court-martialing each other than thinking out some way to win and just make all this stop?

Exhausted, famished, and fatal of mind, he still felt Old Ned stirring in his loins. Had a comely woman been present, or even a hag, he feared he would have rammed her right there, in the rain and mud, while anybody watched who took a mind to.

He understood less and less about life each day. He just knew that he wanted to keep on living it, and that he'd do all the killing that would take.

"No, sir," he told his general. "I believe that's all. And thank you."

"For what?" Law asked.

"Earlier. Standing up and saying it made no sense to charge out and take back those rifle pits."

"I find," Law said, "that the ambition of an order rises in direct proportion to the distance of the issuer from the front." He jiggled his rain cape again, as if doing so might hide its rents from reconnoitering raindrops. "Don't forget to send those skirmishers out."

"No, sir. Fine job for Major Lowther."

"He's back?"

"Been back. I reckon he thought the fighting was about over."

Oates couldn't exactly see for the darkness, but sensed Law shaking his head, deliberately, like a judge plagued by his conscience.

"Man's got powerful friends," Law said. "You watch out for him, William. I need you."

"I can handle Lowther."

"You watch out for him." Although he was the senior officer, Law offered the first salute, a blur in the darkness as good as a pat on the shoulder.

Rain was softening. Half of what was coming down now was drippings from the trees.

Oates had lost his own rain cape sometime back, when he gave it up to fashion a makeshift litter. Didn't mind, really. Getting soaked through at least moved the dirt around on a man's skin. And kept him awake, more or less.

The two men parted, Oates stumbling back through the darkness and slime to his laboring men, heading toward the clanging of shovels and curses almost too tired to come out of a mouth. Yankees were going to come in the morning, sure as the help spit in a hard man's soup. Yankees were coming, at first light, no doubt, and they'd kill a right passel of them.

And then what?

After some doing, he found Lowther. Tucked under a tree.

"Get on up."

"What is it?"

"General Law wants skirmishers out early. I'm sending Feagin with Company B. You'll go along, in overall command."

After a few seconds, Lowther found his voice. "I'm sick. I need to be excused."

"You have a surgeon's certificate? If you don't, you get up right now and follow my orders, Major. You head out there with Feagin. And you make sure that skirmish line is the finest in the Army of Northern Virginia. Now get up."

Lowther rustled and rose. "What time is it? Yankees aren't going to come in this. Not in the dark."

"Well," Oates said, "you just get on out there and let me know when they do come."

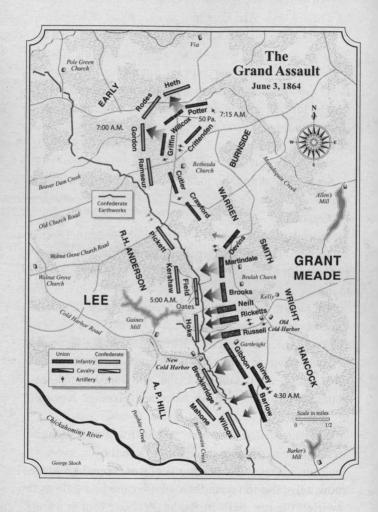

The Grand Assault
June 3, 1864

Via

Pole Green Church

EARLY

Rodes

Heth

Gordon

Griffin Willcox

Potter
50 Pa.

7:15 A.M.

Crittenden

7:00 A.M.

Ramseur

BURNSIDE

Bethesda Church

Manatquin Creek

Beaver Dam Creek

Cutler

Confederate Earthworks

Crawford

WARREN

Allen's Mill

Old Church Road

R.H. ANDERSON

Pickett

Walnut Grove Church Road

Walnut Grove Church

Kershaw

Devins

SMITH

Martindale

GRANT
MEADE

Beulah Church

Field

Brooks

WRIGHT

LEE

5:00 A.M.

Oates

Neill

Kelly

Ricketts

Cold Harbor Road

Gaines' Mill

Hoke

Russell

Old Cold Harbor

Garthright

Gibbon

HANCOCK

Union   Confederate

Infantry

Cavalry

Artillery

New Cold Harbor

Breckinridge

Birney

Barlow

4:30 A.M.

A. P. HILL

Pamunkey Creek

Mahone

Wilcox

Boatswain Creek

Scale in miles

0   1/2

Chickahominy River

Barker's Mill

George Skoch

TWENTY-FIVE

June 3, four fifteen a.m.
Cold Harbor

The men knew.

In the first hint of light, Barlow looked over the waiting lines of soldiers. Their uniforms, and perhaps their spirits, had been dampened by a light rain. He certainly didn't sense ardor in the ranks. Or in himself. The silence was ominous, scratched only by minor skirmishing to the front and slack artillery exchanges. Now and then, a last ramrod clinked home, or a provost guard shouted, "You there, halt!" as cowards attempted to slip away from their duty. The mood had the weight of a sodden overcoat.

Out in the killing space, mist gripped the low ground. Beyond, the only sign of life was the occasional twinkle of a rifle muzzle, or the brief hellfire of an artillery piece. The rounds struck randomly, doing little damage but making men flinch. No one had slept enough.

Barlow had sacrificed a second hour of sleep to bathe his feet. The water delivered by his orderly had been coffee brown swill, but the relief he felt had been sweet. He had scrubbed off the peeling skin that topped his ankles now, relishing the queer mix of pleasure and pain as he swirled the raw flesh in the bucket, one foot at a time. He hoped to gain some peace from his feet, the better to make war.

He had eaten nothing, taking only coffee. Acid gnawed his stomach as thoughts chewed at his mind. He did not want to make this attack, but had prepared his men as best he could. The brigades of Miles and Brooke, his most experienced commanders, formed his assault line, Miles on the left, Brooke on the right, and both reinforced with the green but abundant personnel of heavy artillery regiments. Byrnes, who now had the Irish Brigade, was positioned to follow Miles. MacDougall, of whom Barlow remained uncertain, would follow Brooke, if ordered to go forward. Miles had the best grasp of the ground, after yesterday's skirmishing, and Brooke was set to strike a minor salient, the one place along the Confederate line they all agreed might prove vulnerable. Given the order for a frontal assault, the dispositions were the best Barlow could do.

He took out his pocket watch. The hands tried to hide in the smoky light and he brought the watch close to his eyes. *Four twenty-five.* The attack would begin at four thirty. A signal gun would sound, and Hancock—nowhere to be seen—had ordered a bugler forward to blow the charge.

Clarion-beckoned or not, Miles and Brooke would go forward at four thirty. They had their orders, and Barlow had made them synchronize their watches again that morning. He was not going to chance misunderstandings or signals that went unheard.

The problem of a frontal assault across open ground defied him. Harvard was no help in devising tactics, and a solution eluded him as surely as it did the drunkards and illiterates. All he could do on this unpromising morning was to maintain better control than at Spotsylvania, where success had dissolved into mayhem and thence to butchery. He was *not* going to be swallowed by the excitement of the moment, but would remain near his lines, surrounded by a multitude of couriers, where he could best observe the thing entire. Brooke and Nellie Miles had a surfeit of couriers with them as well: He had ordered them to report each development promptly. He meant to control this fight, to the extent that any fight let itself be controlled. It seemed to him that confusion had become as much of an enemy as the Confederates. Confusion was the beast that had to be tamed. The challenge of command was to stay informed.

The Union guns had been silenced so the whole front could hear the signal shot. Apart from last pricks of skirmishing, the only sounds were of nervous horses and the Latin drone of a priest blessing New York soldiers in the first line of attack. Caps off for a moment, men dipped their heads as the bearded priest marched past. The most devout went briefly to one knee.

Every passing second enriched the light. Barlow watched a New York officer close his eyes and move his lips. The man's neck muscles quivered.

He did not want to make this attack, no more than that poor bugger did. But if it had to be made, and if there was one chance in thirteen Hells to succeed, Francis Channing Barlow meant to do it.

"What are they waiting for?" a courier muttered.

The signal cannon sounded.

All along the Union front, artillery batteries opened, firing over the waiting troops. Even on horseback, Barlow sensed the ground trembling. The air shook.

Confederate guns replied, firing almost blind but compelled to respond.

Miles and Brooke had already stepped off, emerging from the tree line into a field of tall, wet grass and barren patches where the earth looked diseased. Brooke rode out with his lead unit, the massive 7th New York Heavy Artillery, whose soldiers were now infantry in all but name.

Barlow felt a rush of anger. He had told Brooke and Miles to go forward dismounted. He did not want to lose those men.

Looking left, he didn't see anyone on horseback near the

first line of troops, only couriers pausing to their rear. Miles, at least, had listened.

Roping in his temper, Barlow reasoned that Brooke felt a need to inspire the artillerymen, to show confidence. Still, he didn't like being disobeyed.

His lines surged westward in good order, barely annoyed by Confederate artillery. It didn't trick him into confidence: It only meant that the Johnnies had positioned their guns for enfilading fire.

As the blue lines reached the north–south road that cut the field in two, more guns opened, seconded by bright snakes of rifle volleys. Men fell, individually and in clusters. Barlow raised his field glasses, paused to calm his horse, and brought the glasses to his eyes. The road had been worn below the level of the field, creating a shallow trench. Briefly, jarringly, Barlow remembered Antietam, the brief glory and the long recovery from his wound. He snapped his attention back with brutal force.

The 7th New York's flag had threatened to fall more than once, but the green troops had advanced quickly to the road. Now, though, many men didn't want to leave it. Natural enough, Barlow knew, it was the base instinct of the human animal to survive. This would be the test for the 7th's officers. Barlow could see them dashing about, reforming their men, readying them for a charge toward the salient.

They advanced again. The pause had been brief, not enough to break their sense of momentum. As soldiers always did under fire, men began to crouch as they hastened forward, as if struggling through a gale. And it was a gale, but of lead. The Reb entrenchments on the high ground blazed, and cannon double-charged with canister cut swathes through the ranks as the men pressed on. The Heavies had advanced farther and faster than any other regiment on the field.

Something unexpected happened. It made Barlow lower his field glasses, wipe his eyes to uncloud them, and raise the glasses again. Close to the Reb lines, within a few dozen yards, the artillerymen had begun to go to ground.

He figured it out: It was trick terrain, its contours unclear from a distance. Up close to the salient, the sharp rise from the field created a safe harbor for attackers, just below the Reb lines. The Johnnies couldn't see them, couldn't depress their artillery sufficiently to target them, and even Reb infantry would have had to stand atop or emerge from their entrenchments to fire down into them.

"Don't stop," Barlow said aloud. "Don't stop now, damn you."

He saw movement again. Seconds later, he heard a distant hurrah. Before he could raise the glasses, the Heavies had swarmed up the slope to leap the parapet into the Rebel works. They went in with rifles blazing and bayonets. It was simply remarkable, far more than he had expected, under the circumstances.

"Get them," Barlow said, as if the men fighting hand to hand could hear him. "Don't stop. Push deep. Get the bastards. Break it open."

Brooke was still on horseback, near the sunken road, directing men toward the breakthrough.

Good.

Barlow forced his attention to Miles on the left, where the going had been harder from the first. There was no safe ground, nor clear advantage to be seized, and most of the men remained stuck in the ditch the road offered them.

A single regiment continued to advance, although it faced withering fire. Barlow tried to focus the glasses, to read the flag. The unit looked to be a good-sized regiment, by the diminished standards of the campaign. But the dead air wouldn't unfurl the flag sufficiently for him to place the regiment.

"Wave the damn thing," Barlow muttered. He turned to his aide, John Black. "Any idea who those beggars are? To Miles' front?"

"I make it the Fifth New Hampshire. The numbers, the dark uniforms."

Barlow nodded. That made sense. Hapgood was out to prove that his regiment's stint guarding prisoners after Gettysburg hadn't dulled its spirit. And he was headed straight for the southern flank of the salient Brooke's Heavies had just entered.

Good.

One of Brooke's aides galloped over the field, heading for Barlow and his retinue. At least, Brooke seemed to have obeyed the order to report promptly.

Brooke's other units, his veterans, had stopped along their own axes of advance, though.

Resting his field glasses against his saddle, Barlow waited for the man to rein in and shout his report.

"Colonel Brooke's compliments, sir. He's broken into their line."

"I can see that, Lieutenant."

"We've taken colors. And guns."

"But?"

"He can't advance the rest of his line, at present. But he intends to do so, if practicable."

"Tell him to concentrate on the salient. Develop it. Reinforce it." Brooke knew that much, Barlow realized. But he had to say it, to make his intentions absolutely clear. "If the Rebs have any depth at all, they're going to counterattack."

"Yes, sir."

"And Colonel Brooke is to let me know immediately, if and when the breakthrough can accommodate MacDougall. But I don't want that salient turned into a can of sardines like Spotsylvania, understand? He *must* keep control, keep his units from intermingling. Do you understand, Lieutenant?"

The boy nodded.

"Well, what are you waiting for? Doomsday?" Barlow snapped.

The lieutenant saluted and pulled his horse around.

On the left, Miles was still bogged down. But . . . if the penetration could be managed, deepened, widened . . . just perhaps . . .

"Black," Barlow said, "ride to Hancock. Tell him we've entered the enemy's works and taken colors and guns. Don't embellish it. It's hardly a victory yet. Just tell him exactly what I said."

Behind his studied calm, Barlow felt a thrill.

Four thirty a.m.
Confederate center

A multitude of Yankee guns thundered into action, sending their rounds over Oates' raw entrenchments, firing so deep it seemed they were trying to hit Richmond. Wasteful and useless, those fires were, except to wake a man sharply, if he hadn't already been up through the night, walking back and forth to stay awake, telling men already digging to dig a damned sight faster, and finally taking up one of the axes himself, wielding it as much to stay awake as to fell the last trees that needed cutting to clear their fields of fire, ignoring the bite in his bad hip and just swinging that railroad-hammer-heavy ax in the darker-than-darkness night, gripping that rain-slick handle and telling the disembodied whispers all around him, "Stand on back," and then the bone-shaking *thunk* shimmering up the wood, right up to his hands and arms and on through a man's shoulders and into his neck, walloping him like a corn whiskey hangover, even if he wasn't a drinking man and didn't mean to become one, even now.

The first paleness was the gray of their uniforms back when they had been new, so long, long, long ago, a Confederate-gray morning, damp as a woman soured in the sheets, and not even chicory for coffee and nothing to eat. Men like specters, long-eyed ghosts, every one of them that thin, and those Yankee artillery shells flying overhead still—had it been three minutes? five?—and doing no man harm in Oates' small world, just thumping mud somewheres to the rear, the Yankees so blithely ambitious, even now, that they were as like to be trying to hit Montgomery as Richmond.

There came Lowther.

Running up a little hollow, holding on to his cap.

He wasn't alone.

Oates stepped up to the ditch, which was still barely waist-high where it was new made, and he nearly got knocked over by one of his skirmishers vaulting over the mud slop that passed for a parapet, one skirmisher of the many running like Hell, with Captain Feagin among the last, half of the men yelling, "Here they come! Oh, Lordy!"

Yelling wasn't required. Plain was plain. Jesus Christ and the Lord himself, coming on they were, an enormous pack of them rushing through the last gauze of mist. In an instant Oates counted nine deep ranks formed by battalion, their blue so thick it was almost black, and them hurrahing like they'd already won the war.

"Fix bayonets!" Oates shouted, for those blue-bellies were coming on fast, too fast. "Officers, take up those axes!"

And Billy Strickland, baffled, asked him, "Colonel, aren't you going to order the men to load?"

And, Jesus Christ twice over, yes, he'd been so tired and forgetful-stupid that at no time had he told his men to load their rifles, Jesus Christ three times, and only seconds left.

"Load! For God's sake, load, boys!"

Some men had already begun, thrusting ramrods down barrels as though not just their lives but their immortal souls were in question, if such a thing any man had, and the devil pinching them from behind, breathing hot on their dirty necks.

Devils, he knew, existed. They were everywhere now.

Remembering that cannon, so close he could have spit and hit a wheel, he plunged toward it, hollering, "You there! Sergeant! Give 'em double canister! Fire, men, fire!"

Every ready man assumed the command was meant for him, so some early shots popped from his line, not even nibbling at the growling, howling Yankee Leviathan coming their way, not a short cornrow off now.

The artillery crew had been alert, if Oates had not, and fire they did, the canister pre-loaded and ready, and, despite the darkness past, that sergeant had guessed just right how to lay his gun, maybe paced it out while Oates was swinging an ax, and the canister tore into the front Yankee rank and back through the second, blasting bodies and parts of men into one another and into the sky, a great red wash applied to walls of smoke, like a fighting-drunk devil got hold of a paintbrush.

"*Fire!*" Oates shouted, and his men let go an organized volley at last. With the mad-dog, determined, crazy-minded, through-the-canister Yankees thirty paces from the trench.

And down they went, the blue-belly sonsofbitches. It put Oates in mind of the way a fool losing at cards might lose his temper, too, and sweep the table clean before a bullet or knife admonished him.

The Yankees were just gone. No. Men and parts thereof lay on the ground. And yes, damn fools, the Union had bodies to spare and on they came, the second rank, maybe the third already.

Oates' men were packed shoulder to shoulder, so tight they could barely load. On top of that, a passel of Bryan's Georgians came up, boys spying on the hoors in a gypsy camp, wanting to *know.* And Oates told them: "Ain't got no room, dear Jesus, but you can load and pass those rifles up." And they did.

That cannon. The only men who truly understood its language learned it just for that last sliver of an instant before it removed them forever from the discussion. The gun crew leapt about like monkeys in a traveling show, doing that killing dance that culminated twice a minute with a red-gush explanation of eternity.

The foremost Yankees were all down, dead, wounded, or quitting, with the rear ranks running madly back where they'd come from. Five minutes' worth of killing, if that. Oates had never seen such startling destruction.

Fool men stood tall to see, wondering at what they had wrought, until Yankee bullets took down a brace of them.

Blood *steamed* out of that field, sweet Jesus Christ.

Five ten a.m.
The Kelly house

Meade handed the dispatch to the telegrapher:

Lieutenant General Grant:
    General Barlow reports that he has enemy's works with colors and guns. I am at General Wright's head-quarters.

Geo. G. Meade
Major-General

The key began to tap immediately.

Perhaps, just perhaps, Meade thought, there was hope.

Five ten a.m.
Second Corps, Union left

Headed toward the rear, a flock of Rebel prisoners had just passed him by when Barlow saw Union troops trickling back out of the Confederate salient. As he watched through his glasses, the trickle became a rush.

What the devil was going on? Why hadn't Brooke reinforced them? Had the penetration been so shallow, so frail? He wished he could see beyond the crest of that hill, to be there and here at once.

The 5th New Hampshire had broken into the works from the southern flank. But no one from Miles' brigade had followed after them, the others remaining pinned down in the road and taking severe casualties even there. He had sent in Byrnes with the Irish Brigade to add force to Miles' attack, but, thus far, nothing had come of it. The field in front of Miles could not be crossed.

What was the matter with Brooke, though? He hadn't sent back a courier in ten minutes.

More and more men in blue were fleeing the salient.

For God's sake, would it all be for nothing again?

He had ordered MacDougall into the field, holding him short of the road but ready to expand the penetration. It was only a matter of time before the Confederate artillery turned their attention to his ranks, too.

And Gibbon's division, on his right, seemed to have come to a standstill.

Damn it all.

He was about to send a trusty man out to locate Brooke,

if not break his own new rule and ride forward himself, when an officer on foot and hatless came running toward him.

So much for efficient couriers on horseback, Barlow told himself.

"General Barlow," the man puffed, "Colonel Brooke's been wounded."

Damn it *all*.

"Who's in command?"

"Colonel Beaver, sir. He's organizing his men to push into the works."

"A bit late," Barlow said, voice at once cold and scorching. "Can *you* tell me what's going on, Captain?"

The man looked befuddled. "It's not entirely clear, sir. The Heavies are in the Reb lines, though."

"No, they're not. They're coming back."

Thoroughly confused, the captain turned and looked toward the hill. And Barlow realized that the captain had been occupied first with Brooke's wounding, then by his dash to the rear. While Barlow watched the collapse of the penetration, the captain's back had been turned to the crucial event.

And all of it had unfolded in just minutes.

Before raising his glasses to judge the situation again, he asked the captain, "How bad is Brooke?"

The captain shrugged. "He was unconscious. Then he came to. Then he went out again. He's not bleeding much, sir, it seems to be concussion."

Barlow waved him away. No matter what pains you took, war cheated. In fact, it was nothing but one cheat after another. Brooke knocked unconscious precisely when he was needed. It was worse than ill luck. What was the line from beastly old Shakespeare? "As flies to wanton boys, are we to the gods. They kill us for their sport." Something of that ilk.

Black had barely returned from his ride to Hancock's

headquarters—where the poor old bugger seemed unable or unwilling to stir himself—but Barlow trusted no one else to deliver the next set of tidings dispassionately. The last thing they needed now was exaggerated intimations of disaster. It was just another bloody mess, no more, no less. And if he found a chance to redeem it still, he damned well would.

"Black, go back to Hancock. Tell him we could not hold the works reported taken. We've retired a short distance, but Brooke's brigade is about to renew the assault."

"Shall I tell him about Colonel Brooke, sir?"

"Tell him . . . no, not now. Concentrate on the essentials. Hold on a moment." He raised his glasses and saw Jim Beaver's Pennsylvanians giving it another try, rushing back up toward the compromised Rebel lines, flags flying. "Tell him we have colors advancing and near the works."

"Yes, sir."

"Just make sure he understands that we no longer hold the works reported taken. At least, not right now. Exaggeration and absurd expectations have nearly destroyed this army more than once. That's all. Whip that nag of yours."

Black snapped a salute and gee-yawed his horse like a westerner, like one of Grant's bellowing brigands.

He raised his glasses again, sweeping the field. Miles' brigade and the lead regiments belonging to Byrnes hadn't done a damn thing but strew the field with bodies. Along the sunken road and a bit beyond it, men were entrenching, digging deeper where the road gave them a head start.

On the right, though, Beaver's mob had fought its way back to the parapet of the Confederate line. The details were hard to read, but it looked like quite a brawl.

Not a breakthrough, though. And more men flowed rearward, while thousands of their comrades were nailed to the earth by increasingly accurate Rebel fires.

Damn it all, though. Brooke. The worst possible timing.

And Beaver in charge of the brigade, but still acting like a regimental commander, if a brave one, charging with his men and leaving the rest of his command huddled in that roadbed.

Siding with the enemy, his feet began to itch.

He *hated* to come so close and fail again. Briefly, he considered sending in MacDougall to charge over Brooke's men and try one more time to carry the compromised works. But the speed of the Confederate response, the ease with which they'd restored their line, told him that they had reinforcements in plenty, ready and waiting. The Confederates learned quickly. They didn't intend to have another Bloody Angle, either.

When were the glorious professional soldiers going to figure out that frontal attacks against prepared defenses were absolute folly? How many times had Grant and his minions tried the tactic now? If it even deserved to be categorized as a tactic.

It was a bad day already, and he dreaded to see it made worse. Better to do what he could himself than wait for inane orders from on high. He'd keep on trying. To a point.

A courier, bleeding, arrived from Miles' front. As soon as the man opened his mouth, Irish as petty theft, Barlow realized he belonged to Byrnes.

"General Bahrloo, sahr," the man began, slapping gore from his cheek, "'tis Colonel Byrnes, he's wounded and fit to be dying."

Christ.

No, Barlow decided, he was not going to send in Mac-Dougall. Enough was enough.

Five fifteen a.m.
Confederate center

The damned fools were coming again, their third attack, stupidity beyond measure. Brave was all well and good, but Oates saw nothing much to be said for stupid.

On they came, hallooing like damn, drunk fools, like wild boys off on a tear, and one more time his men and those on his flanks, as well as the powder-black artillery-men, just waited out the seconds, infernally cruel in their restraint, and joyful in a place words didn't reach, sublime, and murderous. And the Yankees—Eighteenth Corps men, Oates knew that now—just came on charging like they hadn't seen or even imagined what had happened minutes before to men just the same as them, or maybe not exactly the same, for men weren't that, but same enough for getting killed fast in the dumbest, bravest damned charge Oates had ever witnessed.

"Fire!" he said.

The Yankees got it in front and from both flanks, canister and volleys, with Bryan's Georgians still loading rifles for the Alabamans, men who had almost turned themselves into machines for killing. As Oates gazed through an aperture in the parapet, captivated by the spectacle before him, blue-bellies toppled every which way, some even flying into the air before landing again with a thud you couldn't hear for the racket but felt somewhere down deep, in some even-now-unravaged sympathy-place. Men's chests and shoulders and thighs puffed dust where multiple bullets hit them, and down they went.

Within two minutes of the first shot, the field before the Alabama line was covered with blue, some of that blue rustling and twitching, much of it still as midnight in a graveyard. Had he taken a mind to, Oates believed he could have danced right over that field, old-wound stiffness in hip and thigh no matter, and crossed from one end of the brigade front to the other without touching the earth.

"Cease firing . . . ," Oates said. "I said stop shooting, goddamn it."

Their portion of the field fell quiet enough for a thousand moans to be heard. Men called for their mothers or shouted, in dying-now voices, women's names. As the smoke lifted, the view grew only more frightful. Awesome, with that sense of awe preachers claimed to feel in the presence of the Holy Spirit, an essence in which Oates did not believe and, after this, never would believe, that was dog-certain.

Some of his men, more than a few, were standing, half-exposed, rifles ready to shoot any Yankee who moved a little too much.

Oates raised a paw: *Wait now, y'all just wait.*

"Any man out there . . . any of you Yankees . . . want to come in and surrender, you do that now. Ain't going to shoot you, if you conduct yourself proper. Just leave your rifle lay and come on in, hear?"

In reply, a Yankee sent a bullet close to Oates' head.

His men did not wait for permission to return fire.

Eventually, they got one leg-shot Yankee in, but the rest were afraid now, and they needed to be. Word had just come down the line that despite the negligible casualties in the brigade, General Law had been wounded in the head. The men were fond of Law. As was Oates.

The Yankees were done attacking, but not done dying. After a time, Oates sent a whittled-down company out through a ravine to bring in prisoners, and they herded together a hundred or so.

Returning from the carnage beyond the trench line, the men he had sent out came back with shakes worse than their captives.

Six a.m.
Sixth Corps lines, Union center

Upton was grateful. To the Lord, as always, but also, this time, to General Russell, bandaged but still on the field, and even to General Wright, a man he previously had doubted like Thomas himself. His men had not been forced to join the attack. Russell had seen reason, as had Wright. With the dead two days ripe in the narrow slot between his forward trench and that of the enemy, all could see that the Reb lines were impregnable to his front.

His men did fire into those lines, keeping the Johnnies occupied and preventing them from shifting troops to re-inforce other points under attack. But that was all. He made no charge. His bloodied brigade had been excused from the folly, Lord be praised.

Still, it outraged him that *anyone* could be ordered to attack across open fields against entrenchments perfected for two days and more. Everyone in the army should have learned the lesson by now. Good men, needed men, went to their deaths because the senior generals couldn't think, but relied on soldiers' courage to achieve miracles.

God, not men, made miracles.

He had worked his brain into a heat, spending each spare moment trying to envision a way to break the endless stale-mate. He had listened, avidly, to accounts of Sheridan's horsemen on the field, wondering if it might not be pos-sible to develop large-scale mounted forces that could move so swiftly they kept the enemy off balance, dismounting only to fight when at an advantage. How could the artil-lery problem be solved, the reliance on roads for rapid movement? And a force too large to live off the land would be slowed by its supply train: A contingent moved only as swiftly as its slowest element. A raid might be sustained, but how could you support a lengthy campaign that moved at three or four times the pace of the infantry? How could a force combine speed and firepower, unhinging the enemy's efforts at defense?

Emory Upton could not find the answers. Not yet. But he knew with the firmness he brought to his faith in God that officers had to master the modern age.

He walked among his Heavies. He had rotated the regiment back to build a reserve and grant the men a rest. That morning, the former artillerymen had been skittish as horses new to a battlefield, knowing what war meant now and worried that they, too, would be ordered forward into the maelstrom. They had settled down, but still eyed him and every other officer with distrust. The men understood war better than the generals.

Elsewhere along the corps line, the ruckus of battle had already diminished. Cannon still growled, and many a rifle cracked, but all the hurrahing was done. Other Sixth Corps men had been ordered forward—Wright had stated sourly that "someone has to make this damned attack." Now the staff officers riding to and fro looked as glum as mourners.

Once, not long before, he would have wished to join the battle, any battle, no matter the cost. And he did not believe he had lost his fighting spirit. But squandering lives—and good soldiers—in hopeless attacks seemed criminal.

War? He had acquired a new image of it just the day before, through his field glasses, and he feared it would haunt him forever. Kneeling in an advanced position to scout the narrow strip of ground between his forward line and the enemy parapet, he had seen, magnified, dead men twisted as if consigned to the eternal pit, their bellies swollen to bursting with gas and their upturned faces blackened, the eyes pecked out. He had forced himself to look on, telling himself that the sight was salutary, instructive of the ultimate wages of sin and the inevitable corruption of the flesh.

A particularly jarring sight fixed his attention in mid-survey, making him gag even as he could not stop staring: Black beetles covered a dead man's face, a living mask of them.

As Upton watched, the corpse moved an arm, then settled again.

Six thirty-five a.m.
The Kelly house

Meade handed another message to the telegrapher, to Hancock this time:

> Major General Hancock:
>   Your dispatch received. You will make the attack and support it well, so that in the event of being successful, the advantage gained can be held. If unsuccessful report at once.
>
>   Geo. G. Meade,
>   Major-General.

He could not believe that Hancock, of all people, was giving up so easily. One repulse—after an easy penetration of Lee's works—and then done? Even Wright claimed to be pressing on, if fitfully. Next, he'd hear that Hancock's men were quitting the positions they'd already taken. The lack of resolve was infamous.

Yet, all the while, Meade plagued himself with regrets that he had not engaged more vigorously in preparing the assault. He had not wanted to make this attack. Ordered to execute it, he had sulked, leaving too much to the discretion of his corps commanders, who needed a firm hand

and detailed orders. As a result, matters had gone awry from the very start. As near as one could tell, Warren and Burnside had not even begun their attacks, two hours after the time fixed to step off. Elsewhere, the assault threatened to dissolve. All of it was verging on a shambles.

And Grant, of course, was nowhere to be seen.

He sat down and scribbled the clearest report he could offer of the situation for Grant's review, ending with:

> *I should be glad to have your views as to the continuance of these attacks, if unsuccessful.*

Still, the prospect of defeat, of failure, grated on him. Especially after that scurrilous article Crapsey wrote for the *Philadelphia Inquirer*—a paper his wife and family must see. The scribbler had all but accused him of cowardice, while heaping praise on Grant. As if it all had been fed to the newspaperman by some personal enemy. The claims trumpeted by Crapsey were utterly false, and Grant had already approved the man's public removal from the army . . . although Rawlins had seemed oddly troubled by it all. Meade intended to turn the man's expulsion into a spectacle. A newspaper fellow making an error was one thing, but lying outright endangered the Republic. Such creatures had to be stopped.

But the charge stung deep, and Meade did not want to open himself to the accusation that he had called off this grand assault prematurely. It was Grant's attack, let Grant declare its end. Grant, who was given credit for wonders not one man in the army seemed to have witnessed.

Grant, Grant, Grant, the newspapers were always full of Grant! As if no one else existed. Except, perhaps, Sheridan. Who did they think commanded in the field? Grant and his louts stayed farther to the rear with every battle. Where was Grant now?

The telegraph clattered again. In moments, the operator handed a message directly to Meade:

Major-General Meade,
Commanding the Army of the Potomac:

The moment it becomes certain that an assault cannot succeed, suspend the offensive, but when one does succeed push it vigorously, and if necessary pile in troops at the successful point from wherever they can be taken. I shall go to where you are in the course of an hour.

U. S. Grant
Lieutenant-General

Drivel! Grant had managed to say nothing at all, beyond the most elementary lessons taught new cadets. And, Meade realized, Grant had artfully thrust the decision to continue the attack or halt it back onto his shoulders.

One more try, then. The army had to try.

He wondered how he would put a good face on it all in his next letter to his wife.

Seven a.m.
Second Corps, Union left

Barlow sat his horse facing Hancock, who had come forward at last to see the carnage.

"This is idiocy," the younger man said. "I won't order it."

Hancock, who looked a decade older than he had a month before, nodded and said, "Just make a show of it, Frank. Make some noise. Pretend."

Seven a.m.
Confederate left

Gordon watched them come on in the needling rain. He barely felt excited by the spectacle. Nor was he moved by the prospect of taking revenge on the men who had turned back his attack the evening before. He let their shells whistle overhead and sat on his black stallion as calmly as if surveying field hands working their way down a row.

When he judged the attackers to have reached the proper distance, he waved a hand, the gesture perfunctory. His batteries and regiments opened fire.

He could have closed his eyes and still seen what was happening. His fires would mow them down like wheat ripe for the harvest. They would continue marching forward for another minute, perhaps two, and make a rush, only to falter well short of his works. Then they would withdraw, perhaps to try again and fail again.

And they came on. And fell. One side cheered, then the other. Men died on the spot or dropped to wriggle in pain. Gordon felt as he imagined a stage actor must feel when forced to perform a play that had grown tiresome.

The Yankees bled and withdrew. Those who could walk.

He was more convinced than ever that his epiphany of the night before was the truth: The armies had reached a point at which neither side could decisively defeat the other on a battlefield. One side or the other might lose on a given day, but could not be vanquished.

Gordon saw that the war was far from over. It would be a long time before he slept, in peace, at Fanny's side again.

Seven a.m.
Ninth Corps, Union right

Brown had begun to hope that the 50th would not have to go forward, that the attack on their wing might be canceled. The sky threatened rain again—some looked to be falling already, just to the south—but the only thunder was that of the artillery on the distant flank, and that was much diminished. For an hour or so early on, the sounds of battle had been so intense that it seemed the war's final struggle must be under way. But their brigade had not even been summoned to form up until the worst of the death-storm had passed.

Rain teased, but did no more. He stood in front of the remnants of Company C, twenty-three men, holding his rifle instead of the sword customary to those commanding companies. He wasn't an officer yet, and might never be one, and anyway, a rifle was a great deal more useful in a fight than a fancied-up kitchen knife.

He felt sweat run down his back.

How had they come to this? With him standing where a captain should be, in front of a fraction of the men who had marched beside him when they crossed the Rapidan? He veered between confidence and doubt, between the belief that he could do this work as well as any man, and a sense that he was a corporal pretending to be more, and would be found out and shamed.

"First Sergeant?" a soldier called. He had told the men to continue calling him that, because he didn't know what else they might call him and not be mistaken.

He turned his head, his shoulders.

"What is it, Guertler?"

"I got to take me a leak."

"Do it where you're standing. And hurry up."

"He don't want nobody to see his tiny thing," George Heebner announced.

"Shut up, Heebner," Isaac Eckert ordered. Isaac had been promoted to corporal. Just hadn't been much horseflesh left to choose from.

And they stood, the minutes impossibly long. Surely, some enterprising Reb pickets had spotted the formed-up brigade by now. Whoever waited over there, tucked into that far tree line, would be ready. And, Brown figured, the "whoever" would be the Johnnies they had trounced the night before, in a short, desperate encounter. Their turn now.

"If I had me a big Dutch apple cake, I'd split it with every last one of you, I swear," a soldier said.

No one replied. But Brown saw that apple cake, almost tasted it, and knew every man in his short lines saw it, too.

Frances could make a fine Dutch apple cake. White cake, too, or pink with sugar frosting.

Captain Schwenk walked the regimental line. It didn't take long. He nodded at Brown. Brown nodded back. All of them were just waiting.

To the south, the noise had definitely faded. Both sides were hardly annoying each other. Maybe, just maybe, they'd be spared for one more day.

Brown didn't know whether or not he was afraid. It was surprisingly hard to tell anymore. But he knew he was unhappy. Things that had once made at least a nick of sense just didn't now. What was the word? "Futile." An officer's word. But the right one, as he understood it.

Tired though he had been, though he remained, he wished now that he had written Frances a last letter the night before.

"I swear, they must've forgot us," Heebner said. "Not that I'm complaining."

"Shut up, George," Corporal Eckert told him.

A courier galloped up to the cluster of horsemen in front of the brigade. That was rarely a good sign, Brown knew. But maybe this time it would be a message calling off the attack.

The rider cantered away again. The officers huddled. Then some rode to the rear. Those who remained behind dismounted and passed their horses off to orderlies.

"Guess they didn't forget us, after all," Heebner said.

This time, nobody told him to shut up.

Swords rose skyward. Clouds spit back. Drums began to beat. The line advanced. Behind them, out of sight, a band struck up.

Sure, that's grand, Brown thought. Just tell them we're coming as loud as you can. But stepping through the high, wet grass, he nodded, slightly and briefly, in time with the music. One of the high-up officers liked that song, which an outraged Irishman had told Brown was "The British Grenadiers."

Frances had laughed at his poor ear for music. She played the piano.

At their backs, artillery opened, firing in high arcs, the booming reports interrupting the music, then overwhelming it. Only the drums still carried.

Flag-bearers had no breeze to help them. Now and then, they waved their banners, heavy with the night's rain.

Couldn't see the Rebs, not even their piled-up dirt. They'd placed themselves a few steps back in the trees.

Or what if they weren't there? What if they were gone?

They'd be there.

Brown stepped over a lone body, a grayback. Flies burst into the air.

He looked about. His men were still with him. It seemed they'd follow him, too. Maybe men just followed along by their nature.

Serious fighting erupted off to the left, down toward the

end of the corps line, or maybe past it. He couldn't see a thing and couldn't tell.

What mattered was here, right here.

Rebs were playing coldhearted poker. Clutching their cards tight.

Captain Schwenk pointed the way for the regiment with his sword. Brown wanted him to get on back behind the advancing ranks. He was supposed to be doing a colonel's job now, not a fool captain's.

He wanted Schwenk to survive this, didn't know what would become of them all without him.

There were too many ghosts already, marching beside him, touching him. Brown was neither a superstitious man nor much moved by churchgoing. He sang hymns dutifully, and listened fitfully, and was ever a little relieved when a service ended. He never had the visions others talked of. But the ghosts were there now, always.

It unsettled him, because he loved practical things. He liked ropes tied in good knots, brass polished every day, and the deck of a barge swept clean. A good woman worth the holding. A well-oiled rifle. He had been pleased that morning when he inspected the company's arms, still doing a first sergeant's work, as well as a captain's. The new men had learned. A month's campaigning had left their uniforms in tatters and their shoes as thin as muslin, and they were filthy. But every man's rifle was ready.

What would become of Frances, if he fell? Who might she marry? If he became a ghost?

He could smell her. She smelled like a warm kitchen on a cold day. She played hymns on her piano, but other things, too. She was a sensible woman, churched but not iced over, one who didn't push too hard about anything that made a man uncomfortable, but who had her way of letting you know it was time to stop or keep going.

Had it not been so cold that day in the orchard, when last he had seen her at home . . .

The drums. The guns. Legs brushing through the grass. The brigade had reached the middle of the field.

Brown saw them, the first points of light, and heard the reports. Anxious men over there, too. Unable to hold their fire.

"Steady, boys!" Schwenk called. "Company commanders, maintain your lines."

He was a company commander now, Brown told himself. Responsible for these men. How had it happened?

He turned his head and called, "Noncommissioned officers! Maintain the lines."

Noncommissioned officers? He had two.

"They're straight as a mule's stiff pecker," Corporal Eckert assured him.

Brown could feel the grass, the earth, moist earth, through the new hole in his shoe.

The bearer waved the regimental colors. As if signaling to the Rebs, *Here we are, Johnny. What the dickens are you waiting for?*

The Rebs weren't waiting anymore.

Everything hit them at once, the fire from concealed guns, a staggering rifle volley, a burst of rain.

Men fell. Dozens, it seemed.

Someone called, "Charge!" Then Captain Schwenk was running ahead of them, hollering, "Charge!" himself, and the men followed after, first at the double-quick, then just plain running.

Another Reb volley ripped into them. Schwenk spun about, squirting blood from his side, and fell hard.

No time, no time. Don't think about it.

"Come on!" Brown yelled. "Charge!"

The men stayed with him, even came abreast of him. The

Johnnies were firing on their own now, as fast as they could reload. Maybe even faster, as if they had loaded rifles waiting, or other men reloading for them.

Off to the right, the colors went down. Someone raised them, struggling with an awkward grip. Then Company C was in advance of the colors, with Brown hollering and not even aware of it, just *doing,* another beast trained to his task.

Canister tore a hole in the regiment's center, just to the flank of Company C. The colors had disappeared, left behind, God only knew where.

More shots. Volleys again, from the flank. The guns. Men staggering. Red sprays of blood. Cries of shock, despair. The wounded calling. No officers.

The entire brigade came to a standstill short of the Rebel lines. As if there were an invisible wall they could not push their way through. Men milled like unnerved cattle, directionless, bleeding. More and more of them dropped to the earth, wounded or not. Some ran.

His men were still with him, most of them. Brown raised his rifle in one hand, to rally them, to lead them forward.

More guns opened, from the other flank this time, knocking men over the way a storm wind toppled weakened trees.

And Brown saw it, the madness, the impossibility, the complete, shameless, hopeless swindle.

Men disappeared in clouds of blood. A sergeant from Company B threw his arms wide, embracing an invisible sweetheart, and fell forward. Men trying to withdraw were shot without mercy.

"Down!" Brown shouted. "Company C! Down. Everybody down! Now!"

They obeyed him, the boys who were left. Boys from his hometown, whose father he had become in the midst of war. A twenty-three-year-old father, these perhaps the only children he'd know. These men.

He hugged the ground as rifle balls probed the grass, hunting untouched flesh. Canister snapped overhead, and, at some distance, Brown heard the shriek of Whitworth guns. Farther away, on the other side of the world, men cheered, though he could not say who, or for what.

The earth, wet earth.

Slowly, he inched back toward his men, staying as low as his muscular shoulders allowed, colliding with the shreds of a man from Company D, little more than a head, a few bones, and rags of flesh. The dead man had shared coffee with Brown back on the North Anna. He had told of a wife and children.

He found Isaac Eckert. Or Isaac found him. Their shoulders touched.

"Christ," Isaac said, "where'd they get you?"

"It's not my blood. Get your head down."

"What the bejeezus are we going to do?" Isaac asked him.

"Wait until night," Brown told him. "Then crawl back."

Twelve thirty p.m.
Cold Harbor

Ulysses S. Grant suspended his attack. He had finally seen the battlefield.

EPILOGUE

June 5, four thirty p.m.
Cold Harbor, Hancock's tent

Damn it, Lyman," Hancock said, "can't Meade and Grant even provide their own white flag?" He turned to his body servant, an affected, lowbred Englishman Lyman rather disliked. "Give them something or other they can use. *Not* one of my shirts."

"Of course, sir," the Englishman answered. "*Not* one of your shirts, sir." The man left the tent with all the airs he could muster.

Hancock wheeled back to Lyman, who had learned not to take the general's outbursts personally: Temper was merely a privilege of generalship, if the specimens he had studied were indicative. "Damned disgrace, every bit of it," Hancock roared. "Letting wounded men lie out there for two shit-shaking days." A bull of a man, he snorted. "How many do you think have died already, Professor? While Grant and Meade have been fiddling with their pricks?"

"It's been General Grant, not Meade, sir," Lyman told him. He would *not* hear Meade, a gentleman, unfairly denigrated.

Flies buzzed. Barlow sat on a camp chair, glowering. Lyman knew that Barlow had kicked up the fuss that had, at last, driven Grant to send Lee a note requesting a ceasefire to gather in the wounded. He had been rather surprised at Barlow for showing such concern. Not like Frank at all. But there it was.

Rigorous of eye, Hancock inspected his visitor, tip to toe. Lyman had donned his dress uniform, the finest Boston's tailors could provide, and he held white gloves. Carrying a parley flag had a whiff of medieval pageant in his mind. But Hancock, though he took pains about clothing himself, regarded the elegant outfit with disdain. His stare settled on Lyman's sash.

"Grant, Meade, whoever . . . it's a damned outrage," Hancock growled. "Leaving those men out there. Have you listened to them, Lyman? At night? Have you?"

"Yes, sir. I have." Lyman's voice remained calm: All of this was a fascinating study in humankind. And he had indeed listened to the plaints of the wounded stranded between the lines. Meade had listened as well. Everyone had. Except Grant, who kept to his tent, sulking like Achilles. Meade had pleaded with him to arrange a truce to bring in the wounded, but only Hancock's last telegraphic message, putting things on the record, had finally moved Grant to offer a carefully worded letter to Lee that avoided any hint of a Union defeat.

That was the thing of it, Lyman recognized: Grant did not want to admit that, on that one day, at least, the army he oversaw had been defeated. Meade felt it had to do with the political convention coming in two days and the worry that the Confederate papers would announce Lee's victory in bold type, complicating Lincoln's renomination. For his part, Lyman suspected Grant's rawboned vanity. Despite his homespun manner, Grant had the pride of an emperor. Lyman found it odd that so few saw it.

Another head poked in, that of a colonel Lyman had seen about but couldn't name.

"Ah," Hancock said, bending to stroke his thigh. "Hapgood. You know Lyman here."

In a voice hewn from New England's stone, the colonel said, "Missed the pleasure." He, too, looked over Lyman's uniform. But he held out his hand. Which Lyman took, careful to grip it firmly.

"Hapgood commands what remains of the Fifth New Hampshire," Barlow put in. "Some of the men lying out there belong to his regiment."

"Colonel Hapgood's corps officer of the day," Hancock explained. "He'll see you on your way." And back to Hapgood: "Don't get Lyman killed, if you can help it. Meade's unaccountably fond of him."

A quizzical look had overtaken Hapgood, who seemed to have been summoned without explanation.

"Flag of truce," Barlow told him. "That's why Teddy's dressed up for the ball. Impress our Southern brethren with our plumage." His smile was a silent snicker, just showing his crooked teeth. Even to his friends, Lyman knew, Barlow was only intermittently friendly. One accepted it.

"About damned time," Hapgood said.

"We're just waiting for the general's man to find him a white rag. You, Charlie, are to show Lyman and his equally well-attired cavalry sergeant the way."

Hapgood figured for a pair of seconds. "Have to take him down to the flank. Keep away from the sharpshooters."

Hancock had enough. "Lyman, don't shit this up. Those men are dying." He turned to an orderly who had the gift of making himself nearly invisible in the presence of high rank. "Find Major Mitchell. Tell him to give our imperial emissary two bottles of the best whiskey we've got." Addressing himself a final time to Lyman, he said, "The liquor's not for Dutch courage, Lyman. It's for the Rebs, for goodwill. Maybe they won't shoot you, if you pop out bearing gifts." He stalked out.

"Really, Teddy," Barlow said, "you're the most important man in this army today. Do what you can, old fellow."

"I have no power to negotiate, of course. Grant—"

"Do what you can," Barlow repeated. A trick of the light let Lyman see that his friend's eyes had grown ancient.

Hancock's manservant reappeared. He held out a starched pillowcase, a phenomenon as rare in the camp as a petticoat. Hapgood took it, looked at Lyman, and said, "I'll get this up on a stick."

Lyman was anxious to go. The air in the tent was nastier than the death-smell beyond the flaps. It smelled like rotten feet. Extremely rotten feet.

As Lyman and his escort went out, Barlow called, "Keep him alive, if you can, Charlie. He's not entirely worthless."

Set back a hundred yards from the works, the headquarters of Miles' brigade resembled a termite colony exposed by a lifted plank. Traverses led back from a trench and officers worked in shallow, canvas-topped pits to right and left that served as workplace and sleeping quarters. Everyone and everything was filthy. The stench would not be endured, yet men endured it.

Officers and men alike found Lyman's garb amusing.

Hapgood explained the mission to Miles, who nodded, shrugged, and pointed toward the flank.

The two men rejoined Lyman's cavalry sergeant escort and remounted, nudging their horses through a ravaged grove until the proper entrenchments gave way to rifle pits. Hapgood turned his horse into the sun.

Another colonel, grubby as a tyke who'd been leaping in mud puddles, clambered out of a pit and held up a hand.

"You know where you're going, Hapgood? I've just had two field officers killed out there."

The New Englander, who wore bullet holes through his hat, trousers, and scabbard, drew himself up, insulted.

"I *do* know where I'm going." He nodded. "Some bullets may come through here, but none to hurt."

Lyman was not reassured.

Hapgood led the way through another fringe of trees. Beyond lay open fields.

"You hold that white flag high now," Hapgood told the sergeant.

They emerged into full light, letting their mounts go slowly. Twenty yards out, to the rear of another, sparser line of rifle pits, Hapgood stopped them.

"Stay here," he said, and slipped down from the saddle. "This is as good a point as we're like to find. Let me scare up an officer."

Another interval of waiting began as Hapgood searched out the lieutenant commanding the pickets. Lyman had thought it all might be simpler, more dignified. As in *Henry V,* although Union straits were not as desperate as those of the French had been. He wanted to get on with the business, first because proximity to the wounded had driven home their need for succor still more strongly, and second, because he felt no fear, surprising himself, and wished to complete his mission before pangs of dread unmanned him.

At last, Hapgood flushed out the lieutenant, who edged up and called to the Johnnies to summon an officer of their own. After a bout of jawing on the Confederate side, someone was dispatched. That, too, took time. The brute sun of afternoon began its long decline into the evening.

A Confederate captain haggled a little, then called out for his men to hold their fire. The lieutenant did the same on the Union side, and Hapgood waved Lyman and his sergeant forward. The sergeant made certain the white flag remained visible.

"Best dismount," the New Englander said. "Shoot you just for the horse."

"Are you to come along?" Lyman asked. Tall and flinty, Hapgood gave him confidence.

The colonel shook his head. "Not ordered, not authorized. You're on your own, here on out. But I'll stick by, don't worry. Make sure the boys don't mistake you for a bear, you come back in."

"Thank you." Lyman offered his hand.

Hapgood gripped it hard. "You get this done."

Lyman led the way across the longest field he had ever walked, aiming at the single Confederate standing erect behind the opposing rifle pits. There had been no more than a cavalry skirmish this far to the south, but the dead horses strewn about smelled as foul as dead men.

The Rebel officer stood with folded arms, watching them come. As Lyman passed the first rifle pit, a Johnny looked up from his rifle, expression frozen between spite and laughter. He and all of the other soldiers in evidence looked like beggars from a Hugo novel. Beggars with ready weapons.

"Jaysus," the cavalry sergeant muttered.

Before they closed up to him, the Rebel officer turned on his heel and strode to the rear, around a corner of trees. Lyman followed. Late sun buttered a second field and gilded the oaks beyond. Shielding his eyes, he spotted a pair of officers in frock coats. Perhaps twenty soldiers, all in scavenged uniforms, hunkered along a tree line.

The soldiers took their cue from their officers and did not jeer or smile. Nor did they appear sullen. They were men accustomed to waiting.

One of the officers stepped forward. A major, he noted that Lyman outranked him and saluted. Then he extended his hand, as formally as if at a charity ball.

"Major Wooten," he said. "Fourteenth North Carolina. To whom do I have the pleasure?"

"Lyman." He accepted the Rebel's grip, which was strong without taint of bullying. "Army of the Potomac staff."

"Ah," Wooten said. "And you carry a message, sir?"

Lyman undid two buttons of his tunic to draw out the letter. "For General Lee, from General Grant."

The major's head moved so slightly, it couldn't be called a nod. He did not accept the letter.

"I await word from my superiors . . . whether your dispatch can be received."

Lyman felt a jolt of impatience. Bad enough that it had taken more than two days to move Grant to commit himself to paper . . .

Mastering his pique, he said, "I suppose things must be done properly."

"Yes, sir. These days, many a man has little left, beyond the will to see things properly done."

Viewed close, the major's once fine uniform told of hardship. But the man bore himself as if he would have chosen no other from the grandest wardrobe. Pride shone through the rags of these men like candlelight through torn curtains.

Lyman recalled a conversation with Barlow, who had remarked, much to Lyman's surprise, how he preferred the Confederate officers he'd met during his brief captivity at Gettysburg, when all thought him dying, to the manners and characters of his fellow Yankees. Lyman began to see it now. The Confederate major was utterly without pomposity, yet his dignity was as clean and sharp as a blade. He spoke softly.

Invisible, a horse galloped nearby. Moments later, a captain emerged from the trees. After saluting Major Wooten, he turned to Lyman and said, "I'm permitted the honor of receiving your dispatch, sir."

"Captain," Wooten said to his comrade, "you've forgotten your manners." He raised his hand a few inches, hinting at a salute.

"Your pardon," the captain said, saluting.

Lyman gave him the letter.

"There'll be an answer," the captain said. "You're requested to wait on it, sir."

The evening's gold had turned to orange around them.

No sooner had the captain departed than Lyman remembered the whiskey. He started, as if to run after the courier, then contained himself.

"Sergeant? Our 'peace offering,' if you will?"

It took the cavalryman, who was not at his ease, a moment to grasp the meaning. Then he produced the bottles from his courier bag.

"Compliments of General Hancock," Lyman said, extending the gifts.

Major Wooten did not accept them. Not immediately.

"General Hancock? Must be right fine whiskey, what I hear of the man." He looked down at the proffered bottles, not without, Lyman sensed, a certain longing. Then the major's face brightened. He turned to a man with a sergeant's stripes on what remained of a sleeve. "Uriah, fetch up our best tobacco, see what the boys have." And to Lyman: "If you'll accept an exchange, sir?"

They sat on shot-down leaves on barren ground, the last light phenomenal in its sumptuousness and the air thick as India rubber with the stench of decaying horses. While they waited, Wooten spoke cordially, drawing in two of his subordinates. In a quiet voice not meanly meant, one of them stated, "You can *never* whip us."

To Lyman's disappointment, Major Wooten did not open the whiskey.

The Confederates were not unfriendly, but maintained an edge of reserve and a becoming earnestness of manner. It occurred to Lyman how serious—serious beyond mere death—all this was for these men, whose people and homes were threatened by invasion, who now faced hardships on the best of days. His own people lived in plenty, immune to war.

"Starfish," Wooten said at one point. "Now there's a thing I never thought to study."

As darkness fell, firing broke out along the line back beyond the arc of trees. Wooten and his officers leapt to their feet to quiet things.

When he returned, the major said frankly, "I would offer you the hospitality of our camp, but there's little that suits." His face was blue in the starlit night. Lyman caught the ghost of a smile, and in a voice still softer, Wooten said, "Times I smell the coffee from over your way, it puts me in mind of home. I do miss coffee." He smiled gently. "Of course, a man can't smell nothing but rot these days."

"If I should come again," Lyman assured him, "I'll bring along coffee."

With a gesture as flitting as a bat, Wooten dismissed the promise. "Thank you, Colonel. But we are not reduced to charity."

Neither of them spoke of the wounded men, but Lyman chose to believe that this major thought about them with the same humanity he himself applied.

Just after ten, the major sent a courier to the rear to inquire about the answer to the letter. At eleven, a lieutenant delivered a note. Wooten read it by the light of a match, then passed it to Lyman.

It stated that "General Grant's aide-de-camp need not be delayed further." A response would be passed through the picket line in the morning.

Eleven p.m.
Headquarters, Army of Northern Virginia

No," Lee said.

"Sir," Venable tried again, "it's a matter of common decency. . . ."

Eyes aflame, Lee turned on him. "No, sir! I have said, *'No!'* Do you fail to understand me? General Grant must acknowledge his defeat." He gestured toward the letter on the desk. "His wording is shameless, dishonest. He tries to preserve an illusion of parity, when he has disgraced himself."

"He knows he's been defeated," Marshall tried.

Lee aimed his temper in the military secretary's direction. "He will *admit* defeat. He must not presume upon mercy." Again, he pointed toward the letter. "Read it, Colonel Marshall. No, let me read it to *you,* sir." Animated to a degree that alarmed his aides, Lee snatched up the message from Grant and, voice startlingly harsh, repeated, " 'It is reported to me that there are wounded men, probably of both armies, now lying exposed and suffering between the lines. . . .' " Face heated to a darkling rose, he said, "That . . . is infamous, gentlemen. *My* soldiers are not lying between the lines. Those are *his* soldiers. If he wishes, after so much delay, to ease their suffering at last, General Grant must send out a flag of truce, not a flag of parley. He must admit defeat, and he must adhere to the protocols of war."

"Sir—"

"I will *not* be persuaded!" Lee looked about as if surrounded by enemies. "This country . . . Virginia . . . has suffered . . . suffered. I would not be cruel . . . not cruel, but of necessity. Grant must ask for a formal truce and acknowledge his defeat."

His aides remained silent.

Remembering himself, Lee straightened his spine and mastered his tone. "Colonel Marshall, take up your pen. I will extend to General Grant the courtesy of a reply. You may send it through the picket line in the morning."

Marshall waited. Venable brooded. Taylor looked away.

"General," Lee began, "I have the honor to acknowledge the receipt of your letter . . ."

June 6, seven thirty a.m.
Grant's headquarters

Call his bluff, Grant thought. He understood what Lee wanted. And he didn't mean to give it to him. Not for one more day, anyway. He had calculated the time it would take—not long—for the Richmond papers to declare a victory for Lee, then have the rags pass through the lines. Their claims would spread across the North by telegraphic message.

He did not mean to embarrass Lincoln while the political roosters were crowing up in Baltimore. It was hard enough that the New York papers were printing all too accurate casualty reports, early figures of between five thousand and seventy-five hundred men lost since June first.

The assault on the third had failed. Continuing it had been a mistake. Given. But the army had suffered worse days. And more bad days waited ahead, this kind of war guaranteed it. The political dimension mattered, though. He saw that plain, as he never had before.

He was almost beginning to find politics interesting.

Yet, even as he told himself his delay in requesting a

truce was for Lincoln's benefit, he knew full well it was also a matter of pride. He hated letting Lee believe that, for even a single day, he'd gotten the best of him. Lee's will had to be broken, as surely as his army had to be crushed.

Rawlins looked up from reading the note that Grant had drafted to Lee.

"Well?" Grant asked.

"He won't go for it. He's got us over a barrel. And he knows it."

"I don't know," Grant said. "He likes to play the grand gentleman. This gives him time to think about it, without giving him too much. Proposed cessation of fires, from noon until three." He scratched his beard, which needed trimming. "That should do to get them in."

"Those who are still alive," Rawlins said. "Sam, it was unwise to—"

Grant cut him off. "Don't turn soft on me, John. I can't have you go soft." But he eased his voice. "Give Lee any encouragement, let him think we're weakening, and a lot more men will die than just those boys out there."

"It isn't good for the morale of the army," Rawlins told him. "Listening to them. After three days. Fewer voices calling every day."

"Defeat isn't good for an army's morale, either."

Ten a.m.
Headquarters, Army of Northern Virginia

No," Lee said. "He must admit defeat. Tell him that any parties he sends will be turned back, white flags notwithstanding. Until he asks for a formal truce. Tell him that."

Three p.m.
Headquarters, Army of the Potomac

Meade felt near despair. It was another hot day, fiercely hot. The wounded had been lying in the sun and rain for three and a half days. While Grant and Lee sparred over trivial points of honor. It had struck him that morning that the two of them, the man of Virginia and the man of the West, were two peas from the same pod.

Rawlins came in, coughing from dust and consumption. Humphreys moved to intercept him, but Grant's man was in a hurry and headed straight toward Meade. He waved another letter.

"For God's sake, get this over to Lee quick as you can. He'll . . . he should find this acceptable."

Meade was surprised that Rawlins, who was ailing, had brought the letter himself. It occurred to him, a bit jarringly, that the fellow might actually care about the men. It was a surprising thought.

"What does Grant say this time?" Humphreys asked. The skepticism in his voice was unmistakable.

"He says," Rawlins wheezed, "that he's 'compelled to ask for a suspension of hostilities' and allows Lee to fix the time."

Meade nodded. "That's the proper wording."

Five thirty p.m.
Headquarters, Army of Northern Virginia

No," Lee said. "Not yet. Wait a bit longer, let him worry. I'd prefer General Grant receive the note about seven."

"Sir, that's too late," Venable said. "You specify the hours between eight and ten. They won't have time—"

"I know that, Colonel."

Nine thirty p.m.
Headquarters, Second Corps,
Army of the Potomac

I'm every bit as goddamned mad as you are, Barlow. You think I don't give a damn about those men?"

"It's pitch black out there. And too late, anyway. What the devil good is a truce from eight to ten, if you don't hear a word about it until after nine? I can't send men out there now."

"You might want to watch your tone with General Hancock," Morgan told him.

"Go fuck a mule," Barlow said.

Hancock laughed too loudly. It carried a hint of madness. "I'd like to see that, I think. You're man enough, Morgan."

Barlow shook his head. "I'm feeding shirkers and cowards, safe in the rear, and brave men are abandoned. It's a disgrace beyond comprehension."

"Everything about war's a disgrace," Hancock told him.

June 7, ten thirty a.m.
Grant's headquarters

Send it," Grant said. "I'd shoot the man dead, if I could. 'Virginia gentleman' indeed."

Two p.m.
Headquarters, Army of Northern Virginia

All right," Lee told Marshall and Venable. "But Grant must understand clearly that he is the supplicant, the wording must be precise." A blade-thin smile shaped Lee's mouth. "Tell him his white flags will be recognized between six and eight this evening. Make him jump."

Four p.m.
Headquarters, Army of the Potomac

Thank God," Meade said.

Humphreys curled a corner of his mouth. "Who needs God, when we're blessed with General Grant?"

Eleven p.m.
Barlow's headquarters

They're dead," Nellie Miles told him. "Most of them. Almost all. I suppose it's a wonder we found any still alive."

"Yes," Barlow said. "A wonder."

Midnight
Barlow's tent

She had brought salve and rubbed it, ever so gently, into his feet. First, she had cleaned him with soap, steady-handed, until the scales fell away and the raw flesh cooled. She patted him dry with a towel, then the ointment came out.

"You really must look after yourself," Arabella told him. "This is so much worse."

"I know," he said.

"It could become gangrenous."

He nodded. Then he closed his eyes, the better to feel her touch. It was as well that there was no true privacy. Everything was too grim, too shabby and foul, for deeper intimacies. But it was an immeasurable pleasure just to see her, to briefly feel her touch. He could have gushed thanks to every busybody on the Sanitary Commission for letting her come along on their inspection.

"After the war," he told his wife, "we'll go to Newport. I'll do everything that I'm supposed to do."

She laughed. Gently. "Frank, you'll never do everything you're supposed to do. And I thought we were going to Europe?"

"First Newport, then Europe."

She smiled, as with a child. "And can we afford that?"

"Yes, Belle. We can afford that."

"I should like to do both, that would please me so. Although I dread those wicked old cats in Newport."

"They won't dare be wicked now," Barlow told her. "Not to you, my love."

She smiled. That wry, wise smile that he found irresistible. "Oh, yes. 'The general's wife.' I shall put on airs."

"No, Belle, that's not it. They all know the things you've done. The nursing." Astonishing himself after such a bad day, he smiled back at her. "I hear they call you 'the Scavenger.'"

She stroked his ankle, then fingered more salve from the pot. "I'm sure those old cats called me worse in the past. Frank, do you have any idea what it's like to be a woman with a quarter of a brain? A strumpet fares better."

"I'm dreadfully proud of you, Belle. You know that, I hope?"

And he looked at the woman he loved. Careworn, as weary as any soldier in the army. The nursing, the grimness, an unclean and morbid life. She did not lack courage, his steady Arabella. But the war had aged her fiercely. Ten years older than him, she now looked ten years past that. He loved her all the more.

He felt the urge to embrace her, but she held his foot as tightly as a surgeon's strap.

"Frank?" He recognized her "schoolmarm" voice.

"Yes?"

"I'm told you exposed unarmed men to artillery fire. On purpose. And two were killed."

"They weren't men. They were cowards. Shirkers. Brave men died in their places."

"That was childish of you. And mean."

He straightened his spine. "*You* don't understand—"

He stopped himself. She did understand. The damage he and his kind inflicted dropped into her lap. Like his hideous foot.

"It was childish," she repeated. "Really, you mustn't do things you'll live to regret."

He leaned toward her, earnest as death and loving her unreservedly. His wife, his only true friend. "Belle . . . Bella . . . dear Belle . . . I'll regret *all* of this. You have no idea." Emotions seethed out, tearing holes in his flesh to escape. "Grant . . . Meade . . . the lot of them. They left those men out there for four and a half days. Good men, the best, the finest I had." He could not look at her, but turned his face sideward, gazing down into the shadows cast by the lantern. "I'm going to give it up," he declared. "I'll take that ridiculous job in the darkey bureau, I swear I will." He wanted to stand, but his wife still held his foot. "I *hate* this war."

Arabella released him. Her smile perished. "No," she said. "You won't give it up. Frank, you *love* all this." She struggled to smile again, but the effort faltered. "More than anything."

June 13, ten a.m.
Cold Harbor

Damnedest thing. Yankees just slipped off in the night, just flowed off like water. All the bands playing the evening before should've been a hint that doings were under way, but everybody was trench-tired and glad enough for the music, Yankee or not. Then, come dawn, there weren't enough blue-belly pickets left behind to thumb your nose at, hardly worth the capturing. Nothing left but their death-stink.

Another hot day, bound to be, when a man was sweating dirt like this before noon.

"Get all that busted down," Oates said. "Got to get to marching."

And they would, as soon as the road was clear of the leading regiments. Marching to Lord knew where.

Yankees just disappearing like that. Again. One thing they were good at, anyway. No man took them for quitting, though. They were just gone elsewhere to renew the tribulation. And now the army would run like dogs to hunt them, hoping to run down a fox, but meeting the bear again.

As the sergeants and officers still with the regiment got the men in order—none of it done without the usual grumbling that was as much a part of the army as bullets and beans—Colonel Perry rode up. He had the brigade again, with General Law wounded in the head and sent off.

Perry looked glum.

Oates didn't have much to offer by way of cheer. But he'd

grown to like Perry. Didn't mind taking orders from him, way things turned out.

Perry halted his horse, soothing it in his born-to-it Georgia drawl, although he had adopted Alabama a time back and represented himself as an Alabaman.

The poor devil's face was longer than Abraham's beard. Oates wished he had the gift of humor, would have liked to level a joke, some saucy story, in Perry's direction. But he never possessed the levity required, just never felt or displayed it. He could laugh well enough, but could not make other men laugh.

Was it bad news about the war?

Pulling off his riding gloves, Perry said, "William, we need to talk some."

"Surely."

"Among two men. Two Alabama men. Come off a ways."

Oates felt the first unease. He followed Perry into a grove that had been shot through and shit in, the man-smell compounding the death-smell.

"Don't get fiery now," Perry said. "You have a regiment to march a hard piece today. Just listen to me and hold yourself up like a man."

Oates liked things less and less. He nearly tramped in a pile.

"What do you have to tell me?" he asked. Wondering if, by some strange how, Perry had heard news of his family back home before he heard it himself. Bad news. He was not prepared to lose his mother without seeing her again, that he would not tolerate. He'd even get down on his knees and pray with her, if that was what she wanted, if only she could be cajoled to live on. He'd pray right now, even try to believe in its usefulness.

"Lowther back yet?" Perry asked.

Nothing left to like at all, once that man's name was mentioned.

Oates shook his head. "Not since he run off pretending to be mortally wounded again. Hardly a wood splinter this time. But enough to take him to Richmond."

"I figured he wasn't back," Perry said. He sounded relieved, but in a way that only made Oates wary. "Now you hold yourself up honest and listen to me. Lowther's coming back, all right. Soon. I don't know when exactly. But some things are going to change, and neither you nor me are bound to like it."

"What's that coward done now?"

"It's not what he's done," Perry said, "but what he *got* done."

Oates waited.

"William . . . you know that you can count me among your admirers . . ."

"Ain't looking for a dance partner. What's that sumbitch done? Or got done? Just tell me."

Perry tensed. Preparing himself. As if Oates might strike out at him.

"He's coming back with a commission confirmed by the full Confederate Congress. As a colonel. Backdated more than a year."

"Earlier date than mine?"

Briefly, Perry looked away. Then he steeled himself to his task again. "Yes. You could say that. And he's also going to have a patent to assume command of the Fifteenth Alabama."

Oates had to relearn the English language, one word at a time, to understand. The blow hit harder than that plank his father had laid flat across his shoulders. So long ago.

"That can't be. That . . . can't . . . be."

Perry could not meet Oates' stare. "It's true. I'm telling you because I don't want you surprised. No more than you are right now, anyway. You daren't raise a hand against him."

"I'll kill him."

"And you'd be shot. Or hanged, to save the bullets. Listen to me. I haven't told you all. He's also got a commission for Feagin. As the regiment's lieutenant colonel." Perry hesitated, then dove on in. "And one for you. As a major. As this regiment's major."

"I'm already a goddamned colonel."

"No. You're not. The Congress . . at someone's behest . . . has decided that Law's promotion of you last year was illegal. It was never confirmed in Richmond."

Oates swung. He punched the tree so hard it shivered. It hurt his hand and skinned it. He didn't care.

"This can't be. This damned well can't be." Oates grew frantic, fearful that it might all be true, learning fear for the first time in his life as a grown man. "I've led this regiment since before Gettysburg. Through all"—he swept his bleeding hand toward the battlefield—"all this."

"And you led it well," Perry told him. "Magnificently. Now listen here."

"There's more? You got more? What the Hell more could there be? You're taking my regiment. My men . . ."

"I'm not taking anything. The Congress of the Confederate States of America took it. And God have mercy on their souls for doing it." Perry risked stepping closer. "William, do you have any friends in politics? Friends in the legislature? Anybody?"

Oates shook his head. "Some Alabama boys. One or two."

Perry appeared to have expected that. It wasn't enough.

"I won't serve as major under that cowardly bastard," Oates said.

"I reckoned on that, too. You just march this regiment today. Keep on leading it, for now. I'll try to learn when Lowther's about to grace us with his presence again. When that time comes, General Field's going to write you a pass.

You're going to leave camp before Lowther shows his face. I will have no confrontation, no violence, hear? You'll go when I say go, and that's an order."

"Go where?"

"The pass is for Richmond, to plead your case. I'll try to arrange a meeting with General Lee before you go, get his advice, his recommendation. But"—he reached out as if to take Oates' arm, then stopped himself—"don't expect a miracle. Lee will support you to a degree, but won't contest a decision of the Congress. You're going to need to work the political side."

"I hate politics."

"Well, Lowther doesn't. And he's going to command this regiment. That's how things are."

"No!" Oates shouted, losing control. Burned deep. Raging. Fists clenched to strangle the world. "This is *my* regiment. I've *earned* this command. My brother *died* in this regiment." He gasped for breath, realizing, to his shame, that tears crowded his eyes. "I'll *kill* the man who tries to take it from me. These are my boys."

"No," Perry said. "You won't. And they're not."

June 14, noon
Douthart's plantation, north bank of the James

Meade felt rich with pride. The engineers, *his* engineers, had nearly completed the great pontoon bridge over the James River. And his troops were already crossing by boat from wharf to wharf for miles upstream and down, a great army breaching the obstacle of a wide river with ease. The view from the mansion's lawn on the high spit of land was spectacular, with the troop-bearing vessels steaming below, the engineers quick at their labors, and the roads full of regiments glad to be out where the air was fresh and smelled of water, not death. After the wastes of Cold Harbor, the river seemed as beautiful as he imagined the Nile or the Euphrates.

Grant had given the order, but Meade and Humphreys had moved the army, and Humph had been a genius, a veritable Alexander of logistics. For his part, Meade felt in command again. He still chafed at Grant's presence, but bore it stoically. The past six weeks had been a trial by fire, but their relationship seemed to have settled itself at last.

Now they had to beat Robert E. Lee to Petersburg.

He had mourned the many lost below the Rapidan, and he mourned them still. He doubted he would ever fully forgive Grant those frontal attacks, the slaughter of the army he had nurtured. Nor would he quickly forgive himself his desultory behavior at Cold Harbor. But this day made it hard not to be elated. The army's accomplishment in reaching and crossing the river unmolested was a maneuver to go down in the annals of war.

Even the breeze that rose from the river seemed a glorious thing.

He only wished that he'd been allowed full command, that Grant had remained in Washington, the correct location for a general in chief. He would have done many things differently.

Yet, here they were, crossing one of the South's great rivers, with not one lone Confederate to be seen. The campaign bore a mark of triumph, after all. They had not been dissuaded from their purpose. Discouraged, now and then, it was true. But never deterred.

Biddle, one of his favored aides, approached with a plate covered over with a napkin. Meade smelled bacon.

"Well, Biddle? What do you think of that?" He gestured down toward the busy river.

"We've come a long way, sir."

"And a hard way."

"The boys found quite a larder in the house. It may be late for breakfast, but I thought you'd enjoy a picnic."

"Splendid. What do we have?"

"Bacon thick as a beefsteak. Fresh butter for the biscuits. Eggs."

"Have the men eaten?"

"They're gorging themselves."

"And you?"

"I'll have a plate when I go back in. Not Philadelphia's grandest *petit déjeuner,* but one begins to believe Virginia may not be without virtues."

The breeze lifted the napkin. The fragrance of the food seemed overpowering.

Meade held out his hand for the plate. "My wife and I like picnics, you know. I miss her."

"Yes, sir."

"Well, go and feed yourself, Biddle."

Careful not to tip the plate, Meade lowered himself to the ground and sat on the grass like a child. Out in the river, a steamer blew its horn, a sound so deep it reminded Meade of foghorns and his lighthouses.

The biscuits were fine, but the bacon was truly memorable.

Sitting in the kindly warmth and stroked by the river breeze, with a strip of bacon halfway to his mouth, Meade had a revelation. The obviousness, the simplicity, of it stunned him.

Looking down at the busy array on the river, at the thousands of men ferried to the southern shore, he saw it all:

Grant had no idea how to beat Lee on a battlefield. But Ulysses S. Grant knew how to win the war.

Author's Note

Why waste time on historical fiction? Why not just read history?

Given the inaccuracies, anachronisms, and careless writing that too often infect historical novels, those are legitimate questions. Most readers would answer that they read novels with historical settings simply because they enjoy them, and, in the end, there's no better response. But there is another, compelling answer, as well: If historical fiction is properly done, it can bring history to life. It should be a matter not of either/or, but of complementary roles for historical nonfiction and fiction (and one might argue that today's revisionist historians write more fiction than the sounder historical novelists). Historians provide the indispensable skeleton of facts. Dutiful historical novelists supply warm flesh to give those facts humanity. A historian may tell us that soldiers in wool uniforms marched twenty-two miles in ninety-four-degree heat and many fell out by the roadside. Well-executed historical fiction helps us understand what it *felt* like to make that march.

History tells us what happened. Fiction makes us ask, "What happens next?" History provides the identities. Historical fiction investigates the souls. One descends from Thucydides, the other from Homer.

Of course, historical fiction, poorly done, can become

hysterical fiction (in two senses). Among the routine sins are both dressing up modern, politically correct spirits in antique costumes and simply playing fast and loose with the facts to smooth out the story line. But done well, historical novels can be sublime. Limiting the discussion to our own country, the much-abused genre is redeemed by those rare, magnificent works that resurrect an era with tactile richness—books such as the late Thomas Flanagan's incomparable *The Year of the French,* which made me *see* the Irish rising of 1798; or Joseph Stanley Pennell's haunting *The History of Rome Hanks and Kindred Matters*, an epic that chronicles our Midwest from the Civil War into the twentieth century; or, not least, Wallace Stegner's *Angle of Repose*. These books are so splendid, they frustrate readers conditioned to lesser historical fiction in which every Confederate officer was young, dashing, and raised with a free-black best friend on a progressive plantation, or that features a feisty, clandestinely educated, proto-liberated woman rebelling valiantly against the constricting patriarchal societies of bygone centuries (all the while wearing enthralling dresses). The first sort of novel romanticizes the past, the second euthanizes it.

The past *was* a different place in ways both practical and psychological, even as deep human qualities endure—and it's folly to imagine that those who went before us were somehow nobler creatures en masse. Battlefield leaders and soldiers in our Civil War did not all speak in the sanitized cadences of Victorian-era parsons any more than did Reformation-era *Landsknechte* or the soldiers who marched with Alexander, and the history of the female half of humanity was not populated exclusively by seductive witches concocting medieval granola, secret voracious readers destined for wealthy, enlightened marriages by a novel's end, or Mary Queen of Scots. Most of our ancestors, male or female, would have been happy to keep a few teeth past age thirty.

Getting both the differences and similarities is essential. So is accuracy in each detail. Some years ago, a lazy British novelist caught out with an impossible plot and dubious character constructions responded that he was interested not in historical truth, but simply in the truth of good storytelling. It mattered not to him that his romantic, free-spirited hero had, in fact, been a nasty Nazi agent. I find such liberties with historical facts repugnant. Serious historical fiction doesn't muddle the past for the author's convenience, but makes a sincere effort to *understand,* then to communicate that understanding. If a writer seeks to bring the past to life, he should begin by digging up the right corpse.

Straightforward history and serious historical fiction need never stand in conflict, but should function as a team to help us grip our past . . . for if we do not understand who we were, we will never fully understand who we are. And if we do not understand who we are, the lies of demagogues may all too easily determine what we become.

If nothing else, historical fiction has enticed millions of readers to read straight history. At a time when our education system has abandoned serious history instruction, historical novelists and historians need to embrace each other as allies.

I have tried to make this novel as accurate as possible, down to the local weather at a given time of day. Whenever possible, characters speak the lines they are recorded as having spoken (although one suspects that memoirists did a great deal of sanitizing). But those characters also believe what they believed, not what we wish they would have felt. Just as some were self-sacrificing abolitionists, others reasoned in favor of slavery. Some struggled to lead virtuous lives, while others were merry hellions. In short, they were human.

To us, the answers to yesteryear's doubts seem obvious. But those questions—above all, regarding slavery—were once so fraught that at least 624,000 and perhaps as many as 750,000 Americans died in four years of war to settle them (to the extent that, even now, we may regard them as fully resolved). Whatever an author's personal beliefs, he or she must give a fair hearing to all of the revived characters, to try to understand why they believed as they did and how their beliefs shaped their daily lives as well as the fate of our country. And characters must wield the language of their times, even when it offends us.

There are, however, two instances in which I changed historical details, and the reader must be told of them. First, there is no evidence that Robert E. Lee visited the summit of Clark's Mountain on May 4, 1864. He had ridden up to the signal station in the preceding days, but his midday whereabouts on May 4 are unclear. I placed him atop that mountain for two reasons: First, it made military sense for him to go to the one nearby spot from which he could see the progress of the Army of the Potomac for himself, and second, it was a perfect opportunity to give the reader a panoramic view of the situation through Lee's eyes, to introduce the man through the situation.

The second alteration I made to history was to darken William C. Oates' hair to deepest black to match his presence and personality. It just felt right.

Other factual errors the reader may discover are plain mistakes, not intentional manipulations of history.

One difference between the novel you have in hand and its predecessor, *Cain at Gettysburg,* is that, in *Cain,* every action of the 26th North Carolina or the 26th Wisconsin was accurately portrayed, but the enlisted men from those regiments were fictional characters. In *Hell or Richmond,* the enlisted soldiers of the 50th Pennsylvania Veteran Volunteer Infantry Regiment are historical figures. A treasury of their letters home has survived, and those written by Charles E. Brown, the highly literate John Doudle, Samuel K. Schwenk, and others provided me with a firm foundation for elaborating their personalities. As for Henry Hill, he is mentioned in the letters of other soldiers, but his own letters have not survived. I built his character on my firsthand knowledge of the Hill family, formerly of Schuylkill Haven, my hometown, and my relations through a remarkable aunt's marriage. Each of the Hill males I've known through the generations has been taciturn and stubborn. That stubbornness won Henry Hill a Medal of Honor for his action in the Wilderness, although administrative ineptitude delayed the award until the 1890s. Charles E. Brown, who would end the war as a captain commanding Company C, won the Medal of Honor himself for capturing the flag of the 47th Virginia in the action along the Weldon Railroad, near Petersburg. The personalities attributed to the Eckerts are invented, since I found no evidence of their individual characters beyond names on the regimental roster. Clearly, though, the Eckerts were a patriotic lot, contributing at least half a dozen soldiers to Company C.

And there really were pirates on the Schuylkill Canal.

Napoleon wanted "lucky generals." Good luck matters in publishing, too, and I feel honored and very fortunate that the masterful George Skoch agreed to do the maps for this novel. In the past, George has contributed maps to the finest contemporary Civil War histories, so it was a risk for him to descend to fiction. Making maps for such a book is a significant challenge, since they not only must be accurate, but are limited in number and still must portray, at a glance, the essentials of complex situations. If a map is too detailed, it disrupts the narrative. If crucial details are lacking, the reader's confused. I feel that George got it as right as possible. I hope readers agree.

I also must thank a few of the many individuals who have both supported me and kept me firmly grounded during the maddening process of writing this book. First, my wife, Katherine, a career journalist and executive editor, brings the mercy of Clara Barton to our personal lives, but wields the savagery of Francis Channing Barlow as an editor, her red pen whacking a faltering scribbler with all the force of the flat of Barlow's saber. This is her book, too.

My "real" editor, Bob Gleason, made consistently wise suggestions during the long months of writing, but, more important still, asked penetrating questions that I did my best to answer on the page. A remarkable man whose career began at the door of Henry Miller's almost foreclosed house, Bob knows both the beauty and the business of books as do few others. His alert aide-de-camp, Whitney Ross, also gets a battle star for dealing with my desire to micromanage every step of a book's production.

Regarding production, my thanks to the design and production team at Forge for the splendid work on the jacket design and typeface selections for this book and *Cain at Gettysburg*. People *do* judge books by their covers, and I'm thrilled with the quality of the work the Forge team produces.

Belated thanks go to Scott Miller and Robert Gottlieb, of Trident Media, who have represented me over the decades. Any writer who doesn't think agents are worth their keep is as big a fool as those nineteenth-century officers who insisted that repeating rifles would only waste ammunition. These two men changed my life.

Brigadier General (Retired) Jack Mountcastle, former chief of military history for the U.S. Army, gets a grateful nod, as well, for his selfless assistance over the years and for insisting that John B. Gordon had to be a key figure in this novel. I also am indebted to Andy Waskie for sharing his seemingly endless knowledge of George Gordon Meade. An old redleg vet, Colonel (Retired) Jerry Morelock, of *Armchair General* magazine, has been not only a good friend, but a "fire support provider" over the years; when he is asked for assistance, his prompt reply is always, "On the way!" Eric Weider, scholar, publisher, and friend, has been ineffably generous in support of the work I try to do. Eric's a doggone good man.

Last, but certainly not least, my thanks to our National Battlefield Park historians and Rangers, as well as to the licensed battlefield guides, for all they do for the education of our citizenry and to honor the memories of those who shaped the country we're blessed to live in.

Given space constraints, I can't list the hundreds of reference works that underpin this novel, but I'm obliged to alert readers to key works that either influenced me more powerfully than others or provide excellent texts for those who want to learn more about the men and events of this bloodiest month in American history—and the birth of modern war in Virginia's fields.

The 986 pages of series 1, vol. 36, part 3, of *War of the Rebellion: Official Records of the Union and Confederate Armies* never left my desk during the writing of *Hell or Richmond*. There is no substitute for the actual messages written on the battlefields and the unit reports drafted shortly thereafter (as self-serving as many reports inevitably are). From timelines to temper tantrums, the raw information waits in the *Official Records*. They are indispensable.

Next in importance are the letters, notebooks, and diaries of the participants. My own favorites are the notebooks and letters of Theodore Lyman, who was both a trained scientist with a sharp capacity for critical thought and a talented writer with a tart sense of humor. No one left us better accounts of the campaigns he witnessed or wrote with greater integrity.

Fortunately, ever more letter collections have been published, and I recommend those of Barlow, Meade, Grant, and Upton and the annotated collection of letters home from Company C, 50th Pennsylvania, skillfully assembled by J. Stuart Richards. As for notebooks and diaries, Marsena Patrick's are grumpy and grand, but I've never picked up a Civil War diary that wasn't well worth reading.

Among the memoirs I found useful (and which must, of course, be taken with very large grains of salt), the best were those of John B. Gordon, William C. Oates, Andrew A. Humphreys, Louis Napoleon Beaudry (of the Fifth New York Cavalry, an amazing outfit about which a splendid, stand-alone novel waits to be written), Edward Porter Alexander, and, the finest memoirist of them all, Ulysses S. Grant. Cyrus Comstock's diary is useful for cross-referencing, but Adam Badeau's memoir is fiercely prejudiced against all persons and deeds of the Army of the Potomac. Fitzhugh Lee's biography and memoir of General Lee is useful, if inevitably hagiographic.

Contemporary biographies well worth reading are *Gettysburg Requiem: The Life and Lost Causes of Confederate Colonel William C. Oates,* by Glenn W. LaFantasie; *The Boy General: The Life and Careers of Francis Channing Barlow,* by Richard F. Welch; *John Brown Gordon: Soldier, Southerner, American,* by Ralph Lowell Eckert; *General James Longstreet: The Confederacy's Most Controversial Soldier,* by Jeffry D. Wert; a seemingly inexhaustible supply of Grant biographies (take your pick);

General A. P. Hill: The Story of a Confederate Warrior, by James I. Robertson, Jr.; *Hancock the Superb,* by Glenn Tucker (an oldie but goodie); *Richard S. Ewell: A Soldier's Life,* by Donald C. Pfanz; and the classic Meade biographies by Cleaves and Pennypacker, as well as the fine new *Searching for George Gordon Meade: The Forgotten Victor of Gettysburg,* by Tom Huntington. As for Robert E. Lee, he deserves more scrupulous, less infatuated biographers: His greatness was inseparable from his deficiencies.

For a well-written introduction to several key generals featured in *Hell or Richmond,* I strongly recommend Thomas B. Buell's *The Warrior Generals: Combat Leadership in the Civil War.*

As for books specifically about these battles, the remarkable work of Gordon C. Rhea is brilliant, convincing, and humbling to fellow writers of fiction or nonfiction. His research is impeccable; his analysis is astute; and his writing is compelling. Of all the many contemporary works I consulted, none was of as much value as Rhea's four volumes: *The Battle of the Wilderness, May 5–6, 1864; The Battles for Spotsylvania Court House and the Road to Yellow Tavern, May 7–12, 1864; To the North Anna River: Grant and Lee, May 13–25, 1864;* and *Cold Harbor: Grant and Lee, May 26–June 3, 1864.* This is a magnificent body of work. I do not agree with every one of his conclusions (although I find most inarguable), but I respect the quality of mind that led to each of them. Reportedly, Rhea has been at work on a follow-up volume that moves the armies to Petersburg. His admirers are waiting.

For those who would like a solid one-volume introduction to the Overland Campaign, *Bloody Roads South: The Wilderness to Cold Harbor, May–June 1864,* by Noah Andre Trudeau, is a good place to start. Other worthy and relatively compact volumes are *Into the Wilderness with the Army of the Potomac,* by Robert Garth Scott; *If It Takes All Summer: The Battle of Spotsylvania,* by William D. Matter; and *Not War but Murder: Cold Harbor 1864,* by Ernest B. Furgurson. There are, of course, many more books, old and new, on these battles, with more doubtless on the way for the sesquicentennial. These simply turned out to be my favorites.

I also must mention a book I did not use, but only because I discovered it near the end of my work on *Hell or Richmond.* That is *The 50th Pennsylvania's Civil War Odyssey: The Exciting Life and Hard Times of a Union Volunteer Infantry Regiment: 1861 to 1865,* by Harold B. Birch. This was a fascinating unit composed of deeply committed soldiers, many of whom served from the early months of the war to its final shots.

And then there are the maps to which I referred: With the blessing of the National Park Service, master historian Frank O'Reilly and his team have produced what for me were indispensable map series of the Battles of the Wilderness and Spotsylvania. Painstakingly researched and beautifully executed, these maps, in their dozens, covered the floor of my home office during much of the work on this novel, and when they were not at the foot of my desk, they were in my hands as I walked the battlefields. Of course, the pioneer of such diligent map making was the great, immeasurably influential Edwin C. Bearss, whose Cold Harbor maps of a half century ago set new research standards and whose extensive work on our Civil War remains peerless. A Marine Corps veteran of the Pacific theater in World War II, Ed Bearss still leads a tough and instructive staff ride.

My apologies to any authors who may feel unfairly passed over. I cannot claim to have read everything, nor can my publisher afford me any more space. My purpose here is not to exhaust the resources, but to guide readers who may have developed a deeper interest in these battles toward a few good books to get them started.

History is endless.

Man proposes, God disposes." I like epilogues that tell me what ultimately became of the characters in a historical novel. I did not provide one to this novel for a straightforward reason: I hope to follow the key characters—Barlow and Gordon, Upton and Oates, Grant, Meade, Lee, and the others—through two more novels that will deliver them, at last, to Appomattox or wherever the war's finale overtook them. But I learned long ago that the pride and plans of man are subject to confounding turns of fate. So while I hope to live with these remarkable men for a few years more, I know that depends on everything from accidents of the flesh to sales figures and the state of the publishing industry. God willing, you and I will meet next at Petersburg, on the Monocacy, and in the Valley. Should fate intervene, I hope you will have found the book in hand sufficient in itself.

—Ralph Peters
Advent, 2012

Turn the page for a preview of

VALLEY OF
THE SHADOW

RALPH PETERS

*Available from Tom Doherty Associates
in May 2015*

A FORGE BOOK

"Keep your alignment, men," Lieutenant Colonel Valkenburg called as he rode between their lines. "Keep up your alignment."

The sound of nigh on a thousand men advancing seemed to hush all else in the world. Even the thump of the guns on the far bank faded. Nichols believed he could hear his heart, fearful and no denying it.

The first field they crossed had been stripped bare of crops, leaving a man with his own feeling of nakedness. They were still out of range of the Yankee rifles, but exposed for all to see, and each step brought them closer to whatever the Lord had in mind. Hornhard feet and rough shoes slapped baked earth, raising pale dust to bother throats consigned to the second rank. Sweating untowardly, like a fat man, Nichols felt shrunken.

In the next field, yet uncut, the *shish-shish-shish* of feet and calves pushed through ripe wheat with the sound of a thousand scythes.

The day was hot, bright blue, gold, green-rimmed, marred here and there by smoke. Despite his wash

of sweat, Nichols felt light, with his blanket roll
and haversack left behind in the trees, every man
going forward with just his fighting tools. Still, he
sensed a ghost where the blanket had gripped, the
wet cloth cooling now, despite the sun. He'd learned
so much he hoped he lived to tell it, how a man could
be hot and chilled at once, sick with fear and ready
to kill with fury.

"Keep your alignment, men."

Up ahead, nothing good. Across a dreadful stretch
of fields, flat enough for volleys to sweep them clean,
the Yankees waited, hunkered down, no doubt licking their lips. In between, fences challenged the advance, with haystacks scattered about, as if the
blue-bellies had set out a steeplechase course.

In dead air, flags hung limp. Along the lines the
61st Georgia's officers called out encouragement.
Excepting Colonel Lamar and Lieutenant Colonel
Valkenburg, every one of the officers walked, not
because they'd dismounted to spare themselves, but
because there were no horses to be had, at least not
for the money printed in Richmond. It was a poor
time, a hard time, for rich and poor alike among his
people, with gentry afoot who had ridden all their
lives. Determined they all were, though, every one
of them. Nichols felt that sure as Revelation.

So far still to go, a small eternity. Fresh sweat
popped. Insects rose, clouds of them. He had turned
up the front brim of his hat, the way he always did,
the better to look along the sights when the time
came, and blackflies teased his eyes. He blinked and

blinked again but kept both hands on his rifle. Wasn't no right-shoulder-shift this day, just rifles held at port, the way General Gordon liked things.

Just seemed a mean, long way across those fields. He couldn't figure why the Yankees hadn't let loose with artillery. Unless their guns were already primed with canister, a terrible thing, wrathful.

He fixed his eyes on that first fence. Didn't want to look beyond it.

The day was hot in the nose, hot in the mouth. Field dust, hay dust, peppered his nose, so different from the chalk-cake dust of roads. Breathing almost required an act of will. But his leg had stopped hurting, he barely felt it. He wondered why that was?

A man was a riddle, but the Lord God was a mystery.

Officers pointed the way with their swords and it almost seemed the blades tugged them along. Nichols was glad to bear a rifle, to feel its weight and solidity. Above all, he was glad to feel the smell-close press of his fellow soldiers around him, the presence of others that braved a man up and kept him from shaming himself; glad, too, to see familiar backs in the first line up ahead, to know men not just by their faces, but by their shoulders and signifying movements. Beside him, on his left, marched hard Ive Summerlin, who took every fight personal. To the right, Lem Davis panted, beard alone enough to fright the Yankees, the beard of a Methuselah, though Lem was not so old.

His friends, his kind, his war-kin.

Step forward, step again. Brittle soil crumbled underfoot. A butterfly, confused, fluttered about. His mother said that butterflies brought good luck.

He wanted to be brave inside and out. But he knew that he only could go forward like this, across these endless fields, with his brethren close. He felt himself quiver like a fevered child, the way he was ever inclined to in the moments before he could lose himself in doing.

Men killed hogs kinder than they killed each other.

That fence. A soldier learned to hate fences. Unless they were there for burning when things were quiet.

Them Yanks all tucked in. Waiting. Bits of blue speckled the distance, signs enough for a man to imagine their line, how it would explode.

At that fence. That's where it would start. They'd wait till then.

A part of him wanted to run, a shameful part. His heart raged to burst right out of his chest, to escape his flesh and run off by its own self. Sweat sheathed him.

"Get over that fence!" Colonel Lamar roared. "Company C, open a gap!"

Men rushed from the forward line, ripping at the boards and clubbing the planks with their rifle butts. One fool fellow had cocked his rifle and it shot into the air, a stunning sound that tore right through the day.

As soon as the first rank mounted the fence, the Yankees opened fire. Men splayed their arms and fell—backward, forward—dropping their weapons, casting them off, hats flying, bodies crumpling, some caught halfway, folded over the top rail, rumps in the air, as if awaiting a spanking.

Other men climbed the slats or leapt over. Some paused to help their friends. More and more of the fence simply gave way.

"Come on, boys, come on! Re-form. Re-form and keep moving."

It was hard doings. The first line had become a ragged thing, blundering amid haystacks. It still went forward, though.

"Hold your fire, don't fire. Our time's a-coming. Re-form, and hold your fire!"

Yanks weren't holding theirs. Men dropped.

Nichols crowded through a gap in the broke-down fence, brushing past witch-finger splinters.

Lieutenant Colonel Valkenburg rode through another gap and cantered along the line, calling, "Fill up the first ranks. Sergeants, do your duty!"

"I don't need no sergeant pushing me," Ive Summerlin declared. He trotted forward, toward a hole the Yankees had made in the gray line.

Nichols followed after. Hadn't wanted to, hadn't decided to. Just did. As if Ive pulled him along on a hidden rope.

Lem Davis came after. Big and breathing like a run-out steer.

The Yankees fired as fast as they reloaded.

A few men, very few, paused behind the haystacks, malingering, gripped by fear. Most just stepped along, though, like they couldn't do anything else, and that was that. Both lines were jumbled now.

"Keep going, keep on going!"

Some of the junior officers and sergeants continued to holler about re-forming, but it was as if they did it just to feel better, to keep themselves occupied.

Everyone moved quickly now. Not running, not quite. Forming back up in their accustomed, imperfect way, anxious to get out of the shocks and stacks, craving order as much as they craved safety, needing their comrades stink-close again and ranked up, so a man's chances evened out.

Just as Nichols spotted him again, rounding a haystack, Lieutenant Colonel Valkenburg fell sideward from his horse. As if shoved hard.

"Just keep moving, Georgie," Lem said. "You just look straight ahead."

Wasn't right. It wasn't right. Of all people.

Nichols felt himself tempted by awful words, Satan just a-begging him to utter them.

Men fell on every side.

That second fence. Men couldn't wait, could not just march toward it. One dashed forward, then another. All of them. Amid the wild racket of Yankee volleys.

"Georgia! Georgia!"

Again, men tumbled as they topped the fence, splendid targets for the Yankees now. Nichols spotted Zib Collins, who was supposed to be on stretcher duty and safe, bearing a rifle and fumbling over the obstacle. Then Zib held stone still. For one queer instant. As if at the behest of a man with a camera.

Zib's head just burst, brains splashing everywhere. As if his skull had been struck with a railroad hammer.

"Georgia! Forward!"

Yanks had easy shooting now. But as soon as the bulk of the men were past the fence, Colonel Lamar halted them, cursing those who failed to obey promptly, employing lusty profanity, although the colonel, once a noteworthy sinner, had found his way to Jesus the past winter.

"Form up! Form up, Lord God almighty! Hurry up, boys, hurry!" Nichols shut his ears to the other words blazing by.

They formed back up, right fast. But Lem was on his left now, Ive a few spaces distant on the right.

Eyes hunting the flanks, Lem said, "Seems like we're aiming to take on the Yankees just us'n."

But they were back in solid ranks, instilled again— only the Lord knew how—with order and a refreshed, deepened confidence, going forward as one.

Yanks were little more than a hundred yards off now, not so thick a line, after all.

"At the double-quick . . . forward!"

"Georgia! Georgia!"

"Charge!"

The blue-bellies didn't wait. It was only a bullied-up skirmish line. They fled. Yet, all the dead, the wounded this much had cost . . .

One man shrieked like a woman, a rare thing.

Colonel Lamar steered his horse ahead of the colors. The flags were carried by different soldiers now. The colonel paused just beyond the dip where the skirmish line had lurked.

"Halt and re-form. Halt, boys. Re-form."

"Sure now. Jest let them Yankees have another free

shot," Ive said bitterly, for the hearing of those around him.

But these were dutiful men, ferocious and resigned, and they formed yet again after their brief charge, and they went forward again, and the second Yankee line exploded, so many rifles in play that after two volleys you couldn't see the blue-bellies, just the smoke.

"Forward! Georgia!"

The colors tumbled, the battle flag. New hands reached out. The torn cloth lofted again.

Suddenly, unreasonably, they all began to howl, Nichols and his brethren. It felt wonderful to be a part of this sudden burst of power, to lunge forward again, hallooing, as if their war cry itself must slay the Yankees.

Hundreds of points of light blinked through the smoke. There were bodies underfoot now, from earlier struggles, their own kind, in cavalry jackets and rags.

Another man he knew from home, James Hendrix, clutched his belly and dropped to his knees.

"Onward! Georgia!"

The firing grew so fierce, it felt like walking into a storm wind. Men crouched as they went forward, as if assaulted by a driving rain.

They were close, so close. The racket of the Yankee volleys was ear-busting.

Another man groaned and dropped but paces from Nichols. It was a bewildering thing how any man could stand without being hit.

"Realign. Align on the colors!" Colonel Lamar bellowed. But even as he spoke, the colors fell again. Only to rise a fourth time or a fifth.

The colonel's voice broke off. Men fell. Blood spattered. Nichols found his own face wet without knowing whose blood he wore. His hat was gone.

Another voice called, "Halt. Volley fire. By company. Company officers—"

Then that voice, too, fell away. But the men halted and did as ordered, standing at the edge of the expanding cloud, firing into it on command, then independently, as the smoke engulfed them, too.

A voice reported that Colonel Lamar was dead.

The regiment, the entire brigade, hardly seemed to exist. Nichols was faintly aware that he was shaking. But he dutifully reloaded, fired, and reloaded again, blasting into the smoke, aiming in the direction of those muzzle flames, unwilling to go back one inch.

They crowded together, toward the regimental colors. Before he knew it, Nichols was but a plank length from the single flag remaining. He fought madly, jamming home his ramrod, barely getting the stock back against his shoulder before pulling the trigger again, hating. Nobody was going to take those colors, nobody.

The flag toppled. This time, Lieutenant Mincy dashed forward to raise the staff, only to buckle and drop flat on his face.

The Yankees had been killing all the officers, concentrating on the officers, purposeful and cruel. The revelation made perfect sense to Nichols, but still came as a shock.

He filled up with a hatred less than Christian.

The Yankees didn't come forward, and the remains of the Georgia Brigade would not move back.

The smoke became choking thick.

"Kerenhappuch!" Nichols said. Then he shouted, *"Kerenhappuch!"*

Lem turned. "What the—"

"Job's third daughter! Kerenhappuch!" Nichols began to laugh as he felt for a cartridge.

"Best fix on matters to hand," Lem advised.

They fired into the man-made fog, spotting rough forms now, Yankees no more than thirty yards away. Closer.

"Stand your ground, Georgia!" a grand voice called. "Georgia, hold fast, you're licking them!"

"Well, that's a damned lie," someone said.

"Georgia, stand your ground!"

"That's General Gordon!" The sound of the man's voice, the sense it evoked, the image of the general remembered, filled Nichols with a determination he had not known he could muster. He wanted to rush forward, to go at the Yankees bare-handed. But he stood and fired, obeying the last order he had received, regular as a machine.

Moments later, word passed along the shrinking line that Gordon had been shot.

4:00 p.m.
Thomas farm

Gordon sat up, chasing breath, head hammering and puke dizzy. It had happened fast, the way it always did. Two rounds, maybe three, had struck his horse in a brace of seconds. The animal had reared, throwing him clean, but he'd landed hard.

He tested himself anxiously, checking bones. His vision wouldn't settle and the noise was terrible, terrible. Hands gripped him. He slapped them away.

"I'm all right, damn it," he said. "Give a man his space."

He remembered, looked about. Faces. An aide. "Is York up?"

"Yes, sir. Louisiana's in the fight."

"Tigers," Gordon muttered, meaning to speak firmly.

"Yes, sir. They're right tigers."

"I've got to . . . help me up."

Hands, too many hands, assisted him. "General Evans. I need a report from Evans."

"General Evans has been shot, sir. Your brother has taken temporary command. Until—"

"Colonel Lamar is to command it."

"He's dead, sir."

Gordon bellowed. One wordless howl. Johnny Lamar. Old friend.

The moment of rage cleared his head.

"A horse . . ."

My kingdom for a horse . . . my brigade, my kingdom. Clem Evans, Johnny Lamar . . .

"Take my horse, sir. I'll ride Sergeant Cook's."

"Just give me Cook's horse." He tried to smile toward the sergeant, unsure if he managed it. Then he told all of them: "Georgia must hold its ground. Can't retreat." He looked at the aide. His vision was sharp again. "You said General Evans has been shot. Wounded?"

"Yes, sir. In the side."

"How bad?"

The captain shook his head. "Can't say, sir. Heard he was conscious, though."

"Find my brother. As soon as he can locate a ranking officer, he's to relinquish command. Then find General York. Tell him to keep pressing them, not a step back. Only forward." He tried to find the stirrup with his left boot, but failed twice. Still dizzy, after all.

"Help me."

A sergeant fit the stirrup to Gordon's toe. Gordon gathered the strength to haul his bones up into the saddle.

"Y'all go on now," he told the little crowd. "See to your business."

He rode back through the smoke, sure of his direction, the way he always had been, in the deep forests of north Georgia or on battlefields. His body seemed sound, if aching. And his head was clear enough now. He spurred the strange mount toward the river, where Terry's Brigade had been ordered to halt. He'd sent them forward just far enough to clear out any threat of a flanking maneuver.

The smoke thinned. Noise still clapped his ears, though, a sharp pain. As Gordon emerged from the gray fog into the sunlight, the blaze hit his eyes, his skull, with the force of a mallet. He realized that his hat was gone. But he looked better—fiercer— without it, he fancied.

Alone, he galloped across fields strewn with bodies, most of them in gray or shades of brown. His men, McCausland's. A few Yankees by a fence. The cries of the wounded knew not North or South, only abrupt, unmanageable suffering. But pity was not his dominion. His purpose was to win battles.

Over a rolling crest. Down the far slope, Terry sat his horse, flanked by his staff.

As Gordon reined in, Terry looked him up and down, almost regal, as if condescending to breathe the same air. Yet the fellow was pleasant for all that, as Virginian as fine tobacco and proud women.

"New horse, I do believe," the brigade commander remarked.

The black, dying or dead, had been his favored mount.

"I was inconvenienced," Gordon told him.

"Seems you tired of your hat, as well."

"Never was a proper fit."

"May my brigade be of service, sir? In this heady hour?"

"Yes. You may be of service, Bill. No more time for foolery." He turned in the saddle and pointed to a crest back up the slope and to the left. "Move your men up there. Quick as you can, without disordering them. You're going to roll up the Yankees and put an end to this."

"Bad up top?" Terry asked, serious now.

"Spotsylvania. Smaller, but as bad."

Terry took a moment to swallow that. "And when I get to the top, I'm to—"

"I'll meet you there."

Terry had become faintly unsettled. "But if something should happen? I hear—"

"I'll meet you there," Gordon repeated. "If I don't, you'll see what needs doing, where to attack."

Prepared to ride off, facing myriad tasks, he nonetheless paused before digging in his spurs. Struggling to think like Ulysses, who understood the ways of men like no other: their yearnings, their pride.

"Now we'll see what Virginians are made of," he announced to all who might hear.

4:15 p.m.
Georgetown Pike (Washington road)

Wallace had sent an aide to warn him that his detachment of Vermonters was in retreat, leaping across the girders of the rail bridge, chased by what looked like a full Rebel division. Ricketts pictured men shot in the back and plunging into the river. Who had been in command? Young Davis, was it? Few officers left his senior, far too few. The Wilderness, Spotsylvania, Cold Harbor. Well, Davis had done yeoman's work, holding out with his pitiful handful. But the fact that mattered now was that the Rebs would soon be in his division's rear.

Ricketts felt he was playing poker with disappearing cards.

Wallace had claimed he could hold another half hour, but that had been almost fifteen minutes back. Ricketts imagined the Home Brigade men—who had not done badly at all—losing their courage in one fateful instant and starting to run. He knew how that contagion went. This was the hour for veterans, with all hell bubbling up. But even veterans would hold only so long before they broke.

He was tired. Growing too old for this. But he remained determined to stay at the table to play this final hand. Wallace had authorized him to retreat whenever he deemed it necessary, but Ricketts disliked quitting. Stubborn, all his life. Far more than was politic. One of the reasons he had remained a lieutenant for epochs, then a captain for ages.

And the one time he had softened his principles, at that damnable court-martial, he had marked himself with an odor that wouldn't wash off. Better to be stubborn and pay the price.

He could no longer see the brick house, although it stood but a few hundred yards away. A cloud had grown around it, spreading along the crest, dense as a nightmare. The noise told him his men were holding, though. A few skedaddlers wandered back, and a multitude of wounded men had withdrawn, but the fight was not yet over, not just yet.

And the dead? The lives he was betting in a hopeless game?

He would not order a retreat while Truex held that ridge. He just would not do it. But he had directed his Second Brigade to swing back, now that the river was lost and their flank turned. He intended to firm up a third, last line on the Pike.

Perhaps he could bring off an orderly withdrawal? Even now? With the First Brigade falling back upon the Second, and the Second withdrawing again.

Things would need to go smoothly, more smoothly than battle generally allowed, but there was a chance: Hold the Rebs while the Home Brigade men cleared off and Wallace saved the guns, then withdraw in stages, making any Rebel pursuit pay a premium.

He had been taught, many years before, that a fighting withdrawal was the most difficult military feat, and he doubted things would go nicely. But if you held a poor hand, you had to play boldly.

"Over there," he greeted a Second Brigade officer he recognized. "Put your men over there, when they come up. Build a firing line this side of the road."

Black with smoke and powder, the major stared in bewilderment. "Sir . . . I have no men . . . I don't know where . . ."

Before Ricketts could shape a useful question, Truex's aide, Captain Lanius, emerged out of the smoke, galloping down from the shrouded battle line and nearly riding over a wounded man. One of the many, many wounded men.

Before Ricketts could admonish him, Lanius called from the saddle, "Colonel Truex's compliments, he needs help. Right now, sir. They're breaking our center, Louisiana Brigade. We're holding up on the left, it's a bloody mess, but we're holding. It's the center that's cracking."

Ricketts made an instant decision that changed his plans again.

"Tell Colonel Truex I'm sending him my reserve. No. Wait. You can guide them up yourself."

His "reserve." Two bloodied, played-out regiments,

with several companies already stripped away. His best hope of a last defense of the Pike.

After he had spoken, Ricketts felt a rush of doubt. But it was too late. He had promised help for Truex.

Ricketts played the last card in his hand.

4:25 p.m.
Thomas farm

Brigadier General Terry hurried his troops along, all but giving each man a boot in the haunches. Getting them up to that crest in good order, if a tad breathless.

No sign of Gordon. As Terry approached the high ground, all he could see was bald dirt and a world of smoke beyond it, set to the noise of all the devils in Hell banging pots and pans.

Spotsylvania? Bad as that? My, oh my. Terry believed he had glimpsed a spot of alarm in Gordon's eyes. And Gordon was the most confident creature, man or beast, that Terry had ever met. Oh, surely Gordon had known doubts, the man was human. But Terry had never seen a sign until that afternoon.

If he *had* seen it. With Gordon, a man could be certain without being sure.

Surprising him, the leading men in his brigade began to growl as they neared the ridgetop. Climbing blindly, with the fighting still hidden from view, marching up toward the smoke and sky, they just started in to snarling, like animals that had put up with all they meant to stand. It was an uncanny sound, one Terry did not recall from previous battles.

Had to wonder what men sensed, how they came to that wordless knowing that enthralled them all at once, melting them into one big pot of mischief.

Terry heard cheering, Southern cheering, from down along the river, off toward those bridges, loud enough to compete with the roar of battle. Sounded like Ramseur might have got up from his daybed.

Growling and snarling, rabid, his men were ready to savage all in their way. It filled him with pride.

Terry reached the true crest, horse high-stepping again, and there was Gordon. Sitting upright on that borrowed nag, cool as branch water, as if he had nothing more to do than wait on old Virginia.

It was Gordon restored. In that red shirt, and still without a hat.

When the first rank spotted Gordon, the soldiers sent up a cheer.

"Hurry on, now. Hurry on," Gordon called. His regular voice of command was back upon him, ordering men to their deaths in a tone that was downright affable.

Riding up to that "inexplicable paragon of mystifying, exasperating manliness"—as Zeb York once had put it—Terry said, "Virginia is at your service, sir."

A fence ahead. Then a field. Another fence lower down, broken. Beyond it, the battle, with all the sparks and smoke of Vulcan's forge.

As the two generals watched, a pair of Yankee regiments marched up from the low ground, oblivious to their presence, headed into the maelstrom and exposing meager flanks.

Terry's men surged forward on their own. Growling again. The sound seemed to take even Gordon aback.

"Hold on now, hold on!" Gordon called, princely even on that borrowed nag. "You'll get your chance, boys, your time's going to come. Just get through that fence and form back up."

"Something's got into them," Terry said. "Not sure they'll be bridled again, once we turn 'em loose."

The men rushed the fence, funneling through a gap, breaking down more gaps, or climbing over the rails in their impatience.

Hurrying to assuage some terrible need, the Yankees marching into the fight still showed no awareness that they were about to be gobbled. The bluecoats were formed up smartly, advancing at right-shoulder-shift, as if on parade.

"So much for all those reports of militia and mules," Gordon said. "Let those Federals clear the slope, then advance, once you're formed up."

But the time for orders had passed. A pack of hungry dogs smelling fresh meat, Terry's men began to run down the slope toward the Yankees. Somebody yelled "Charge!"

"What the devil?" Terry demanded.

Hundreds of men poured over and through the fence, joining the attack. It was the wildest thing that Terry had ever seen. But he had his orders, his sense of how things should go, and he rode forward to halt them, to beat them back into their proper formation.

Gordon caught up with him.

"Not going to stop them now," he said. "You were right, they won't be bridled."

Terry's Virginians raised a Rebel yell.

4:40 p.m.
Thomas farm

Yanks are running," Ive Summerlin hollered.

Nichols saw it, too, the sudden breaking up of the line of shadows, the individual flights.

He felt relief, immense relief, as if he had just stopped running after ten miles. Exhausted. He wanted to sit down. His leg decided to hurt again.

"Let's go. Get them sumbitches!" somebody shouted. And they all plunged forward, into the torn smoke, howling. Nichols screamed, too, running along with the others.

It was all so sudden, so reasonless. They had stood there killing each other, as though they would just keep shooting until all but a last one was dead and maybe him, too. Then the Yanks broke.

Some tried to resist even now, but were clubbed down, shot down, run through. Others raised their hands where they stood, faces fearful—faces that surely had worn murderous looks spare minutes before. Ive Summerlin shot a Yank in the belly before the man could get his hands high enough. And they kept running, stumbling over the wounded and dead, even kicking them out of the way, charging down the slope through drifts of smoke. Ahead: a confusion of Yankees, shrieking horses, stray commands.

"Git 'em, git 'em!"

The Yanks weren't done, not quite. Nichols ran past herded prisoners, men made sheep, past individual combats like wrestling matches at the fair, only without rules, and he came up short just as a Federal line, ragged but still standing, fired from the far side of a road.

The volley felled Rebs and their prisoners alike.

The blue-bellies yelled, "Pennsylvania! Pennsylvania!"

A nearby voice, Louisiana-toned, said, "I'll give them shit-eating bastards Pennsylvania. . . ."

Nichols' own kind formed up again, with amazing rapidity, even though no officers were near. He joined a line of strangers and near strangers, faces he knew but couldn't quite slap a name on. In seconds, men had reloaded, raised their rifles, and fired into the blue line, just as the Yankees unleashed a volley of their own.

Men fell. The smoke thickened again.

A Yankee officer rode right between the two lines, galloping up the road, crazed, or perhaps carried along by a runaway horse. Men fired at him, but he eluded the bullets. Then he was gone, a wisp, and the men on foot went back to slaying one another.

Nichols loaded and fired, reached down into his cartridge box again—and found it empty. He knelt to snatch cartridges from a Federal lying open-eyed and still, but had no sooner bent than a fresh volley felled the soldiers who had stood to either side of him.

Nichols looked from one fallen man to the other, a broom-bearded sergeant pawing the air and a fair boy writhing. It made him want to stand up and shout at the Yankees, "You're *whipped*. We whipped you, fair and square. Why don't you quit?"

As if his outrage had willed it, the last Yankee line began to dissolve. Brave men ran. Men in gray seemed to be everywhere now, rushing up from the left, even appearing behind the last clots of resisting Yankees.

Men threw down their rifles and raised their hands. Wherever a Yankee officer tried to bring off his men, he was quickly shot. Still, the killing dragged on down in the hollows.

It was over, though. Some men just didn't have the sense to see it. Or the Christian strength to bear defeat. But for all the shooting and shouting that continued, a fellow just knew that things had finished up, the way you knew the blood was all drained out of a strung-up hog.

Nichols stood. Dumbly. Out of worldly ambition of any kind.

There were Yankee prisoners in numbers enough to work all the fields in Georgia. Powder-blackened men with sour expressions, some weeping, though not from fright or weakness, a man could tell that. Their fear of death had passed, replaced by lesser dreads.

A broken-toothed fellow in brown homespun came smiling up to Nichols, long, greased hair gone thin and hanging below a black hat a witch might have worn in a picture book.

"Who're you with, there, sonny?"

"Sixty-first Georgia," Nichols said proudly, defiantly. "Evans' Brigade, General Gordon's Division."

The ugly mouth cackled and formed new words: "Bet y'all glad Ramseur come to save you, ain't you now?"

Nichols knocked the man down.

5:30 p.m.
Thomas farm

Early dismounted on the crest, amid the dead and dying.

"Stay in the saddle, Sandie," he said. His voice carried no hint of sorrow or remorse, only cold determination. "You ride off yourself, send out couriers. Tell all of them—Gordon, Ramseur, Rodes–I said not to get carried away. No more prisoners, I can't herd any more. Let them run off, I don't choose to be encumbered. This army already favors a band of gypsies."

"Yes, sir. Anything else?"

"Tell McCausland he may find the road to Washington open now, if he cares to look. And if he doesn't mind too awfully much, I'd appreciate him doing what I goddamned well ordered that fool to do this morning. He's to get on down that road and keep on going."

"I believe he's already dispatched most of his command, sir."

"Tell him to send off the rest."

"They're caring for their wounded."

"Let somebody else do it. God almighty, I'm going to get some use out of his clapped-up jockeys yet." He chewed a cud that wasn't there, a ghost of old tobacco. "Any word from Johnson?"

"No, sir. But he should be a good ways along now, putting a scare in folks."

Early tested a fallen Yankee with the tip of his boot. "He won't get within fifty miles of Point Lookout." He pondered for a moment. "Crazy idea. No sense being too hard on Johnson on that count, fool though he may be. You go on now."

Early squatted. The way common soldiers did when they were about to loot a corpse. But he didn't touch the body, only looked at it—the hole in the temple nearly the size of a dollar, the blood darkened almost brown, the lazy flies, gorged, feasted, surfeited.

"Damned Sixth Corps. Looks like someone in Washington done woke up." He lifted his eyes to the staff men gathered around. "Going to have to get an early start tomorrow morning."

5:30 p.m.
Baltimore road, east of the Stone Bridge

Wallace could not speak at first, but needed to calm himself and catch his breath from the pounding ride. He had been relieved to find General Tyler and his men exactly where they were supposed to be, but

the level of firing just across the river, toward Frederick, suggested that few were apt to be there much
longer.

Wearing a harried look, Erastus Tyler waited for
his superior to speak first.

"Well, we've lost," Wallace said.

Tyler nodded.

"We've lost, but we cost them a day. A full day."

"Yes, sir."

"Ras, you *must* hold the bridge, keep the Rebels
from crossing. This road's all we have left. Ricketts
put up a remarkable fight, we can't let his survivors
be cut off."

Tyler, too, appeared wearied. Stained. Not just
with the salt that collected from a man's sweat, but
by life. They all were.

"Do my best, sir. Men held fine all day. Only a
few ran off. But they're tired now. Unsteady."

"We're all tired."

"Just telling you the truth, sir. They will not hold
against a determined attack. Some will fight, but not
enough. And not long enough. Not with everybody
else running. Panic's catching, you know that."

And running his men were, Wallace had to face
it. He had waited too long to withdraw, zealous for
each additional minute, tallying the hours as a child
might, selfish, blinded. When he left the battlefield,
with Ross tugging his mount's bridle to make him
go, he had fled a debacle, with his own men disappearing and Ricketts' remaining soldiers all but surrounded.

Ricketts. The Republic owed that man a debt.

And Alexander had brought off his guns. Even that howitzer.

Not everyone had quit, there had been heroes. Many of them. And officers were still out there, along the line of retreat, attempting to lead the remnants of companies and regiments amid the confusion and the Rebel pursuit, to save what could be saved.

Wallace knew that he needed to move on himself, to rally as many men as he could, to gather numbers sufficient to block the road to Baltimore at whatever point presented itself, to fight again. In case he had been wrong about that, too, and Early planned on burning the docks and warehouses, the rail yards and the arsenal.

He had to see to countless tasks, but he only slumped in the saddle, allowing himself a stolen moment of rest, overtaken by the day, overwhelmed at last. He just wanted to sleep. Between clean sheets.

How many men had his obstinacy killed? And how many of those deaths had been unnecessary, offerings made too late to affect the result, men left to die when he should have begun to clear the field and spare what lives he could?

Selfishness. Pride. Vainglory. So many sins were disguised by the fine word *duty*.

Waking himself, Wallace told Tyler, "I'm depending on you, Ras. Hold the bridge. As long as you can. Do your best. Give me two hours. One hour."

And Wallace turned back toward his shattered army.

7:00 p.m.
The Baltimore and Ohio Railroad,
east of Monocacy Junction

Ricketts and his staff followed the rail line. The Reb pursuit appeared to have slackened and the men let their winded horses slow to a walk for a stretch.

He had waited too long, making the wrong guesses toward the end. The Rebs had overwhelmed them, that was true. But Ricketts already saw the things he might have done differently. *Would* do differently. Another time.

Would he be allowed another time? With his wrecked division?

He hoped that Wallace had escaped the Rebs. The damned fool. A damned fool, and a good man. For any blunders he might have made, Wallace had done a dozen and more things right. He had seen what needed doing and had done it, where a timid man, one thinking of his career, would have found excuses so convincing they were sure to get him promoted. Together, they had bought a day for Washington. *And* bloodied Early's army.

His own losses were terrible, though. He would not know the true numbers for days, as soldiers left to save themselves filtered back in to their commands, as they always did. But the numbers would be grim, not least those taken prisoner. He barely had escaped himself, refusing his staff's entreaties to ride off until the Rebels had almost boxed them in.

He believed that Truex had gotten off the field, too. But the toll of regimental officers looked to be crippling.

They passed a slump-shouldered group of soldiers—his men, judging by their hard-worn uniforms. Most had brought off their rifles, but not all of them.

"You men gave them the devil today," Ricketts told them. "And we'll give them the devil again, when we have the chance."

"Strikes me the Devil got his own both ways," a wag called out. "Any of you officers got a spare beefsteak?"

That was all right. When men could joke, it meant they were not broken. The division had been shattered, but not destroyed. The men would come in. And those two missing regiments would be found, with hell to pay when he found the man responsible for their absence from the field.

He worried a bit about his future, but not overly much. He had been the subordinate, and his division had fought handsomely. He was unlikely to bear any blame. But it had been, after all, a defeat—no matter its contribution—and the entire effort might be portrayed as foolhardy by those safe behind mahogany desks in Washington.

He was unlikely to suffer any consequences. But Wallace? No breed of man was more vindictive than those who shied from battle in the rear. If Wallace had enemies, this would be their hour.

Off to the right, ahead of them, firing erupted.

"Best pick up the pace, sir," an aide counseled.

9:30 p.m.
Thomas farm

Nichols sat. It was all he could do, all he wanted to do, to the extent he felt any least desire to do anything. He had eaten, Yankee food, of which there was plenty. Brined pork, beans, and crackers without weevils. He had eaten like a machine, spooning up the food steadily, not tasting much, filling the empty space in his belly as if that might fill the other emptiness.

After he had knocked down Ramseur's man, the 61st Georgia and the 12th Georgia Battalion were ordered to stop where they were and leave chasing Yankees to others. Wandering back a stretch over the field, he had come upon Tom Nichols of Company A, a namesake but no kin. Tom's brains were hanging out of his temple, and the wounded man pawed one-handed at the slops, either trying to shove them back in or brush them away from his skull. Nichols knelt down to see if there was anything he could do, trying not to show the horror he felt, and helped Tom to a drink from his canteen. It was almost as if Tom had already turned hant, for he seemed to feel no pain. He still had a scrap of his wits, though.

"If I can get back to Virginia," the dying man declared, "just get back to Virginia . . . get me a horse . . ." His eyes met Nichols', but it was beyond knowing what Tom really saw. "Never going to cross the Potomac again, never going to cross the Potomac again, never." He went back to smearing his brains across his temple.

Nichols sat with him until a pair of litter bearers appeared to take him to a field surgery. It was clear from their looks, from any expertise they had acquired, that Tom was a goner. But Nichols had already known that.

". . . a horse . . . ," Tom said, the last words Nichols heard from him.

He meant to pray thereafter, to thank the Lord for delivering him this day, but he kept putting it off. After trying to banter with him, to cheer him, Lem Davis and Dan Frawley had let him alone, just keeping watch on his doings from a distance. He didn't resent that, didn't feel anything about it. When Tom Boyet fetched his blanket roll and haversack for him, setting both down by his side, he had lacked the means, the courtesy, to thank him.

Nichols wanted to see his mother again. He wanted to live that long. Tom would not live that long.

He knew he should be thankful that so many of his brethren, his close brethren, had survived. But he felt the death of Lieutenant Colonel Valkenburg unreasonably, deeply, seeing him fall from his saddle again and again, until it was maddening. And Colonel Lamar, too, it didn't seem fair. He hoped the colonel had died in grace, forgiven his last profanities. Lieutenant Mincy stuck in his thoughts as well, although it was told he might live to drink coffee again, surviving his third wound, a blessing. Nichols meant to pray for Mincy, too. And for General

Evans, who also promised to live. But it was just too hard to move, to part his lips.

He sat in the gloaming, shirking his duty to help out with the wounded, his own kind and the Yankees.

"It's a terrible thing," he said suddenly, speaking out loud. "It's a terrible thing."

But had a man asked, he could not have told him what that terrible thing was.

When the roll was called, in the virgin dark, the 61st Georgia, which had gone into battle with one hundred and fifty men, answered with fifty-two voices.